Baroness Emmuska Orczy was born in 1865, in Tarnaors, Heves county, Hungary. She was the daughter of Baron Felix Orczy de Orczu, who was a composer, and Countess Emma Wass von Szentegyed und Czege. In 1868 they fled Hungary with a three-year-old Emmuska, to avoid the upheaval of a peasant revolution.

The family lived in Budapest, Brussels and Paris, and during this time Orczy studied music. The family settled in London in 1880, where Orczy studied art. Some of her paintings have been shown at the Royal Academy in London. When she was at school, she met her future husband, Montague Barstow, a young illustrator.

To augment the couple's small income, Orczy worked as a translator and illustrator with her husband. In 1903 they coauthored a play, *The Scarlet Pimpernel*. It was slow to gain popularity, but eventually it set stage records. It was also translated, and performed in other countries.

Orczy completed her novel, *The Scarlet Pimpernel*, in 1905. The success of the play extended to the book and it became wildly popular. She continued to write throughout her life, adding to The Scarlet Pimpernel series, and writing other historical fiction. However, none sold as well as *The Scarlet Pimpernel*.

During World War I, Baroness Orczy was active in the Women of England's Active Service League, an organization she had started. The members set out to persuade every man they knew to serve his country in the military. The group eventually grew to 20,000 members.

Baroness Orczy died in Henley-on-Thames, in 1947.

Baroness Emmuska Magdolna Rozália Mária Jozefa Borbála Emmuska
Orczy de Orczi, *The Scarlet Pimpernel Anthology Volume II*
*El Dorado, Lord Tony's Wife, The League of The Scarlet Pimpernel*

This reprint edition, Copyright © 2014,
WilliamsBookseller.com,
Printed in the United States of America
ISBN-13: 978-1479249726
SBN-10:1479249726

# THE SCARLET
# PIMPERNEL ANTHOLOGY
## VOLUME II

# THE SCARLET PIMPERNEL ANTHOLOGY

## VOLUME II

### ELDORADO, LORD TONY'S WIFE, AND THE LEAGUE OF THE SCARLET PIMPERNEL

BY BARONESS EMMUSKA ORCZY

# CONTENTS

# ELDORADO

BARONESS EMMUSKA ORCZY

# FORWARD

There has of late years crept so much confusion into the mind of the student as well as of the general reader as to the identity of the Scarlet Pimpernel with that of the Gascon Royalist plotter known to history as the Baron de Batz, that the time seems opportune for setting all doubts on that subject at rest.

The identity of the Scarlet Pimpernel is in no way whatever connected with that of the Baron de Batz, and even superficial reflection will soon bring the mind to the conclusion that great fundamental differences existed in these two men, in their personality, in their character, and, above all, in their aims.

According to one or two enthusiastic historians, the Baron de Batz was the chief agent in a vast network of conspiracy, entirely supported by foreign money—both English and Austrian—and which had for its object the overthrow of the Republican Government and the restoration of the monarchy in France.

In order to attain this political goal, it is averred that he set himself the task of pitting the members of the revolutionary Government one against the other, and bringing hatred and dissensions amongst them, until the cry of "Traitor!" resounded from one end of the Assembly of the Convention to the other, and the Assembly itself became as one vast den of wild beasts wherein wolves and hyenas devoured one another and, still unsatiated, licked their streaming jaws hungering for more prey.

Those same enthusiastic historians, who have a firm belief in the so-called "Foreign Conspiracy," ascribe every important event of the Great Revolution—be that event the downfall of the Girondins, the escape of the Dauphin from the Temple, or the death of Robespierre—to the intrigues of Baron de Batz. He it was, so they say, who egged the Jacobins on against the Mountain, Robespierre against Danton, Hebert against Robespierre. He it was who instigated the massacres of September, the atrocities of Nantes, the horrors of Thermidor, the sacrileges, the noyades: all with the view of causing every section of the National Assembly to vie with the other in excesses and in cruelty, until the makers of the Revolution, satiated with their own lust, turned on one another, and Sardanapalus-like buried themselves and their orgies in the vast hecatomb of a self-consumed anarchy.

Whether the power thus ascribed to Baron de Batz by his historians is real or imaginary it is not the purpose of this preface to investigate. Its sole object is to point out the difference between the career of this plotter and that of the Scarlet Pimpernel.

The Baron de Batz himself was an adventurer without

substance, save that which he derived from abroad. He was one of those men who have nothing to lose and everything to gain by throwing themselves headlong in the seething cauldron of internal politics.

Though he made several attempts at rescuing King Louis first, and then the Queen and Royal Family from prison and from death, he never succeeded, as we know, in any of these undertakings, and he never once so much as attempted the rescue of other equally innocent, if not quite so distinguished, victims of the most bloodthirsty revolution that has ever shaken the foundations of the civilised world.

Nay more; when on the 29th Prairial those unfortunate men and women were condemned and executed for alleged complicity in the so-called "Foreign Conspiracy," de Batz, who is universally admitted to have been the head and prime-mover of that conspiracy—if, indeed, conspiracy there was—never made either the slightest attempt to rescue his confederates from the guillotine, or at least the offer to perish by their side if he could not succeed in saving them.

And when we remember that the martyrs of the 29th Prairial included women like Grandmaison, the devoted friend of de Batz, the beautiful Emilie de St. Amaranthe, little Cecile Renault—a mere child not sixteen years of age—also men like Michonis and Roussell, faithful servants of de Batz, the Baron de Lezardiere, and the Comte de St. Maurice, his friends, we no longer can have the slightest doubt that the Gascon plotter and the English gentleman are indeed two very different persons. The latter's aims were absolutely non-political. He never intrigued for the restoration of the monarchy, or even for the overthrow of that Republic which he loathed.

His only concern was the rescue of the innocent, the stretching out of a saving hand to those unfortunate creatures who had fallen into the nets spread out for them by their fellow-men; by those who—godless, lawless, penniless themselves—had sworn to exterminate all those who clung to their belongings, to their religion, and to their beliefs.

The Scarlet Pimpernel did not take it upon himself to punish the guilty; his care was solely of the helpless and of the innocent.

For this aim he risked his life every time that he set foot on French soil, for it he sacrificed his fortune, and even his personal happiness, and to it he devoted his entire existence.

Moreover, whereas the French plotter is said to have had confederates even in the Assembly of the Convention, confederates who were sufficiently influential and powerful to secure his own immunity, the Englishman when he was bent on his errands of mercy had the whole of France against him.

The Baron de Batz was a man who never justified either his own ambitions or even his existence; the Scarlet Pimpernel was a personality of whom an entire nation might justly be proud.

# PART I
## CHAPTER 1: IN THE THEATRE NATIONAL

And yet people found the opportunity to amuse themselves, to dance and to go to the theatre, to enjoy music and open-air cafes and promenades in the Palais Royal.

New fashions in dress made their appearance, milliners produced fresh "creations," and jewellers were not idle. A grim sense of humour, born of the very intensity of ever-present danger, had dubbed the cut of certain tunics "*tete tranche*," or a favourite ragout was called "*a la guillotine*."

On three evenings only during the past memorable four and a half years did the theatres close their doors, and these evenings were the ones immediately following that terrible 2nd of September the day of the butchery outside the Abbaye prison, when Paris herself was aghast with horror, and the cries of the massacred might have drowned the calls of the audience whose hands upraised for plaudits would still be dripping with blood.

On all other evenings of these same four and a half years the theatres in the Rue de Richelieu, in the Palais Royal, the Luxembourg, and others, had raised their curtains and taken money at their doors. The same audience that earlier in the day had whiled away the time by witnessing the ever-recurrent dramas of the Place de la Revolution assembled here in the evenings and filled stalls, boxes, and tiers, laughing over the satires of Voltaire or weeping over the sentimental tragedies of persecuted Romeos and innocent Juliets.

Death knocked at so many doors these days! He was so constant a guest in the houses of relatives and friends that those who had merely shaken him by the hand, those on whom he had smiled, and whom he, still smiling, had passed indulgently by, looked on him with that subtle contempt born of familiarity, shrugged their shoulders at his passage, and envisaged his probable visit on the morrow with lighthearted indifference.

Paris—despite the horrors that had stained her walls had remained a city of pleasure, and the knife of the guillotine did scarce descend more often than did the drop-scenes on the stage.

On this bitterly cold evening of the 27th Nivose, in the second year of the Republic—or, as we of the old style still persist in calling it, the 16th of January, 1794—the auditorium of the Theatre National was filled with a very brilliant company.

The appearance of a favourite actress in the part of one of Moliere's volatile heroines had brought pleasure-loving Paris to witness this revival of "Le Misanthrope," with new scenery, dresses, and the aforesaid charming actress to add piquancy to the master's mordant wit.

The Moniteur, which so impartially chronicles the events of those times, tells us under that date that the Assembly of the Convention voted on that same day a new law giving fuller power to its spies, enabling them to effect domiciliary searches at their discretion without previous reference to the Committee of General Security, authorising them to proceed against all enemies of public happiness, to send them to prison at their own discretion, and assuring them the sum of thirty-five livres "for every piece of game thus beaten up for the guillotine." Under that same date the Moniteur also puts it on record that the Theatre National was filled to its utmost capacity for the revival of the late citoyen Moliere's comedy.

The Assembly of the Convention having voted the new law which placed the lives of thousands at the mercy of a few human bloodhounds, adjourned its sitting and proceeded to the Rue de Richelieu.

Already the house was full when the fathers of the people made their way to the seats which had been reserved for them. An awed hush descended on the throng as one by one the men whose very names inspired horror and dread filed in through the narrow gangways of the stalls or took their places in the tiny boxes around.

Citizen Robespierre's neatly bewigged head soon appeared in one of these; his bosom friend St. Just was with him, and also his sister Charlotte. Danton, like a big, shaggy-coated lion, elbowed his way into the stalls, whilst Sauterre, the handsome butcher and idol of the people of Paris, was loudly acclaimed as his huge frame, gorgeously clad in the uniform of the National Guard, was sighted on one of the tiers above.

The public in the parterre and in the galleries whispered excitedly; the awe-inspiring names flew about hither and thither on the wings of the overheated air. Women craned their necks to catch sight of heads which mayhap on the morrow would roll into the gruesome basket at the foot of the guillotine.

In one of the tiny avant-scene boxes two men had taken their seats long before the bulk of the audience had begun to assemble in the house. The inside of the box was in complete darkness, and the narrow opening which allowed but a sorry view of one side of the stage helped to conceal rather than display the occupants.

The younger one of these two men appeared to be something of a stranger in Paris, for as the public men and the well-known members of the Government began to arrive he often turned to his companion for information regarding these notorious personalities.

"Tell me, de Batz," he said, calling the other's attention to a group of men who had just entered the house, "that creature there in the green coat—with his hand up to his face now—who is he?"

"Where? Which do you mean?"

"There! He looks this way now, and he has a playbill in his hand. The man with the protruding chin and the convex forehead, a face like a marmoset, and eyes like a jackal. What?"

The other leaned over the edge of the box, and his small, restless eyes wandered over the now closely-packed auditorium.

"Oh!" he said as soon as he recognised the face which his friend had pointed out to him, "that is citizen Foucquier-Tinville."

"The Public Prosecutor?"

"Himself. And Heron is the man next to him."

"Heron?" said the younger man interrogatively.

"Yes. He is chief agent to the Committee of General Security now."

"What does that mean?"

Both leaned back in their chairs, and their sombrely-clad figures were once more merged in the gloom of the narrow box. Instinctively, since the name of the Public Prosecutor had been mentioned between them, they had allowed their voices to sink to a whisper.

The older man—a stoutish, florid-looking individual, with small, keen eyes, and skin pitted with small-pox—shrugged his shoulders at his friend's question, and then said with an air of contemptuous indifference:

"It means, my good St. Just, that these two men whom you see down there, calmly conning the programme of this evening's entertainment, and preparing to enjoy themselves to-night in the company of the late M. de Moliere, are two hell-hounds as powerful as they are cunning."

"Yes, yes," said St. Just, and much against his will a slight shudder ran through his slim figure as he spoke. "Foucquier-Tinville I know; I know his cunning, and I know his power—but the other?"

"The other?" retorted de Batz lightly. "Heron? Let me tell you, my friend, that even the might and lust of that damned Public Prosecutor pale before the power of Heron!"

"But how? I do not understand."

"Ah! you have been in England so long, you lucky dog, and though no doubt the main plot of our hideous tragedy has reached your ken, you have no cognisance of the actors who play the principal parts on this arena flooded with blood and carpeted with hate. They come and go, these actors, my good St. Just—they come and go. Marat is already the man of yesterday, Robespierre is the man of to-morrow. To-day we still have Danton and Foucquier-Tinville; we still have Pere Duchesne, and your own good cousin Antoine St. Just, but Heron and his like are with us always."

"Spies, of course?"

"Spies," assented the other. "And what spies! Were you present at the sitting of the Assembly to-day?"

"I was. I heard the new decree which already has passed into law. Ah! I tell you, friend, that we do not let the grass grow under our feet these days. Robespierre wakes up one morning with a whim; by the afternoon that whim has become law, passed by a servile body of men too terrified to run counter to his will, fearful lest they be accused of moderation or of humanity—the greatest crimes that can be committed nowadays."

"But Danton?"

"Ah! Danton? He would wish to stem the tide that his own passions have let loose; to muzzle the raging beasts whose fangs he himself has sharpened. I told you that Danton is still the man of to-day; to-morrow he will be accused of moderation. Danton and moderation! —ye gods! Eh? Danton, who thought the guillotine too slow in its work, and armed thirty soldiers with swords, so that thirty heads might fall at one and the same time. Danton, friend, will perish to-morrow accused of treachery against the Revolution, of moderation towards her enemies; and curs like Heron will feast on the blood of lions like Danton and his crowd."

He paused a moment, for he dared not raise his voice, and his whispers were being drowned by the noise in the auditorium. The curtain, timed to be raised at eight o'clock, was still down, though it was close on half-past, and the public was growing impatient. There was loud stamping of feet, and a few shrill whistles of disapproval proceeded from the gallery.

"If Heron gets impatient," said de Batz lightly, when the noise had momentarily subsided, "the manager of this theatre and mayhap his leading actor and actress will spend an unpleasant day to-morrow."

"Always Heron!" said St. Just, with a contemptuous smile.

"Yes, my friend," rejoined the other imperturbably, "always Heron. And he has even obtained a longer lease of existence this afternoon."

"By the new decree?"

"Yes. The new decree. The agents of the Committee of General Security, of whom Heron is the chief, have from to-day powers of domiciliary search; they have full powers to proceed against all enemies of public welfare. Isn't that beautifully vague? And they have absolute discretion; every one may become an enemy of public welfare, either by spending too much money or by spending too little, by laughing to-day or crying to-morrow, by mourning for one dead relative or rejoicing over the execution of another. He may be a bad example to the public by the cleanliness of his person or by the filth upon his clothes, he may offend by walking to-day and by riding in a carriage next week; the agents of the Committee of General Security shall alone decide what constitutes enmity against public welfare. All prisons are to be opened at their bidding to receive those whom they choose to denounce; they have henceforth the right to examine prisoners privately and without witnesses, and to send them to trial without further warrants; their duty is clear—they must 'beat up game for the guillotine.' Thus is the decree worded; they must furnish the Public Prosecutor with work to do, the tribunals with victims to condemn, the Place de la Revolution with death-scenes to amuse the people, and for their work they will be rewarded thirty-five livres for every head that falls under the guillotine Ah! if Heron and his like and his myrmidons work hard and well they can make a comfortable income of four or five thousand livres a week. We are getting on, friend St. Just—we are getting on."

He had not raised his voice while he spoke, nor in the recounting of such inhuman monstrosity, such vile and bloodthirsty conspiracy against the liberty, the dignity, the very life of an entire nation, did he appear to feel the slightest indignation; rather did a tone of amusement and even of triumph strike through his speech; and now he laughed good-humouredly like an indulgent parent who is watching the naturally cruel antics of a spoilt boy.

"Then from this hell let loose upon earth," exclaimed St. Just hotly, "must we rescue those who refuse to ride upon this tide of blood."

His cheeks were glowing, his eyes sparkled with enthusiasm. He looked very young and very eager. Armand St. Just, the brother of Lady Blakeney, had something of the refined beauty of his lovely sister, but the features though manly—had not the latent strength expressed in them which characterised every line of Marguerite's exquisite face. The forehead suggested a dreamer rather than a thinker, the blue-grey eyes were those of an idealist rather than of a man of action.

De Batz's keen piercing eyes had no doubt noted this, even whilst he gazed at his young friend with that same look of good-humoured indulgence which seemed habitual to him.

"We have to think of the future, my good St. Just," he said after a slight pause, and speaking slowly and decisively, like a father rebuking a hot-headed child, "not of the present. What are a few lives worth beside the great principles which we have at stake?"

"The restoration of the monarchy—I know," retorted St. Just, still unsobered, "but, in the meanwhile—"

"In the meanwhile," rejoined de Batz earnestly, "every victim to the lust of these men is a step towards the restoration of law and order—that is to say, of the monarchy. It is only through these violent excesses perpetrated in its name that the nation will realise how it is being fooled by a set of men who have only their own power and their own advancement in view, and who imagine that the only way to that power is over the dead bodies of those who stand in their way. Once the nation is sickened by these orgies of ambition and of hate, it will turn against these savage brutes, and gladly acclaim the restoration of all that they are striving to destroy. This is our only hope for the future, and, believe me, friend, that every head snatched from the guillotine by your romantic hero, the Scarlet Pimpernel, is a stone laid for the consolidation of this infamous Republic."

"I'll not believe it," protested St. Just emphatically.

De Batz, with a gesture of contempt indicative also of complete self-satisfaction and unalterable self-belief, shrugged his broad shoulders. His short fat fingers, covered with rings, beat a tattoo upon the ledge of the box.

Obviously, he was ready with a retort. His young friend's attitude irritated even more than it amused him. But he said nothing for the moment, waiting while the traditional three knocks on the floor of the stage proclaimed the rise of the curtain. The growing impatience of the audience subsided as if by magic at the welcome call; everybody settled down again comfortably in their seats, they gave up the contemplation of the fathers of the people, and turned their full attention to the actors on the boards.

# CHAPTER 2: WIDELY DIVERGENT AIMS

This was Armand S. Just's first visit to Paris since that memorable day when first he decided to sever his connection from the Republican party, of which he and his beautiful sister Marguerite had at one time been amongst the most noble, most enthusiastic followers. Already a year and a half ago the excesses of the party had horrified him, and that was long before they had degenerated into the sickening orgies which were culminating to-day in wholesale massacres and bloody hecatombs of innocent victims.

With the death of Mirabeau the moderate Republicans, whose sole and entirely pure aim had been to free the people of France from the autocratic tyranny of the Bourbons, saw the power go from their clean hands to the grimy ones of lustful demagogues, who knew no law save their own passions of bitter hatred against all classes that were not as self-seeking, as ferocious as themselves.

It was no longer a question of a fight for political and religious liberty only, but one of class against class, man against man, and let the weaker look to himself. The weaker had proved himself to be, firstly, the man of property and substance, then the law-abiding citizen, lastly the man of action who had obtained for the people that very same liberty of thought and of belief which soon became so terribly misused.

Armand St. Just, one of the apostles of liberty, fraternity, and equality, soon found that the most savage excesses of tyranny were being perpetrated in the name of those same ideals which he had worshipped.

His sister Marguerite, happily married in England, was the final temptation which caused him to quit the country the destinies of which he no longer could help to control. The spark of enthusiasm which he and the followers of Mirabeau had tried to kindle in the hearts of an oppressed people had turned to raging tongues of unquenchable flames. The taking of the Bastille had been the prelude to the massacres of September, and even the horror of these had since paled beside the holocausts of to-day.

Armand, saved from the swift vengeance of the revolutionaries by the devotion of the Scarlet Pimpernel, crossed over to England and enrolled himself under the banner of the heroic chief. But he had been unable hitherto to be an active member of the League. The chief was loath to allow him to run foolhardy risks. The St. Justs—both Marguerite and Armand—were still very well-known in Paris. Marguerite was not a woman easily forgotten, and her marriage with an English "*aristo*" did not please those republican circles who had looked upon her as their queen. Armand's secession from his party into the ranks of the emigres had singled him out for special reprisals, if and whenever he could be got hold of, and both brother and sister had an unusually bitter enemy in their cousin Antoine St. Just—once an aspirant to Marguerite's hand, and now a servile adherent and imitator of Robespierre, whose ferocious cruelty he tried to emulate with a view to ingratiating himself with the most powerful man of the day.

Nothing would have pleased Antoine St. Just more than the opportunity of showing his zeal and his patriotism by denouncing his own kith and kin to the Tribunal of the Terror, and the Scarlet Pimpernel, whose own slender fingers were held on the pulse of that reckless revolution, had no wish to sacrifice Armand's life deliberately, or even to expose it to unnecessary dangers.

Thus it was that more than a year had gone by before Armand St. Just—an enthusiastic member of the League of the Scarlet Pimpernel—was able to do aught for its service. He had chafed under the enforced restraint placed upon him by the prudence of his chief, when, indeed, he was longing to risk his life with the comrades whom he loved and beside the leader whom he revered.

At last, in the beginning of '94 he persuaded Blakeney to allow him to join the next expedition to France. What the principal aim of that expedition was the members of the League did not know as yet, but what they did know was that perils—graver even than hitherto—would attend them on their way.

The circumstances had become very different of late. At first the impenetrable mystery which had surrounded the personality of the chief had been a full measure of safety, but now one tiny corner of that veil of mystery had been lifted by two rough pairs of hands at least; Chauvelin, ex-ambassador at the English Court, was no longer in any doubt as to the identity of the Scarlet Pimpernel, whilst Collot d'Herbois had seen him at Boulogne, and had there been effectually foiled by him.

Four months had gone by since that day, and the Scarlet Pimpernel was hardly ever out of France now; the massacres in Paris and in the provinces had multiplied with appalling rapidity, the necessity for the selfless devotion of that small band of heroes had become daily, hourly more pressing. They rallied round their chief with unbounded enthusiasm, and let it be admitted at once that the sporting instinct—inherent in these English gentlemen—made them all the more keen, all the more eager now that the dangers which beset their expeditions were increased tenfold.

At a word from the beloved leader, these young men—the spoilt darlings of society—would leave the gaieties, the pleasures, the luxuries of London or of Bath, and, taking their lives in their hands, they placed them, together with their fortunes, and even their good names, at the service of the innocent and helpless victims of merciless tyranny. The married men—Ffoulkes, my Lord Hastings, Sir Jeremiah Wallescourt—left wife and children at a call from the chief, at the cry of the wretched. Armand—unattached and enthusiastic—had the right to demand that he should no longer be left behind.

He had only been away a little over fifteen months, and yet he found Paris a different city from the one he had left immediately after the terrible massacres of September. An air of grim loneliness seemed to hang over her despite the crowds that thronged her streets; the men whom he was wont to meet in public places fifteen months ago—friends and political allies—were no longer to be seen; strange faces surrounded him on every side—sullen, glowering faces, all wearing a certain air of horrified surprise and of vague, terrified wonder, as if life had become one awful puzzle, the answer to which must be found in the brief interval between the swift passages of death.

Armand St. Just, having settled his few simple belongings in the squalid lodgings which had been assigned to him, had started out after dark to wander somewhat aimlessly through the streets. Instinctively he seemed to be searching for a familiar face, some one who would come to him out of that merry past which he had spent with Marguerite in their pretty apartment in the Rue St. Honore.

For an hour he wandered thus and met no one whom he knew. At times it appeared to him as if he did recognise a face or figure that passed him swiftly by in the gloom, but even before he could fully make up his mind to that, the face or figure had already disappeared, gliding furtively down some narrow unlighted by-street, without turning to look to right or left, as if dreading fuller recognition. Armand felt a total stranger in his own native city.

The terrible hours of the execution on the Place de la Revolution were fortunately over, the tumbrils no longer rattled along the uneven pavements, nor did the death-cry of the unfortunate victims resound through the deserted streets. Armand was, on this first day of his arrival, spared the sight of this degradation of the once lovely city; but her desolation, her general appearance of shamefaced indigence and of cruel aloofness struck a chill in the young man's heart.

It was no wonder, therefore, when anon he was wending his way slowly back to his lodging he was accosted by a pleasant, cheerful voice, that he responded to it with alacrity. The voice, of a smooth, oily timbre, as if the owner kept it well greased for purposes of amiable speech, was like an echo of the past, when jolly, irresponsible Baron de Batz, erst-while officer of the Guard in the service of the late King, and since then known to be the most inveterate conspirator for the restoration of the monarchy, used to amuse Marguerite by his vapid, senseless plans for the overthrow of the newly-risen power of the people.

Armand was quite glad to meet him, and when de Batz

suggested that a good talk over old times would be vastly agreeable, the younger man gladly acceded. The two men, though certainly not mistrustful of one another, did not seem to care to reveal to each other the place where they lodged. De Batz at once proposed the avant-scene box of one of the theatres as being the safest place where old friends could talk without fear of spying eyes or ears.

"There is no place so safe or so private nowadays, believe me, my young friend," he said "I have tried every sort of nook and cranny in this accursed town, now riddled with spies, and I have come to the conclusion that a small avant-scene box is the most perfect den of privacy there is in the entire city. The voices of the actors on the stage and the hum among the audience in the house will effectually drown all individual conversation to every ear save the one for whom it is intended."

It is not difficult to persuade a young man who feels lonely and somewhat forlorn in a large city to while away an evening in the companionship of a cheerful talker, and de Batz was essentially good company. His vapourings had always been amusing, but Armand now gave him credit for more seriousness of purpose; and though the chief had warned him against picking up acquaintances in Paris, the young man felt that that restriction would certainly not apply to a man like de Batz, whose hot partisanship of the Royalist cause and hare-brained schemes for its restoration must make him at one with the League of the Scarlet Pimpernel.

Armand accepted the other's cordial invitation. He, too, felt that he would indeed be safer from observation in a crowded theatre than in the streets. Among a closely packed throng bent on amusement the sombrely-clad figure of a young man, with the appearance of a student or of a journalist, would easily pass unperceived.

But somehow, after the first ten minutes spent in de Batz' company within the gloomy shelter of the small avant-scene box, Armand already repented of the impulse which had prompted him to come to the theatre to-night, and to renew acquaintanceship with the ex-officer of the late King's Guard. Though he knew de Batz to be an ardent Royalist, and even an active adherent of the monarchy, he was soon conscious of a vague sense of mistrust of this pompous, self-complacent individual, whose every utterance breathed selfish aims rather than devotion to a forlorn cause.

Therefore, when the curtain rose at last on the first act of Moliere's witty comedy, St. Just turned deliberately towards the stage and tried to interest himself in the wordy quarrel between Philinte and Alceste.

But this attitude on the part of the younger man did not seem to suit his newly-found friend. It was clear that de Batz did not consider the topic of conversation by any means exhausted, and that it had been more with a view to a discussion like the present interrupted one that he had invited St. Just to come to the theatre with him to-night, rather than for the purpose of witnessing Mlle. Lange's debut in the part of Celimene.

The presence of St. Just in Paris had as a matter of fact astonished de Batz not a little, and had set his intriguing brain busy on conjectures. It was in order to turn these conjectures into certainties that he had desired private talk with the young man.

He waited silently now for a moment or two, his keen, small eyes resting with evident anxiety on Armand's averted head, his fingers still beating the impatient tattoo upon the velvet-covered cushion of the box. Then at the first movement of St. Just towards him he was ready in an instant to re-open the subject under discussion.

With a quick nod of his head he called his young friend's attention back to the men in the auditorium.

"Your good cousin Antoine St. Just is hand and glove with Robespierre now," he said. "When you left Paris more than a year ago you could afford to despise him as an empty-headed windbag; now, if you desire to remain in France, you will have to fear him as a power and a menace."

"Yes, I knew that he had taken to herding with the wolves," rejoined Armand lightly. "At one time he was in love with my sister. I thank God that she never cared for him."

"They say that he herds with the wolves because of this disappointment," said de Batz. "The whole pack is made up of men who have been disappointed, and who have nothing more to lose. When all these wolves will have devoured one another, then and then only can we hope for the restoration of the monarchy in France. And they will not turn on one another whilst prey for their greed lies ready to their jaws. Your friend the Scarlet Pimpernel should feed this bloody revolution of ours rather than starve it, if indeed he hates it as he seems to do."

His restless eyes peered with eager interrogation into those of the younger man. He paused as if waiting for a reply; then, as St. Just remained silent, he reiterated slowly, almost in the tones of a challenge:

"If indeed he hates this bloodthirsty revolution of ours as he seems to do."

The reiteration implied a doubt. In a moment St. Just's loyalty was up in arms.

"The Scarlet Pimpernel," he said, "cares naught for your political aims. The work of mercy that he does, he does for justice and for humanity."

"And for sport," said de Batz with a sneer, "so I've been told."

"He is English," assented St. Just, "and as such will never own to sentiment. Whatever be the motive, look at the result!

"Yes! a few lives stolen from the guillotine."

"Women and children—innocent victims—would have perished but for his devotion."

"The more innocent they were, the more helpless, the more pitiable, the louder would their blood have cried for reprisals against the wild beasts who sent them to their death."

St. Just made no reply. It was obviously useless to attempt to argue with this man, whose political aims were as far apart from those of the Scarlet Pimpernel as was the North Pole from the South.

"If any of you have influence over that hot-headed leader of yours," continued de Batz, unabashed by the silence of his friend, "I wish to God you would exert it now."

"In what way?" queried St. Just, smiling in spite of himself at the thought of his or any one else's control over Blakeney and his plans.

It was de Batz' turn to be silent. He paused for a moment or two, then he asked abruptly:

"Your Scarlet Pimpernel is in Paris now, is he not?"

"I cannot tell you," replied Armand.

"Bah! there is no necessity to fence with me, my friend. The moment I set eyes on you this afternoon I knew that you had not come to Paris alone."

"You are mistaken, my good de Batz," rejoined the young man earnestly; "I came to Paris alone."

"Clever parrying, on my word—but wholly wasted on my unbelieving ears. Did I not note at once that you did not seem overpleased to-day when I accosted you?"

"Again you are mistaken. I was very pleased to meet you, for I had felt singularly lonely all day, and was glad to shake a friend by the hand. What you took for displeasure was only surprise."

"Surprise? Ah, yes! I don't wonder that you were surprised to see me walking unmolested and openly in the streets of Paris—whereas you had heard of me as a dangerous conspirator, eh?—and as a man who has the entire police of his country at his heels—on whose head there is a price—what?"

"I knew that you had made several noble efforts to rescue the unfortunate King and Queen from the hands of these brutes."

"All of which efforts were unsuccessful," assented de Batz imperturbably, "every one of them having been either betrayed by some d——d confederate or ferreted out by some astute spy eager for gain. Yes, my friend, I made several efforts to rescue King Louis and Queen Marie Antoinette from the scaffold, and every time I was foiled, and yet here I am, you see, unscathed and free. I walk about the streets boldly, and talk to my friends as I meet them."

"You are lucky," said St. Just, not without a tinge of sarcasm.

"I have been prudent," retorted de Batz. "I have taken the

trouble to make friends there where I thought I needed them most—the mammon of unrighteousness, you know-what?"

And he laughed a broad, thick laugh of perfect self-satisfaction.

"Yes, I know," rejoined St. Just, with the tone of sarcasm still more apparent in his voice now. "You have Austrian money at your disposal."

"Any amount," said the other complacently, "and a great deal of it sticks to the grimy fingers of these patriotic makers of revolutions. Thus do I ensure my own safety. I buy it with the Emperor's money, and thus am I able to work for the restoration of the monarchy in France."

Again St. Just was silent. What could he say? Instinctively now, as the fleshy personality of the Gascon Royalist seemed to spread itself out and to fill the tiny box with his ambitious schemes and his far-reaching plans, Armand's thoughts flew back to that other plotter, the man with the pure and simple aims, the man whose slender fingers had never handled alien gold, but were ever there ready stretched out to the helpless and the weak, whilst his thoughts were only of the help that he might give them, but never of his own safety.

De Batz, however, seemed blandly unconscious of any such disparaging thoughts in the mind of his young friend, for he continued quite amiably, even though a note of anxiety seemed to make itself felt now in his smooth voice:

"We advance slowly, but step by step, my good St. Just," he said. "I have not been able to save the monarchy in the person of the King or the Queen, but I may yet do it in the person of the Dauphin."

"The Dauphin," murmured St. Just involuntarily.

That involuntary murmur, scarcely audible, so soft was it, seemed in some way to satisfy de Batz, for the keenness of his gaze relaxed, and his fat fingers ceased their nervous, intermittent tattoo on the ledge of the box.

"Yes! the Dauphin," he said, nodding his head as if in answer to his own thoughts, "or rather, let me say, the reigning King of France— Louis XVII, by the grace of God—the most precious life at present upon the whole of this earth."

"You are right there, friend de Batz," assented Armand fervently, "the most precious life, as you say, and one that must be saved at all costs."

"Yes," said de Batz calmly, "but not by your friend the Scarlet Pimpernel."

"Why not?"

Scarce were those two little words out of St. Just's mouth than he repented of them. He bit his lip, and with a dark frown upon his face he turned almost defiantly towards his friend.

But de Batz smiled with easy bonhomie.

"Ah, friend Armand," he said, "you were not cut out for diplomacy, nor yet for intrigue. So then," he added more seriously, "that gallant hero, the Scarlet Pimpernel, has hopes of rescuing our young King from the clutches of Simon the cobbler and of the herd of hyenas on the watch for his attenuated little corpse, eh?"

"I did not say that," retorted St. Just sullenly.

"No. But I say it. Nay! nay! do not blame yourself, my over-loyal young friend. Could I, or any one else, doubt for a moment that sooner or later your romantic hero would turn his attention to the most pathetic sight in the whole of Europe—the child-martyr in the Temple prison? The wonder were to me if the Scarlet Pimpernel ignored our little King altogether for the sake of his subjects. No, no; do not think for a moment that you have betrayed your friend's secret to me. When I met you so luckily today I guessed at once that you were here under the banner of the enigmatical little red flower, and, thus guessing, I even went a step further in my conjecture. The Scarlet Pimpernel is in Paris now in the hope of rescuing Louis XVII from the Temple prison."

"If that is so, you must not only rejoice but should be able to help."

"And yet, my friend, I do neither the one now nor mean to do the other in the future," said de Batz placidly. "I happen to be a Frenchman, you see."

"What has that to do with such a question?"

"Everything; though you, Armand, despite that you are a Frenchman too, do not look through my spectacles. Louis XVII is King of France, my good St. Just; he must owe his freedom and his life to us Frenchmen, and to no one else."

"That is sheer madness, man," retorted Armand. "Would you have the child perish for the sake of your own selfish ideas?"

"You may call them selfish if you will; all patriotism is in a measure selfish. What does the rest of the world care if we are a republic or a monarchy, an oligarchy or hopeless anarchy? We work for ourselves and to please ourselves, and I for one will not brook foreign interference."

"Yet you work with foreign money!"

"That is another matter. I cannot get money in France, so I get it where I can; but I can arrange for the escape of Louis XVII is King of France, my good St. Just; he must of France should belong the honour and glory of having saved our King."

For the third time now St. Just allowed the conversation to drop; he was gazing wide-eyed, almost appalled at this impudent display of well-nigh ferocious selfishness and vanity. De Batz, smiling and complacent, was leaning back in his chair, looking at his young friend with perfect contentment expressed in every line of his pock-marked face and in the very attitude of his well-fed body. It was easy enough now to understand the remarkable immunity which this man was enjoying, despite the many foolhardy plots which he hatched, and which had up to now invariably come to naught.

A regular braggart and empty windbag, he had taken but one good care, and that was of his own skin. Unlike other less fortunate Royalists of France, he neither fought in the country nor braved dangers in town. He played a safer game—crossed the frontier and constituted himself agent of Austria; he succeeded in gaining the Emperor's money for the good of the Royalist cause, and for his own most especial benefit.

Even a less astute man of the world than was Armand St. Just would easily have guessed that de Batz' desire to be the only instrument in the rescue of the poor little Dauphin from the Temple was not actuated by patriotism, but solely by greed. Obviously there was a rich reward waiting for him in Vienna the day that he brought Louis XVII safely into Austrian territory; that reward he would miss if a meddlesome Englishman interfered in this affair. Whether in this wrangle he risked the life of the child-King or not mattered to him not at all. It was de Batz who was to get the reward, and whose welfare and prosperity mattered more than the most precious life in Europe.

St. Just would have given much to be back in his lonely squalid lodgings now. Too late did he realise how wise had been the dictum which had warned him against making or renewing friendships in France.

Men had changed with the times. How terribly they had changed! Personal safety had become a fetish with most—a goal so difficult to attain that it had to be fought for and striven for, even at the expense of humanity and of self-respect.

Selfishness—the mere, cold-blooded insistence for self-advancement—ruled supreme. De Batz, surfeited with foreign money, used it firstly to ensure his own immunity, scattering it to right and left to still the ambition of the Public Prosecutor or to satisfy the greed of innumerable spies.

What was left over he used for the purpose of pitting the bloodthirsty demagogues one against the other, making of the National Assembly a gigantic bear-den, wherein wild beasts could rend one another limb from limb.

In the meanwhile, what cared he—he said it himself—whether hundreds of innocent martyrs perished miserably and uselessly? They were the necessary food whereby the Revolution was to be satiated and de Batz' schemes enabled to mature. The most precious life in Europe even was only to be saved if its price went to swell the pockets of de Batz, or to further his future ambitions.

Times had indeed changed an entire nation. St. Just felt as sickened with this self-seeking Royalist as he did with the savage brutes who struck to right or left for their own delectation. He was meditating immediate flight back to his lodgings, with a hope of finding there a word for him from the chief—a word to remind him that men did live nowadays who had other aims besides their own advancement—other ideals besides the deification of self.

The curtain had descended on the first act, and traditionally, as the works of M. de Moliere demanded it, the three knocks were heard again without any interval. St. Just rose ready with a pretext for parting with his friend. The curtain was being slowly drawn up on the second act, and disclosed Alceste in wrathful conversation with Celimene.

Alceste's opening speech is short. Whilst the actor spoke it Armand had his back to the stage; with hand outstretched, he was murmuring what he hoped would prove a polite excuse for thus leaving his amiable host while the entertainment had only just begun.

De Batz—vexed and impatient—had not by any means finished with his friend yet. He thought that his specious arguments—delivered with boundless conviction—had made some impression on the mind of the young man. That impression, however, he desired to deepen, and whilst Armand was worrying his brain to find a plausible excuse for going away, de Batz was racking his to find one for keeping him here.

Then it was that the wayward demon Chance intervened. Had St. Just risen but two minutes earlier, had his active mind suggested the desired excuse more readily, who knows what unspeakable sorrow, what heartrending misery, what terrible shame might have been spared both him and those for whom he cared? Those two minutes—did he but know it—decided the whole course of his future life. The excuse hovered on his lips, de Batz reluctantly was preparing to bid him good-bye, when Celimene, speaking common-place words enough in answer to her quarrelsome lover, caused him to drop the hand which he was holding out to his friend and to turn back towards the stage.

It was an exquisite voice that had spoken—a voice mellow and tender, with deep tones in it that betrayed latent power. The voice had caused Armand to look, the lips that spoke forged the first tiny link of that chain which riveted him forever after to the speaker.

It is difficult to say if such a thing really exists as love at first sight. Poets and romancists will have us believe that it does; idealists swear by it as being the only true love worthy of the name.

I do not know if I am prepared to admit their theory with regard to Armand St. Just. Mlle. Lange's exquisite voice certainly had charmed him to the extent of making him forget his mistrust of de Batz and his desire to get away. Mechanically almost he sat down again, and leaning both elbows on the edge of the box, he rested his chin in his hand, and listened. The words which the late M. de Moliere puts into the mouth of Celimene are trite and flippant enough, yet every time that Mlle. Lange's lips moved Armand watched her, entranced.

There, no doubt, the matter would have ended: a young man fascinated by a pretty woman on the stage—'tis a small matter, and one from which there doth not often spring a weary trail of tragic circumstances. Armand, who had a passion for music, would have worshipped at the shrine of Mlle. Lange's perfect voice until the curtain came down on the last act, had not his friend de Batz seen the keen enchantment which the actress had produced on the young enthusiast.

Now de Batz was a man who never allowed an opportunity to slip by, if that opportunity led towards the furtherance of his own desires. He did not want to lose sight of Armand just yet, and here the good demon Chance had given him an opportunity for obtaining what he wanted.

He waited quietly until the fall of the curtain at the end of Act II.; then, as Armand, with a sigh of delight, leaned back in his chair, and closing his eyes appeared to be living the last half-hour all over again, de Batz remarked with well-assumed indifference:

"Mlle. Lange is a promising young actress. Do you not think so, my friend?"

"She has a perfect voice—it was exquisite melody to the ear," replied Armand. "I was conscious of little else."

"She is a beautiful woman, nevertheless," continued de Batz with a smile. "During the next act, my good St. Just, I would suggest that you open your eyes as well as your ears."

Armand did as he was bidden. The whole appearance of Mlle. Lange seemed in harmony with her voice. She was not very tall, but eminently graceful, with a small, oval face and slender, almost childlike figure, which appeared still more so above the wide hoops and draped panniers of the fashions of Moliere's time.

Whether she was beautiful or not the young man hardly knew. Measured by certain standards, she certainly was not so, for her mouth was not small, and her nose anything but classical in outline. But the eyes were brown, and they had that half-veiled look in them—shaded with long lashes that seemed to make a perpetual tender appeal to the masculine heart: the lips, too, were full and moist, and the teeth dazzling white. Yes!—on the whole we might easily say that she was exquisite, even though we did not admit that she was beautiful.

Painter David has made a sketch of her; we have all seen it at the Musee Carnavalet, and all wondered why that charming, if irregular, little face made such an impression of sadness.

There are five acts in "Le Misanthrope," during which Celimene is almost constantly on the stage. At the end of the fourth act de Batz said casually to his friend:

"I have the honour of personal acquaintanceship with Mlle. Lange. An you care for an introduction to her, we can go round to the green room after the play."

Did prudence then whisper, "Desist"? Did loyalty to the leader murmur, "Obey"? It were indeed difficult to say. Armand St. Just was not five-and-twenty, and Mlle. Lange's melodious voice spoke louder than the whisperings of prudence or even than the call of duty.

He thanked de Batz warmly, and during the last half-hour, while the misanthropical lover spurned repentant Celimene, he was conscious of a curious sensation of impatience, a tingling of his nerves, a wild, mad longing to hear those full moist lips pronounce his name, and have those large brown eyes throw their half-veiled look into his own.

# CHAPTER 4: MADEMOISELLE LANGE

The green-room was crowded when de Batz and St. Just arrived there after the performance. The older man cast a hasty glance through the open door. The crowd did not suit his purpose, and he dragged his companion hurriedly away from the contemplation of Mlle. Lange, sitting in a far corner of the room, surrounded by an admiring throng, and by innumerable floral tributes offered to her beauty and to her success.

De Batz without a word led the way back towards the stage. Here, by the dim light of tallow candles fixed in sconces against the surrounding walls, the scene-shifters were busy moving drop-scenes, back cloths and wings, and paid no heed to the two men who strolled slowly up and down silently, each wrapped in his own thoughts.

Armand walked with his hands buried in his breeches pockets, his head bent forward on his chest; but every now and again he threw quick, apprehensive glances round him whenever a firm step echoed along the empty stage or a voice rang clearly through the now deserted theatre.

"Are we wise to wait here?" he asked, speaking to himself rather than to his companion.

He was not anxious about his own safety; but the words of de Batz had impressed themselves upon his mind: "Heron and his spies we have always with us."

From the green-room a separate foyer and exit led directly out into the street. Gradually the sound of many voices, the loud laughter and occasional snatches of song which for the past half-hour had proceeded from that part of the house, became more subdued and more rare. One by one the friends of the artists were leaving the theatre, after having paid the usual banal compliments to those whom they favoured, or presented the accustomed offering of flowers to the brightest star of the night.

The actors were the first to retire, then the older actresses, the ones who could no longer command a court of admirers round them. They all filed out of the greenroom and crossed the stage to where, at the back, a narrow, rickety wooden stairs led to their so-called dressing-rooms—tiny, dark cubicles, ill-lighted, unventilated, where some half-dozen of the lesser stars tumbled over one another while removing wigs and grease-paint.

Armand and de Batz watched this exodus, both with equal impatience. Mlle. Lange was the last to leave the green-room. For some time, since the crowd had become thinner round her, Armand had contrived to catch glimpses of her slight, elegant figure. A short passage led from the stage to the green-room door, which was wide open, and at the corner of this passage the young man had paused from time to time in his walk, gazing with earnest admiration at the dainty outline of the young girl's head, with its wig of powdered curls that seemed scarcely whiter than the creamy brilliance of her skin.

De Batz did not watch Mlle. Lange beyond casting impatient looks in the direction of the crowd that prevented her leaving the green-room. He did watch Armand, however—noted his eager look, his brisk and alert movements, the obvious glances of admiration which he cast in the direction of the young actress, and this seemed to afford him a considerable amount of contentment.

The best part of an hour had gone by since the fall of the curtain before Mlle. Lange finally dismissed her many admirers, and de Batz had the satisfaction of seeing her running down the passage, turning back occasionally in order to bid gay "good-nights" to the loiterers who were loath to part from her. She was a child in all her movements, quite unconscious of self or of her own charms, but frankly delighted with her success. She was still dressed in the ridiculous hoops and panniers pertaining to her part, and the powdered peruke hid the charm of her own hair; the costume gave a certain stilted air to her unaffected personality, which, by this very sense of contrast, was essentially fascinating.

In her arms she held a huge sheaf of sweet-scented narcissi, the spoils of some favoured spot far away in the South. Armand thought that never in his life had he seen anything so winsome or so charming.

Having at last said the positively final adieu, Mlle. Lange with a happy little sigh turned to run down the passage.

She came face to face with Armand, and gave a sudden little gasp of terror. It was not good these days to come on any loiterer unawares.

But already de Batz had quickly joined his friend, and his smooth, pleasant voice, and podgy, beringed hand extended towards Mlle. Lange, were sufficient to reassure her.

"You were so surrounded in the green-room, mademoiselle," he said courteously, "I did not venture to press in among the crowd of your admirers. Yet I had the great wish to present my respectful congratulations in person."

"Ah! c'est ce cher de Batz!" exclaimed mademoiselle gaily, in that exquisitely rippling voice of hers. "And where in the world do you spring from, my friend?

"Hush-sh-sh!" he whispered, holding her small bemittened hand in his, and putting one finger to his lips with an urgent entreaty for discretion; "not my name, I beg of you, fair one."

"Bah!" she retorted lightly, even though her full lips trembled now as she spoke and belied her very words. "You need have no fear whilst you are in this part of the house. It is an understood thing that the Committee of General Security does not send its spies behind the curtain of a theatre. Why, if all of us actors and actresses were sent to the guillotine there would be no play on the morrow. Artistes are not replaceable in a few hours; those that are in existence must perforce be spared, or the citizens who govern us now would not know where to spend their evenings."

But though she spoke so airily and with her accustomed gaiety, it was easily perceived that even on this childish mind the dangers which beset every one these days had already imprinted their mark of suspicion and of caution.

"Come into my dressing-room," she said. "I must not tarry here any longer, for they will be putting out the lights. But I have a room to myself, and we can talk there quite agreeably."

She led the way across the stage towards the wooden stairs. Armand, who during this brief colloquy between his friend and the young girl had kept discreetly in the background, felt undecided what to do. But at a peremptory sign from de Batz he, too, turned in the wake of the gay little lady, who ran swiftly up the rickety steps, humming snatches of popular songs the while, and not turning to see if indeed the two men were following her.

She had the sheaf of narcissi still in her arms, and the door of her tiny dressing-room being open, she ran straight in and threw the flowers down in a confused, sweet-scented mass upon the small table that stood at one end of the room, littered with pots and bottles, letters, mirrors, powder-puffs, silk stockings, and cambric handkerchiefs.

Then she turned and faced the two men, a merry look of unalterable gaiety dancing in her eyes.

"Shut the door, mon ami," she said to de Batz, "and after that sit down where you can, so long as it is not on my most precious pot of unguent or a box of costliest powder."

While de Batz did as he was told, she turned to Armand and said with a pretty tone of interrogation in her melodious voice:

"Monsieur?"

"St. Just, at your service, mademoiselle," said Armand, bowing very low in the most approved style obtaining at the English Court.

"St. Just?" she repeated, a look of puzzlement in her brown eyes. "Surely—"

"A kinsman of citizen St. Just, whom no doubt you know, mademoiselle," he exclaimed.

"My friend Armand St. Just," interposed de Batz, "is practically a new-comer in Paris. He lives in England habitually."

"In England?" she exclaimed. "Oh! do tell me all about England. I would love to go there. Perhaps I may have to go some day. Oh! do sit down, de Batz," she continued, talking rather volubly, even as a delicate blush heightened the colour in her cheeks under the look of obvious admiration from Armand St. Just's expressive eyes.

She swept a handful of delicate cambric and silk from off a chair, making room for de Batz' portly figure. Then she sat upon the sofa, and with an inviting gesture and a call from the eyes she bade Armand sit down next to her. She leaned back against the cushions, and the table being close by, she stretched out a hand and once more took up the bunch of narcissi, and while she talked to Armand she held the snow-white blooms quite close to her face—so close, in fact, that he could not see her mouth and chin, only her dark eyes shone across at him over the heads of the blossoms.

"Tell me all about England," she reiterated, settling herself down among the cushions like a spoilt child who is about to listen to an oft-told favourite story.

Armand was vexed that de Batz was sitting there. He felt he could have told this dainty little lady quite a good deal about England if only his pompous, fat friend would have had the good sense to go away.

As it was, he felt unusually timid and gauche, not quite knowing what to say, a fact which seemed to amuse Mlle. Lange not a little.

"I am very fond of England," he said lamely; "my sister is married to an Englishman, and I myself have taken up my permanent residence there."

"Among the society of emigres?" she queried.

Then, as Armand made no reply, de Batz interposed quickly:

"Oh! you need not fear to admit it, my good Armand; Mademoiselle Lange, has many friends among the emigres—have you not, mademoiselle?"

"Yes, of course," she replied lightly; "I have friends everywhere. Their political views have nothing to do with me. Artistes, I think, should have naught to do with politics. You see, citizen St. Just, I never inquired of you what were your views. Your name and kinship would proclaim you a partisan of citizen Robespierre, yet I find you in the company of M. de Batz; and you tell me that you live in England."

"He is no partisan of citizen Robespierre," again interposed de Batz; "in fact, mademoiselle, I may safely tell you, I think, that my friend has but one ideal on this earth, whom he has set up in a shrine, and whom he worships with all the ardour of a Christian for his God."

"How romantic!" she said, and she looked straight at Armand. "Tell me, monsieur, is your ideal a woman or a man?"

His look answered her, even before he boldly spoke the two words:

"A woman."

She took a deep draught of sweet, intoxicating scent from the narcissi, and his gaze once more brought blushes to her cheeks. De Batz' good-humoured laugh helped her to hide this unwonted access of confusion.

"That was well turned, friend Armand," he said lightly; "but I assure you, mademoiselle, that before I brought him here to-night his ideal was a man."

"A man!" she exclaimed, with a contemptuous little pout. "Who was it?"

"I know no other name for him but that of a small, insignificant flower—the Scarlet Pimpernel," replied de Batz.

"The Scarlet Pimpernel!" she ejaculated, dropping the flowers suddenly, and gazing on Armand with wide, wondering eyes. "And do you know him, monsieur?"

He was frowning despite himself, despite the delight which he felt at sitting so close to this charming little lady, and feeling that in a measure his presence and his personality interested her. But he felt irritated with de Batz, and angered at what he considered the latter's indiscretion. To him the very name of his leader was almost a sacred one; he was one of those enthusiastic devotees who only care to name the idol of their dreams with bated breath, and only in the ears of those who would understand and sympathise.

Again he felt that if only he could have been alone with mademoiselle he could have told her all about the Scarlet Pimpernel, knowing that in her he would find a ready listener, a helping and a loving heart; but as it was he merely replied tamely enough:

"Yes, mademoiselle, I do know him."

"You have seen him?" she queried eagerly; "spoken to him?"

"Yes."

"Oh! do tell me all about him. You know quite a number of us in France have the greatest possible admiration for your national hero. We know, of course, that he is an enemy of our Government—but, oh! we feel that he is not an enemy of France because of that. We are a nation of heroes, too, monsieur," she added with a pretty, proud toss of the head; "we can appreciate bravery and resource, and we love the mystery that surrounds the personality of your Scarlet Pimpernel. But since you know him, monsieur, tell me what is he like?"

Armand was smiling again. He was yielding himself up wholly to the charm which emanated from this young girl's entire being, from her gaiety and her unaffectedness, her enthusiasm, and that obvious artistic temperament which caused her to feel every sensation with superlative keenness and thoroughness.

"What is he like?" she insisted.

"That, mademoiselle," he replied, "I am not at liberty to tell you."

"Not at liberty to tell me!" she exclaimed; "but monsieur, if I command you—"

"At risk of falling forever under the ban of your displeasure, mademoiselle, I would still remain silent on that subject."

She gazed on him with obvious astonishment. It was quite an unusual thing for this spoilt darling of an admiring public to be thus openly thwarted in her whims.

"How tiresome and pedantic!" she said, with a shrug of her pretty shoulders and a moue of discontent. "And, oh! how ungallant! You have learnt ugly, English ways, monsieur; for there, I am told, men hold their womenkind in very scant esteem. There!" she added, turning with a mock air of hopelessness towards de Batz, "am I not a most unlucky woman? For the past two years I have used my best endeavours to catch sight of that interesting Scarlet Pimpernel; here do I meet monsieur, who actually knows him (so he says), and he is so ungallant that he even refuses to satisfy the first cravings of my just curiosity."

"Citizen St. Just will tell you nothing now, mademoiselle," rejoined de Batz with his good-humoured laugh; "it is my presence, I assure you, which is setting a seal upon his lips. He is, believe me, aching to confide in you, to share in your enthusiasm, and to see your beautiful eyes glowing in response to his ardour when he describes to you the exploits of that prince of heroes. En tete-a-tete one day, you will, I know, worm every secret out of my discreet friend Armand."

Mademoiselle made no comment on this—that is to say, no audible comment—but she buried the whole of her face for a few seconds among the flowers, and Armand from amongst those flowers caught sight of a pair of very bright brown eyes which shone on him with a puzzled look.

She said nothing more about the Scarlet Pimpernel or about England just then, but after awhile she began talking of more indifferent subjects: the state of the weather, the price of food, the discomforts of her own house, now that the servants had been put on perfect equality with their masters.

Armand soon gathered that the burning questions of the day, the horrors of massacres, the raging turmoil of politics, had not affected her very deeply as yet. She had not troubled her pretty head very much about the social and humanitarian aspect of the present seething revolution. She did not really wish to think about it at all. An artiste to her finger-tips, she was spending her young life in earnest work, striving to attain perfection in her art, absorbed in study during the day, and in the expression of what she had learnt in the evenings.

The terrors of the guillotine affected her a little, but somewhat vaguely still. She had not realised that any dangers could assail her whilst she worked for the artistic delectation of the public.

It was not that she did not understand what went on around her, but that her artistic temperament and her environment had kept her aloof from it all. The horrors of the Place de la Revolution made her shudder, but only in the same way as the tragedies of M. Racine or of

Sophocles which she had studied caused her to shudder, and she had exactly the same sympathy for poor Queen Marie Antoinette as she had for Mary Stuart, and shed as many tears for King Louis as she did for Polyeucte.

Once de Batz mentioned the Dauphin, but mademoiselle put up her hand quickly and said in a trembling voice, whilst the tears gathered in her eyes:

"Do not speak of the child to me, de Batz. What can I, a lonely, hard-working woman, do to help him? I try not to think of him, for if I did, knowing my own helplessness, I feel that I could hate my countrymen, and speak my bitter hatred of them across the footlights; which would be more than foolish," she added naively, "for it would not help the child, and I should be sent to the guillotine. But oh sometimes I feel that I would gladly die if only that poor little child-martyr were restored to those who love him and given back once more to joy and happiness. But they would not take my life for his, I am afraid," she concluded, smiling through her tears. "My life is of no value in comparison with his."

Soon after this she dismissed her two visitors. De Batz, well content with the result of this evening's entertainment, wore an urbane, bland smile on his rubicund face. Armand, somewhat serious and not a little in love, made the hand-kiss with which he took his leave last as long as he could.

"You will come and see me again, citizen St. Just?" she asked after that preliminary leave-taking.

"At your service, mademoiselle," he replied with alacrity.

"How long do you stay in Paris?"

"I may be called away at any time."

"Well, then, come to-morrow. I shall be free towards four o'clock. Square du Roule. You cannot miss the house. Any one there will tell you where lives citizeness Lange."

"At your service, mademoiselle," he replied.

The words sounded empty and meaningless, but his eyes, as they took final leave of her, spoke the gratitude and the joy which he felt.

# Chapter 5: The Temple Prison

It was close on midnight when the two friends finally parted company outside the doors of the theatre. The night air struck with biting keenness against them when they emerged from the stuffy, overheated building, and both wrapped their caped cloaks tightly round their shoulders. Armand—more than ever now—was anxious to rid himself of de Batz. The Gascon's platitudes irritated him beyond the bounds of forbearance, and he wanted to be alone, so that he might think over the events of this night, the chief event being a little lady with an enchanting voice and the most fascinating brown eyes he had ever seen.

Self-reproach, too, was fighting a fairly even fight with the excitement that had been called up by that same pair of brown eyes. Armand for the past four or five hours had acted in direct opposition to the earnest advice given to him by his chief; he had renewed one friendship which had been far better left in oblivion, and he had made an acquaintance which already was leading him along a path that he felt sure his comrade would disapprove. But the path was so profusely strewn with scented narcissi that Armand's sensitive conscience was quickly lulled to rest by the intoxicating fragrance.

Looking neither to right nor left, he made his way very quickly up the Rue Richelieu towards the Montmartre quarter, where he lodged.

De Batz stood and watched him for as long as the dim lights of the street lamps illuminated his slim, soberly-clad figure; then he turned on his heel and walked off in the opposite direction.

His florid, pock-marked face wore an air of contentment not altogether unmixed with a kind of spiteful triumph.

"So, my pretty Scarlet Pimpernel," he muttered between his closed lips, "you wish to meddle in my affairs, to have for yourself and your friends the credit and glory of snatching the golden prize from the clutches of these murderous brutes. Well, we shall see! We shall see which is the wiliest—the French ferret or the English fox."

He walked deliberately away from the busy part of the town, turning his back on the river, stepping out briskly straight before him, and swinging his gold-beaded cane as he walked.

The streets which he had to traverse were silent and deserted, save occasionally where a drinking or an eating house had its swing-doors still invitingly open. From these places, as de Batz strode rapidly by, came sounds of loud voices, rendered raucous by outdoor oratory; volleys of oaths hurled irreverently in the midst of impassioned speeches; interruptions from rowdy audiences that vied with the speaker in invectives and blasphemies; wordy war-fares that ended in noisy vituperations; accusations hurled through the air heavy with tobacco smoke and the fumes of cheap wines and of raw spirits.

De Batz took no heed of these as he passed, anxious only that the crowd of eating-house politicians did not, as often was its wont, turn out pele-mele into the street, and settle its quarrel by the weight of fists. He did not wish to be embroiled in a street fight, which invariably ended in denunciations and arrests, and was glad when presently he had left the purlieus of the Palais Royal behind him, and could strike on his left toward the lonely Faubourg du Temple.

From the dim distance far away came at intervals the mournful sound of a roll of muffled drums, half veiled by the intervening hubbub of the busy night life of the great city. It proceeded from the Place de la Revolution, where a company of the National Guard were on night watch round the guillotine. The dull, intermittent notes of the drum came as a reminder to the free people of France that the watchdog of a vengeful revolution was alert night and day, never sleeping, ever wakeful, "beating up game for the guillotine," as the new decree framed to-day by the Government of the people had ordered that it should do.

From time to time now the silence of this lonely street was broken by a sudden cry of terror, followed by the clash of arms, the inevitable volley of oaths, the call for help, the final moan of anguish. They were the ever-recurring brief tragedies which told of denunciations, of domiciliary search, of sudden arrests, of an agonising desire for life and for freedom—for life under these same horrible conditions of brutality and of servitude, for freedom to breathe, if only a day or two longer, this air, polluted by filth and by blood.

De Batz, hardened to these scenes, paid no heed to them. He had heard it so often, that cry in the night, followed by death-like silence; it came from comfortable bourgeois houses, from squalid lodgings, or lonely cul-de-sac, wherever some hunted quarry was run to earth by the newly-organised spies of the Committee of General Security.

Five and thirty livres for every head that falls trunkless into the basket at the foot of the guillotine! Five and thirty pieces of silver, now as then, the price of innocent blood. Every cry in the night, every call for help, meant game for the guillotine, and five and thirty livres in the hands of a Judas.

And de Batz walked on unmoved by what he saw and heard, swinging his cane and looking satisfied. Now he struck into the Place de la Victoire, and looked on one of the open-air camps that had recently been established where men, women, and children were working to provide arms and accoutrements for the Republican army that was fighting the whole of Europe.

The people of France were up in arms against tyranny; and on the open places of their mighty city they were encamped day and night forging those arms which were destined to make them free, and in the meantime were bending under a yoke of tyranny more complete, more grinding and absolute than any that the most despotic kings had ever dared to inflict.

Here by the light of resin torches, at this late hour of the night, raw lads were being drilled into soldiers, half-naked under the cutting blast of the north wind, their knees shaking under them, their arms and legs blue with cold, their stomachs empty, and their teeth chattering with fear; women were sewing shirts for the great improvised army, with eyes straining to see the stitches by the flickering light of the torches, their throats parched with the continual inhaling of smoke-laden air; even children, with weak, clumsy little fingers, were picking rags to be woven into cloth again all, all these slaves were working far into the night, tired, hungry, and cold, but working unceasingly, as the country had demanded it: "the people of France in arms against tyranny!" The people of France had to set to work to make arms, to clothe the soldiers, the defenders of the people's liberty.

And from this crowd of people—men, women, and children—there came scarcely a sound, save raucous whispers, a moan or a sigh quickly suppressed. A grim silence reigned in this thickly-peopled camp; only the crackling of the torches broke that silence now and then, or the flapping of canvas in the wintry gale. They worked on sullen, desperate, and starving, with no hope of payment save the miserable rations wrung from poor tradespeople or miserable farmers, as wretched, as oppressed as themselves; no hope of payment, only fear of punishment, for that was ever present.

The people of France in arms against tyranny were not allowed to forget that grim taskmaster with the two great hands stretched upwards, holding the knife which descended mercilessly, indiscriminately on necks that did not bend willingly to the task.

A grim look of gratified desire had spread over de Batz' face as he skirted the open-air camp. Let them toil, let them groan, let them starve! The more these clouts suffer, the more brutal the heel that grinds them down, the sooner will the Emperor's money accomplish its work, the sooner will these wretches be clamoring for the monarchy, which would mean a rich reward in de Batz' pockets.

To him everything now was for the best: the tyranny, the brutality, the massacres. He gloated in the holocausts with as much satisfaction as did the most bloodthirsty Jacobin in the Convention. He would with his own hands have wielded the guillotine that worked too slowly for his ends. Let that end justify the means, was his motto. What matter if the future King of France walked up to his throne over steps made of headless corpses and rendered slippery with the blood of martyrs?

The ground beneath de Batz' feet was hard and white with the frost. Overhead the pale, wintry moon looked down serene and placid on this giant city wallowing in an ocean of misery.There, had been but little snow as yet this year, and the cold was intense. On his right now the Cimetiere des SS. Innocents lay peaceful and still beneath the wan light of the moon. A thin covering of snow lay evenly alike on grass mounds and smooth stones. Here and there a broken cross with chipped arms still held pathetically outstretched, as if in a final appeal for human love, bore mute testimony to senseless excesses and spiteful desire for destruction.

But here within the precincts of the dwelling of the eternal Master a solemn silence reigned; only the cold north wind shook the branches of the yew, causing them to send forth a melancholy sigh into the night, and to shed a shower of tiny crystals of snow like the frozen tears of the dead.

And round the precincts of the lonely graveyard, and down narrow streets or open places, the night watchmen went their rounds, lanthorn in hand, and every five minutes their monotonous call rang clearly out in the night:

"Sleep, citizens! everything is quiet and at peace!"

We may take it that de Batz did not philosophise over-much on what went on around him. He had walked swiftly up the Rue St. Martin, then turning sharply to his right he found himself beneath the tall, frowning walls of the Temple prison, the grim guardian of so many secrets, such terrible despair, such unspeakable tragedies.

Here, too, as in the Place de la Revolution, an intermittent roll of muffled drums proclaimed the ever-watchful presence of the National Guard. But with that exception not a sound stirred round the grim and stately edifice; there were no cries, no calls, no appeals around its walls. All the crying and wailing was shut in by the massive stone that told no tales.

Dim and flickering lights shone behind several of the small windows in the facade of the huge labyrinthine building. Without any hesitation de Batz turned down the Rue du Temple, and soon found himself in front of the main gates which gave on the courtyard beyond. The sentinel challenged him, but he had the pass-word, and explained that he desired to have speech with citizen Heron.

With a surly gesture the guard pointed to the heavy bell-pull up against the gate, and de Batz pulled it with all his might. The long clang of the brazen bell echoed and re-echoed round the solid stone walls. Anon a tiny judas in the gate was cautiously pushed open, and a peremptory voice once again challenged the midnight intruder.

De Batz, more peremptorily this time, asked for citizen Heron, with whom he had immediate and important business, and a glimmer of a piece of silver which he held up close to the judas secured him the necessary admittance.

The massive gates slowly swung open on their creaking hinges, and as de Batz passed beneath the archway they closed again behind him. The concierge's lodge was immediately on his left. Again he was challenged, and again gave the pass-word. But his face was apparently known here, for no serious hindrance to proceed was put in his way.

A man, whose wide, lean frame was but ill-covered by a threadbare coat and ragged breeches, and with soleless shoes on his feet, was told off to direct the citoyen to citizen Heron's rooms. The man walked slowly along with bent knees and arched spine, and shuffled his feet as he walked; the bunch of keys which he carried rattled ominously in his long, grimy hands; the passages were badly lighted, and he also carried a lanthorn to guide himself on the way.

Closely followed by de Batz, he soon turned into the central corridor, which is open to the sky above, and was spectrally alight now with flag-stones and walls gleaming beneath the silvery sheen of the moon, and throwing back the fantastic elongated shadows of the two men as they walked.

On the left, heavily barred windows gave on the corridor, as did here and there the massive oaken doors, with their gigantic hinges and bolts, on the steps of which squatted groups of soldiers wrapped in their cloaks, with wild, suspicious eyes beneath their capotes, peering at the midnight visitor as he passed.

There was no thought of silence here. The very walls seemed alive with sounds, groans and tears, loud wails and murmured prayers; they exuded from the stones and trembled on the frost-laden air.

Occasionally at one of the windows a pair of white hands would appear, grasping the heavy iron bar, trying to shake it in its socket, and mayhap, above the hands, the dim vision of a haggard face, a man's or a woman's, trying to get a glimpse of the outside world, a final look at the sky, before the last journey to the place of death to-morrow. Then one of the soldiers, with a loud, angry oath, would struggle to his feet, and with the butt-end of his gun strike at the thin, wan fingers till their hold on the iron bar relaxed, and the pallid face beyond would sink back into the darkness with a desperate cry of pain.

A quick, impatient sigh escaped de Batz' lips. He had skirted the wide courtyard in the wake of his guide, and from where he was he could see the great central tower, with its tiny windows lighted from within, the grim walls behind which the descendant of the world's conquerors, the bearer of the proudest name in Europe, and wearer of its most ancient crown, had spent the last days of his brilliant life in abject shame, sorrow, and degradation. The memory had swiftly surged up before him of that night when he all but rescued King Louis and his family from this same miserable prison: the guard had been bribed, the keeper corrupted, everything had been prepared, save the reckoning with the one irresponsible factor—chance!

He had failed then and had tried again, and again had failed; a fortune had been his reward if he had succeeded. He had failed, but even now, when his footsteps echoed along the flagged courtyard, over which an unfortunate King and Queen had walked on their way to their last ignominious Calvary, he hugged himself with the satisfying thought that where he had failed at least no one else had succeeded.

Whether that meddlesome English adventurer, who called himself the Scarlet Pimpernel, had planned the rescue of King Louis or of Queen Marie Antoinette at any time or not—that he did not know; but on one point at least he was more than ever determined, and that was that no power on earth should snatch from him the golden prize offered by Austria for the rescue of the little Dauphin.

"I would sooner see the child perish, if I cannot save him myself," was the burning thought in this man's tortuous brain. "And let that accursed Englishman look to himself and to his d——d confederates," he added, muttering a fierce oath beneath his breath.

A winding, narrow stone stair, another length or two of corridor, and his guide's shuffling footsteps paused beside a low iron-studded door let into the solid stone. De Batz dismissed his ill-clothed guide and pulled the iron bell-handle which hung beside the door.

The bell gave forth a dull and broken clang, which seemed like an echo of the wails of sorrow that peopled the huge building with their weird and monotonous sounds.

De Batz—a thoroughly unimaginative person—waited patiently beside the door until it was opened from within, and he was confronted by a tall stooping figure, wearing a greasy coat of snuff-brown cloth, and holding high above his head a lanthorn that threw its feeble light on de Batz' jovial face and form.

"It is even I, citizen Heron," he said, breaking in swiftly on the other's ejaculation of astonishment, which threatened to send his name echoing the whole length of corridors and passages, until round every corner of the labyrinthine house of sorrow the murmur would be borne on the wings of the cold night breeze: "Citizen Heron is in parley with *ci-devant* Baron de Batz!"

A fact which would have been equally unpleasant for both these worthies.

"Enter!" said Heron curtly.

He banged the heavy door to behind his visitor; and de Batz, who seemed to know his way about the place, walked straight across the narrow landing to where a smaller door stood invitingly open. He stepped boldly in, the while citizen Heron put the lanthorn down on the floor of the *couloir*, and then followed his nocturnal visitor into the room.

# CHAPTER 6: THE COMMITTEE'S AGENT

It was a narrow, ill-ventilated place, with but one barred window that gave on the courtyard. An evil-smelling lamp hung by a chain from the grimy ceiling, and in a corner of the room a tiny iron stove shed more unpleasant vapour than warm glow around.

There was but little furniture: two or three chairs, a table which was littered with papers, and a corner-cupboard—the open doors of which revealed a miscellaneous collection—bundles of papers, a tin saucepan, a piece of cold sausage, and a couple of pistols. The fumes of stale tobacco-smoke hovered in the air, and mingled most unpleasantly with those of the lamp above, and of the mildew that penetrated through the walls just below the roof.

Heron pointed to one of the chairs, and then sat down on the other, close to the table, on which he rested his elbow. He picked up a short-stemmed pipe, which he had evidently laid aside at the sound of the bell, and having taken several deliberate long-drawn puffs from it, he said abruptly:

"Well, what is it now?"

In the meanwhile de Batz had made himself as much at home in this uncomfortable room as he possibly could. He had deposited his hat and cloak on one rickety rush-bottomed chair, and drawn another close to the fire. He sat down with one leg crossed over the other, his podgy be-ringed hand wandering with loving gentleness down the length of his shapely calf.

He was nothing if not complacent, and his complacency seemed highly to irritate his friend Heron.

"Well, what is it?" reiterated the latter, drawing his visitor's attention roughly to himself by banging his fist on the table. "Out with it! What do you want? Why have you come at this hour of the night to compromise me, I suppose—bring your own d—d neck and mine into the same noose—what?"

"Easy, easy, my friend," responded de Batz imperturbably; "waste not so much time in idle talk. Why do I usually come to see you? Surely you have had no cause to complain hitherto of the unprofitableness of my visits to you?"

"They will have to be still more profitable to me in the future," growled the other across the table. "I have more power now."

"I know you have," said de Batz suavely. "The new decree? What? You may denounce whom you please, search whom you please, arrest whom you please, and send whom you please to the Supreme Tribunal without giving them the slightest chance of escape."

"Is it in order to tell me all this that you have come to see me at this hour of the night?" queried Heron with a sneer.

"No; I came at this hour of the night because I surmised that in the future you and your hell-hounds would be so busy all day 'beating up game for the guillotine' that the only time you would have at the disposal of your friends would be the late hours of the night. I saw you at the theatre a couple of hours ago, friend Heron; I didn't think to find you yet abed."

"Well, what do you want?"

"Rather," retorted de Batz blandly, "shall we say, what do *you* want, citizen Heron?"

"For what?

"For my continued immunity at the hands of yourself and your pack?"

Heron pushed his chair brusquely aside and strode across the narrow room deliberately facing the portly figure of de Batz, who with head slightly inclined on one side, his small eyes narrowed till they appeared mere slits in his pockmarked face, was steadily and quite placidly contemplating this inhuman monster who had this very day been given uncontrolled power over hundreds of thousands of human lives.

Heron was one of those tall men who look mean in spite of their height. His head was small and narrow, and his hair, which was sparse and lank, fell in untidy strands across his forehead. He stooped slightly from the neck, and his chest, though wide, was hollow between the shoulders. But his legs were big and bony, slightly bent at the knees, like those of an ill-conditioned horse.

The face was thin and the cheeks sunken; the eyes, very large and prominent, had a look in them of cold and ferocious cruelty, a look which contrasted strangely with the weakness and petty greed apparent in the mouth, which was flabby, with full, very red lips, and chin that sloped away to the long thin neck.

Even at this moment as he gazed on de Batz the greed and the cruelty in him were fighting one of those battles the issue of which is always uncertain in men of his stamp.

"I don't know," he said slowly, "that I am prepared to treat with you any longer. You are an intolerable bit of vermin that has annoyed the Committee of General Security for over two years now. It would be excessively pleasant to crush you once and for all, as one would a buzzing fly."

"Pleasant, perhaps, but immeasurably foolish," rejoined de Batz coolly; "you would only get thirty-five livres for my head, and I offer you ten times that amount for the self-same commodity."

"I know, I know; but the whole thing has become too dangerous."

"Why? I am very modest. I don't ask a great deal. Let your hounds keep off my scent."

"You have too many d—d confederates."

"Oh! Never mind about the others. I am not bargaining about them. Let them look after themselves."

"Every time we get a batch of them, one or the other denounces you."

"Under torture, I know," rejoined de Batz placidly, holding his podgy hands to the warm glow of the fire. "For you have started torture in your house of Justice now, eh, friend Heron? You and your friend the Public Prosecutor have gone the whole gamut of devilry—eh?"

"What's that to you?" retorted the other gruffly.

"Oh, nothing, nothing! I was even proposing to pay you three thousand five hundred livres for the privilege of taking no further interest in what goes on inside this prison!"

"Three thousand five hundred!" ejaculated Heron involuntarily, and this time even his eyes lost their cruelty; they joined issue with the mouth in an expression of hungering avarice.

"Two little zeros added to the thirty-five, which is all you would get for handing me over to your accursed Tribunal," said de Batz, and, as if thoughtlessly, his hand wandered to the inner pocket of his coat, and a slight rustle as of thin crisp paper brought drops of moisture to the lips of Heron.

"Leave me alone for three weeks and the money is yours," concluded de Batz pleasantly.

There was silence in the room now. Through the narrow barred window the steely rays of the moon fought with the dim yellow light of the oil lamp, and lit up the pale face of the Committee's agent with its lines of cruelty in sharp conflict with those of greed.

"Well! is it a bargain?" asked de Batz at last in his usual smooth, oily voice, as he half drew from out his pocket that tempting little bundle of crisp printed paper. "You have only to give me the usual receipt for the money and it is yours."

Heron gave a vicious snarl.

"It is dangerous, I tell you. That receipt, if it falls into some cursed meddler's hands, would send me straight to the guillotine."

"The receipt could only fall into alien hands," rejoined de Batz blandly, "if I happened to be arrested, and even in that case they could but fall into those of the chief agent of the Committee of General Security, and he hath name Heron. You must take some risks, my friend. I take them too. We are each in the other's hands. The bargain is quite fair."

For a moment or two longer Heron appeared to be hesitating whilst de Batz watched him with keen intentness. He had no doubt himself as to the issue. He had tried most of these patriots in his own golden crucible, and had weighed their patriotism against Austrian money, and had never found the latter wanting.

He had not been here to-night if he were not quite sure. This inveterate conspirator in the Royalist cause never took personal risks. He looked on Heron now, smiling to himself the while with perfect satisfaction.

"Very well," said the Committee's agent with sudden decision, "I'll take the money. But on one condition."

"What is it?"

"That you leave little Capet alone."

"The Dauphin!"

"Call him what you like," said Heron, taking a step nearer to de Batz, and from his great height glowering down in fierce hatred and rage upon his accomplice; "call the young devil what you like, but leave us to deal with him."

"To kill him, you mean? Well, how can I prevent it, my friend?"

"You and your like are always plotting to get him out of here. I won't have it. I tell you I won't have it. If the brat disappears I am a dead man. Robespierre and his gang have told me as much. So you leave him alone, or I'll not raise a finger to help you, but will lay my own hands on your accursed neck."

He looked so ferocious and so merciless then, that despite himself, the selfish adventurer, the careless self-seeking intriguer, shuddered with a quick wave of unreasoning terror. He turned away from Heron's piercing gaze, the gaze of a hyena whose prey is being snatched from beneath its nails. For a moment he stared thoughtfully into the fire.

He heard the other man's heavy footsteps cross and re-cross the narrow room, and was conscious of the long curved shadow creeping up the mildewed wall or retreating down upon the carpetless floor.

Suddenly, without any warning he felt a grip upon his shoulder. He gave a start and almost uttered a cry of alarm which caused Heron to laugh. The Committee's agent was vastly amused at his friend's obvious access of fear. There was nothing that he liked better than that he should inspire dread in the hearts of all those with whom he came in contact.

"I am just going on my usual nocturnal round," he said abruptly. "Come with me, citizen de Batz."

A certain grim humour was apparent in his face as he proffered this invitation, which sounded like a rough command. As de Batz seemed to hesitate he nodded peremptorily to him to follow. Already he had gone into the hall and picked up his lanthorn. From beneath his waistcoat he drew forth a bunch of keys, which he rattled impatiently, calling to his friend to come.

"Come, citizen," he said roughly. "I wish to show you the one treasure in this house which your d—d fingers must not touch."

Mechanically de Batz rose at last. He tried to be master of the terror which was invading his very bones. He would not own to himself even that he was afraid, and almost audibly he kept murmuring to himself that he had no cause for fear.

Heron would never touch him. The spy's avarice, his greed of money were a perfect safeguard for any man who had the control of millions, and Heron knew, of course, that he could make of this inveterate plotter a comfortable source of revenue for himself. Three weeks would soon be over, and fresh bargains could be made time and again, while de Batz was alive and free.

Heron was still waiting at the door, even whilst de Batz wondered what this nocturnal visitation would reveal to him of atrocity and of outrage. He made a final effort to master his nervousness, wrapped his cloak tightly around him, and followed his host out of the room.

# CHAPTER 7: THE MOST PRECIOUS LIFE IN EUROPE

Once more he was being led through the interminable corridors of the gigantic building. Once more from the narrow, barred windows close by him he heard the heart-breaking sighs, the moans, the curses which spoke of tragedies that he could only guess.

Heron was walking on ahead of him, preceding him by some fifty metres or so, his long legs covering the distances more rapidly than de Batz could follow them. The latter knew his way well about the old prison. Few men in Paris possessed that accurate knowledge of its intricate passages and its network of cells and halls which de Batz had acquired after close and persevering study.

He himself could have led Heron to the doors of the tower where the little Dauphin was being kept imprisoned, but unfortunately he did not possess the keys that would open all the doors which led to it. There were sentinels at every gate, groups of soldiers at each end of every corridor, the great—now empty—courtyards, thronged with prisoners in the daytime, were alive with soldiery even now. Some walked up and down with fixed bayonet on shoulder, others sat in groups on the stone copings or squatted on the ground, smoking or playing cards, but all of them were alert and watchful.

Heron was recognised everywhere the moment he appeared, and though in these days of equality no one presented arms, nevertheless every guard stood aside to let him pass, or when necessary opened a gate for the powerful chief agent of the Committee of General Security.

Indeed, de Batz had no keys such as these to open the way for him to the presence of the martyred little King.

Thus the two men wended their way on in silence, one preceding the other. De Batz walked leisurely, thought-fully, taking stock of everything he saw—the gates, the barriers, the positions of sentinels and warders, of everything in fact that might prove a help or a hindrance presently, when the great enterprise would be hazarded. At last—still in the wake of Heron—he found himself once more behind the main entrance gate, underneath the archway on which gave the guichet of the concierge.

Here, too, there seemed to be an unnecessary number of soldiers: two were doing sentinel outside the guichet, but there were others in a file against the wall.

Heron rapped with his keys against the door of the concierge's lodge, then, as it was not immediately opened from within, he pushed it open with his foot.

"The concierge?" he queried peremptorily.

From a corner of the small panelled room there came a grunt and a reply:

"Gone to bed, *quoi!*"

The man who previously had guided de Batz to Heron's door slowly struggled to his feet. He had been squatting somewhere in the gloom, and had been roused by Heron's rough command. He slouched forward now still carrying a boot in one hand and a blacking brush in the other.

"Take this lanthorn, then," said the chief agent with a snarl directed at the sleeping concierge, "and come along. Why are you still here?" he added, as if in after-thought.

"The citizen concierge was not satisfied with the way I had done his boots," muttered the man, with an evil leer as he spat contemptuously on the floor; "*an aristo, quoi?* A hell of a place this . . . twenty cells to sweep out every day . . . and boots to clean for every *aristo* of a concierge or warder who demands it. . . . Is that work for a free born patriot, I ask?"

"Well, if you are not satisfied, citoyen Dupont," retorted Heron dryly, "you may go when you like, you know there are plenty of others ready to do your work..."

"Nineteen hours a day, and nineteen sous by way of payment . . . . I have had fourteen days of this convict work . . ."

He continued to mutter under his breath, whilst Heron, paying no further heed to him, turned abruptly towards a group of soldiers stationed outside.

"*En avant*, corporal!" he said; "bring four men with you . . . we go up to the tower."

The small procession was formed. On ahead the lanthorn-bearer, with arched spine and shaking knees, dragging shuffling footsteps along the corridor, then the corporal with two of his soldiers, then Heron closely followed by de Batz, and finally two more soldiers bringing up the rear.

Heron had given the bunch of keys to the man Dupont. The latter, on ahead, holding the lanthorn aloft, opened one gate after another. At each gate he waited for the little procession to file through, then he re-locked the gate and passed on.

Up two or three flights of winding stairs set in the solid stone, and the final heavy door was reached.

De Batz was meditating. Heron's precautions for the safe-guarding of the most precious life in Europe were more complete than he had anticipated. What lavish liberality would be required! what superhuman ingenuity and boundless courage in order to break down all the barriers that had been set up round that young life that flickered inside this grim tower!

Of these three requisites the corpulent, complacent intriguer possessed only the first in a considerable degree. He could be exceedingly liberal with the foreign money which he had at his disposal. As for courage and ingenuity, he believed that he possessed both, but these qualities had not served him in very good stead in the attempts which he had made at different times to rescue the unfortunate members of the Royal Family from prison. His overwhelming egotism would not admit for a moment that in ingenuity and pluck the Scarlet Pimpernel and his English followers could outdo him, but he did wish to make quite sure that they would not interfere with him in the highly remunerative work of saving the Dauphin.

Heron's impatient call roused him from these meditations. The little party had come to a halt outside a massive iron-studded door.

At a sign from the chief agent the soldiers stood at attention. He then called de Batz and the lanthorn-bearer to him.

He took a key from his breeches pocket, and with his own hand unlocked the massive door. He curtly ordered the lanthorn-bearer and de Batz to go through, then he himself went in, and finally once more re-locked the door behind him, the soldiers remaining on guard on the landing outside.

Now the three men were standing in a square antechamber, dank and dark, devoid of furniture save for a large cupboard that filled the whole of one wall; the others, mildewed and stained, were covered with a greyish paper, which here and there hung away in strips.

Heron crossed this ante-chamber, and with his knuckles rapped against a small door opposite.

"*Hola!*" he shouted, "*Simon, mon vieux, tu es la?*"

From the inner room came the sound of voices, a man's and a woman's, and now, as if in response to Heron's call, the shrill tones of a child. There was some shuffling, too, of footsteps, and some pushing about of furniture, then the door was opened, and a gruff voice invited the belated visitors to enter.

The atmosphere in this further room was so thick that at first de Batz was only conscious of the evil smells that pervaded it; smells which were made up of the fumes of tobacco, of burning coke, of a smoky lamp, and of stale food, and mingling through it all the pungent odour of raw spirits.

Heron had stepped briskly in, closely followed by de Batz. The man Dupont with a mutter of satisfaction put down his lanthorn and curled himself up in a corner of the antechamber. His interest in the spectacle so favoured by citizen Heron had apparently been exhausted by constant repetition.

De Batz looked round him with keen curiosity with which

disgust was ready enough to mingle.

The room itself might have been a large one; it was almost impossible to judge of its size, so crammed was it with heavy and light furniture of every conceivable shape and type. There was a monumental wooden bedstead in one corner, a huge sofa covered in black horsehair in another. A large table stood in the centre of the room, and there were at least four capacious armchairs round it. There were wardrobes and cabinets, a diminutive washstand and a huge pier-glass, there were innumerable boxes and packing-cases, cane-bottomed chairs and what-nots every-where. The place looked like a depot for second-hand furniture.

In the midst of all the litter de Batz at last became conscious of two people who stood staring at him and at Heron. He saw a man before him, somewhat fleshy of build, with smooth, mouse-coloured hair brushed away from a central parting, and ending in a heavy curl above each ear; the eyes were wide open and pale in colour, the lips unusually thick and with a marked downward droop. Close beside him stood a youngish-looking woman, whose unwieldy bulk, however, and pallid skin revealed the sedentary life and the ravages of ill-health.

Both appeared to regard Heron with a certain amount of awe, and de Batz with a vast measure of curiosity.

Suddenly the woman stood aside, and in the far corner of the room there was displayed to the Gascon Royalist's cold, calculating gaze the pathetic figure of the uncrowned King of France.

"How is it Capet is not yet in bed?" queried Heron as soon as he caught sight of the child.

"He wouldn't say his prayers this evening," replied Simon with a coarse laugh, "and wouldn't drink his medicine. Bah!" he added with a snarl, "this is a place for dogs and not for human folk."

"If you are not satisfied, mon vieux," retorted Heron curtly, "you can send in your resignation when you like. There are plenty who will be glad of the place."

The ex-cobbler gave another surly growl and expectorated on the floor in the direction where stood the child.

"Little vermin," he said, "he is more trouble than man or woman can bear."

The boy in the meanwhile seemed to take but little notice of the vulgar insults put upon him by his guardian. He stood, a quaint, impassive little figure, more interested apparently in de Batz, who was a stranger to him, than in the three others whom he knew. De Batz noted that the child looked well nourished, and that he was warmly clad in a rough woollen shirt and cloth breeches, with coarse grey stockings and thick shoes; but he also saw that the clothes were indescribably filthy, as were the child's hands and face. The golden curls, among which a young and queenly mother had once loved to pass her slender perfumed fingers, now hung bedraggled, greasy, and lank round the little face, from the lines of which every trace of dignity and of simplicity had long since been erased.

There was no look of the martyr about this child now, even though, mayhap, his small back had often smarted under his vulgar tutor's rough blows; rather did the pale young face wear the air of sullen indifference, and an abject desire to please, which would have appeared heart-breaking to any spectator less self-seeking and egotistic than was this Gascon conspirator.

Madame Simon had called him to her while her man and the citizen Heron were talking, and the child went readily enough, without any sign of fear. She took the corner of her coarse dirty apron in her hand, and wiped the boy's mouth and face with it.

"I can't keep him clean," she said with an apologetic shrug of the shoulders and a look at de Batz. "There now," she added, speaking once more to the child, "drink like a good boy, and say your lesson to please *maman*, and then you shall go to bed."

She took a glass from the table, which was filled with a clear liquid that de Batz at first took to be water, and held it to the boy's lips. He turned his head away and began to whimper.

"Is the medicine very nasty?" queried de Batz.

"*Mon Dieu!* but no, citizen," exclaimed the woman, "it is good strong eau de vie, the best that can be procured. Capet likes it really— don't you, Capet? It makes you happy and cheerful, and sleep well of nights. Why, you had a glassful yesterday and enjoyed it. Take it now," she added in a quick whisper, seeing that Simon and Heron were in close conversation together; "you know it makes papa angry if you don't have at least half a glass now and then."

The child wavered for a moment longer, making a quaint little grimace of distaste. But at last he seemed to make up his mind that it was wisest to yield over so small a matter, and he took the glass from Madame Simon.

And thus did de Batz see the descendant of St. Louis quaffing a glass of raw spirit at the bidding of a rough cobbler's wife, whom he called by the fond and foolish name sacred to childhood, *maman!*

Selfish egoist though he was, de Batz turned away in loathing.

Simon had watched the little scene with obvious satisfaction. He chuckled audibly when the child drank the spirit, and called Heron's attention to him, whilst a look of triumph lit up his wide, pale eyes.

"And now, *mon petit*," he said jovially, "let the citizen hear you say your prayers!"

He winked toward de Batz, evidently anticipating a good deal of enjoyment for the visitor from what was coming. From a heap of litter in a corner of the room he fetched out a greasy red bonnet adorned with a tricolour cockade, and a soiled and tattered flag, which had once been white, and had golden fleur-de-lys embroidered upon it.

The cap he set on the child's head, and the flag he threw upon the floor.

"Now, Capet—your prayers!" he said with another chuckle of amusement.

All his movements were rough, and his speech almost ostentatiously coarse. He banged against the furniture as he moved about the room, kicking a footstool out of the way or knocking over a chair. De Batz instinctively thought of the perfumed stillness of the rooms at Versailles, of the army of elegant high-born ladies who had ministered to the wants of this child, who stood there now before him, a cap on his yellow hair, and his shoulder held up to his ear with that gesture of careless indifference peculiar to children when they are sullen or uncared for.

Obediently, quite mechanically it seemed, the boy trod on the flag which Henri IV had borne before him at Ivry, and le Roi Soleil had flaunted in the face of the armies of Europe. The son of the Bourbons was spitting on their flag, and wiping his shoes upon its tattered folds. With shrill cracked voice he sang the Carmagnole, "*Ca ira! ca ira! les aristos a la lanterne!*" until de Batz himself felt inclined to stop his ears and to rush from the place in horror.

Louis XVII, whom the hearts of many had proclaimed King of France by the grace of God, the child of the Bourbons, the eldest son of the Church, was stepping a vulgar dance over the flag of St. Louis, which he had been taught to defile. His pale cheeks glowed as he danced, his eyes shone with the unnatural light kindled in them by the intoxicating liquor; with one slender hand he waved the red cap with the tricolour cockade, and shouted "*Vive la Republique!*"

Madame Simon was clapping her hands, looking on the child with obvious pride, and a kind of rough maternal affection. Simon was gazing on Heron for approval, and the latter nodded his head, murmuring words of encouragement and of praise.

"Thy catechism now, Capet—thy catechism," shouted Simon in a hoarse voice.

The boy stood at attention, cap on head, hands on his hips, legs wide apart, and feet firmly planted on the fleur-de-lys, the glory of his forefathers.

"Thy name?" queried Simon.

"Louis Capet," replied the child in a clear, high-pitched voice.

"What art thou?"

"A citizen of the Republic of France."

"What was thy father?"

"Louis Capet, *ci-devant* king, a tyrant who perished by the will of the people!"

"What was thy mother?"

"A ——"

De Batz involuntarily uttered a cry of horror. Whatever the man's private character was, he had been born a gentleman, and his every instinct revolted against what he saw and heard. The scene had positively sickened him. He turned precipitately towards the door.

"How now, citizen?" queried the Committee's agent with a sneer. "Are you not satisfied with what you see?"

"Mayhap the citizen would like to see Capet sitting in a golden chair," interposed Simon the cobbler with a sneer, "and me and my wife kneeling and kissing his hand—what?"

"'Tis the heat of the room," stammered de Batz, who was fumbling with the lock of the door; "my head began to swim."

"Spit on their accursed flag, then, like a good patriot, like Capet," retorted Simon gruffly. "Here, Capet, my son," he added, pulling the boy by the arm with a rough gesture, "get thee to bed; thou art quite drunk enough to satisfy any good Republican."

By way of a caress he tweaked the boy's ear and gave him a prod in the back with his bent knee. He was not wilfully unkind, for just now he was not angry with the lad; rather was he vastly amused with the effect Capet's prayer and Capet's recital of his catechism had had on the visitor.

As to the lad, the intensity of excitement in him was immediately followed by an overwhelming desire for sleep. Without any preliminary of undressing or of washing, he tumbled, just as he was, on to the sofa. Madame Simon, with quite pleasing solicitude, arranged a pillow under his head, and the very next moment the child was fast asleep.

"'Tis well, *citoyen* Simon," said Heron in his turn, going towards the door. "I'll report favourably on you to the Committee of Public Security. As for the *citoyenne*, she had best be more careful," he added, turning to the woman Simon with a snarl on his evil face. "There was no cause to arrange a pillow under the head of that vermin's spawn. Many good patriots have no pillows to put under their heads. Take that pillow away; and I don't like the shoes on the brat's feet; sabots are quite good enough."

*Citoyenne* Simon made no reply. Some sort of retort had apparently hovered on her lips, but had been checked, even before it was uttered, by a peremptory look from her husband. Simon the cobbler, snarling in speech but obsequious in manner, prepared to accompany the citizen agent to the door.

De Batz was taking a last look at the sleeping child; the uncrowned King of France was wrapped in a drunken sleep, with the last spoken insult upon his dead mother still hovering on his childish lips.

# Chapter 8: Arcades Ambo

"That is the way we conduct our affairs, citizen," said Heron gruffly, as he once more led his guest back into his office.

It was his turn to be complacent now. De Batz, for once in his life cowed by what he had seen, still wore a look of horror and disgust upon his florid face.

"What devils you all are!" he said at last.

"We are good patriots," retorted Heron, "and the tyrant's spawn leads but the life that hundreds of thousands of children led whilst his father oppressed the people. Nay! what am I saying? He leads a far better, far happier life. He gets plenty to eat and plenty of warm clothes. Thousands of innocent children, who have not the crimes of a despot father upon their conscience, have to starve whilst he grows fat."

The leer in his face was so evil that once more de Batz felt that eerie feeling of terror creeping into his bones. Here were cruelty and bloodthirsty ferocity personified to their utmost extent. At thought of the Bourbons, or of all those whom he considered had been in the past the oppressors of the people, Heron was nothing but a wild and ravenous beast, hungering for revenge, longing to bury his talons and his fangs into the body of those whose heels had once pressed on his own neck.

And de Batz knew that even with millions or countless money at his command he could not purchase from this carnivorous brute the life and liberty of the son of King Louis. No amount of bribery would accomplish that; it would have to be ingenuity pitted against animal force, the wiliness of the fox against the power of the wolf.

Even now Heron was darting savagely suspicious looks upon him.

"I shall get rid of the Simons," he said; "there's something in that woman's face which I don't trust. They shall go within the next few hours, or as soon as I can lay my hands upon a better patriot than that mealy-mouthed cobbler. And it will be better not to have a woman about the place. Let me see—to-day is Thursday, or else Friday morning. By Sunday I'll get those Simons out of the place. Methought I saw you ogling that woman," he added, bringing his bony fist crashing down on the table so that papers, pen, and inkhorn rattled loudly; "and if I thought that you—"

De Batz thought it well at this point to finger once more nonchalantly the bundle of crisp paper in the pocket of his coat.

"Only on that one condition," reiterated Heron in a hoarse voice; "if you try to get at Capet, I'll drag you to the Tribunal with my own hands."

"Always presuming that you can get me, my friend," murmured de Batz, who was gradually regaining his accustomed composure.

Already his active mind was busily at work. One or two things which he had noted in connection with his visit to the Dauphin's prison had struck him as possibly useful in his schemes. But he was disappointed that Heron was getting rid of the Simons. The woman might have been very useful and more easily got at than a man. The avarice of the French bourgeoise would have proved a promising factor. But this, of course, would now be out of the question. At the same time it was not because Heron raved and stormed and uttered cries like a hyena that he, de Batz, meant to give up an enterprise which, if successful, would place millions into his own pocket.

As for that meddling Englishman, the Scarlet Pimpernel, and his crack-brained followers, they must be effectually swept out of the way first of all. De Batz felt that they were the real, the most likely hindrance to his schemes. He himself would have to go very cautiously to work, since apparently Heron would not allow him to purchase immunity for himself in that one matter, and whilst he was laying his plans with necessary deliberation so as to ensure his own safety, that accursed Scarlet Pimpernel would mayhap snatch the golden prize from the Temple prison right under his very nose.

When he thought of that the Gascon Royalist felt just as vindictive as did the chief agent of the Committee of General Security.

While these thoughts were coursing through de Batz' head, Heron had been indulging in a volley of vituperation.

"If that little vermin escapes," he said, "my life will not be worth an hour's purchase. In twenty-four hours I am a dead man, thrown to the guillotine like those dogs of aristocrats! You say I am a night-bird, citizen. I tell you that I do not sleep night or day thinking of that brat and the means to keep him safely under my hand. I have never trusted those Simons—"

"Not trusted them!" exclaimed de Batz; "surely you could not find anywhere more inhuman monsters!"

"Inhuman monsters?" snarled Heron. "Bah! they don't do their business thoroughly; we want the tyrant's spawn to become a true Republican and a patriot—aye! to make of him such a one that even if you and your cursed confederates got him by some hellish chance, he would be no use to you as a king, a tyrant to set above the people, to set up in your Versailles, your Louvre, to eat off golden plates and wear satin clothes. You have seen the brat! By the time he is a man he should forget how to eat save with his fingers, and get roaring drunk every night. That's what we want!—to make him so that he shall be no use to you, even if you did get him away; but you shall not! You shall not, not if I have to strangle him with my own hands."

He picked up his short-stemmed pipe and pulled savagely at it for awhile. De Batz was meditating.

"My friend," he said after a little while, "you are agitating yourself quite unnecessarily, and gravely jeopardising your prospects of getting a comfortable little income through keeping your fingers off my person. Who said I wanted to meddle with the child?"

"You had best not," growled Heron.

"Exactly. You have said that before. But do you not think that you would be far wiser, instead of directing your undivided attention to my unworthy self, to turn your thoughts a little to one whom, believe me, you have far greater cause to fear?"

"Who is that?"

"The Englishman."

"You mean the man they call the Scarlet Pimpernel?"

"Himself. Have you not suffered from his activity, friend Heron? I fancy that citizen Chauvelin and citizen Collot would have quite a tale to tell about him."

"They ought both to have been guillotined for that blunder last autumn at Boulogne."

"Take care that the same accusation be not laid at your door this year, my friend," commented de Batz placidly.

"Bah!"

"The Scarlet Pimpernel is in Paris even now."

"The devil he is!"

"And on what errand, think you?"

There was a moment's silence, and then de Batz continued with slow and dramatic emphasis:

"That of rescuing your most precious prisoner from the Temple."

"How do you know?" Heron queried savagely.

"I guessed."

"How?"

"I saw a man in the Theatre National to-day . . . "

"Well?"

"Who is a member of the League of the Scarlet Pimpernel."

"D—— him! Where can I find him?"

"Will you sign a receipt for the three thousand five hundred livres, which I am pining to hand over to you, my friend, and I will tell you?"

"Where's the money?"

"In my pocket."

Without further words Heron dragged the inkhorn and a sheet of paper towards him, took up a pen, and wrote a few words rapidly in a loose, scrawly hand. He strewed sand over the writing, then handed it across the table to de Batz.

"Will that do?" he asked briefly.

The other was reading the note through carefully.

"I see you only grant me a fortnight," he remarked casually.

"For that amount of money it is sufficient. If you want an extension you must pay more."

"So be it," assented de Batz coolly, as he folded the paper across. "On the whole a fortnight's immunity in France these days is quite a pleasant respite. And I prefer to keep in touch with you, friend Heron. I'll call on you again this day fortnight."

He took out a letter-case from his pocket. Out of this he drew a packet of bank-notes, which he laid on the table in front of Heron, then he placed the receipt carefully into the letter-case, and this back into his pocket.

Heron in the meanwhile was counting over the banknotes. The light of ferocity had entirely gone from his eyes; momentarily the whole expression of the face was one of satisfied greed.

"Well!" he said at last when he had assured himself that the number of notes was quite correct, and he had transferred the bundle of crisp papers into an inner pocket of his coat—"well, what about your friend?"

"I knew him years ago," rejoined de Batz coolly; "he is a kinsman of citizen St. Just. I know that he is one of the confederates of the Scarlet Pimpernel."

"Where does he lodge?"

"That is for you to find out. I saw him at the theatre, and afterwards in the green-room; he was making himself agreeable to the citizeness Lange. I heard him ask for leave to call on her to-morrow at four o'clock. You know where she lodges, of course!"

He watched Heron while the latter scribbled a few words on a scrap of paper, then he quietly rose to go. He took up his cloak and once again wrapped it round his shoulders. There was nothing more to be said, and he was anxious to go.

The leave-taking between the two men was neither cordial nor more than barely courteous. De Batz nodded to Heron, who escorted him to the outside door of his lodging, and there called loudly to a soldier who was doing sentinel at the further end of the corridor.

"Show this citizen the way to the guichet," he said curtly. "Good-night, citizen," he added finally, nodding to de Batz.

Ten minutes later the Gascon once more found himself in the Rue du Temple between the great outer walls of the prison and the silent little church and convent of St. Elizabeth. He looked up to where in the central tower a small grated window lighted from within showed the place where the last of the Bourbons was being taught to desecrate the traditions of his race, at the bidding of a mender of shoes—a naval officer cashiered for misconduct and fraud.

Such is human nature in its self-satisfied complacency that de

Batz, calmly ignoring the vile part which he himself had played in the last quarter of an hour of his interview with the Committee's agent, found it in him to think of Heron with loathing, and even of the cobbler Simon with disgust.

Then with a self-righteous sense of duty performed, and an indifferent shrug of the shoulders, he dismissed Heron from his mind.

"That meddlesome Scarlet Pimpernel will find his hands over-full to-morrow, and mayhap will not interfere in my affairs for some time to come," he mused; "meseems that that will be the first time that a member of his precious League has come within the clutches of such unpleasant people as the sleuth-hounds of my friend Heron!"

# CHAPTER 9: WHAT LOVE CAN DO

"Yesterday you were unkind and ungallant. How could I smile when you seemed so stern?"

"Yesterday I was not alone with you. How could I say what lay next my heart, when indifferent ears could catch the words that were meant only for you?"

"Ah, monsieur, do they teach you in England how to make pretty speeches?"

"No, mademoiselle, that is an instinct that comes into birth by the fire of a woman's eyes."

Mademoiselle Lange was sitting upon a small sofa of antique design, with cushions covered in faded silks heaped round her pretty head. Armand thought that she looked like that carved cameo which his sister Marguerite possessed.

He himself sat on a low chair at some distance from her. He had brought her a large bunch of early violets, for he knew that she was fond of flowers, and these lay upon her lap, against the opalescent grey of her gown.

She seemed a little nervous and agitated, his obvious admiration bringing a ready blush to her cheeks.

The room itself appeared to Armand to be a perfect frame for the charming picture which she presented. The furniture in it was small and old; tiny tables of antique Vernis-Martin, softly faded tapestries, a pale-toned Aubusson carpet. Everything mellow and in a measure pathetic. Mademoiselle Lange, who was an orphan, lived alone under the duennaship of a middle-aged relative, a penniless hanger-on of the successful young actress, who acted as her chaperone, housekeeper, and maid, and kept unseemly or over-bold gallants at bay.

She told Armand all about her early life, her childhood in the backshop of Maitre Meziere, the jeweller, who was a relative of her mother's; of her desire for an artistic career, her struggles with the middle-class prejudices of her relations, her bold defiance of them, and final independence.

She made no secret of her humble origin, her want of education in those days; on the contrary, she was proud of what she had accomplished for herself. She was only twenty years of age, and already held a leading place in the artistic world of Paris.

Armand listened to her chatter, interested in everything she said, questioning her with sympathy and discretion. She asked him a good deal about himself, and about his beautiful sister Marguerite, who, of course, had been the most brilliant star in that most brilliant constellation, the Comedie Francaise. She had never seen Marguerite

St. Just act, but, of course, Paris still rang with her praises, and all art-lovers regretted that she should have married and left them to mourn for her.

Thus the conversation drifted naturally back to England. Mademoiselle professed a vast interest in the citizen's country of adoption.

"I had always," she said, "thought it an ugly country, with the noise and bustle of industrial life going on everywhere, and smoke and fog to cover the landscape and to stunt the trees."

"Then, in future, mademoiselle," he replied, "must you think of it as one carpeted with verdure, where in the spring the orchard trees covered with delicate blossom would speak to you of fairyland, where the dewy grass stretches its velvety surface in the shadow of ancient monumental oaks, and ivy-covered towers rear their stately crowns to the sky."

"And the Scarlet Pimpernel? Tell me about him, monsieur."

"Ah, mademoiselle, what can I tell you that you do not already know? The Scarlet Pimpernel is a man who has devoted his entire existence to the benefit of suffering mankind. He has but one thought, and that is for those who need him; he hears but one sound the cry of the oppressed."

"But they do say, monsieur, that philanthropy plays but a sorry part in your hero's schemes. They aver that he looks on his own efforts and the adventures through which he goes only in the light of sport."

"Like all Englishmen, mademoiselle, the Scarlet Pimpernel is a little ashamed of sentiment. He would deny its very existence with his lips, even whilst his noble heart brimmed over with it. Sport? Well! mayhap the sporting instinct is as keen as that of charity—the race for lives, the tussle for the rescue of human creatures, the throwing of a life on the hazard of a die."

"They fear him in France, monsieur. He has saved so many whose death had been decreed by the Committee of Public Safety."

"Please God, he will save many yet."

"Ah, monsieur, the poor little boy in the Temple prison!"

"He has your sympathy, mademoiselle?"

"Of every right-minded woman in France, monsieur. Oh!" she added with a pretty gesture of enthusiasm, clasping her hands together, and looking at Armand with large eyes filled with tears, "if your noble Scarlet Pimpernel will do aught to save that poor innocent lamb, I would indeed bless him in my heart, and help him with all my humble might if I could."

"May God's saints bless you for those words, mademoiselle," he said, whilst, carried away by her beauty, her charm, her perfect femininity, he stooped towards her until his knee touched the carpet at her feet. "I had begun to lose my belief in my poor misguided country, to think all men in France vile, and all women base. I could thank you on my knees for your sweet words of sympathy, for the expression of tender motherliness that came into your eyes when you spoke of the poor forsaken Dauphin in the Temple."

She did not restrain her tears; with her they came very easily, just as with a child, and as they gathered in her eyes and rolled down her fresh cheeks they in no way marred the charm of her face. One hand lay in her lap fingering a diminutive bit of cambric, which from time to time she pressed to her eyes. The other she had almost unconsciously yielded to Armand.

The scent of the violets filled the room. It seemed to emanate from her, a fitting attribute of her young, wholly unsophisticated girlhood. The citizen was goodly to look at; he was kneeling at her feet, and his lips were pressed against her hand.

Armand was young and he was an idealist. I do not for a moment imagine that just at this moment he was deeply in love. The stronger feeling had not yet risen up in him; it came later when tragedy encompassed him and brought passion to sudden maturity. Just now he was merely yielding himself up to the intoxicating moment, with all the abandonment, all the enthusiasm of the Latin race. There was no reason why he should not bend the knee before this exquisite little cameo, that by its very presence was giving him an hour of perfect pleasure and of aesthetic joy.

Outside the world continued its hideous, relentless way; men butchered one another, fought and hated. Here in this small old-world salon, with its faded satins and bits of ivory-tinted lace, the outer universe had never really penetrated. It was a tiny world—quite apart from the rest of mankind, perfectly peaceful and absolutely beautiful.

If Armand had been allowed to depart from here now, without having been the cause as well as the chief actor in the events that followed, no doubt that Mademoiselle Lange would always have remained a charming memory with him, an exquisite bouquet of violets pressed reverently between the leaves of a favourite book of poems, and the scent of spring flowers would in after years have ever brought her dainty picture to his mind.

He was murmuring pretty words of endearment; carried away by emotion, his arm stole round her waist; he felt that if another tear came like a dewdrop rolling down her cheek he must kiss it away at its very source. Passion was not sweeping them off their feet—not yet, for they were very young, and life had not as yet presented to them its most unsolvable problem.

But they yielded to one another, to the springtime of their life, calling for Love, which would come presently hand in hand with his grim attendant, Sorrow.

Even as Armand's glowing face was at last lifted up to hers

asking with mute lips for that first kiss which she already was prepared to give, there came the loud noise of men's heavy footsteps tramping up the old oak stairs, then some shouting, a woman's cry, and the next moment Madame Belhomme, trembling, wide-eyed, and in obvious terror, came rushing into the room.

"Jeanne! Jeanne! My child! It is awful! It is awful! Mon Dieu— *mon Dieu!* What is to become of us?"

She was moaning and lamenting even as she ran in, and now she threw her apron over her face and sank into a chair, continuing her moaning and her lamentations.

Neither Mademoiselle nor Armand had stirred. They remained like graven images, he on one knee, she with large eyes fixed upon his face. They had neither of them looked on the old woman; they seemed even now unconscious of her presence. But their ears had caught the sound of that measured tramp of feet up the stairs of the old house, and the halt upon the landing; they had heard the brief words of command:

"Open, in the name of the people!"

They knew quite well what it all meant; they had not wandered so far in the realms of romance that reality—the grim, horrible reality of the moment—had not the power to bring them back to earth.

That peremptory call to open in the name of the people was the prologue these days to a drama which had but two concluding acts: arrest, which was a certainty; the guillotine, which was more than probable. Jeanne and Armand, these two young people who but a moment ago had tentatively lifted the veil of life, looked straight into each other's eyes and saw the hand of death interposed between them: they looked straight into each other's eyes and knew that nothing but the hand of death would part them now. Love had come with its attendant, Sorrow; but he had come with no uncertain footsteps. Jeanne looked on the man before her, and he bent his head to imprint a glowing kiss upon her hand.

"Aunt Marie!"

It was Jeanne Lange who spoke, but her voice was no longer that of an irresponsible child; it was firm, steady and hard. Though she spoke to the old woman, she did not look at her; her luminous brown eyes rested on the bowed head of Armand St. Just.

"Aunt Marie!" she repeated more peremptorily, for the old woman, with her apron over her head, was still moaning, and unconscious of all save an overmastering fear.

"Open, in the name of the people!" came in a loud harsh voice once more from the other side of the front door.

"Aunt Marie, as you value your life and mine, pull yourself together," said Jeanne firmly.

"What shall we do? Oh! what shall we do?" moaned Madame Belhomme. But she had dragged the apron away from her face, and was looking with some puzzlement at meek, gentle little Jeanne, who had suddenly become so strange, so dictatorial, all unlike her habitual somewhat diffident self.

"You need not have the slightest fear, Aunt Marie, if you will only do as I tell you," resumed Jeanne quietly; "if you give way to fear, we are all of us undone. As you value your life and mine," she now repeated authoritatively, "pull yourself together, and do as I tell you."

The girl's firmness, her perfect quietude had the desired effect. Madame Belhomme, though still shaken up with sobs of terror, made a great effort to master herself; she stood up, smoothed down her apron, passed her hand over her ruffled hair, and said in a quaking voice:

"What do you think we had better do?"

"Go quietly to the door and open it."

"But—the soldiers—"

"If you do not open quietly they will force the door open within the next two minutes," interposed Jeanne calmly. "Go quietly and open the door. Try and hide your fears, grumble in an audible voice at being interrupted in your cooking, and tell the soldiers at once that they will find mademoiselle in the boudoir. Go, for God's sake!" she added, whilst suppressed emotion suddenly made her young voice vibrate; "go, before they break open that door!"

Madame Belhomme, impressed and cowed, obeyed like an automaton. She turned and marched fairly straight out of the room. It was not a minute too soon. From outside had already come the third and final summons:

"Open, in the name of the people!"

After that a crowbar would break open the door.

Madame Belhomme's heavy footsteps were heard crossing the ante-chamber. Armand still knelt at Jeanne's feet, holding her trembling little hand in his.

"A love-scene," she whispered rapidly, "a love-scene—quick—do you know one?"

And even as he had tried to rise she held him back, down on his knees.

He thought that fear was making her distracted.

"Mademoiselle—" he murmured, trying to soothe her.

"Try and understand," she said with wonderful calm, "and do as I tell you. Aunt Marie has obeyed. Will you do likewise?"

"To the death!" he whispered eagerly.

"Then a love-scene," she entreated. "Surely you know one. Rodrigue and Chimène! Surely—surely," she urged, even as tears of anguish rose into her eyes, "you—you must, or, if not that, something else. Quick! The very seconds are precious!"

They were indeed! Madame Belhomme, obedient as a frightened dog, had gone to the door and opened it; even her well-feigned grumblings could now be heard and the rough interrogations from the soldiery.

"Citizeness Lange!" said a gruff voice.

"In her boudoir, *quoi!*"

Madame Belhomme, braced up apparently by fear, was playing her part remarkably well.

"Bothering good citizens! On baking day, too!" she went on grumbling and muttering.

"Oh, think—think!" murmured Jeanne now in an agonised whisper, her hot little hand grasping his so tightly that her nails were driven into his flesh. "You must know something, that will do—anything—for dear life's sake. . . . Armand!"

His name—in the tense excitement of this terrible moment—had escaped her lips.

All in a flash of sudden intuition he understood what she wanted, and even as the door of the boudoir was thrown violently open Armand—still on his knees, but with one hand pressed to his heart, the other stretched upwards to the ceiling in the most approved dramatic style, was loudly declaiming:

> *"Pour venger son honneur il perdit son amour,*
> *Pour venger sa maitresse il a quitte le jour!"*

Whereupon Mademoiselle Lange feigned the most perfect impatience.

"No, no, my good cousin," she said with a pretty moue of disdain, "that will never do! You must not thus emphasise the end of every line; the verses should flow more evenly, as thus. . . . "

Heron had paused at the door. It was he who had thrown it open—he who, followed by a couple of his sleuth-hounds, had thought to find here the man denounced by de Batz as being one of the followers of that irrepressible Scarlet Pimpernel. The obviously Parisian intonation of the man kneeling in front of citizeness Lange in an attitude no ways suggestive of personal admiration, and coolly reciting verses out of a play, had somewhat taken him aback.

"What does this mean?" he asked gruffly, striding forward into the room and glaring first at mademoiselle, then at Armand.

Mademoiselle gave a little cry of surprise.

"Why, if it isn't citizen Heron!" she cried, jumping up with a dainty movement of coquetry and embarrassment. "Why did not Aunt Marie announce you? . . . It is indeed remiss of her, but she is so ill-tempered on baking days I dare not even rebuke her. Won't you sit down, citizen Heron? And you, cousin," she added, looking down airily on Armand, "I pray you maintain no longer that foolish attitude."

The febrileness of her manner, the glow in her cheeks were

easily attributable to natural shyness in face of this unexpected visit. Heron, completely bewildered by this little scene, which was so unlike what he expected, and so unlike those to which he was accustomed in the exercise of his horrible duties, was practically speechless before the little lady who continued to prattle along in a simple, unaffected manner.

"Cousin," she said to Armand, who in the meanwhile had risen to his knees, "this is citizen Heron, of whom you have heard me speak. My cousin Belhomme," she continued, once more turning to Heron, "is fresh from the country, citizen. He hails from Orleans, where he has played leading parts in the tragedies of the late citizen Corneille. But, ah me! I fear that he will find Paris audiences vastly more critical than the good Orleanese. Did you hear him, citizen, declaiming those beautiful verses just now? He was murdering them, say I—yes, murdering them—the gaby!"

Then only did it seem as if she realised that there was something amiss, that citizen Heron had come to visit her, not as an admirer of her talent who would wish to pay his respects to a successful actress, but as a person to be looked on with dread.

She gave a quaint, nervous little laugh, and murmured in the tones of a frightened child:

"La, citizen, how glum you look! I thought you had come to compliment me on my latest success. I saw you at the theatre last night, though you did not afterwards come to see me in the green-room. Why! I had a regular ovation! Look at my flowers!" she added more gaily, pointing to several bouquets in vases about the room. "Citizen Danton brought me the violets himself, and citizen Santerre the narcissi, and that laurel wreath—is it not charming?—that was a tribute from citizen Robespierre himself."

She was so artless, so simple, and so natural that Heron was completely taken off his usual mental balance. He had expected to find the usual setting to the dramatic episodes which he was wont to conduct—screaming women, a man either at bay, sword in hand, or hiding in a linen cupboard or up a chimney.

Now everything puzzled him. De Batz—he was quite sure—had spoken of an Englishman, a follower of the Scarlet Pimpernel; every thinking French patriot knew that all the followers of the Scarlet Pimpernel were Englishmen with red hair and prominent teeth, whereas this man. . . .

Armand—who deadly danger had primed in his improvised role —was striding up and down the room declaiming with ever-varying intonations:

*"Joignez tous vos efforts contre un espoir si doux*
*Pour en venir a bout, c'est trop peu que de vous."*

"No! no!" said mademoiselle impatiently; "you must not make that ugly pause midway in the last line: '*pour en venir a bout, c'est trop peu que de vous!*'"

She mimicked Armand's diction so quaintly, imitating his stride, his awkward gesture, and his faulty phraseology with such funny exaggeration that Heron laughed in spite of himself.

"So that is a cousin from Orleans, is it?" he asked, throwing his lanky body into an armchair, which creaked dismally under his weight.

"Yes! a regular gaby—what?" she said archly. "Now, citizen Heron, you must stay and take coffee with me. Aunt Marie will be bringing it in directly. Hector," she added, turning to Armand, "come down from the clouds and ask Aunt Marie to be quick."

This certainly was the first time in the whole of his experience that Heron had been asked to stay and drink coffee with the quarry he was hunting down. Mademoiselle's innocent little ways, her desire for the prolongation of his visit, further addled his brain. De Batz had undoubtedly spoken of an Englishman, and the cousin from Orleans was certainly a Frenchman every inch of him.

Perhaps had the denunciation come from any one else but de Batz, Heron might have acted and thought more circumspectly; but, of course, the chief agent of the Committee of General Security was more suspicious of the man from whom he took a heavy bribe than of any one else in France. The thought had suddenly crossed his mind that mayhap de Batz had sent him on a fool's errand in order to get him safely out of the way of the Temple prison at a given hour of the day.

The thought took shape, crystallised, caused him to see a rapid vision of de Batz sneaking into his lodgings and stealing his keys, the guard being slack, careless, inattentive, allowing the adventurer to pass barriers that should have been closed against all comers.

Now Heron was sure of it; it was all a conspiracy invented by de Batz. He had forgotten all about his theories that a man under arrest is always safer than a man that is free. Had his brain been quite normal, and not obsessed, as it always was now by thoughts of the Dauphin's escape from prison, no doubt he would have been more suspicious of Armand, but all his worst suspicions were directed against de Batz. Armand seemed to him just a fool, an actor *quoi?* and so obviously not an Englishman.

He jumped to his feet, curtly declining mademoiselle's offers of hospitality. He wanted to get away at once. Actors and actresses were always, by tacit consent of the authorities, more immune than the rest of the community. They provided the only amusement in the intervals of the horrible scenes around the scaffolds; they were irresponsible, harmless creatures who did not meddle in politics.

Jeanne the while was gaily prattling on, her luminous eyes fixed upon the all-powerful enemy, striving to read his thoughts, to understand what went on behind those cruel, prominent eyes, the chances that Armand had of safety and of life.

She knew, of course, that the visit was directed against Armand —some one had betrayed him, that odious de Batz mayhap—and she was fighting for Armand's safety, for his life. Her armoury consisted of her presence of mind, her cool courage, her self-control; she used all these weapons for his sake, though at times she felt as if the strain on her nerves would snap the thread of life in her. The effort seemed more than she could bear.

But she kept up her part, rallying Heron for the shortness of his visit, begging him to tarry for another five minutes at least, throwing out—with subtle feminine intuition—just those very hints anent little Capet's safety that were most calculated to send him flying back towards the Temple.

"I felt so honoured last night, citizen," she said coquettishly, "that you even forgot little Capet in order to come and watch my debut as Celimene."

"Forget him!" retorted Heron, smothering a curse, "I never forget the vermin. I must go back to him; there are too many cats nosing round my mouse. Good day to you, citizeness. I ought to have brought flowers, I know; but I am a busy man—a harassed man."

"*Je te crois*," she said with a grave nod of the head; "but do come to the theatre to-night. I am playing Camille—such a fine part! one of my greatest successes."

"Yes, yes, I'll come—mayhap, mayhap—but I'll go now—glad to have seen you, citizeness. Where does your cousin lodge?" he asked abruptly.

"Here," she replied boldly, on the spur of the moment.

"Good. Let him report himself to-morrow morning at the Conciergerie, and get his certificate of safety. It is a new decree, and you should have one, too."

"Very well, then. Hector and I will come together, and perhaps Aunt Marie will come too. Don't send us to *maman* guillotine yet awhile, citizen," she said lightly; "you will never get such another Camille, nor yet so good a Celimene."

She was gay, artless to the last. She accompanied Heron to the door herself, chaffing him about his escort.

"You are an *aristo*, citizen," she said, gazing with well-feigned admiration on the two sleuth-hounds who stood in wait in the anteroom; "it makes me proud to see so many citizens at my door. Come and see me play Camille—come to-night, and don't forget the green-room door—it will always be kept invitingly open for you."

She bobbed him a curtsey, and he walked out, closely followed by his two men; then at last she closed the door behind them. She stood there for a while, her ear glued against the massive panels, listening for their measured tread down the oak staircase. At last it rang more sharply against the flagstones of the courtyard below; then she was satisfied that they had gone, and went slowly back to the boudoir.

# CHAPTER 10: SHADOWS

The tension on her nerves relaxed; there was the inevitable reaction. Her knees were shaking under her, and she literally staggered into the room.

But Armand was already near her, down on both his knees this time, his arms clasping the delicate form that swayed like the slender stems of narcissi in the breeze.

"Oh! you must go out of Paris at once—at once," she said through sobs which no longer would be kept back.

"He'll return—I know that he will return—and you will not be safe until you are back in England."

But he could not think of himself or of anything in the future. He had forgotten Heron, Paris, the world; he could only think of her.

"I owe my life to you!" he murmured. "Oh, how beautiful you are—how brave! How I love you!"

It seemed that he had always loved her, from the moment that first in his boyish heart he had set up an ideal to worship, and then, last night, in the box of the theatre—he had his back turned toward the stage, and was ready to go—her voice had called him back; it had held him spellbound; her voice, and also her eyes. . . . He did not know then that it was Love which then and there had enchained him. Oh, how foolish he had been! for now he knew that he had loved her with all his might, with all his soul, from the very instant that his eyes had rested upon her.

He babbled along—incoherently—in the intervals of covering her hands and the hem of her gown with kisses. He stooped right down to the ground and kissed the arch of her instep; he had become a devotee worshipping at the shrine of his saint, who had performed a great and a wonderful miracle.

Armand the idealist had found his ideal in a woman. That was the great miracle which the woman herself had performed for him. He found in her all that he had admired most, all that he had admired in the leader who hitherto had been the only personification of his ideal. But Jeanne possessed all those qualities which had roused his enthusiasm in the noble hero whom he revered. Her pluck, her ingenuity, her calm devotion which had averted the threatened danger from him!

What had he done that she should have risked her own sweet life for his sake?

But Jeanne did not know. She could not tell. Her nerves now were somewhat unstrung, and the tears that always came so readily to her eyes flowed quite unchecked. She could not very well move, for he held her knees imprisoned in his arms, but she was quite content to remain like this, and to yield her hands to him so that he might cover them with kisses.

Indeed, she did not know at what precise moment love for him had been born in her heart. Last night, perhaps . . . she could not say . . . but when they parted she felt that she must see him again . . . and then today . . . perhaps it was the scent of the violets . . . they were so exquisitely sweet . . . perhaps it was his enthusiasm and his talk about England . . . but when Heron came she knew that she must save Armand's life at all cost . . . that she would die if they dragged him away to prison.

Thus these two children philosophised, trying to understand the mystery of the birth of Love. But they were only children; they did not really understand. Passion was sweeping them off their feet, because a common danger had bound them irrevocably to one another. The womanly instinct to save and to protect had given the young girl strength to bear a difficult part, and now she loved him for the dangers from which she had rescued him, and he loved her because she had risked her life for him.

The hours sped on; there was so much to say, so much that was exquisite to listen to. The shades of evening were gathering fast; the room, with its pale-toned hangings and faded tapestries, was sinking into the arms of gloom. Aunt Marie was no doubt too terrified to stir out of her kitchen; she did not bring the lamps, but the darkness suited Armand's mood, and Jeanne was glad that the gloaming effectually hid the perpetual blush in her cheeks.

In the evening air the dying flowers sent their heady fragrance around. Armand was intoxicated with the perfume of violets that clung to Jeanne's fingers, with the touch of her satin gown that brushed his cheek, with the murmur of her voice that quivered through her tears.

No noise from the ugly outer world reached this secluded spot. In the tiny square outside a street lamp had been lighted, and its feeble rays came peeping in through the lace curtains at the window. They caught the dainty silhouette of the young girl, playing with the loose tendrils of her hair around her forehead, and outlining with a thin band of light the contour of neck and shoulder, making the satin of her gown shimmer with an opalescent glow.

Armand rose from his knees. Her eyes were calling to him, her lips were ready to yield.

"*Tu m'aimes?*" he whispered.

And like a tired child she sank upon his breast.

He kissed her hair, her eyes, her lips; her skin was fragrant as the flowers of spring, the tears on her cheeks glistened like morning dew.

Aunt Marie came in at last, carrying the lamp. She found them sitting side by side, like two children, hand in hand, mute with the eloquence which comes from boundless love. They were under a spell, forgetting even that they lived, knowing nothing except that they loved.

The lamp broke the spell, and Aunt Marie's still trembling voice:

"Oh, my dear! how did you manage to rid yourself of those brutes?"

But she asked no other question, even when the lamp showed up quite clearly the glowing cheeks of Jeanne and the ardent eyes of Armand. In her heart, long since atrophied, there were a few memories, carefully put away in a secret cell, and those memories caused the old woman to understand.

Neither Jeanne nor Armand noticed what she did; the spell had been broken, but the dream lingered on; they did not see Aunt Marie putting the room tidy, and then quietly tiptoeing out by the door.

But through the dream, reality was struggling for recognition. After Armand had asked for the hundredth time: "*Tu m'aimes?*" and Jeanne for the hundredth time had replied mutely with her eyes, her fears for him suddenly returned.

Something had awakened her from her trance—a heavy footstep, mayhap, in the street below, the distant roll of a drum, or only the clash of steel saucepans in Aunt Marie's kitchen. But suddenly Jeanne was alert, and with her alertness came terror for the beloved.

"Your life," she said—for he had called her his life just then, "your life—and I was forgetting that it is still in danger . . . your dear, your precious life!"

"Doubly dear now," he replied, "since I owe it to you."

"Then I pray you, I entreat you, guard it well for my sake—make all haste to leave Paris . . . oh, this I beg of you!" she continued more earnestly, seeing the look of demur in his eyes; "every hour you spend in it brings danger nearer to your door."

"I could not leave Paris while you are here."

"But I am safe here," she urged; "quite, quite safe, I assure you. I am only a poor actress, and the Government takes no heed of us mimes. Men must be amused, even between the intervals of killing one another. Indeed, indeed, I should be far safer here now, waiting quietly for awhile, while you make preparations to go . . . . My hasty departure at this moment would bring disaster on us both."

There was logic in what she said. And yet how could he leave her? now that he had found this perfect woman—this realisation of his highest ideals, how could he go and leave her in this awful Paris, with brutes like Heron forcing their hideous personality into her sacred presence, threatening that very life he would gladly give his own to keep inviolate?

"Listen, sweetheart," he said after awhile, when presently

reason struggled back for first place in his mind. "Will you allow me to consult with my chief, with the Scarlet Pimpernel, who is in Paris at the present moment? I am under his orders; I could not leave France just now. My life, my entire person are at his disposal. I and my comrades are here under his orders, for a great undertaking which he has not yet unfolded to us, but which I firmly believe is framed for the rescue of the Dauphin from the Temple."

She gave an involuntary exclamation of horror.

"No, no!" she said quickly and earnestly; "as far as you are concerned, Armand, that has now become an impossibility. Some one has betrayed you, and you are henceforth a marked man. I think that odious de Batz had a hand in Heron's visit of this afternoon. We succeeded in putting these spies off the scent, but only for a moment . . . within a few hours—less perhaps—Heron will repent him of his carelessness; he'll come back—I know that he will come back. He may leave me, personally, alone; but he will be on your track; he'll drag you to the Conciergerie to report yourself, and there your true name and history are bound to come to light. If you succeed in evading him, he will still be on your track. If the Scarlet Pimpernel keeps you in Paris now, your death will be at his door."

Her voice had become quite hard and trenchant as she said these last words; womanlike, she was already prepared to hate the man whose mysterious personality she had hitherto admired, now that the life and safety of Armand appeared to depend on the will of that elusive hero.

"You must not be afraid for me, Jeanne," he urged. "The Scarlet Pimpernel cares for all his followers; he would never allow me to run unnecessary risks."

She was unconvinced, almost jealous now of his enthusiasm for that unknown man. Already she had taken full possession of Armand; she had purchased his life, and he had given her his love. She would share neither treasure with that nameless leader who held Armand's allegiance.

"It is only for a little while, sweetheart," he reiterated again and again. "I could not, anyhow, leave Paris whilst I feel that you are here, maybe in danger. The thought would be horrible. I should go mad if I had to leave you."

Then he talked again of England, of his life there, of the happiness and peace that were in store for them both.

"We will go to England together," he whispered, "and there we will be happy together, you and I. We will have a tiny house among the Kentish hills, and its walls will be covered with honeysuckle and roses. At the back of the house there will be an orchard, and in May, when the fruit-blossom is fading and soft spring breezes blow among the trees, showers of sweet-scented petals will envelop us as we walk along, falling on us like fragrant snow. You will come, sweetheart, will you not?"

"If you still wish it, Armand," she murmured.

Still wish it! He would gladly go to-morrow if she would come with him. But, of course, that could not be arranged. She had her contract to fulfil at the theatre, then there would be her house and furniture to dispose of, and there was Aunt Marie. . . . But, of course, Aunt Marie would come too . . . She thought that she could get away some time before the spring; and he swore that he could not leave Paris until she came with him.

It seemed a terrible deadlock, for she could not bear to think of him alone in those awful Paris streets, where she knew that spies would always be tracking him. She had no illusions as to the impression which she had made on Heron; she knew that it could only be a momentary one, and that Armand would henceforth be in daily, hourly danger.

At last she promised him that she would take the advice of his chief; they would both be guided by what he said. Armand would confide in him to-night, and if it could be arranged she would hurry on her preparations and, mayhap, be ready to join him in a week.

"In the meanwhile, that cruel man must not risk your dear life," she said. "Remember, Armand, your life belongs to me. Oh, I could hate him for the love you bear him!"

"Sh—sh—sh!" he said earnestly. "Dear heart, you must not speak like that of the man whom, next to your perfect self, I love most upon earth."

"You think of him more than of me. I shall scarce live until I know that you are safely out of Paris."

Though it was horrible to part, yet it was best, perhaps, that he should go back to his lodgings now, in case Heron sent his spies back to her door, and since he meant to consult with his chief. She had a vague hope that if the mysterious hero was indeed the noble-hearted man whom Armand represented him to be, surely he would take compassion on the anxiety of a sorrowing woman, and release the man she loved from bondage.

This thought pleased her and gave her hope. She even urged Armand now to go.

"When may I see you to-morrow?" he asked.

"But it will be so dangerous to meet," she argued.

"I must see you. I could not live through the day without seeing you."

"The theatre is the safest place."

"I could not wait till the evening. May I not come here?"

"No, no. Heron's spies may be about."

"Where then?"

She thought it over for a moment.

"At the stage-door of the theatre at one o'clock," she said at last. "We shall have finished rehearsal. Slip into the guichet of the concierge. I will tell him to admit you, and send my dresser to meet you there; she will bring you along to my room, where we shall be undisturbed for at least half an hour."

He had perforce to be content with that, though he would so much rather have seen her here again, where the faded tapestries and soft-toned hangings made such a perfect background for her delicate charm. He had every intention of confiding in Blakeney, and of asking his help for getting Jeanne out of Paris as quickly as may be.

Thus this perfect hour was past; the most pure, the fullest of joy that these two young people were ever destined to know. Perhaps they felt within themselves the consciousness that their great love would rise anon to yet greater, fuller perfection when Fate had crowned it with his halo of sorrow. Perhaps, too, it was that consciousness that gave to their kisses now the solemnity of a last farewell.

# CHAPTER 11: THE LEAGUE OF THE SCARLET PIMPERNEL

Armand never could say definitely afterwards whither he went when he left the Square du Roule that evening. No doubt he wandered about the streets for some time in an absent, mechanical way, paying no heed to the passers-by, none to the direction in which he was going.

His mind was full of Jeanne, her beauty, her courage, her attitude in face of the hideous bloodhound who had come to pollute that charming old-world boudoir by his loathsome presence. He recalled every word she uttered, every gesture she made.

He was a man in love for the first time—wholly, irremediably in love.

I suppose that it was the pangs of hunger that first recalled him to himself. It was close on eight o'clock now, and he had fed on his imaginings—first on anticipation, then on realisation, and lastly on memory—during the best part of the day. Now he awoke from his day-dream to find himself tired and hungry, but fortunately not very far from that quarter of Paris where food is easily obtainable.

He was somewhere near the Madeleine—a quarter he knew well. Soon he saw in front of him a small eating-house which looked fairly clean and orderly. He pushed open its swing-door, and seeing an empty table in a secluded part of the room, he sat down and ordered some supper.

The place made no impression upon his memory. He could not have told you an hour later where it was situated, who had served him, what he had eaten, or what other persons were present in the dining-room at the time that he himself entered it.

Having eaten, however, he felt more like his normal self—more conscious of his actions. When he finally left the eating-house, he realised, for instance, that it was very cold—a fact of which he had for the past few hours been totally unaware. The snow was falling in thin close flakes, and a biting north-easterly wind was blowing those flakes into his face and down his collar. He wrapped his cloak tightly around him. It was a good step yet to Blakeney's lodgings, where he knew that he was expected.

He struck quickly into the Rue St. Honore, avoiding the great open places where the grim horrors of this magnificent city in revolt against civilisation were displayed in all their grim nakedness—on the Place de la Revolution the guillotine, on the Carrousel the open-air camps of workers under the lash of slave-drivers more cruel than the uncivilised brutes of the Far West.

And Armand had to think of Jeanne in the midst of all these horrors. She was still a petted actress to-day, but who could tell if on the morrow the terrible law of the "suspect" would not reach her in order to drag her before a tribunal that knew no mercy, and whose sole justice was a condemnation?

The young man hurried on; he was anxious to be among his own comrades, to hear his chief's pleasant voice, to feel assured that by all the sacred laws of friendship Jeanne henceforth would become the special care of the Scarlet Pimpernel and his league.

Blakeney lodged in a small house situated on the Quai de l'Ecole, at the back of St. Germain l'Auxerrois, from whence he had a clear and uninterrupted view across the river, as far as the irregular block of buildings of the Chatelet prison and the house of Justice.

The same tower-clock that two centuries ago had tolled the signal for the massacre of the Huguenots was even now striking nine. Armand slipped through the half-open *porte cochere*, crossed the narrow dark courtyard, and ran up two flights of winding stone stairs. At the top of these, a door on his right allowed a thin streak of light to filtrate between its two folds. An iron bell handle hung beside it; Armand gave it a pull.

Two minutes later he was amongst his friends. He heaved a great sigh of content and relief. The very atmosphere here seemed to be different. As far as the lodging itself was concerned, it was as bare, as devoid of comfort as those sort of places—so-called *chambres garnies* —usually were in these days. The chairs looked rickety and uninviting, the sofa was of black horsehair, the carpet was threadbare, and in places in actual holes; but there was a certain something in the air which revealed, in the midst of all this squalor, the presence of a man of fastidious taste.

To begin with, the place was spotlessly clean; the stove, highly polished, gave forth a pleasing warm glow, even whilst the window, slightly open, allowed a modicum of fresh air to enter the room. In a rough earthenware jug on the table stood a large bunch of Christmas roses, and to the educated nostril the slight scent of perfumes that hovered in the air was doubly pleasing after the fetid air of the narrow streets.

Sir Andrew Ffoulkes was there, also my Lord Tony, and Lord Hastings. They greeted Armand with whole-hearted cheeriness.

"Where is Blakeney?" asked the young man as soon as he had shaken his friends by the hand.

"Present!" came in loud, pleasant accents from the door of an inner room on the right.

And there he stood under the lintel of the door, the man against whom was raised the giant hand of an entire nation—the man for whose head the revolutionary government of France would gladly pay out all the savings of its Treasury—the man whom human bloodhounds were tracking, hot on the scent—for whom the nets of a bitter revenge and relentless reprisals were constantly being spread.

Was he unconscious of it, or merely careless? His closest friend, Sir Andrew Ffoulkes, could not say. Certain it is that, as he now appeared before Armand, picturesque as ever in perfectly tailored clothes, with priceless lace at throat and wrists, his slender fingers holding an enamelled snuff-box and a handkerchief of delicate cambric, his whole personality that of a dandy rather than a man of action, it seemed impossible to connect him with the foolhardy escapades which had set one nation glowing with enthusiasm and another clamouring for revenge.

But it was the magnetism that emanated from him that could not be denied; the light that now and then, swift as summer lightning, flashed out from the depths of the blue eyes usually veiled by heavy, lazy lids, the sudden tightening of firm lips, the setting of the square jaw, which in a moment—but only for the space of a second—transformed the entire face, and revealed the born leader of men.

Just now there was none of that in the debonnair, easy-going man of the world who advanced to meet his friend. Armand went quickly up to him, glad to grasp his hand, slightly troubled with remorse, no doubt, at the recollection of his adventure of to-day. It almost seemed to him that from beneath his half-closed lids Blakeney had shot a quick inquiring glance upon him. The quick flash seemed to light up the young man's soul from within, and to reveal it, naked, to his friend.

It was all over in a moment, and Armand thought that mayhap his conscience had played him a trick: there was nothing apparent in him—of this he was sure—that could possibly divulge his secret just yet.

"I am rather late, I fear," he said. "I wandered about the streets in the late afternoon and lost my way in the dark. I hope I have not kept you all waiting."

They all pulled chairs closely round the fire, except Blakeney, who preferred to stand. He waited awhile until they were all comfortably settled, and all ready to listen, then:

"It is about the Dauphin," he said abruptly without further preamble.

They understood. All of them had guessed it, almost before the summons came that had brought them to Paris two days ago. Sir Andrew Ffoulkes had left his young wife because of that, and Armand had demanded it as a right to join hands in this noble work. Blakeney had not left France for over three months now. Backwards and forwards between Paris, or Nantes, or Orleans to the coast, where his friends would meet him to receive those unfortunates whom one man's whole-hearted devotion had rescued from death; backwards and forwards into the very hearts of those cities wherein an army of sleuth-hounds were on his track, and the guillotine was stretching out her arms to catch the foolhardy adventurer.

Now it was about the Dauphin. They all waited, breathless and eager, the fire of a noble enthusiasm burning in their hearts. They waited in silence, their eyes fixed on the leader, lest one single word from him should fail to reach their ears.

The full magnetism of the man was apparent now. As he held these four men at this moment, he could have held a crowd. The man of the world—the fastidious dandy—had shed his mask; there stood the leader, calm, serene in the very face of the most deadly danger that had ever encompassed any man, looking that danger fully in the face, not striving to belittle it or to exaggerate it, but weighing it in the balance with what there was to accomplish: the rescue of a martyred, innocent child from the hands of fiends who were destroying his very soul even more completely than his body.

"Everything, I think, is prepared," resumed Sir Percy after a slight pause. "The Simons have been summarily dismissed; I learned that to-day. They remove from the Temple on Sunday next, the nineteenth. Obviously that is the one day most likely to help us in our operations. As far as I am concerned, I cannot make any hard-and-fast plans. Chance at the last moment will have to dictate. But from every one of you I must have co-operation, and it can only be by your following my directions implicitly that we can even remotely hope to succeed."

He crossed and recrossed the room once or twice before he spoke again, pausing now and again in his walk in front of a large map of Paris and its environs that hung upon the wall, his tall figure erect, his hands behind his back, his eyes fixed before him as if he saw right through the walls of this squalid room, and across the darkness that overhung the city, through the grim bastions of the mighty building far away, where the descendant of an hundred kings lived at the mercy of human fiends who worked for his abasement.

The man's face now was that of a seer and a visionary; the firm lines were set and rigid as those of an image carved in stone—the statue of heart-whole devotion, with the self-imposed task beckoning sternly to follow, there where lurked danger and death.

"The way, I think, in which we could best succeed would be this," he resumed after a while, sitting now on the edge of the table and directly facing his four friends. The light from the lamp which stood upon the table behind him fell full upon those four glowing faces fixed eagerly upon him, but he himself was in shadow, a massive silhouette broadly cut out against the light-coloured map on the wall beyond.

"I remain here, of course, until Sunday," he said, "and will closely watch my opportunity, when I can with the greatest amount of safety enter the Temple building and take possession of the child. I shall, of course choose the moment when the Simons are actually on the move, with their successors probably coming in at about the same time. God alone knows," he added earnestly, "how I shall contrive to get possession of the child; at the moment I am just as much in the dark about that as you are."

He paused a moment, and suddenly his grave face seemed flooded with sunshine, a kind of lazy merriment danced in his eyes, effacing all trace of solemnity within them.

"La!" he said lightly, "on one point I am not at all in the dark, and that is that His Majesty King Louis XVII will come out of that ugly house in my company next Sunday, the nineteenth day of January in this year of grace seventeen hundred and ninety-four; and this, too, do I know—that those murderous blackguards shall not lay hands on me whilst that precious burden is in my keeping. So I pray you, my good Armand, do not look so glum," he added with his pleasant, merry laugh; "you'll need all your wits about you to help us in our undertaking."

"What do you wish me to do, Percy?" said the young man simply.

"In one moment I will tell you. I want you all to understand the situation first. The child will be out of the Temple on Sunday, but at what hour I know not. The later it will be the better would it suit my purpose, for I cannot get him out of Paris before evening with any chance of safety. Here we must risk nothing; the child is far better off as he is now than he would be if he were dragged back after an abortive attempt at rescue. But at this hour of the night, between nine and ten o'clock, I can arrange to get him out of Paris by the Villette gate, and that is where I want you, Ffoulkes, and you, Tony, to be, with some kind of covered cart, yourselves in any disguise your ingenuity will suggest. Here are a few certificates of safety; I have been making a collection of them for some time, as they are always useful."

He dived into the wide pocket of his coat and drew forth a number of cards, greasy, much-fingered documents of the usual pattern which the Committee of General Security delivered to the free citizens of the new republic, and without which no one could enter or leave any town or country commune without being detained as "suspect." He glanced at them and handed them over to Ffoulkes.

"Choose your own identity for the occasion, my good friend," he said lightly; "and you too, Tony. You may be stonemasons or coal-carriers, chimney-sweeps or farm-labourers, I care not which so long as you look sufficiently grimy and wretched to be unrecognisable, and so long as you can procure a cart without arousing suspicions, and can wait for me punctually at the appointed spot."

Ffoulkes turned over the cards, and with a laugh handed them over to Lord Tony. The two fastidious gentlemen discussed for awhile the respective merits of a chimney-sweep's uniform as against that of a coal-carrier.

"You can carry more grime if you are a sweep," suggested Blakeney; "and if the soot gets into your eyes it does not make them smart like coal does."

"But soot adheres more closely," argued Tony solemnly, "and I know that we shan't get a bath for at least a week afterwards."

"Certainly you won't, you sybarite!" asserted Sir Percy with a laugh.

"After a week soot might become permanent," mused Sir Andrew, wondering what, under the circumstance, my lady would say to him.

"If you are both so fastidious," retorted Blakeney, shrugging his broad shoulders, "I'll turn one of you into a reddleman, and the other into a dyer. Then one of you will be bright scarlet to the end of his days, as the reddle never comes off the skin at all, and the other will have to soak in turpentine before the dye will consent to move. . . . In either case . . . oh, my dear Tony! . . . the smell. . . . "

He laughed like a schoolboy in anticipation of a prank, and held his scented handkerchief to his nose. My Lord Hastings chuckled audibly, and Tony punched him for this unseemly display of mirth.

Armand watched the little scene in utter amazement. He had been in England over a year, and yet he could not understand these Englishmen. Surely they were the queerest, most inconsequent people in the world. Here were these men, who were engaged at this very moment in an enterprise which for cool-headed courage and foolhardy daring had probably no parallel in history. They were literally taking their lives in their hands, in all probability facing certain death; and yet they now sat chaffing and fighting like a crowd of third-form schoolboys, talking utter, silly nonsense, and making foolish jokes that would have shamed a Frenchman in his teens. Vaguely he wondered what fat, pompous de Batz would think of this discussion if he could overhear it. His contempt, no doubt, for the Scarlet Pimpernel and his followers would be increased tenfold.

Then at last the question of the disguise was effectually dismissed. Sir Andrew Ffoulkes and Lord Anthony Dewhurst had settled their differences of opinion by solemnly agreeing to represent two over-grimy and overheated coal-heavers. They chose two certificates of safety that were made out in the names of Jean Lepetit and Achille Grospierre, labourers.

"Though you don't look at all like an Achille, Tony," was Blakeney's parting shot to his friend.

Then without any transition from this schoolboy nonsense to the serious business of the moment, Sir Andrew Ffoulkes said abruptly:

"Tell us exactly, Blakeney, where you will want the cart to stand on Sunday."

Blakeney rose and turned to the map against the wall, Ffoulkes and Tony following him. They stood close to his elbow whilst his slender, nervy hand wandered along the shiny surface of the varnished paper. At last he placed his finger on one spot.

"Here you see," he said, "is the Villette gate. Just outside it a narrow street on the right leads down in the direction of the canal. It is just at the bottom of that narrow street at its junction with the tow-path there that I want you two and the cart to be. It had better be a coal-car by the way; they will be unloading coal close by there to-morrow," he added with one of his sudden irrepressible outbursts of merriment. "You and Tony can exercise your muscles coal-heaving, and incidentally make yourselves known in the neighbourhood as good if somewhat grimy patriots."

"We had better take up our parts at once then," said Tony. "I'll take a fond farewell of my clean shirt to-night."

"Yes, you will not see one again for some time, my good Tony. After your hard day's work to-morrow you will have to sleep either inside your cart, if you have already secured one, or under the arches of the canal bridge, if you have not."

"I hope you have an equally pleasant prospect for Hastings," was my Lord Tony's grim comment.

It was easy to see that he was as happy as a schoolboy about to start for a holiday. Lord Tony was a true sportsman. Perhaps there was in him less sentiment for the heroic work which he did under the guidance of his chief than an inherent passion for dangerous adventures. Sir Andrew Ffoulkes, on the other hand, thought perhaps a little less of the adventure, but a great deal of the martyred child in the Temple. He was just as buoyant, just as keen as his friend, but the leaven of sentiment raised his sporting instincts to perhaps a higher plane of self-devotion.

"Well, now, to recapitulate," he said, in turn following with his finger the indicated route on the map. "Tony and I and the coal-cart will await you on this spot, at the corner of the towpath on Sunday evening at nine o'clock."

"And your signal, Blakeney?" asked Tony.

"The usual one," replied Sir Percy, "the seamew's cry thrice repeated at brief intervals. But now," he continued, turning to Armand and Hastings, who had taken no part in the discussion hitherto, "I want your help a little further afield."

"I thought so," nodded Hastings.

"The coal-cart, with its usual miserable nag, will carry us a distance of fifteen or sixteen kilometres, but no more. My purpose is to cut along the north of the city, and to reach St. Germain, the nearest point where we can secure good mounts. There is a farmer just outside the commune; his name is Achard. He has excellent horses, which I have borrowed before now; we shall want five, of course, and he has one powerful beast that will do for me, as I shall have, in addition to my own weight, which is considerable, to take the child with me on the pillion. Now you, Hastings and Armand, will have to start early to-morrow morning, leave Paris by the Neuilly gate, and from there make your way to St. Germain by any conveyance you can contrive to obtain. At St. Germain you must at once find Achard's farm; disguised as labourers you will not arouse suspicion by so doing. You will find the farmer quite amenable to money, and you must secure the best horses you can get for our own use, and, if possible, the powerful mount I spoke of just now. You are both excellent horse-men, therefore I selected you amongst the others for this special errand, for you two, with the five horses, will have to come and meet our coal-cart some seventeen kilometres out of St. Germain, to where the first sign-post indicates the road to Courbevoie. Some two hundred metres down this road on the right there is a small spinney, which will afford splendid shelter for yourselves and your horses. We hope to be there at about one o'clock after midnight of Monday morning. Now, is all that quite clear, and are you both satisfied?"

"It is quite clear," exclaimed Hastings placidly; "but I, for one, am not at all satisfied."

"And why·not?"

"Because it is all too easy. We get none of the danger."

"Oho! I thought that you would bring that argument forward, you incorrigible grumbler," laughed Sir Percy good-humouredly. "Let me tell you that if you start to-morrow from Paris in that spirit you will run your head and Armand's into a noose long before you reach the gate of Neuilly. I cannot allow either of you to cover your faces with too much grime; an honest farm labourer should not look over-dirty, and your chances of being discovered and detained are, at the outset, far greater than those which Ffoulkes and Tony will run—"

Armand had said nothing during this time. While Blakeney was unfolding his plan for him and for Lord Hastings—a plan which practically was a command—he had sat with his arms folded across his chest, his head sunk upon his breast. When Blakeney had asked if they were satisfied, he had taken no part in Hastings' protest nor responded to his leader's good-humoured banter.

Though he did not look up even now, yet he felt that Percy's eyes were fixed upon him, and they seemed to scorch into his soul. He made a great effort to appear eager like the others, and yet from the first a chill had struck at his heart. He could not leave Paris before he had seen Jeanne.

He looked up suddenly, trying to seem unconcerned; he even

looked his chief fully in the face.

"When ought we to leave Paris?" he asked calmly.

"You *must* leave at daybreak," replied Blakeney with a slight, almost imperceptible emphasis on the word of command. "When the gates are first opened, and the work-people go to and fro at their work, that is the safest hour. And you must be at St. Germain as soon as may be, or the farmer may not have a sufficiency of horses available at a moment's notice. I want you to be spokesman with Achard, so that Hastings' British accent should not betray you both. Also you might not get a conveyance for St. Germain immediately. We must think of every eventuality, Armand. There is so much at stake."

Armand made no further comment just then. But the others looked astonished. Armand had but asked a simple question, and Blakeney's reply seemed almost like a rebuke—so circumstantial too, and so explanatory. He was so used to being obeyed at a word, so accustomed that the merest wish, the slightest hint from him was understood by his band of devoted followers, that the long explanation of his orders which he gave to Armand struck them all with a strange sense of unpleasant surprise.

Hastings was the first to break the spell that seemed to have fallen over the party.

"We leave at daybreak, of course," he said, "as soon as the gates are open. We can, I know, get one of the carriers to give us a lift as far as St. Germain. There, how do we find Achard?"

"He is a well-known farmer," replied Blakeney. "You have but to ask."

"Good. Then we bespeak five horses for the next day, find lodgings in the village that night, and make a fresh start back towards Paris in the evening of Sunday. Is that right?"

"Yes. One of you will have two horses on the lead, the other one. Pack some fodder on the empty saddles and start at about ten o'clock. Ride straight along the main road, as if you were making back for Paris, until you come to four cross-roads with a sign-post pointing to Courbevoie. Turn down there and go along the road until you meet a close spinney of fir-trees on your right. Make for the interior of that. It gives splendid shelter, and you can dismount there and give the horses a feed. We'll join you one hour after midnight. The night will be dark, I hope, and the moon anyhow will be on the wane."

"I think I understand. Anyhow, it's not difficult, and we'll be as careful as may be."

"You will have to keep your heads clear, both of you," concluded Blakeney.

He was looking at Armand as he said this; but the young man had not made a movement during this brief colloquy between Hastings and the chief. He still sat with arms folded, his head falling on his breast.

Silence had fallen on them all. They all sat round the fire buried in thought. Through the open window there came from the quay beyond the hum of life in the open-air camp; the tramp of the sentinels around it, the words of command from the drill-sergeant, and through it all the moaning of the wind and the beating of the sleet against the window-panes.

A whole world of wretchedness was expressed by those sounds! Blakeney gave a quick, impatient sigh, and going to the window he pushed it further open, and just then there came from afar the muffled roll of drums, and from below the watchman's cry that seemed such dire mockery:

"Sleep, citizens! Everything is safe and peaceful."

"Sound advice," said Blakeney lightly. "Shall we also go to sleep? What say you all—eh?"

He had with that sudden rapidity characteristic of his every action, already thrown off the serious air which he had worn a moment ago when giving instructions to Hastings. His usual debonnair manner was on him once again, his laziness, his careless insouciance. He was even at this moment deeply engaged in flicking off a grain of dust from the immaculate Mechlin ruff at his wrist. The heavy lids had fallen over the tell-tale eyes as if weighted with fatigue, the mouth appeared ready for the laugh which never was absent from it very long.

It was only Ffoulkes's devoted eyes that were sharp enough to pierce the mask of light-hearted gaiety which enveloped the soul of his leader at the present moment. He saw—for the first time in all the years that he had known Blakeney—a frown across the habitually smooth brow, and though the lips were parted for a laugh, the lines round mouth and chin were hard and set.

With that intuition born of whole-hearted friendship Sir Andrew guessed what troubled Percy. He had caught the look which the latter had thrown on Armand, and knew that some explanation would have to pass between the two men before they parted to-night. Therefore he gave the signal for the breaking up of the meeting.

"There is nothing more to say, is there, Blakeney?" he asked.

"No, my good fellow, nothing," replied Sir Percy. "I do not know how you all feel, but I am demmed fatigued."

"What about the rags for to-morrow?" queried Hastings.

"You know where to find them. In the room below. Ffoulkes has the key. Wigs and all are there. But don't use false hair if you can help it —it is apt to shift in a scrimmage."

He spoke jerkily, more curtly than was his wont. Hastings and Tony thought that he was tired. They rose to say good night. Then the three men went away together, Armand remaining behind.

# Chapter 12: What Love Is

"Well, now, Armand, what is it?" asked Blakeney, the moment the footsteps of his friends had died away down the stone stairs, and their voices had ceased to echo in the distance.

"You guessed, then, that there was . . . something?" said the younger man, after a slight hesitation.

"Of course."

Armand rose, pushing the chair away from him with an impatient nervy gesture. Burying his hands in the pockets of his breeches, he began striding up and down the room, a dark, troubled expression in his face, a deep frown between his eyes.

Blakeney had once more taken up his favourite position, sitting on the corner of the table, his broad shoulders interposed between the lamp and the rest of the room. He was apparently taking no notice of Armand, but only intent on the delicate operation of polishing his nails.

Suddenly the young man paused in his restless walk and stood in front of his friend—an earnest, solemn, determined figure.

"Blakeney," he said, "I cannot leave Paris to-morrow."

Sir Percy made no reply. He was contemplating the polish which he had just succeeded in producing on his thumbnail.

"I must stay here for a while longer," continued Armand firmly. "I may not be able to return to England for some weeks. You have the three others here to help you in your enterprise outside Paris. I am entirely at your service within the compass of its walls."

Still no comment from Blakeney, not a look from beneath the fallen lids. Armand continued, with a slight tone of impatience apparent in his voice:

"You must want some one to help you here on Sunday. I am entirely at your service . . . here or anywhere in Paris . . . but I cannot leave this city . . . at any rate, not just yet. . . . "

Blakeney was apparently satisfied at last with the result of his polishing operations. He rose, gave a slight yawn, and turned toward the door.

"Good night, my dear fellow," he said pleasantly; "it is time we were all abed. I am so demmed fatigued."

"Percy!" exclaimed the young man hotly.

"Eh? What is it?" queried the other lazily.

"You are not going to leave me like this—without a word?"

"I have said a great many words, my good fellow. I have said 'good night,' and remarked that I was demmed fatigued."

He was standing beside the door which led to his bedroom, and now he pushed it open with his hand.

"Percy, you cannot go and leave me like this!" reiterated Armand with rapidly growing irritation.

"Like what, my dear fellow?" queried Sir Percy with good-humoured impatience.

"Without a word—without a sign. What have I done that you should treat me like a child, unworthy even of attention?"

Blakeney had turned back and was now facing him, towering above the slight figure of the younger man. His face had lost none of its gracious air, and beneath their heavy lids his eyes looked down not unkindly on his friend.

"Would you have preferred it, Armand," he said quietly, "if I had said the word that your ears have heard even though my lips have not uttered it?"

"I don't understand," murmured Armand defiantly.

"What sign would you have had me make?" continued Sir Percy, his pleasant voice falling calm and mellow on the younger man's supersensitive consciousness: "That of branding you, Marguerite's brother, as a liar and a cheat?"

"Blakeney!" retorted the other, as with flaming cheeks and wrathful eyes he took a menacing step toward his friend; "had any man but you dared to speak such words to me—"

"I pray to God, Armand, that no man but I has the right to speak them."

"You have no right."

"Every right, my friend. Do I not hold your oath? . . . Are you not prepared to break it?"

"I'll not break my oath to you. I'll serve and help you in every way you can command . . . my life I'll give to the cause . . . give me the most dangerous—the most difficult task to perform. . . . I'll do it—I'll do it gladly."

"I have given you an over-difficult and dangerous task."

"Bah! To leave Paris in order to engage horses, while you and the others do all the work. That is neither difficult nor dangerous."

"It will be difficult for you, Armand, because your head is not sufficiently cool to foresee serious eventualities and to prepare against them. It is dangerous, because you are a man in love, and a man in love is apt to run his head—and that of his friends—blindly into a noose."

"Who told you that I was in love?"

"You yourself, my good fellow. Had you not told me so at the outset," he continued, still speaking very quietly and deliberately and never raising his voice, "I would even now be standing over you, dog-whip in hand, to thrash you as a defaulting coward and a perjurer. . . . Bah!" he added with a return to his habitual bonhomie, "I would no doubt even have lost my temper with you. Which would have been purposeless and excessively bad form. Eh?"

A violent retort had sprung to Armand's lips. But fortunately at that very moment his eyes, glowing with anger, caught those of Blakeney fixed with lazy good-nature upon his. Something of that irresistible dignity which pervaded the whole personality of the man checked Armand's hotheaded words on his lips.

"I cannot leave Paris to-morrow," he reiterated more calmly.

"Because you have arranged to see her again?"

"Because she saved my life to-day, and is herself in danger."

"She is in no danger," said Blakeney simply, "since she saved the life of my friend."

"Percy!"

The cry was wrung from Armand St. Just's very soul. Despite the tumult of passion which was raging in his heart, he was conscious again of the magnetic power which bound so many to this man's service. The words he had said—simple though they were—had sent a thrill through Armand's veins. He felt himself disarmed. His resistance fell before the subtle strength of an unbendable will; nothing remained in his heart but an overwhelming sense of shame and of impotence.

He sank into a chair and rested his elbows on the table, burying his face in his hands. Blakeney went up to him and placed a kindly hand upon his shoulder.

"The difficult task, Armand," he said gently.

"Percy, cannot you release me? She saved my life. I have not thanked her yet."

"There will be time for thanks later, Armand. Just now over yonder the son of kings is being done to death by savage brutes."

"I would not hinder you if I stayed."

"God knows you have hindered us enough already."

"How?"

"You say she saved your life... then you were in danger . . . Heron and his spies have been on your track; your track leads to mine, and I have sworn to save the Dauphin from the hands of thieves. . . . A man in love, Armand, is a deadly danger among us. . . . Therefore at daybreak you must leave Paris with Hastings on your difficult and dangerous task."

"And if I refuse?" retorted Armand.

"My good fellow," said Blakeney earnestly, "in that admirable lexicon which the League of the Scarlet Pimpernel has compiled for itself there is no such word as refuse."

"But if I do refuse?" persisted the other.

"You would be offering a tainted name and tarnished honour to the woman you pretend to love."

"And you insist upon my obedience?"

"By the oath which I hold from you."

"But this is cruel—inhuman!"

"Honour, my good Armand, is often cruel and seldom human. He is a godlike taskmaster, and we who call ourselves men are all of us his slaves."

"The tyranny comes from you alone. You could release me an you would."

"And to gratify the selfish desire of immature passion, you would wish to see me jeopardise the life of those who place infinite trust in me."

"God knows how you have gained their allegiance, Blakeney. To me now you are selfish and callous."

"There is the difficult task you craved for, Armand," was all the answer that Blakeney made to the taunt—"to obey a leader whom you no longer trust."

But this Armand could not brook. He had spoken hotly, impetuously, smarting under the discipline which thwarted his desire, but his heart was loyal to the chief whom he had reverenced for so long.

"Forgive me, Percy," he said humbly; "I am distracted. I don't think I quite realised what I was saying. I trust you, of course . . . . implicitly . . . and you need not even fear . . . I shall not break my oath, though your orders now seem to me needlessly callous and selfish. . . . I will obey . . . you need not be afraid."

"I was not afraid of that, my good fellow."

"Of course, you do not understand . . . you cannot. To you, your honour, the task which you have set yourself, has been your only fetish . . . Love in its true sense does not exist for you. . . . I see it now . . . you do not know what it is to love."

Blakeney made no reply for the moment. He stood in the centre of the room, with the yellow light of the lamp falling full now upon his tall powerful frame, immaculately dressed in perfectly-tailored clothes, upon his long, slender hands half hidden by filmy lace, and upon his face, across which at this moment a heavy strand of curly hair threw a curious shadow. At Armand's words his lips had imperceptibly tightened, his eyes had narrowed as if they tried to see something that was beyond the range of their focus.

Across the smooth brow the strange shadow made by the hair seemed to find a reflex from within. Perhaps the reckless adventurer, the careless gambler with life and liberty, saw through the walls of this squalid room, across the wide, ice-bound river, and beyond even the gloomy pile of buildings opposite, a cool, shady garden at Richmond, a velvety lawn sweeping down to the river's edge, a bower of clematis and roses, with a carved stone seat half covered with moss. There sat an exquisitely beautiful woman with great sad eyes fixed on the far-distant horizon. The setting sun was throwing a halo of gold all round her hair, her white hands were clasped idly on her lap.

She gazed out beyond the river, beyond the sunset, toward an unseen bourne of peace and happiness, and her lovely face had in it a look of utter hopelessness and of sublime self-abnegation. The air was still. It was late autumn, and all around her the russet leaves of beech and chestnut fell with a melancholy hush-sh-sh about her feet.

She was alone, and from time to time heavy tears gathered in her eyes and rolled slowly down her cheeks.

Suddenly a sigh escaped the man's tightly-pressed lips. With a strange gesture, wholly unusual to him, he passed his hand right across his eyes.

"Mayhap you are right, Armand," he said quietly; "mayhap I do not know what it is to love."

Armand turned to go. There was nothing more to be said. He knew Percy well enough by now to realise the finality of his pronouncements. His heart felt sore, but he was too proud to show his hurt again to a man who did not understand. All thoughts of disobedience he had put resolutely aside; he had never meant to break his oath. All that he had hoped to do was to persuade Percy to release him from it for awhile.

That by leaving Paris he risked to lose Jeanne he was quite convinced, but it is nevertheless a true fact that in spite of this he did not withdraw his love and trust from his chief. He was under the influence of that same magnetism which enchained all his comrades to the will of this man; and though his enthusiasm for the great cause had somewhat waned, his allegiance to its leader was no longer tottering.

But he would not trust himself to speak again on the subject.

"I will find the others downstairs," was all he said, "and will arrange with Hastings for to-morrow. Good night, Percy."

"Good night, my dear fellow. By the way, you have not told me yet who she is."

"Her name is Jeanne Lange," said St. Just half reluctantly. He had not meant to divulge his secret quite so fully as yet.

"The young actress at the Theatre National?"

"Yes. Do you know her?"

"Only by name."

"She is beautiful, Percy, and she is an angel . . . Think of my sister Marguerite. . . . she, too, was an actress. . . . Good night, Percy."

"Good night."

The two men grasped one another by the hand. Armand's eyes proffered a last desperate appeal. But Blakeney's eyes were impassive and unrelenting, and Armand with a quick sigh finally took his leave.

For a long while after he had gone Blakeney stood silent and motionless in the middle of the room. Armand's last words lingered in his ear:

"Think of Marguerite!"

The walls had fallen away from around him—the window, the

river below, the Temple prison had all faded away, merged in the chaos of his thoughts.

Now he was no longer in Paris; he heard nothing of the horrors that even at this hour of the night were raging around him; he did not hear the call of murdered victims, of innocent women and children crying for help; he did not see the descendant of St. Louis, with a red cap on his baby head, stamping on the fleur-de-lys, and heaping insults on the memory of his mother. All that had faded into nothingness.

He was in the garden at Richmond, and Marguerite was sitting on the stone seat, with branches of the rambler roses twining themselves in her hair.

He was sitting on the ground at her feet, his head pillowed in her lap, lazily dreaming whilst at his feet the river wound its graceful curves beneath overhanging willows and tall stately elms.

A swan came sailing majestically down the stream, and Marguerite, with idle, delicate hands, threw some crumbs of bread into the water. Then she laughed, for she was quite happy, and anon she stooped, and he felt the fragrance of her lips as she bent over him and savoured the perfect sweetness of her caress. She was happy because her husband was by her side. He had done with adventures, with risking his life for others' sake. He was living only for her.

The man, the dreamer, the idealist that lurked behind the adventurous soul, lived an exquisite dream as he gazed upon that vision. He closed his eyes so that it might last all the longer, so that through the open window opposite he should not see the great gloomy walls of the labyrinthine building packed to overflowing with innocent men, women, and children waiting patiently and with a smile on their lips for a cruel and unmerited death; so that he should not see even through the vista of houses and of streets that grim Temple prison far away, and the light in one of the tower windows, which illumined the final martyrdom of a boy-king.

Thus he stood for fully five minutes, with eyes deliberately closed and lips tightly set. Then the neighbouring tower-clock of St. Germain l'Auxerrois slowly tolled the hour of midnight. Blakeney woke from his dream. The walls of his lodging were once more around him, and through the window the ruddy light of some torch in the street below fought with that of the lamp.

He went deliberately up to the window and looked out into the night. On the quay, a little to the left, the outdoor camp was just breaking up for the night. The people of France in arms against tyranny were allowed to put away their work for the day and to go to their miserable homes to gather rest in sleep for the morrow. A band of soldiers, rough and brutal in their movements, were hustling the women and children. The little ones, weary, sleepy, and cold, seemed too dazed to move. One woman had two little children clinging to her skirts; a soldier suddenly seized one of them by the shoulders and pushed it along roughly in front of him to get it out of the way. The woman struck at the soldier in a stupid, senseless, useless way, and then gathered her trembling chicks under her wing, trying to look defiant.

In a moment she was surrounded. Two soldiers seized her, and two more dragged the children away from her. She screamed and the children cried, the soldiers swore and struck out right and left with their bayonets. There was a general melee, calls of agony rent the air, rough oaths drowned the shouts of the helpless. Some women, panic-stricken, started to run.

And Blakeney from his window looked down upon the scene. He no longer saw the garden at Richmond, the lazily-flowing river, the bowers of roses; even the sweet face of Marguerite, sad and lonely, appeared dim and far away.

He looked across the ice-bound river, past the quay where rough soldiers were brutalising a number of wretched defenceless women, to that grim Chatelet prison, where tiny lights shining here and there behind barred windows told the sad tale of weary vigils, of watches through the night, when dawn would bring martyrdom and death.

And it was not Marguerite's blue eyes that beckoned to him now, it was not her lips that called, but the wan face of a child with matted curls hanging above a greasy forehead, and small hands covered in grime that had once been fondled by a Queen.

The adventurer in him had chased away the dream.

"While there is life in me I'll cheat those brutes of prey," he murmured.

# CHAPTER 13: THEN EVERYTHING WAS DARK

The night that Armand St. Just spent tossing about on a hard, narrow bed was the most miserable, agonising one he had ever passed in his life. A kind of fever ran through him, causing his teeth to chatter and the veins in his temples to throb until he thought that they must burst.

Physically he certainly was ill; the mental strain caused by two great conflicting passions had attacked his bodily strength, and whilst his brain and heart fought their battles together, his aching limbs found no repose.

His love for Jeanne! His loyalty to the man to whom he owed his life, and to whom he had sworn allegiance and implicit obedience!

These superacute feelings seemed to be tearing at his very heartstrings, until he felt that he could no longer lie on the miserable palliasse which in these squalid lodgings did duty for a bed.

He rose long before daybreak, with tired back and burning eyes, but unconscious of any pain save that which tore at his heart.

The weather, fortunately, was not quite so cold—a sudden and very rapid thaw had set in; and when after a hurried toilet Armand, carrying a bundle under his arm, emerged into the street, the mild south wind struck pleasantly on his face.

It was then pitch dark. The street lamps had been extinguished long ago, and the feeble January sun had not yet tinged with pale colour the heavy clouds that hung over the sky.

The streets of the great city were absolutely deserted at this hour. It lay, peaceful and still, wrapped in its mantle of gloom. A thin rain was falling, and Armand's feet, as he began to descend the heights of Montmartre, sank ankle deep in the mud of the road. There was but scanty attempt at pavements in this outlying quarter of the town, and Armand had much ado to keep his footing on the uneven and intermittent stones that did duty for roads in these parts. But this discomfort did not trouble him just now. One thought—and one alone —was clear in his mind: he must see Jeanne before he left Paris.

He did not pause to think how he could accomplish that at this hour of the day. All he knew was that he must obey his chief, and that he must see Jeanne. He would see her, explain to her that he must leave Paris immediately, and beg her to make her preparations quickly, so that she might meet him as soon as maybe, and accompany him to England straight away.

He did not feel that he was being disloyal by trying to see Jeanne. He had thrown prudence to the winds, not realising that his imprudence would and did jeopardise, not only the success of his chief's plans, but also his life and that of his friends. He had before parting from Hastings last night arranged to meet him in the neighbourhood of the Neuilly Gate at seven o'clock; it was only six now. There was plenty of time for him to rouse the concierge at the house of the Square du Roule, to see Jeanne for a few moments, to slip into Madame Belhomme's kitchen, and there into the labourer's clothes which he was carrying in the bundle under his arm, and to be at the gate at the appointed hour.

The Square du Roule is shut off from the Rue St. Honore, on which it abuts, by tall iron gates, which a few years ago, when the secluded little square was a fashionable quarter of the city, used to be kept closed at night, with a watchman in uniform to intercept midnight prowlers. Now these gates had been rudely torn away from their sockets, the iron had been sold for the benefit of the ever-empty Treasury, and no one cared if the homeless, the starving, or the evil-doer found shelter under the porticoes of the houses, from whence wealthy or aristocratic owners had long since thought it wise to flee.

No one challenged Armand when he turned into the square, and though the darkness was intense, he made his way fairly straight for the house where lodged Mademoiselle Lange.

So far he had been wonderfully lucky. The foolhardiness with which he had exposed his life and that of his friends by wandering about the streets of Paris at this hour without any attempt at disguise, though carrying one under his arm, had not met with the untoward fate which it undoubtedly deserved. The darkness of the night and the thin sheet of rain as it fell had effectually wrapped his progress through the lonely streets in their beneficent mantle of gloom; the soft mud below had drowned the echo of his footsteps. If spies were on his track, as Jeanne had feared and Blakeney prophesied, he had certainly succeeded in evading them.

He pulled the concierge's bell, and the latch of the outer door, manipulated from within, duly sprang open in response. He entered, and from the lodge the concierge's voice emerging, muffled from the depths of pillows and blankets, challenged him with an oath directed at the unseemliness of the hour.

"Mademoiselle Lange," said Armand boldly, as without hesitation he walked quickly past the lodge making straight for the stairs.

It seemed to him that from the concierge's room loud vituperations followed him, but he took no notice of these; only a short flight of stairs and one more door separated him from Jeanne.

He did not pause to think that she would in all probability be still in bed, that he might have some difficulty in rousing Madame Belhomme, that the latter might not even care to admit him; nor did he reflect on the glaring imprudence of his actions. He wanted to see Jeanne, and she was the other side of that wall.

"He, citizen! *Hola!* Here! Curse you! Where are you?" came in a gruff voice to him from below.

He had mounted the stairs, and was now on the landing just outside Jeanne's door. He pulled the bell-handle, and heard the pleasing echo of the bell that would presently wake Madame Belhomme and bring her to the door.

"Citizen! *Hola!* Curse you for an *aristo!* What are you doing there?"

The concierge, a stout, elderly man, wrapped in a blanket, his feet thrust in slippers, and carrying a guttering tallow candle, had appeared upon the landing.

He held the candle up so that its feeble flickering rays fell on Armand's pale face, and on the damp cloak which fell away from his shoulders.

"What are you doing there?" reiterated the concierge with another oath from his prolific vocabulary.

"As you see, citizen," replied Armand politely, "I am ringing Mademoiselle Lange's front door bell."

"At this hour of the morning?" queried the man with a sneer.

"I desire to see her."

"Then you have come to the wrong house, citizen," said the concierge with a rude laugh.

"The wrong house? What do you mean?" stammered Armand, a little bewildered.

"She is not here—*quoi!*" retorted the concierge, who now turned deliberately on his heel. "Go and look for her, citizen; it'll take you some time to find her."

He shuffled off in the direction of the stairs. Armand was vainly trying to shake himself free from a sudden, an awful sense of horror.

He gave another vigorous pull at the hell, then with one bound he overtook the concierge, who was preparing to descend the stairs, and gripped him peremptorily by the arm.

"Where is Mademoiselle Lange?" he asked.

His voice sounded quite strange in his own ear; his throat felt parched, and he had to moisten his lips with his tongue before he was able to speak.

"Arrested," replied the man.

"Arrested? When? Where? How?"

"When—late yesterday evening. Where?—here in her room. How?—by the agents of the Committee of General Security. She and the old woman! Basta! that's all I know. Now I am going back to bed, and you clear out of the house. You are making a disturbance, and I shall be reprimanded. I ask you, is this a decent time for rousing honest patriots out of their morning sleep?"

He shook his arm free from Armand's grasp and once more

began to descend.

Armand stood on the landing like a man who has been stunned by a blow on the head. His limbs were paralysed. He could not for the moment have moved or spoken if his life had depended on a sign or on a word. His brain was reeling, and he had to steady himself with his hand against the wall or he would have fallen headlong on the floor. He had lived in a whirl of excitement for the past twenty-four hours; his nerves during that time had been kept at straining point. Passion, joy, happiness, deadly danger, and moral fights had worn his mental endurance threadbare; want of proper food and a sleepless night had almost thrown his physical balance out of gear. This blow came at a moment when he was least able to bear it.

Jeanne had been arrested! Jeanne was in the hands of those brutes, whom he, Armand, had regarded yesterday with insurmountable loathing! Jeanne was in prison—she was arrested—she would be tried, condemned, and all because of him!

The thought was so awful that it brought him to the verge of mania. He watched as in a dream the form of the concierge shuffling his way down the oak staircase; his portly figure assumed Gargantuan proportions, the candle which he carried looked like the dancing flames of hell, through which grinning faces, hideous and contortioned, mocked at him and leered.

Then suddenly everything was dark. The light had disappeared round the bend of the stairs; grinning faces and ghoulish visions vanished; he only saw Jeanne, his dainty, exquisite Jeanne, in the hands of those brutes. He saw her as he had seen a year and a half ago the victims of those bloodthirsty wretches being dragged before a tribunal that was but a mockery of justice; he heard the quick interrogatory, and the responses from her perfect lips, that exquisite voice of hers veiled by tones of anguish. He heard the condemnation, the rattle of the tumbril on the ill-paved streets—saw her there with hands clasped together, her eyes—

Great God! he was really going mad!

Like a wild creature driven forth he started to run down the stairs, past the concierge, who was just entering his lodge, and who now turned in surly anger to watch this man running away like a lunatic or a fool, out by the front door and into the street. In a moment he was out of the little square; then like a hunted hare he still ran down the Rue St. Honore, along its narrow, interminable length. His hat had fallen from his head, his hair was wild all round his face, the rain weighted the cloak upon his shoulders; but still he ran.

His feet made no noise on the muddy pavement. He ran on and on, his elbows pressed to his sides, panting, quivering, intent but upon one thing—the goal which he had set himself to reach.

Jeanne was arrested. He did not know where to look for her,

but he did know whither he wanted to go now as swiftly as his legs would carry him.

It was still dark, but Armand St. Just was a born Parisian, and he knew every inch of this quarter, where he and Marguerite had years ago lived. Down the Rue St. Honore, he had reached the bottom of the interminably long street at last. He had kept just a sufficiency of reason —or was it merely blind instinct?—to avoid the places where the night patrols of the National Guard might be on the watch. He avoided the Place du Carrousel, also the quay, and struck sharply to his right until he reached the facade of St. Germain l'Auxerrois.

Another effort; round the corner, and there was the house at last. He was like the hunted creature now that has run to earth. Up the two flights of stone stairs, and then the pull at the bell; a moment of tense anxiety, whilst panting, gasping, almost choked with the sustained effort and the strain of the past half-hour, he leaned against the wall, striving not to fall.

Then the well-known firm step across the rooms beyond, the open door, the hand upon his shoulder.

After that he remembered nothing more.

# Chapter 14: The Chief

He had not actually fainted, but the exertion of that long run had rendered him partially unconscious. He knew now that he was safe, that he was sitting in Blakeney's room, and that something hot and vivifying was being poured down his throat.

"Percy, they have arrested her!" he said, panting, as soon as speech returned to his paralysed tongue.

"All right. Don't talk now. Wait till you are better."

With infinite care and gentleness Blakeney arranged some cushions under Armand's head, turned the sofa towards the fire, and anon brought his friend a cup of hot coffee, which the latter drank with avidity.

He was really too exhausted to speak. He had contrived to tell Blakeney, and now Blakeney knew, so everything would be all right. The inevitable reaction was asserting itself; the muscles had relaxed, the nerves were numbed, and Armand lay back on the sofa with eyes half closed, unable to move, yet feeling his strength gradually returning to him, his vitality asserting itself, all the feverish excitement of the past twenty-four hours yielding at last to a calmer mood.

Through his half-closed eyes he could see his brother-in-law moving about the room. Blakeney was fully dressed. In a sleepy kind of way Armand wondered if he had been to bed at all; certainly his clothes set on him with their usual well-tailored perfection, and there was no suggestion in his brisk step and alert movements that he had passed a sleepless night.

Now he was standing by the open window. Armand, from where he lay, could see his broad shoulders sharply outlined against the grey background of the hazy winter dawn. A wan light was just creeping up from the east over the city; the noises of the streets below came distinctly to Armand's ear.

He roused himself with one vigorous effort from his lethargy, feeling quite ashamed of himself and of this breakdown of his nervous system. He looked with frank admiration on Sir Percy, who stood immovable and silent by the window—a perfect tower of strength, serene and impassive, yet kindly in distress.

"Percy," said the young man, "I ran all the way from the top of the Rue St. Honore. I was only breathless. I am quite all right. May I tell you all about it?"

Without a word Blakeney closed the window and came across to the sofa; he sat down beside Armand, and to all outward appearances he was nothing now but a kind and sympathetic listener to a friend's tale of woe. Not a line in his face or a look in his eyes betrayed the thoughts of the leader who had been thwarted at the outset of a dangerous enterprise, or of the man, accustomed to command, who had been so flagrantly disobeyed.

Armand, unconscious of all save of Jeanne and of her immediate need, put an eager hand on Percy's arm.

"Heron and his hell-hounds went back to her lodgings last night," he said, speaking as if he were still a little out of breath. "They hoped to get me, no doubt; not finding me there, they took her. Oh, my God!"

It was the first time that he had put the whole terrible circumstance into words, and it seemed to gain in reality by the recounting. The agony of mind which he endured was almost unbearable; he hid his face in his hands lest Percy should see how terribly he suffered.

"I knew that," said Blakeney quietly. Armand looked up in surprise.

"How? When did you know it?" he stammered.

"Last night when you left me. I went down to the Square du Roule. I arrived there just too late."

"Percy!" exclaimed Armand, whose pale face had suddenly flushed scarlet, "you did that?—last night you—"

"Of course," interposed the other calmly; "had I not promised you to keep watch over her? When I heard the news it was already too late to make further inquiries, but when you arrived just now I was on the point of starting out, in order to find out in what prison Mademoiselle Lange is being detained. I shall have to go soon, Armand, before the guard is changed at the Temple and the Tuileries. This is the safest time, and God knows we are all of us sufficiently compromised already."

The flush of shame deepened in St. Just's cheek. There had not been a hint of reproach in the voice of his chief, and the eyes which regarded him now from beneath the half-closed lids showed nothing but lazy bonhomie.

In a moment now Armand realised all the harm which his recklessness had done, was still doing to the work of the League. Every one of his actions since his arrival in Paris two days ago had jeopardised a plan or endangered a life: his friendship with de Batz, his connection with Mademoiselle Lange, his visit to her yesterday afternoon, the repetition of it this morning, culminating in that wild run through the streets of Paris, when at any moment a spy lurking round a corner might either have barred his way, or, worse still, have followed him to Blakeney's door. Armand, without a thought of any one save of his beloved, might easily this morning have brought an agent of the Committee of General Security face to face with his chief.

"Percy," he murmured, "can you ever forgive me?"

"Pshaw, man!" retorted Blakeney lightly; "there is naught to forgive, only a great deal that should no longer be forgotten; your duty to the others, for instance, your obedience, and your honour."

"I was mad, Percy. Oh! if you only could understand what she means to me!"

Blakeney laughed, his own light-hearted careless laugh, which so often before now had helped to hide what he really felt from the eyes of the indifferent, and even from those of his friends.

"No! no!" he said lightly, "we agreed last night, did we not? that in matters of sentiment I am a cold-blooded fish. But will you at any rate concede that I am a man of my word? Did I not pledge it last night that Mademoiselle Lange would be safe? I foresaw her arrest the moment I heard your story. I hoped that I might reach her before that brute Heron's return; unfortunately he forestalled me by less than half an hour. Mademoiselle Lange has been arrested, Armand; but why should you not trust me on that account? Have we not succeeded, I and the others, in worse cases than this one? They mean no harm to Jeanne Lange," he added emphatically; "I give you my word on that. They only want her as a decoy. It is you they want. You through her, and me through you. I pledge you my honour that she will be safe. You must try and trust me, Armand. It is much to ask, I know, for you will have to trust me with what is most precious in the world to you; and you will have to obey me blindly, or I shall not be able to keep my word."

"What do you wish me to do?"

"Firstly, you must be outside Paris within the hour. Every minute that you spend inside the city now is full of danger—oh, no! not for you," added Blakeney, checking with a good-humoured gesture Armand's words of protestation, "danger for the others—and for our scheme tomorrow."

"How can I go to St. Germain, Percy, knowing that she—"

"Is under my charge?" interposed the other calmly. "That should not be so very difficult. Come," he added, placing a kindly hand on the other's shoulder, "you shall not find me such an inhuman monster after all. But I must think of the others, you see, and of the child whom I have sworn to save. But I won't send you as far as St. Germain. Go down to the room below and find a good bundle of rough clothes that will serve you as a disguise, for I imagine that you have lost those which you had on the landing or the stairs of the house in the Square du Roule. In a tin box with the clothes downstairs you will find the packet of miscellaneous certificates of safety. Take an appropriate one, and then start out immediately for Villette. You understand?"

"Yes, yes!" said Armand eagerly. "You want me to join Ffoulkes and Tony."

"Yes! You'll find them probably unloading coal by the canal. Try and get private speech with them as early as may be, and tell Tony to set out at once for St. Germain, and to join Hastings there, instead of you, whilst you take his place with Ffoulkes."

"Yes, I understand; but how will Tony reach St. Germain?"

"La, my good fellow," said Blakeney gaily, "you may safely trust Tony to go where I send him. Do you but do as I tell you, and leave him to look after himself. And now," he added, speaking more earnestly, "the sooner you get out of Paris the better it will be for us all. As you see, I am only sending you to La Villette, because it is not so far, but that I can keep in personal touch with you. Remain close to the gates for an hour after nightfall. I will contrive before they close to bring you news of Mademoiselle Lange."

Armand said no more. The sense of shame in him deepened with every word spoken by his chief. He felt how untrustworthy he had been, how undeserving of the selfless devotion which Percy was showing him even now. The words of gratitude died on his lips; he knew that they would be unwelcome. These Englishmen were so devoid of sentiment, he thought, and his brother-in-law, with all his unselfish and heroic deeds, was, he felt, absolutely callous in matters of the heart.

But Armand was a noble-minded man, and with the true sporting instinct in him, despite the fact that he was a creature of nerves, highly strung and imaginative. He could give ungrudging admiration to his chief, even whilst giving himself up entirely to the sentiment for Jeanne.

He tried to imbue himself with the same spirit that actuated my Lord Tony and the other members of the League. How gladly would he have chaffed and made senseless schoolboy jokes like those which—in face of their hazardous enterprise and the dangers which they all ran—had horrified him so much last night.

But somehow he knew that jokes from him would not ring true. How could he smile when his heart was brimming over with his love for Jeanne, and with solicitude on her account? He felt that Percy was regarding him with a kind of indulgent amusement; there was a look of suppressed merriment in the depths of those lazy blue eyes.

So he braced up his nerves, trying his best to look cool and unconcerned, but he could not altogether hide from his friend the burning anxiety which was threatening to break his heart.

"I have given you my word, Armand," said Blakeney in answer to the unspoken prayer; "cannot you try and trust me—as the others do? Then with sudden transition he pointed to the map behind him.

"Remember the gate of Villette, and the corner by the towpath. Join Ffoulkes as soon as may be and send Tony on his way, and wait for news of Mademoiselle Lange some time to-night."

"God bless you, Percy!" said Armand involuntarily. "Good-bye!"

"Good-bye, my dear fellow. Slip on your disguise as quickly as you can, and be out of the house in a quarter of an hour."

He accompanied Armand through the ante-room, and finally closed the door on him. Then he went back to his room and walked up to the window, which he threw open to the humid morning air. Now that he was alone the look of trouble on his face deepened to a dark, anxious frown, and as he looked out across the river a sigh of bitter impatience and disappointment escaped his lips.

# CHAPTER 15: THE GATE OF LA VILLETTE

And now the shades of evening had long since yielded to those of night. The gate of La Villette, at the northeast corner of the city, was about to close. Armand, dressed in the rough clothes of a labouring man, was leaning against a low wall at the angle of the narrow street which abuts on the canal at its further end; from this point of vantage he could command a view of the gate and of the life and bustle around it.

He was dog-tired. After the emotions of the past twenty-four hours, a day's hard manual toil to which he was unaccustomed had caused him to ache in every limb. As soon as he had arrived at the canal wharf in the early morning he had obtained the kind of casual work that ruled about here, and soon was told off to unload a cargo of coal which had arrived by barge overnight. He had set-to with a will, half hoping to kill his anxiety by dint of heavy bodily exertion. During the course of the morning he had suddenly become aware of Sir Andrew Ffoulkes and of Lord Anthony Dewhurst working not far away from him, and as fine a pair of coalheavers as any shipper could desire.

It was not very difficult in the midst of the noise and activity that reigned all about the wharf for the three men to exchange a few words together, and Armand soon communicated the chief's new instructions to my Lord Tony, who effectually slipped away from his work some time during the day. Armand did not even see him go, it had all been so neatly done.

Just before five o'clock in the afternoon the labourers were paid off. It was then too dark to continue work. Armand would have liked to talk to Sir Andrew, if only for a moment. He felt lonely and desperately anxious. He had hoped to tire out his nerves as well as his body, but in this he had not succeeded. As soon as he had given up his tools, his brain began to work again more busily than ever. It followed Percy in his peregrinations through the city, trying to discover where those brutes were keeping Jeanne.

That task had suddenly loomed up before Armand's mind with all its terrible difficulties. How could Percy—a marked man if ever there was one—go from prison to prison to inquire about Jeanne? The very idea seemed preposterous. Armand ought never to have consented to such an insensate plan. The more he thought of it, the more impossible did it seem that Blakeney could find anything out.

Sir Andrew Ffoulkes was nowhere to be seen. St. Just wandered about in the dark, lonely streets of this outlying quarter vainly trying to find the friend in whom he could confide, who, no doubt, would reassure him as to Blakeney's probable movements in Paris. Then as the hour approached for the closing of the city gates Armand took up his stand at an angle of the street from whence he could see both the gate on one side of him and the thin line of the canal intersecting the street at its further end.

Unless Percy came within the next five minutes the gates would be closed and the difficulties of crossing the barrier would be increased a hundredfold. The market gardeners with their covered carts filed out of the gate one by one; the labourers on foot were returning to their homes; there was a group of stonemasons, a few road-makers, also a number of beggars, ragged and filthy, who herded somewhere in the neighbourhood of the canal.

In every form, under every disguise, Armand hoped to discover Percy. He could not stand still for very long, but strode up and down the road that skirts the fortifications at this point.

There were a good many idlers about at this hour; some men who had finished their work, and meant to spend an hour or so in one of the drinking shops that abounded in the neighbourhood of the wharf; others who liked to gather a small knot of listeners around them, whilst they discoursed on the politics of the day, or rather raged against the Convention, which was all made up of traitors to the people's welfare.

Armand, trying manfully to play his part, joined one of the groups that stood gaping round a street orator. He shouted with the best of them, waved his cap in the air, and applauded or hissed in unison with the majority. But his eyes never wandered for long away from the gate whence Percy must come now at any moment—now or not at all.

At what precise moment the awful doubt took birth in his mind the young man could not afterwards have said. Perhaps it was when he heard the roll of drums proclaiming the closing of the gates, and witnessed the changing of the guard.

Percy had not come. He could not come now, and he (Armand) would have the night to face without news of Jeanne. Something, of course, had detained Percy; perhaps he had been unable to get definite information about Jeanne; perhaps the information which he had obtained was too terrible to communicate.

If only Sir Andrew Ffoulkes had been there, and Armand had had some one to talk to, perhaps then he would have found sufficient strength of mind to wait with outward patience, even though his nerves were on the rack.

Darkness closed in around him, and with the darkness came the full return of the phantoms that had assailed him in the house of the Square du Roule when first he had heard of Jeanne's arrest. The open place facing the gate had transformed itself into the Place de la Revolution, the tall rough post that held a flickering oil lamp had become the gaunt arm of the guillotine, the feeble light of the lamp was the knife that gleamed with the reflection of a crimson light.

And Armand saw himself, as in a vision, one of a vast and noisy throng—they were all pressing round him so that he could not move; they were brandishing caps and tricolour flags, also pitchforks and scythes. He had seen such a crowd four years ago rushing towards the Bastille. Now they were all assembled here around him and around the guillotine.

Suddenly a distant rattle caught his subconscious ear: the rattle of wheels on rough cobble-stones. Immediately the crowd began to cheer and to shout; some sang the "*Ca ira!*" and others screamed:

"*Les aristos! a la lanterne! a mort! a mort! les aristos!*"

He saw it all quite plainly, for the darkness had vanished, and the vision was more vivid than even reality could have been. The rattle of wheels grew louder, and presently the cart debouched on the open place.

Men and women sat huddled up in the cart; but in the midst of them a woman stood, and her eyes were fixed upon Armand. She wore her pale-grey satin gown, and a white kerchief was folded across her bosom. Her brown hair fell in loose soft curls all round her head. She looked exactly like the exquisite cameo which Marguerite used to wear. Her hands were tied with cords behind her back, but between her fingers she held a small bunch of violets.

Armand saw it all. It was, of course, a vision, and he knew that it was one, but he believed that the vision was prophetic. No thought of the chief whom he had sworn to trust and to obey came to chase away these imaginings of his fevered fancy. He saw Jeanne, and only Jeanne, standing on the tumbril and being led to the guillotine. Sir Andrew was not there, and Percy had not come. Armand believed that a direct message had come to him from heaven to save his beloved.

Therefore he forgot his promise—his oath; he forgot those very things which the leader had entreated him to remember—his duty to the others, his loyalty, his obedience. Jeanne had first claim on him. It were the act of a coward to remain in safety whilst she was in such deadly danger.

Now he blamed himself severely for having quitted Paris. Even Percy must have thought him a coward for obeying quite so readily. Maybe the command had been but a test of his courage, of the strength of his love for Jeanne.

A hundred conjectures flashed through his brain; a hundred plans presented themselves to his mind. It was not for Percy, who did not know her, to save Jeanne or to guard her. That task was Armand's, who worshipped her, and who would gladly die beside her if he failed to rescue her from threatened death.

Resolution was not slow in coming. A tower clock inside the city struck the hour of six, and still no sign of Percy.

Armand, his certificate of safety in his hand, walked boldly up to the gate.

The guard challenged him, but he presented the certificate. There was an agonising moment when the card was taken from him, and he was detained in the guard-room while it was being examined by the sergeant in command.

But the certificate was in good order, and Armand, covered in coal-dust, with the perspiration streaming down his face, did certainly not look like an aristocrat in disguise. It was never very difficult to enter the great city; if one wished to put one's head in the lion's mouth, one was welcome to do so; the difficulty came when the lion thought fit to close his jaws.

Armand, after five minutes of tense anxiety, was allowed to cross the barrier, but his certificate of safety was detained. He would have to get another from the Committee of General Security before he would be allowed to leave Paris again.

The lion had thought fit to close his jaws.

# Chapter 16: The Weary Search

Blakeney was not at his lodgings when Armand arrived there that evening, nor did he return, whilst the young man haunted the precincts of St. Germain l'Auxerrois and wandered along the quays hours and hours at a stretch, until he nearly dropped under the portico of a house, and realised that if he loitered longer he might lose consciousness completely, and be unable on the morrow to be of service to Jeanne.

He dragged his weary footsteps back to his own lodgings on the heights of Montmartre. He had not found Percy, he had no news of Jeanne; it seemed as if hell itself could hold no worse tortures than this intolerable suspense.

He threw himself down on the narrow palliasse and, tired nature asserting herself, at last fell into a heavy, dreamless torpor, like the sleep of a drunkard, deep but without the beneficent aid of rest.

It was broad daylight when he awoke. The pale light of a damp, wintry morning filtered through the grimy panes of the window. Armand jumped out of bed, aching of limb but resolute of mind. There was no doubt that Percy had failed in discovering Jeanne's whereabouts; but where a mere friend had failed a lover was more likely to succeed.

The rough clothes which he had worn yesterday were the only ones he had. They would, of course, serve his purpose better than his own, which he had left at Blakeney's lodgings yesterday. In half an hour he was dressed, looking a fairly good imitation of a labourer out of work.

He went to a humble eating house of which he knew, and there, having ordered some hot coffee with a hunk of bread, he set himself to think.

It was quite a usual thing these days for relatives and friends of prisoners to go wandering about from prison to prison to find out where the loved ones happened to be detained. The prisons were over full just now; convents, monasteries, and public institutions had all been requisitioned by the Government for the housing of the hundreds of so-called traitors who had been arrested on the barest suspicion, or at the mere denunciation of an evil-wisher.

There were the Abbaye and the Luxembourg, the erstwhile convents of the Visitation and the Sacre-Coeur, the cloister of the Oratorians, the Salpetriere, and the St. Lazare hospitals, and there was, of course, the Temple, and, lastly, the Conciergerie, to which those prisoners were brought whose trial would take place within the next few days, and whose condemnation was practically assured. Persons under arrest at some of the other prisons did sometimes come out of them alive, but the Conciergerie was only the ante-chamber of the guillotine.

Therefore Armand's idea was to visit the Conciergerie first. The sooner he could reassure himself that Jeanne was not in immediate danger the better would he be able to endure the agony of that heart-breaking search, that knocking at every door in the hope of finding his beloved.

If Jeanne was not in the Conciergerie, then there might be some hope that she was only being temporarily detained, and through Armand's excited brain there had already flashed the thought that mayhap the Committee of General Security would release her if he gave himself up.

These thoughts, and the making of plans, fortified him mentally and physically; he even made a great effort to eat and drink, knowing that his bodily strength must endure if it was going to be of service to Jeanne.

He reached the Quai de l'Horloge soon after nine. The grim, irregular walls of the Chatelet and the house of Justice loomed from out the mantle of mist that lay on the river banks. Armand skirted the square clock-tower, and passed through the monumental gateways of the house of Justice.

He knew that his best way to the prison would be through the halls and corridors of the Tribunal, to which the public had access whenever the court was sitting. The sittings began at ten, and already the usual crowd of idlers were assembling—men and women who apparently had no other occupation save to come day after day to this theatre of horrors and watch the different acts of the heartrending dramas that were enacted here with a kind of awful monotony.

Armand mingled with the crowd that stood about the courtyard, and anon moved slowly up the gigantic flight of stone steps, talking lightly on indifferent subjects. There was quite a goodly sprinkling of workingmen amongst this crowd, and Armand in his toil-stained clothes attracted no attention.

Suddenly a word reached his ear—just a name flippantly spoken by spiteful lips—and it changed the whole trend of his thoughts. Since he had risen that morning he had thought of nothing but of Jeanne, and—in connection with her—of Percy and his vain quest of her. Now that name spoken by some one unknown brought his mind back to more definite thoughts of his chief.

"Capet!" the name—intended as an insult, but actually merely irrelevant—whereby the uncrowned little King of France was designated by the revolutionary party.

Armand suddenly recollected that to-day was Sunday, the 19th of January. He had lost count of days and of dates lately, but the name, "Capet," had brought everything back: the child in the Temple; the conference in Blakeney's lodgings; the plans for the rescue of the boy. That was to take place to-day—Sunday, the 19th. The Simons would be moving from the Temple, at what hour Blakeney did not know, but it would be today, and he would be watching his opportunity.

Now Armand understood everything; a great wave of bitterness swept over his soul. Percy had forgotten Jeanne! He was busy thinking of the child in the Temple, and whilst Armand had been eating out his heart with anxiety, the Scarlet Pimpernel, true only to his mission, and impatient of all sentiment that interfered with his schemes, had left Jeanne to pay with her life for the safety of the uncrowned King.

But the bitterness did not last long; on the contrary, a kind of wild exultation took its place. If Percy had forgotten, then Armand could stand by Jeanne alone. It was better so! He would save the loved one; it was his duty and his right to work for her sake. Never for a moment did he doubt that he could save her, that his life would be readily accepted in exchange for hers.

The crowd around him was moving up the monumental steps, and Armand went with the crowd. It lacked but a few minutes to ten now; soon the court would begin to sit. In the olden days, when he was studying for the law, Armand had often wandered about at will along the corridors of the house of Justice. He knew exactly where the different prisons were situated about the buildings, and how to reach the courtyards where the prisoners took their daily exercise.

To watch those *aristos* who were awaiting trial and death taking their recreation in these courtyards had become one of the sights of Paris. Country cousins on a visit to the city were brought hither for entertainment. Tall iron gates stood between the public and the prisoners, and a row of sentinels guarded these gates; but if one was enterprising and eager to see, one could glue one's nose against the ironwork and watch the *ci-devant* aristocrats in threadbare clothes trying to cheat their horror of death by acting a farce of light-heartedness which their wan faces and tear-dimmed eyes effectually belied.

All this Armand knew, and on this he counted. For a little while he joined the crowd in the Salle des Pas Perdus, and wandered idly up and down the majestic colonnaded hall. He even at one time formed part of the throng that watched one of those quick tragedies that were enacted within the great chamber of the court. A number of prisoners brought in, in a batch; hurried interrogations, interrupted answers, a quick indictment, monstrous in its flaring injustice, spoken by Foucquier-Tinville, the public prosecutor, and listened to in all seriousness by men who dared to call themselves judges of their fellows.

The accused had walked down the Champs Elysees without wearing a tricolour cockade; the other had invested some savings in an

English industrial enterprise; yet another had sold public funds, causing them to depreciate rather suddenly in the market!

Sometimes from one of these unfortunates led thus wantonly to butchery there would come an excited protest, or from a woman screams of agonised entreaty. But these were quickly silenced by rough blows from the butt-ends of muskets, and condemnations—wholesale sentences of death—were quickly passed amidst the cheers of the spectators and the howls of derision from infamous jury and judge.

Oh! the mockery of it all—the awful, the hideous ignominy, the blot of shame that would forever sully the historic name of France. Armand, sickened with horror, could not bear more than a few minutes of this monstrous spectacle. The same fate might even now be awaiting Jeanne. Among the next batch of victims to this sacrilegious butchery he might suddenly spy his beloved with her pale face and cheeks stained with her tears.

He fled from the great chamber, keeping just a sufficiency of presence of mind to join a knot of idlers who were drifting leisurely towards the corridors. He followed in their wake and soon found himself in the long Galerie des Prisonniers, along the flagstones of which two days ago de Batz had followed his guide towards the lodgings of Heron.

On his left now were the arcades shut off from the courtyard beyond by heavy iron gates. Through the ironwork Armand caught sight of a number of women walking or sitting in the courtyard. He heard a man next to him explaining to his friend that these were the female prisoners who would be brought to trial that day, and he felt that his heart must burst at the thought that mayhap Jeanne would be among them.

He elbowed his way cautiously to the front rank. Soon he found himself beside a sentinel who, with a good-humoured jest, made way for him that he might watch the *aristos*. Armand leaned against the grating, and his every sense was concentrated in that of sight.

At first he could scarcely distinguish one woman from another amongst the crowd that thronged the courtyard, and the close ironwork hindered his view considerably. The women looked almost like phantoms in the grey misty air, gliding slowly along with noiseless tread on the flag-stones.

Presently, however, his eyes, which mayhap were somewhat dim with tears, became more accustomed to the hazy grey light and the moving figures that looked so like shadows. He could distinguish isolated groups now, women and girls sitting together under the colonnaded arcades, some reading, others busy, with trembling fingers, patching and darning a poor, torn gown. Then there were others who were actually chatting and laughing together, and—oh, the pity of it! the pity and the shame!—a few children, shrieking with delight, were playing hide and seek in and out amongst the columns.

And, between them all, in and out like the children at play, unseen, yet familiar to all, the spectre of Death, scythe and hour-glass in hand, wandered, majestic and sure.

Armand's very soul was in his eyes. So far he had not yet caught sight of his beloved, and slowly—very slowly—a ray of hope was filtering through the darkness of his despair.

The sentinel, who had stood aside for him, chaffed him for his intentness.

"Have you a sweetheart among these *aristos*, citizen?" he asked. "You seem to be devouring them with your eyes."

Armand, with his rough clothes soiled with coal-dust, his face grimy and streaked with sweat, certainly looked to have but little in common with the *ci-devant aristos* who formed the hulk of the groups in the courtyard. He looked up; the soldier was regarding him with obvious amusement, and at sight of Armand's wild, anxious eyes he gave vent to a coarse jest.

"Have I made a shrewd guess, citizen?" he said. "Is she among that lot?"

"I do not know where she is," said Armand almost involuntarily.

"Then why don't you find out?" queried the soldier.

The man was not speaking altogether unkindly. Armand, devoured with the maddening desire to know, threw the last fragment of prudence to the wind. He assumed a more careless air, trying to look as like a country bumpkin in love as he could.

"I would like to find out," he said, "but I don't know where to inquire. My sweetheart has certainly left her home," he added lightly; "some say that she has been false to me, but I think that, mayhap, she has been arrested."

"Well, then, you gaby," said the soldier good-humouredly, "go straight to La Tournelle; you know where it is?"

Armand knew well enough, but thought it more prudent to keep up the air of the ignorant lout.

"Straight down that first corridor on your right," explained the other, pointing in the direction which he had indicated, "you will find the guichet of La Tournelle exactly opposite to you. Ask the concierge for the register of female prisoners—every freeborn citizen of the Republic has the right to inspect prison registers. It is a new decree framed for safeguarding the liberty of the people. But if you do not press half a livre in the hand of the concierge," he added, speaking confidentially, "you will find that the register will not be quite ready for your inspection."

"Half a livre!" exclaimed Armand, striving to play his part to the end. "How can a poor devil of a labourer have half a livre to give away?"

"Well! a few sous will do in that case; a few sous are always welcome these hard times."

Armand took the hint, and as the crowd had drifted away momentarily to a further portion of the corridor, he contrived to press a few copper coins into the hand of the obliging soldier.

Of course, he knew his way to La Tournelle, and he would have covered the distance that separated him from the guichet there with steps flying like the wind, but, commending himself for his own prudence, he walked as slowly as he could along the interminable corridor, past the several minor courts of justice, and skirting the courtyard where the male prisoners took their exercise.

At last, having struck sharply to his left and ascended a short flight of stairs, he found himself in front of the guichet—a narrow wooden box, wherein the clerk in charge of the prison registers sat nominally at the disposal of the citizens of this free republic.

But to Armand's almost overwhelming chagrin he found the place entirely deserted. The guichet was closed down; there was not a soul in sight. The disappointment was doubly keen, coming as it did in the wake of hope that had refused to be gainsaid. Armand himself did not realise how sanguine he had been until he discovered that he must wait and wait again—wait for hours, all day mayhap, before he could get definite news of Jeanne.

He wandered aimlessly in the vicinity of that silent, deserted, cruel spot, where a closed trapdoor seemed to shut off all his hopes of a speedy sight of Jeanne. He inquired of the first sentinels whom he came across at what hour the clerk of the registers would be back at his post; the soldiers shrugged their shoulders and could give no information. Then began Armand's aimless wanderings round La Tournelle, his fruitless inquiries, his wild, excited search for the hide-bound official who was keeping from him the knowledge of Jeanne.

He went back to his sentinel well-wisher by the women's courtyard, but found neither consolation nor encouragement there.

"It is not the hour—*quoi?*" the soldier remarked with laconic philosophy.

It apparently was not the hour when the prison registers were placed at the disposal of the public. After much fruitless inquiry, Armand at last was informed by a bon bourgeois, who was wandering about the house of Justice and who seemed to know its multifarious rules, that the prison registers all over Paris could only be consulted by the public between the hours of six and seven in the evening.

There was nothing for it but to wait. Armand, whose temples were throbbing, who was footsore, hungry, and wretched, could gain nothing by continuing his aimless wanderings through the labyrinthine building. For close upon another hour he stood with his face glued against the ironwork which separated him from the female prisoners' courtyard. Once it seemed to him as if from its further end he caught the sound of that exquisitely melodious voice which had rung forever in his ear since that memorable evening when Jeanne's dainty footsteps had first crossed the path of his destiny. He strained his eyes to look in the direction whence the voice had come, but the centre of the courtyard was planted with a small garden of shrubs, and Armand could not see across it. At last, driven forth like a wandering and lost soul, he turned back and out into the streets. The air was mild and damp. The sharp thaw had persisted through the day, and a thin, misty rain was falling and converting the ill-paved roads into seas of mud.

But of this Armand was wholly unconscious. He walked along the quay holding his cap in his hand, so that the mild south wind should cool his burning forehead.

How he contrived to kill those long, weary hours he could not afterwards have said. Once he felt very hungry, and turned almost mechanically into an eating-house, and tried to eat and drink. But most of the day he wandered through the streets, restlessly, unceasingly, feeling neither chill nor fatigue. The hour before six o'clock found him on the Quai de l'Horloge in the shadow of the great towers of the Hall of Justice, listening for the clang of the clock that would sound the hour of his deliverance from this agonising torture of suspense.

He found his way to La Tournelle without any hesitation. There before him was the wooden box, with its guichet open at last, and two stands upon its ledge, on which were placed two huge leather-bound books.

Though Armand was nearly an hour before the appointed time, he saw when he arrived a number of people standing round the guichet. Two soldiers were there keeping guard and forcing the patient, long-suffering inquirers to stand in a queue, each waiting his or her turn at the books.

It was a curious crowd that stood there, in single file, as if waiting at the door of the cheaper part of a theatre; men in substantial cloth clothes, and others in ragged blouse and breeches; there were a few women, too, with black shawls on their shoulders and kerchiefs round their wan, tear-stained faces.

They were all silent and absorbed, submissive under the rough handling of the soldiery, humble and deferential when anon the clerk of the registers entered his box, and prepared to place those fateful books at the disposal of those who had lost a loved one—father, brother, mother, or wife—and had come to search through those cruel pages.

From inside his box the clerk disputed every inquirer's right to consult the books; he made as many difficulties as he could, demanding the production of certificates of safety, or permits from the section. He was as insolent as he dared, and Armand from where he stood could see that a continuous if somewhat thin stream of coppers flowed from the hands of the inquirers into those of the official.

It was quite dark in the passage where the long queue continued to swell with amazing rapidity. Only on the ledge in front of the guichet there was a guttering tallow candle at the disposal of the inquirers.

Now it was Armand's turn at last. By this time his heart was beating so strongly and so rapidly that he could not have trusted himself to speak. He fumbled in his pocket, and without unnecessary preliminaries he produced a small piece of silver, and pushed it towards the clerk, then he seized on the register marked "Femmes" with voracious avidity.

The clerk had with stolid indifference pocketed the half-livre; he looked on Armand over a pair of large bone-rimmed spectacles, with the air of an old hawk that sees a helpless bird and yet is too satiated to eat. He was apparently vastly amused at Armand's trembling hands, and the clumsy, aimless way with which he fingered the book and held up the tallow candle.

"What date?" he asked curtly in a piping voice.

"What date?" reiterated Armand vaguely.

"What day and hour was she arrested?" said the man, thrusting his beak-like nose closer to Armand's face. Evidently the piece of silver had done its work well; he meant to be helpful to this country lout.

"On Friday evening," murmured the young man.

The clerk's hands did not in character gainsay the rest of his appearance; they were long and thin, with nails that resembled the talons of a hawk. Armand watched them fascinated as from above they turned over rapidly the pages of the book; then one long, grimy finger pointed to a row of names down a column.

"If she is here," said the man curtly, "her name should be amongst these."

Armand's vision was blurred. He could scarcely see. The row of names was dancing a wild dance in front of his eyes; perspiration stood out on his forehead, and his breath came in quick, stertorous gasps.

He never knew afterwards whether he actually saw Jeanne's name there in the book, or whether his fevered brain was playing his aching senses a cruel and mocking trick. Certain it is that suddenly amongst a row of indifferent names hers suddenly stood clearly on the page, and to him it seemed as if the letters were writ out in blood.

> 582. Belhomme, Louise, aged sixty. Discharged.
> And just below, the other entry:
> 583. Lange, Jeanne, aged twenty, actress. Square du Roule
> No.5. Suspected of harbouring traitors and ci-devants.
> Transferred 29th Nivose to the Temple, cell 29.

He saw nothing more, for suddenly it seemed to him as if some one held a vivid scarlet veil in front of his eyes, whilst a hundred claw-like hands were tearing at his heart and at his throat.

"Clear out now! it is my turn—what? Are you going to stand there all night?"

A rough voice seemed to be speaking these words; rough hands apparently were pushing him out of the way, and some one snatched the candle out of his hand; but nothing was real. He stumbled over a corner of a loose flagstone, and would have fallen, but something seemed to catch bold of him and to lead him away for a little distance, until a breath of cold air blew upon his face.

This brought him back to his senses.

Jeanne was a prisoner in the Temple; then his place was in the prison of the Temple, too. It could not be very difficult to run one's head into the noose that caught so many necks these days. A few cries of "*Vive le roi!*" or "*A bas la republique!*" and more than one prison door would gape invitingly to receive another guest.

The hot blood had rushed into Armand's head. He did not see clearly before him, nor did he hear distinctly. There was a buzzing in his ears as of myriads of mocking birds' wings, and there was a veil in front of his eyes—a veil through which he saw faces and forms flitting ghost-like in the gloom, men and women jostling or being jostled, soldiers, sentinels; then long, interminable corridors, more crowd and more soldiers, winding stairs, courtyards and gates; finally the open street, the quay, and the river beyond.

An incessant hammering went on in his temples, and that veil never lifted from before his eyes. Now it was lurid and red, as if stained with blood; anon it was white like a shroud but it was always there.

Through it he saw the Pont-au-Change, which he crossed, then far down on the Quai de l'Ecole to the left the corner house behind St. Germain l'Auxerrois, where Blakeney lodged—Blakeney, who for the sake of a stranger had forgotten all about his comrade and Jeanne.

Through it he saw the network of streets which separated him from the neighbourhood of the Temple, the gardens of ruined habitations, the closely-shuttered and barred windows of ducal houses, then the mean streets, the crowded drinking bars, the tumble-down shops with their dilapidated awnings.

He saw with eyes that did not see, heard the tumult of daily life round him with ears that did not hear. Jeanne was in the Temple prison, and when its grim gates closed finally for the night, he— Armand, her chevalier, her lover, her defender—would be within its walls as near to cell No. 29 as bribery, entreaty, promises would help him to attain.

Ah! there at last loomed the great building, the pointed bastions cut through the surrounding gloom as with a sable knife.

Armand reached the gate; the sentinels challenged him; he replied:

"*Vive le roi!*" shouting wildly like one who is drunk.

He was hatless, and his clothes were saturated with moisture. He tried to pass, but crossed bayonets barred the way. Still he shouted:

"*Vive le roi!*" and "*A bas la republique!*"

"*Allons!* the fellow is drunk!" said one of the soldiers.

Armand fought like a madman; he wanted to reach that gate. He shouted, he laughed, and he cried, until one of the soldiers in a fit of rage struck him heavily on the head.

Armand fell backwards, stunned by the blow; his foot slipped on the wet pavement. Was he indeed drunk, or was he dreaming? He put his hand up to his forehead; it was wet, but whether with the rain or with blood he did not know; but for the space of one second he tried to collect his scattered wits.

"Citizen St. Just!" said a quiet voice at his elbow.

Then, as he looked round dazed, feeling a firm, pleasant grip on his arm, the same quiet voice continued calmly:

"Perhaps you do not remember me, citizen St. Just. I had not the honour of the same close friendship with you as I had with your charming sister. My name is Chauvelin. Can I be of any service to you?"

# CHAPTER 17: CHAUVELIN

Chauvelin! The presence of this man here at this moment made the events of the past few days seem more absolutely like a dream. Chauvelin!—the most deadly enemy he, Armand, and his sister Marguerite had in the world. Chauvelin!—the evil genius that presided over the Secret Service of the Republic. Chauvelin—the aristocrat turned revolutionary, the diplomat turned spy, the baffled enemy of the Scarlet Pimpernel.

He stood there vaguely outlined in the gloom by the feeble rays of an oil lamp fixed into the wall just above. The moisture on his sable clothes glistened in the flickering light like a thin veil of crystal; it clung to the rim of his hat, to the folds of his cloak; the ruffles at his throat and wrist hung limp and soiled.

He had released Armand's arm, and held his hands now underneath his cloak; his pale, deep-set eyes rested gravely on the younger man's face.

"I had an idea, somehow," continued Chauvelin calmly, "that you and I would meet during your sojourn in Paris. I heard from my friend Heron that you had been in the city; he, unfortunately, lost your track almost as soon as he had found it, and I, too, had begun to fear that our mutual and ever enigmatical friend, the Scarlet Pimpernel, had spirited you away, which would have been a great disappointment to me."

Now he once more took hold of Armand by the elbow, but quite gently, more like a comrade who is glad to have met another, and is preparing to enjoy a pleasant conversation for a while. He led the way back to the gate, the sentinel saluting at sight of the tricolour scarf which was visible underneath his cloak. Under the stone rampart Chauvelin paused.

It was quiet and private here. The group of soldiers stood at the further end of the archway, but they were out of hearing, and their forms were only vaguely discernible in the surrounding darkness.

Armand had followed his enemy mechanically like one bewitched and irresponsible for his actions. When Chauvelin paused he too stood still, not because of the grip on his arm, but because of that curious numbing of his will.

Vague, confused thoughts were floating through his brain, the most dominant one among them being that Fate had effectually ordained everything for the best. Here was Chauvelin, a man who hated him, who, of course, would wish to see him dead. Well, surely it must be an easier matter now to barter his own life for that of Jeanne; she had only been arrested on suspicion of harbouring him, who was a known traitor to the Republic; then, with his capture and speedy death, her supposed guilt would, he hoped, be forgiven. These people could have no ill-will against her, and actors and actresses were always leniently dealt with when possible. Then surely, surely, he could serve Jeanne best by his own arrest and condemnation, than by working to rescue her from prison.

In the meanwhile Chauvelin shook the damp from off his cloak, talking all the time in his own peculiar, gently ironical manner.

"Lady Blakeney?" he was saying—"I hope that she is well!"

"I thank you, sir," murmured Armand mechanically.

"And my dear friend, Sir Percy Blakeney? I had hoped to meet him in Paris. Ah! but no doubt he has been busy very busy; but I live in hopes—I live in hopes. See how kindly Chance has treated me," he continued in the same bland and mocking tones. "I was taking a stroll in these parts, scarce hoping to meet a friend, when, passing the postern-gate of this charming hostelry, whom should I see but my amiable friend St. Just striving to gain admission. But, la! here am I talking of myself, and I am not re-assured as to your state of health. You felt faint just now, did you not? The air about this building is very dank and close. I hope you feel better now. Command me, pray, if I can be of service to you in any way."

Whilst Chauvelin talked he had drawn Armand after him into the lodge of the concierge. The young man now made a great effort to pull himself vigorously together and to steady his nerves.

He had his wish. He was inside the Temple prison now, not far from Jeanne, and though his enemy was older and less vigorous than himself, and the door of the concierge's lodge stood wide open, he knew that he was in-deed as effectually a prisoner already as if the door of one of the numerous cells in this gigantic building had been bolted and barred upon him.

This knowledge helped him to recover his complete presence of mind. No thought of fighting or trying to escape his fate entered his head for a moment. It had been useless probably, and undoubtedly it was better so. If he only could see Jeanne, and assure himself that she would be safe in consequence of his own arrest, then, indeed, life could hold no greater happiness for him.

Above all now he wanted to be cool and calculating, to curb the excitement which the Latin blood in him called forth at every mention of the loved one's name. He tried to think of Percy, of his calmness, his easy banter with an enemy; he resolved to act as Percy would act under these circumstances.

Firstly, he steadied his voice, and drew his well-knit, slim figure upright. He called to mind all his friends in England, with their rigid manners, their impassiveness in the face of trying situations. There was

Lord Tony, for instance, always ready with some boyish joke, with boyish impertinence always hovering on his tongue. Armand tried to emulate Lord Tony's manner, and to borrow something of Percy's calm impudence.

"Citizen Chauvelin," he said, as soon as he felt quite sure of the steadiness of his voice and the calmness of his manner, "I wonder if you are quite certain that that light grip which you have on my arm is sufficient to keep me here walking quietly by your side instead of knocking you down, as I certainly feel inclined to do, for I am a younger, more vigorous man than you."

"H'm!" said Chauvelin, who made pretence to ponder over this difficult problem; "like you, citizen St. Just, I wonder—"

"It could easily be done, you know."

"Fairly easily," rejoined the other; "but there is the guard; it is numerous and strong in this building, and—"

"The gloom would help me; it is dark in the corridors, and a desperate man takes risks, remember—"

"Quite so! And you, citizen St. Just, are a desperate man just now."

"My sister Marguerite is not here, citizen Chauvelin. You cannot barter my life for that of your enemy."

"No! no! no!" rejoined Chauvelin blandly; "not for that of my enemy, I know, but—"

Armand caught at his words like a drowning man at a reed.

"For hers!" he exclaimed.

"For hers?" queried the other with obvious puzzlement.

"Mademoiselle Lange," continued Armand with all the egoistic ardour of the lover who believes that the attention of the entire world is concentrated upon his beloved.

"Mademoiselle Lange! You will set her free now that I am in your power."

Chauvelin smiled, his usual suave, enigmatical smile.

"Ah, yes!" he said. "Mademoiselle Lange. I had forgotten."

"Forgotten, man?—forgotten that those murderous dogs have arrested her?—the best, the purest, this vile, degraded country has ever produced. She sheltered me one day just for an hour. I am a traitor to the Republic—I own it. I'll make full confession; but she knew nothing of this. I deceived her; she is quite innocent, you understand? I'll make full confession, but you must set her free."

He had gradually worked himself up again to a state of feverish excitement. Through the darkness which hung about in this small room he tried to peer in Chauvelin's impassive face.

"Easy, easy, my young friend," said the other placidly; "you seem to imagine that I have something to do with the arrest of the lady in whom you take so deep an interest. You forget that now I am but a discredited servant of the Republic whom I failed to serve in her need. My life is only granted me out of pity for my efforts, which were genuine if not successful. I have no power to set any one free."

"Nor to arrest me now, in that case!" retorted Armand.

Chauvelin paused a moment before he replied with a deprecating smile:

"Only to denounce you, perhaps. I am still an agent of the Committee of General Security."

"Then all is for the best!" exclaimed St. Just eagerly. "You shall denounce me to the Committee. They will be glad of my arrest, I assure you. I have been a marked man for some time. I had intended to evade arrest and to work for the rescue of Mademoiselle Lange; but I will give up all thought of that—I will deliver myself into your hands absolutely; nay, more, I will give you my most solemn word of honour that not only will I make no attempt at escape, but that I will not allow any one to help me to do so. I will be a passive and willing prisoner if you, on the other hand, will effect Mademoiselle Lange's release."

"H'm!" mused Chauvelin again, "it sounds feasible."

"It does! it does!" rejoined Armand, whose excitement was at fever-pitch. "My arrest, my condemnation, my death, will be of vast deal more importance to you than that of a young and innocent girl against whom unlikely charges would have to be tricked up, and whose acquittal mayhap public feeling might demand. As for me, I shall be an easy prey; my known counter-revolutionary principles, my sister's marriage with a foreigner—"

"Your connection with the Scarlet Pimpernel," suggested Chauvelin blandly.

"Quite so. I should not defend myself—"

"And your enigmatical friend would not attempt your rescue. C'est entendu," said Chauvelin with his wonted blandness. "Then, my dear, enthusiastic young friend, shall we adjourn to the office of my colleague, citizen Heron, who is chief agent of the Committee of General Security, and will receive your—did you say confession?—and note the conditions under which you place yourself absolutely in the hands of the Public Prosecutor and subsequently of the executioner. Is that it?"

Armand was too full of schemes, too full of thoughts of Jeanne to note the tone of quiet irony with which Chauvelin had been speaking all along. With the unreasoning egoism of youth he was quite convinced that his own arrest, his own affairs were as important to this entire nation in revolution as they were to himself. At moments like these it is difficult to envisage a desperate situation clearly, and to a young man in love the fate of the beloved never seems desperate whilst he himself is alive and ready for every sacrifice for her sake. "My life for hers" is the sublime if often foolish battle-cry that has so often resulted in whole-sale destruction. Armand at this moment, when he fondly believed that he was making a bargain with the most astute, most unscrupulous spy this revolutionary Government had in its pay— Armand just then had absolutely forgotten his chief, his friends, the league of mercy and help to which he belonged.

Enthusiasm and the spirit of self-sacrifice were carrying him away. He watched his enemy with glowing eyes as one who looks on the arbiter of his fate.

Chauvelin, without another word, beckoned to him to follow. He led the way out of the lodge, then, turning sharply to his left, he reached the wide quadrangle with the covered passage running right round it, the same which de Batz had traversed two evenings ago when he went to visit Heron.

Armand, with a light heart and springy step, followed him as if he were going to a feast where he would meet Jeanne, where he would kneel at her feet, kiss her hands, and lead her triumphantly to freedom and to happiness.

# Chapter 18: The Removal

Chauvelin no longer made any pretence to hold Armand by the arm. By temperament as well as by profession a spy, there was one subject at least which he had mastered thoroughly: that was the study of human nature. Though occasionally an exceptionally complex mental organisation baffled him—as in the case of Sir Percy Blakeney—he prided himself, and justly, too, on reading natures like that of Armand St. Just as he would an open book.

The excitable disposition of the Latin races he knew out and out; he knew exactly how far a sentimental situation would lead a young Frenchman like Armand, who was by disposition chivalrous, and by temperament essentially passionate. Above all things, he knew when and how far he could trust a man to do either a sublime action or an essentially foolish one.

Therefore he walked along contentedly now, not even looking back to see whether St. Just was following him. He knew that he did.

His thoughts only dwelt on the young enthusiast—in his mind he called him the young fool—in order to weigh in the balance the mighty possibilities that would accrue from the present sequence of events. The fixed idea ever working in the man's scheming brain had already transformed a vague belief into a certainty. That the Scarlet Pimpernel was in Paris at the present moment Chauvelin had now become convinced. How far he could turn the capture of Armand St. Just to the triumph of his own ends remained to be seen.

But this he did know: the Scarlet Pimpernel—the man whom he had learned to know, to dread, and even in a grudging manner to admire—was not like to leave one of his followers in the lurch. Marguerite's brother in the Temple would be the surest decoy for the elusive meddler who still, and in spite of all care and precaution, continued to baffle the army of spies set upon his track.

Chauvelin could hear Armand's light, elastic footsteps resounding behind him on the flagstones. A world of intoxicating possibilities surged up before him. Ambition, which two successive dire failures had atrophied in his breast, once more rose up buoyant and hopeful. Once he had sworn to lay the Scarlet Pimpernel by the heels, and that oath was not yet wholly forgotten; it had lain dormant after the catastrophe of Boulogne, but with the sight of Armand St. Just it had re-awakened and confronted him again with the strength of a likely fulfilment.

The courtyard looked gloomy and deserted. The thin drizzle which still fell from a persistently leaden sky effectually held every outline of masonry, of column, or of gate hidden as beneath a shroud.

The corridor which skirted it all round was ill-lighted save by an occasional oil-lamp fixed in the wall.

But Chauvelin knew his way well. Heron's lodgings gave on the second courtyard, the Square du Nazaret, and the way thither led past the main square tower, in the top floor of which the uncrowned King of France eked out his miserable existence as the plaything of a rough cobbler and his wife.

Just beneath its frowning bastions Chauvelin turned back towards Armand. He pointed with a careless hand up-wards to the central tower.

"We have got little Capet in there," he said dryly. "Your chivalrous Scarlet Pimpernel has not ventured in these precincts yet, you see."

Armand was silent. He had no difficulty in looking unconcerned; his thoughts were so full of Jeanne that he cared but little at this moment for any Bourbon king or for the destinies of France.

Now the two men reached the postern gate. A couple of sentinels were standing by, but the gate itself was open, and from within there came the sound of bustle and of noise, of a good deal of swearing, and also of loud laughter.

The guard-room gave on the left of the gate, and the laughter came from there. It was brilliantly lighted, and Armand, peering in, in the wake of Chauvelin, could see groups of soldiers sitting and standing about. There was a table in the centre of the room, and on it a number of jugs and pewter mugs, packets of cards, and overturned boxes of dice.

But the bustle did not come from the guard-room; it came from the landing and the stone stairs beyond.

Chauvelin, apparently curious, had passed through the gate, and Armand followed him. The light from the open door of the guard-room cut sharply across the landing, making the gloom beyond appear more dense and almost solid. From out the darkness, fitfully intersected by a lanthorn apparently carried to and fro, moving figures loomed out ghost-like and weirdly gigantic. Soon Armand distinguished a number of large objects that encumbered the landing, and as he and Chauvelin left the sharp light of the guard-room 'behind them, he could see that the large objects were pieces of furniture of every shape and size; a wooden bedstead—dismantled—leaned against the wall, a black horsehair sofa blocked the way to the tower stairs, and there were numberless chairs and several tables piled one on the top of the other.

In the midst of this litter a stout, flabby-cheeked man stood, apparently giving directions as to its removal to persons at present unseen.

"Hola, Papa Simon!" exclaimed Chauvelin jovially; "moving out to-day? What?"

"Yes, thank the Lord!—if there be a Lord!" retorted the other curtly. "Is that you, citizen Chauvelin?"

"In person, citizen. I did not know you were leaving quite so soon. Is citizen Heron anywhere about?"

"Just left," replied Simon. "He had a last look at Capet just before my wife locked the brat up in the inner room. Now he's gone back to his lodgings."

A man carrying a chest, empty of its drawers, on his back now came stumbling down the tower staircase. Madame Simon followed close on his heels, steadying the chest with one hand.

"We had better begin to load up the cart," she called to her husband in a high-pitched querulous voice; "the corridor is getting too much encumbered."

She looked suspiciously at Chauvelin and at Armand, and when she encountered the former's bland, unconcerned gaze she suddenly shivered and drew her black shawl closer round her shoulders.

"Bah!" she said, "I shall be glad to get out of this God-forsaken hole. I hate the very sight of these walls."

"Indeed, the citizeness does not look over robust in health," said Chauvelin with studied politeness. "The stay in the tower did not, mayhap, bring forth all the fruits of prosperity which she had anticipated."

The woman eyed him with dark suspicion lurking in her hollow eyes.

"I don't know what you mean, citizen," she said with a shrug of her wide shoulders.

"Oh! I meant nothing," rejoined Chauvelin, smiling. "I am so interested in your removal; busy man as I am, it has amused me to watch you. Whom have you got to help you with the furniture?"

"Dupont, the man-of-all-work, from the concierge," said Simon curtly. "Citizen Heron would not allow any one to come in from the outside."

"Rightly too. Have the new commissaries come yet?

"Only citizen Cochefer. He is waiting upstairs for the others."

"And Capet?"

"He is all safe. Citizen Heron came to see him, and then he told me to lock the little vermin up in the inner room. Citizen Cochefer had just arrived by that time, and he has remained in charge."

During all this while the man with the chest on his back was waiting for orders. Bent nearly double, he was grumbling audibly at his uncomfortable position.

"Does the citizen want to break my back?" he muttered.

"We had best get along—*quoi?*"

He asked if he should begin to carry the furniture out into the street.

"Two sous have I got to pay every ten minutes to the lad who holds my nag," he said, muttering under his breath; "we shall be all night at this rate."

"Begin to load then," commanded Simon gruffly. "Here!—begin with this sofa."

"You'll have to give me a hand with that," said the man. "Wait a bit; I'll just see that everything is all right in the cart. I'll be back directly."

"Take something with you then as you are going down," said Madame Simon in her querulous voice.

The man picked up a basket of linen that stood in the angle by the door. He hoisted it on his back and shuffled away with it across the landing and out through the gate.

"How did Capet like parting from his papa and *maman?*" asked Chauvelin with a laugh.

"H'm!" growled Simon laconically. "He will find out soon enough how well off he was under our care."

"Have the other commissaries come yet?"

"No. But they will be here directly. Citizen Cochefer is upstairs mounting guard over Capet."

"Well, good-bye, Papa Simon," concluded Chauvelin jovially. "Citizeness, your servant!"

He bowed with unconcealed irony to the cobbler's wife, and nodded to Simon, who expressed by a volley of motley oaths his exact feelings with regard to all the agents of the Committee of General Security.

"Six months of this penal servitude have we had," he said roughly, "and no thanks or pension. I would as soon serve a *ci-devant aristo* as your accursed Committee."

The man Dupont had returned. Stolidly, after the fashion of his kind, he commenced the removal of citizen Simon's goods. He seemed a clumsy enough creature, and Simon and his wife had to do most of the work themselves.

Chauvelin watched the moving forms for a while, then he shrugged his shoulders with a laugh of indifference, and turned on his heel.

# CHAPTER 19: IT IS ABOUT THE DAUPHIN

Heron was not at his lodgings when, at last, after vigorous pulls at the bell, a great deal of waiting and much cursing, Chauvelin, closely followed by Armand, was introduced in the chief agent's office.

The soldier who acted as servant said that citizen Heron had gone out to sup, but would surely be home again by eight o'clock. Armand by this time was so dazed with fatigue that he sank on a chair like a log, and remained there staring into the fire, unconscious of the flight of time.

Anon Heron came home. He nodded to Chauvelin, and threw but a cursory glance on Armand.

"Five minutes, citizen," he said, with a rough attempt at an apology. "I am sorry to keep you waiting, but the new commissaries have arrived who are to take charge of Capet. The Simons have just gone, and I want to assure myself that everything is all right in the Tower. Cochefer has been in charge, but I like to cast an eye over the brat every day myself."

He went out again, slamming the door behind him. His heavy footsteps were heard treading the flagstones of the corridor, and gradually dying away in the distance. Armand had paid no heed either to his entrance or to his exit. He was only conscious of an intense weariness, and would at this moment gladly have laid his head on the scaffold if on it he could find rest.

A white-faced clock on the wall ticked off the seconds one by one. From the street below came the muffled sounds of wheeled traffic on the soft mud of the road; it was raining more heavily now, and from time to time a gust of wind rattled the small windows in their dilapidated frames, or hurled a shower of heavy drops against the panes. The heat from the stove had made Armand drowsy; his head fell forward on his chest. Chauvelin, with his hands held behind his back, paced ceaselessly up and down the narrow room.

Suddenly Armand started—wide awake now. Hurried footsteps on the flagstones outside, a hoarse shout, a banging of heavy doors, and the next moment Heron stood once more on the threshold of the room. Armand, with wide-opened eyes, gazed on him in wonder. The whole appearance of the man had changed. He looked ten years older, with lank, dishevelled hair hanging matted over a moist forehead, the cheeks ashen-white, the full lips bloodless and hanging, flabby and parted, displaying both rows of yellow teeth that shook against each other. The whole figure looked bowed, as if shrunk within itself.

Chauvelin had paused in his restless walk. He gazed on his

colleague, a frown of puzzlement on his pale, set face.

"Capet!" he exclaimed, as soon as he had taken in every detail of Heron's altered appearance, and seen the look of wild terror that literally distorted his face.

Heron could not speak; his teeth were chattering in his mouth, and his tongue seemed paralysed. Chauvelin went up to him. He was several inches shorter than his colleague, but at this moment he seemed to be towering over him like an avenging spirit. He placed a firm hand on the other's bowed shoulders.

"Capet has gone—is that it?" he queried peremptorily.

The look of terror increased in Heron's eyes, giving its mute reply.

"How? When?"

But for the moment the man was speechless. An almost maniacal fear seemed to hold him in its grip. With an impatient oath Chauvelin turned away from him.

"Brandy!" he said curtly, speaking to Armand.

A bottle and glass were found in the cupboard. It was St. Just who poured out the brandy and held it to Heron's lips. Chauvelin was once more pacing up and down the room in angry impatience.

"Pull yourself together, man," he said roughly after a while, "and try and tell me what has occurred."

Heron had sunk into a chair. He passed a trembling hand once or twice over his forehead.

"Capet has disappeared," he murmured; "he must have been spirited away while the Simons were moving their furniture. That accursed Cochefer was completely taken in."

Heron spoke in a toneless voice, hardly above a whisper, and like one whose throat is dry and mouth parched. But the brandy had revived him somewhat, and his eyes lost their former glassy look.

"How?" asked Chauvelin curtly.

"I was just leaving the Tower when he arrived. I spoke to him at the door. I had seen Capet safely installed in the room, and gave orders to the woman Simon to let citizen Cochefer have a look at him, too, and then to lock up the brat in the inner room and install Cochefer in the antechamber on guard. I stood talking to Cochefer for a few moments in the antechamber. The woman Simon and the man-of-all-work, Dupont—whom I know well—were busy with the furniture. There could not have been any one else concealed about the place—that I'll swear. Cochefer, after he took leave of me, went straight into the room; he found the woman Simon in the act of turning the key in the door of the inner chamber. I have locked Capet in there,' she said, giving the key to Cochefer; 'he will be quite safe until to-night; when the other commissaries come.'

"Didn't Cochefer go into the room and ascertain whether the

woman was lying?"

"Yes, he did! He made the woman re-open the door and peeped in over her shoulder. She said the child was asleep. He vows that he saw the child lying fully dressed on a rug in the further corner of the room. The room, of course, was quite empty of furniture and only lighted by one candle, but there was the rug and the child asleep on it. Cochefer swears he saw him, and now—when I went up—"

"Well?"

"The commissaries were all there—Cochefer and Lasniere, Lorinet and Legrand. We went into the inner room, and I had a candle in my hand. We saw the child lying on the rug, just as Cochefer had seen him, and for a while we took no notice of it. Then some one—I think it was Lorinet—went to have a closer look at the brat. He took up the candle and went up to the rug. Then he gave a cry, and we all gathered round him. The sleeping child was only a bundle of hair and of clothes, a dummy—what?"

There was silence now in the narrow room, while the white-faced clock continued to tick off each succeeding second of time. Heron had once more buried his head in his hands; a trembling—like an attack of ague—shook his wide, bony shoulders. Armand had listened to the narrative with glowing eyes and a beating heart. The details which the two Terrorists here could not probably understand he had already added to the picture which his mind had conjured up.

He was back in thought now in the small lodging in the rear of St. Germain l'Auxerrois; Sir Andrew Ffoulkes was there, and my Lord Tony and Hastings, and a man was striding up and down the room, looking out into the great space beyond the river with the eyes of a seer, and a firm voice said abruptly:

"It is about the Dauphin!"

"Have you any suspicions?" asked Chauvelin now, pausing in his walk beside Heron, and once more placing a firm, peremptory hand on his colleague's shoulder.

"Suspicions!" exclaimed the chief agent with a loud oath. "Suspicions! Certainties, you mean. The man sat here but two days ago, in that very chair, and bragged of what he would do. I told him then that if he interfered with Capet I would wring his neck with my own hands."

And his long, talon-like fingers, with their sharp, grimy nails, closed and unclosed like those of feline creatures when they hold the coveted prey.

"Of whom do you speak?" queried Chauvelin curtly.

"Of whom? Of whom but that accursed de Batz? His pockets are bulging with Austrian money, with which, no doubt, he has bribed the Simons and Cochefer and the sentinels—"

"And Lorinet and Lasniere and you," interposed Chauvelin

dryly.

"It is false!" roared Heron, who already at the suggestion was foaming at the mouth, and had jumped up from his chair, standing at bay as if prepared to fight for his life.

"False, is it?" retorted Chauvelin calmly; "then be not so quick, friend Heron, in slashing out with senseless denunciations right and left. You'll gain nothing by denouncing any one just now. This is too intricate a matter to be dealt with a sledge-hammer. Is any one up in the Tower at this moment?" he asked in quiet, business-like tones.

"Yes. Cochefer and the others are still there. They are making wild schemes to cover their treachery. Cochefer is aware of his own danger, and Lasniere and the others know that they arrived at the Tower several hours too late. They are all at fault, and they know it. As for that de Batz," he continued with a voice rendered raucous with bitter passion, "I swore to him two days ago that he should not escape me if he meddled with Capet. I'm on his track already. I'll have him before the hour of midnight, and I'll torture him—yes! I'll torture him— the Tribunal shall give me leave. We have a dark cell down below here where my men know how to apply tortures worse than the rack—where they know just how to prolong life long enough to make it unendurable. I'll torture him! I'll torture him!"

But Chauvelin abruptly silenced the wretch with a curt command; then, without another word, he walked straight out of the room. In thought Armand followed him. The wild desire was suddenly born in him to run away at this moment, while Heron, wrapped in his own meditations, was paying no heed to him. Chauvelin's footsteps had long ago died away in the distance; it was a long way to the upper floor of the Tower, and some time would be spent, too, in interrogating the commissaries. This was Armand's opportunity. After all, if he were free himself he might more effectually help to rescue Jeanne. He knew, too, now where to join his leader. The corner of the street by the canal, where Sir Andrew Ffoulkes would be waiting with the coal-cart; then there was the spinney on the road to St. Germain. Armand hoped that, with good luck, he might yet overtake his comrades, tell them of Jeanne's plight, and entreat them to work for her rescue.

He had forgotten that now he had no certificate of safety, that undoubtedly he would be stopped at the gates at this hour of the night; that his conduct proving suspect he would in all probability he detained, and, mayhap, be brought back to this self-same place within an hour. He had forgotten all that, for the primeval instinct for freedom had suddenly been aroused. He rose softly from his chair and crossed the room. Heron paid no attention to him. Now he had traversed the antechamber and unlatched the outer door.

Immediately a couple of bayonets were crossed in front of him, two more further on ahead scintillated feebly in the flickering light.

Chauvelin had taken his precautions. There was no doubt that Armand St. Just was effectually a prisoner now. With a sigh of disappointment he went back to his place beside the fire. Heron had not even moved whilst he had made this futile attempt at escape. Five minutes later Chauvelin re-entered the room.

# CHAPTER 20: THE CERTIFICATE OF SAFETY

"You can leave de Batz and his gang alone, citizen Heron," said Chauvelin, as soon as he had closed the door behind him; "he had nothing to do with the escape of the Dauphin."

Heron growled out a few words of incredulity. But Chauvelin shrugged his shoulders and looked with unutterable contempt on his colleague. Armand, who was watching him closely, saw that in his hand he held a small piece of paper, which he had crushed into a shapeless mass.

"Do not waste your time, citizen," he said, "in raging against an empty wind-bag. Arrest de Batz if you like, or leave him alone an you please—we have nothing to fear from that braggart."

With nervous, slightly shaking fingers he set to work to smooth out the scrap of paper which he held. His hot hands had soiled it and pounded it until it was a mere rag and the writing on it illegible. But, such as it was, he threw it down with a blasphemous oath on the desk in front of Heron's eyes.

"It is that accursed Englishman who has been at work again," he said more calmly; "I guessed it the moment I heard your story. Set your whole army of sleuth-hounds on his track, citizen; you'll need them all."

Heron picked up the scrap of torn paper and tried to decipher the writing on it by the light from the lamp. He seemed almost dazed now with the awful catastrophe that had befallen him, and the fear that his own wretched life would have to pay the penalty for the disappearance of the child.

As for Armand—even in the midst of his own troubles, and of his own anxiety for Jeanne, he felt a proud exultation in his heart. The Scarlet Pimpernel had succeeded; Percy had not failed in his self-imposed undertaking. Chauvelin, whose piercing eyes were fixed on him at that moment, smiled with contemptuous irony.

"As you will find your hands overfull for the next few hours, citizen Heron," he said, speaking to his colleague and nodding in the direction of Armand, "I'll not trouble you with the voluntary confession this young citizen desired to make to you. All I need tell you is that he is an adherent of the Scarlet Pimpernel—I believe one of his most faithful, most trusted officers."

Heron roused himself from the maze of gloomy thoughts that were again paralysing his tongue. He turned bleary, wild eyes on Armand.

"We have got one of them, then?" he murmured incoherently, babbling like a drunken man.

"M'yes!" replied Chauvelin lightly; "but it is too late now for a formal denunciation and arrest. He cannot leave Paris anyhow, and all that your men need to do is to keep a close look-out on him. But I should send him home to-night if I were you."

Heron muttered something more, which, however, Armand did not understand. Chauvelin's words were still ringing in his ear. Was he, then, to be set free to-night? Free in a measure, of course, since spies were to be set to watch him—but free, nevertheless? He could not understand Chauvelin's attitude, and his own self-love was not a little wounded at the thought that he was of such little account that these men could afford to give him even this provisional freedom. And, of course, there was still Jeanne.

"I must, therefore, bid you good-night, citizen," Chauvelin was saying in his bland, gently ironical manner. "You will be glad to return to your lodgings. As you see, the chief agent of the Committee of General Security is too much occupied just now to accept the sacrifice of your life which you were prepared so generously to offer him."

"I do not understand you, citizen," retorted Armand coldly, "nor do I desire indulgence at your hands. You have arrested an innocent woman on the trumped-up charge that she was harbouring me. I came here to-night to give myself up to justice so that she might be set free."

"But the hour is somewhat late, citizen," rejoined Chauvelin urbanely. "The lady in whom you take so fervent an interest is no doubt asleep in her cell at this hour. It would not be fitting to disturb her now. She might not find shelter before morning, and the weather is quite exceptionally unpropitious."

"Then, sir," said Armand, a little bewildered, "am I to understand that if I hold myself at your disposition Mademoiselle Lange will be set free as early to-morrow morning as may be?"

"No doubt, sir—no doubt," replied Chauvelin with more than his accustomed blandness; "if you will hold yourself entirely at our disposition, Mademoiselle Lange will be set free to-morrow. I think that we can safely promise that, citizen Heron, can we not?" he added, turning to his colleague.

But Heron, overcome with the stress of emotions, could only murmur vague, unintelligible words.

"Your word on that, citizen Chauvelin?" asked Armand.

"My word on it an you will accept it."

"No, I will not do that. Give me an unconditional certificate of safety and I will believe you."

"Of what use were that to you?" asked Chauvelin.

"I believe my capture to be of more importance to you than that of Mademoiselle Lange," said Armand quietly.

"I will use the certificate of safety for myself or one of my friends if you break your word to me anent Mademoiselle Lange."

"H'm! the reasoning is not illogical, citizen," said Chauvelin, whilst a curious smile played round the corners of his thin lips. "You are quite right. You are a more valuable asset to us than the charming lady who, I hope, will for many a day and year to come delight pleasure-loving Paris with her talent and her grace."

"Amen to that, citizen," said Armand fervently.

"Well, it will all depend on you, sir! Here," he added, coolly running over some papers on Heron's desk until he found what he wanted, "is an absolutely unconditional certificate of safety. The Committee of General Security issue very few of these. It is worth the cost of a human life. At no barrier or gate of any city can such a certificate be disregarded, nor even can it be detained. Allow me to hand it to you, citizen, as a pledge of my own good faith."

Smiling, urbane, with a curious look that almost expressed amusement lurking in his shrewd, pale eyes, Chauvelin handed the momentous document to Armand.

The young man studied it very carefully before he slipped it into the inner pocket of his coat.

"How soon shall I have news of Mademoiselle Lange?" he asked finally.

"In the course of to-morrow. I myself will call on you and redeem that precious document in person. You, on the other hand, will hold yourself at my disposition. That's understood, is it not?"

"I shall not fail you. My lodgings are—"

"Oh! do not trouble," interposed Chauvelin, with a polite bow; "we can find that out for ourselves."

Heron had taken no part in this colloquy. Now that Armand prepared to go he made no attempt to detain him, or to question his colleague's actions. He sat by the table like a log; his mind was obviously a blank to all else save to his own terrors engendered by the events of this night.

With bleary, half-veiled eyes he followed Armand's progress through the room, and seemed unaware of the loud slamming of the outside door. Chauvelin had escorted the young man past the first line of sentry, then he took cordial leave of him.

"Your certificate will, you will find, open every gate to you. Good-night, citizen. A demain."

"Good-night."

Armand's slim figure disappeared in the gloom. Chauvelin watched him for a few moments until even his footsteps had died away in the distance; then he turned back towards Heron's lodgings.

"A nous deux," he muttered between tightly clenched teeth; "a *nous deux* once more, my enigmatical Scarlet Pimpernel."

# CHAPTER 21: BACK TO PARIS

It was an exceptionally dark night, and the rain was falling in torrents. Sir Andrew Ffoulkes, wrapped in a piece of sacking, had taken shelter right underneath the coal-cart; even then he was getting wet through to the skin.

He had worked hard for two days coal-heaving, and the night before he had found a cheap, squalid lodging where at any rate he was protected from the inclemencies of the weather; but to-night he was expecting Blakeney at the appointed hour and place. He had secured a cart of the ordinary ramshackle pattern used for carrying coal. Unfortunately there were no covered ones to be obtained in the neighbourhood, and equally unfortunately the thaw had set in with a blustering wind and diving rain, which made waiting in the open air for hours at a stretch and in complete darkness excessively unpleasant.

But for all these discomforts Sir Andrew Ffoulkes cared not one jot. In England, in his magnificent Suffolk home, he was a confirmed sybarite, in whose service every description of comfort and luxury had to be enrolled. Here tonight in the rough and tattered clothes of a coal-heaver, drenched to the skin, and crouching under the body of a cart that hardly sheltered him from the rain, he was as happy as a schoolboy out for a holiday.

Happy, but vaguely anxious.

He had no means of ascertaining the time. So many of the church-bells and clock towers had been silenced recently that not one of those welcome sounds penetrated to the dreary desolation of this canal wharf, with its abandoned carts standing ghostlike in a row. Darkness had set in very early in the afternoon, and the heavers had given up work soon after four o'clock.

For about an hour after that a certain animation had still reigned round the wharf, men crossing and going, one or two of the barges moving in or out alongside the quay. But for some time now darkness and silence had been the masters in this desolate spot, and that time had seemed to Sir Andrew an eternity. He had hobbled and tethered his horse, and stretched himself out at full length under the cart. Now and again he had crawled out from under this uncomfortable shelter and walked up and down in ankle-deep mud, trying to restore circulation in his stiffened limbs; now and again a kind of torpor had come over him, and he had fallen into a brief and restless sleep. He would at this moment have given half his fortune for knowledge of the exact time.

But through all this weary waiting he was never for a moment in doubt. Unlike Armand St. Just, he had the simplest, most perfect faith in his chief. He had been Blakeney's constant companion in all these adventures for close upon four years now; the thought of failure, however vague, never once entered his mind.

He was only anxious for his chief's welfare. He knew that he would succeed, but he would have liked to have spared him much of the physical fatigue and the nerve-racking strain of these hours that lay between the daring deed and the hope of safety. Therefore he was conscious of an acute tingling of his nerves, which went on even during the brief patches of fitful sleep, and through the numbness that invaded his whole body while the hours dragged wearily and slowly along.

Then, quite suddenly, he felt wakeful and alert; quite a while—even before he heard the welcome signal—he knew, with a curious, subtle sense of magnetism, that the hour had come, and that his chief was somewhere near by, not very far.

Then he heard the cry—a seamew's call—repeated thrice at intervals, and five minutes later something loomed out of the darkness quite close to the hind wheels of the cart.

"Hist! Ffoulkes!" came in a soft whisper, scarce louder than the wind.

"Present!" came in quick response.

"Here, help me to lift the child into the cart. He is asleep, and has been a dead weight on my arm for close on an hour now. Have you a dry bit of sacking or something to lay him on?"

"Not very dry, I am afraid."

With tender care the two men lifted the sleeping little King of France into the rickety cart. Blakeney laid his cloak over him, and listened for awhile to the slow regular breathing of the child.

"St. Just is not here—you know that?" said Sir Andrew after a while.

"Yes, I knew it," replied Blakeney curtly.

It was characteristic of these two men that not a word about the adventure itself, about the terrible risks and dangers of the past few hours, was exchanged between them. The child was here and was safe, and Blakeney knew the whereabouts of St. Just—that was enough for Sir Andrew Ffoulkes, the most devoted follower, the most perfect friend the Scarlet Pimpernel would ever know.

Ffoulkes now went to the horse, detached the nose-bag, and undid the nooses of the hobble and of the tether.

"Will you get in now, Blakeney?" he said; "we are ready."

And in unbroken silence they both got into the cart; Blakeney sitting on its floor beside the child, and Ffoulkes gathering the reins in his hands.

The wheels of the cart and the slow jog-trot of the horse made scarcely any noise in the mud of the roads, what noise they did make was effectually drowned by the soughing of the wind in the bare branches of the stunted acacia trees that edged the towpath along the line of the canal.

Sir Andrew had studied the topography of this desolate neighbourhood well during the past twenty-four hours; he knew of a detour that would enable him to avoid the La Villette gate and the neighbourhood of the fortifications, and yet bring him out soon on the road leading to St. Germain.

Once he turned to ask Blakeney the time.

"It must be close on ten now," replied Sir Percy. "Push your nag along, old man. Tony and Hastings will be waiting for us."

It was very difficult to see clearly even a metre or two ahead, but the road was a straight one, and the old nag seemed to know it almost as well and better than her driver. She shambled along at her own pace, covering the ground very slowly for Ffoulkes's burning impatience. Once or twice he had to get down and lead her over a rough piece of ground. They passed several groups of dismal, squalid houses, in some of which a dim light still burned, and as they skirted St. Ouen the church clock slowly tolled the hour of midnight.

But for the greater part of the way derelict, uncultivated spaces of terrains vagues, and a few isolated houses lay between the road and the fortifications of the city. The darkness of the night, the late hour, the soughing of the wind, were all in favour of the adventurers; and a coal-cart slowly trudging along in this neighbourhood, with two labourers sitting in it, was the least likely of any vehicle to attract attention.

Past Clichy, they had to cross the river by the rickety wooden bridge that was unsafe even in broad daylight. They were not far from their destination now. Half a dozen kilometres further on they would be leaving Courbevoie on their left, and then the sign-post would come in sight. After that the spinney just off the road, and the welcome presence of Tony, Hastings, and the horses. Ffoulkes got down in order to make sure of the way. He walked at the horse's head now, fearful lest he missed the cross-roads and the sign-post.

The horse was getting over-tired; it had covered fifteen kilometres, and it was close on three o'clock of Monday morning.

Another hour went by in absolute silence. Ffoulkes and Blakeney took turns at the horse's head. Then at last they reached the cross-roads; even through the darkness the sign-post showed white against the surrounding gloom.

"This looks like it," murmured Sir Andrew. He turned the horse's head sharply towards the left, down a narrower road, and leaving the sign-post behind him. He walked slowly along for another quarter of an hour, then Blakeney called a halt.

"The spinney must be sharp on our right now," he said.

He got down from the cart, and while Ffoulkes remained beside the horse, he plunged into the gloom. A moment later the cry of the seamew rang out three times into the air. It was answered almost immediately.

The spinney lay on the right of the road. Soon the soft sounds that to a trained ear invariably betray the presence of a number of horses reached Ffoulkes' straining senses. He took his old nag out of the shafts, and the shabby harness from off her, then he turned her out on the piece of waste land that faced the spinney. Some one would find her in the morning, her and the cart with the shabby harness laid in it, and, having wondered if all these things had perchance dropped down from heaven, would quietly appropriate them, and mayhap thank much-maligned heaven for its gift.

Blakeney in the meanwhile had lifted the sleeping child out of the cart. Then he called to Sir Andrew and led the way across the road and into the spinney.

Five minutes later Hastings received the uncrowned King of France in his arms.

Unlike Ffoulkes, my Lord Tony wanted to hear all about the adventure of this afternoon. A thorough sportsman, he loved a good story of hairbreadth escapes, of dangers cleverly avoided, risks taken and conquered.

"Just in ten words, Blakeney," he urged entreatingly; "how did you actually get the boy away?"

Sir Percy laughed—despite himself—at the young man's eagerness.

"Next time we meet, Tony," he begged; "I am so demmed fatigued, and there's this beastly rain—"

"No, no—now! while Hastings sees to the horses. I could not exist long without knowing, and we are well sheltered from the rain under this tree."

"Well, then, since you will have it," he began with a laugh, which despite the weariness and anxiety of the past twenty-four hours had forced itself to his lips, "I have been sweeper and man-of-all-work at the Temple for the past few weeks, you must know—"

"No!" ejaculated my Lord Tony lustily. "By gum!"

"Indeed, you old sybarite, whilst you were enjoying yourself heaving coal on the canal wharf, I was scrubbing floors, lighting fires, and doing a number of odd jobs for a lot of demmed murdering villains, and"—he added under his breath—"incidentally, too, for our league. Whenever I had an hour or two off duty I spent them in my lodgings, and asked you all to come and meet me there."

"By Gad, Blakeney! Then the day before yesterday?—when we all met—"

"I had just had a bath—sorely needed, I can tell you. I had been cleaning boots half the day, but I had heard that the Simons were removing from the Temple on the Sunday, and had obtained an order from them to help them shift their furniture."

"Cleaning boots!" murmured my Lord Tony with a chuckle. "Well! and then?"

"Well, then everything worked out splendidly. You see by that time I was a well-known figure in the Temple. Heron knew me well. I used to be his lanthorn-bearer when at nights he visited that poor mite in his prison. It was 'Dupont, here! Dupont there!' all day long. 'Light the fire in the office, Dupont! Dupont, brush my coat! Dupont, fetch me a light!' When the Simons wanted to move their household goods they called loudly for Dupont. I got a covered laundry cart, and I brought a dummy with me to substitute for the child. Simon himself knew nothing of this, but Madame was in my pay. The dummy was just splendid, with real hair on its head; Madame helped me to substitute it for the child; we laid it on the sofa and covered it over with a rug, even while those brutes Heron and Cochefer were on the landing outside, and we stuffed His Majesty the King of France into a linen basket. The room was badly lighted, and any one would have been deceived. No one was suspicious of that type of trickery, so it went off splendidly. I moved the furniture of the Simons out of the Tower. His Majesty King Louis XVII was still concealed in the linen basket. I drove the Simons to their new lodgings—the man still suspects nothing—and there I helped them to unload the furniture—with the exception of the linen basket, of course. After that I drove my laundry cart to a house I knew of and collected a number of linen baskets, which I had arranged should be in readiness for me. Thus loaded up I left Paris by the Vincennes gate, and drove as far as Bagnolet, where there is no road except past the octroi, where the officials might have proved unpleasant. So I lifted His Majesty out of the basket and we walked on hand in hand in the darkness and the rain until the poor little feet gave out. Then the little fellow—who has been wonderfully plucky throughout, indeed, more a Capet than a Bourbon—snuggled up in my arms and went fast asleep, and—and—well, I think that's all, for here we are, you see."

"But if Madame Simon had not been amenable to bribery?" suggested Lord Tony after a moment's silence.

"Then I should have had to think of something else."

"If during the removal of the furniture Heron had remained resolutely in the room?"

"Then, again, I should have had to think of something else; but remember that in life there is always one supreme moment when Chance—who is credited to have but one hair on her head—stands by you for a brief space of time; sometimes that space is infinitesimal—one minute, a few seconds—just the time to seize Chance by that one hair. So I pray you all give me no credit in this or any other matter in which we all work together, but the quickness of seizing Chance by the hair during the brief moment when she stands by my side. If Madame Simon had been un-amenable, if Heron had remained in the room all the time, if Cochefer had had two looks at the dummy instead of one—well, then, something else would have helped me, something would have occurred; something—I know not what—but surely something which Chance meant to be on our side, if only we were quick enough to seize it—and so you see how simple it all is."

So simple, in fact, that it was sublime. The daring, the pluck, the ingenuity and, above all, the super-human heroism and endurance which rendered the hearers of this simple narrative, simply told, dumb with admiration.

Their thoughts now were beyond verbal expression.

"How soon was the hue and cry for the child about the streets?" asked Tony, after a moment's silence.

"It was not out when I left the gates of Paris," said Blakeney meditatively; "so quietly has the news of the escape been kept, that I am wondering what devilry that brute Heron can be after. And now no more chattering," he continued lightly; "all to horse, and you, Hastings, have a care. The destinies of France, mayhap, will be lying asleep in your arms."

"But you, Blakeney?" exclaimed the three men almost simultaneously.

"I am not going with you. I entrust the child to you. For God's sake guard him well! Ride with him to Mantes. You should arrive there at about ten o'clock. One of you then go straight to No.9 Rue la Tour. Ring the bell; an old man will answer it. Say the one word to him, '*Enfant*'; he will reply, '*De roi!*' Give him the child, and may Heaven bless you all for the help you have given me this night!"

"But you, Blakeney?" reiterated Tony with a note of deep anxiety in his fresh young voice.

"I am straight for Paris," he said quietly.

"Impossible!"

"Therefore feasible."

"But why? Percy, in the name of Heaven, do you realise what you are doing?"

"Perfectly."

"They'll not leave a stone unturned to find you—they know by now, believe me, that your hand did this trick."

"I know that."

"And yet you mean to go back?"

"And yet I am going back."

"Blakeney!"

"It's no use, Tony. Armand is in Paris. I saw him in the corridor of the Temple prison in the company of Chauvelin."

"Great God!" exclaimed Lord Hastings.

The others were silent. What was the use of arguing? One of themselves was in danger. Armand St. Just, the brother of Marguerite Blakeney! Was it likely that Percy would leave him in the lurch.

"One of us will stay with you, of course?" asked Sir Andrew after awhile.

"Yes! I want Hastings and Tony to take the child to Mantes, then to make all possible haste for Calais, and there to keep in close touch with the Day-Dream; the skipper will contrive to open communication. Tell him to remain in Calais waters. I hope I may have need of him soon.

"And now to horse, both of you," he added gaily. "Hastings, when you are ready, I will hand up the child to you. He will be quite safe on the pillion with a strap round him and you."

Nothing more was said after that. The orders were given, there was nothing to do but to obey; and the uncrowned King of France was not yet out of danger. Hastings and Tony led two of the horses out of the spinney; at the roadside they mounted, and then the little lad for whose sake so much heroism, such selfless devotion had been expended, was hoisted up, still half asleep, on the pillion in front of my Lord Hastings.

"Keep your arm round him," admonished Blakeney; "your horse looks quiet enough. But put on speed as far as Mantes, and may Heaven guard you both!"

The two men pressed their heels to their horses' flanks, the beasts snorted and pawed the ground anxious to start. There were a few whispered farewells, two loyal hands were stretched out at the last, eager to grasp the leader's hand.

Then horses and riders disappeared in the utter darkness which comes before the dawn.

Blakeney and Ffoulkes stood side by side in silence for as long as the pawing of hoofs in the mud could reach their ears, then Ffoulkes asked abruptly:

"What do you want me to do, Blakeney?"

"Well, for the present, my dear fellow, I want you to take one of the three horses we have left in the spinney, and put him into the shafts of our old friend the coal-cart; then I am afraid that you must go back the way we came."

"Yes?"

"Continue to heave coal on the canal wharf by La Villette; it is the best way to avoid attention. After your day's work keep your cart and horse in readiness against my arrival, at the same spot where you were last night. If after having waited for me like this for three consecutive nights you neither see nor hear anything from me, go back to England and tell Marguerite that in giving my life for her brother I gave it for her!"

"Blakeney—!"

"I spoke differently to what I usually do, is that it?" he interposed, placing his firm hand on his friend's shoulder. "I am degenerating, Ffoulkes—that's what it is. Pay no heed to it. I suppose that carrying that sleeping child in my arms last night softened some nerves in my body. I was so infinitely sorry for the poor mite, and vaguely wondered if I had not saved it from one misery only to plunge it in another. There was such a fateful look on that wan little face, as if destiny had already writ its veto there against happiness. It came on me then how futile were our actions, if God chooses to interpose His will between us and our desires."

Almost as he left off speaking the rain ceased to patter down against the puddles in the road. Overhead the clouds flew by at terrific speed, driven along by the blustering wind. It was less dark now, and Sir Andrew, peering through the gloom, could see his leader's face. It was singularly pale and hard, and the deep-set lazy eyes had in them just that fateful look which he himself had spoken of just now.

"You are anxious about Armand, Percy?" asked Ffoulkes softly.

"Yes. He should have trusted me, as I had trusted him. He missed me at the Villette gate on Friday, and without a thought left me —left us all in the lurch; he threw himself into the lion's jaws, thinking that he could help the girl he loved. I knew that I could save her. She is in comparative safety even now. The old woman, Madame Belhomme, had been freely released the day after her arrest, but Jeanne Lange is still in the house in the Rue de Charonne. You know it, Ffoulkes. I got her there early this morning. It was easy for me, of course: 'Hola, Dupont! my boots, Dupont!' 'One moment, citizen, my daughter—' 'Curse thy daughter, bring me my boots!' and Jeanne Lange walked out of the Temple prison her hand in that of that lout Dupont."

"But Armand does not know that she is in the Rue de Charonne?"

"No. I have not seen him since that early morning on Saturday when he came to tell me that she had been arrested. Having sworn that he would obey me, he went to meet you and Tony at La Villette, but returned to Paris a few hours later, and drew the undivided attention of all the committees on Jeanne Lange by his senseless, foolish inquiries. But for his action throughout the whole of yesterday I could have smuggled Jeanne out of Paris, got her to join you at Villette, or Hastings in St. Germain. But the barriers were being closely watched for her, and I had the Dauphin to think of. She is in comparative safety; the people in the Rue de Charonne are friendly for the moment; but for how long? Who knows? I must look after her of course. And Armand! Poor old Armand! The lion's jaws have snapped over him, and they hold him tight. Chauvelin and his gang are using him as a decoy to trap me, of course. All that had not happened if Armand had trusted me."

He sighed a quick sigh of impatience, almost of regret. Ffoulkes was the one man who could guess the bitter disappointment that this had meant. Percy had longed to be back in England soon, back to Marguerite, to a few days of unalloyed happiness and a few days of peace.

Now Armand's actions had retarded all that; they were a deliberate bar to the future as it had been mapped out by a man who foresaw everything, who was prepared for every eventuality.

In this case, too, he had been prepared, but not for the want of trust which had brought on disobedience akin to disloyalty. That absolutely unforeseen eventuality had changed Blakeney's usual irresponsible gaiety into a consciousness of the inevitable, of the inexorable decrees of Fate.

With an anxious sigh, Sir Andrew turned away from his chief and went back to the spinney to select for his own purpose one of the three horses which Hastings and Tony had unavoidably left behind.

"And you, Blakeney—how will you go back to that awful Paris?" he said, when he had made his choice and was once more back beside Percy.

"I don't know yet," replied Blakeney, "but it would not be safe to ride. I'll reach one of the gates on this side of the city and contrive to slip in somehow. I have a certificate of safety in my pocket in case I need it.

"We'll leave the horses here," he said presently, whilst he was helping Sir Andrew to put the horse in the shafts of the coal-cart; "they cannot come to much harm. Some poor devil might steal them, in order to escape from those vile brutes in the city. If so, God speed him, say I. I'll compensate my friend the farmer of St. Germain for their loss at an early opportunity. And now, good-bye, my dear fellow! Some time to-night, if possible, you shall hear direct news of me—if not, then to-morrow or the day after that. Good-bye, and Heaven guard you!"

"God guard you, Blakeney!" said Sir Andrew fervently.

He jumped into the cart and gathered up the reins. His heart was heavy as lead, and a strange mist had gathered in his eyes, blurring the last dim vision which he had of his chief standing all alone in the gloom, his broad, magnificent figure looking almost weirdly erect and defiant, his head thrown back, and his kind, lazy eyes watching the final departure of his most faithful comrade and friend.

# Chapter 22: Of That There Could Be No Question

Blakeney had more than one *pied-a-terre* in Paris, and never stayed longer than two or three days in any of these. It was not difficult for a single man, be he labourer or bourgeois, to obtain a night's lodging, even in these most troublous times, and in any quarter of Paris, provided the rent—out of all proportion to the comfort and accommodation given—was paid ungrudgingly and in advance.

Emigration and, above all, the enormous death-roll of the past eighteen months, had emptied the apartment houses of the great city, and those who had rooms to let were only too glad of a lodger, always providing they were not in danger of being worried by the committees of their section.

The laws framed by these same committees now demanded that all keepers of lodging or apartment houses should within twenty-four hours give notice at the bureau of their individual sections of the advent of new lodgers, together with a description of the personal appearance of such lodgers, and an indication of their presumed civil status and occupation. But there was a margin of twenty-four hours, which could on pressure be extended to forty-eight, and, therefore, any one could obtain shelter for forty-eight hours, and have no questions asked, provided he or she was willing to pay the exorbitant sum usually asked under the circumstances.

Thus Blakeney had no difficulty in securing what lodgings he wanted when he once more found himself inside Paris at somewhere about noon of that same Monday.

The thought of Hastings and Tony speeding on towards Mantes with the royal child safely held in Hastings' arms had kept his spirits buoyant and caused him for a while to forget the terrible peril in which Armand St. Just's thoughtless egoism had placed them both.

Blakeney was a man of abnormal physique and iron nerve, else he could never have endured the fatigues of the past twenty-four hours, from the moment when on the Sunday afternoon he began to play his part of furniture-remover at the Temple, to that when at last on Monday at noon he succeeded in persuading the sergeant at the Maillot gate that he was an honest stonemason residing at Neuilly, who was come to Paris in search of work.

After that matters became more simple. Terribly foot-sore, though he would never have admitted it, hungry and weary, he turned into an unpretentious eating-house and ordered some dinner. The place when he entered was occupied mostly by labourers and workmen, dressed very much as he was himself, and quite as grimy as he had become after having driven about for hours in a laundry-cart and in a coal-cart, and having walked twelve kilometres, some of which he had covered whilst carrying a sleeping child in his arms.

Thus, Sir Percy Blakeney, Bart., the friend and companion of the Prince of Wales, the most fastidious fop the salons of London and Bath had ever seen, was in no way distinguishable outwardly from the tattered, half-starved, dirty, and out-at-elbows products of this fraternising and equalising Republic.

He was so hungry that the ill-cooked, badly-served meal tempted him to eat; and he ate on in silence, seemingly more interested in boiled beef than in the conversation that went on around him. But he would not have been the keen and daring adventurer that he was if he did not all the while keep his ears open for any fragment of news that the desultory talk of his fellow-diners was likely to yield to him.

Politics were, of course, discussed; the tyranny of the sections, the slavery that this free Republic had brought on its citizens. The names of the chief personages of the day were all mentioned in turns Focquier-Tinville, Santerre, Danton, Robespierre. Heron and his sleuth-hounds were spoken of with execrations quickly suppressed, but of little Capet not one word.

Blakeney could not help but infer that Chauvelin, Heron and the commissaries in charge were keeping the escape of the child a secret for as long as they could.

He could hear nothing of Armand's fate, of course. The arrest— if arrest there had been—was not like to be bruited abroad just now. Blakeney having last seen Armand in Chauvelin's company, whilst he himself was moving the Simons' furniture, could not for a moment doubt that the young man was imprisoned,—unless, indeed, he was being allowed a certain measure of freedom, whilst his every step was being spied on, so that he might act as a decoy for his chief.

At thought of that all weariness seemed to vanish from Blakeney's powerful frame. He set his lips firmly together, and once again the light of irresponsible gaiety danced in his eyes.

He had been in as tight a corner as this before now; at Boulogne his beautiful Marguerite had been used as a decoy, and twenty-four hours later he had held her in his arms on board his yacht the Day-Dream. As he would have put it in his own forcible language:

"Those d—d murderers have not got me yet."

The battle mayhap would this time be against greater odds than before, but Blakeney had no fear that they would prove overwhelming.

There was in life but one odd that was overwhelming, and that was treachery.

But of that there could be no question.

In the afternoon Blakeney started off in search of lodgings for the night. He found what would suit him in the Rue de l'Arcade, which was equally far from the House of Justice as it was from his former lodgings. Here he would be safe for at least twenty-four hours, after which he might have to shift again. But for the moment the landlord of the miserable apartment was over-willing to make no fuss and ask no questions, for the sake of the money which this *aristo* in disguise dispensed with a lavish hand.

Having taken possession of his new quarters and snatched a few hours of sound, well-deserved rest, until the time when the shades of evening and the darkness of the streets would make progress through the city somewhat more safe, Blakeney sallied forth at about six o'clock having a threefold object in view.

Primarily, of course, the threefold object was concentrated on Armand. There was the possibility of finding out at the young man's lodgings in Montmartre what had become of him; then there were the usual inquiries that could be made from the registers of the various prisons; and, thirdly, there was the chance that Armand had succeeded in sending some kind of message to Blakeney's former lodgings in the Rue St. Germain l'Auxerrois.

On the whole, Sir Percy decided to leave the prison registers alone for the present. If Armand had been actually arrested, he would almost certainly be confined in the Chatelet prison, where he would be closer to hand for all the interrogatories to which, no doubt, he would be subjected.

Blakeney set his teeth and murmured a good, sound, British oath when he thought of those interrogatories. Armand St. Just, highly strung, a dreamer and a bundle of nerves—how he would suffer under the mental rack of questions and cross-questions, cleverly-laid traps to catch information from him unawares!

His next objective, then, was Armand's former lodging, and from six o'clock until close upon eight Sir Percy haunted the slopes of Montmartre, and more especially the neighbourhood of the Rue de la Croix Blanche, where Armand had lodged these former days. At the house itself he could not inquire as yet; obviously it would not have been safe; tomorrow, perhaps, when he knew more, but not tonight. His keen eyes had already spied at least two figures clothed in the rags of out-of-work labourers like himself, who had hung with suspicious persistence in this same neighbourhood, and who during the two hours that he had been in observation had never strayed out of sight of the house in the Rue de la Croix Blanche.

That these were two spies on the watch was, of course, obvious; but whether they were on the watch for St. Just or for some other unfortunate wretch it was at this stage impossible to conjecture.

Then, as from the Tour des Dames close by the clock solemnly struck the hour of eight, and Blakeney prepared to wend his way back to another part of the city, he suddenly saw Armand walking slowly up the street.

The young man did not look either to right or left; he held his head forward on his chest, and his hands were hidden underneath his cloak. When he passed immediately under one of the street lamps Blakeney caught sight of his face; it was pale and drawn. Then he turned his head, and for the space of two seconds his eyes across the narrow street encountered those of his chief. He had the presence of mind not to make a sign or to utter a sound; he was obviously being followed, but in that brief moment Sir Percy had seen in the young man's eyes a look that reminded him of a hunted creature.

"What have those brutes been up to with him, I wonder?" he muttered between clenched teeth.

Armand soon disappeared under the doorway of the same house where he had been lodging all along. Even as he did so Blakeney saw the two spies gather together like a pair of slimy lizards, and whisper excitedly one to another. A third man, who obviously had been dogging Armand's footsteps, came up and joined them after a while.

Blakeney could have sworn loudly and lustily, had it been possible to do so without attracting attention. The whole of Armand's history in the past twenty-four hours was perfectly clear to him. The young man had been made free that he might prove a decoy for more important game.

His every step was being watched, and he still thought Jeanne Lange in immediate danger of death. The look of despair in his face proclaimed these two facts, and Blakeney's heart ached for the mental torture which his friend was enduring. He longed to let Armand know that the woman he loved was in comparative safety.

Jeanne Lange first, and then Armand himself; and the odds would be very heavy against the Scarlet Pimpernel! But that Marguerite should not have to mourn an only brother, of that Sir Percy made oath.

He now turned his steps towards his own former lodgings by St. Germain l'Auxerrois. It was just possible that Armand had succeeded in leaving a message there for him. It was, of course, equally possible that when he did so Heron's men had watched his movements, and that spies would be stationed there, too, on the watch.

But that risk must, of course, be run. Blakeney's former lodging was the one place that Armand would know of to which he could send a message to his chief, if he wanted to do so. Of course, the unfortunate young man could not have known until just now that Percy would come back to Paris, but he might guess it, or wish it, or only vaguely hope for it; he might want to send a message, he might long to communicate with his brother-in-law, and, perhaps, feel sure that the latter would not leave him in the lurch.

With that thought in his mind, Sir Percy was not likely to give up the attempt to ascertain for himself whether Armand had tried to communicate with him or not. As for spies—well, he had dodged some of them often enough in his time—the risks that he ran to-night were no worse than the ones to which he had so successfully run counter in the Temple yesterday.

Still keeping up the slouchy gait peculiar to the out-at-elbows working man of the day, hugging the houses as he walked along the streets, Blakeney made slow progress across the city. But at last he reached the facade of St. Germain l'Auxerrois, and turning sharply to his right he soon came in sight of the house which he had only quitted twenty-four hours ago.

We all know that house—all of us who are familiar with the Paris of those terrible days. It stands quite detached—a vast quadrangle, facing the Quai de l'Ecole and the river, backing on the Rue St. Germain l'Auxerrois, and shouldering the Carrefour des Trois Manes. The porte-cochere, so-called, is but a narrow doorway, and is actually situated in the Rue St. Germain l'Auxerrois.

Blakeney made his way cautiously right round the house; he peered up and down the quay, and his keen eyes tried to pierce the dense gloom that hung at the corners of the Pont Neuf immediately opposite. Soon he assured himself that for the present, at any rate, the house was not being watched.

Armand presumably had not yet left a message for him here; but he might do so at any time now that he knew that his chief was in Paris and on the look-out for him.

Blakeney made up his mind to keep this house in sight. This art of watching he had acquired to a masterly extent, and could have taught Heron's watch-dogs a remarkable lesson in it. At night, of course, it was a comparatively easy task. There were a good many unlighted doorways along the quay, whilst a street lamp was fixed on a bracket in the wall of the very house which he kept in observation.

Finding temporary shelter under various doorways, or against the dank walls of the houses, Blakeney set himself resolutely to a few hours' weary waiting. A thin, drizzly rain fell with unpleasant persistence, like a damp mist, and the thin blouse which he wore soon became wet through and clung hard and chilly to his shoulders.

It was close on midnight when at last he thought it best to give up his watch and to go back to his lodgings for a few hours' sleep; but at seven o'clock the next morning he was back again at his post.

The porte-cochere of his former lodging-house was not yet open; he took up his stand close beside it. His woollen cap pulled well over his forehead, the grime cleverly plastered on his hair and face, his lower jaw thrust forward, his eyes looking lifeless and bleary, all gave him an expression of sly villainy, whilst the short clay pipe struck at a sharp angle in his mouth, his hands thrust into the pockets of his ragged breeches, and his bare feet in the mud of the road, gave the final touch to his representation of an out-of-work, ill-conditioned, and supremely discontented loafer.

He had not very long to wait. Soon the porte-cochere of the house was opened, and the concierge came out with his broom, making a show of cleaning the pavement in front of the door. Five minutes later a lad, whose clothes consisted entirely of rags, and whose feet and head were bare, came rapidly up the street from the quay, and walked along looking at the houses as he went, as if trying to decipher their number. The cold grey dawn was just breaking, dreary and damp, as all the past days had been. Blakeney watched the lad as he approached, the small, naked feet falling noiselessly on the cobblestones of the road. When the boy was quite close to him and to the house, Blakeney shifted his position and took the pipe out of his mouth.

"Up early, my son!" he said gruffly.

"Yes," said the pale-faced little creature; "I have a message to deliver at No. 9 Rue St. Germain l'Auxerrois. It must be somewhere near here."

"It is. You can give me the message."

"Oh, no, citizen!" said the lad, into whose pale, circled eyes a look of terror had quickly appeared. "It is for one of the lodgers in No. 9. I must give it to him."

With an instinct which he somehow felt could not err at this moment, Blakeney knew that the message was one from Armand to himself; a written message, too, since—instinctively when he spoke—the boy clutched at his thin shirt, as if trying to guard something precious that had been entrusted to him.

"I will deliver the message myself, sonny," said Blakeney gruffly. "I know the citizen for whom it is intended. He would not like the concierge to see it."

"Oh! I would not give it to the concierge," said the boy. "I would take it upstairs myself."

"My son," retorted Blakeney, "let me tell you this. You are going to give that message up to me and I will put five whole livres into your hand."

Blakeney, with all his sympathy aroused for this poor pale-faced lad, put on the airs of a ruffianly bully. He did not wish that message to be taken indoors by the lad, for the concierge might get hold of it, despite the boy's protests and tears, and after that Blakeney would perforce have to disclose himself before it would be given up to him. During the past week the concierge had been very amenable to bribery. Whatever suspicions he had had about his lodger he had kept to himself for the sake of the money which he received; but it was impossible to gauge any man's trend of thought these days from one hour to the next. Something—for aught Blakeney knew—might have occurred in the past twenty-four hours to change an amiable and accommodating lodging-house keeper into a surly or dangerous spy.

Fortunately, the concierge had once more gone within; there was no one abroad, and if there were, no one probably would take any notice of a burly ruffian brow-beating a child.

"*Allons!*" he said gruffly, "give me the letter, or that five livres goes back into my pocket."

"Five livres!" exclaimed the child with pathetic eagerness. "Oh, citizen!"

The thin little hand fumbled under the rags, but it reappeared again empty, whilst a faint blush spread over the hollow cheeks.

"The other citizen also gave me five livres," he said humbly. "He lodges in the house where my mother is concierge. It is in the Rue de la Croix Blanche. He has been very kind to my mother. I would rather do as he bade me."

"Bless the lad," murmured Blakeney under his breath; "his loyalty redeems many a crime of this God-forsaken city. Now I suppose I shall have to bully him, after all."

He took his hand out of his breeches pocket; between two very dirty fingers he held a piece of gold. The other hand he placed quite roughly on the lad's chest.

"Give me the letter," he said harshly, "or—"

He pulled at the ragged blouse, and a scrap of soiled paper soon fell into his hand. The lad began to cry.

"Here," said Blakeney, thrusting the piece of gold into the thin small palm, "take this home to your mother, and tell your lodger that a big, rough man took the letter away from you by force. Now run, before I kick you out of the way."

The lad, terrified out of his poor wits, did not wait for further commands; he took to his heels and ran, his small hand clutching the piece of gold. Soon he had disappeared round the corner of the street.

Blakeney did not at once read the paper; he thrust it quickly into his breeches pocket and slouched away slowly down the street, and thence across the Place du Carrousel, in the direction of his new lodgings in the Rue de l'Arcade.

It was only when he found himself alone in the narrow, squalid room which he was occupying that he took the scrap of paper from his pocket and read it slowly through. It said:

Percy, you cannot forgive me, nor can I ever forgive myself, but if you only knew what I have suffered for the past two days you would, I think, try and forgive. I am free and yet a prisoner; my every footstep is dogged. What they ultimately mean to do with me I do not know. And when I think of Jeanne I long for the power to end mine own miserable existence. Percy! she is still in the hands of those fiends. . . . I saw the prison register; her name written there has been like a burning brand on my heart ever since. She was still in prison the day that you left Paris; to-morrow, to-night mayhap, they will try her, condemn her, torture her, and I dare not go to see you, for I would only be bringing spies to your door. But will you come to me, Percy? It should be safe in the hours of the night, and the concierge is devoted to me. To-night at ten o'clock she will leave the *porte-cochere* unlatched. If you find it so, and if on the ledge of the window immediately on your left as you enter you find a candle alight, and beside it a scrap of paper with your initials S. P. traced on it, then it will be quite safe for you to come up to my room. It is on the second landing—a door on your right—that too I will leave on the latch. But in the name of the woman you love best in all the world come at once to me then, and bear in mind, Percy, that the woman I love is threatened with immediate death, and that I am powerless to save her. Indeed, believe me, I would gladly die even now but for the thought of Jeanne, whom I should be leaving in the hands of those fiends. For God's sake, Percy, remember that Jeanne is all the world to me.

"Poor old Armand," murmured Blakeney with a kindly smile directed at the absent friend, "he won't trust me even now. He won't trust his Jeanne in my hands. Well," he added after a while, "after all, I would not entrust Marguerite to anybody else either."

# CHAPTER 23: THE OVERWHELMING ODDS

At half-past ten that same evening, Blakeney, still clad in a workman's tattered clothes, his feet bare so that he could tread the streets unheard, turned into the Rue de la Croix Blanche.

The *porte-cochère* of the house where Armand lodged had been left on the latch; not a soul was in sight. Peering cautiously round, he slipped into the house. On the ledge of the window, immediately on his left when he entered, a candle was left burning, and beside it there was a scrap of paper with the initials S. P. roughly traced in pencil. No one challenged him as he noiselessly glided past it, and up the narrow stairs that led to the upper floor. Here, too, on the second landing the door on the right had left on the latch. He pushed it open and entered.

As is usual even in the meanest lodgings in Paris houses, a small antechamber gave between the front door and the main room. When Percy entered the antechamber was unlighted, but the door into the inner room beyond was ajar. Blakeney approached it with noiseless tread, and gently pushed it open.

That very instant he knew that the game was up; he heard the footsteps closing up behind him, saw Armand, deathly pale, leaning against the wall in the room in front of him, and Chauvelin and Heron standing guard over him.

The next moment the room and the antechamber were literally alive with soldiers—twenty of them to arrest one man.

It was characteristic of that man that when hands were laid on him from every side he threw back his head and laughed—laughed mirthfully, light-heartedly, and the first words that escaped his lips were:

"Well, I am d—d!"

"The odds are against you, Sir Percy," said Chauvelin to him in English, whilst Heron at the further end of the room was growling like a contented beast.

"By the Lord, sir," said Percy with perfect *sang-froid*, "I do believe that for the moment they are."

"Have done, my men—have done!" he added, turning good-humouredly to the soldiers round him. "I never fight against overwhelming odds. Twenty to one, eh? I could lay four of you out easily enough, perhaps even six, but what then?"

But a kind of savage lust seemed to have rendered these men temporarily mad, and they were being egged on by Heron. The mysterious Englishman, about whom so many eerie tales were told! Well, he had supernatural powers, and twenty to one might be nothing to him if the devil was on his side. Therefore a blow on his forearm with the butt-end of a bayonet was useful for disabling his right hand, and soon the left arm with a dislocated shoulder hung limp by his side. Then he was bound with cords.

The vein of luck had given out. The gambler had staked more than usual and had lost; but he knew how to lose, just as he had always known how to win.

"Those d—d brutes are trussing me like a fowl," he murmured with irrepressible gaiety at the last.

Then the wrench on his bruised arms as they were pulled roughly back by the cords caused the veil of unconsciousness to gather over his eyes.

"And Jeanne was safe, Armand," he shouted with a last desperate effort; "those devils have lied to you and tricked you into this . . . . Since yesterday she is out of prison . . . in the house . . . you know . . . "

After that he lost consciousness.

And this occurred on Tuesday, January 21st, in the year 1794, or, in accordance with the new calendar, on the 2nd Pluviose, year II of the Republic.

It is chronicled in the Moniteur of the 3rd Pluviose that, "on the previous evening, at half-past ten of the clock, the Englishman known as the Scarlet Pimpernel, who for three years has conspired against the safety of the Republic, was arrested through the patriotic exertions of citizen Chauvelin, and conveyed to the Conciergerie, where he now lies —sick, but closely guarded. Long live the Republic!"

# PART II

## CHAPTER 24: THE NEWS

The grey January day was falling, drowsy, and dull into the arms of night.

Marguerite, sitting in the dusk beside the fire in her small boudoir, shivered a little as she drew her scarf closer round her shoulders.

Edwards, the butler, entered with the lamp. The room looked peculiarly cheery now, with the delicate white panelling of the wall glowing under the soft kiss of the flickering firelight and the steadier glow of the rose-shaded lamp.

"Has the courier not arrived yet, Edwards?" asked Marguerite, fixing the impassive face of the well-drilled servant with her large purple-rimmed eyes.

"Not yet, m'lady," he replied placidly.

"It is his day, is it not?"

"Yes, m'lady. And the forenoon is his time. But there have been heavy rains, and the roads must be rare muddy. He must have been delayed, m'lady."

"Yes, I suppose so," she said listlessly. "That will do, Edwards. No, don't close the shutters. I'll ring presently."

The man went out of the room as automatically as he had come. He closed the door behind him, and Marguerite was once more alone.

She picked up the book which she had fingered idly before the light gave out. She tried once more to fix her attention on this tale of love and adventure written by Mr. Fielding; but she had lost the thread of the story, and there was a mist between her eyes and the printed pages.

With an impatient gesture she threw down the book and passed her hand across her eyes, then seemed astonished to find that her hand was wet.

She rose and went to the window. The air outside had been singularly mild all day; the thaw was persisting, and a south wind came across the Channel—from France.

Marguerite threw open the casement and sat down on the wide sill, leaning her head against the window-frame, and gazing out into the fast gathering gloom. From far away, at the foot of the gently sloping lawns, the river murmured softly in the night; in the borders to the right and left a few snowdrops still showed like tiny white specks through the surrounding darkness. Winter had begun the process of slowly shedding its mantle, coquetting with Spring, who still lingered in the land of Infinity. Gradually the shadows drew closer and closer; the reeds and rushes on the river bank were the first to sink into their embrace, then the big cedars on the lawn, majestic and defiant, but yielding still unconquered to the power of night.

The tiny stars of snowdrop blossoms vanished one by one, and at last the cool, grey ribbon of the river surface was wrapped under the mantle of evening.

Only the south wind lingered on, soughing gently in the drowsy reeds, whispering among the branches of the cedars, and gently stirring the tender corollas of the sleeping snowdrops.

Marguerite seemed to open out her lungs to its breath. It had come all the way from France, and on its wings had brought something of Percy—a murmur as if he had spoken—a memory that was as intangible as a dream.

She shivered again, though of a truth it was not cold. The courier's delay had completely unsettled her nerves. Twice a week he came especially from Dover, and always he brought some message, some token which Percy had contrived to send from Paris. They were like tiny scraps of dry bread thrown to a starving woman, but they did just help to keep her heart alive—that poor, aching, disappointed heart that so longed for enduring happiness which it could never get.

The man whom she loved with all her soul, her mind and her body, did not belong to her; he belonged to suffering humanity over there in terror-stricken France, where the cries of the innocent, the persecuted, the wretched called louder to him than she in her love could do.

He had been away three months now, during which time her starving heart had fed on its memories, and the happiness of a brief visit from him six weeks ago, when—quite unexpectedly—he had appeared before her . . . home between two desperate adventures that had given life and freedom to a number of innocent people, and nearly cost him his—and she had lain in his arms in a swoon of perfect happiness.

But he had gone away again as suddenly as he had come, and for six weeks now she had lived partly in anticipation of the courier with messages from him, and partly on the fitful joy engendered by these messages. To-day she had not even that, and the disappointment seemed just now more than she could bear.

She felt unaccountably restless, and could she but have analysed her feelings—had she dared so to do—she would have realised that the weight which oppressed her heart so that she could hardly breathe, was one of vague yet dark foreboding.

She closed the window and returned to her seat by the fire, taking up her hook with the strong resolution not to allow her nerves to get the better of her. But it was difficult to pin one's attention down to the adventures of Master Tom Jones when one's mind was fully engrossed with those of Sir Percy Blakeney.

The sound of carriage wheels on the gravelled forecourt in the front of the house suddenly awakened her drowsy senses. She threw down the book, and with trembling hands clutched the arms of her chair, straining her ears to listen. A carriage at this hour—and on this damp winter's evening! She racked her mind wondering who it could be.

Lady Ffoulkes was in London, she knew. Sir Andrew, of course, was in Paris. His Royal Highness, ever a faithful visitor, would surely not venture out to Richmond in this inclement weather—and the courier always came on horseback.

There was a murmur of voices; that of Edwards, mechanical and placid, could be heard quite distinctly saying:

"I'm sure that her ladyship will be at home for you, m'lady. But I'll go and ascertain."

Marguerite ran to the door and with joyful eagerness tore it open.

"Suzanne!" she called "my little Suzanne! I thought you were in London. Come up quickly! In the boudoir—yes. Oh! what good fortune hath brought you?"

Suzanne flew into her arms, holding the friend whom she loved so well close and closer to her heart, trying to hide her face, which was wet with tears, in the folds of Marguerite's kerchief.

"Come inside, my darling," said Marguerite. "Why, how cold your little hands are!"

She was on the point of turning back to her boudoir, drawing Lady Ffoulkes by the hand, when suddenly she caught sight of Sir Andrew, who stood at a little distance from her, at the top of the stairs.

"Sir Andrew!" she exclaimed with unstinted gladness.

Then she paused. The cry of welcome died on her lips, leaving them dry and parted. She suddenly felt as if some fearful talons had gripped her heart and were tearing at it with sharp, long nails; the blood flew from her cheeks and from her limbs, leaving her with a sense of icy numbness.

She backed into the room, still holding Suzanne's hand, and drawing her in with her. Sir Andrew followed them, then closed the door behind him. At last the word escaped Marguerite's parched lips:

"Percy! Something has happened to him! He is dead?"

"No, no!" exclaimed Sir Andrew quickly.

Suzanne put her loving arms round her friend and drew her down into the chair by the fire. She knelt at her feet on the hearthrug, and pressed her own burning lips on Marguerite's icy-cold hands. Sir Andrew stood silently by, a world of loving friendship, of heart-broken sorrow, in his eyes.

There was silence in the pretty white-panelled room for a while.

Marguerite sat with her eyes closed, bringing the whole armoury of her will power to bear her up outwardly now.

"Tell me!" she said at last, and her voice was toneless and dull, like one that came from the depths of a grave—"tell me—exactly—everything. Don't be afraid. I can bear it. Don't be afraid."

Sir Andrew remained standing, with bowed head and one hand resting on the table. In a firm, clear voice he told her the events of the past few days as they were known to him. All that he tried to hide was Armand's disobedience, which, in his heart, he felt was the primary cause of the catastrophe. He told of the rescue of the Dauphin from the Temple, the midnight drive in the coal-cart, the meeting with Hastings and Tony in the spinney. He only gave vague explanations of Armand's stay in Paris which caused Percy to go back to the city, even at the moment when his most daring plan had been so successfully carried through.

"Armand, I understand, has fallen in love with a beautiful woman in Paris, Lady Blakeney," he said, seeing that a strange, puzzled look had appeared in Marguerite's pale face. "She was arrested the day before the rescue of the Dauphin from the Temple. Armand could not join us. He felt that he could not leave her. I am sure that you will understand."

Then as she made no comment, he resumed his narrative:

"I had been ordered to go back to La Villette, and there to resume my duties as a labourer in the day-time, and to wait for Percy during the night. The fact that I had received no message from him for two days had made me somewhat worried, but I have such faith in him, such belief in his good luck and his ingenuity, that I would not allow myself to be really anxious. Then on the third day I heard the news."

"What news?" asked Marguerite mechanically.

"That the Englishman who was known as the Scarlet Pimpernel had been captured in a house in the Rue de la Croix Blanche, and had been imprisoned in the Conciergerie."

"The Rue de la Croix Blanche? Where is that?"

"In the Montmartre quarter. Armand lodged there. Percy, I imagine, was working to get him away; and those brutes captured him."

"Having heard the news, Sir Andrew, what did you do?"

"I went into Paris and ascertained its truth."

"And there is no doubt of it?"

"Alas, none! I went to the house in the Rue de la Croix Blanche. Armand had disappeared. I succeeded in inducing the concierge to talk. She seems to have been devoted to her lodger. Amidst tears she told me some of the details of the capture. Can you bear to hear them, Lady Blakeney?"

"Yes—tell me everything—don't be afraid," she reiterated with the same dull monotony.

"It appears that early on the Tuesday morning the son of the concierge—a lad about fifteen—was sent off by her lodger with a message to No. 9 Rue St. Germain l'Auxerrois. That was the house where Percy was staying all last week, where he kept disguises and so on for us all, and where some of our meetings were held. Percy evidently expected that Armand would try and communicate with him at that address, for when the lad arrived in front of the house he was accosted—so he says—by a big, rough workman, who browbeat him into giving up the lodger's letter, and finally pressed a piece of gold into his hand. The workman was Blakeney, of course. I imagine that Armand, at the time that he wrote the letter, must have been under the belief that Mademoiselle Lange was still in prison; he could not know then that Blakeney had already got her into comparative safety. In the letter he must have spoken of the terrible plight in which he stood, and also of his fears for the woman whom he loved. Percy was not the man to leave a comrade in the lurch! He would not be the man whom we all love and admire, whose word we all obey, for whose sake we would gladly all of us give our life—he would not be that man if he did not brave even certain dangers in order to be of help to those who call on him. Armand called and Percy went to him. He must have known that Armand was being spied upon, for Armand, alas! was already a marked man, and the watch-dogs of those infernal committees were already on his heels. Whether these sleuth-hounds had followed the son of the concierge and seen him give the letter to the workman in the Rue St. Germain l'Auxerrois, or whether the concierge in the Rue de la Croix Blanche was nothing but a spy of Heron's, or, again whether the Committee of General Security kept a company of soldiers in constant alert in that house, we shall, of course, never know. All that I do know is that Percy entered that fatal house at half-past ten, and that a quarter of an hour later the concierge saw some of the soldiers descending the stairs, carrying a heavy burden. She peeped out of her lodge, and by the light in the corridor she saw that the heavy burden was the body of a man bound closely with ropes: his eyes were closed, his clothes were stained with blood. He was seemingly unconscious. The next day the official organ of the Government proclaimed the capture of the Scarlet Pimpernel, and there was a public holiday in honour of the event."

Marguerite had listened to this terrible narrative dry-eyed and silent. Now she still sat there, hardly conscious of what went on around her—of Suzanne's tears, that fell unceasingly upon her fingers—of Sir Andrew, who had sunk into a chair, and buried his head in his hands. She was hardly conscious that she lived; the universe seemed to have stood still before this awful, monstrous cataclysm.

But, nevertheless, she was the first to return to the active realities of the present.

"Sir Andrew," she said after a while, "tell me, where are my

Lords Tony and Hastings?"

"At Calais, madam," he replied. "I saw them there on my way hither. They had delivered the Dauphin safely into the hands of his adherents at Mantes, and were awaiting Blakeney's further orders, as he had commanded them to do."

"Will they wait for us there, think you?"

"For us, Lady Blakeney?" he exclaimed in puzzlement.

"Yes, for us, Sir Andrew," she replied, whilst the ghost of a smile flitted across her drawn face; "you had thought of accompanying me to Paris, had you not?"

"But Lady Blakeney—"

"Ah! I know what you would say, Sir Andrew. You will speak of dangers, of risks, of death, mayhap; you will tell me that I as a woman can do nothing to help my husband—that I could be but a hindrance to him, just as I was in Boulogne. But everything is so different now. Whilst those brutes planned his capture he was clever enough to outwit them, but now they have actually got him, think you they'll let him escape? They'll watch him night and day, my friend, just as they watched the unfortunate Queen; but they'll not keep him months, weeks, or even days in prison—even Chauvelin now will no longer attempt to play with the Scarlet Pimpernel. They have him, and they will hold him until such time as they take him to the guillotine."

Her voice broke in a sob; her self-control was threatening to leave her. She was but a woman, young and passionately in love with the man who was about to die an ignominious death, far away from his country, his kindred, his friends.

"I cannot let him die alone, Sir Andrew; he will be longing for me, and—and, after all, there is you, and my Lord Tony, and Lord Hastings and the others; surely—surely we are not going to let him die, not like that, and not alone."

"You are right, Lady Blakeney," said Sir Andrew earnestly; "we are not going to let him die, if human agency can do aught to save him. Already Tony, Hastings and I have agreed to return to Paris. There are one or two hidden places in and around the city known only to Percy and to the members of the League where he must find one or more of us if he succeeds in getting away. All the way between Paris and Calais we have places of refuge, places where any of us can hide at a given moment; where we can find disguises when we want them, or horses in an emergency. No! no! we are not going to despair, Lady Blakeney; there are nineteen of us prepared to lay down our lives for the Scarlet Pimpernel. Already I, as his lieutenant, have been selected as the leader of as determined a gang as has ever entered on a work of rescue before. We leave for Paris to-morrow, and if human pluck and devotion can destroy mountains then we'll destroy them. Our watchword is: 'God save the Scarlet Pimpernel.'"

He knelt beside her chair and kissed the cold fingers which, with a sad little smile, she held out to him.

"And God bless you all!" she murmured.

Suzanne had risen to her feet when her husband knelt; now he stood up beside her. The dainty young woman hardly more than a child —was doing her best to restrain her tears.

"See how selfish I am," said Marguerite. "I talk calmly of taking your husband from you, when I myself know the bitterness of such partings."

"My husband will go where his duty calls him," said Suzanne with charming and simple dignity. "I love him with all my heart, because he is brave and good. He could not leave his comrade, who is also his chief, in the lurch. God will protect him, I know. I would not ask him to play the part of a coward."

Her brown eyes glowed with pride. She was the true wife of a soldier, and with all her dainty ways and childlike manners she was a splendid woman and a staunch friend. Sir Percy Blakeney bad saved her entire family from death, the Comte and Comtesse de Tournai, the Vicomte, her brother, and she herself all owed their lives to the Scarlet Pimpernel.

This she was not like to forget.

"There is but little danger for us, I fear me," said Sir Andrew lightly; "the revolutionary Government only wants to strike at a head, it cares nothing for the limbs. Perhaps it feels that without our leader we are enemies not worthy of persecution. If there are any dangers, so much the better," he added; "but I don't anticipate any, unless we succeed in freeing our chief; and having freed him, we fear nothing more."

"The same applies to me, Sir Andrew," rejoined Marguerite earnestly. "Now that they have captured Percy, those human fiends will care naught for me. If you succeed in freeing Percy I, like you, will have nothing more to fear, and if you fail—"

She paused and put her small, white hand on Sir Andrew's arm.

"Take me with you, Sir Andrew," she entreated; "do not condemn me to the awful torture of weary waiting, day after day, wondering, guessing, never daring to hope, lest hope deferred be more hard to bear than dreary hopelessness."

Then as Sir Andrew, very undecided, yet half inclined to yield, stood silent and irresolute, she pressed her point, gently but firmly insistent.

"I would not be in the way, Sir Andrew; I would know how to efface myself so as not to interfere with your plans. But, oh!" she added, while a quivering note of passion trembled in her voice, "can't you see that I must breathe the air that he breathes else I shall stifle or mayhap go mad?"

Sir Andrew turned to his wife, a mute query in his eyes.

"You would do an inhuman and a cruel act," said Suzanne with seriousness that sat quaintly on her baby face, "if you did not afford your protection to Marguerite, for I do believe that if you did not take her with you to-morrow she would go to Paris alone."

Marguerite thanked her friend with her eyes. Suzanne was a child in nature, but she had a woman's heart. She loved her husband, and, therefore, knew and understood what Marguerite must be suffering now.

Sir Andrew no longer could resist the unfortunate woman's earnest pleading. Frankly, he thought that if she remained in England while Percy was in such deadly peril she ran the grave risk of losing her reason before the terrible strain of suspense. He knew her to be a woman of courage, and one capable of great physical endurance; and really he was quite honest when he said that he did not believe there would be much danger for the headless League of the Scarlet Pimpernel unless they succeeded in freeing their chief. And if they did succeed, then indeed there would be nothing to fear, for the brave and loving wife who, like every true woman does, and has done in like circumstances since the beginning of time, was only demanding with passionate insistence the right to share the fate, good or ill, of the man whom she loved.

# CHAPTER 25: PARIS ONCE MORE

Sir Andrew had just come in. He was trying to get a little warmth into his half-frozen limbs, for the cold had set in again, and this time with renewed vigour, and Marguerite was pouring out a cup of hot coffee which she had been brewing for him. She had not asked for news. She knew that he had none to give her, else he had not worn that wearied, despondent look in his kind face.

"I'll just try one more place this evening," he said as soon as he had swallowed some of the hot coffee—"a restaurant in the Rue de la Harpe; the members of the Cordeliers' Club often go there for supper, and they are usually well informed. I might glean something definite there."

"It seems very strange that they are so slow in bringing him to trial," said Marguerite in that dull, toneless voice which had become habitual to her. "When you first brought me the awful news that... I made sure that they would bring him to trial at once, and was in terror lest we arrived here too late to—to see him."

She checked herself quickly, bravely trying to still the quiver of her voice.

"And of Armand?" she asked.

He shook his head sadly.

"With regard to him I am at a still greater loss," he said: "I cannot find his name on any of the prison registers, and I know that he is not in the Conciergerie. They have cleared out all the prisoners from there; there is only Percy—"

"Poor Armand!" she sighed; "it must be almost worse for him than for any of us; it was his first act of thoughtless disobedience that brought all this misery upon our heads."

She spoke sadly but quietly. Sir Andrew noted that there was no bitterness in her tone. But her very quietude was heart-breaking; there was such an infinity of despair in the calm of her eyes.

"Well! though we cannot understand it all, Lady Blakeney," he said with forced cheerfulness, "we must remember one thing—that whilst there is life there is hope."

"Hope!" she exclaimed with a world of pathos in her sigh, her large eyes dry and circled, fixed with indescribable sorrow on her friend's face.

Ffoulkes turned his head away, pretending to busy himself with the coffee-making utensils. He could not bear to see that look of hopelessness in her face, for in his heart he could not find the wherewithal to cheer her. Despair was beginning to seize on him too, and this he would not let her see.

They had been in Paris three days now, and it was six days since Blakeney had been arrested. Sir Andrew and Marguerite had found temporary lodgings inside Paris, Tony and Hastings were just outside the gates, and all along the route between Paris and Calais, at St. Germain, at Mantes, in the villages between Beauvais and Amiens, wherever money could obtain friendly help, members of the devoted League of the Scarlet Pimpernel lay in hiding, waiting to aid their chief.

Ffoulkes had ascertained that Percy was kept a close prisoner in the Conciergerie, in the very rooms occupied by Marie Antoinette during the last months of her life. He left poor Marguerite to guess how closely that elusive Scarlet Pimpernel was being guarded, the precautions surrounding him being even more minute than those which bad made the unfortunate Queen's closing days a martyrdom for her.

But of Armand he could glean no satisfactory news, only the negative probability that he was not detained in any of the larger prisons of Paris, as no register which he, Ffoulkes, so laboriously consulted bore record of the name of St. Just.

Haunting the restaurants and drinking booths where the most advanced Jacobins and Terrorists were wont to meet, he had learned one or two details of Blakeney's incarceration which he could not possibly impart to Marguerite. The capture of the mysterious Englishman known as the Scarlet Pimpernel had created a great deal of popular satisfaction; but it was obvious that not only was the public mind not allowed to associate that capture with the escape of little Capet from the Temple, but it soon became clear to Ffoulkes that the news of that escape was still being kept a profound secret.

On one occasion he had succeeded in spying on the Chief Agent of the Committee of General Security, whom he knew by sight, while the latter was sitting at dinner in the company of a stout, florid man with pock-marked face and podgy hands covered with rings.

Sir Andrew marvelled who this man might be. Heron spoke to him in ambiguous phrases that would have been unintelligible to any one who did not know the circumstances of the Dauphin's escape and the part that the League of the Scarlet Pimpernel had played in it. But to Sir Andrew Ffoulkes, who—cleverly disguised as a farrier, grimy after his day's work—was straining his ears to listen whilst apparently consuming huge slabs of boiled beef, it soon became clear that the chief agent and his fat friend were talking of the Dauphin and of Blakeney.

"He won't hold out much longer, citizen," the chief agent was saying in a confident voice; "our men are absolutely unremitting in their task. Two of them watch him night and day; they look after him well, and practically never lose sight of him, but the moment he tries to get any sleep one of them rushes into the cell with a loud banging of bayonet and sabre, and noisy tread on the flagstones, and shouts at the top of his voice: 'Now then, *aristo*, where's the brat? Tell us now, and you shall be down and go to sleep.' I have done it myself all through one day just for the pleasure of it. It's a little tiring for you to have to shout a good deal now, and sometimes give the cursed Englishman a good shake-up. He has had five days of it, and not one wink of sleep during that time—not one single minute of rest—and he only gets enough food to keep him alive. I tell you he can't last. Citizen Chauvelin had a splendid idea there. It will all come right in a day or two."

"H'm!" grunted the other sulkily; "those Englishmen are tough."

"Yes!" retorted Heron with a grim laugh and a leer of savagery that made his gaunt face look positively hideous—"you would have given out after three days, friend de Batz, would you not? And I warned you, didn't I? I told you if you tampered with the brat I would make you cry in mercy to me for death."

"And I warned you," said the other imperturbably, "not to worry so much about me, but to keep your eyes open for those cursed Englishmen."

"I am keeping my eyes open for you, nevertheless, my friend. If I thought you knew where the vermin's spawn was at this moment I would—"

"You would put me on the same rack that you or your precious friend, Chauvelin, have devised for the Englishman. But I don't know where the lad is. If I did I would not be in Paris."

"I know that," assented Heron with a sneer; "you would soon be after the reward—over in Austria, what?—but I have your movements tracked day and night, my friend. I dare say you are as anxious as we are as to the whereabouts of the child. Had he been taken over the frontier you would have been the first to hear of it, eh? No," he added confidently, and as if anxious to reassure himself, "my firm belief is that the original idea of these confounded Englishmen was to try and get the child over to England, and that they alone know where he is. I tell you it won't be many days before that very withered Scarlet Pimpernel will order his followers to give little Capet up to us. Oh! they are hanging about Paris some of them, I know that; citizen Chauvelin is convinced that the wife isn't very far away. Give her a sight of her husband now, say I, and she'll make the others give the child up soon enough."

The man laughed like some hyena gloating over its prey. Sir Andrew nearly betrayed himself then. He had to dig his nails into his own flesh to prevent himself from springing then and there at the throat of that wretch whose monstrous ingenuity had invented torture for the fallen enemy far worse than any that the cruelties of medieval Inquisitions had devised.

So they would not let him sleep! A simple idea born in the brain of a fiend. Heron had spoken of Chauvelin as the originator of the devilry; a man weakened deliberately day by day by insufficient food, and the horrible process of denying him rest. It seemed inconceivable that human, sentient beings should have thought of such a thing. Perspiration stood up in beads on Sir Andrew's brow when he thought of his friend, brought down by want of sleep to—what? His physique was splendidly powerful, but could it stand against such racking torment for long? And the clear, the alert mind, the scheming brain, the reckless daring—how soon would these become enfeebled by the slow, steady torture of an utter want of rest?

Ffoulkes had to smother a cry of horror, which surely must have drawn the attention of that fiend on himself had he not been so engrossed in the enjoyment of his own devilry. As it is, he ran out of the stuffy eating-house, for he felt as if its fetid air must choke him.

For an hour after that he wandered about the streets, not daring to face Marguerite, lest his eyes betrayed some of the horror which was shaking his very soul.

That was twenty-four hours ago. To-day he had learnt little else. It was generally known that the Englishman was in the Conciergerie prison, that he was being closely watched, and that his trial would come on within the next few days; but no one seemed to know exactly when. The public was getting restive, demanding that trial and execution to which every one seemed to look forward as to a holiday. In the meanwhile the escape of the Dauphin had been kept from the knowledge of the public; Heron and his gang, fearing for their lives, had still hopes of extracting from the Englishman the secret of the lad's hiding-place, and the means they employed for arriving at this end was worthy of Lucifer and his host of devils in hell.

From other fragments of conversation which Sir Andrew Ffoulkes had gleaned that same evening, it seemed to him that in order to hide their defalcations Heron and the four commissaries in charge of little Capet had substituted a deaf and dumb child for the escaped little prisoner. This miserable small wreck of humanity was reputed to be sick and kept in a darkened room, in bed, and was in that condition exhibited to any member of the Convention who had the right to see him. A partition had been very hastily erected in the inner room once occupied by the Simons, and the child was kept behind that partition, and no one was allowed to come too near to him. Thus the fraud was succeeding fairly well. Heron and his accomplices only cared to save their skins, and the wretched little substitute being really ill, they firmly hoped that he would soon die, when no doubt they would bruit abroad the news of the death of Capet, which would relieve them of further responsibility.

That such ideas, such thoughts, such schemes should have engendered in human minds it is almost impossible to conceive, and yet we know from no less important a witness than Madame Simon herself that the child who died in the Temple a few weeks later was a poor little imbecile, a deaf and dumb child brought hither from one of the asylums and left to die in peace. There was nobody but kindly Death to take him out of his misery, for the giant intellect that had planned and carried out the rescue of the uncrowned King of France, and which alone might have had the power to save him too, was being broken on the rack of enforced sleeplessness.

# CHAPTER 26: THE BITTEREST FOE

That same evening Sir Andrew Ffoulkes, having announced his intention of gleaning further news of Armand, if possible, went out shortly after seven o'clock, promising to be home again about nine.

Marguerite, on the other hand, had to make her friend a solemn promise that she would try and eat some supper which the landlady of these miserable apartments had agreed to prepare for her. So far they had been left in peaceful occupation of these squalid lodgings in a tumble-down house on the Quai de la Ferraille, facing the house of Justice, the grim walls of which Marguerite would watch with wide-open dry eyes for as long as the grey wintry light lingered over them.

Even now, though the darkness had set in, and snow, falling in close, small flakes, threw a thick white veil over the landscape, she sat at the open window long after Sir Andrew had gone out, watching the few small flicks of light that blinked across from the other side of the river, and which came from the windows of the Chatelet towers. The windows of the Conciergerie she could not see, for these gave on one of the inner courtyards; but there was a melancholy consolation even in the gazing on those walls that held in their cruel, grim embrace all that she loved in the world.

It seemed so impossible to think of Percy—the laughter-loving, irresponsible, light-hearted adventurer—as the prey of those fiends who would revel in their triumph, who would crush him, humiliate him, insult him—ye gods alive! even torture him, perhaps—that they might break the indomitable spirit that would mock them even on the threshold of death.

Surely, surely God would never allow such monstrous infamy as the deliverance of the noble soaring eagle into the hands of those preying jackals! Marguerite—though her heart ached beyond what human nature could endure, though her anguish on her husband's account was doubled by that which she felt for her brother—could not bring herself to give up all hope. Sir Andrew said it rightly; while there was life there was hope. While there was life in those vigorous limbs, spirit in that daring mind, how could puny, rampant beasts gain the better of the immortal soul? As for Armand—why, if Percy were free she would have no cause to fear for Armand.

She sighed a sigh of deep, of passionate regret and longing. If she could only see her husband; if she could only look for one second into those laughing, lazy eyes, wherein she alone knew how to fathom the infinity of passion that lay within their depths; if she could but once feel his—ardent kiss on her lips, she could more easily endure this agonising suspense, and wait confidently and courageously for the issue.

She turned away from the window, for the night was getting bitterly cold. From the tower of St. Germain l'Auxerrois the clock slowly struck eight. Even as the last sound of the historic bell died away in the distance she heard a timid knocking at the door.

"Enter!" she called unthinkingly.

She thought it was her landlady, come up with more wood, mayhap, for the fire, so she did not turn to the door when she heard it being slowly opened, then closed again, and presently a soft tread on the threadbare carpet.

"May I crave your kind attention, Lady Blakeney?" said a harsh voice, subdued to tones of ordinary courtesy.

She quickly repressed a cry of terror. How well she knew that voice! When last she heard it it was at Boulogne, dictating that infamous letter—the weapon wherewith Percy had so effectually foiled his enemy. She turned and faced the man who was her bitterest foe— hers in the person of the man she loved.

"Chauvelin!" she gasped.

"Himself at your service, dear lady," he said simply.

He stood in the full light of the lamp, his trim, small figure boldly cut out against the dark wall beyond. He wore the usual sable-coloured clothes which he affected, with the primly-folded jabot and cuffs edged with narrow lace.

Without waiting for permission from her he quietly and deliberately placed his hat and cloak on a chair. Then he turned once more toward her, and made a movement as if to advance into the room; but instinctively she put up a hand as if to ward off the calamity of his approach.

He shrugged his shoulders, and the shadow of a smile, that had neither mirth nor kindliness in it, hovered round the corners of his thin lips.

"Have I your permission to sit?" he asked.

"As you will," she replied slowly, keeping her wide-open eyes fixed upon him as does a frightened bird upon the serpent whom it loathes and fears.

"And may I crave a few moments of your undivided attention, Lady Blakeney?" he continued, taking a chair, and so placing it beside the table that the light of the lamp when he sat remained behind him and his face was left in shadow.

"Is it necessary?" asked Marguerite.

"It is," he replied curtly, "if you desire to see and speak with your husband—to be of use to him before it is too late."

"Then, I pray you, speak, citizen, and I will listen."

She sank into a chair, not heeding whether the light of the lamp fell on her face or not, whether the lines in her haggard cheeks, or her tear-dimmed eyes showed plainly the sorrow and despair that had traced them. She had nothing to hide from this man, the cause of all the tortures which she endured. She knew that neither courage nor sorrow would move him, and that hatred for Percy—personal deadly hatred for the man who had twice foiled him—had long crushed the last spark of humanity in his heart.

"Perhaps, Lady Blakeney," he began after a slight pause and in his smooth, even voice, "it would interest you to hear how I succeeded in procuring for myself this pleasure of an interview with you?"

"Your spies did their usual work, I suppose," she said coldly.

"Exactly. We have been on your track for three days, and yesterday evening an unguarded movement on the part of Sir Andrew Ffoulkes gave us the final clue to your whereabouts."

"Of Sir Andrew Ffoulkes?" she asked, greatly puzzled.

"He was in an eating-house, cleverly disguised, I own, trying to glean information, no doubt as to the probable fate of Sir Percy Blakeney. As chance would have it, my friend Heron, of the Committee of General Security, chanced to be discussing with reprehensible openness—er—certain—what shall I say?—certain measures which, at my advice, the Committee of Public Safety have been forced to adopt with a view to—"

"A truce on your smooth-tongued speeches, citizen Chauvelin," she interposed firmly. "Sir Andrew Ffoulkes has told me naught of this —so I pray you speak plainly and to the point, if you can."

He bowed with marked irony.

"As you please," he said. "Sir Andrew Ffoulkes, hearing certain matters of which I will tell you anon, made a movement which betrayed him to one of our spies. At a word from citizen Heron this man followed on the heels of the young farrier who had shown such interest in the conversation of the Chief Agent. Sir Andrew, I imagine, burning with indignation at what he had heard, was perhaps not quite so cautious as he usually is. Anyway, the man on his track followed him to this door. It was quite simple, as you see. As for me, I had guessed a week ago that we would see the beautiful Lady Blakeney in Paris before long. When I knew where Sir Andrew Ffoulkes lodged, I had no difficulty in guessing that Lady Blakeney would not be far off."

"And what was there in citizen Heron's conversation last night," she asked quietly, "that so aroused Sir Andrew's indignation?"

"He has not told you?" "Oh! it is very simple. Let me tell you, Lady Blakeney, exactly how matters stand. Sir Percy Blakeney—before lucky chance at last delivered him into our hands—thought fit, as no doubt you know, to meddle with our most important prisoner of State."

"A child. I know it, sir—the son of a murdered father whom you and your friends were slowly doing to death."

"That is as it may be, Lady Blakeney," rejoined Chauvelin calmly; "but it was none of Sir Percy Blakeney's business. This, however, he chose to disregard. He succeeded in carrying little Capet from the Temple, and two days later we had him under lock, and key."

"Through some infamous and treacherous trick, sir," she retorted.

Chauvelin made no immediate reply; his pale, inscrutable eyes were fixed upon her face, and the smile of irony round his mouth appeared more strongly marked than before.

"That, again, is as it may be," he said suavely; "but anyhow for the moment we have the upper hand. Sir Percy is in the Conciergerie, guarded day and night, more closely than Marie Antoinette even was guarded."

"And he laughs at your bolts and bars, sir," she rejoined proudly. "Remember Calais, remember Boulogne. His laugh at your discomfiture, then, must resound in your ear even to-day."

"Yes; but for the moment laughter is on our side. Still we are willing to forego even that pleasure, if Sir Percy will but move a finger towards his own freedom."

"Again some infamous letter?" she asked with bitter contempt; "some attempt against his honour?"

"No, no, Lady Blakeney," he interposed with perfect blandness. "Matters are so much simpler now, you see. We hold Sir Percy at our mercy. We could send him to the guillotine to-morrow, but we might be willing—remember, I only say we might—to exercise our prerogative of mercy if Sir Percy Blakeney will on his side accede to a request from us."

"And that request?"

"Is a very natural one. He took Capet away from us, and it is but credible that he knows at the present moment exactly where the child is. Let him instruct his followers—and I mistake not, Lady Blakeney, there are several of them not very far from Paris just now—let him, I say, instruct these followers of his to return the person of young Capet to us, and not only will we undertake to give these same gentlemen a safe conduct back to England, but we even might be inclined to deal somewhat less harshly with the gallant Scarlet Pimpernel himself."

She laughed a harsh, mirthless, contemptuous laugh.

"I don't think that I quite understand," she said after a moment or two, whilst he waited calmly until her out-break of hysterical mirth had subsided. "You want my husband—the Scarlet Pimpernel, citizen—to deliver the little King of France to you after he has risked his life to save the child out of your clutches? Is that what you are trying to say?"

"It is," rejoined Chauvelin complacently, "just what we have been saying to Sir Percy Blakeney for the past six days, madame."

"Well! then you have had your answer, have you not?"

"Yes," he replied slowly; "but the answer has become weaker day by day."

"Weaker? I don't understand."

"Let me explain, Lady Blakeney," said Chauvelin, now with measured emphasis. He put both elbows on the table and leaned well forward, peering into her face, lest one of its varied expressions escaped him. "Just now you taunted me with my failure in Calais, and again at Boulogne, with a proud toss of the head, which I own is excessive becoming; you threw the name of the Scarlet Pimpernel in my face like a challenge which I no longer dare to accept. 'The Scarlet Pimpernel,' you would say to me, 'stands for loyalty, for honour, and for indomitable courage. Think you he would sacrifice his honour to obtain your mercy? Remember Boulogne and your discomfiture!' All of which, dear lady, is perfectly charming and womanly and enthusiastic, and I, bowing my humble head, must own that I was fooled in Calais and baffled in Boulogne. But in Boulogne I made a grave mistake, and one from which I learned a lesson, which I am putting into practice now."

He paused a while as if waiting for her reply. His pale, keen eyes had already noted that with every phrase he uttered the lines in her beautiful face became more hard and set. A look of horror was gradually spreading over it, as if the icy-cold hand of death had passed over her eyes and cheeks, leaving them rigid like stone.

"In Boulogne," resumed Chauvelin quietly, satisfied that his words were hitting steadily at her heart—"in Boulogne Sir Percy and I did not fight an equal fight. Fresh from a pleasant sojourn in his own magnificent home, full of the spirit of adventure which puts the essence of life into a man's veins, Sir Percy Blakeney's splendid physique was pitted against my feeble powers. Of course I lost the battle. I made the mistake of trying to subdue a man who was in the zenith of his strength, whereas now—"

"Yes, citizen Chauvelin," she said, "whereas now—"

"Sir Percy Blakeney has been in the prison of the Conciergerie for exactly one week, Lady Blakeney," he replied, speaking very slowly, and letting every one of his words sink individually into her mind. "Even before he had time to take the bearings of his cell or to plan on his own behalf one of those remarkable escapes for which he is so justly famous, our men began to work on a scheme which I am proud to say originated with myself. A week has gone by since then, Lady Blakeney, and during that time a special company of prison guard, acting under the orders of the Committee of General Security and of Public Safety, have questioned the prisoner unremittingly—unremittingly, remember —day and night. Two by two these men take it in turns to enter the prisoner's cell every quarter of an hour—lately it has had to be more often—and ask him the one question, 'Where is little Capet?' Up to now we have received no satisfactory reply, although we have explained to Sir Percy that many of his followers are honouring the neighbourhood of Paris with their visit, and that all we ask for from him are instructions to those gallant gentlemen to bring young Capet back to us. It is all very simple, unfortunately the prisoner is somewhat obstinate. At first, even, the idea seemed to amuse him; he used to laugh and say that he always had the faculty of sleeping with his eyes open. But our soldiers are untiring in their efforts, and the want of sleep as well as of a sufficiency of food and of fresh air is certainly beginning to tell on Sir Percy Blakeney's magnificent physique. I don't think that it will be very long before he gives way to our gentle persuasions; and in any case now, I assure you, dear lady, that we need not fear any attempt on his part to escape. I doubt if he could walk very steadily across this room—"

Marguerite had sat quite silent and apparently impassive all the while that Chauvelin had been speaking; even now she scarcely stirred. Her face expressed absolutely nothing but deep puzzlement. There was a frown between her brows, and her eyes, which were always of such liquid blue, now looked almost black. She was trying to visualise that which Chauvelin had put before her: a man harassed day and night, unceasingly, unremittingly, with one question allowed neither respite nor sleep—his brain, soul, and body fagged out at every hour, every moment of the day and night, until mind and body and soul must inevitably give way under anguish ten thousand times more unendurable than any physical torment invented by monsters in barbaric times.

That man thus harassed, thus fagged out, thus martyrised at all hours of the day and night, was her husband, whom she loved with every fibre of her being, with every throb of her heart.

Torture? Oh, no! these were advanced and civilised times that could afford to look with horror on the excesses of medieval days. This was a revolution that made for progress, and challenged the opinion of the world. The cells of the Temple of La Force or the Conciergerie held no secret inquisition with iron maidens and racks and thumbscrews; but a few men had put their tortuous brains together, and had said one to another: "We want to find out from that man where we can lay our hands on little Capet, so we won't let him sleep until he has told us. It is not torture—oh, no! Who would dare to say that we torture our prisoners? It is only a little horseplay, worrying to the prisoner, no doubt; but, after all, he can end the unpleasantness at any moment. He need but to answer our question, and he can go to sleep as comfortably as a little child. The want of sleep is very trying, the want of proper food and of fresh air is very weakening; the prisoner must give way sooner or later—"

So these fiends had decided it between them, and they had put

their idea into execution for one whole week. Marguerite looked at
Chauvelin as she would on some monstrous, inscrutable Sphinx,
marveling if God—even in His anger—could really have created such a
fiendish brain, or, having created it, could allow it to wreak such devilry
unpunished.

Even now she felt that he was enjoying the mental anguish
which he had put upon her, and she saw his thin, evil lips curled into a
smile.

"So you came to-night to tell me all this?" she asked as soon as
she could trust herself to speak. Her impulse was to shriek out her
indignation, her horror of him, into his face. She longed to call down
God's eternal curse upon this fiend; but instinctively she held herself in
check. Her indignation, her words of loathing would only have added to
his delight.

"You have had your wish," she added coldly; "now, I pray you,
go."

"Your pardon, Lady Blakeney," he said with all his habitual
blandness; "my object in coming to see you tonight was twofold.
Methought that I was acting as your friend in giving you authentic news
of Sir Percy, and in suggesting the possibility of your adding your
persuasion to ours."

"My persuasion? You mean that I—"

"You would wish to see your husband, would you not, Lady
Blakeney?"

"Yes."

"Then I pray you command me. I will grant you the permission
whenever you wish to go."

"You are in the hope, citizen," she said, "that I will do my best
to break my husband's spirit by my tears or my prayers—is that it?"

"Not necessarily," he replied pleasantly. "I assure you that we
can manage to do that ourselves, in time."

"You devil!" The cry of pain and of horror was involuntarily
wrung from the depths of her soul. "Are you not afraid that God's hand
will strike you where you stand?"

"No," he said lightly; "I am not afraid, Lady Blakeney. You see, I
do not happen to believe in God. Come!" he added more seriously,
"have I not proved to you that my offer is disinterested? Yet I repeat it
even now. If you desire to see Sir Percy in prison, command me, and
the doors shall be open to you."

She waited a moment, looking him straight and quite
dispassionately in the face; then she said coldly:

"Very well! I will go."

"When?" he asked.

"This evening."

"Just as you wish. I would have to go and see my friend Heron first, and arrange with him for your visit."

"Then go. I will follow in half an hour."

"*C'est entendu.* Will you be at the main entrance of the Conciergerie at half-past nine? You know it, perhaps—no? It is in the Rue de la Barillerie, immediately on the right at the foot of the great staircase of the house of Justice."

"Of the house of Justice!" she exclaimed involuntarily, a world of bitter contempt in her cry. Then she added in her former matter-of-fact tones:

"Very good, citizen. At half-past nine I will be at the entrance you name."

"And I will be at the door prepared to escort you."

He took up his hat and coat and bowed ceremoniously to her. Then he turned to go. At the door a cry from her—involuntarily enough, God knows!—made him pause.

"My interview with the prisoner," she said, vainly trying, poor soul! to repress that quiver of anxiety in her voice, "it will be private?"

"Oh, yes! Of course," he replied with a reassuring smile. "*Au revoir*, Lady Blakeney! Half-past nine, remember—"

She could no longer trust herself to look on him as he finally took his departure. She was afraid—yes, absolutely afraid that her fortitude would give way—meanly, despicably, uselessly give way; that she would suddenly fling herself at the feet of that sneering, inhuman wretch, that she would pray, implore—Heaven above! what might she not do in the face of this awful reality, if the last lingering shred of vanishing reason, of pride, and of courage did not hold her in check?

Therefore she forced herself not to look on that departing, sable-clad figure, on that evil face, and those hands that held Percy's fate in their cruel grip; but her ears caught the welcome sound of his departure—the opening and shutting of the door, his light footstep echoing down the stone stairs.

When at last she felt that she was really alone she uttered a loud cry like a wounded doe, and falling on her knees she buried her face in her hands in a passionate fit of weeping. Violent sobs shook her entire frame; it seemed as if an overwhelming anguish was tearing at her heart—the physical pain of it was almost unendurable. And yet even through this paroxysm of tears her mind clung to one root idea: when she saw Percy she must be brave and calm, be able to help him if he wanted her, to do his bidding if there was anything that she could do, or any message that she could take to the others. Of hope she had none. The last lingering ray of it had been extinguished by that fiend when he said, "We need not fear that he will escape. I doubt if he could walk very steadily across this room now."

# CHAPTER 27: IN THE CONCIERGERIE

Marguerite, accompanied by Sir Andrew Ffoulkes, walked rapidly along the quay. It lacked ten minutes to the half hour; the night was dark and bitterly cold. Snow was still falling in sparse, thin flakes, and lay like a crisp and glittering mantle over the parapets of the bridges and the grim towers of the Chatelet prison.

They walked on silently now. All that they had wanted to say to one another had been said inside the squalid room of their lodgings when Sir Andrew Ffoulkes had come home and learned that Chauvelin had been.

"They are killing him by inches, Sir Andrew," had been the heartrending cry which burst from Marguerite's oppressed heart as soon as her hands rested in the kindly ones of her best friend. "Is there aught that we can do?"

There was, of course, very little that could be done. One or two fine steel files which Sir Andrew gave her to conceal beneath the folds of her kerchief; also a tiny dagger with sharp, poisoned blade, which for a moment she held in her hand hesitating, her eyes filling with tears, her heart throbbing with unspeakable sorrow.

Then slowly—very slowly—she raised the small, death-dealing instrument to her lips, and reverently kissed the narrow blade.

"If it must be!" she murmured, "God in His mercy will forgive!"

She sheathed the dagger, and this, too, she hid in the folds of her gown.

"Can you think of anything else, Sir Andrew, that he might want?" she asked. "I have money in plenty, in case those soldiers—"

Sir Andrew sighed, and turned away from her so as to hide the hopelessness which he felt. Since three days now he had been exhausting every conceivable means of getting at the prison guard with bribery and corruption. But Chauvelin and his friends had taken excellent precautions. The prison of the Conciergerie, situated as it was in the very heart of the labyrinthine and complicated structure of the Chatelet and the house of Justice, and isolated from every other group of cells in the building, was inaccessible save from one narrow doorway which gave on the guard-room first, and thence on the inner cell beyond. Just as all attempts to rescue the late unfortunate Queen from that prison had failed, so now every attempt to reach the imprisoned Scarlet Pimpernel was equally doomed to bitter disappointment.

The guard-room was filled with soldiers day and night; the windows of the inner cell, heavily barred, were too small to admit of the passage of a human body, and they were raised twenty feet from the corridor below. Sir Andrew had stood in the corridor two days ago, he had looked on the window behind which he knew that his friend must be eating out his noble heart in a longing for liberty, and he had realised then that every effort at help from the outside was foredoomed to failure.

"Courage, Lady Blakeney," he said to Marguerite, when anon they had crossed the Pont au Change, and were wending their way slowly along the Rue de la Barillerie; "remember our proud dictum: the Scarlet Pimpernel never fails! and also this, that whatever messages Blakeney gives you for us, whatever he wishes us to do, we are to a man ready to do it, and to give our lives for our chief. Courage! Something tells me that a man like Percy is not going to die at the hands of such vermin as Chauvelin and his friends."

They had reached the great iron gates of the house of Justice. Marguerite, trying to smile, extended her trembling band to this faithful, loyal comrade.

"I'll not be far," he said. "When you come out do not look to the right or left, but make straight for home; I'll not lose sight of you for a moment, and as soon as possible will overtake you. God bless you both."

He pressed his lips on her cold little hand, and watched her tall, elegant figure as she passed through the great gates until the veil of falling snow hid her from his gaze. Then with a deep sigh of bitter anguish and sorrow he turned away and was soon lost in the gloom.

Marguerite found the gate at the bottom of the monumental stairs open when she arrived. Chauvelin was standing immediately inside the building waiting for her.

"We are prepared for your visit, Lady Blakeney," he said, "and the prisoner knows that you are coming."

He led the way down one of the numerous and interminable corridors of the building, and she followed briskly, pressing her hand against her bosom there where the folds of her kerchief hid the steel files and the precious dagger.

Even in the gloom of these ill-lighted passages she realised that she was surrounded by guards. There were soldiers everywhere; two had stood behind the door when first she entered, and had immediately closed it with a loud clang behind her; and all the way down the corridors, through the half-light engendered by feebly flickering lamps, she caught glimpses of the white facings on the uniforms of the town guard, or occasionally the glint of steel of a bayonet. Presently Chauvelin paused beside a door, which he had just reached. His hand was on the latch, for it did not appear to be locked, and he turned toward Marguerite.

"I am very sorry, Lady Blakeney," he said in simple, deferential tones, "that the prison authorities, who at my request are granting you this interview at such an unusual hour, have made a slight condition to your visit."

"A condition?" she asked. "What is it?"

"You must forgive me," he said, as if purposely evading her question, "for I give you my word that I had nothing to do with a regulation that you might justly feel was derogatory to your dignity. If you will kindly step in here a wardress in charge will explain to you what is required."

He pushed open the door, and stood aside ceremoniously in order to allow her to pass in. She looked on him with deep puzzlement and a look of dark suspicion in her eyes. But her mind was too much engrossed with the thought of her meeting with Percy to worry over any trifle that might—as her enemy had inferred—offend her womanly dignity.

She walked into the room, past Chauvelin, who whispered as she went by:

"I will wait for you here. And, I pray you, if you have aught to complain of summon me at once."

Then he closed the door behind her. The room in which Marguerite now found herself was a small unventilated quadrangle, dimly lighted by a hanging lamp. A woman in a soiled cotton gown and lank grey hair brushed away from a parchment-like forehead rose from the chair in which she had been sitting when Marguerite entered, and put away some knitting on which she had apparently been engaged.

"I was to tell you, citizeness," she said the moment the door had been closed and she was alone with Marguerite, "that the prison authorities have given orders that I should search you before you visit the prisoner."

She repeated this phrase mechanically like a child who has been taught to say a lesson by heart. She was a stoutish middle-aged woman, with that pasty, flabby skin peculiar to those who live in want of fresh air; but her small, dark eyes were not unkindly, although they shifted restlessly from one object to another as if she were trying to avoid looking the other woman straight in the face.

"That you should search me!" reiterated Marguerite slowly, trying to understand.

"Yes," replied the woman. "I was to tell you to take off your clothes, so that I might look them through and through. I have often had to do this before when visitors have been allowed inside the prison, so it is no use your trying to deceive me in any way. I am very sharp at finding out if any one has papers, or files or ropes concealed in an underpetticoat. Come," she added more roughly, seeing that Marguerite had remained motionless in the middle of the room; "the quicker you are about it the sooner you will be taken to see the prisoner."

These words had their desired effect. The proud Lady Blakeney, inwardly revolting at the outrage, knew that resistance would be worse than useless. Chauvelin was the other side of the door. A call from the woman would bring him to her assistance, and Marguerite was only longing to hasten the moment when she could be with her husband.

She took off her kerchief and her gown and calmly submitted to the woman's rough hands as they wandered with sureness and accuracy to the various pockets and folds that might conceal prohibited articles. The woman did her work with peculiar stolidity; she did not utter a word when she found the tiny steel files and placed them on a table beside her. In equal silence she laid the little dagger beside them, and the purse which contained twenty gold pieces. These she counted in front of Marguerite and then replaced them in the purse. Her face expressed neither surprise, nor greed nor pity. She was obviously beyond the reach of bribery—just a machine paid by the prison authorities to do this unpleasant work, and no doubt terrorised into doing it conscientiously.

When she had satisfied herself that Marguerite had nothing further concealed about her person, she allowed her to put her dress on once more. She even offered to help her on with it. When Marguerite was fully dressed she opened the door for her. Chauvelin was standing in the passage waiting patiently. At sight of Marguerite, whose pale, set face betrayed nothing of the indignation which she felt, he turned quick, inquiring eyes on the woman.

"Two files, a dagger and a purse with twenty louis," said the latter curtly.

Chauvelin made no comment. He received the information quite placidly, as if it had no special interest for him. Then he said quietly:

"This way, citizeness!"

Marguerite followed him, and two minutes later he stood beside a heavy nail-studded door that had a small square grating let into one of the panels, and said simply:

"This is it."

Two soldiers of the National Guard were on sentry at the door, two more were pacing up and down outside it, and had halted when citizen Chauvelin gave his name and showed his tricolour scarf of office. From behind the small grating in the door a pair of eyes peered at the newcomers.

"*Qui va la?*" came the quick challenge from the guard-room within.

"Citizen Chauvelin of the Committee of Public Safety," was the prompt reply.

There was the sound of grounding of arms, of the drawing of bolts and the turning of a key in a complicated lock. The prison was kept locked from within, and very heavy bars had to be moved ere the ponderous door slowly swung open on its hinges.

Two steps led up into the guard-room. Marguerite mounted them with the same feeling of awe and almost of reverence as she would have mounted the steps of a sacrificial altar.

The guard-room itself was more brilliantly lighted than the corridor outside. The sudden glare of two or three lamps placed about the room caused her momentarily to close her eyes that were aching with many shed and unshed tears. The air was rank and heavy with the fumes of tobacco, of wine and stale food. A large barred window gave on the corridor immediately above the door.

When Marguerite felt strong enough to look around her, she saw that the room was filled with soldiers. Some were sitting, others standing, others lay on rugs against the wall, apparently asleep. There was one who appeared to be in command, for with a word he checked the noise that was going on in the room when she entered, and then he said curtly:

"This way, citizeness!"

He turned to an opening in the wall on the left, the stone-lintel of a door, from which the door itself had been removed; an iron bar ran across the opening, and this the sergeant now lifted, nodding to Marguerite to go within.

Instinctively she looked round for Chauvelin.

But he was nowhere to be seen.

# CHAPTER 28: THE CAGED LION

Was there some instinct of humanity left in the soldier who allowed Marguerite through the barrier into the prisoner's cell? Had the wan face of this beautiful woman stirred within his heart the last chord of gentleness that was not wholly atrophied by the constant cruelties, the excesses, the mercilessness which his service under this fraternising republic constantly demanded of him?

Perhaps some recollection of former years, when first he served his King and country, recollection of wife or sister or mother pleaded within him in favour of this sorely-stricken woman with the look of unspeakable sorrow in her large blue eyes.

Certain it is that as soon as Marguerite passed the barrier he put himself on guard against it with his back to the interior of the cell and to her.

Marguerite had paused on the threshold.

After the glaring light of the guard-room the cell seemed dark, and at first she could hardly see. The whole length of the long, narrow cubicle lay to her left, with a slight recess at its further end, so that from the threshold of the doorway she could not see into the distant corner. Swift as a lightning flash the remembrance came back to her of proud Marie Antoinette narrowing her life to that dark corner where the insolent eyes of the rabble soldiery could not spy her every movement.

Marguerite stepped further into the room. Gradually by the dim light of an oil lamp placed upon a table in the recess she began to distinguish various objects: one or two chairs, another table, and a small but very comfortable-looking camp bedstead.

Just for a few seconds she only saw these inanimate things, then she became conscious of Percy's presence.

He sat on a chair, with his left arm half-stretched out upon the table, his head hidden in the bend of the elbow.

Marguerite did not utter a cry; she did not even tremble. Just for one brief instant she closed her eyes, so as to gather up all her courage before she dared to look again. Then with a steady and noiseless step she came quite close to him. She knelt on the flagstones at his feet and raised reverently to her lips the hand that hung nerveless and limp by his side.

He gave a start; a shiver seemed to go right through him; he half raised his head and murmured in a hoarse whisper:

"I tell you that I do not know, and if I did—"

She put her arms round him and pillowed her head upon his breast. He turned his head slowly toward her, and now his eyes

—hollowed and rimmed with purple—looked straight into hers.

"My beloved," he said, "I knew that you would come." His arms closed round her. There was nothing of lifelessness or of weariness in the passion of that embrace; and when she looked up again it seemed to her as if that first vision which she had had of him with weary head bent, and wan, haggard face was not reality, only a dream born of her own anxiety for him, for now the hot, ardent blood coursed just as swiftly as ever through his veins, as if life—strong, tenacious, pulsating life—throbbed with unabated vigour in those massive limbs, and behind that square, clear brow as though the body, but half subdued, had transferred its vanishing strength to the kind and noble heart that was beating with the fervour of self-sacrifice.

"Percy," she said gently, "they will only give us a few moments together. They thought that my tears would break your spirit where their devilry had failed."

He held her glance with his own, with that close, intent look which binds soul to soul, and in his deep blue eyes there danced the restless flames of his own undying mirth:

"La! little woman," he said with enforced lightness, even whilst his voice quivered with the intensity of passion engendered by her presence, her nearness, the perfume of her hair, "how little they know you, eh? Your brave, beautiful, exquisite soul, shining now through your glorious eyes, would defy the machinations of Satan himself and his horde. Close your dear eyes, my love. I shall go mad with joy if I drink their beauty in any longer."

He held her face between his two hands, and indeed it seemed as if he could not satiate his soul with looking into her eyes. In the midst of so much sorrow, such misery and such deadly fear, never had Marguerite felt quite so happy, never had she felt him so completely her own. The inevitable bodily weakness, which of necessity had invaded even his splendid physique after a whole week's privations, had made a severe breach in the invincible barrier of self-control with which the soul of the inner man was kept perpetually hidden behind a mask of indifference and of irresponsibility.

And yet the agony of seeing the lines of sorrow so plainly writ on the beautiful face of the woman he worshipped must have been the keenest that the bold adventurer had ever experienced in the whole course of his reckless life. It was he—and he alone—who was making her suffer; her for whose sake he would gladly have shed every drop of his blood, endured every torment, every misery and every humiliation; her whom he worshipped only one degree less than he worshipped his honour and the cause which he had made his own.

Yet, in spite of that agony, in spite of the heartrending pathos of her pale wan face, and through the anguish of seeing her tears, the ruling passion—strong in death—the spirit of adventure, the mad, wild, devil-may-care irresponsibility was never wholly absent.

"Dear heart," he said with a quaint sigh, whilst he buried his face in the soft masses of her hair, "until you came I was so d—d fatigued."

He was laughing, and the old look of boyish love of mischief illumined his haggard face.

"Is it not lucky, dear heart," he said a moment or two later, "that those brutes do not leave me unshaved? I could not have faced you with a week's growth of beard round my chin. By dint of promises and bribery I have persuaded one of that rabble to come and shave me every morning. They will not allow me to handle a razor my-self. They are afraid I should cut my throat—or one of theirs. But mostly I am too d—d sleepy to think of such a thing."

"Percy!" she exclaimed with tender and passionate reproach.

"I know—I know, dear," he murmured, "what a brute I am! Ah, God did a cruel thing the day that He threw me in your path. To think that once—not so very long ago—we were drifting apart, you and I. You would have suffered less, dear heart, if we had continued to drift."

Then as he saw that his bantering tone pained her, he covered her hands with kisses, entreating her forgiveness.

"Dear heart," he said merrily, "I deserve that you should leave me to rot in this abominable cage. They haven't got me yet, little woman, you know; I am not yet dead—only d—d sleepy at times. But I'll cheat them even now, never fear."

"How, Percy—how?" she moaned, for her heart was aching with intolerable pain; she knew better than he did the precautions which were being taken against his escape, and she saw more clearly than he realised it himself the terrible barrier set up against that escape by ever encroaching physical weakness.

"Well, dear," he said simply, "to tell you the truth I have not yet thought of that all-important 'how.' I had to wait, you see, until you came. I was so sure that you would come! I have succeeded in putting on paper all my instructions for Ffoulkes and the others. I will give them to you anon. I knew that you would come, and that I could give them to you; until then I had but to think of one thing, and that was of keeping body and soul together. My chance of seeing you was to let them have their will with me. Those brutes were sure, sooner or later, to bring you to me, that you might see the caged fox worn down to imbecility, eh? That you might add your tears to their persuasion, and succeed where they have failed."

He laughed lightly with an unstrained note of gaiety, only Marguerite's sensitive ears caught the faint tone of bitterness which rang through the laugh.

"Once I know that the little King of France is safe," he said, "I can think of how best to rob those d—d murderers of my skin."

Then suddenly his manner changed. He still held her with one arm closely to, him, but the other now lay across the table, and the slender, emaciated hand was tightly clutched. He did not look at her, but straight ahead; the eyes, unnaturally large now, with their deep purple rims, looked far ahead beyond the stone walls of this grim, cruel prison.

The passionate lover, hungering for his beloved, had vanished; there sat the man with a purpose, the man whose firm hand had snatched men and women and children from death, the reckless enthusiast who tossed his life against an ideal.

For a while he sat thus, while in his drawn and haggard face she could trace every line formed by his thoughts—the frown of anxiety, the resolute setting of the lips, the obstinate look of will around the firm jaw. Then he turned again to her.

"My beautiful one," he said softly, "the moments are very precious. God knows I could spend eternity thus with your dear form nestling against my heart. But those d—d murderers will only give us half an hour, and I want your help, my beloved, now that I am a helpless cur caught in their trap. Will you listen attentively, dear heart, to what I am going to say?

"Yes, Percy, I will listen," she replied.

"And have you the courage to do just what I tell you, dear?"

"I would not have courage to do aught else," she said simply.

"It means going from hence to-day, dear heart, and perhaps not meeting again. Hush-sh-sh, my beloved," he said, tenderly placing his thin hand over her mouth, from which a sharp cry of pain had well-nigh escaped; "your exquisite soul will be with me always. Try—try not to give way to despair. Why! your love alone, which I see shining from your dear eyes, is enough to make a man cling to life with all his might. Tell me! will you do as I ask you?"

And she replied firmly and courageously:

"I will do just what you ask, Percy."

"God bless you for your courage, dear. You will have need of it."

# CHAPTER 29: FOR THE SAKE OF
# THAT HELPLESS INNOCENT

The next instant he was kneeling on the floor and his hands were wandering over the small, irregular flagstones immediately underneath the table. Marguerite had risen to her feet; she watched her husband with intent and puzzled eyes; she saw him suddenly pass his slender fingers along a crevice between two flagstones, then raise one of these slightly and from beneath it extract a small bundle of papers, each carefully folded and sealed. Then he replaced the stone and once more rose to his knees.

He gave a quick glance toward the doorway. That corner of his cell, the recess wherein stood the table, was invisible to any one who had not actually crossed the threshold. Reassured that his movements could not have been and were not watched, he drew Marguerite closer to him.

"Dear heart," he whispered, "I want to place these papers in your care. Look upon them as my last will and testament. I succeeded in fooling those brutes one day by pretending to be willing to accede to their will. They gave me pen and ink and paper and wax, and I was to write out an order to my followers to bring the Dauphin hither. They left me in peace for one quarter of an hour, which gave me time to write three letters—one for Armand and the other two for Ffoulkes, and to hide them under the flooring of my cell. You see, dear, I knew that you would come and that I could give them to you then."

He paused, and that, ghost of a smile once more hovered round his lips. He was thinking of that day when he had fooled Heron and Chauvelin into the belief that their devilry had succeeded, and that they had brought the reckless adventurer to his knees. He smiled at the recollection of their wrath when they knew that they had been tricked, and after a quarter of an hour's anxious waiting found a few sheets of paper scribbled over with incoherent words or satirical verse, and the prisoner having apparently snatched ten minutes' sleep, which seemingly had restored to him quite a modicum of his strength.

But of this he told Marguerite nothing, nor of the insults and the humiliation which he had had to bear in consequence of that trick. He did not tell her that directly afterwards the order went forth that the prisoner was to be kept on bread and water in the future, nor that Chauvelin had stood by laughing and jeering while . . .

No! he did not tell her all that; the recollection of it all had still the power to make him laugh; was it not all a part and parcel of that great gamble for human lives wherein he had held the winning cards himself for so long?

"It is your turn now," he had said even then to his bitter enemy.

"Yes!" Chauvelin had replied, "our turn at last. And you will not bend my fine English gentleman, we'll break you yet, never fear."

It was the thought of it all, of that hand to hand, will to will, spirit to spirit struggle that lighted up his haggard face even now, gave him a fresh zest for life, a desire to combat and to conquer in spite of all, in spite of the odds that had martyred his body but left the mind, the will, the power still unconquered.

He was pressing one of the papers into her hand, holding her fingers tightly in his, and compelling her gaze with the ardent excitement of his own.

"This first letter is for Ffoulkes," he said. "It relates to the final measures for the safety of the Dauphin. They are my instructions to those members of the League who are in or near Paris at the present moment. Ffoulkes, I know, must be with you—he was not likely, God bless his loyalty, to let you come to Paris alone. Then give this letter to him, dear heart, at once, to-night, and tell him that it is my express command that he and the others shall act in minute accordance with my instructions."

"But the Dauphin surely is safe now," she urged. "Ffoulkes and the others are here in order to help you."

"To help me, dear heart?" he interposed earnestly. "God alone can do that now, and such of my poor wits as these devils do not succeed in crushing out of me within the next ten days."

Ten days!

"I have waited a week, until this hour when I could place this packet in your hands; another ten days should see the Dauphin out of France—after that, we shall see."

"Percy," she exclaimed in an agony of horror, "you cannot endure this another day—and live!"

"Nay!" he said in a tone that was almost insolent in its proud defiance, "there is but little that a man cannot do an he sets his mind to it. For the rest, 'tis in God's hands!" he added more gently. "Dear heart! you swore that you would be brave. The Dauphin is still in France, and until he is out of it he will not really be safe; his friends wanted to keep him inside the country. God only knows what they still hope; had I been free I should not have allowed him to remain so long; now those good people at Mantes will yield to my letter and to Ffoulkes' earnest appeal—they will allow one of our League to convey the child safely out of France, and I'll wait here until I know that he is safe. If I tried to get away now, and succeeded—why, Heaven help us! the hue and cry might turn against the child, and he might be captured before I could get to him. Dear heart! dear, dear heart! try to understand. The safety of that child is bound with mine honour, but I swear to you, my sweet love, that the day on which I feel that that safety is assured I will save mine own skin—what there is left of it—if I can!"

"Percy!" she cried with a sudden outburst of passionate revolt, "you speak as if the safety of that child were of more moment than your own. Ten days!—but, God in Heaven! have you thought how I shall live these ten days, whilst slowly, inch by inch, you give your dear, your precious life for a forlorn cause?

"I am very tough, m'dear," he said lightly; "'tis not a question of life. I shall only be spending a few more very uncomfortable days in this d—d hole; but what of that?"

Her eyes spoke the reply; her eyes veiled with tears, that wandered with heart-breaking anxiety from the hollow circles round his own to the lines of weariness about the firm lips and jaw. He laughed at her solicitude.

"I can last out longer than these brutes have any idea of," he said gaily.

"You cheat yourself, Percy," she rejoined with quiet earnestness. "Every day that you spend immured between these walls, with that ceaseless nerve-racking torment of sleeplessness which these devils have devised for the breaking of your will—every day thus spent diminishes your power of ultimately saving yourself. You see, I speak calmly—dispassionately—I do not even urge my claims upon your life. But what you must weigh in the balance is the claim of all those for whom in the past you have already staked your life, whose lives you have purchased by risking your own. What, in comparison with your noble life, is that of the puny descendant of a line of decadent kings? Why should it be sacrificed—ruthlessly, hopelessly sacrificed that a boy might live who is as nothing to the world, to his country—even to his own people?"

She had tried to speak calmly, never raising her voice beyond a whisper. Her hands still clutched that paper, which seemed to sear her fingers, the paper which she felt held writ upon its smooth surface the death-sentence of the man she loved.

But his look did not answer her firm appeal; it was fixed far away beyond the prison walls, on a lonely country road outside Paris, with the rain falling in a thin drizzle, and leaden clouds overhead chasing one another, driven by the gale.

"Poor mite," he murmured softly; "he walked so bravely by my side, until the little feet grew weary; then he nestled in my arms and slept until we met Ffoulkes waiting with the cart. He was no King of France just then, only a helpless innocent whom Heaven aided me to save."

Marguerite bowed her head in silence. There was nothing more that she could say, no plea that she could urge. Indeed, she had understood, as he had begged her to understand. She understood that long ago he had mapped out the course of his life, and now that that course happened to lead up a Calvary of humiliation and of suffering he was not likely to turn back, even though, on the summit, death already was waiting and beckoning with no uncertain hand; not until he could murmur, in the wake of the great and divine sacrifice itself, the sublime words:

"It is accomplished."

"But the Dauphin is safe enough now," was all that she said, after that one moment's silence when her heart, too, had offered up to God the supreme abnegation of self, and calmly faced a sorrow which threatened to break it at last.

"Yes!" he rejoined quietly, "safe enough for the moment. But he would be safer still if he were out of France. I had hoped to take him one day with me to England. But in this plan damnable Fate has interfered. His adherents wanted to get him to Vienna, and their wish had best be fulfilled now. In my instructions to Ffoulkes I have mapped out a simple way for accomplishing the journey. Tony will be the one best suited to lead the expedition, and I want him to make straight for Holland; the Northern frontiers are not so closely watched as are the Austrian ones. There is a faithful adherent of the Bourbon cause who lives at Delft, and who will give the shelter of his name and home to the fugitive King of France until he can be conveyed to Vienna. He is named Nauudorff. Once I feel that the child is safe in his hands I will look after myself, never fear."

He paused, for his strength, which was only factitious, born of the excitement that Marguerite's presence had called forth, was threatening to give way. His voice, though he had spoken in a whisper all along, was very hoarse, and his temples were throbbing with the sustained effort to speak.

"If those friends had only thought of denying me food instead of sleep," he murmured involuntarily, "I could have held out until—"

Then with characteristic swiftness his mood changed in a moment. His arms closed round Marguerite once more with a passion of self-reproach.

"Heaven forgive me for a selfish brute," he said, whilst the ghost of a smile once more lit up the whole of his face. "Dear soul, I must have forgotten your sweet presence, thus brooding over my own troubles, whilst your loving heart has a graver burden—God help me!— than it can possibly bear. Listen, my beloved, for I don't know how many minutes longer they intend to give us, and I have not yet spoken to you about Armand—"

"Armand!" she cried.

A twinge of remorse had gripped her. For fully ten minutes now she had relegated all thoughts of her brother to a distant cell of her memory.

"We have no news of Armand," she said. "Sir Andrew has searched all the prison registers. Oh! were not my heart atrophied by all that it has endured this past sennight it would feel a final throb of agonising pain at every thought of Armand."

A curious look, which even her loving eyes failed to interpret, passed like a shadow over her husband's face. But the shadow lifted in a moment, and it was with a reassuring smile that he said to her:

"Dear heart! Armand is comparatively safe for the moment. Tell Ffoulkes not to search the prison registers for him, rather to seek out Mademoiselle Lange. She will know where to find Armand."

"Jeanne Lange!" she exclaimed with a world of bitterness in the tone of her voice, "the girl whom Armand loved, it seems, with a passion greater than his loyalty. Oh! Sir Andrew tried to disguise my brother's folly, but I guessed what he did not choose to tell me. It was his disobedience, his want of trust, that brought this unspeakable misery on us all."

"Do not blame him overmuch, dear heart. Armand was in love, and love excuses every sin committed in its name. Jeanne Lange was arrested and Armand lost his reason temporarily. The very day on which I rescued the Dauphin from the Temple I had the good fortune to drag the little lady out of prison. I had given my promise to Armand that she should be safe, and I kept my word. But this Armand did not know—or else—"

He checked himself abruptly, and once more that strange, enigmatical look crept into his eyes.

"I took Jeanne Lange to a place of comparative safety," he said after a slight pause, "but since then she has been set entirely free."

"Free?"

"Yes. Chauvelin himself brought me the news," he replied with a quick, mirthless laugh, wholly unlike his usual light-hearted gaiety. "He had to ask me where to find Jeanne, for I alone knew where she was. As for Armand, they'll not worry about him whilst I am here. Another reason why I must bide a while longer. But in the meanwhile, dear, I pray you find Mademoiselle Lange; she lives at No. 5 Square du Roule. Through her I know that you can get to see Armand. This second letter," he added, pressing a smaller packet into her hand, "is for him. Give it to him, dear heart; it will, I hope, tend to cheer him. I fear me the poor lad frets; yet he only sinned because he loved, and to me he will always be your brother—the man who held your affection for all the years before I came into your life. Give him this letter, dear; they are my instructions to him, as the others are for Ffoulkes; but tell him to read them when he is all alone. You will do that, dear heart, will you not?"

"Yes, Percy," she said simply. "I promise."

Great joy, and the expression of intense relief, lit up his face, whilst his eyes spoke the gratitude which he felt.

"Then there is one thing more," he said. "There are others in this cruel city, dear heart, who have trusted me, and whom I must not fail—Marie de Marmontel and her brother, faithful servants of the late queen; they were on the eve of arrest when I succeeded in getting them to a place of comparative safety; and there are others there, too all of these poor victims have trusted me implicitly. They are waiting for me there, trusting in my promise to convey them safely to England. Sweetheart, you must redeem my promise to them. You will?—you will? Promise me that you will—"

"I promise, Percy," she said once more.

"Then go, dear, to-morrow, in the late afternoon, to No. 98, Rue de Charonne. It is a narrow house at the extreme end of that long street which abuts on the fortifications. The lower part of the house is occupied by a dealer in rags and old clothes. He and his wife and family are wretchedly poor, but they are kind, good souls, and for a consideration and a minimum of risk to themselves they will always render service to the English milors, whom they believe to be a band of inveterate smugglers. Ffoulkes and all the others know these people and know the house; Armand by the same token knows it too. Marie de Marmontel and her brother are there, and several others; the old Comte de Lezardiere, the Abbe de Firmont; their names spell suffering, loyalty, and hopelessness. I was lucky enough to convey them safely to that hidden shelter. They trust me implicitly, dear heart. They are waiting for me there, trusting in my promise to them. Dear heart, you will go, will you not?"

"Yes, Percy," she replied. "I will go; I have promised."

"Ffoulkes has some certificates of safety by him, and the old clothes dealer will supply the necessary disguises; he has a covered cart which he uses for his business, and which you can borrow from him. Ffoulkes will drive the little party to Achard's farm in St. Germain, where other members of the League should be in waiting for the final journey to England. Ffoulkes will know how to arrange for everything; he was always my most able lieutenant. Once everything is organised he can appoint Hastings to lead the party. But you, dear heart, must do as you wish. Achard's farm would be a safe retreat for you and for Ffoulkes: if... I know—I know, dear," he added with infinite tenderness. "See I do not even suggest that you should leave me. Ffoulkes will be with you, and I know that neither he nor you would go even if I commanded. Either Achard's farm, or even the house in the Rue de Charonne, would be quite safe for you, dear, under Ffoulkes's protection, until the time when I myself can carry you back—you, my precious burden—to England in mine own arms, or until... Hush-sh-sh, dear heart," he entreated, smothering with a passionate kiss the low moan of pain which had escaped her lips; "it is all in God's hands now; I am in a tight corner—tighter than ever I have been before; but I am not dead yet, and those brutes have not yet paid the full price for my life. Tell me, dear heart, that you have understood—that you will do all that I asked. Tell me again, my dear, dear love; it is the very essence of life to hear your sweet lips murmur this promise now."

And for the third time she reiterated firmly:

"I have understood every word that you said to me, Percy, and I promise on your precious life to do what you ask."

He sighed a deep sigh of satisfaction, and even at that moment there came from the guard-room beyond the sound of a harsh voice, saying peremptorily:

"That half-hour is nearly over, sergeant; 'tis time you interfered."

"Three minutes more, citizen," was the curt reply.

"Three minutes, you devils," murmured Blakeney between set teeth, whilst a sudden light which even Marguerite's keen gaze failed to interpret leapt into his eyes. Then he pressed the third letter into her hand.

Once more his close, intent gaze compelled hers; their faces were close one to the other, so near to him did he draw her, so tightly did he hold her to him. The paper was in her hand and his fingers were pressed firmly on hers.

"Put this in your kerchief, my beloved," he whispered. "Let it rest on your exquisite bosom where I so love to pillow my head. Keep it there until the last hour when it seems to you that nothing more can come between me and shame. . . . Hush-sh-sh, dear," he added with passionate tenderness, checking the hot protest that at the word "shame" had sprung to her lips, "I cannot explain more fully now. I do not know what may happen. I am only a man, and who knows what subtle devilry those brutes might not devise for bringing the untamed adventurer to his knees. For the next ten days the Dauphin will be on the high roads of France, on his way to safety. Every stage of his journey will be known to me. I can from between these four walls follow him and his escort step by step. Well, dear, I am but a man, already brought to shameful weakness by mere physical discomfort— the want of sleep—such a trifle after all; but in case my reason tottered —God knows what I might do—then give this packet to Ffoulkes—it contains my final instructions—and he will know how to act. Promise me, dear heart, that you will not open the packet unless—unless mine own dishonour seems to you imminent—unless I have yielded to these brutes in this prison, and sent Ffoulkes or one of the others orders to exchange the Dauphin's life for mine; then, when mine own handwriting hath proclaimed me a coward, then and then only, give this packet to Ffoulkes. Promise me that, and also that when you and he have mastered its contents you will act exactly as I have commanded. Promise me that, dear, in your own sweet name, which may God bless, and in that of Ffoulkes, our loyal friend."

Through the sobs that well-nigh choked her she murmured the promise he desired.

His voice had grown hoarser and more spent with the inevitable reaction after the long and sustained effort, but the vigour of the spirit was untouched, the fervour, the enthusiasm.

"Dear heart," he murmured, "do not look on me with those dear, scared eyes of yours. If there is aught that puzzles you in what I said, try and trust me a while longer. Remember, I must save the Dauphin at all costs; mine honour is bound with his safety. What happens to me after that matters but little, yet I wish to live for your dear sake."

He drew a long breath which had naught of weariness in it. The haggard look had completely vanished from his face, the eyes were lighted up from within, the very soul of reckless daring and immortal gaiety illumined his whole personality.

"Do not look so sad, little woman," he said with a strange and sudden recrudescence of power; "those d—d murderers have not got me yet—even now."

Then he went down like a log.

The effort had been too prolonged—weakened nature reasserted her rights and he lost consciousness. Marguerite, helpless and almost distraught with grief, had yet the strength of mind not to call for assistance. She pillowed the loved one's head upon her breast, she kissed the dear, tired eyes, the poor throbbing temples. The unutterable pathos of seeing this man, who was always the personification of extreme vitality, energy, and boundless endurance and pluck, lying thus helpless, like a tired child, in her arms, was perhaps the saddest moment of this day of sorrow. But in her trust she never wavered for one instant. Much that he had said had puzzled her; but the word "shame" coming from his own lips as a comment on himself never caused her the slightest pang of fear. She had quickly hidden the tiny packet in her kerchief. She would act point by point exactly as he had ordered her to do, and she knew that Ffoulkes would never waver either.

Her heart ached well-nigh to breaking point. That which she could not understand had increased her anguish tenfold. If she could only have given way to tears she could have borne this final agony more easily. But the solace of tears was not for her; when those loved eyes once more opened to consciousness they should see hers glowing with courage and determination.

There had been silence for a few minutes in the little cell. The soldiery outside, inured to their hideous duty, thought no doubt that

the time had come for them to interfere. The iron bar was raised and
thrown back with a loud crash, the butt-ends of muskets were
grounded against the floor, and two soldiers made noisy irruption into
the cell.

"Hola, citizen! Wake up," shouted one of the men; "you have
not told us yet what you have done with Capet!"

Marguerite uttered a cry of horror. Instinctively her arms were
interposed between the unconscious man and these inhuman
creatures, with a beautiful gesture of protecting motherhood.

"He has fainted," she said, her voice quivering with indignation.
"My God! are you devils that you have not one spark of manhood in
you?"

The men shrugged their shoulders, and both laughed brutally.
They had seen worse sights than these, since they served a Republic
that ruled by bloodshed and by terror. They were own brothers in
callousness and cruelty to those men who on this self-same spot a few
months ago had watched the daily agony of a martyred Queen, or to
those who had rushed into the Abbaye prison on that awful day in
September, and at a word from their infamous leaders had put eighty
defenceless prisoners—men, women, and children—to the sword.

"Tell him to say what he has done with Capet," said one of the
soldiers now, and this rough command was accompanied with a coarse
jest that sent the blood flaring up into Marguerite's pale cheeks.

The brutal laugh, the coarse words which accompanied it, the
insult flung at Marguerite, had penetrated to Blakeney's slowly
returning consciousness. With sudden strength, that appeared almost
supernatural, he jumped to his feet, and before any of the others could
interfere he had with clenched fist struck the soldier a full blow on the
mouth.

The man staggered back with a curse, the other shouted for
help; in a moment the narrow place swarmed with soldiers; Marguerite
was roughly torn away from the prisoner's side, and thrust into the far
corner of the cell, from where she only saw a confused mass of blue
coats and white belts, and—towering for one brief moment above what
seemed to her fevered fancy like a veritable sea of heads—the pale face
of her husband, with wide dilated eyes searching the gloom for hers.

"Remember!" he shouted, and his voice for that brief moment
rang out clear and sharp above the din.

Then he disappeared behind the wall of glistening bayonets, of
blue coats and uplifted arms; mercifully for her she remembered
nothing more very clearly.

She felt herself being dragged out of the cell, the iron bar being
thrust down behind her with a loud clang. Then in a vague, dreamy
state of semi-unconsciousness she saw the heavy bolts being drawn
back from the outer door, heard the grating of the key in the

monumental lock, and the next moment a breath of fresh air brought the sensation of renewed life into her.

# CHAPTER 30: AFTERWARDS

"I am sorry, Lady Blakeney," said a harsh, dry voice close to her; "the incident at the end of your visit was none of our making, remember."

She turned away, sickened with horror at thought of contact with this wretch. She had heard the heavy oaken door swing to behind her on its ponderous hinges, and the key once again turn in the lock. She felt as if she had suddenly been thrust into a coffin, and that clods of earth were being thrown upon her breast, oppressing her heart so that she could not breathe.

Had she looked for the last time on the man whom she loved beyond everything else on earth, whom she worshipped more ardently day by day? Was she even now carrying within the folds of her kerchief a message from a dying man to his comrades?

Mechanically she followed Chauvelin down the corridor and along the passages which she had traversed a brief half-hour ago. From some distant church tower a clock tolled the hour of ten. It had then really only been little more than thirty brief minutes since first she had entered this grim building, which seemed less stony than the monsters who held authority within it; to her it seemed that centuries had gone over her head during that time. She felt like an old woman, unable to straighten her back or to steady her limbs; she could only dimly see some few paces ahead the trim figure of Chauvelin walking with measured steps, his hands held behind his back, his head thrown up with what looked like triumphant defiance.

At the door of the cubicle where she had been forced to submit to the indignity of being searched by a wardress, the latter was now standing, waiting with characteristic stolidity. In her hand she held the steel files, the dagger and the purse which, as Marguerite passed, she held out to her.

"Your property, citizeness," she said placidly.

She emptied the purse into her own hand, and solemnly counted out the twenty pieces of gold. She was about to replace them all into the purse, when Marguerite pressed one of them back into her wrinkled hand.

"Nineteen will be enough, citizeness," she said; "keep one for yourself, not only for me, but for all the poor women who come here with their heart full of hope, and go hence with it full of despair."

The woman turned calm, lack-lustre eyes on her, and silently pocketed the gold piece with a grudgingly muttered word of thanks.

Chauvelin during this brief interlude, had walked thoughtlessly on ahead. Marguerite, peering down the length of the narrow corridor, spied his sable-clad figure some hundred metres further on as it crossed the dim circle of light thrown by one of the lamps.

She was about to follow, when it seemed to her as if some one was moving in the darkness close beside her. The wardress was even now in the act of closing the door of her cubicle, and there were a couple of soldiers who were disappearing from view round one end of the passage, whilst Chauvelin's retreating form was lost in the gloom at the other.

There was no light close to where she herself was standing, and the blackness around her was as impenetrable as a veil; the sound of a human creature moving and breathing close to her in this intense darkness acted weirdly on her overwrought nerves.

"*Qui va la?*" she called.

There was a more distinct movement among the shadows this time, as of a swift tread on the flagstones of the corridor. All else was silent round, and now she could plainly hear those footsteps running rapidly down the passage away from her. She strained her eyes to see more clearly, and anon in one of the dim circles of light on ahead she spied a man's figure—slender and darkly clad—walking quickly yet furtively like one pursued. As he crossed the light the man turned to look back. It was her brother Armand.

Her first instinct was to call to him; the second checked that call upon her lips.

Percy had said that Armand was in no danger; then why should he be sneaking along the dark corridors of this awful house of Justice if he was free and safe?

Certainly, even at a distance, her brother's movements suggested to Marguerite that he was in danger of being seen. He cowered in the darkness, tried to avoid the circles of light thrown by the lamps in the passage. At all costs Marguerite felt that she must warn him that the way he was going now would lead him straight into Chauvelin's arms, and she longed to let him know that she was close by.

Feeling sure that he would recognise her voice, she made pretence to turn back to the cubicle through the door of which the wardress had already disappeared, and called out as loudly as she dared:

"Good-night, citizeness!"

But Armand—who surely must have heard—did not pause at the sound. Rather was he walking on now more rapidly than before. In less than a minute he would be reaching the spot where Chauvelin stood waiting for Marguerite. That end of the corridor, however, received no light from any of the lamps; strive how she might, Marguerite could see nothing now either of Chauvelin or of Armand.

Blindly, instinctively, she ran forward, thinking only to reach Armand, and to warn him to turn back before it was too late; before he found himself face to face with the most bitter enemy he and his nearest and dearest had ever had. But as she at last came to a halt at the end of the corridor, panting with the exertion of running and the fear for Armand, she almost fell up against Chauvelin, who was standing there alone and imperturbable, seemingly having waited patiently for her. She could only dimly distinguish his face, the sharp features and thin cruel mouth, but she felt—more than she actually saw —his cold steely eyes fixed with a strange expression of mockery upon her.

But of Armand there was no sign, and she—poor soul!—had difficulty in not betraying the anxiety which she felt for her brother. Had the flagstones swallowed him up? A door on the right was the only one that gave on the corridor at this point; it led to the concierge's lodge, and thence out into the courtyard. Had Chauvelin been dreaming, sleeping with his eyes open, whilst he stood waiting for her, and had Armand succeeded in slipping past him under cover of the darkness and through that door to safety that lay beyond these prison walls?

Marguerite, miserably agitated, not knowing what to think, looked somewhat wild-eyed on Chauvelin; he smiled, that inscrutable, mirthless smile of his, and said blandly:

"Is there aught else that I can do for you, citizeness? This is your nearest way out. No doubt Sir Andrew will be waiting to escort you home."

Then as she—not daring either to reply or to question—walked straight up to the door, he hurried forward, prepared to open it for her. But before he did so he turned to her once again:

"I trust that your visit has pleased you, Lady Blakeney," he said suavely. "At what hour do you desire to repeat it to-morrow?"

"To-morrow?" she reiterated in a vague, absent manner, for she was still dazed with the strange incident of Armand's appearance and his flight.

"Yes. You would like to see Sir Percy again to-morrow, would you not? I myself would gladly pay him a visit from time to time, but he does not care for my company. My colleague, citizen Heron, on the other hand, calls on him four times in every twenty-four hours; he does so a few moments before the changing of the guard, and stays chatting with Sir Percy until after the guard is changed, when he inspects the men and satisfies himself that no traitor has crept in among them. All the men are personally known to him, you see. These hours are at five in the morning and again at eleven, and then again at five and eleven in the evening. My friend Heron, as you see, is zealous and assiduous, and, strangely enough, Sir Percy does not seem to view his visit with any displeasure. Now at any other hour of the day, Lady Blakeney, I pray you command me and I will arrange that citizen Heron grant you a second interview with the prisoner."

Marguerite had only listened to Chauvelin's lengthy speech with half an ear; her thoughts still dwelt on the past half-hour with its bitter joy and its agonising pain; and fighting through her thoughts of Percy there was the recollection of Armand which so disquieted her. But though she had only vaguely listened to what Chauvelin was saying, she caught the drift of it.

Madly she longed to accept his suggestion. The very thought of seeing Percy on the morrow was solace to her aching heart; it could feed on hope to-night instead of on its own bitter pain. But even during this brief moment of hesitancy, and while her whole being cried out for this joy that her enemy was holding out to her, even then in the gloom ahead of her she seemed to see a vision of a pale face raised above a crowd of swaying heads, and of the eyes of the dreamer searching for her own, whilst the last sublime cry of perfect self-devotion once more echoed in her ear:

"Remember!"

The promise which she had given him, that would she fulfill. The burden which he had laid on her shoulders she would try to bear as heroically as he was bearing his own. Aye, even at the cost of the supreme sorrow of never resting again in the haven of his arms.

But in spite of sorrow, in spite of anguish so terrible that she could not imagine Death itself to have a more cruel sting, she wished above all to safeguard that final, attenuated thread of hope which was wound round the packet that lay hidden on her breast.

She wanted, above all, not to arouse Chauvelin's suspicions by markedly refusing to visit the prisoner again—suspicions that might lead to her being searched once more and the precious packet filched from her. Therefore she said to him earnestly now:

"I thank you, citizen, for your solicitude on my behalf, but you will understand, I think, that my visit to the prisoner has been almost more than I could bear. I cannot tell you at this moment whether to-morrow I should be in a fit state to repeat it."

"As you please," he replied urbanely. "But I pray you to remember one thing, and that is—"

He paused a moment while his restless eyes wandered rapidly over her face, trying, as it were, to get at the soul of this woman, at her innermost thoughts, which he felt were hidden from him.

"Yes, citizen," she said quietly; "what is it that I am to remember?"

"That it rests with you, Lady Blakeney, to put an end to the present situation."

"How?"

"Surely you can persuade Sir Percy's friends not to leave their chief in durance vile. They themselves could put an end to his troubles to-morrow."

"By giving up the Dauphin to you, you mean?" she retorted coldly.

"Precisely."

"And you hoped—you still hope that by placing before me the picture of your own fiendish cruelty against my husband you will induce me to act the part of a traitor towards him and a coward before his followers?"

"Oh!" he said deprecatingly, "the cruelty now is no longer mine. Sir Percy's release is in your hands, Lady Blakeney—in that of his followers. I should only be too willing to end the present intolerable situation. You and your friends are applying the last turn of the thumbscrew, not I—"

She smothered the cry of horror that had risen to her lips. The man's cold-blooded sophistry was threatening to make a breach in her armour of self-control.

She would no longer trust herself to speak, but made a quick movement towards the door.

He shrugged his shoulders as if the matter were now entirely out of his control. Then he opened the door for her to pass out, and as her skirts brushed against him he bowed with studied deference, murmuring a cordial "Good-night!"

"And remember, Lady Blakeney," he added politely, "that should you at any time desire to communicate with me at my rooms, 19, Rue Dupuy, I hold myself entirely at your service."

Then as her tall, graceful figure disappeared in the outside gloom he passed his thin hand over his mouth as if to wipe away the last lingering signs of triumphant irony:

"The second visit will work wonders, I think, my fine lady," he murmured under his breath.

# CHAPTER 31: AN INTERLUDE

It was close on midnight now, and still they sat opposite one another, he the friend and she the wife, talking over that brief half-hour that had meant an eternity to her.

Marguerite had tried to tell Sir Andrew everything; bitter as it was to put into actual words the pathos and misery which she had witnessed, yet she would hide nothing from the devoted comrade whom she knew Percy would trust absolutely. To him she repeated every word that Percy had uttered, described every inflection of his voice, those enigmatical phrases which she had not understood, and together they cheated one another into the belief that hope lingered somewhere hidden in those words.

"I am not going to despair, Lady Blakeney," said Sir Andrew firmly; "and, moreover, we are not going to disobey. I would stake my life that even now Blakeney has some scheme in his mind which is embodied in the various letters which he has given you, and which—Heaven help us in that case!—we might thwart by disobedience. Tomorrow in the late afternoon I will escort you to the Rue de Charonne. It is a house that we all know well, and which Armand, of course, knows too. I had already inquired there two days ago to ascertain whether by chance St. Just was not in hiding there, but Lucas, the landlord and old-clothes dealer, knew nothing about him."

Marguerite told him about her swift vision of Armand in the dark corridor of the house of Justice.

"Can you understand it, Sir Andrew?" she asked, fixing her deep, luminous eyes inquiringly upon him.

"No, I cannot," he said, after an almost imperceptible moment of hesitancy; "but we shall see him to-morrow. I have no doubt that Mademoiselle Lange will know where to find him; and now that we know where she is, all our anxiety about him, at any rate, should soon be at an end."

He rose and made some allusion to the lateness of the hour. Somehow it seemed to her that her devoted friend was trying to hide his innermost thoughts from her. She watched him with an anxious, intent gaze.

"Can you understand it all, Sir Andrew?" she reiterated with a pathetic note of appeal.

"No, no!" he said firmly. "On my soul, Lady Blakeney, I know no more of Armand than you do yourself. But I am sure that Percy is right. The boy frets because remorse must have assailed him by now. Had he but obeyed implicitly that day, as we all did—"

But he could not frame the whole terrible proposition in words.

Bitterly as he himself felt on the subject of Armand, he would not add yet another burden to this devoted woman's heavy load of misery.

"It was Fate, Lady Blakeney," he said after a while. "Fate! a damnable fate which did it all. Great God! to think of Blakeney in the hands of those brutes seems so horrible that at times I feel as if the whole thing were a nightmare, and that the next moment we shall both wake hearing his merry voice echoing through this room."

He tried to cheer her with words of hope that he knew were but chimeras. A heavy weight of despondency lay on his heart. The letter from his chief was hidden against his breast; he would study it anon in the privacy of his own apartment so as to commit every word to memory that related to the measures for the ultimate safety of the child-King. After that it would have to be destroyed, lest it fell into inimical hands.

Soon he bade Marguerite good-night. She was tired out, body and soul, and he—her faithful friend—vaguely wondered how long she would be able to withstand the strain of so much sorrow, such unspeakable misery.

When at last she was alone Marguerite made brave efforts to compose her nerves so as to obtain a certain modicum of sleep this night. But, strive how she might, sleep would not come. How could it, when before her wearied brain there rose constantly that awful vision of Percy in the long, narrow cell, with weary head bent over his arm, and those friends shouting persistently in his ear:

"Wake up, citizen! Tell us, where is Capet?"

The fear obsessed her that his mind might give way; for the mental agony of such intense weariness must be well-nigh impossible to bear. In the dark, as she sat hour after hour at the open window, looking out in the direction where through the veil of snow the grey walls of the Chatelet prison towered silent and grim, she seemed to see his pale, drawn face with almost appalling reality; she could see every line of it, and could study it with the intensity born of a terrible fear.

How long would the ghostly glimmer of merriment still linger in the eyes? When would the hoarse, mirthless laugh rise to the lips, that awful laugh that proclaims madness? Oh! she could have screamed now with the awfulness of this haunting terror. Ghouls seemed to be mocking her out of the darkness, every flake of snow that fell silently on the window-sill became a grinning face that taunted and derided; every cry in the silence of the night, every footstep on the quay below turned to hideous jeers hurled at her by tormenting fiends.

She closed the window quickly, for she feared that she would go mad. For an hour after that she walked up and down the room making violent efforts to control her nerves, to find a glimmer of that courage which she promised Percy that she would have.

# CHAPTER 32: SISTERS

The morning found her fagged out, but more calm. Later on she managed to drink some coffee, and having washed and dressed, she prepared to go out.

Sir Andrew appeared in time to ascertain her wishes.

"I promised Percy to go to the Rue de Charonne in the late afternoon," she said. "I have some hours to spare, and mean to employ them in trying to find speech with Mademoiselle Lange."

"Blakeney has told you where she lives?"

"Yes. In the Square du Roule. I know it well. I can be there in half an hour."

He, of course, begged to be allowed to accompany her, and anon they were walking together quickly up toward the Faubourg St. Honore. The snow had ceased falling, but it was still very cold, but neither Marguerite nor Sir Andrew were conscious of the temperature or of any outward signs around them. They walked on silently until they reached the torn-down gates of the Square du Roule; there Sir Andrew parted from Marguerite after having appointed to meet her an hour later at a small eating-house he knew of where they could have some food together, before starting on their long expedition to the Rue de Charonne.

Five minutes later Marguerite Blakeney was shown in by worthy Madame Belhomme, into the quaint and pretty drawing-room with its soft-toned hangings and old-world air of faded grace. Mademoiselle Lange was sitting there, in a capacious armchair, which encircled her delicate figure with its frame-work of dull old gold.

She was ostensibly reading when Marguerite was announced, for an open book lay on a table beside her; but it seemed to the visitor that mayhap the young girl's thoughts had played truant from her work, for her pose was listless and apathetic, and there was a look of grave trouble upon the childlike face.

She rose when Marguerite entered, obviously puzzled at the unexpected visit, and somewhat awed at the appearance of this beautiful woman with the sad look in her eyes.

"I must crave your pardon, mademoiselle," said Lady Blakeney as soon as the door had once more closed on Madame Belhomme, and she found herself alone with the young girl. "This visit at such an early hour must seem to you an intrusion. But I am Marguerite St. Just, and —"

Her smile and outstretched hand completed the sentence.

"St. Just!" exclaimed Jeanne.

"Yes. Armand's sister!"

A swift blush rushed to the girl's pale cheeks; her brown eyes expressed unadulterated joy. Marguerite, who was studying her closely, was conscious that her poor aching heart went out to this exquisite child, the far-off innocent cause of so much misery.

Jeanne, a little shy, a little confused and nervous in her movements, was pulling a chair close to the fire, begging Marguerite to sit. Her words came out all the while in short jerky sentences, and from time to time she stole swift shy glances at Armand's sister.

"You will forgive me, mademoiselle," said Marguerite, whose simple and calm manner quickly tended to soothe Jeanne Lange's confusion; "but I was so anxious about my brother—I do not know where to find him."

"And so you came to me, madame?"

"Was I wrong?"

"Oh, no! But what made you think that—that I would know?"

"I guessed," said Marguerite with a smile. "You had heard about me then?"

"Oh, yes!"

"Through whom? Did Armand tell you about me?"

"No, alas! I have not seen him this past fortnight, since you, mademoiselle, came into his life; but many of Armand's friends are in Paris just now; one of them knew, and he told me."

The soft blush had now overspread the whole of the girl's face, even down to her graceful neck. She waited to see Marguerite comfortably installed in an armchair, then she resumed shyly:

"And it was Armand who told me all about you. He loves you so dearly."

"Armand and I were very young children when we lost our parents," said Marguerite softly, "and we were all in all to each other then. And until I married he was the man I loved best in all the world."

"He told me you were married—to an Englishman."

"Yes?"

"He loves England too. At first he always talked of my going there with him as his wife, and of the happiness we should find there together."

"Why do you say 'at first'?"

"He talks less about England now."

"Perhaps he feels that now you know all about it, and that you understand each other with regard to the future."

"Perhaps."

Jeanne sat opposite to Marguerite on a low stool by the fire. Her elbows were resting on her knees, and her face just now was half-hidden by the wealth of her brown curls. She looked exquisitely pretty sitting like this, with just the suggestion of sadness in the listless pose. Marguerite had come here to-day prepared to hate this young girl, who in a few brief days had stolen not only Armand's heart, but his allegiance to his chief, and his trust in him. Since last night, when she had seen her brother sneak silently past her like a thief in the night, she had nurtured thoughts of ill-will and anger against Jeanne.

But hatred and anger had melted at the sight of this child. Marguerite, with the perfect understanding born of love itself, had soon realised the charm which a woman like Mademoiselle Lange must of necessity exercise over a chivalrous, enthusiastic nature like Armand's. The sense of protection—the strongest perhaps that exists in a good man's heart—would draw him irresistibly to this beautiful child, with the great, appealing eyes, and the look of pathos that pervaded the entire face. Marguerite, looking in silence on the—dainty picture before her, found it in her heart to forgive Armand for disobeying his chief when those eyes beckoned to him in a contrary direction.

How could he, how could any chivalrous man endure the thought of this delicate, fresh flower lying crushed and drooping in the hands of monsters who respected neither courage nor purity? And Armand had been more than human, or mayhap less, if he had indeed consented to leave the fate of the girl whom he had sworn to love and protect in other hands than his own.

It seemed almost as if Jeanne was conscious of the fixity of Marguerite's gaze, for though she did not turn to look at her, the flush gradually deepened in her cheeks.

"Mademoiselle Lange," said Marguerite gently, "do you not feel that you can trust me?"

She held out her two hands to the girl, and Jeanne slowly turned to her. The next moment she was kneeling at Marguerite's feet, and kissing the beautiful kind hands that had been stretched out to her with such sisterly love.

"Indeed, indeed, I do trust you," she said, and looked with tear-dimmed eyes in the pale face above her. "I have longed for some one in whom I could confide. I have been so lonely lately, and Armand—"

With an impatient little gesture she brushed away the tears which had gathered in her eyes.

"What has Armand been doing?" asked Marguerite with an encouraging smile.

"Oh, nothing to grieve me!" replied the young girl eagerly, "for he is kind and good, and chivalrous and noble. Oh, I love him with all my heart! I loved him from the moment that I set eyes on him, and then he came to see me—perhaps you know! And he talked so beautiful about England, and so nobly about his leader the Scarlet Pimpernel— have you heard of him?"

"Yes," said Marguerite, smiling. "I have heard of him."

"It was that day that citizen Heron came with his soldiers! Oh! you do not know citizen Heron. He is the most cruel man in France. In

Paris he is hated by every one, and no one is safe from his spies. He
came to arrest Armand, but I was able to fool him and to save Armand.
And after that," she added with charming naivete, "I felt as if, having
saved Armand's life, he belonged to me—and his love for me had made
me his."

"Then I was arrested," she continued after a slight pause, and at
the recollection of what she had endured then her fresh voice still
trembled with horror.

"They dragged me to prison, and I spent two days in a dark cell,
where—"

She hid her face in her hands, whilst a few sobs shook her
whole frame; then she resumed more calmly:

"I had seen nothing of Armand. I wondered where he was, and I
knew that he would be eating out his heart with anxiety for me. But
God was watching over me. At first I was transferred to the Temple
prison, and there a kind creature—a sort of man-of-all work in the
prison took compassion on me. I do not know how he contrived it, but
one morning very early he brought me some filthy old rags which he
told me to put on quickly, and when I had done that he bade me follow
him. Oh! he was a very dirty, wretched man himself, but he must have
had a kind heart. He took me by the hand and made me carry his
broom and brushes. Nobody took much notice of us, the dawn was only
just breaking, and the passages were very dark and deserted; only once
some soldiers began to chaff him about me: '*C'est ma fille—quoi?*' he
said roughly. I very nearly laughed then, only I had the good sense to
restrain myself, for I knew that my freedom, and perhaps my life,
depended on my not betraying myself. My grimy, tattered guide took
me with him right through the interminable corridors of that awful
building, whilst I prayed fervently to God for him and for myself. We
got out by one of the service stairs and exit, and then he dragged me
through some narrow streets until we came to a corner where a covered
cart stood waiting. My kind friend told me to get into the cart, and then
he bade the driver on the box take me straight to a house in the Rue St.
Germain l'Auxerrois. Oh! I was infinitely grateful to the poor creature
who had helped me to get out of that awful prison, and I would gladly
have given him some money, for I am sure he was very poor; but I had
none by me. He told me that I should be quite safe in the house in the
Rue St. Germain l'Auxerrois, and begged me to wait there patiently for
a few days until I heard from one who had my welfare at heart, and
who would further arrange for my safety."

Marguerite had listened silently to this narrative so naively told
by this child, who obviously had no idea to whom she owed her
freedom and her life. While the girl talked, her mind could follow with
unspeakable pride and happiness every phase of that scene in the early
dawn, when that mysterious, ragged man-of-all-work, unbeknown even

to the woman whom he was saving, risked his own noble life for the sake of her whom his friend and comrade loved.

"And did you never see again the kind man to whom you owe your life?" she asked.

"No!" replied Jeanne. "I never saw him since; but when I arrived at the Rue St. Germain l'Auxerrois I was told by the good people who took charge of me that the ragged man-of-all-work had been none other than the mysterious Englishman whom Armand reveres, he whom they call the Scarlet Pimpernel."

"But you did not stay very long in the Rue St. Germain l'Auxerrois, did you?"

"No. Only three days. The third day I received a communique from the Committee of General Security, together with an unconditional certificate of safety. It meant that I was free—quite free. Oh! I could scarcely believe it. I laughed and I cried until the people in the house thought that I had gone mad. The past few days had been such a horrible nightmare."

"And then you saw Armand again?"

"Yes. They told him that I was free. And he came here to see me. He often comes; he will be here anon."

"But are you not afraid on his account and your own? He is—he must be still—'suspect'; a well-known adherent of the Scarlet Pimpernel, he would be safer out of Paris."

"No! oh, no! Armand is in no danger. He, too, has an unconditional certificate of safety."

"An unconditional certificate of safety?" asked Marguerite, whilst a deep frown of grave puzzlement appeared between her brows. "What does that mean?"

"It means that he is free to come and go as he likes; that neither he nor I have anything to fear from Heron and his awful spies. Oh! but for that sad and careworn look on Armand's face we could be so happy; but he is so unlike himself. He is Armand and yet another; his look at times quite frightens me."

"Yet you know why he is so sad," said Marguerite in a strange, toneless voice which she seemed quite unable to control, for that tonelessness came from a terrible sense of suffocation, of a feeling as if her heart-strings were being gripped by huge, hard hands.

"Yes, I know," said Jeanne half hesitatingly, as if knowing, she was still unconvinced.

"His chief, his comrade, the friend of whom you speak, the Scarlet Pimpernel, who risked his life in order to save yours, mademoiselle, is a prisoner in the hands of those that hate him."

Marguerite had spoken with sudden vehemence. There was almost an appeal in her voice now, as if she were trying not to convince Jeanne only, but also herself, of something that was quite simple, quite straightforward, and yet which appeared to be receding from her, an intangible something, a spirit that was gradually yielding to a force as yet unborn, to a phantom that had not yet emerged from out chaos.

But Jeanne seemed unconscious of all this. Her mind was absorbed in Armand, the man whom she loved in her simple, whole-hearted way, and who had seemed so different of late.

"Oh, yes!" she said with a deep, sad sigh, whilst the ever-ready tears once more gathered in her eyes, "Armand is very unhappy because of him. The Scarlet Pimpernel was his friend; Armand loved and revered him. Did you know," added the girl, turning large, horror-filled eyes on Marguerite, "that they want some information from him about the Dauphin, and to force him to give it they—they—"

"Yes, I know," said Marguerite.

"Can you wonder, then, that Armand is unhappy. Oh! last night, after he went from me, I cried for hours, just because he had looked so sad. He no longer talks of happy England, of the cottage we were to have, and of the Kentish orchards in May. He has not ceased to love me, for at times his love seems so great that I tremble with a delicious sense of fear. But oh! his love for me no longer makes him happy."

Her head had gradually sunk lower and lower on her breast, her voice died down in a murmur broken by heartrending sighs. Every generous impulse in Marguerite's noble nature prompted her to take that sorrowing child in her arms, to comfort her if she could, to reassure her if she had the power. But a strange icy feeling had gradually invaded her heart, even whilst she listened to the simple unsophisticated talk of Jeanne Lange. Her hands felt numb and clammy, and instinctively she withdrew away from the near vicinity of the girl. She felt as if the room, the furniture in it, even the window before her were dancing a wild and curious dance, and that from everywhere around strange whistling sounds reached her ears, which caused her head to whirl and her brain to reel.

Jeanne had buried her head in her hands. She was crying—softly, almost humbly at first, as if half ashamed of her grief; then, suddenly it seemed, as if she could not contain herself any longer, a heavy sob escaped her throat and shook her whole delicate frame with its violence. Sorrow no longer would be gainsaid, it insisted on physical expression—that awful tearing of the heart-strings which leaves the body numb and panting with pain.

In a moment Marguerite had forgotten; the dark and shapeless phantom that had knocked at the gate of her soul was relegated back into chaos. It ceased to be, it was made to shrivel and to burn in the great seething cauldron of womanly sympathy. What part this child had played in the vast cataclysm of misery which had dragged a noble-hearted enthusiast into the dark torture-chamber, whence the only outlet led to the guillotine, she—Marguerite Blakeney—did not know;

what part Armand, her brother, had played in it, that she would not dare to guess; all that she knew was that here was a loving heart that was filled with pain—a young, inexperienced soul that was having its first tussle with the grim realities of life—and every motherly instinct in Marguerite was aroused.

She rose and gently drew the young girl up from her knees, and then closer to her; she pillowed the grief-stricken head against her shoulder, and murmured gentle, comforting words into the tiny ear.

"I have news for Armand," she whispered, "that will comfort him, a message—a letter from his friend. You will see, dear, that when Armand reads it he will become a changed man; you see, Armand acted a little foolishly a few days ago. His chief had given him orders which he disregarded—he was so anxious about you—he should have obeyed; and now, mayhap, he feels that his disobedience may have been the—the innocent cause of much misery to others; that is, no doubt, the reason why he is so sad. The letter from his friend will cheer him, you will see."

"Do you really think so, madame?" murmured Jeanne, in whose tear-stained eyes the indomitable hopefulness of youth was already striving to shine.

"I am sure of it," assented Marguerite.

And for the moment she was absolutely sincere. The phantom had entirely vanished. She would even, had he dared to re-appear, have mocked and derided him for his futile attempt at turning the sorrow in her heart to a veritable hell of bitterness.

# CHAPTER 33: LITTLE MOTHER

The two women, both so young still, but each of them with a mark of sorrow already indelibly graven in her heart, were clinging to one another, bound together by the strong bond of sympathy. And but for the sadness of it all it were difficult to conjure up a more beautiful picture than that which they presented as they stood side by side; Marguerite, tall and stately as an exquisite lily, with the crown of her ardent hair and the glory of her deep blue eyes, and Jeanne Lange, dainty and delicate, with the brown curls and the child-like droop of the soft, moist lips.

Thus Armand saw them when, a moment or two later, entered unannounced. He had pushed open the door and looked on the two women silently for a second or two; on the girl whom he loved so dearly, for whose sake he had committed the great, the unpardonable sin which would send him forever henceforth, Cain-like, a wanderer on the face of the earth; and the other, his sister, her whom a Judas act would condemn to lonely sorrow and widowhood.

He could have cried out in an agony of remorse, and it was the groan of acute soul anguish which escaped his lips that drew Marguerite's attention to his presence.

Even though many things that Jeanne Lange had said had prepared her for a change in her brother, she was immeasurably shocked by his appearance. He had always been slim and rather below the average in height, but now his usually upright and trim figure seemed to have shrunken within itself; his clothes hung baggy on his shoulders, his hands appeared waxen and emaciated, but the greatest change was in his face, in the wide circles round the eyes, that spoke of wakeful nights, in the hollow cheeks, and the mouth that had wholly forgotten how to smile.

Percy after a week's misery immured in a dark and miserable prison, deprived of food and rest, did not look such a physical wreck as did Armand St. Just, who was free.

Marguerite's heart reproached her for what she felt had been neglect, callousness on her part. Mutely, within herself, she craved his forgiveness for the appearance of that phantom which should never have come forth from out that chaotic hell which had engendered it.

"Armand!" she cried.

And the loving arms that had guided his baby footsteps long ago, the tender hands that had wiped his boyish tears, were stretched out with unalterable love toward him.

"I have a message for you, dear," she said gently—"a letter from him. Mademoiselle Jeanne allowed me to wait here for you until you came."

Silently, like a little shy mouse, Jeanne had slipped out of the room. Her pure love for Armand had ennobled every one of her thoughts, and her innate kindliness and refinement had already suggested that brother and sister would wish to be alone. At the door she had turned and met Armand's look. That look had satisfied her; she felt that in it she had read the expression of his love, and to it she had responded with a glance that spoke of hope for a future meeting.

As soon as the door had closed on Jeanne Lange, Armand, with an impulse that refused to be checked, threw himself into his sister's arms. The present, with all its sorrows, its remorse and its shame, had sunk away; only the past remained—the unforgettable past, when Marguerite was "little mother"—the soother, the comforter, the healer, the ever-willing receptacle wherein he had been wont to pour the burden of his childish griefs, of his boyish escapades.

Conscious that she could not know everything—not yet, at any rate—he gave himself over to the rapture of this pure embrace, the last time, mayhap, that those fond arms would close round him in unmixed tenderness, the last time that those fond lips would murmur words of affection and of comfort.

To-morrow those same lips would, perhaps, curse the traitor, and the small hand be raised in wrath, pointing an avenging finger on the Judas.

"Little mother," he whispered, babbling like a child, "it is good to see you again."

"And I have brought you a message from Percy," she said, "a letter which he begged me to give you as soon as may be."

"You have seen him?" he asked.

She nodded silently, unable to speak. Not now, not when her nerves were strung to breaking pitch, would she trust herself to speak of that awful yesterday. She groped in the folds of her gown and took the packet which Percy had given her for Armand. It felt quite bulky in her hand.

"There is quite a good deal there for you to read, dear," she said. "Percy begged me to give you this, and then to let you read it when you were alone."

She pressed the packet into his hand. Armand's face was ashen pale. He clung to her with strange, nervous tenacity; the paper which he held in one hand seemed to sear his fingers as with a branding-iron.

"I will slip away now," she said, for strangely enough since Percy's message had been in Armand's hands she was once again conscious of that awful feeling of iciness round her heart, a sense of numbness that paralysed her very thoughts.

"You will make my excuses to Mademoiselle Lange," she said, trying to smile. "When you have read, you will wish to see her alone."

Gently she disengaged herself from Armand's grasp and made for the door. He appeared dazed, staring down at that paper which was scorching his fingers. Only when her hand was on the latch did he seem to realise that she was going.

"Little mother," came involuntarily to his lips.

She came straight back to him and took both his wrists in her small hands. She was taller than he, and his head was slightly bent forward. Thus she towered over him, loving but strong, her great, earnest eyes searching his soul.

"When shall I see you again, little mother?" he asked.

"Read your letter, dear," she replied, "and when you have read it, if you care to impart its contents to me, come to-night to my lodgings, Quai de la Ferraille, above the saddler's shop. But if there is aught in it that you do not wish me to know, then do not come; I shall understand. Good-bye, dear."

She took his head between her two cold hands, and as it was still bowed she placed a tender kiss, as of a long farewell, upon his hair.

Then she went out of the room.

# CHAPTER 34: THE LETTER

Armand sat in the armchair in front of the fire. His head rested against one hand; in the other he held the letter written by the friend whom he had betrayed.

Twice he had read it now, and already was every word of that minute, clear writing graven upon the innermost fibres of his body, upon the most secret cells of his brain.

Armand, I know. I knew even before Chauvelin came to me, and stood there hoping to gloat over the soul-agony a man who finds that he has been betrayed by his dearest friend. But that d—d reprobate did not get that satisfaction, for I was prepared. Not only do I know, Armand, but *I* understand. I, who do not know what love is, have realised how small a thing is honour, loyalty, or friendship when weighed in the balance of a loved one's need.

To save Jeanne you sold me to Heron and his crowd. We are men, Armand, and the word forgiveness has only been spoken once these past two thousand years, and then it was spoken by Divine lips. But Marguerite loves you, and mayhap soon you will be all that is left her to love on this earth. Because of this she must never know. . . . As for you, Armand—well, God help you! But meseems that the hell which you are enduring now is ten thousand times worse than mine. I have heard your furtive footsteps in the corridor outside the grated window of this cell, and would not then have exchanged my hell for yours. Therefore, Armand, and because Marguerite loves you, I would wish to turn to you in the hour that I need help. I am in a tight corner, but the hour may come when a comrade's hand might mean life to me. I have thought of you, Armand partly because having taken more than my life, your own belongs to me, and partly because the plan which I have in my mind will carry with it grave risks for the man who stands by me.

I swore once that never would I risk a comrade's life to save mine own; but matters are so different now . . . we are both in hell, Armand, and I in striving to get out of mine will be showing you a way out of yours.

Will you retake possession of your lodgings in the Rue de la Croix Blanche? I should always know then where to find you in an emergency. But if at any time you receive another letter from me, be its contents what they may, act in accordance with the letter, and send a copy of it at once to Ffoulkes or to Marguerite. Keep in close touch with them both. Tell her I so far forgave your disobedience (there was nothing more) that I may yet trust my life and mine honour in your hands.

I shall have no means of ascertaining definitely whether you will do all that I ask; but somehow, Armand, I know that you will.

For the third time Armand read the letter through.

"But, Armand," he repeated, murmuring the words softly under his breath, "I know that you will."

Prompted by some indefinable instinct, moved by a force that compelled, he allowed himself to glide from the chair on to the floor, on to his knees.

All the pent-up bitterness, the humiliation, the shame of the past few days, surged up from his heart to his lips in one great cry of pain.

"My God!" he whispered, "give me the chance of giving my life for him."

Alone and unwatched, he gave himself over for a few moments to the almost voluptuous delight of giving free rein to his grief. The hot Latin blood in him, tempestuous in all its passions, was firing his heart and brain now with the glow of devotion and of self-sacrifice.

The calm, self-centred Anglo-Saxon temperament—the almost fatalistic acceptance of failure without reproach yet without despair, which Percy's letter to him had evidenced in so marked a manner—was, mayhap, somewhat beyond the comprehension of this young enthusiast, with pure Gallic blood in his veins, who was ever wont to allow his most elemental passions to sway his actions. But though he did not altogether understand, Armand St. Just could fully appreciate. All that was noble and loyal in him rose triumphant from beneath the devastating ashes of his own shame.

Soon his mood calmed down, his look grew less wan and haggard. Hearing Jeanne's discreet and mouselike steps in the next room, he rose quickly and hid the letter in the pocket of his coat.

She came in and inquired anxiously about Marguerite; a hurriedly expressed excuse from him, however, satisfied her easily enough. She wanted to be alone with Armand, happy to see that he held his head more erect to-day, and that the look as of a hunted creature had entirely gone from his eyes.

She ascribed this happy change to Marguerite, finding it in her heart to be grateful to the sister for having accomplished what the fiancee had failed to do.

For awhile they remained together, sitting side by side, speaking at times, but mostly silent, seeming to savour the return of truant happiness. Armand felt like a sick man who has obtained a sudden surcease from pain. He looked round him with a kind of melancholy delight on this room which he had entered for the first time less than a fortnight ago, and which already was so full of memories.

Those first hours spent at the feet of Jeanne Lange, how exquisite they had been, how fleeting in the perfection of their happiness! Now they seemed to belong to a far distant past, evanescent like the perfume of violets, swift in their flight like the winged steps of youth. Blakeney's letter had effectually taken the bitter sting from out his remorse, but it had increased his already over-heavy load of inconsolable sorrow.

Later in the day he turned his footsteps in the direction of the river, to the house in the Quai de la Ferraille above the saddler's shop. Marguerite had returned alone from the expedition to the Rue de Charonne. Whilst Sir Andrew took charge of the little party of fugitives and escorted them out of Paris, she came back to her lodgings in order to collect her belongings, preparatory to taking up her quarters in the house of Lucas, the old-clothes dealer. She returned also because she hoped to see Armand.

"If you care to impart the contents of the letter to me, come to my lodgings to-night," she had said.

All day a phantom had haunted her, the phantom of an agonising suspicion.

But now the phantom had vanished never to return. Armand was sitting close beside her, and he told her that the chief had selected him amongst all the others to stand by him inside the walls of Paris until the last.

"I shall mayhap," thus closed that precious document, "have no means of ascertaining definitely whether you will act in accordance with this letter. But somehow, Armand, I know that you will."

"I know that you will, Armand," reiterated Marguerite fervently.

She had only been too eager to be convinced; the dread and dark suspicion which had been like a hideous poisoned sting had only vaguely touched her soul; it had not gone in very deeply. How could it, when in its death-dealing passage it encountered the rampart of tender, almost motherly love?

Armand, trying to read his sister's thoughts in the depths of her blue eyes, found the look in them limpid and clear. Percy's message to Armand had reassured her just as he had intended that it should do. Fate had dealt over harshly with her as it was, and Blakeney's remorse for the sorrow which he had already caused her, was scarcely less keen than Armand's. He did not wish her to bear the intolerable burden of hatred against her brother; and by binding St. Just close to him at the supreme hour of danger he hoped to prove to the woman whom he loved so passionately that Armand was worthy of trust.

# Part III

## Chapter 35: The Last Phase

"Well? How is it now?"

"The last phase, I think."

"He will yield?"

"He must."

"Bah! you have said it yourself often enough; those English are tough."

"It takes time to hack them to pieces, perhaps. In this case even you, citizen Chauvelin, said that it would take time. Well, it has taken just seventeen days, and now the end is in sight."

It was close on midnight in the guard-room which gave on the innermost cell of the Conciergerie. Heron had just visited the prisoner as was his wont at this hour of the night. He had watched the changing of the guard, inspected the night-watch, questioned the sergeant in charge, and finally he had been on the point of retiring to his own new quarters in the house of Justice, in the near vicinity of the Conciergerie, when citizen Chauvelin entered the guard-room unexpectedly and detained his colleague with the peremptory question:

"How is it now?"

"If you are so near the end, citizen Heron," he now said, sinking his voice to a whisper, "why not make a final effort and end it to-night?"

"I wish I could; the anxiety is wearing me out more'n him," added with a jerky movement of the head in direction of the inner cell.

"Shall I try?" rejoined Chauvelin grimly.

"Yes, an you wish."

Citizen Heron's long limbs were sprawling on a guard-room chair. In this low narrow room he looked like some giant whose body had been carelessly and loosely put together by a 'prentice hand in the art of manufacture. His broad shoulders were bent, probably under the weight of anxiety to which he had referred, and his head, with the lank, shaggy hair overshadowing the brow, was sunk deep down on his chest.

Chauvelin looked on his friend and associate with no small measure of contempt. He would no doubt have preferred to conclude the present difficult transaction entirely in his own way and alone; but equally there was no doubt that the Committee of Public Safety did not trust him quite so fully as it used to do before the fiasco at Calais and the blunders of Boulogne. Heron, on the other hand, enjoyed to its outermost the confidence of his colleagues; his ferocious cruelty and his callousness were well known, whilst physically, owing to his great height and bulky if loosely knit frame, he had a decided advantage over his trim and slender friend.

As far as the bringing of prisoners to trial was concerned, the chief agent of the Committee of General Security had been given a perfectly free hand by the decree of the 27th Nivose. At first, therefore, he had experienced no difficulty when he desired to keep the Englishman in close confinement for a time without hurrying on that summary trial and condemnation which the populace had loudly demanded, and to which they felt that they were entitled to as a public holiday. The death of the Scarlet Pimpernel on the guillotine had been a spectacle promised by every demagogue who desired to purchase a few votes by holding out visions of pleasant doings to come; and during the first few days the mob of Paris was content to enjoy the delights of expectation.

But now seventeen days had gone by and still the Englishman was not being brought to trial. The pleasure-loving public was waxing impatient, and earlier this evening, when citizen Heron had shown himself in the stalls of the national theatre, he was greeted by a crowded audience with decided expressions of disapproval and open mutterings of:

"What of the Scarlet Pimpernel?"

It almost looked as if he would have to bring that accursed Englishman to the guillotine without having wrested from him the secret which he would have given a fortune to possess. Chauvelin, who had also been present at the theatre, had heard the expressions of discontent; hence his visit to his colleague at this late hour of the night.

"Shall I try?" he had queried with some impatience, and a deep sigh of satisfaction escaped his thin lips when the chief agent, wearied and discouraged, had reluctantly agreed.

"Let the men make as much noise as they like," he added with an enigmatical smile. "The Englishman and I will want an accompaniment to our pleasant conversation."

Heron growled a surly assent, and without another word Chauvelin turned towards the inner cell. As he stepped in he allowed the iron bar to fall into its socket behind him. Then he went farther into the room until the distant recess was fully revealed to him. His tread had been furtive and almost noiseless. Now he paused, for he had caught sight the prisoner. For a moment he stood quite still, with hands clasped behind his back in his wonted attitude—still save for a strange, involuntary twitching of his mouth, and the nervous clasping and interlocking of his fingers behind his back. He was savouring to its utmost fulsomeness the supremest joy which animal man can ever know—the joy of looking on a fallen enemy.

Blakeney sat at the table with one arm resting on it, the emaciated hand tightly clutched, the body leaning forward, the eyes looking into nothingness.

For the moment he was unconscious of Chauvelin's presence, and the latter could gaze on him to the full content of his heart.

Indeed, to all outward appearances there sat a man whom privations of every sort and kind, the want of fresh air, of proper food, above all, of rest, had worn down physically to a shadow. There was not a particle of colour in cheeks or lips, the skin was grey in hue, the eyes looked like deep caverns, wherein the glow of fever was all that was left of life.

Chauvelin looked on in silence, vaguely stirred by something that he could not define, something that right through his triumphant satisfaction, his hatred and final certainty of revenge, had roused in him a sense almost of admiration.

He gazed on the noiseless figure of the man who had endured so much for an ideal, and as he gazed it seemed to him as if the spirit no longer dwelt in the body, but hovered round in the dank, stuffy air of the narrow cell above the head of the lonely prisoner, crowning it with glory that was no longer of this earth.

Of this the looker-on was conscious despite himself, of that and of the fact that stare as he might, and with perception rendered doubly keen by hate, he could not, in spite of all, find the least trace of mental weakness in that far-seeing gaze which seemed to pierce the prison walls, nor could he see that bodily weakness had tended to subdue the ruling passions.

Sir Percy Blakeney—a prisoner since seventeen days in close, solitary confinement, half-starved, deprived of rest, and of that mental and physical activity which had been the very essence of life to him hitherto—might be outwardly but a shadow of his former brilliant self, but nevertheless he was still that same elegant English gentleman, that prince of dandies whom Chauvelin had first met eighteen months ago at the most courtly Court in Europe. His clothes, despite constant wear and the want of attention from a scrupulous valet, still betrayed the perfection of London tailoring; he had put them on with meticulous care, they were free from the slightest particle of dust, and the filmy folds of priceless Mechlin still half-veiled the delicate whiteness of his shapely hands.

And in the pale, haggard face, in the whole pose of body and of arm, there was still the expression of that indomitable strength of will, that reckless daring, that almost insolent challenge to Fate; it was there untamed, uncrushed. Chauvelin himself could not deny to himself its presence or its force. He felt that behind that smooth brow, which looked waxlike now, the mind was still alert, scheming, plotting, striving for freedom, for conquest and for power, and rendered even doubly keen and virile by the ardour of supreme self-sacrifice.

Chauvelin now made a slight movement and suddenly Blakeney became conscious of his presence, and swift as a flash a smile lit up his wan face.

"Why! if it is not my engaging friend Monsieur Chambertin," he said gaily.

He rose and stepped forward in the most approved fashion prescribed by the elaborate etiquette of the time. But Chauvelin smiled grimly and a look of almost animal lust gleamed in his pale eyes, for he had noted that as he rose Sir Percy had to seek the support of the table, even whilst a dull film appeared to gather over his eyes.

The gesture had been quick and cleverly disguised, but it had been there nevertheless—that and the livid hue that overspread the face as if consciousness was threatening to go. All of which was sufficient still further to assure the looker-on that that mighty physical strength was giving way at last, that strength which he had hated in his enemy almost as much as he had hated the thinly veiled insolence of his manner.

"And what procures me, sir, the honour of your visit?" continued Blakeney, who had—at any rate, outwardly soon recovered himself, and whose voice, though distinctly hoarse and spent, rang quite cheerfully across the dank narrow cell.

"My desire for your welfare, Sir Percy," replied Chauvelin with equal pleasantry.

"La, sir; but have you not gratified that desire already, to an extent which leaves no room for further solicitude? But I pray you, will you not sit down?" he continued, turning back toward the table. "I was about to partake of the lavish supper which your friends have provided for me. Will you not share it, sir? You are most royally welcome, and it will mayhap remind you of that supper we shared together in Calais, eh? when you, Monsieur Chambertin, were temporarily in holy orders."

He laughed, offering his enemy a chair, and pointed with inviting gesture to the hunk of brown bread and the mug of water which stood on the table.

"Such as it is, sir," he said with a pleasant smile, "it is yours to command."

Chauvelin sat down. He held his lower lip tightly between his teeth, so tightly that a few drops of blood appeared upon its narrow surface. He was making vigorous efforts to keep his temper under control, for he would not give his enemy the satisfaction of seeing him resent his insolence. He could afford to keep calm now that victory was at last in sight, now that he knew that he had but to raise a finger, and those smiling, impudent lips would be closed forever at last.

"Sir Percy," he resumed quietly, "no doubt it affords you a certain amount of pleasure to aim your sarcastic shafts at me. I will not begrudge you that pleasure; in your present position, sir, your shafts have little or no sting."

"And I shall have but few chances left to aim them at your

charming self," interposed Blakeney, who had drawn another chair close to the table and was now sitting opposite his enemy, with the light of the lamp falling full on his own face, as if he wished his enemy to know that he had nothing to hide, no thought, no hope, no fear.

"Exactly," said Chauvelin dryly. "That being the case, Sir Percy, what say you to no longer wasting the few chances which are left to you for safety? The time is getting on. You are not, I imagine, quite as hopeful as you were even a week ago, . . . you have never been over-comfortable in this cell, why not end this unpleasant state of affairs now—once and for all? You'll not have cause to regret it. My word on it."

Sir Percy leaned back in his chair. He yawned loudly and ostentatiously.

"I pray you, sir, forgive me," he said. "Never have I been so d—d fatigued. I have not slept for more than a fortnight."

"Exactly, Sir Percy. A night's rest would do you a world of good."

"A night, sir?" exclaimed Blakeney with what seemed like an echo of his former inimitable laugh. "La! I should want a week."

"I am afraid we could not arrange for that, but one night would greatly refresh you."

"You are right, sir, you are right; but those d—d fellows in the next room make so much noise."

"I would give strict orders that perfect quietude reigned in the guard-room this night," said Chauvelin, murmuring softly, and there was a gentle purr in his voice, "and that you were left undisturbed for several hours. I would give orders that a comforting supper be served to you at once, and that everything be done to minister to your wants."

"That sounds d—d alluring, sir. Why did you not suggest this before?"

"You were so—what shall I say—so obstinate, Sir Percy?"

"Call it pig-headed, my dear Monsieur Chambertin," retorted Blakeney gaily, "truly you would oblige me."

"In any case you, sir, were acting in direct opposition to your own interests."

"Therefore you came," concluded Blakeney airily, "like the good Samaritan to take compassion on me and my troubles, and to lead me straight away to comfort, a good supper and a downy bed."

"Admirably put, Sir Percy," said Chauvelin blandly; "that is exactly my mission."

"How will you set to work, Monsieur Chambertin?"

"Quite easily, if you, Sir Percy, will yield to the persuasion of my friend citizen Heron."

"Ah!"

"Why, yes! He is anxious to know where little Capet is. A

reasonable whim, you will own, considering that the disappearance of the child is causing him grave anxiety."

"And you, Monsieur Chambertin?" queried Sir Percy with that suspicion of insolence in his manner which had the power to irritate his enemy even now. "And yourself, sir; what are your wishes in the matter?"

"Mine, Sir Percy?" retorted Chauvelin. "Mine? Why, to tell you the truth, the fate of little Capet interests me but little. Let him rot in Austria or in our prisons, I care not which. He'll never trouble France overmuch, I imagine. The teachings of old Simon will not tend to make a leader or a king out of the puny brat whom you chose to drag out of our keeping. My wishes, sir, are the annihilation of your accursed League, and the lasting disgrace, if not the death, of its chief."

He had spoken more hotly than he had intended, but all the pent-up rage of the past eighteen months, the recollections of Calais and of Boulogne, had all surged up again in his mind, because despite the closeness of these prison walls, despite the grim shadow of starvation and of death that beckoned so close at hand, he still encountered a pair of mocking eyes, fixed with relentless insolence upon him.

Whilst he spoke Blakeney had once more leaned forward, resting his elbows upon the table. Now he drew nearer to him the wooden platter on which reposed that very uninviting piece of dry bread. With solemn intentness he proceeded to break the bread into pieces; then he offered the platter to Chauvelin.

"I am sorry," he said pleasantly, "that I cannot offer you more dainty fare, sir, but this is all that your friends have supplied me with to-day."

He crumbled some of the dry bread in his slender fingers, then started munching the crumbs with apparent relish. He poured out some water into the mug and drank it. Then he said with a light laugh:

"Even the vinegar which that ruffian Brogard served us at Calais was preferable to this, do you not imagine so, my good Monsieur Chambertin?"

Chauvelin made no reply. Like a feline creature on the prowl, he was watching the prey that had so nearly succumbed to his talons. Blakeney's face now was positively ghastly. The effort to speak, to laugh, to appear unconcerned, was apparently beyond his strength. His cheeks and lips were livid in hue, the skin clung like a thin layer of wax to the bones of cheek and jaw, and the heavy lids that fell over the eyes had purple patches on them like lead.

To a system in such an advanced state of exhaustion the stale water and dusty bread must have been terribly nauseating, and Chauvelin himself callous and thirsting for vengeance though he was, could hardly bear to look calmly on the martyrdom of this man whom he and his colleagues were torturing in order to gain their own ends.

An ashen hue, which seemed like the shadow of the hand of death, passed over the prisoner's face. Chauvelin felt compelled to avert his gaze. A feeling that was almost akin to remorse had stirred a hidden chord in his heart. The feeling did not last—the heart had been too long atrophied by the constantly recurring spectacles of cruelties, massacres, and wholesale hecatombs perpetrated in the past eighteen months in the name of liberty and fraternity to be capable of a sustained effort in the direction of gentleness or of pity. Any noble instinct in these revolutionaries had long ago been drowned in a whirlpool of exploits that would forever sully the records of humanity; and this keeping of a fellow-creature on the rack in order to wring from him a Judas-like betrayal was but a complement to a record of infamy that had ceased by its very magnitude to weigh upon their souls.

Chauvelin was in no way different from his colleagues; the crimes in which he had had no hand he had condoned by continuing to serve the Government that had committed them, and his ferocity in the present case was increased a thousandfold by his personal hatred for the man who had so often fooled and baffled him.

When he looked round a second or two later that ephemeral fit of remorse did its final vanishing; he had once more encountered the pleasant smile, the laughing if ashen-pale face of his unconquered foe.

"Only a passing giddiness, my dear sir," said Sir Percy lightly. "As you were saying—"

At the airily-spoken words, at the smile that accompanied them, Chauvelin had jumped to his feet. There was something almost supernatural, weird, and impish about the present situation, about this dying man who, like an impudent schoolboy, seemed to be mocking Death with his tongue in his cheek, about his laugh that appeared to find its echo in a widely yawning grave.

"In the name of God, Sir Percy," he said roughly, as he brought his clenched fist crashing down upon the table, "this situation is intolerable. Bring it to an end to-night!"

"Why, sir?" retorted Blakeney, "methought you and your kind did not believe in God."

"No. But you English do."

"We do. But we do not care to hear His name on your lips."

"Then in the name of the wife whom you love—"

But even before the words had died upon his lips, Sir Percy, too, had risen to his feet.

"Have done, man—have done," he broke in hoarsely, and despite weakness, despite exhaustion and weariness, there was such a dangerous look in his hollow eyes as he leaned across the table that Chauvelin drew back a step or two, and—vaguely fearful—looked furtively towards the opening into the guard-room. "Have done," he reiterated for the third time; "do not name her, or by the living God whom you dared to invoke I'll find strength yet to smite you in the face."

But Chauvelin, after that first moment of almost superstitious fear, had quickly recovered his *sang-froid*.

"Little Capet, Sir Percy," he said, meeting the other's threatening glance with an imperturbable smile, "tell me where to find him, and you may yet live to savour the caresses of the most beautiful woman in England."

He had meant it as a taunt, the final turn of the thumb-screw applied to a dying man, and he had in that watchful, keen mind of his well weighed the full consequences of the taunt.

The next moment he had paid to the full the anticipated price. Sir Percy had picked up the pewter mug from the table—it was half-filled with brackish water—and with a hand that trembled but slightly he hurled it straight at his opponent's face.

The heavy mug did not hit citizen Chauvelin; it went crashing against the stone wall opposite. But the water was trickling from the top of his head all down his eyes and cheeks. He shrugged his shoulders with a look of benign indulgence directed at his enemy, who had fallen back into his chair exhausted with the effort.

Then he took out his handkerchief and calmly wiped the water from his face.

"Not quite so straight a shot as you used to be, Sir Percy," he said mockingly.

"No, sir—apparently—not."

The words came out in gasps. He was like a man only partly conscious. The lips were parted, the eyes closed, the head leaning against the high back of the chair. For the space of one second Chauvelin feared that his zeal had outrun his prudence, that he had dealt a death-blow to a man in the last stage of exhaustion, where he had only wished to fan the flickering flame of life. Hastily—for the seconds seemed precious—he ran to the opening that led into the guard-room.

"Brandy—quick!" he cried.

Heron looked up, roused from the semi-somnolence in which he had lain for the past half-hour. He disentangled his long limbs from out the guard-room chair.

"Eh?" he queried. "What is it?"

"Brandy," reiterated Chauvelin impatiently; "the prisoner has fainted."

"Bah!" retorted the other with a callous shrug of the shoulders, "you are not going to revive him with brandy, I imagine."

"No. But you will, citizen Heron," rejoined the other dryly, "for if you do not he'll be dead in an hour!"

"Devils in hell!" exclaimed Heron, "you have not killed him? You—you d—d fool!"

He was wide awake enough now; wide awake and shaking with fury. Almost foaming at the mouth and uttering volleys of the choicest oaths, he elbowed his way roughly through the groups of soldiers who were crowding round the centre table of the guard-room, smoking and throwing dice or playing cards. They made way for him as hurriedly as they could, for it was not safe to thwart the citizen agent when he was in a rage.

Heron walked across to the opening and lifted the iron bar. With scant ceremony he pushed his colleague aside and strode into the cell, whilst Chauvelin, seemingly not resenting the other's ruffianly manners and violent language, followed close upon his heel.

In the centre of the room both men paused, and Heron turned with a surly growl to his friend.

"You vowed he would be dead in an hour," he said reproachfully.

The other shrugged his shoulders.

"It does not look like it now certainly," he said dryly.

Blakeney was sitting—as was his wont—close to the table, with one arm leaning on it, the other, tightly clenched, resting upon his knee. A ghost of a smile hovered round his lips.

"Not in an hour, citizen Heron," he said, and his voice flow was scarce above a whisper, "nor yet in two."

"You are a fool, man," said Heron roughly. "You have had seventeen days of this. Are you not sick of it?"

"Heartily, my dear friend," replied Blakeney a little more firmly.

"Seventeen days," reiterated the other, nodding his shaggy head; "you came here on the 2nd of Pluviose, today is the 19th."

"The 19th Pluviose?" interposed Sir Percy, and a strange gleam suddenly flashed in his eyes. "Demn it, sir, and in Christian parlance what may that day be?"

"The 7th of February at your service, Sir Percy," replied Chauvelin quietly.

"I thank you, sir. In this d—d hole I had lost count of time."

Chauvelin, unlike his rough and blundering colleague, had been watching the prisoner very closely for the last moment or two, conscious of a subtle, undefinable change that had come over the man during those few seconds while he, Chauvelin, had thought him dying. The pose was certainly the old familiar one, the head erect, the hand clenched, the eyes looking through and beyond the stone walls; but there was an air of listlessness in the stoop of the shoulders, and— except for that one brief gleam just now—a look of more complete weariness round the hollow eyes! To the keen watcher it appeared as if that sense of living power, of unconquered will and defiant mind was no longer there, and as if he himself need no longer fear that almost supersensual thrill which had a while ago kindled in him a vague sense of admiration—almost of remorse.

Even as he gazed, Blakeney slowly turned his eyes full upon him. Chauvelin's heart gave a triumphant bound.

With a mocking smile he met the wearied look, the pitiable appeal. His turn had come at last—his turn to mock and to exult. He knew that what he was watching now was no longer the last phase of a long and noble martyrdom; it was the end—the inevitable end—that for which he had schemed and striven, for which he had schooled his heart to ferocity and callousness that were devilish in their intensity. It was the end indeed, the slow descent of a soul from the giddy heights of attempted self-sacrifice, where it had striven to soar for a time, until the body and the will both succumbed together and dragged it down with them into the abyss of submission and of irreparable shame.

# CHAPTER 36: SUBMISSION

Silence reigned in the narrow cell for a few moments, whilst two human jackals stood motionless over their captured prey.

A savage triumph gleamed in Chauvelin's eyes, and even Heron, dull and brutal though he was, had become vaguely conscious of the great change that had come over the prisoner.

Blakeney, with a gesture and a sigh of hopeless exhaustion had once more rested both his elbows on the table; his head fell heavy and almost lifeless downward in his arms.

"Curse you, man!" cried Heron almost involuntarily. "Why in the name of hell did you wait so long?"

Then, as the prisoner made no reply, but only raised his head slightly, and looked on the other two men with dulled, wearied eyes, Chauvelin interposed calmly:

"More than a fortnight has been wasted in useless obstinacy, Sir Percy. Fortunately it is not too late."

"Capet?" said Heron hoarsely, "tell us, where is Capet?"

He leaned across the table, his eyes were bloodshot with the keenness of his excitement, his voice shook with the passionate desire for the crowning triumph.

"If you'll only not worry me," murmured the prisoner; and the whisper came so laboriously and so low that both men were forced to bend their ears close to the scarcely moving lips; "if you will let me sleep and rest, and leave me in peace—"

"The peace of the grave, man," retorted Chauvelin roughly; "if you will only speak. Where is Capet?"

"I cannot tell you; the way is long, the road—intricate."

"Bah!"

"I'll lead you to him, if you will give me rest."

"We don't want you to lead us anywhere," growled Heron with a smothered curse; "tell us where Capet is; we'll find him right enough."

"I cannot explain; the way is intricate; the place off the beaten track, unknown except to me and my friends."

Once more that shadow, which was so like the passing of the hand of Death, overspread the prisoner's face; his head rolled back against the chair.

"He'll die before he can speak," muttered Chauvelin under his breath. "You usually are well provided with brandy, citizen Heron."

The latter no longer demurred. He saw the danger as clearly as did his colleague. It had been hell's own luck if the prisoner were to die now when he seemed ready to give in. He produced a flask from the pocket of his coat, and this he held to Blakeney's lips.

"Beastly stuff," murmured the latter feebly. "I think I'd sooner faint—than drink."

"Capet? where is Capet?" reiterated Heron impatiently. "One—two—three hundred leagues from here.

I must let one of my friends know; he'll communicate with the others; they must be prepared," replied the prisoner slowly.

Heron uttered a blasphemous oath.

"Where is Capet? Tell us where Capet is, or—"

He was like a raging tiger that had thought to hold its prey and suddenly realised that it was being snatched from him. He raised his fist, and without doubt the next moment he would have silenced forever the lips that held the precious secret, but Chauvelin fortunately was quick enough to seize his wrist.

"Have a care, citizen," he said peremptorily; "have a care! You called me a fool just now when you thought I had killed the prisoner. It is his secret we want first; his death can follow afterwards."

"Yes, but not in this d—d hole," murmured Blakeney.

"On the guillotine if you'll speak," cried Heron, whose exasperation was getting the better of his self-interest, "but if you'll not speak then it shall be starvation in this hole—yes, starvation," he growled, showing a row of large and uneven teeth like those of some mongrel cur, "for I'll have that door walled in to-night, and not another living soul shall cross this threshold again until your flesh has rotted on your bones and the rats have had their fill of you."

The prisoner raised his head slowly, a shiver shook him as if caused by ague, and his eyes, that appeared almost sightless, now looked with a strange glance of horror on his enemy.

"I'll die in the open," he whispered, "not in this d—d hole."

"Then tell us where Capet is."

"I cannot; I wish to God I could. But I'll take you to him, I swear I will. I'll make my friends give him up to you. Do you think that I would not tell you now, if I could."

Heron, whose every instinct of tyranny revolted against this thwarting of his will, would have continued to heckle the prisoner even now, had not Chauvelin suddenly interposed with an authoritative gesture.

"You'll gain nothing this way, citizen," he said quietly; "the man's mind is wandering; he is probably quite unable to give you clear directions at this moment."

"What am I to do, then?" muttered the other roughly.

"He cannot live another twenty-four hours now, and would only grow more and more helpless as time went on."

"Unless you relax your strict regime with him."

"And if I do we'll only prolong this situation indefinitely; and in the meanwhile how do we know that the brat is not being spirited away out of the country?"

The prisoner, with his head once more buried in his arms, had fallen into a kind of torpor, the only kind of sleep that the exhausted system would allow. With a brutal gesture Heron shook him by the shoulder.

"He," he shouted, "none of that, you know. We have not settled the matter of young Capet yet."

Then, as the prisoner made no movement, and the chief agent indulged in one of his favourite volleys of oaths, Chauvelin placed a peremptory hand on his colleague's shoulder.

"I tell you, citizen, that this is no use," he said firmly. "Unless you are prepared to give up all thoughts of finding Capet, you must try and curb your temper, and try diplomacy where force is sure to fail."

"Diplomacy?" retorted the other with a sneer. "Bah! it served you well at Boulogne last autumn, did it not, citizen Chauvelin?"

"It has served me better now," rejoined the other imperturbably. "You will own, citizen, that it is my diplomacy which has placed within your reach the ultimate hope of finding Capet."

"H'm!" muttered the other, "you advised us to starve the prisoner. Are we any nearer to knowing his secret?"

"Yes. By a fortnight of weariness, of exhaustion and of starvation, you are nearer to it by the weakness of the man whom in his full strength you could never hope to conquer."

"But if the cursed Englishman won't speak, and in the meanwhile dies on my hands—"

"He won't do that if you will accede to his wish. Give him some good food now, and let him sleep till dawn."

"And at dawn he'll defy me again. I believe now that he has some scheme in his mind, and means to play us a trick."

"That, I imagine, is more than likely," retorted Chauvelin dryly; "though," he added with a contemptuous nod of the head directed at the huddled-up figure of his once brilliant enemy, "neither mind nor body seem to me to be in a sufficiently active state just now for hatching plot or intrigue; but even if—vaguely floating through his clouded mind—there has sprung some little scheme for evasion, I give you my word, citizen Heron, that you can thwart him completely, and gain all that you desire, if you will only follow my advice."

There had always been a great amount of persuasive power in citizen Chauvelin, ex-envoy of the revolutionary Government of France at the Court of St. James, and that same persuasive eloquence did not fail now in its effect on the chief agent of the Committee of General Security. The latter was made of coarser stuff than his more brilliant colleague. Chauvelin was like a wily and sleek panther that is furtive in its movements, that will lure its prey, watch it, follow it with stealthy footsteps, and only pounce on it when it is least wary, whilst Heron was more like a raging bull that tosses its head in a blind, irresponsible fashion, rushes at an obstacle without gauging its resisting powers, and allows its victim to slip from beneath its weight through the very clumsiness and brutality of its assault.

Still Chauvelin had two heavy black marks against him—those of his failures at Calais and Boulogne. Heron, rendered cautious both by the deadly danger in which he stood and the sense of his own incompetence to deal with the present situation, tried to resist the other's authority as well as his persuasion.

"Your advice was not of great use to citizen Collot last autumn at Boulogne," he said, and spat on the ground by way of expressing both his independence and his contempt.

"Still, citizen Heron," retorted Chauvelin with unruffled patience, "it is the best advice that you are likely to get in the present emergency. You have eyes to see, have you not? Look on your prisoner at this moment. Unless something is done, and at once, too, he will be past negotiating with in the next twenty-four hours; then what will follow?"

He put his thin hand once more on his colleague's grubby coat-sleeve, he drew him closer to himself away from the vicinity of that huddled figure, that captive lion, wrapped in a torpid somnolence that looked already so like the last long sleep.

"What will follow, citizen Heron?" he reiterated, sinking his voice to a whisper; "sooner or later some meddlesome busybody who sits in the Assembly of the Convention will get wind that little Capet is no longer in the Temple prison, that a pauper child was substituted for him, and that you, citizen Heron, together with the commissaries in charge, have thus been fooling the nation and its representatives for over a fortnight. What will follow then, think you?"

And he made an expressive gesture with his outstretched fingers across his throat.

Heron found no other answer but blasphemy.

"I'll make that cursed Englishman speak yet," he said with a fierce oath.

"You cannot," retorted Chauvelin decisively. "In his present state he is incapable of it, even if he would, which also is doubtful."

"Ah! then you do think that he still means to cheat us?"

"Yes, I do. But I also know that he is no longer in a physical state to do it. No doubt he thinks that he is. A man of that type is sure to overvalue his own strength; but look at him, citizen Heron. Surely you must see that we have nothing to fear from him now."

Heron now was like a voracious creature that has two victims lying ready for his gluttonous jaws. He was loath to let either of them go. He hated the very thought of seeing the Englishman being led out of this narrow cell, where he had kept a watchful eye over him night and day for a fortnight, satisfied that with every day, every hour, the chances of escape became more improbable and more rare; at the same time there was the possibility of the recapture of little Capet, a possibility which made Heron's brain reel with the delightful vista of it, and which might never come about if the prisoner remained silent to the end.

"I wish I were quite sure," he said sullenly, "that you were body and soul in accord with me."

"I am in accord with you, citizen Heron," rejoined the other earnestly—"body and soul in accord with you. Do you not believe that I hate this man—aye! hate him with a hatred ten thousand times more strong than yours? I want his death—Heaven or hell alone know how I long for that—but what I long for most is his lasting disgrace. For that I have worked, citizen Heron—for that I advised and helped you. When first you captured this man you wanted summarily to try him, to send him to the guillotine amidst the joy of the populace of Paris, and crowned with a splendid halo of martyrdom. That man, citizen Heron, would have baffled you, mocked you, and fooled you even on the steps of the scaffold. In the zenith of his strength and of insurmountable good luck you and all your myrmidons and all the assembled guard of Paris would have had no power over him. The day that you led him out of this cell in order to take him to trial or to the guillotine would have been that of your hopeless discomfiture. Having once walked out of this cell hale, hearty and alert, be the escort round him ever so strong, he never would have re-entered it again. Of that I am as convinced as that I am alive. I know the man; you don't. Mine are not the only fingers through which he has slipped. Ask citizen Collot d'Herbois, ask Sergeant Bibot at the barrier of Menilmontant, ask General Santerre and his guards. They all have a tale to tell. Did I believe in God or the devil, I should also believe that this man has supernatural powers and a host of demons at his beck and call."

"Yet you talk now of letting him walk out of this cell to-morrow?"

"He is a different man now, citizen Heron. On my advice you placed him on a regime that has counteracted the supernatural power by simple physical exhaustion, and driven to the four winds the host of demons who no doubt fled in the face of starvation."

"If only I thought that the recapture of Capet was as vital to you as it is to me," said Heron, still unconvinced.

"The capture of Capet is just as vital to me as it is to you," rejoined Chauvelin earnestly, "if it is brought about through the instrumentality of the Englishman."

He paused, looking intently on his colleague, whose shifty eyes encountered his own. Thus eye to eye the two men at last understood one another.

"Ah!" said Heron with a snort, "I think I understand."

"I am sure that you do," responded Chauvelin dryly. "The disgrace of this cursed Scarlet Pimpernel and his League is as vital to me, and more, as the capture of Capet is to you. That is why I showed you the way how to bring that meddlesome adventurer to his knees; that is why I will help you now both to find Capet and with his aid and to wreak what reprisals you like on him in the end."

Heron before he spoke again cast one more look on the prisoner. The latter had not stirred; his face was hidden, but the hands, emaciated, nerveless and waxen, like those of the dead, told a more eloquent tale, mayhap, then than the eyes could do. The chief agent of the Committee of General Security walked deliberately round the table until he stood once more close beside the man from whom he longed with passionate ardour to wrest an all-important secret. With brutal, grimy hand he raised the head that lay, sunken and inert, against the table; with callous eyes he gazed attentively on the face that was then revealed to him, he looked on the waxen flesh, the hollow eyes, the bloodless lips; then he shrugged his wide shoulders, and with a laugh that surely must have caused joy in hell, he allowed the wearied head to fall back against the outstretched arms, and turned once again to his colleague.

"I think you are right, citizen Chauvelin," he said; "there is not much supernatural power here. Let me hear your advice."

# CHAPTER 37: CHAUVELIN'S ADVICE

Citizen Chauvelin had drawn his colleague with him to the end of the cell that was farthest away from the recess, and the table at which the prisoner was sitting.

Here the noise and hubbub that went on constantly in the guard room would effectually drown a whispered conversation. Chauvelin called to the sergeant to hand him a couple of chairs over the barrier. These he placed against the wall opposite the opening, and beckoning Heron to sit down, he did likewise, placing himself close to his colleague.

From where the two men now sat they could see both into the guard-room opposite them and into the recess at the furthermost end of the cell.

"First of all," began Chauvelin after a while, and sinking his voice to a whisper, "let me understand you thoroughly, citizen Heron. Do you want the death of the Englishman, either to-day or to-morrow, either in this prison or on the guillotine? For that now is easy of accomplishment; or do you want, above all, to get hold of little Capet?"

"It is Capet I want," growled Heron savagely under his breath. "Capet! Capet! My own neck is dependent on my finding Capet. Curse you, have I not told you that clearly enough?"

"You have told it me very clearly, citizen Heron; but I wished to make assurance doubly sure, and also make you understand that I, too, want the Englishman to betray little Capet into your hands. I want that more even than I do his death."

"Then in the name of hell, citizen, give me your advice."

"My advice to you, citizen Heron, is this: Give your prisoner now just a sufficiency of food to revive him—he will have had a few moments' sleep—and when he has eaten, and, mayhap, drunk a glass of wine, he will, no doubt, feel a recrudescence of strength, then give him pen and ink and paper. He must, as he says, write to one of his followers, who, in his turn, I suppose, will communicate with the others, bidding them to be prepared to deliver up little Capet to us; the letter must make it clear to that crowd of English gentlemen that their beloved chief is giving up the uncrowned King of France to us in exchange for his own safety. But I think you will agree with me, citizen Heron, that it would not be over-prudent on our part to allow that same gallant crowd to be forewarned too soon of the pro-posed doings of their chief. Therefore, I think, we'll explain to the prisoner that his follower, whom he will first apprise of his intentions, shall start with us to-morrow on our expedition, and accompany us until its last stage, when, if it is found necessary, he may be sent on ahead, strongly escorted of course, and with personal messages from the gallant Scarlet Pimpernel to the members of his League."

"What will be the good of that?" broke in Heron viciously. "Do you want one of his accursed followers to be ready to give him a helping hand on the way if he tries to slip through our fingers?

"Patience, patience, my good Heron!" rejoined Chauvelin with a placid smile. "Hear me out to the end. Time is precious. You shall offer what criticism you will when I have finished, but not before."

"Go on, then. I listen."

"I am not only proposing that one member of the Scarlet Pimpernel League shall accompany us to-morrow," continued Chauvelin, "but I would also force the prisoner's wife—Marguerite Blakeney—to follow in our train."

"A woman? Bah! What for?"

"I will tell you the reason of this presently. In her case I should not let the prisoner know beforehand that she too will form a part of our expedition. Let this come as a pleasing surprise for him. She could join us on our way out of Paris."

"How will you get hold of her?"

"Easily enough. I know where to find her. I traced her myself a few days ago to a house in the Rue de Charonne, and she is not likely to have gone away from Paris while her husband was at the Conciergerie. But this is a digression, let me proceed more consecutively. The letter, as I have said, being written to-night by the prisoner to one of his followers, I will myself see that it is delivered into the right hands. You, citizen Heron, will in the meanwhile make all arrangements for the journey. We ought to start at dawn, and we ought to be prepared, especially during the first fifty leagues of the way, against organised attack in case the Englishman leads us into an ambush."

"Yes. He might even do that, curse him!" muttered Heron.

"He might, but it is unlikely. Still it is best to be prepared. Take a strong escort, citizen, say twenty or thirty men, picked and trained soldiers who would make short work of civilians, however well-armed they might be. There are twenty members—including the chief—in that Scarlet Pimpernel League, and I do not quite see how from this cell the prisoner could organise an ambuscade against us at a given time. Anyhow, that is a matter for you to decide. I have still to place before you a scheme which is a measure of safety for ourselves and our men against ambush as well as against trickery, and which I feel sure you will pronounce quite adequate."

"Let me hear it, then!"

"The prisoner will have to travel by coach, of course. You can travel with him, if you like, and put him in irons, and thus avert all chances of his escaping on the road. But"—and here Chauvelin made a long pause, which had the effect of holding his colleague's attention still more closely—"remember that we shall have his wife and one of his friends with us. Before we finally leave Paris tomorrow we will explain to the prisoner that at the first attempt to escape on his part, at the slightest suspicion that he has tricked us for his own ends or is leading us into an ambush—at the slightest suspicion, I say—you, citizen Heron, will order his friend first, and then Marguerite Blakeney herself, to be summarily shot before his eyes."

Heron gave a long, low whistle. Instinctively he threw a furtive, backward glance at the prisoner, then he raised his shifty eyes to his colleague.

There was unbounded admiration expressed in them. One blackguard had met another—a greater one than himself—and was proud to acknowledge him as his master.

"By Lucifer, citizen Chauvelin," he said at last, "I should never have thought of such a thing myself."

Chauvelin put up his hand with a gesture of self-deprecation.

"I certainly think that measure ought to be adequate," he said with a gentle air of assumed modesty, "unless you would prefer to arrest the woman and lodge her here, keeping her here as an hostage."

"No, no!" said Heron with a gruff laugh; "that idea does not appeal to me nearly so much as the other. I should not feel so secure on the way. . . . I should always be thinking that that cursed woman had been allowed to escape. . . . No! no! I would rather keep her under my own eye—just as you suggest, citizen Chauvelin... and under the prisoner's, too," he added with a coarse jest. "If he did not actually see her, he might be more ready to try and save himself at her expense. But, of course, he could not see her shot before his eyes. It is a perfect plan, citizen, and does you infinite credit; and if the Englishman tricked us," he concluded with a fierce and savage oath, "and we did not find Capet at the end of the journey, I would gladly strangle his wife and his friend with my own hands."

"A satisfaction which I would not begrudge you, citizen," said Chauvelin dryly. "Perhaps you are right . . . the woman had best be kept under your own eye . . . the prisoner will never risk her safety on that, I would stake my life. We'll deliver our final 'either—or' the moment that she has joined our party, and before we start further on our way. Now, citizen Heron, you have heard my advice; are you prepared to follow it?"

"To the last letter," replied the other.

And their two hands met in a grasp of mutual understanding—two hands already indelibly stained with much innocent blood, more deeply stained now with seventeen past days of inhumanity and miserable treachery to come.

# CHAPTER 38: CAPITULATION

What occurred within the inner cell of the Conciergerie prison within the next half-hour of that 16th day of Pluviose in the year II of the Republic is, perhaps, too well known to history to need or bear overfull repetition.

Chroniclers intimate with the inner history of those infamous days have told us how the chief agent of the Committee of General Security gave orders one hour after midnight that hot soup, white bread and wine be served to the prisoner, who for close on fourteen days previously had been kept on short rations of black bread and water; the sergeant in charge of the guard-room watch for the night also received strict orders that that same prisoner was on no account to be disturbed until the hour of six in the morning, when he was to be served with anything in the way of breakfast that he might fancy.

All this we know, and also that citizen Heron, having given all necessary orders for the morning's expedition, returned to the Conciergerie, and found his colleague Chauvelin waiting for him in the guard-room.

"Well?" he asked with febrile impatience—"the prisoner?"

"He seems better and stronger," replied Chauvelin.

"Not too well, I hope?"

"No, no, only just well enough."

"You have seen him—since his supper?"

"Only from the doorway. It seems he ate and drank hardly at all, and the sergeant had some difficulty in keeping him awake until you came."

"Well, now for the letter," concluded Heron with the same marked feverishness of manner which sat so curiously on his uncouth personality. "Pen, ink and paper, sergeant!" he commanded.

"On the table, in the prisoner's cell, citizen," replied the sergeant.

He preceded the two citizens across the guard-room to the doorway, and raised for them the iron bar, lowering it back after them.

The next moment Heron and Chauvelin were once more face to face with their prisoner.

Whether by accident or design the lamp had been so placed that as the two men approached its light fell full upon their faces, while that of the prisoner remained in shadow. He was leaning forward with both elbows on the table, his thin, tapering fingers toying with the pen and ink-horn which had been placed close to his hand.

"I trust that everything has been arranged for your comfort, Sir Percy?" Chauvelin asked with a sarcastic little smile.

"I thank you, sir," replied Blakeney politely.

"You feel refreshed, I hope?"

"Greatly so, I assure you. But I am still demmed sleepy; and if you would kindly be brief—"

"You have not changed your mind, sir?" queried Chauvelin, and a note of anxiety, which he vainly tried to conceal, quivered in his voice.

"No, my good M. Chambertin," replied Blakeney with the same urbane courtesy, "I have not changed my mind."

A sigh of relief escaped the lips of both the men. The prisoner certainly had spoken in a clearer and firmer voice; but whatever renewed strength wine and food had imparted to him he apparently did not mean to employ in renewed obstinacy. Chauvelin, after a moment's pause, resumed more calmly:

"You are prepared to direct us to the place where little Capet lies hidden?"

"I am prepared to do anything, sir, to get out of this d—d hole."

"Very well. My colleague, citizen Heron, has arranged for an escort of twenty men picked from the best regiment of the Garde de Paris to accompany us—yourself, him and me—to wherever you will direct us. Is that clear?"

"Perfectly, sir."

"You must not imagine for a moment that we, on the other hand, guarantee to give you your life and freedom even if this expedition prove unsuccessful."

"I would not venture on suggesting such a wild proposition, sir," said Blakeney placidly.

Chauvelin looked keenly on him. There was something in the tone of that voice that he did not altogether like—something that reminded him of an evening at Calais, and yet again of a day at Boulogne. He could not read the expression in the eyes, so with a quick gesture he pulled the lamp forward so that its light now fell full on the face of the prisoner.

"Ah! that is certainly better, is it not, my dear M. Chambertin?" said Sir Percy, beaming on his adversary with a pleasant smile.

His face, though still of the same ashen hue, looked serene if hopelessly wearied; the eyes seemed to mock. But this Chauvelin decided in himself must have been a trick of his own overwrought fancy. After a brief moment's pause he resumed dryly:

"If, however, the expedition turns out successful in every way— if little Capet, without much trouble to our escort, falls safe and sound into our hands—if certain contingencies which I am about to tell you all fall out as we wish—then, Sir Percy, I see no reason why the Government of this country should not exercise its prerogative of mercy towards you after all."

"An exercise, my dear M. Chambertin, which must have

wearied through frequent repetition," retorted Blakeney with the same imperturbable smile.

"The contingency at present is somewhat remote; when the time comes we'll talk this matter over. . . . I will make no promise . . . and, anyhow, we can discuss it later."

"At present we are but wasting our valuable time over so trifling a matter. . . . If you'll excuse me, sir. . . . I am so demmed fatigued—"

"Then you will be glad to have everything settled quickly, I am sure."

"Exactly, sir."

Heron was taking no part in the present conversation. He knew that his temper was not likely to remain within bounds, and though he had nothing but contempt for his colleague's courtly manners, yet vaguely in his stupid, blundering way he grudgingly admitted that mayhap it was better to allow citizen Chauvelin to deal with the Englishman. There was always the danger that if his own violent temper got the better of him, he might even at this eleventh hour order this insolent prisoner to summary trial and the guillotine, and thus lose the final chance of the more important capture.

He was sprawling on a chair in his usual slouching manner with his big head sunk between his broad shoulders, his shifty, prominent eyes wandering restlessly from the face of his colleague to that of the other man.

But now he gave a grunt of impatience.

"We are wasting time, citizen Chauvelin," he muttered. "I have still a great deal to see to if we are to start at dawn. Get the d—d letter written, and—"

The rest of the phrase was lost in an indistinct and surly murmur. Chauvelin, after a shrug of the shoulders, paid no further heed to him; he turned, bland and urbane, once more to the prisoner.

"I see with pleasure, Sir Percy," he said, "that we thoroughly understand one another. Having had a few hours' rest you will, I know, feel quite ready for the expedition. Will you kindly indicate to me the direction in which we will have to travel?"

"Northwards all the way."

"Towards the coast?"

"The place to which we must go is about seven leagues from the sea."

"Our first objective then will be Beauvais, Amiens, Abbeville, Crecy, and so on?"

"Precisely."

"As far as the forest of Boulogne, shall we say?"

"Where we shall come off the beaten track, and you will have to trust to my guidance."

"We might go there now, Sir Percy, and leave you here."

"You might. But you would not then find the child. Seven leagues is not far from the coast. He might slip through your fingers."

"And my colleague Heron, being disappointed, would inevitably send you to the guillotine."

"Quite so," rejoined the prisoner placidly. "Methought, sir, that we had decided that I should lead this little expedition? Surely," he added, "it is not so much the Dauphin whom you want as my share in this betrayal."

"You are right as usual, Sir Percy. Therefore let us take that as settled. We go as far as Crecy, and thence place ourselves entirely in your hands."

"The journey should not take more than three days, sir."

"During which you will travel in a coach in the company of my friend Heron."

"I could have chosen pleasanter company, sir; still, it will serve."

"This being settled, Sir Percy. I understand that you desire to communicate with one of your followers."

"Some one must let the others know . . . those who have the Dauphin in their charge."

"Quite so. Therefore I pray you write to one of your friends that you have decided to deliver the Dauphin into our hands in exchange for your own safety."

"You said just now that this you would not guarantee," interposed Blakeney quietly.

"If all turns out well," retorted Chauvelin with a show of contempt, "and if you will write the exact letter which I shall dictate, we might even give you that guarantee."

"The quality of your mercy, sir, passes belief."

"Then I pray you write. Which of your followers will have the honour of the communication?"

"My brother-in-law, Armand St. Just; he is still in Paris, I believe. He can let the others know."

Chauvelin made no immediate reply. He paused awhile, hesitating. Would Sir Percy Blakeney be ready—if his own safety demanded it—to sacrifice the man who had betrayed him? In the momentous "either—or" that was to be put to him, by-and-by, would he choose his own life and leave Armand St. Just to perish? It was not for Chauvelin—or any man of his stamp—to judge of what Blakeney would do under such circumstances, and had it been a question of St. Just alone, mayhap Chauvelin would have hesitated still more at the present juncture.

But the friend as hostage was only destined to be a minor leverage for the final breaking-up of the League of the Scarlet Pimpernel through the disgrace of its chief. There was the wife—

Marguerite Blakeney—sister of St. Just, joint and far more important hostage, whose very close affection for her brother might prove an additional trump card in that handful which Chauvelin already held.

Blakeney paid no heed seemingly to the other's hesitation. He did not even look up at him, but quietly drew pen and paper towards him, and made ready to write.

"What do you wish me to say?" he asked simply.

"Will that young blackguard answer your purpose, citizen Chauvelin?" queried Heron roughly.

Obviously the same doubt had crossed his mind. Chauvelin quickly re-assured him.

"Better than any one else," he said firmly. "Will you write at my dictation, Sir Percy?

"I am waiting to do so, my dear sir."

"Begin your letter as you wish, then; now continue."

And he began to dictate slowly, watching every word as it left Blakeney's pen.

"'I cannot stand my present position any longer. Citizen Heron, and also M. Chauvelin—' Yes, Sir Percy, Chauvelin, not Chambertin . . . C, H, A, U, V, E, L, I, N. . . . That is quite right— 'have made this prison a perfect hell for me.'"

Sir Percy looked up from his writing, smiling.

"You wrong yourself, my dear M. Chambertin!" he said; "I have really been most comfortable."

"I wish to place the matter before your friends in as indulgent a manner as I can," retorted Chauvelin dryly.

"I thank you, sir. Pray proceed."

" . . . a perfect hell for me,'" resumed the other. "Have you that? . . . 'and I have been forced to give way. To-morrow we start from here at dawn; and I will guide citizen Heron to the place where he can find the Dauphin. But the authorities demand that one of my followers, one who has once been a member of the League of the Scarlet Pimpernel, shall accompany me on this expedition. I therefore ask you'—or 'desire you' or 'beg you'—whichever you prefer, Sir Percy..."

"'Ask you' will do quite nicely. This is really very interesting, you know."

" . . . 'to be prepared to join the expedition. We start at dawn, and you would be required to be at the main gate of the house of Justice at six o'clock precisely. I have an assurance from the authorities that your life should be in-violate, but if you refuse to accompany me, the guillotine will await me on the morrow.'"

"'The guillotine will await me on the morrow.' That sounds quite cheerful, does it not, M. Chambertin?" said the prisoner, who had not evinced the slightest surprise at the wording of the letter whilst he wrote at the other's dictation. "Do you know, I quite enjoyed writing this letter; it so reminded me of happy days in Boulogne."

Chauvelin pressed his lips together. Truly now he felt that a retort from him would have been undignified, more especially as just at this moment there came from the guard room the sound of men's voices talking and laughing, the occasional clang of steel, or of a heavy boot against the tiled floor, the rattling of dice, or a sudden burst of laughter—sounds, in fact, that betokened the presence of a number of soldiers close by.

Chauvelin contented himself with a nod in the direction of the guard-room.

"The conditions are somewhat different now," he said placidly, "from those that reigned in Boulogne. But will you not sign your letter, Sir Percy?"

"With pleasure, sir," responded Blakeney, as with an elaborate flourish of the pen he appended his name to the missive.

Chauvelin was watching him with eyes that would have shamed a lynx by their keenness. He took up the completed letter, read it through very carefully, as if to find some hidden meaning behind the very words which he himself had dictated; he studied the signature, and looked vainly for a mark or a sign that might convey a different sense to that which he had intended. Finally, finding none, he folded the letter up with his own hand, and at once slipped it in the pocket of his coat.

"Take care, M. Chambertin," said Blakeney lightly; "it will burn a hole in that elegant vest of yours."

"It will have no time to do that, Sir Percy," retorted Chauvelin blandly; "an you will furnish me with citizen St. Just's present address, I will myself convey the letter to him at once."

"At this hour of the night? Poor old Armand, he'll be abed. But his address, sir, is No. 32, Rue de la Croix Blanche, on the first floor, the door on your right as you mount the stairs; you know the room well, citizen Chauvelin; you have been in it before. And now," he added with a loud and ostentatious yawn, "shall we all to bed? We start at dawn, you said, and I am so d—d fatigued."

Frankly, he did not look it now. Chauvelin himself, despite his matured plans, despite all the precautions that he meant to take for the success of this gigantic scheme, felt a sudden strange sense of fear creeping into his bones. Half an hour ago he had seen a man in what looked like the last stage of utter physical exhaustion, a hunched up figure, listless and limp, hands that twitched nervously, the face as of a dying man. Now those outward symptoms were still there certainly; the face by the light of the lamp still looked livid, the lips bloodless, the hands emaciated and waxen, but the eyes!—they were still hollow, with heavy lids still purple, but in their depths there was a curious, mysterious light, a look that seemed to see something that was hidden to natural sight.

Citizen Chauvelin thought that Heron, too, must be conscious of this, but the Committee's agent was sprawling on a chair, sucking a short-stemmed pipe, and gazing with entire animal satisfaction on the prisoner.

"The most perfect piece of work we have ever accomplished, you and I, citizen Chauvelin," he said complacently.

"You think that everything is quite satisfactory?" asked the other with anxious stress on his words.

"Everything, of course. Now you see to the letter. I will give final orders for to-morrow, but I shall sleep in the guard-room."

"And I on that inviting bed," interposed the prisoner lightly, as he rose to his feet. "Your servant, citizens!"

He bowed his head slightly, and stood by the table whilst the two men prepared to go. Chauvelin took a final long look at the man whom he firmly believed he had at last brought down to abject disgrace.

Blakeney was standing erect, watching the two retreating figures—one slender hand was on the table. Chauvelin saw that it was leaning rather heavily, as if for support, and that even whilst a final mocking laugh sped him and his colleague on their way, the tall figure of the conquered lion swayed like a stalwart oak that is forced to bend to the mighty fury of an all-compelling wind.

With a sigh of content Chauvelin took his colleague by the arm, and together the two men walked out of the cell.

# CHAPTER 39: KILL HIM!

Two hours after midnight Armand St. Just was wakened from sleep by a peremptory pull at his bell. In these days in Paris but one meaning could as a rule be attached to such a summons at this hour of the night, and Armand, though possessed of an unconditional certificate of safety, sat up in bed, quite convinced that for some reason which would presently be explained to him he had once more been placed on the list of the "suspect," and that his trial and condemnation on a trumped-up charge would follow in due course.

Truth to tell, he felt no fear at the prospect, and only a very little sorrow. The sorrow was not for himself; he regretted neither life nor happiness. Life had become hateful to him since happiness had fled with it on the dark wings of dishonour; sorrow such as he felt was only for Jeanne! She was very young, and would weep bitter tears. She would be unhappy, because she truly loved him, and because this would be the first cup of bitterness which life was holding out to her. But she was very young, and sorrow would not be eternal. It was better so. He, Armand St. Just, though he loved her with an intensity of passion that had been magnified and strengthened by his own overwhelming shame, had never really brought his beloved one single moment of unalloyed happiness.

From the very first day when he sat beside her in the tiny boudoir of the Square du Roule, and the heavy foot fall of Heron and his bloodhounds broke in on their first kiss, down to this hour which he believed struck his own death-knell, his love for her had brought more tears to her dear eyes than smiles to her exquisite mouth.

Her he had loved so dearly, that for her sweet sake he had sacrificed honour, friendship and truth; to free her, as he believed, from the hands of impious brutes he had done a deed that cried Cain-like for vengeance to the very throne of God. For her he had sinned, and because of that sin, even before it was committed, their love had been blighted, and happiness had never been theirs.

Now it was all over. He would pass out of her life, up the steps of the scaffold, tasting as he mounted them the most entire happiness that he had known since that awful day when he became a Judas.

The peremptory summons, once more repeated, roused him from his meditations. He lit a candle, and without troubling to slip any of his clothes on, he crossed the narrow ante-chamber, and opened the door that gave on the landing.

"In the name of the people!"

He had expected to hear not only those words, but also the

grounding of arms and the brief command to halt. He had expected to see before him the white facings of the uniform of the Garde de Paris, and to feel himself roughly pushed back into his lodging preparatory to the search being made of all his effects and the placing of irons on his wrists.

Instead of this, it was a quiet, dry voice that said without undue harshness:

"In the name of the people!"

And instead of the uniforms, the bayonets and the scarlet caps with tricolour cockades, he was confronted by a slight, sable-clad figure, whose face, lit by the flickering light of the tallow candle, looked strangely pale and earnest.

"Citizen Chauvelin!" gasped Armand, more surprised than frightened at this unexpected apparition.

"Himself, citizen, at your service," replied Chauvelin with his quiet, ironical manner. "I am the bearer of a letter for you from Sir Percy Blakeney. Have I your permission to enter?"

Mechanically Armand stood aside, allowing the other man to pass in. He closed the door behind his nocturnal visitor, then, taper in hand, he preceded him into the inner room.

It was the same one in which a fortnight ago a fighting lion had been brought to his knees. Now it lay wrapped in gloom, the feeble light of the candle only lighting Armand's face and the white frill of his shirt. The young man put the taper down on the table and turned to his visitor.

"Shall I light the lamp?" he asked.

"Quite unnecessary," replied Chauvelin curtly. "I have only a letter to deliver, and after that to ask you one brief question."

From the pocket of his coat he drew the letter which Blakeney had written an hour ago.

"The prisoner wrote this in my presence," he said as he handed the letter over to Armand. "Will you read it?"

Armand took it from him, and sat down close to the table; leaning forward he held the paper near the light, and began to read. He read the letter through very slowly to the end, then once again from the beginning. He was trying to do that which Chauvelin had wished to do an hour ago; he was trying to find the inner meaning which he felt must inevitably lie behind these words which Percy had written with his own hand.

That these bare words were but a blind to deceive the enemy Armand never doubted for a moment. In this he was as loyal as Marguerite would have been herself. Never for a moment did the suspicion cross his mind that Blakeney was about to play the part of a coward, but he, Armand, felt that as a faithful friend and follower he ought by instinct to know exactly what his chief intended, what he meant him to do.

Swiftly his thoughts flew back to that other letter, the one which Marguerite had given him—the letter full of pity and of friendship which had brought him hope and a joy and peace which he had thought at one time that he would never know again. And suddenly one sentence in that letter stood out so clearly before his eyes that it blurred the actual, tangible ones on the paper which even now rustled in his hand.

But if at any time you receive another letter from me—be its contents what they may—act in accordance with the letter, but send a copy of it at once to Ffoulkes or to Marguerite.

Now everything seemed at once quite clear; his duty, his next actions, every word that he would speak to Chauvelin. Those that Percy had written to him were already indelibly graven on his memory.

Chauvelin had waited with his usual patience, silent and imperturbable, while the young man read. Now when he saw that Armand had finished, he said quietly:

"Just one question, citizen, and I need not detain you longer. But first will you kindly give me back that letter? It is a precious document which will for ever remain in the archives of the nation."

But even while he spoke Armand, with one of those quick intuitions that come in moments of acute crisis, had done just that which he felt Blakeney would wish him to do. He had held the letter close to the candle. A corner of the thin crisp paper immediately caught fire, and before Chauvelin could utter a word of anger, or make a movement to prevent the conflagration, the flames had licked up fully one half of the letter, and Armand had only just time to throw the remainder on the floor and to stamp out the blaze with his foot.

"I am sorry, citizen," he said calmly; "an accident."

"A useless act of devotion," interposed Chauvelin, who already had smothered the oath that had risen to his lips. "The Scarlet Pimpernel's actions in the present matter will not lose their merited publicity through the foolish destruction of this document."

"I had no thought, citizen," retorted the young man, "of commenting on the actions of my chief, or of trying to deny them that publicity which you seem to desire for them almost as much as I do."

"More, citizen, a great deal more! The impeccable Scarlet Pimpernel, the noble and gallant English gentleman, has agreed to deliver into our hands the uncrowned King of France—in exchange for his own life and freedom. Methinks that even his worst enemy would not wish for a better ending to a career of adventure, and a reputation for bravery unequalled in Europe. But no more of this, time is pressing, I must help citizen Heron with his final preparations for his journey. You, of course, citizen St. Just, will act in accordance with Sir Percy Blakeney's wishes?"

"Of course," replied Armand.

"You will present yourself at the main entrance of the house of Justice at six o'clock this morning."

"I will not fail you."

"A coach will be provided for you. You will follow the expedition as hostage for the good faith of your chief."

"I quite understand."

"H'm! That's brave! You have no fear, citizen St. Just?"

"Fear of what, sir?

"You will be a hostage in our hands, citizen; your life a guarantee that your chief has no thought of playing us false. Now I was thinking of—of certain events—which led to the arrest of Sir Percy Blakeney."

"Of my treachery, you mean," rejoined the young man calmly, even though his face had suddenly become pale as death. "Of the damnable lie wherewith you cheated me into selling my honour, and made me what I am—a creature scarce fit to walk upon this earth."

"Oh!" protested Chauvelin blandly.

"The damnable lie," continued Armand more vehemently, "that hath made me one with Cain and the Iscariot. When you goaded me into the hellish act, Jeanne Lange was already free."

"Free—but not safe."

"A lie, man! A lie! For which you are thrice accursed. Great God, is it not you that should have cause for fear? Methinks were I to strangle you now I should suffer less of remorse."

"And would be rendering your ex-chief but a sorry service," interposed Chauvelin with quiet irony. "Sir Percy Blakeney is a dying man, citizen St. Just; he'll be a dead man at dawn if I do not put in an appearance by six o'clock this morning. This is a private understanding between citizen Heron and myself. We agreed to it before I came to see you."

"Oh, you take care of your own miserable skin well enough! But you need not be afraid of me—I take my orders from my chief, and he has not ordered me to kill you."

"That was kind of him. Then we may count on you? You are not afraid?"

"Afraid that the Scarlet Pimpernel would leave me in the lurch because of the immeasurable wrong I have done to him?" retorted Armand, proud and defiant in the name of his chief. "No, sir, I am not afraid of that; I have spent the last fortnight in praying to God that my life might yet be given for his."

"H'm! I think it most unlikely that your prayers will be granted, citizen; prayers, I imagine, so very seldom are; but I don't know, I never pray myself. In your case, now, I should say that you have not the slightest chance of the Deity interfering in so pleasant a manner. Even were Sir Percy Blakeney prepared to wreak personal revenge on you, he would scarcely be so foolish as to risk the other life which we shall also hold as hostage for his good faith."

"The other life?"

"Yes. Your sister, Lady Blakeney, will also join the expedition to-morrow. This Sir Percy does not yet know; but it will come as a pleasant surprise for him. At the slightest suspicion of false play on Sir Percy's part, at his slightest attempt at escape, your life and that of your sister are forfeit; you will both be summarily shot before his eyes. I do not think that I need be more precise, eh, citizen St. Just?"

The young man was quivering with passion. A terrible loathing for himself, for his crime which had been the precursor of this terrible situation, filled his soul to the verge of sheer physical nausea. A red film gathered before his eyes, and through it he saw the grinning face of the inhuman monster who had planned this hideous, abominable thing. It seemed to him as if in the silence and the hush of the night, above the feeble, flickering flame that threw weird shadows around, a group of devils were surrounding him, and were shouting, "Kill him! Kill him now! Rid the earth of this hellish brute!"

No doubt if Chauvelin had exhibited the slightest sign of fear, if he had moved an inch towards the door, Armand, blind with passion, driven to madness by agonising remorse more even than by rage, would have sprung at his enemy's throat and crushed the life out of him as he would out of a venomous beast. But the man's calm, his immobility, recalled St. Just to himself. Reason, that had almost yielded to passion again, found strength to drive the enemy back this time, to whisper a warning, an admonition, even a reminder. Enough harm, God knows, had been done by tempestuous passion already. And God alone knew what terrible consequences its triumph now might bring in its trial, and striking on Armand's buzzing ears Chauvelin's words came back as a triumphant and mocking echo:

"He'll be a dead man at dawn if I do not put in an appearance by six o'clock."

The red film lifted, the candle flickered low, the devils vanished, only the pale face of the Terrorist gazed with gentle irony out of the gloom.

"I think that I need not detain you any longer, citizen, St. Just," he said quietly; "you can get three or four hours' rest yet before you need make a start, and I still have a great many things to see to. I wish you good-night, citizen."

"Good-night," murmured Armand mechanically.

He took the candle and escorted his visitor back to the door. He waited on the landing, taper in hand, while Chauvelin descended the narrow, winding stairs.

There was a light in the concierge's lodge. No doubt the woman had struck it when the nocturnal visitor had first demanded admittance. His name and tricolour scarf of office had ensured him the full measure of her attention, and now she was evidently sitting up waiting to let him out.

St. Just, satisfied that Chauvelin had finally gone, now turned back to his own rooms.

# CHAPTER 40: GOD HELP US ALL

He carefully locked the outer door. Then he lit the lamp, for the candle gave but a flickering light, and he had some important work to do.

Firstly, he picked up the charred fragment of the letter, and smoothed it out carefully and reverently as he would a relic. Tears had gathered in his eyes, but he was not ashamed of them, for no one saw them; but they eased his heart, and helped to strengthen his resolve. It was a mere fragment that had been spared by the flame, but Armand knew every word of the letter by heart.

He had pen, ink and paper ready to his hand, and from memory wrote out a copy of it. To this he added a covering letter from himself to Marguerite:

This—which I had from Percy through the hands of Chauvelin—I neither question nor understand. . . . He wrote the letter, and I have no thought but to obey. In his previous letter to me he enjoined me, if ever he wrote to me again, to obey him implicitly, and to communicate with you. To both these commands do I submit with a glad heart. But of this must I give you warning, little mother—Chauvelin desires you also to accompany us to-morrow. . . . Percy does not know this yet, else he would never start. But those fiends fear that his readiness is a blind... and that he has some plan in his head for his own escape and the continued safety of the Dauphin. . . . This plan they hope to frustrate through holding you and me as hostages for his good faith. God only knows how gladly I would give my life for my chief... but your life, dear little mother... is sacred above all. . . . I think that I do right in warning you. God help us all.

Having written the letter, he sealed it, together with the copy of Percy's letter which he had made. Then he took up the candle and went downstairs.

There was no longer any light in the concierge's lodge, and Armand had some difficulty in making himself heard. At last the woman came to the door. She was tired and cross after two interruptions of her night's rest, but she had a partiality for her young lodger, whose pleasant ways and easy liberality had been like a pale ray of sunshine through the squalor of every-day misery.

"It is a letter, citoyenne," said Armand, with earnest entreaty, "for my sister. She lives in the Rue de Charonne, near the fortifications, and must have it within an hour; it is a matter of life and death to her, to me, and to another who is very dear to us both."

The concierge threw up her hands in horror.

"Rue de Charonne, near the fortifications," she exclaimed, "and within an hour! By the Holy Virgin, citizen, that is impossible. Who will take it? There is no way."

"A way must be found, citoyenne," said Armand firmly, "and at once; it is not far, and there are five golden louis waiting for the messenger!"

Five golden louis! The poor, hardworking woman's eyes gleamed at the thought. Five louis meant food for at least two months if one was careful, and—

"Give me the letter, citizen," she said, "time to slip on a warm petticoat and a shawl, and I'll go myself. It's not fit for the boy to go at this hour."

"You will bring me back a line from my sister in reply to this," said Armand, whom circumstances had at last rendered cautious. "Bring it up to my rooms that I may give you the five louis in exchange."

He waited while the woman slipped back into her room. She heard him speaking to her boy; the same lad who a fortnight ago had taken the treacherous letter which had lured Blakeney to the house into the fatal ambuscade that had been prepared for him. Everything reminded Armand of that awful night, every hour that he had since spent in the house had been racking torture to him. Now at last he was to leave it, and on an errand which might help to ease the load of remorse from his heart.

The woman was soon ready. Armand gave her final directions as to how to find the house; then she took the letter and promised to be very quick, and to bring back a reply from the lady.

Armand accompanied her to the door. The night was dark, a thin drizzle was falling; he stood and watched until the woman's rapidly walking figure was lost in the misty gloom.

Then with a heavy sigh he once more went within.

# CHAPTER 41: WHEN HOPE WAS DEAD

In a small upstairs room in the Rue de Charonne, above the shop of Lucas the old-clothes dealer, Marguerite sat with Sir Andrew Ffoulkes. Armand's letter, with its message and its warning, lay open on the table between them, and she had in her hand the sealed packet which Percy had given her just ten days ago, and which she was only to open if all hope seemed to be dead, if nothing appeared to stand any longer between that one dear life and irretrievable shame.

A small lamp placed on the table threw a feeble yellow light on the squalid, ill-furnished room, for it lacked still an hour or so before dawn. Armand's concierge had brought her lodger's letter, and Marguerite had quickly despatched a brief reply to him, a reply that held love and also encouragement.

Then she had summoned Sir Andrew. He never had a thought of leaving her during these days of dire trouble, and he had lodged all this while in a tiny room on the top-most floor of this house in the Rue de Charonne.

At her call he had come down very quickly, and now they sat together at the table, with the oil-lamp illumining their pale, anxious faces; she the wife and he the friend holding a consultation together in this most miserable hour that preceded the cold wintry dawn.

Outside a thin, persistent rain mixed with snow pattered against the small window panes, and an icy wind found out all the crevices in the worm-eaten woodwork that would afford it ingress to the room. But neither Marguerite nor Ffoulkes was conscious of the cold. They had wrapped their cloaks round their shoulders, and did not feel the chill currents of air that caused the lamp to flicker and to smoke.

"I can see now," said Marguerite in that calm voice which comes so naturally in moments of infinite despair—"I can see now exactly what Percy meant when he made me promise not to open this packet until it seemed to me—to me and to you, Sir Andrew—that he was about to play the part of a coward. A coward! Great God!" She checked the sob that had risen to her throat, and continued in the same calm manner and quiet, even voice:

"You do think with me, do you not, that the time has come, and that we must open this packet?"

"Without a doubt, Lady Blakeney," replied Ffoulkes with equal earnestness. "I would stake my life that already a fortnight ago Blakeney had that same plan in his mind which he has now matured. Escape from that awful Conciergerie prison with all the precautions so carefully taken against it was impossible. I knew that alas! from the first. But in the open all might yet be different. I'll not believe it that a man like Blakeney is destined to perish at the hands of those curs."

She looked on her loyal friend with tear-dimmed eyes through which shone boundless gratitude and heart-broken sorrow.

He had spoken of a fortnight! It was ten days since she had seen Percy. It had then seemed as if death had already marked him with its grim sign. Since then she had tried to shut away from her mind the terrible visions which her anguish constantly conjured up before her of his growing weakness, of the gradual impairing of that brilliant intellect, the gradual exhaustion of that mighty physical strength.

"God bless you, Sir Andrew, for your enthusiasm and for your trust," she said with a sad little smile; "but for you I should long ago have lost all courage, and these last ten days—what a cycle of misery they represent—would have been maddening but for your help and your loyalty. God knows I would have courage for everything in life, for everything save one, but just that, his death; that would be beyond my strength—neither reason nor body could stand it. Therefore, I am so afraid, Sir Andrew," she added piteously.

"Of what, Lady Blakeney?"

"That when he knows that I too am to go as hostage, as Armand says in his letter, that my life is to be guarantee his, I am afraid that he will draw back—that he will—my God!" she cried with sudden fervour, "tell me what to do!"

"Shall we open the packet?" asked Ffoulkes gently, "and then just make up our minds to act exactly as Blakeney has enjoined us to do, neither more nor less, but just word for word, deed for deed, and I believe that that will be right—whatever may betide—in the end."

Once more his quiet strength, his earnestness and his faith comforted her. She dried her eyes and broke open the seal. There were two separate letters in the packet, one unaddressed, obviously intended for her and Ffoulkes, the other was addressed to M. le baron Jean de Batz, 15, Rue St. Jean de Latran a Paris.

"A letter addressed to that awful Baron de Batz," said Marguerite, looking with puzzled eyes on the paper as she turned it over and over in her hand, "to that bombastic windbag! I know him and his ways well! What can Percy have to say to him?"

Sir Andrew too looked puzzled. But neither of them had the mind to waste time in useless speculations. Marguerite unfolded the letter which was intended for her, and after a final look on her friend, whose kind face was quivering with excitement, she began slowly to read aloud:

I need not ask either of you two to trust me, knowing that you will. But I could not die inside this hole like a rat in a trap—I had to try and free myself, at the worst to die in the open beneath God's sky. You two will understand, and understanding you will trust me to the end.

Send the enclosed letter at once to its address. And you, Ffoulkes, my most sincere and most loyal friend, I beg with all my soul to see to the safety of Marguerite. Armand will stay by me—but you, Ffoulkes, do not leave her, stand by her. As soon as you read this letter—and you will not read it until both she and you have felt that hope has fled and I myself am about to throw up the sponge—try and persuade her to make for the coast as quickly as may be. . . . At Calais you can open up communications with the Day-Dream in the usual way, and embark on her at once. Let no member of the League remain on French soil one hour longer after that. Then tell the skipper to make for Le Portel—the place which he knows—and there to keep a sharp outlook for another three nights. After that make straight for home, for it will be no use waiting any longer. I shall not come. These measures are for Marguerite's safety, and for you all who are in France at this moment. Comrade, I entreat you to look on these measures as on my dying wish. To de Batz I have given rendezvous at the Chapelle of the Holy Sepulchre, just outside the park of the Chateau d'Ourde. He will help me to save the Dauphin, and if by good luck he also helps me to save myself I shall be within seven leagues of Le Portel, and with the Liane frozen as she is I could reach the coast.

But Marguerite's safety I leave in your hands, Ffoulkes. Would that I could look more clearly into the future, and know that those devils will not drag her into danger. Beg her to start at once for Calais immediately you have both read this. I only beg, I do not command. I know that you, Ffoulkes, will stand by her whatever she may wish to do. God's blessing be for ever on you both.

Marguerite's voice died away in the silence that still lay over this deserted part of the great city and in this squalid house where she and Sir Andrew Ffoulkes had found shelter these last ten days. The agony of mind which they had here endured, never doubting, but scarcely ever hoping, had found its culmination at last in this final message, which almost seemed to come to them from the grave.

It had been written ten days ago. A plan had then apparently formed in Percy's mind which he had set forth during the brief half-hour's respite which those fiends had once given him. Since then they had never given him ten consecutive minutes' peace; since then ten days had gone by how much power, how much vitality had gone by too on the leaden wings of all those terrible hours spent in solitude and in misery?

"We can but hope, Lady Blakeney," said Sir Andrew Ffoulkes after a while, "that you will be allowed out of Paris; but from what Armand says—"

"And Percy does not actually send me away," she rejoined with a pathetic little smile.

"No. He cannot compel you, Lady Blakeney. You are not a

member of the League."

"Oh, yes, I am!" she retorted firmly; "and I have sworn obedience, just as all of you have done. I will go, just as he bids me, and you, Sir Andrew, you will obey him too?"

"My orders are to stand by you. That is an easy task."

"You know where this place is?" she asked—"the Chateau d'Ourde?"

"Oh, yes, we all know it! It is empty, and the park is a wreck; the owner fled from it at the very outbreak of the revolution; he left some kind of steward nominally in charge, a curious creature, half imbecile; the chateau and the chapel in the forest just outside the grounds have oft served Blakeney and all of us as a place of refuge on our way to the coast."

"But the Dauphin is not there?" she said.

"No. According to the first letter which you brought me from Blakeney ten days ago, and on which I acted, Tony, who has charge of the Dauphin, must have crossed into Holland with his little Majesty to-day."

"I understand," she said simply. "But then—this letter to de Batz?"

"Ah, there I am completely at sea! But I'll deliver it, and at once too, only I don't like to leave you. Will you let me get you out of Paris first? I think just before dawn it could be done. We can get the cart from Lucas, and if we could reach St. Germain before noon, I could come straight back then and deliver the letter to de Batz. This, I feel, I ought to do myself; but at Achard's farm I would know that you were safe for a few hours."

"I will do whatever you think right, Sir Andrew," she said simply; "my will is bound up with Percy's dying wish. God knows I would rather follow him now, step by step,—as hostage, as prisoner— any way so long as I can see him, but—"

She rose and turned to go, almost impassive now in that great calm born of despair.

A stranger seeing her now had thought her indifferent. She was very pale, and deep circles round her eyes told of sleepless nights and days of mental misery, but otherwise there was not the faintest outward symptom of that terrible anguish which was rending her heartstrings. Her lips did not quiver, and the source of her tears had been dried up ten days ago.

"Ten minutes and I'll be ready, Sir Andrew," she said. "I have but few belongings. Will you the while see Lucas about the cart?"

He did as she desired. Her calm in no way deceived him; he knew that she must be suffering keenly, and would suffer more keenly still while she would be trying to efface her own personal feelings all through that coming dreary journey to Calais.

He went to see the landlord about the horse and cart, and a quarter of an hour later Marguerite came downstairs ready to start. She found Sir Andrew in close converse with an officer of the Garde de Paris, whilst two soldiers of the same regiment were standing at the horse's head.

When she appeared in the doorway Sir Andrew came at once up to her.

"It is just as I feared, Lady Blakeney," he said; "this man has been sent here to take charge of you. Of course, he knows nothing beyond the fact that his orders are to convey you at once to the guard-house of the Rue Ste. Anne, where he is to hand you over to citizen Chauvelin of the Committee of Public Safety."

Sir Andrew could not fail to see the look of intense relief which, in the midst of all her sorrow, seemed suddenly to have lighted up the whole of Marguerite's wan face. The thought of wending her own way to safety whilst Percy, mayhap, was fighting an uneven fight with death had been well-nigh intolerable; but she had been ready to obey without a murmur. Now Fate and the enemy himself had decided otherwise. She felt as if a load had been lifted from her heart.

"I will at once go and find de Batz," Sir Andrew contrived to whisper hurriedly. "As soon as Percy's letter is safely in his hands I will make my way northwards and communicate with all the members of the League, on whom the chief has so strictly enjoined to quit French soil immediately. We will proceed to Calais first and open up communication with the Day-Dream in the usual way. The others had best embark on board her, and the skipper shall then make for the known spot of Le Portel, of which Percy speaks in his letter. I myself will go by land to Le Portel, and thence, if I have no news of you or of the expedition, I will slowly work southwards in the direction of the Chateau d'Ourde. That is all that I can do. If you can contrive to let Percy or even Armand know my movements, do so by all means. I know that I shall be doing right, for, in a way, I shall be watching over you and arranging for your safety, as Blakeney begged me to do. God bless you, Lady Blakeney, and God save the Scarlet Pimpernel!"

He stooped and kissed her hand, and she intimated to the officer that she was ready. He had a hackney coach waiting for her lower down the street. To it she walked with a firm step, and as she entered it she waved a last farewell to Sir Andrew Ffoulkes.

# CHAPTER 42: THE GUARD-HOUSE
## THE RUE STE. ANNE

The little cortege was turning out of the great gates of the house of Justice. It was intensely cold; a bitter north-easterly gale was blowing from across the heights of Montmartre, driving sleet and snow and half-frozen rain into the faces of the men, and finding its way up their sleeves, down their collars and round the knees of their threadbare breeches.

Armand, whose fingers were numb with the cold, could scarcely feel the reins in his hands. Chauvelin was riding close beside him, but the two men had not exchanged one word since the moment when the small troop of some twenty mounted soldiers had filed up inside the courtyard, and Chauvelin, with a curt word of command, had ordered one of the troopers to take Armand's horse on the lead.

A hackney coach brought up the rear of the cortege, with a man riding at either door and two more following at a distance of twenty paces. Heron's gaunt, ugly face, crowned with a battered, sugar-loaf hat, appeared from time to time at the window of the coach. He was no horseman, and, moreover, preferred to keep the prisoner closely under his own eye. The corporal had told Armand that the prisoner was with citizen Heron inside the coach—in irons. Beyond that the soldiers could tell him nothing; they knew nothing of the object of this expedition. Vaguely they might have wondered in their dull minds why this particular prisoner was thus being escorted out of the Conciergerie prison with so much paraphernalia and such an air of mystery, when there were thousands of prisoners in the city and the provinces at the present moment who anon would be bundled up wholesale into carts to be dragged to the guillotine like a flock of sheep to the butchers.

But even if they wondered they made no remarks among themselves. Their faces, blue with the cold, were the perfect mirrors of their own unconquerable stolidity.

The tower clock of Notre Dame struck seven when the small cavalcade finally moved slowly out of the monumental gates. In the east the wan light of a February morning slowly struggled out of the surrounding gloom. Now the towers of many churches loomed ghostlike against the dull grey sky, and down below, on the right, the frozen river, like a smooth sheet of steel, wound its graceful curves round the islands and past the facade of the Louvres palace, whose walls looked grim and silent, like the mausoleum of the dead giants of the past.

All around the great city gave signs of awakening; the business of the day renewed its course every twenty-four hours, despite the tragedies of death and of dishonour that walked with it hand in hand. From the Place de La Revolution the intermittent roll of drums came from time to time with its muffled sound striking the ear of the passer-by. Along the quay opposite an open-air camp was already astir; men, women, and children engaged in the great task of clothing and feeding the people of France, armed against tyranny, were bending to their task, even before the wintry dawn had spread its pale grey tints over the narrower streets of the city.

Armand shivered under his cloak. This silent ride beneath the laden sky, through the veil of half-frozen rain and snow, seemed like a dream to him. And now, as the outriders of the little cavalcade turned to cross the Pont au Change, he saw spread out on his left what appeared like the living panorama of these three weeks that had just gone by. He could see the house of the Rue St. Germain l'Auxerrois where Percy had lodged before he carried through the rescue of the little Dauphin. Armand could even see the window at which the dreamer had stood, weaving noble dreams that his brilliant daring had turned into realities, until the hand of a traitor had brought him down to—to what? Armand would not have dared at this moment to look back at that hideous, vulgar hackney coach wherein that proud, reckless adventurer, who had defied Fate and mocked Death, sat, in chains, beside a loathsome creature whose very propinquity was an outrage.

Now they were passing under the very house on the Quai de La Ferraille, above the saddler's shop, the house where Marguerite had lodged ten days ago, whither Armand had come, trying to fool himself into the belief that the love of "little mother" could be deceived into blindness against his own crime. He had tried to draw a veil before those eyes which he had scarcely dared encounter, but he knew that that veil must lift one day, and then a curse would send him forth, outlawed and homeless, a wanderer on the face of the earth.

Soon as the little cortege wended its way northwards it filed out beneath the walls of the Temple prison; there was the main gate with its sentry standing at attention, there the archway with the guichet of the concierge, and beyond it the paved courtyard. Armand closed his eyes deliberately; he could not bear to look.

No wonder that he shivered and tried to draw his cloak closer around him. Every stone, every street corner was full of memories. The chill that struck to the very marrow of his bones came from no outward cause; it was the very hand of remorse that, as it passed over him, froze the blood in his veins and made the rattle of those wheels behind him sound like a hellish knell.

At last the more closely populated quarters of the city were left behind. On ahead the first section of the guard had turned into the Rue

St. Anne. The houses became more sparse, intersected by narrow pieces of terrains vagues, or small weed-covered bits of kitchen garden.

Then a halt was called.

It was quite light now. As light as it would ever be beneath this leaden sky. Rain and snow still fell in gusts, driven by the blast.

Some one ordered Armand to dismount. It was probably Chauvelin. He did as he was told, and a trooper led him to the door of an irregular brick building that stood isolated on the right, extended on either side by a low wall, and surrounded by a patch of uncultivated land, which now looked like a sea of mud.

On ahead was the line of fortifications dimly outlined against the grey of the sky, and in between brown, sodden earth, with here and there a detached house, a cabbage patch, a couple of windmills deserted and desolate.

The loneliness of an unpopulated outlying quarter of the great mother city, a useless limb of her active body, an ostracised member of her vast family.

Mechanically Armand had followed the soldier to the door of the building. Here Chauvelin was standing, and bade him follow. A smell of hot coffee hung in the dark narrow passage in front. Chauvelin led the way to a room on the left.

Still that smell of hot coffee. Ever after it was associated in Armand's mind with this awful morning in the guard-house of the Rue Ste. Anne, when the rain and snow beat against the windows, and he stood there in the low guard-room shivering and half-numbed with cold.

There was a table in the middle of the room, and on it stood cups of hot coffee. Chauvelin bade him drink, suggesting, not unkindly, that the warm beverage would do him good. Armand advanced further into the room, and saw that there were wooden benches all round against the wall. On one of these sat his sister Marguerite.

When she saw him she made a sudden, instinctive movement to go to him, but Chauvelin interposed in his usual bland, quiet manner.

"Not just now, citizeness," he said.

She sat down again, and Armand noted how cold and stony seemed her eyes, as if life within her was at a stand-still, and a shadow that was almost like death had atrophied every emotion in her.

"I trust you have not suffered too much from the cold, Lady Blakeney," resumed Chauvelin politely; "we ought not to have kept you waiting here for so long, but delay at departure is sometimes inevitable."

She made no reply, only acknowledging his reiterated inquiry as to her comfort with an inclination of the head.

Armand had forced himself to swallow some coffee, and for the moment he felt less chilled. He held the cup between his two hands, and gradually some warmth crept into his bones.

"Little mother," he said in English, "try and drink some of this, it will do you good."

"Thank you, dear," she replied. "I have had some. I am not cold."

Then a door at the end of the room was pushed open, and Heron stalked in.

"Are we going to be all day in this confounded hole?" he queried roughly.

Armand, who was watching his sister very closely, saw that she started at the sight of the wretch, and seemed immediately to shrink still further within herself, whilst her eyes, suddenly luminous and dilated, rested on him like those of a captive bird upon an approaching cobra.

But Chauvelin was not to be shaken out of his suave manner.

"One moment, citizen Heron," he said; "this coffee is very comforting. Is the prisoner with you?" he added lightly.

Heron nodded in the direction of the other room.

"In there," he said curtly.

"Then, perhaps, if you will be so good, citizen, to invite him thither, I could explain to him his future position and our own."

Heron muttered something between his fleshy lips, then he turned back towards the open door, solemnly spat twice on the threshold, and nodded his gaunt head once or twice in a manner which apparently was understood from within.

"No, sergeant, I don't want you," he said gruffly; "only the prisoner."

A second or two later Sir Percy Blakeney stood in the doorway; his hands were behind his back, obviously hand-cuffed, but he held himself very erect, though it was clear that this caused him a mighty effort. As soon as he had crossed the threshold his quick glance had swept right round the room.

He saw Armand, and his eyes lit up almost imperceptibly.

Then he caught sight of Marguerite, and his pale face took on suddenly a more ashen hue.

Chauvelin was watching him with those keen, light-coloured eyes of his. Blakeney, conscious of this, made no movement, only his lips tightened, and the heavy lids fell over the hollow eyes, completely hiding their glance.

But what even the most astute, most deadly enemy could not see was that subtle message of understanding that passed at once between Marguerite and the man she loved; it was a magnetic current, intangible, invisible to all save to her and to him. She was prepared to see him, prepared to see in him all that she had feared; the weakness, the mental exhaustion, the submission to the inevitable. Therefore she had also schooled her glance to express to him all that she knew she would not be allowed to say—the reassurance that she had read his last letter, that she had obeyed it to the last word, save where Fate and her enemy had interfered with regard to herself.

With a slight, imperceptible movement—imperceptible to every one save to him, she had seemed to handle a piece of paper in her kerchief, then she had nodded slowly, with her eyes—steadfast, reassuring—fixed upon him, and his glance gave answer that he had understood.

But Chauvelin and Heron had seen nothing of this. They were satisfied that there had been no communication between the prisoner and his wife and friend.

"You are no doubt surprised, Sir Percy," said Chauvelin after a while, "to see Lady Blakeney here. She, as well as citizen St. Just, will accompany our expedition to the place where you will lead us. We none of us know where that place is—citizen Heron and myself are entirely in your hands—you might be leading us to certain death, or again to a spot where your own escape would be an easy matter to yourself. You will not be surprised, therefore, that we have thought fit to take certain precautions both against any little ambuscade which you may have prepared for us, or against your making one of those daring attempts at escape for which the noted Scarlet Pimpernel is so justly famous."

He paused, and only Heron's low chuckle of satisfaction broke the momentary silence that followed. Blakeney made no reply. Obviously he knew exactly what was coming. He knew Chauvelin and his ways, knew the kind of tortuous conception that would find origin in his brain; the moment that he saw Marguerite sitting there he must have guessed that Chauvelin once more desired to put her precious life in the balance of his intrigues.

"Citizen Heron is impatient, Sir Percy," resumed Chauvelin after a while, "so I must be brief. Lady Blakeney, as well as citizen St. Just, will accompany us on this expedition to whithersoever you may lead us. They will be the hostages which we will hold against your own good faith. At the slightest suspicion—a mere suspicion perhaps—that you have played us false, at a hint that you have led us into an ambush, or that the whole of this expedition has been but a trick on your part to effect your own escape, or if merely our hope of finding Capet at the end of our journey is frustrated, the lives of our two hostages belong to us, and your friend and your wife will be summarily shot before your eyes."

Outside the rain pattered against the window-panes, the gale whistled mournfully among the stunted trees, but within this room not a sound stirred the deadly stillness of the air, and yet at this moment hatred and love, savage lust and sublime self-abnegation—the most power full passions the heart of man can know—held three men here enchained; each a slave to his dominant passion, each ready to stake his all for the satisfaction of his master. Heron was the first to speak.

"Well!" he said with a fierce oath, "what are we waiting for? The prisoner knows how he stands. Now we can go."

"One moment, citizen," interposed Chauvelin, his quiet manner contrasting strangely with his colleague's savage mood. "You have quite understood, Sir Percy," he continued, directly addressing the prisoner, "the conditions under which we are all of us about to proceed on this journey?"

"All of us?" said Blakeney slowly. "Are you taking it for granted then that I accept your conditions and that I am prepared to proceed on the journey?"

"If you do not proceed on the journey," cried Heron with savage fury, "I'll strangle that woman with my own hands—now!"

Blakeney looked at him for a moment or two through half-closed lids, and it seemed then to those who knew him well, to those who loved him and to the man who hated him, that the mighty sinews almost cracked with the passionate desire to kill. Then the sunken eyes turned slowly to Marguerite, and she alone caught the look—it was a mere flash, of a humble appeal for pardon.

It was all over in a second; almost immediately the tension on the pale face relaxed, and into the eyes there came that look of acceptance—nearly akin to fatalism—an acceptance of which the strong alone are capable, for with them it only comes in the face of the inevitable.

Now he shrugged his broad shoulders, and once more turning to Heron he said quietly:

"You leave me no option in that case. As you have remarked before, citizen Heron, why should we wait any longer? Surely we can now go."

# CHAPTER 43: THE DREARY JOURNEY

Rain! Rain! Rain! Incessant, monotonous and dreary! The wind had changed round to the southwest. It blew now in great gusts that sent weird, sighing sounds through the trees, and drove the heavy showers into the faces of the men as they rode on, with heads bent forward against the gale.

The rain-sodden bridles slipped through their hands, bringing out sores and blisters on their palms; the horses were fidgety, tossing their heads with wearying persistence as the wet trickled into their ears, or the sharp, intermittent hailstones struck their sensitive noses.

Three days of this awful monotony, varied only by the halts at wayside inns, the changing of troops at one of the guard-houses on the way, the reiterated commands given to the fresh squad before starting on the next lap of this strange, momentous way; and all the while, audible above the clatter of horses' hoofs, the rumbling of coach-wheels —two closed carriages, each drawn by a pair of sturdy horses; which were changed at every halt. A soldier on each box urged them to a good pace to keep up with the troopers, who were allowed to go at an easy canter or light jog-trot, whatever might prove easiest and least fatiguing. And from time to time Heron's shaggy, gaunt head would appear at the window of one of the coaches, asking the way, the distance to the next city or to the nearest wayside inn; cursing the troopers, the coachman, his colleague and every one concerned, blaspheming against the interminable length of the road, against the cold and against the wet.

Early in the evening on the second day of the journey he had met with an accident. The prisoner, who presumably was weak and weary, and not over steady on his feet, had fallen up against him as they were both about to re-enter the coach after a halt just outside Amiens, and citizen Heron had lost his footing in the slippery mud of the road. His head came in violent contact with the step, and his right temple was severely cut. Since then he had been forced to wear a bandage across the top of his face, under his sugar-loaf hat, which had added nothing to his beauty, but a great deal to the violence of his temper. He wanted to push the men on, to force the pace, to shorten the halts; but Chauvelin knew better than to allow slackness and discontent to follow in the wake of over-fatigue.

The soldiers were always well rested and well fed, and though the delay caused by long and frequent halts must have been just as irksome to him as it was to Heron, yet he bore it imperturbably, for he would have had no use on this momentous journey for a handful of men whose enthusiasm and spirit had been blown away by the roughness of the gale, or drowned in the fury of the constant downpour of rain.

Of all this Marguerite had been conscious in a vague, dreamy kind of way. She seemed to herself like the spectator in a moving panoramic drama, unable to raise a finger or to do aught to stop that final, inevitable ending, the cataclysm of sorrow and misery that awaited her, when the dreary curtain would fall on the last act, and she and all the other spectators—Armand, Chauvelin, Heron, the soldiers— would slowly wend their way home, leaving the principal actor behind the fallen curtain, which never would be lifted again.

After that first halt in the guard-room of the Rue Ste. Anne she had been bidden to enter a second hackney coach, which, followed the other at a distance of fifty metres or so, and was, like that other, closely surrounded by a squad of mounted men.

Armand and Chauvelin rode in this carriage with her; all day she sat looking out on the endless monotony of the road, on the drops of rain that pattered against the window-glass, and ran down from it like a perpetual stream of tears.

There were two halts called during the day—one for dinner and one midway through the afternoon—when she and Armand would step out of the coach and be led—always with soldiers close around them— to some wayside inn, where some sort of a meal was served, where the atmosphere was close and stuffy and smelt of onion soup and of stale cheese.

Armand and Marguerite would in most cases have a room to themselves, with sentinels posted outside the door, and they would try and eat enough to keep body and soul together, for they would not allow their strength to fall away before the end of the journey was reached.

For the night halt—once at Beauvais and the second night at Abbeville—they were escorted to a house in the interior of the city, where they were accommodated with moderately clean lodgings. Sentinels, however, were always at their doors; they were prisoners in all but name, and had little or no privacy; for at night they were both so tired that they were glad to retire immediately, and to lie down on the hard beds that had been provided for them, even if sleep fled from their eyes, and their hearts and souls were flying through the city in search of him who filled their every thought.

Of Percy they saw little or nothing. In the daytime food was evidently brought to him in the carriage, for they did not see him get down, and on those two nights at Beauvais and Abbeville, when they caught sight of him stepping out of the coach outside the gates of the barracks, he was so surrounded by soldiers that they only saw the top of his head and his broad shoulders towering above those of the men.

Once Marguerite had put all her pride, all her dignity by, and asked citizen Chauvelin for news of her husband.

"He is well and cheerful, Lady Blakeney," he had replied with his sarcastic smile. "Ah!" he added pleasantly, "those English are remarkable people. We, of Gallic breed, will never really understand them. Their fatalism is quite Oriental in its quiet resignation to the decree of Fate. Did you know, Lady Blakeney, that when Sir Percy was arrested he did not raise a hand. I thought, and so did my colleague, that he would have fought like a lion. And now, that he has no doubt realised that quiet submission will serve him best in the end, he is as calm on this journey as I am myself. In fact," he concluded complacently, "whenever I have succeeded in peeping into the coach I have invariably found Sir Percy Blakeney fast asleep."

"He—" she murmured, for it was so difficult to speak to this callous wretch, who was obviously mocking her in her misery—"he—you—you are not keeping him in irons?"

"No! Oh no!" replied Chauvelin with perfect urbanity. "You see, now that we have you, Lady Blakeney, and citizen St. Just with us we have no reason to fear that that elusive Pimpernel will spirit himself away."

A hot retort had risen to Armand's lips. The warm Latin blood in him rebelled against this intolerable situation, the man's sneers in the face of Marguerite's anguish. But her restraining, gentle hand had already pressed his. What was the use of protesting, of insulting this brute, who cared nothing for the misery which he had caused so long as he gained his own ends?

And Armand held his tongue and tried to curb his temper, tried to cultivate a little of that fatalism which Chauvelin had said was characteristic of the English. He sat beside his sister, longing to comfort her, yet feeling that his very presence near her was an outrage and a sacrilege. She spoke so seldom to him, even when they were alone, that at times the awful thought which had more than once found birth in his weary brain became crystallised and more real. Did Marguerite guess? Had she the slightest suspicion that the awful cataclysm to which they were tending with every revolution of the creaking coach-wheels had been brought about by her brother's treacherous hand?

And when that thought had lodged itself quite snugly in his mind he began to wonder whether it would not be far more simple, far more easy, to end his miserable life in some manner that might suggest itself on the way. When the coach crossed one of those dilapidated, parapetless bridges, over abysses fifty metres deep, it might be so easy to throw open the carriage door and to take one final jump into eternity.

So easy—but so damnably cowardly.

Marguerite's near presence quickly brought him back to himself. His life was no longer his own to do with as he pleased; it belonged to the chief whom he had betrayed, to the sister whom he must endeavour to protect.

Of Jeanne now he thought but little. He had put even the memory of her by—tenderly, like a sprig of lavender pressed between the faded leaves of his own happiness. His hand was no longer fit to hold that of any pure woman—his hand had on it a deep stain, immutable, like the brand of Cain.

Yet Marguerite beside him held his hand and together they looked out on that dreary, dreary road and listened to of the patter of the rain and the rumbling of the wheels of that other coach on ahead—and it was all so dismal and so horrible, the rain, the soughing of the wind in the stunted trees, this landscape of mud and desolation, this eternally grey sky.

# CHAPTER 44: THE HALT AT CRECY

"Now, then, citizen, don't go to sleep; this is Crecy, our last halt!"

Armand woke up from his last dream. They had been moving steadily on since they left Abbeville soon after dawn; the rumble of the wheels, the swaying and rocking of the carriage, the interminable patter of the rain had lulled him into a kind of wakeful sleep.

Chauvelin had already alighted from the coach. He was helping Marguerite to descend. Armand shook the stiffness from his limbs and followed in the wake of his sister. Always those miserable soldiers round them, with their dank coats of rough blue cloth, and the red caps on their heads! Armand pulled Marguerite's hand through his arm, and dragged her with him into the house.

The small city lay damp and grey before them; the rough pavement of the narrow street glistened with the wet, reflecting the dull, leaden sky overhead; the rain beat into the puddles; the slate-roofs shone in the cold wintry light.

This was Crecy! The last halt of the journey, so Chauvelin had said. The party had drawn rein in front of a small one-storied building that had a wooden verandah running the whole length of its front.

The usual low narrow room greeted Armand and Marguerite as they entered; the usual mildewed walls, with the colour wash flowing away in streaks from the unsympathetic beam above; the same device, "*Liberte, Egalite, Fraternite!*" scribbled in charcoal above the black iron stove; the usual musty, close atmosphere, the usual smell of onion and stale cheese, the usual hard straight benches and central table with its soiled and tattered cloth.

Marguerite seemed dazed and giddy; she had been five hours in that stuffy coach with nothing to distract her thoughts except the rain-sodden landscape, on which she had ceaselessly gazed since the early dawn.

Armand led her to the bench, and she sank down on it, numb and inert, resting her elbows on the table and her head in her hands.

"If it were only all over!" she sighed involuntarily. "Armand, at times now I feel as if I were not really sane—as if my reason had already given way! Tell me, do I seem mad to you at times?"

He sat down beside her and tried to chafe her little cold hands.

There was a knock at the door, and without waiting for permission Chauvelin entered the room.

"My humble apologies to you, Lady Blakeney," he said in his usual suave manner, "but our worthy host informs me that this is the only room in which he can serve a meal. Therefore I am forced to intrude my presence upon you."

Though he spoke with outward politeness, his tone had become more peremptory, less bland, and he did not await Marguerite's reply before he sat down opposite to her and continued to talk airily.

"An ill-conditioned fellow, our host," he said—"quite reminds me of our friend Brogard at the Chat Gris in Calais. You remember him, Lady Blakeney?"

"My sister is giddy and over-tired," interposed Armand firmly. "I pray you, citizen, to have some regard for her."

"All regard in the world, citizen St. Just," protested Chauvelin jovially. "Methought that those pleasant reminiscences would cheer her. Ah! here comes the soup," he added, as a man in blue blouse and breeches, with sabots on his feet, slouched into the room, carrying a tureen which he incontinently placed upon the table. "I feel sure that in England Lady Blakeney misses our excellent *croutes-au-pot*, the glory of our bourgeois cookery—Lady Blakeney, a little soup?"

"I thank you, sir," she murmured.

"Do try and eat something, little mother," Armand whispered in her ear; "try and keep up your strength for his sake, if not for mine."

She turned a wan, pale face to him, and tried to smile.

"I'll try, dear," she said.

"You have taken bread and meat to the citizens in the coach?" Chauvelin called out to the retreating figure of mine host.

"H'm!" grunted the latter in assent.

"And see that the citizen soldiers are well fed, or there will be trouble."

"H'm!" grunted the man again. After which he banged the door to behind him.

"Citizen Heron is loath to let the prisoner out of his sight," explained Chauvelin lightly, "now that we have reached the last, most important stage of our journey, so he is sharing Sir Percy's mid-day meal in the interior of the coach."

He ate his soup with a relish, ostentatiously paying many small attentions to Marguerite all the time. He ordered meat for her—bread, butter—asked if any dainties could be got. He was apparently in the best of tempers.

After he had eaten and drunk he rose and bowed ceremoniously to her.

"Your pardon, Lady Blakeney," he said, "but I must confer with the prisoner now, and take from him full directions for the continuance of our journey. After that I go to the guard-house, which is some distance from here, right at the other end of the city. We pick up a fresh squad here, twenty hardened troopers from a cavalry regiment usually stationed at Abbeville. They have had work to do in this town, which is a hot-bed of treachery. I must go inspect the men and the sergeant who will be in command. Citizen Heron leaves all these inspections to me;

he likes to stay by his prisoner. In the meanwhile you will be escorted back to your coach, where I pray you to await my arrival, when we change guard first, then proceed on our way."

Marguerite was longing to ask him many questions; once again she would have smothered her pride and begged for news of her husband, but Chauvelin did not wait. He hurried out of the room, and Armand and Marguerite could hear him ordering the soldiers to take them forthwith back to the coach.

As they came out of the inn they saw the other coach some fifty metres further up the street. The horses that had done duty since leaving Abbeville had been taken out, and two soldiers in ragged shirts, and with crimson caps set jauntily over their left ear, were leading the two fresh horses along. The troopers were still mounting guard round both the coaches; they would be relieved presently.

Marguerite would have given ten years of her life at this moment for the privilege of speaking to her husband, or even of seeing him—of seeing that he was well. A quick, wild plan sprang up in her mind that she would bribe the sergeant in command to grant her wish while citizen Chauvelin was absent. The man had not an unkind face, and he must be very poor—people in France were very poor these days, though the rich had been robbed and luxurious homes devastated ostensibly to help the poor.

She was about to put this sudden thought into execution when Heron's hideous face, doubly hideous now with that bandage of doubtful cleanliness cutting across his brow, appeared at the carriage window.

He cursed violently and at the top of his voice.

"What are those d—d *aristos* doing out there?" he shouted.

"Just getting into the coach, citizen," replied the sergeant promptly.

And Armand and Marguerite were immediately ordered back into the coach.

Heron remained at the window for a few moments longer; he had a toothpick in his hand which he was using very freely.

"How much longer are we going to wait in this cursed hole?" he called out to the sergeant.

"Only a few moments longer, citizen. Citizen Chauvelin will be back soon with the guard."

A quarter of an hour later the clatter of cavalry horses on the rough, uneven pavement drew Marguerite's attention. She lowered the carriage window and looked out. Chauvelin had just returned with the new escort. He was on horseback; his horse's bridle, since he was but an indifferent horseman, was held by one of the troopers.

Outside the inn he dismounted; evidently he had taken full command of the expedition, and scarcely referred to Heron, who spent

most of his time cursing at the men or the weather when he was not
lying half-asleep and partially drunk in the inside of the carriage.

The changing of the guard was now accomplished quietly and in
perfect order. The new escort consisted of twenty mounted men,
including a sergeant and a corporal, and of two drivers, one for each
coach. The cortege now was filed up in marching order; ahead a small
party of scouts, then the coach with Marguerite and Armand closely
surrounded by mounted men, and at a short distance the second coach
with citizen Heron and the prisoner equally well guarded.

Chauvelin superintended all the arrangements himself. He
spoke for some few moments with the sergeant, also with the driver of
his own coach. He went to the window of the other carriage, probably
in order to consult with citizen Heron, or to take final directions from
the prisoner, for Marguerite, who was watching him, saw him standing
on the step and leaning well forward into the interior, whilst apparently
he was taking notes on a small tablet which he had in his hand.

A small knot of idlers had congregated in the narrow street;
men in blouses and boys in ragged breeches lounged against the
verandah of the inn and gazed with inexpressive, stolid eyes on the
soldiers, the coaches, the citizen who wore the tricolour scarf. They had
seen this sort of thing before now—*aristos* being conveyed to Paris
under arrest, prisoners on their way to or from Amiens. They saw
Marguerite's pale face at the carriage window. It was not the first
woman's face they had seen under like circumstances, and there was no
special interest about this *aristo*. They were smoking or spitting, or just
lounging idly against the balustrade. Marguerite wondered if none of
them had wife, sister, or mother, or child; if every sympathy, every kind
of feeling in these poor wretches had been atrophied by misery or by
fear.

At last everything was in order and the small party ready to
start.

"Does any one here know the Chapel of the Holy Sepulchre,
close by the park of the Chateau d'Ourde?" asked Chauvelin, vaguely
addressing the knot of gaffers that stood closest to him.

The men shook their heads. Some had dimly heard of the
Chateau d'Ourde; it was some way in the interior of the forest of
Boulogne, but no one knew about a chapel; people did not trouble
about chapels nowadays. With the indifference so peculiar to local
peasantry, these men knew no more of the surrounding country than
the twelve or fifteen league circle that was within a walk of their sleepy
little town.

One of the scouts on ahead turned in his saddle and spoke to
citizen Chauvelin:

"I think I know the way pretty well; citizen Chauvelin," he said;
"at any rate, I know it as far as the forest of Boulogne."

Chauvelin referred to his tablets.

"That's good," he said; "then when you reach the mile-stone that stands on this road at the confine of the forest, bear sharply to your right and skirt the wood until you see the hamlet of—Le—something. Le—Le—yes—Le Crocq—that's it in the valley below."

"I know Le Crocq, I think," said the trooper.

"Very well, then; at that point it seems that a wide road strikes at right angles into the interior of the forest; you follow that until a stone chapel with a colonnaded porch stands before you on your left, and the walls and gates of a park on your right. That is so, is it not, Sir Percy?" he added, once more turning towards the interior of the coach.

Apparently the answer satisfied him, for he gave the quick word of command, "*En avant!*" then turned back towards his own coach and finally entered it.

"Do you know the Chateau d'Ourde, citizen St. Just?" he asked abruptly as soon as the carriage began to move.

Armand woke—as was habitual with him these days—from some gloomy reverie.

"Yes, citizen," he replied. "I know it."

"And the Chapel of the Holy Sepulchre?"

"Yes. I know it too."

Indeed, he knew the chateau well, and the little chapel in the forest, whither the fisher-folk from Portel and Boulogne came on a pilgrimage once a year to lay their nets on the miracle-working relic. The chapel was disused now. Since the owner of the chateau had fled no one had tended it, and the fisher-folk were afraid to wander out, lest their superstitious faith be counted against them by the authorities, who had abolished *le bon Dieu.*

But Armand had found refuge there eighteen months ago, on his way to Calais, when Percy had risked his life in order to save him—Armand—from death. He could have groaned aloud with the anguish of this recollection. But Marguerite's aching nerves had thrilled at the name.

The Chateau d'Ourde! The Chapel of the Holy Sepulchre! That was the place which Percy had mentioned in his letter, the place where he had given rendezvous to de Batz. Sir Andrew had said that the Dauphin could not possibly be there, yet Percy was leading his enemies thither, and had given the rendezvous there to de Batz. And this despite that whatever plans, whatever hopes, had been born in his mind when he was still immured in the Conciergerie prison must have been set at naught by the clever counter plot of Chauvelin and Heron.

"At the merest suspicion that you have played us false, at a hint that you have led us into an ambush, or if merely our hopes of finding Capet at the end of the journey are frustrated, the lives of your wife and of your friend are forfeit to us, and they will both be shot before your eyes."

With these words, with this precaution, those cunning fiends had effectually not only tied the schemer's hands, but forced him either to deliver the child to them or to sacrifice his wife and his friend.

The impasse was so horrible that she could not face it even in her thoughts. A strange, fever-like heat coursed through her veins, yet left her hands icy-cold; she longed for, yet dreaded, the end of the journey—that awful grappling with the certainty of coming death. Perhaps, after all, Percy, too, had given up all hope. Long ago he had consecrated his life to the attainment of his own ideals; and there was a vein of fatalism in him; perhaps he had resigned himself to the inevitable, and his only desire now was to give up his life, as he had said, in the open, beneath God's sky, to draw his last breath with the storm-clouds tossed through infinity above him, and the murmur of the wind in the trees to sing him to rest.

Crecy was gradually fading into the distance, wrapped in a mantle of damp and mist. For a long while Marguerite could see the sloping slate roofs glimmering like steel in the grey afternoon light, and the quaint church tower with its beautiful lantern, through the pierced stonework of which shone patches of the leaden sky.

Then a sudden twist of the road hid the city from view; only the outlying churchyard remained in sight, with its white monuments and granite crosses, over which the dark yews, wet with the rain and shaken by the gale, sent showers of diamond-like sprays.

# CHAPTER 45: THE FOREST OF BOULOGNE

Progress was not easy, and very slow along the muddy road; the two coaches moved along laboriously, with wheels creaking and sinking deeply from time to time in the quagmire.

When the small party finally reached the edge of the wood the greyish light of this dismal day had changed in the west to a dull reddish glow—a glow that had neither brilliance nor incandescence in it; only a weird tint that hung over the horizon and turned the distance into lines of purple.

The nearness of the sea made itself already felt; there was a briny taste in the damp atmosphere, and the trees all turned their branches away in the same direction against the onslaught of the prevailing winds.

The road at this point formed a sharp fork, skirting the wood on either side, the forest lying like a black close mass of spruce and firs on the left, while the open expanse of country stretched out on the right. The south-westerly gale struck with full violence against the barrier of forest trees, bending the tall crests of the pines and causing their small dead branches to break and fall with a sharp, crisp sound like a cry of pain.

The squad had been fresh at starting; now the men had been four hours in the saddle under persistent rain and gusty wind; they were tired, and the atmosphere of the close, black forest so near the road was weighing upon their spirits.

Strange sounds came to them from out the dense network of trees—the screeching of night-birds, the weird call of the owls, the swift and furtive tread of wild beasts on the prowl. The cold winter and lack of food had lured the wolves from their fastnesses—hunger had emboldened them, and now, as gradually the grey light fled from the sky, dismal howls could be heard in the distance, and now and then a pair of eyes, bright with the reflection of the lurid western glow, would shine momentarily out of the darkness like tiny glow-worms, and as quickly vanish away.

The men shivered—more with vague superstitious fear than with cold. They would have urged their horses on, but the wheels of the coaches stuck persistently in the mud, and now and again a halt had to be called so that the spokes and axles might be cleared.

They rode on in silence. No one had a mind to speak, and the mournful soughing of the wind in the pine-trees seemed to check the words on every lip. The dull thud of hoofs in the soft road, the clang of steel bits and buckles, the snorting of the horses alone answered the wind, and also the monotonous creaking of the wheels ploughing through the ruts.

Soon the ruddy glow in the west faded into soft-toned purple and then into grey; finally that too vanished. Darkness was drawing in on every side like a wide, black mantle pulled together closer and closer overhead by invisible giant hands.

The rain still fell in a thin drizzle that soaked through caps and coats, made the bridles slimy and the saddles slippery and damp. A veil of vapour hung over the horses' cruppers, and was rendered fuller and thicker every moment with the breath that came from their nostrils. The wind no longer blew with gusty fury—its strength seemed to have been spent with the grey light of day—but now and then it would still come sweeping across the open country, and dash itself upon the wall of forest trees, lashing against the horses' ears, catching the corner of a mantle here, an ill-adjusted cap there, and wreaking its mischievous freak for a while, then with a sigh of satisfaction die, murmuring among the pines.

Suddenly there was a halt, much shouting, a volley of oaths from the drivers, and citizen Chauvelin thrust his head out of the carriage window.

"What is it?" he asked.

"The scouts, citizen," replied the sergeant, who had been riding close to the coach door all this while; "they have returned."

"Tell one man to come straight to me and report."

Marguerite sat quite still. Indeed, she had almost ceased to live momentarily, for her spirit was absent from her body, which felt neither fatigue, nor cold, nor pain. But she heard the snorting of the horse close by as its rider pulled him up sharply beside the carriage door.

"Well?" said Chauvelin curtly.

"This is the cross-road, citizen," replied the man; "it strikes straight into the wood, and the hamlet of Le Crocq lies down in the valley on the right."

"Did you follow the road in the wood?"

"Yes, citizen. About two leagues from here there is a clearing with a small stone chapel, more like a large shrine, nestling among the trees. Opposite to it the angle of a high wall with large wrought-iron gates at the corner, and from these a wide drive leads through a park."

"Did you turn into the drive?"

"Only a little way, citizen. We thought we had best report first that all is safe."

"You saw no one?"

"No one."

"The chateau, then, lies some distance from the gates?"

"A league or more, citizen. Close to the gates there are outhouses and stabling, the disused buildings of the home farm, I should say."

"Good! We are on the right road, that is clear. Keep ahead with your men now, but only some two hundred metres or so. Stay!" he added, as if on second thoughts. "Ride down to the other coach and ask the prisoner if we are on the right track."

The rider turned his horse sharply round. Marguerite heard-the clang of metal and the sound of retreating hoofs.

A few moments later the man returned.

"Yes, citizen," he reported, "the prisoner says it is quite right. The Chateau d'Ourde lies a full league from its gates. This is the nearest road to the chapel and the chateau. He says we should reach the former in half an hour. It will be very dark in there," he added with a significant nod in the direction of the wood.

Chauvelin made no reply, but quietly stepped out of the coach. Marguerite watched him, leaning out of the window, following his small trim figure as he pushed his way past the groups of mounted men, catching at a horse's bit now and then, or at a bridle, making a way for himself amongst the restless, champing animals, without the slightest hesitation or fear.

Soon his retreating figure lost its sharp outline silhouetted against the evening sky. It was enfolded in the veil of vapour which was blown out of the horses' nostrils or rising from their damp cruppers; it became more vague, almost ghost-like, through the mist and the fast-gathering gloom.

Presently a group of troopers hid him entirely from her view, but she could hear his thin, smooth voice quite clearly as he called to citizen Heron.

"We are close to the end of our journey now, citizen," she heard him say. "If the prisoner has not played us false little Capet should be in our charge within the hour."

A growl not unlike those that came from out the mysterious depths of the forest answered him.

"If he is not," and Marguerite recognised the harsh tones of citizen Heron—"if he is not, then two corpses will be rotting in this wood tomorrow for the wolves to feed on, and the prisoner will be on his way back to Paris with me."

Some one laughed. It might have been one of the troopers, more callous than his comrades, but to Marguerite the laugh had a strange, familiar ring in it, the echo of something long since past and gone.

Then Chauvelin's voice once more came clearly to her ear:

"My suggestion, citizen," he was saying, "is that the prisoner shall now give me an order—couched in whatever terms he may think necessary—but a distinct order to his friends to give up Capet to me without any resistance. I could then take some of the men with me, and ride as quickly as the light will allow up to the chateau, and take possession of it, of Capet, and of those who are with him. We could get along faster thus. One man can give up his horse to me and continue the journey on the box of your coach. The two carriages could then follow at foot pace. But I fear that if we stick together complete darkness will overtake us and we might find ourselves obliged to pass a very uncomfortable night in this wood."

"I won't spend another night in this suspense—it would kill me," growled Heron to the accompaniment of one of his choicest oaths.

"You must do as you think right—you planned the whole of this affair—see to it that it works out well in the end."

"How many men shall I take with me? Our advance guard is here, of course."

"I couldn't spare you more than four more men—I shall want the others to guard the prisoners."

"Four men will be quite sufficient, with the four of the advance guard. That will leave you twelve men for guarding your prisoners, and you really only need to guard the woman—her life will answer for the others."

He had raised his voice when he said this, obviously intending that Marguerite and Armand should hear.

"Then I'll ahead," he continued, apparently in answer to an assent from his colleague. "Sir Percy, will you be so kind as to scribble the necessary words on these tablets?"

There was a long pause, during which Marguerite heard plainly the long and dismal cry of a night bird that, mayhap, was seeking its mate. Then Chauvelin's voice was raised again.

"I thank you," he said; "this certainly should be quite effectual. And now, citizen Heron, I do not think that under the circumstances we need fear an ambuscade or any kind of trickery—you hold the hostages. And if by any chance I and my men are attacked, or if we encounter armed resistance at the chateau, I will despatch a rider back straightway to you, and—well, you will know what to do."

His voice died away, merged in the soughing of the wind, drowned by the clang of metal, of horses snorting, of men living and breathing. Marguerite felt that beside her Armand had shuddered, and that in the darkness his trembling hand had sought and found hers.

She leaned well out of the window, trying to see. The gloom had gathered more closely in, and round her the veil of vapour from the horses' steaming cruppers hung heavily in the misty air. In front of her the straight lines of a few fir trees stood out dense and black against the greyness beyond, and between these lines purple tints of various tones and shades mingled one with the other, merging the horizon line with the sky. Here and there a more solid black patch indicated the tiny houses of the hamlet of Le Crocq far down in the valley below; from some of these houses small lights began to glimmer like blinking yellow eyes. Marguerite's gaze, however, did not rest on the distant landscape —it tried to pierce the gloom that hid her immediate surroundings; the mounted men were all round the coach—more closely round her than the trees in the forest. But the horses were restless, moving all the time, and as they moved she caught glimpses of that other coach and of Chauvelin's ghostlike figure, walking rapidly through the mist. Just for one brief moment she saw the other coach, and Heron's head and shoulders leaning out of the window. If his sugar-loaf hat was on his head, and the bandage across his brow looked like a sharp, pale streak below it.

"Do not doubt it, citizen Chauvelin," he called out loudly in his harsh, raucous voice, "I shall know what to do; the wolves will have their meal to-night, and the guillotine will not be cheated either."

Armand put his arm round his sister's shoulders and gently drew her back into the carriage.

"Little mother," he said, "if you can think of a way whereby my life would redeem Percy's and yours, show me that way now."

But she replied quietly and firmly:

"There is no way, Armand. If there is, it is in the hands of God."

# CHAPTER 46: OTHERS IN THE PARK

Chauvelin and his picked escort had in the meanwhile detached themselves from the main body of the squad. Soon the dull thud of their horses' hoofs treading the soft ground came more softly—then more softly still as they turned into the wood, and the purple shadows seemed to enfold every sound and finally to swallow them completely.

Armand and Marguerite from the depth of the carriage heard Heron's voice ordering his own driver now to take the lead. They sat quite still and watched, and presently the other coach passed them slowly on the road, its silhouette standing out ghostly and grim for a moment against the indigo tones of the distant country.

Heron's head, with its battered sugar-loaf hat, and the soiled bandage round the brow, was as usual out of the carriage window. He leered across at Marguerite when he saw the outline of her face framed by the window of the carriage.

"Say all the prayers you have ever known, citizeness," he said with a loud laugh, "that my friend Chauvelin may find Capet at the chateau, or else you may take a last look at the open country, for you will not see the sun rise on it to-morrow. It is one or the other, you know."

She tried not to look at him; the very sight of him filled her with horror—that blotched, gaunt face of his, the fleshy lips, that hideous bandage across his face that hid one of his eyes! She tried not to see him and not to hear him laugh.

Obviously he too laboured under the stress of great excitement. So far everything had gone well; the prisoner had made no attempt at escape, and apparently did not mean to play a double game. But the crucial hour had come, and with it darkness and the mysterious depths of the forest with their weird sounds and sudden flashes of ghostly lights. They naturally wrought on the nerves of men like Heron, whose conscience might have been dormant, but whose ears were nevertheless filled with the cries of innocent victims sacrificed to their own lustful ambitions and their blind, unreasoning hates.

He gave sharp orders to the men to close up round the carriages, and then gave the curt word of command:

"*En avant!*"

Marguerite could but strain her ears to listen. All her senses, all her faculties had merged into that of hearing, rendering it doubly keen. It seemed to her that she could distinguish the faint sound—that even as she listened grew fainter and fainter yet—of Chauvelin and his squad moving away rapidly into the thickness of the wood some distance already ahead.

Close to her there was the snorting of horses, the clanging and noise of moving mounted men. Heron's coach had taken the lead; she could hear the creaking of its wheels, the calls of the driver urging his beasts.

The diminished party was moving at foot-pace in the darkness that seemed to grow denser at every step, and through that silence which was so full of mysterious sounds.

The carriage rolled and rocked on its springs; Marguerite, giddy and overtired, lay back with closed eyes, her hand resting in that of Armand. Time, space and distance had ceased to be; only Death, the great Lord of all, had remained; he walked on ahead, scythe on skeleton shoulder, and beckoned patiently, but with a sure, grim hand.

There was another halt, the coach-wheels groaned and creaked on their axles, one or two horses reared with the sudden drawing up of the curb.

"What is it now?" came Heron's hoarse voice through the darkness.

"It is pitch-dark, citizen," was the response from ahead. "The drivers cannot see their horses' ears. They wait to know if they may light their lanthorns and then lead their horses."

"They can lead their horses," replied Heron roughly, "but I'll have no lanthorns lighted. We don't know what fools may be lurking behind trees, hoping to put a bullet through my head—or yours, sergeant—we don't want to make a lighted target of ourselves—what? But let the drivers lead their horses, and one or two of you who are riding greys might dismount too and lead the way—the greys would show up perhaps in this cursed blackness."

While his orders were being carried out, he called out once more:

"Are we far now from that confounded chapel?"

"We can't be far, citizen; the whole forest is not more than six leagues wide at any point, and we have gone two since we turned into it."

"Hush!" Heron's voice suddenly broke in hoarsely. "What was that? Silence, I say. Damn you—can't you hear?"

There was a hush—every ear straining to listen; but the horses were not still—they continued to champ their bits, to paw the ground, and to toss their heads, impatient to get on. Only now and again there would come a lull even through these sounds—a second or two, mayhap, of perfect, unbroken silence—and then it seemed as if right through the darkness a mysterious echo sent back those same sounds— the champing of bits, the pawing of soft ground, the tossing and snorting of animals, human life that breathed far out there among the trees.

"It is citizen Chauvelin and his men," said the sergeant after a while, and speaking in a whisper.

"Silence—I want to hear," came the curt, hoarsely-whispered command.

Once more every one listened, the men hardly daring to breathe, clinging to their bridles and pulling on their horses' mouths, trying to keep them still, and again through the night there came like a faint echo which seemed to throw back those sounds that indicated the presence of men and of horses not very far away.

"Yes, it must be citizen Chauvelin," said Heron at last; but the tone of his voice sounded as if he were anxious and only half convinced; "but I thought he would be at the chateau by now."

"He may have had to go at foot-pace; it is very dark, citizen Heron," remarked the sergeant.

"*En avant*, then," quoth the other; "the sooner we come up with him the better."

And the squad of mounted men, the two coaches, the drivers and the advance section who were leading their horses slowly restarted on the way. The horses snorted, the bits and stirrups clanged, and the springs and wheels of the coaches creaked and groaned dismally as the ramshackle vehicles began once more to plough the carpet of pine-needles that lay thick upon the road.

But inside the carriage Armand and Marguerite held one another tightly by the hand.

"It is de Batz—with his friends," she whispered scarce above her breath.

"De Batz?" he asked vaguely and fearfully, for in the dark he could not see her face, and as he did not understand why she should suddenly be talking of de Batz he thought with horror that mayhap her prophecy anent herself had come true, and that her mind wearied and over-wrought—had become suddenly unhinged.

"Yes, de Batz," she replied. "Percy sent him a message, through me, to meet him—here. I am not mad, Armand," she added more calmly. "Sir Andrew took Percy's letter to de Batz the day that we started from Paris."

"Great God!" exclaimed Armand, and instinctively, with a sense of protection, he put his arms round his sister. "Then, if Chauvelin or the squad is attacked—if—"

"Yes," she said calmly; "if de Batz makes an attack on Chauvelin, or if he reaches the chateau first and tries to defend it, they will shoot us... Armand, and Percy."

"But is the Dauphin at the Chateau d'Ourde?"

"No, no! I think not."

"Then why should Percy have invoked the aid of de Batz? Now, when—"

"I don't know," she murmured helplessly. "Of course, when he wrote the letter he could not guess that they would hold us as hostages. He may have thought that under cover of darkness and of an unexpected attack he might have saved himself had he been alone; but now—now that you and I are here—Oh! it is all so horrible, and I cannot understand it all."

"Hark!" broke in Armand, suddenly gripping her arm more tightly.

"Halt!" rang the sergeant's voice through the night.

This time there was no mistaking the sound; already it came from no far distance. It was the sound of a man running and panting, and now and again calling out as he ran.

For a moment there was stillness in the very air, the wind itself was hushed between two gusts, even the rain had ceased its incessant pattering. Heron's harsh voice was raised in the stillness.

"What is it now?" he demanded.

"A runner, citizen," replied the sergeant, "coming through the wood from the right."

"From the right?" and the exclamation was accompanied by a volley of oaths; "the direction of the chateau? Chauvelin has been attacked; he is sending a messenger back to me. Sergeant—sergeant, close up round that coach; guard your prisoners as you value your life, and—"

The rest of his words were drowned in a yell of such violent fury that the horses, already over-nervous and fidgety, reared in mad terror, and the men had the greatest difficulty in holding them in. For a few minutes noisy confusion prevailed, until the men could quieten their quivering animals with soft words and gentle pattings.

Then the troopers obeyed, closing up round the coach wherein brother and sister sat huddled against one another.

One of the men said under his breath:

"Ah! but the citizen agent knows how to curse! One day he will break his gullet with the fury of his oaths."

In the meanwhile the runner had come nearer, always at the same breathless speed.

The next moment he was challenged:

"*Qui va la?*"

"A friend!" he replied, panting and exhausted. "Where is citizen Heron?"

"Here!" came the reply in a voice hoarse with passionate excitement. "Come up, damn you. Be quick!"

"A lanthorn, citizen," suggested one of the drivers.

"No—no—not now. Here! Where the devil are we?"

"We are close to the chapel on our left, citizen," said the

sergeant.

The runner, whose eyes were no doubt accustomed to the gloom, had drawn nearer to the carriage.

"The gates of the chateau," he said, still somewhat breathlessly, "are just opposite here on the right, citizen. I have just come through them."

"Speak up, man!" and Heron's voice now sounded as if choked with passion. "Citizen Chauvelin sent you?"

"Yes. He bade me tell you that he has gained access to the chateau, and that Capet is not there."

A series of citizen Heron's choicest oaths interrupted the man's speech. Then he was curtly ordered to proceed, and he resumed his report.

"Citizen Chauvelin rang at the door of the chateau; after a while he was admitted by an old servant, who appeared to be in charge, but the place seemed otherwise absolutely deserted—only—"

"Only what? Go on; what is it?"

"As we rode through the park it seemed to us as if we were being watched, and followed. We heard distinctly the sound of horses behind and around us, but we could see nothing; and now, when I ran back, again I heard. There are others in the park to-night besides us, citizen."

There was silence after that. It seemed as if the flood of Heron's blasphemous eloquence had spent itself at last.

"Others in the park!" And now his voice was scarcely above a whisper, hoarse and trembling. "How many? Could you see?"

"No, citizen, we could not see; but there are horsemen lurking round the chateau now. Citizen Chauvelin took four men into the house with him and left the others on guard outside. He bade me tell you that it might be safer to send him a few more men if you could spare them. There are a number of disused farm buildings quite close to the gates, and he suggested that all the horses be put up there for the night, and that the men come up to the chateau on foot; it would be quicker and safer, for the darkness is intense."

Even while the man spoke the forest in the distance seemed to wake from its solemn silence, the wind on its wings brought sounds of life and movement different from the prowling of beasts or the screeching of night-birds. It was the furtive advance of men, the quick whispers of command, of encouragement, of the human animal preparing to attack his kind. But all in the distance still, all muffled, all furtive as yet.

"Sergeant!" It was Heron's voice, but it too was subdued, and almost calm now; "can you see the chapel?"

"More clearly, citizen," replied the sergeant. "It is on our left; quite a small building, I think."

"Then dismount, and walk all round it. See that there are no windows or door in the rear."

There was a prolonged silence, during which those distant sounds of men moving, of furtive preparations for attack, struck distinctly through the night.

Marguerite and Armand, clinging to one another, not knowing what to think, nor yet what to fear, heard the sounds mingling with those immediately round them, and Marguerite murmured under her breath:

"It is de Batz and some of his friends; but what can they do? What can Percy hope for now?"

But of Percy she could hear and see nothing. The darkness and the silence had drawn their impenetrable veil between his unseen presence and her own consciousness. She could see the coach in which he was, but Heron's hideous personality, his head with its battered hat and soiled bandage, had seemed to obtrude itself always before her gaze, blotting out from her mind even the knowledge that Percy was there not fifty yards away from her.

So strong did this feeling grow in her that presently the awful dread seized upon her that he was no longer there; that he was dead, worn out with fatigue and illness brought on by terrible privations, or if not dead that he had swooned, that he was unconscious—his spirit absent from his body. She remembered that frightful yell of rage and hate which Heron had uttered a few minutes ago. Had the brute vented his fury on his helpless, weakened prisoner, and stilled forever those lips that, mayhap, had mocked him to the last?

Marguerite could not guess. She hardly knew what to hope. Vaguely, when the thought of Percy lying dead beside his enemy floated through her aching brain, she was almost conscious of a sense of relief at the thought that at least he would be spared the pain of the final, inevitable cataclysm.

# CHAPTER 47: THE CHAPEL
# OF THE HOLY SEPULCHRE

The sergeant's voice broke in upon her misery.

The man had apparently done as the citizen agent had ordered, and had closely examined the little building that stood on the left—a vague, black mass more dense than the surrounding gloom.

"It is all solid stone, citizen," he said; "iron gates in front, closed but not locked, rusty key in the lock, which turns quite easily; no windows or door in the rear."

"You are quite sure?"

"Quite certain, citizen; it is plain, solid stone at the back, and the only possible access to the interior is through the iron gate in front."

"Good."

Marguerite could only just hear Heron speaking to the sergeant. Darkness enveloped every form and deadened every sound. Even the harsh voice which she had learned to loathe and to dread sounded curiously subdued and unfamiliar. Heron no longer seemed inclined to storm, to rage, or to curse. The momentary danger, the thought of failure, the hope of revenge, had apparently cooled his temper, strengthened his determination, and forced his voice down to a little above a whisper. He gave his orders clearly and firmly, and the words came to Marguerite on the wings of the wind with strange distinctness, borne to her ears by the darkness itself, and the hush that lay over the wood.

"Take half a dozen men with you, sergeant," she beard him say, "and join citizen Chauvelin at the chateau. You can stable your horses in the farm buildings close by, as he suggests and run to him on foot. You and your men should quickly get the best of a handful of midnight prowlers; you are well armed and they only civilians. Tell citizen Chauvelin that I in the meanwhile will take care of our prisoners. The Englishman I shall put in irons and lock up inside the chapel, with five men under the command of your corporal to guard him, the other two I will drive myself straight to Crecy with what is left of the escort. You understand?"

"Yes, citizen."

"We may not reach Crecy until two hours after midnight, but directly I arrive I will send citizen Chauvelin further reinforcements, which, however, I hope may not necessary, but which will reach him in the early morning. Even if he is seriously attacked, he can, with fourteen men he will have with him, hold out inside the castle through the night. Tell him also that at dawn two prisoners who will be with me will be shot in the courtyard of the guard-house at Crecy, but that whether he has got hold of Capet or not he had best pick up the Englishman in the chapel in the morning and bring him straight to Crecy, where I shall be awaiting him ready to return to Paris. You understand?"

"Yes, citizen."

"Then repeat what I said."

"I am to take six men with me to reinforce citizen Chauvelin now."

"Yes."

"And you, citizen, will drive straight back to Crecy, and will send us further reinforcements from there, which will reach us in the early morning."

"Yes."

"We are to hold the chateau against those unknown marauders if necessary until the reinforcements come from Crecy. Having routed them, we return here, pick up the Englishman whom you will have locked up in the chapel under a strong guard commanded by Corporal Cassard, and join you forthwith at Crecy."

"This, whether citizen Chauvelin has got hold of Capet or not."

"Yes, citizen, I understand," concluded the sergeant imperturbably; "and I am also to tell citizen Chauvelin that the two prisoners will be shot at dawn in the courtyard of the guard-house at Crecy."

"Yes. That is all. Try to find the leader of the attacking party, and bring him along to Crecy with the Englishman; but unless they are in very small numbers do not trouble about the others. Now *en avant*; citizen Chauvelin might be glad of your help. And—stay—order all the men to dismount, and take the horses out of one of the coaches, then let the men you are taking with you each lead a horse, or even two, and stable them all in the farm buildings. I shall not need them, and could not spare any of my men for the work later on. Remember that, above all, silence is the order. When you are ready to start, come back to me here."

The sergeant moved away, and Marguerite heard him transmitting the citizen agent's orders to the soldiers. The dismounting was carried on in wonderful silence—for silence had been one of the principal commands—only one or two words reached her ears.

"First section and first half of second section fall in, right wheel. First section each take two horses on the lead. Quietly now there; don't tug at his bridle—let him go."

And after that a simple report:

"All ready, citizen!"

"Good!" was the response. "Now detail your corporal and two

men to come here to me, so that we may put the Englishman in irons, and take him at once to the chapel, and four men to stand guard at the doors of the other coach."

The necessary orders were given, and after that there came the curt command:

"*En avant!*"

The sergeant, with his squad and all the horses, was slowly moving away in the night. The horses' hoofs hardly made a noise on the soft carpet of pine-needles and of dead fallen leaves, but the champing of the bits was of course audible, and now and then the snorting of some poor, tired horse longing for its stable.

Somehow in Marguerite's fevered mind this departure of a squad of men seemed like the final flitting of her last hope; the slow agony of the familiar sounds, the retreating horses and soldiers moving away amongst the shadows, took on a weird significance. Heron had given his last orders. Percy, helpless and probably unconscious, would spend the night in that dank chapel, while she and Armand would be taken back to Crecy, driven to death like some insentient animals to the slaughter.

When the grey dawn would first begin to peep through the branches of the pines Percy would be led back to Paris and the guillotine, and she and Armand will have been sacrificed to the hatred and revenge of brutes.

The end had come, and there was nothing more to be done. Struggling, fighting, scheming, could be of no avail now; but she wanted to get to her husband; she wanted to be near him now that death was so imminent both for him and for her.

She tried to envisage it all, quite calmly, just as she knew that Percy would wish her to do. The inevitable end was there, and she would not give to these callous wretches here the gratuitous spectacle of a despairing woman fighting blindly against adverse Fate.

But she wanted to go to her husband. She felt that she could face death more easily on the morrow if she could but see him once, if she could but look once more into the eyes that had mirrored so much enthusiasm, such absolute vitality and whole-hearted self-sacrifice, and such an intensity of love and passion; if she could but kiss once more those lips that had smiled through life, and would smile, she knew, even in the face of death.

She tried to open the carriage door, but it was held from without, and a harsh voice cursed her, ordering her to sit still.

But she could lean out of the window and strain her eyes to see. They were by now accustomed to the gloom, the dilated pupils taking in pictures of vague forms moving like ghouls in the shadows. The other coach was not far, and she could hear Heron's voice, still subdued and calm, and the curses of the men. But not a sound from Percy.

"I think the prisoner is unconscious," she heard one of the men say.

"Lift him out of the carriage, then," was Heron's curt command; "and you go and throw open the chapel gates."

Marguerite saw it all. The movement, the crowd of men, two vague, black forms lifting another one, which appeared heavy and inert, out of the coach, and carrying it staggering up towards the chapel.

Then the forms disappeared, swallowed up by the more dense mass of the little building, merged in with it, immovable as the stone itself.

Only a few words reached her now.

"He is unconscious."

"Leave him there, then; he'll not move!"

"Now close the gates!"

There was a loud clang, and Marguerite gave a piercing scream. She tore at the handle of the carriage door.

"Armand, Armand, go to him!" she cried; and all her self-control, all her enforced calm, vanished in an outburst of wild, agonising passion. "Let me get to him, Armand! This is the end; get me to him, in the name of God!"

"Stop that woman screaming," came Heron's voice clearly through the night. "Put her and the other prisoner in irons—quick!"

But while Marguerite expended her feeble strength in a mad, pathetic effort to reach her husband, even now at this last hour, when all hope was dead and Death was so nigh, Armand had already wrenched the carriage door from the grasp of the soldier who was guarding it. He was of the South, and knew the trick of charging an unsuspecting adversary with head thrust forward like a bull inside a ring. Thus he knocked one of the soldiers down and made a quick rush for the chapel gates.

The men, attacked so suddenly and in such complete darkness, did not wait for orders. They closed in round Armand; one man drew his sabre and hacked away with it in aimless rage.

But for the moment he evaded them all, pushing his way through them, not heeding the blows that came on him from out the darkness. At last he reached the chapel. With one bound he was at the gate, his numb fingers fumbling for the lock, which he could not see.

It was a vigorous blow from Heron's fist that brought him at last to his knees, and even then his hands did not relax their hold; they gripped the ornamental scroll of the gate, shook the gate itself in its rusty hinges, pushed and pulled with the unreasoning strength of despair. He had a sabre cut across his brow, and the blood flowed in a warm, trickling stream down his face. But of this he was unconscious; all that he wanted, all that he was striving for with agonising heart-beats and cracking sinews, was to get to his friend, who was lying in there unconscious, abandoned—dead, perhaps.

"Curse you," struck Heron's voice close to his ear. "Cannot some of you stop this raving maniac?"

Then it was that the heavy blow on his head caused him a sensation of sickness, and he fell on his knees, still gripping the ironwork.

Stronger hands than his were forcing him to loosen his hold; blows that hurt terribly rained on his numbed fingers; he felt himself dragged away, carried like an inert mass further and further from that gate which he would have given his lifeblood to force open.

And Marguerite heard all this from the inside of the coach where she was imprisoned as effectually as was Percy's unconscious body inside that dark chapel. She could hear the noise and scramble, and Heron's hoarse commands, the swift sabre strokes as they cut through the air.

Already a trooper had clapped irons on her wrists, two others held the carriage doors. Now Armand was lifted back into the coach, and she could not even help to make him comfortable, though as he was lifted in she heard him feebly moaning. Then the carriage doors were banged to again.

"Do not allow either of the prisoners out again, on peril of your lives!" came with a vigorous curse from Heron.

After which there was a moment's silence; whispered commands came spasmodically in deadened sound to her ear.

"Will the key turn?"

"Yes, citizen."

"All secure?"

"Yes, citizen. The prisoner is groaning."

"Let him groan."

"The empty coach, citizen? The horses have been taken out."

"Leave it standing where it is, then; citizen Chauvelin will need it in the morning."

"Armand," whispered Marguerite inside the coach, "did you see Percy?"

"It was so dark," murmured Armand feebly; "but I saw him, just inside the gates, where they had laid him down. I heard him groaning. Oh, my God!"

"Hush, dear!" she said. "We can do nothing more, only die, as he lived, bravely and with a smile on our lips, in memory of him."

"Number 35 is wounded, citizen," said one of the men.

"Curse the fool who did the mischief," was the placid response. "Leave him here with the guard."

"How many of you are there left, then?" asked the same voice a moment later.

"Only two, citizen; if one whole section remains with me at the chapel door, and also the wounded man."

"Two are enough for me, and five are not too many at the chapel door." And Heron's coarse, cruel laugh echoed against the stone walls of the little chapel. "Now then, one of you get into the coach, and the other go to the horses' heads; and remember, Corporal Cassard, that you and your men who stay here to guard that chapel door are answerable to the whole nation with your lives for the safety of the Englishman."

The carriage door was thrown open, and a soldier stepped in and sat down opposite Marguerite and Armand. Heron in the meanwhile was apparently scrambling up the box. Marguerite could hear him muttering curses as he groped for the reins, and finally gathered them into his hand.

The springs of the coach creaked and groaned as the vehicle slowly swung round; the wheels ploughed deeply through the soft carpet of dead leaves.

Marguerite felt Armand's inert body leaning heavily against her shoulder.

"Are you in pain, dear?" she asked softly.

He made no reply, and she thought that he had fainted. It was better so; at least the next dreary hours would flit by for him in the blissful state of unconsciousness. Now at last the heavy carriage began to move more evenly. The soldier at the horses' heads was stepping along at a rapid pace.

Marguerite would have given much even now to look back once more at the dense black mass, blacker and denser than any shadow that had ever descended before on God's earth, which held between its cold, cruel walls all that she loved in the world.

But her wrists were fettered by the irons, which cut into her flesh when she moved. She could no longer lean out of the window, and she could not even hear. The whole forest was hushed, the wind was lulled to rest; wild beasts and night-birds were silent and still. And the wheels of the coach creaked in the ruts, bearing Marguerite with every turn further and further away from the man who lay helpless in the chapel of the Holy Sepulchre.

# CHAPTER 48: THE WANING MOON

Armand had wakened from his attack of faintness, and brother and sister sat close to one another, shoulder touching shoulder. That sense of nearness was the one tiny spark of comfort to both of them on this dreary, dreary way.

The coach had lumbered on unceasingly since all eternity—so it seemed to them both. Once there had been a brief halt, when Heron's rough voice had ordered the soldier at the horses' heads to climb on the box beside him, and once—it had been a very little while ago—a terrible cry of pain and terror had rung through the stillness of the night. Immediately after that the horses had been put at a more rapid pace, but it had seemed to Marguerite as if that one cry of pain had been repeated by several others which sounded more feeble and soon appeared to be dying away in the distance behind.

The soldier who sat opposite to them must have heard the cry too, for he jumped up, as if wakened from sleep, and put his head out of the window.

"Did you hear that cry, citizen?" he asked.

But only a curse answered him, and a peremptory command not to lose sight of the prisoners by poking his head out of the window.

"Did you hear the cry?" asked the soldier of Marguerite as he made haste to obey.

"Yes! What could it be?" she murmured.

"It seems dangerous to drive so fast in this darkness," muttered the soldier.

After which remark he, with the stolidity peculiar to his kind, figuratively shrugged his shoulders, detaching himself, as it were, of the whole affair.

"We should be out of the forest by now," he remarked in an undertone a little while later; "the way seemed shorter before."

Just then the coach gave an unexpected lurch to one side, and after much groaning and creaking of axles and springs it came to a standstill, and the citizen agent was heard cursing loudly and then scrambling down from the box.

The next moment the carriage-door was pulled open from without, and the harsh voice called out peremptorily:

"Citizen soldier, here—quick!—quick!—curse you!—we'll have one of the horses down if you don't hurry!"

The soldier struggled to his feet; it was never good to be slow in obeying the citizen agent's commands. He was half-asleep and no doubt numb with cold and long sitting still; to accelerate his movements he was suddenly gripped by the arm and dragged incontinently out of the coach.

Then the door was slammed to again, either by a rough hand or a sudden gust of wind, Marguerite could not tell; she heard a cry of rage and one of terror, and Heron's raucous curses. She cowered in the corner of the carriage with Armand's head against her shoulder, and tried to close her ears to all those hideous sounds.

Then suddenly all the sounds were hushed and all around everything became perfectly calm and still—so still that at first the silence oppressed her with a vague, nameless dread. It was as if Nature herself had paused, that she might listen; and the silence became more and more absolute, until Marguerite could hear Armand's soft, regular breathing close to her ear.

The window nearest to her was open, and as she leaned forward with that paralysing sense of oppression a breath of pure air struck full upon her nostrils and brought with it a briny taste as if from the sea.

It was not quite so dark; and there was a sense as of open country stretching out to the limits of the horizon. Overhead a vague greyish light suffused the sky, and the wind swept the clouds in great rolling banks right across that light.

Marguerite gazed upward with a more calm feeling that was akin to gratitude. That pale light, though so wan and feeble, was thrice welcome after that inky blackness wherein shadows were less dark than the lights. She watched eagerly the bank of clouds driven by the dying gale.

The light grew brighter and faintly golden, now the banks of clouds—storm-tossed and fleecy—raced past one another, parted and reunited like veils of unseen giant dancers waved by hands that controlled infinite space—advanced and rushed and slackened speed again—united and finally torn asunder to reveal the waning moon, honey-coloured and mysterious, rising as if from an invisible ocean far away.

The wan pale light spread over the wide stretch of country, throwing over it as it spread dull tones of indigo and of blue. Here and there sparse, stunted trees with fringed gaunt arms bending to prevailing winds proclaimed the neighbourhood of the sea.

Marguerite gazed on the picture which the waning moon had so suddenly revealed; but she gazed with eyes that knew not what they saw. The moon had risen on her right—there lay the east—and the coach must have been travelling due north, whereas Crecy . . .

In the absolute silence that reigned she could perceive from far, very far away, the sound of a church clock striking the midnight hour; and now it seemed to her supersensitive senses that a firm footstep was treading the soft earth, a footstep that drew nearer—and then nearer still.

Nature did pause to listen. The wind was hushed, the night-birds in the forest had gone to rest. Marguerite's heart beat so fast that its throbbings choked her, and a dizziness clouded her consciousness.

But through this state of torpor she heard the opening of the carriage door, she felt the onrush of that pure, briny air, and she felt a long, burning kiss upon her hands.

She thought then that she was really dead, and that God in His infinite love had opened to her the outer gates of Paradise.

"My love!" she murmured.

She was leaning back in the carriage and her eyes were closed, but she felt that firm fingers removed the irons from her wrists, and that a pair of warm lips were pressed there in their stead.

"There, little woman, that's better so—is it not? Now let me get hold of poor old Armand!"

It was Heaven, of course, else how could earth hold such heavenly joy?

"Percy!" exclaimed Armand in an awed voice.

"Hush, dear!" murmured Marguerite feebly; "we are in Heaven you and I—"

Whereupon a ringing laugh woke the echoes of the silent night.

"In Heaven, dear heart!" And the voice had a delicious earthly ring in its whole-hearted merriment. "Please God, you'll both be at Portel with me before dawn."

Then she was indeed forced to believe. She put out her hands and groped for him, for it was dark inside the carriage; she groped, and felt his massive shoulders leaning across the body of the coach, while his fingers busied themselves with the irons on Armand's wrist.

"Don't touch that brute's filthy coat with your dainty fingers, dear heart," he said gaily. "Great Lord! I have worn that wretch's clothes for over two hours; I feel as if the dirt had penetrated to my bones."

Then with that gesture so habitual to him he took her head between his two hands, and drawing her to him until the wan light from without lit up the face that he worshipped, he gazed his fill into her eyes.

She could only see the outline of his head silhouetted against the wind-tossed sky; she could not see his eyes, nor his lips, but she felt his nearness, and the happiness of that almost caused her to swoon.

"Come out into the open, my lady fair," he murmured, and though she could not see, she could feel that he smiled; "let God's pure air blow through your hair and round your dear head. Then, if you can walk so far, there's a small half-way house close by here. I have knocked up the none too amiable host. You and Armand could have half an hour's rest there before we go further on our way."

"But you, Percy?—are you safe?"

"Yes, m'dear, we are all of us safe until morning-time enough to reach Le Portel, and to be aboard the Day-Dream before mine amiable friend M. Chambertin has discovered his worthy colleague lying gagged and bound inside the chapel of the Holy Sepulchre. By Gad! how old Heron will curse—the moment he can open his mouth!"

He half helped, half lifted her out of the carriage. The strong pure air suddenly rushing right through to her lungs made her feel faint, and she almost fell. But it was good to feel herself falling, when one pair of arms amongst the millions on the earth were there to receive her.

"Can you walk, dear heart?" he asked. "Lean well on me—it is not far, and the rest will do you good."

"But you, Percy—"

He laughed, and the most complete joy of living seemed to resound through that laugh. Her arm was in his, and for one moment he stood still while his eyes swept the far reaches of the country, the mellow distance still wrapped in its mantle of indigo, still untouched by the mysterious light of the waning moon.

He pressed her arm against his heart, but his right hand was stretched out towards the black wall of the forest behind him, towards the dark crests of the pines in which the dying wind sent its last mournful sighs.

"Dear heart," he said, and his voice quivered with the intensity of his excitement, "beyond the stretch of that wood, from far away over there, there are cries and moans of anguish that come to my ear even now. But for you, dear, I would cross that wood to-night and re-enter Paris to-morrow. But for you, dear—but for you," he reiterated earnestly as he pressed her closer to him, for a bitter cry had risen to her lips.

She went on in silence. Her happiness was great—as great as was her pain. She had found him again, the man whom she worshipped, the husband whom she thought never to see again on earth. She had found him, and not even now—not after those terrible weeks of misery and suffering unspeakable—could she feel that love had triumphed over the wild, adventurous spirit, the reckless enthusiasm, the ardour of self-sacrifice.

# CHAPTER 49: THE LAND OF ELDORADO

It seems that in the pocket of Heron's coat there was a letter-case with some few hundred francs. It was amusing to think that the brute's money helped to bribe the ill-tempered keeper of the half-way house to receive guests at midnight, and to ply them well with food, drink, and the shelter of a stuffy coffee-room.

Marguerite sat silently beside her husband, her hand in his. Armand, opposite to them, had both elbows on the table. He looked pale and wan, with a bandage across his forehead, and his glowing eyes were resting on his chief.

"Yes! you demmed young idiot," said Blakeney merrily, "you nearly upset my plan in the end, with your yelling and screaming outside the chapel gates."

"I wanted to get to you, Percy. I thought those brutes had got you there inside that building."

"Not they!" he exclaimed. "It was my friend Heron whom they had trussed and gagged, and whom my amiable friend M. Chambertin will find in there to-morrow morning. By Gad! I would go back if only for the pleasure of hearing Heron curse when first the gag is taken from his mouth."

"But how was it all done, Percy? And there was de Batz—"

"De Batz was part of the scheme I had planned for mine own escape before I knew that those brutes meant to take Marguerite and you as hostages for my good behaviour. What I hoped then was that under cover of a tussle or a fight I could somehow or other contrive to slip through their fingers. It was a chance, and you know my belief in bald-headed Fortune, with the one solitary hair. Well, I meant to grab that hair; and at the worst I could but die in the open and not caged in that awful hole like some noxious vermin. I knew that de Batz would rise to the bait. I told him in my letter that the Dauphin would be at the Chateau d'Ourde this night, but that I feared the revolutionary Government had got wind of this fact, and were sending an armed escort to bring the lad away. This letter Ffoulkes took to him; I knew that he would make a vigorous effort to get the Dauphin into his hands, and that during the scuffle that one hair on Fortune's head would for one second only, mayhap, come within my reach. I had so planned the expedition that we were bound to arrive at the forest of Boulogne by nightfall, and night is always a useful ally. But at the guard-house of the Rue Ste. Anne I realised for the first time that those brutes had pressed me into a tighter corner than I had pre-conceived."

He paused, and once again that look of recklessness swept over his face, and his eyes—still hollow and circled—shone with the excitement of past memories.

"I was such a weak, miserable wretch, then," he said, in answer to Marguerite's appeal. "I had to try and build up some strength, when —Heaven forgive me for the sacrilege—I had unwittingly risked your precious life, dear heart, in that blind endeavour to save mine own. By Gad! it was no easy task in that jolting vehicle with that noisome wretch beside me for sole company; yet I ate and I drank and I slept for three days and two nights, until the hour when in the darkness I struck Heron from behind, half-strangled him first, then gagged him, and finally slipped into his filthy coat and put that loathsome bandage across my head, and his battered hat above it all. The yell he gave when first I attacked him made every horse rear—you must remember it—the noise effectually drowned our last scuffle in the coach. Chauvelin was the only man who might have suspected what had occurred, but he had gone on ahead, and bald-headed Fortune had passed by me, and I had managed to grab its one hair. After that it was all quite easy. The sergeant and the soldiers had seen very little of Heron and nothing of me; it did not take a great effort to deceive them, and the darkness of the night was my most faithful friend. His raucous voice was not difficult to imitate, and darkness always muffles and changes every tone. Anyway, it was not likely that those loutish soldiers would even remotely suspect the trick that was being played on them. The citizen agent's orders were promptly and implicitly obeyed. The men never even thought to wonder that after insisting on an escort of twenty he should drive off with two prisoners and only two men to guard them. If they did wonder, it was not theirs to question. Those two troopers are spending an uncomfortable night somewhere in the forest of Boulogne, each tied to a tree, and some two leagues apart one from the other. And now," he added gaily, "en voiture, my fair lady; and you, too, Armand. 'Tis seven leagues to Le Portel, and we must be there before dawn."

"Sir Andrew's intention was to make for Calais first, there to open communication with the *Day Dream* and then for Le Portel," said Marguerite; "after that he meant to strike back for the Chateau d'Ourde in search of me."

"Then we'll still find him at Le Portel—I shall know how to lay hands on him; but you two must get aboard the Day-Dream at once, for Ffoulkes and I can always look after ourselves."

It was one hour after midnight when—refreshed with food and rest—Marguerite, Armand and Sir Percy left the half-way house. Marguerite was standing in the doorway ready to go. Percy and Armand had gone ahead to bring the coach along.

"Percy," whispered Armand, "Marguerite does not know?"

"Of course she does not, you young fool," retorted Percy lightly. "If you try and tell her I think I would smash your head."

"But you—" said the young man with sudden vehemence; "can

you bear the sight of me? My God! when I think—"

"Don't think, my good Armand—not of that anyway. Only think of the woman for whose sake you committed a crime—if she is pure and good, woo her and win her—not just now, for it were foolish to go back to Paris after her, but anon, when she comes to England and all these past days are forgotten—then love her as much as you can, Armand. Learn your lesson of love better than I have learnt mine; do not cause Jeanne Lange those tears of anguish which my mad spirit brings to your sister's eyes. You were right, Armand, when you said that I do not know how to love!"

But on board the *Day Dream*, when all danger was past, Marguerite felt that he did.

# LORD TONY'S WIFE

BARONESS EMMUSKA ORCZY

# PROLOGUE
## NANTES, 1789

### I

"Tyrant! tyrant! tyrant!"

It was Pierre who spoke, his voice was hardly raised above a murmur, but there was such an intensity of passion expressed in his face, in the fingers of his hand which closed slowly and convulsively as if they were clutching the throat of a struggling viper, there was so much hate in those muttered words, so much power, such compelling and awesome determination that an ominous silence fell upon the village lads and the men who sat with him in the low narrow room of the *auberge des* Trois Vertus.

Even the man in the tattered coat and threadbare breeches, who—perched upon the centre table—had been haranguing the company on the subject of the Rights of Man, paused in his peroration and looked down on Pierre half afraid of that fierce flame of passionate hate which his own words had helped to kindle.

The silence, however, had only lasted a few moments, the next Pierre was on his feet, and a cry like that of a bull in a slaughter-house escaped his throat.

"In the name of God!" he shouted, "let us cease all that senseless talking. Haven't we planned enough and talked enough to satisfy our puling consciences? The time has come to strike, *mes amis*, to strike I say, to strike at those cursed aristocrats, who have made us what we are—ignorant, wretched, downtrodden—senseless clods to work our fingers to the bone, our bodies till they break so that they may wallow in their pleasures and their luxuries! Strike, I say!" he reiterated while his eyes glowed and his breath came and went through his throat with a hissing sound. "Strike! as the men and women struck in Paris on that great day in July. To them the Bastille stood for tyranny, and they struck at it as they would at the head of a tyrant—and the tyrant cowered, cringed, made terms—he was frightened at the wrath of the people! That is what happened in Paris! That is what must happen in Nantes. The *château* of the duc de Kernogan is our Bastille! Let us strike at it to-night, and if the arrogant aristocrat resists, we'll raze his house to the ground. The hour, the day, the darkness are all propitious. The arrangements hold good. The neighbours are ready. Strike, I say!"

He brought his hard fist crashing down upon the table, so that mugs and bottles rattled: his enthusiasm had fired all his hearers: his hatred and his lust of revenge had done more in five minutes than all the tirades of the agitators sent down from Paris to instil revolutionary ideas into the slow-moving brains of village lads.

"Who will give the signal?" queried one of the older men quietly.

"I will!" came a lusty response from Pierre.

He strode to the door, and all the men jumped to their feet, ready to follow him, dragged into this hot-headed venture by the mere force of one man's towering passion. They followed Pierre like sheep—sheep that have momentarily become intoxicated—sheep that have become fierce—a strange sight truly—and yet one that the man in the tattered coat who had done so much speechifying lately, watched with eager interest and presently related with great wealth of detail to M. de Mirabeau the champion of the people.

"It all came about through the death of a pair of pigeons," he said.

The death of the pigeons, however, was only the spark which set all these turbulent passions ablaze. They had been smouldering for half a century, and had been ready to burst into flames for the past decade.

Antoine Melun, the wheelwright, who was to have married Louise, Pierre's sister, had trapped a pair of pigeons in the woods of M. le duc de Kernogan. He had done it to assert his rights as a man—he did not want the pigeons. Though he was a poor man, he was no poorer than hundreds of peasants for miles around: but he paid imposts and taxes until every particle of profit which he gleaned from his miserable little plot of land went into the hands of the collectors, whilst M. le duc de Kernogan paid not one sou towards the costs of the State, and he had to live on what was left of his own rye and wheat after M. le duc's pigeons had had their fill of them.

Antoine Melun did not want to eat the pigeons which he had trapped, but he desired to let M. le duc de Kernogan know that God and Nature had never intended all the beasts and birds of the woods to be the exclusive property of one man, rather than another. So he trapped and killed two pigeons and M. le duc's head-bailiff caught him in the act of carrying those pigeons home.

Whereupon Antoine was arrested for poaching and thieving: he was tried at Nantes under the presidency of M. le duc de Kernogan, and ten minutes ago, while the man in the tattered coat was declaiming to a number of peasant lads in the coffee-room of the auberge des Trois Vertus on the subject of their rights as men and citizens, some one brought the news that Antoine Melun had just been condemned to death and would be hanged on the morrow.

That was the spark which had fanned Pierre Adet's hatred of the aristocrats to a veritable conflagration: the news of Antoine Melun's fate was the bleat which rallied all those human sheep around their leader. For Pierre had naturally become their leader because his hatred of M. le duc was more tangible, more powerful than theirs. Pierre had

had more education than they. His father, Jean Adet the miller, had
sent him to a school in Nantes, and when Pierre came home M. le curé
of Vertou took an interest in him and taught him all he knew himself—
which was not much—in the way of philosophy and the classics. But
later on Pierre took to reading the writings of M. Jean-Jacques
Rousseau and soon knew the Contrat Social almost by heart. He had
also read the articles in M. Marat's newspaper *L'ami du Peuple!* and,
like Antoine Melun, the wheelwright, he had got it into his head that it
was not God, nor yet Nature who had intended one man to starve while
another gorged himself on all the good things of this world.

He did not, however, speak of these matters, either to his father
or to his sister or to M. le curé, but he brooded over them, and when
the price of bread rose to four sous he muttered curses against M. le
duc de Kernogan, and when famine prices ruled throughout the district
those curses became overt threats; and by the time that the pinch of
hunger was felt in Vertou Pierre's passion of fury against the duc de
Kernogan had turned to a frenzy of hate against the entire noblesse of
France.

Still he said nothing to his father, nothing to his mother and
sister. But his father knew. Old Jean would watch the storm-clouds
which gathered on Pierre's lowering brow; he heard the muttered
curses which escaped from Pierre's lips whilst he worked for the liege-
lord whom he hated. But Jean was a wise man and knew how useless it
is to put out a feeble hand in order to stem the onrush of a torrent. He
knew how useless are the words of wisdom from an old man to quell
the rebellious spirit of the young.

Jean was on the watch. And evening after evening when the
work on the farm was done, Pierre would sit in the small low room of
the auberge with other lads from the village talking, talking of their
wrongs, of the arrogance of the aristocrats, the sins of M. le duc and his
family, the evil conduct of the King and the immorality of the Queen:
and men in ragged coats and tattered breeches came in from Nantes,
and even from Paris, in order to harangue these village lads and told
them yet further tales of innumerable wrongs suffered by the people at
the hands of the *aristos,* and stuffed their heads full of schemes for
getting even once and for all with those men and women who fattened
on the sweat of the poor and drew their luxury from the hunger and the
toil of the peasantry.

Pierre sucked in these harangues through every pore: they were
meat and drink to him. His hate and passions fed upon these effusions
till his whole being was consumed by a maddening desire for reprisals,
for vengeance—for the lust of triumph over those whom he had been
taught to fear.

And in the low, narrow room of the *auberge* the fevered heads
of village lads were bent together in conclave, and the ravings and

shoutings of a while ago were changed to whisperings and low murmurings behind barred doors and shuttered windows. Men exchanged cryptic greetings when they met in the village street, enigmatical signs passed between them while they worked: strangers came and went at dead of night to and from the neighbouring villages. M. le duc's overseers saw nothing, heard nothing, guessed nothing. M. le curé saw much and old Jean Adet guessed a great deal, but they said nothing, for nothing then would have availed.

Then came the catastrophe.

## II

Pierre pushed open the outer door of the *auberge des* Trois Vertus and stepped out under the porch. A gust of wind caught him in the face. The night, so the chronicles of the time tell us, was as dark as pitch: on ahead lay the lights of the city flickering in the gale: to the left the wide tawny ribbon of the river wound its turbulent course toward the ocean, the booming of the waters swollen by the recent melting of the snow sounded like the weird echoes of invisible cannons far away.

Without hesitation Pierre advanced. His little troop followed him in silence. They were a little sobered now that they came out into the open and that the fumes of cider and of hot, perspiring humanity no longer obscured their vision or inflamed their brain.

They knew whither Pierre was going. It had all been pre-arranged—throughout this past summer, in the musty parlour of the *auberge*, behind barred doors and shuttered windows—all they had to do was to follow Pierre, whom they had tacitly chosen as their leader. They walked on behind him, their hands buried in the pockets of their thin, tattered breeches, their heads bent forward against the fury of the gale.

Pierre made straight for the mill—his home—where his father lived and where Louise was even now crying her eyes out because Antoine Melun, her sweetheart, had been condemned to be hanged for killing two pigeons.

At the back of the mill was the dwelling house and beyond it a small farmery, for Jean Adet owned a little bit of land and would have been fairly well off if the taxes had not swallowed up all the money that he made out of the sale of his rye and his hay. Just here the ground rose sharply to a little hillock which dominated the flat valley of the Loire and commanded a fine view over the more distant villages.

Pierre skirted the mill and without looking round to see if the others followed him he struck squarely to the right up a narrow lane bordered by tall poplars, and which led upwards to the summit of the little hillock around which clustered the tumble-down barns of his father's farmery.

The gale lashed the straight, tall stems of the poplars until they bent nearly double, and each tiny bare twig sighed and whispered as if in pain. Pierre strode on and the others followed in silence. They were chilled to the bone under their scanty clothes, but they followed on with grim determination, set teeth, and anger and hate seething in their hearts.

The top of the rising ground was reached. It was pitch dark, and the men when they halted fell up against one another trying to get a foothold on the sodden ground. But Pierre seemed to have eyes like a cat. He only paused one moment to get his bearings, then—still without a word—he set to work. A large barn and a group of small circular straw ricks loomed like solid masses out of the darkness—black, silhouetted against the black of the stormy sky. Pierre turned toward the barn: those of his comrades who were in the forefront of the small crowd saw him disappearing inside one of those solid shadowy masses that looked so ghostlike in the night.

Anon those who watched and who happened to be facing the interior of the barn saw sparks from a tinder flying in every direction: the next moment they could see Pierre himself quite clearly. He was standing in the middle of the barn and intent on lighting a roughly-fashioned torch with his tinder: soon the resin caught a spark and Pierre held the torch inclined toward the ground so that the flames could lick their way up the shaft. The flickering light cast a weird glow and deep grotesque shadows upon the face and figure of the young man. His hair, lanky and dishevelled, fell over his eyes; his mouth and jaw, illumined from below by the torch, looked unnaturally large, and showed his teeth gleaming white, like the fangs of a beast of prey. His shirt was torn open at the neck, and the sleeves of his coat were rolled up to the elbow. He seemed not to feel either the cold from without or the scorching heat of the flaming torch in his hand. But he worked deliberately and calmly, without haste or febrile movements: grim determination held his excitement in check.

At last his work was done. The men who had pressed forward, in order to watch him, fell back as he advanced, torch in hand. They knew exactly what he was going to do, they had thought it all out, planned it, spoken of it till even their unimaginative minds had visualised this coming scene with absolutely realistic perception. And yet, now that the supreme hour had come, now that they saw Pierre—torch in hand—prepared to give the signal which would set ablaze the seething revolt of the countryside, their heart seemed to stop its beating within their body; they held their breath, their toil-worn hands went up to their throats as if to repress that awful choking sensation which was so like fear.

But Pierre had no such hesitations; if his breath seemed to choke him as it reached his throat, if it escaped through his set teeth with a strange whistling sound, it was because his excitement was that of a hungry beast who had sighted his prey and is ready to spring and devour. His hand did not shake, his step was firm: the gusts of wind caught the flame of his torch till the sparks flew in every direction and scorched his hair and his hands, and while the others recoiled he strode on, to the straw-rick that was nearest.

For one moment he held the torch aloft. There was triumph now in his eyes, in his whole attitude. He looked out into the darkness far away which seemed all the more impenetrable beyond the restricted circle of flickering torchlight. It seemed as if he would wrest from that inky blackness all the secrets which it hid—all the enthusiasm, the excitement, the passions, the hatred which he would have liked to set ablaze as he would the straw-ricks anon.

"Are you ready, *mes amis?*" he called.

"Aye! aye!" they replied—not gaily, not lustily, but calmly and under their breath.

One touch of the torch and the dry straw began to crackle; a gust of wind caught the flame and whipped it into energy; it crept up the side of the little rick like a glowing python that wraps its prey in its embrace. Another gust of wind, and the flame leapt joyously up to the pinnacle of the rick, and sent forth other tongues to lick and to lick, to enfold the straw, to devour, to consume.

But Pierre did not wait to see the consummation of his work of destruction. Already with a few rapid strides he had reached his father's second straw-rick, and this too he set alight, and then another and another, until six blazing furnaces sent their lurid tongues of flames, twisting and twirling, writhing and hissing through the stormy night.

Within the space of two minutes the whole summit of the hillock seemed to be ablaze, and Pierre, like a god of fire, torch in hand, seemed to preside over and command a multitude of ever-spreading flames to his will. Excitement had overmastered him now, the lust to destroy was upon him, and excitement had seized all the others too.

There was shouting and cursing, and laughter that sounded mirthless and forced, and calls to Pierre, and oaths of revenge. Memory, like an evil-intentioned witch, was riding invisibly in the darkness, and she touched each seething brain with her fever-giving wand. Every man had an outrage to remember, an injustice to recall, and strong, brown fists were shaken aloft in the direction of the *château* Kernogan, whose lights glimmered feebly in the distance beyond the Loire.

"Death to the tyrant! *A la lanterne les aristos!* The people's hour has come at last! No more starvation! No more injustice! Equality! Liberty! *A mort les aristos!*"

The shouts, the curses, the crackling flames, the howling of the wind, the soughing of the trees, made up a confusion of sounds which seemed hardly of this earth; the blazing ricks, the flickering, red light of the flames had finally transformed the little hillock behind the mill into another Brocken on whose summit witches and devils do of a truth hold their revels.

"*A moi!*" shouted Pierre again, and he threw his torch down upon the ground and once more made for the barn. The others followed him. In the barn were such weapons as these wretched, penniless peasants had managed to collect—scythes, poles, axes, saws, anything that would prove useful for the destruction of the *château* Kernogan and the proposed brow-beating of M. le duc and his family. All the men trooped in in the wake of Pierre. The entire hillock was now a blaze of light—lurid and red and flickering—alternately teased and fanned and subdued by the gale, so that at times every object stood out clearly cut, every blade of grass, every stone in bold relief, and in the ruts and fissures, every tiny pool of muddy water shimmered like strings of fire-opals: whilst at others, a pall of inky darkness, smoke-laden and impenetrable would lie over the ground and erase the outline of farm-buildings and distant mill and of the pushing and struggling mass of humanity inside the barn.

But Pierre, heedless of light and darkness, of heat or of cold, proceeded quietly and methodically to distribute the primitive implements of warfare to this crowd of ignorant men, who were by now over ready for mischief: and with every weapon which he placed in willing hands, he found the right words for willing ears—words which would kindle passion and lust of vengeance most readily where they lay dormant, or would fan them into greater vigour where they smouldered.

"For thee this scythe, Hector Lebrun," he would say to a tall, lanky youth whose emaciated arms and bony hands were stretched with longing toward the bright piece of steel; "remember last year's harvest, the heavy tax thou wert forced to pay, so that not one sou of profit went into thy pocket, and thy mother starved whilst M. le duc and his brood feasted and danced, and shiploads of corn were sunk in the Loire lest abundance made bread too cheap for the poor!

"For thee this pick-axe, Henri Meunier! Remember the new roof on thy hut, which thou didst build to keep the wet off thy wife's bed, who was crippled with ague—and the heavy impost levied on thee by the tax-collector for this improvement to thy miserable hovel.

"This pole for thee, Charles Blanc! Remember the beating administered to thee by the duc's bailiff for daring to keep a tame rabbit to amuse thy children!

"Remember! Remember, *mes amis!*" he added exultantly, "remember every wrong you have endured, every injustice, every blow! remember your poverty and his wealth, your crusts of dry bread and his succulent meals, your rags and his silks and velvets, remember your

starving children and ailing mother, your care-laden wife and toil-worn
daughters! Forget nothing, *mes amis*, to-night, and at the gates of the
*château* Kernogan demand of its arrogant owner wrong for wrong and
outrage for outrage."

A deafening cry of triumph greeted this peroration, scythes and
sickles and axes and poles were brandished in the air and several scores
of hands were stretched out to Pierre and clasped in this newly-formed
bond of vengeful fraternity.

### III

Then it was that with vigorous play of the elbows, Jean Adet,
the miller, forced his way through the crowd till he stood face to face
with his son.

"Unfortunate!" he cried, "what is all this? What dost thou
propose to do? Whither are ye all going?"

"To Kernogan!" they all shouted in response.

"*En avant*, Pierre! we follow!" cried some of them impatiently.

But Jean Adet—who was a powerful man despite his years—had
seized Pierre by the arm and dragged him to a distant corner of the
barn:

"Pierre!" he said in tones of command, "I forbid thee in the
name of thy duty and the obedience which thou dost owe to me and to
thy mother, to move another step in this hot-headed adventure. I was
on the high-road, walking homewards, when that conflagration and the
senseless cries of these poor lads warned me that some awful mischief
was afoot. Pierre! my son! I command thee to lay that weapon down."

But Pierre—who in his normal state was a dutiful son and
sincerely fond of his father—shook himself free from Jean Adet's grasp.

"Father!" he said loudly and firmly, "this is no time for
interference. We are all of us men here and know our own minds. What
we mean to do to-night we have thought on and planned for weeks and
months. I pray you, father, let me be! I am not a child and I have work
to do."

"Not a child?" exclaimed the old man as he turned appealingly
to the lads who had stood by, silent and sullen during this little scene.
"Not a child? But you are all only children, my lads. You don't know
what you are doing. You don't know what terrible consequences this
mad escapade will bring upon us all, upon the whole village, aye! and
the country-side. Do you suppose for one moment that the *château* of
Kernogan will fall at the mercy of a few ignorant unarmed lads like
yourselves? Why! four hundred of you would not succeed in forcing
your way even as far as the courtyard of the palace. M. le duc has had
wind for some time of your turbulent meetings at the *auberge*: he has
kept an armed guard inside his castle yard for weeks past, a company of

artillery with two guns hoisted upon his walls. My poor lads! you are running straight to ruin! Go home, I beg of you! Forget this night's escapade! Nothing but misery to you and yours can result from it."

They listened quietly, if surlily, to Jean Adet's impassioned words. Far be it from their thoughts to flout or to mock him. Paternal authority commanded respect even among the most rough; but they all felt that they had gone too far now to draw back: the savour of anticipated revenge had been too sweet to be forgone quite so readily, and Pierre with his vigorous personality, his glowing eloquence, his compelling power had more influence over them than the sober counsels of prudence and the wise admonitions of old Jean Adet. Not one word was spoken, but with an instinctive gesture every man grasped his weapon more firmly and then turned to Pierre, thus electing him their spokesman.

Pierre too had listened in silence to all that his father said, striving to hide the burning anxiety which was gnawing at his heart, lest his comrades allowed themselves to be persuaded by the old man's counsels and their ardour be cooled by the wise dictates of prudence. But when Jean Adet had finished speaking, and Pierre saw each man thus grasping his weapon all the more firmly and in silence, a cry of triumph escaped his lips.

"It is all in vain, father," he cried, "our minds are made up. A host of angels from heaven would not bar our way now to victory and to vengeance."

"Pierre!" admonished the old man.

"It is too late, my father," said Pierre firmly, "*en avant*, lads!"

"Yes! *en avant! en avant!*" assented some, "we have wasted too much time as it is."

"But, unfortunate lads," admonished the old man, "what are you going to do?—a handful of you—where are you going?"

"We go straight to the cross-roads now, father," said Pierre, firmly. "The firing of your ricks—for which I humbly crave your pardon —is the preconcerted signal which will bring the lads from all the neighbouring villages—from Goulaine and les Sorinières and Doulon and Tourne-Bride to our meeting place. Never you fear! There will be more than four hundred of us and a company of paid soldiers is not like to frighten us. Eh, lads?"

"No! no! *en avant!*" they shouted and murmured impatiently, "there has been too much talking already and we have wasted precious time."

"Pierre!" entreated the miller.

But no one listened to the old man now. A general movement down the hillock had already begun and Pierre, turning his back on his father, had pushed his way to the front of the crowd and was now leading the way down the slope. Up on the summit the fire was already burning low; only from time to time an imprisoned tongue of flame would dart out of the dying embers and leap fitfully up into the night. A dull red glow illumined the small farmery and the mill and the slowly moving mass of men along the narrow road, whilst clouds of black, dense smoke were tossed about by the gale. Pierre walked with head erect. He ceased to think of his father and he never looked back to see if the others followed him. He knew that they did: like the straw-ricks a while ago, they had become the prey of a consuming fire: the fire of their own passion which had caught them and held them and would not leave them now until their ardour was consumed in victory or defeat.

IV

M. le duc de Kernogan had just finished dinner when Jacques Labrunière, his head-bailiff, came to him with the news that a rabble crowd, composed of the peasantry of Goulaine and Vertou and the neighbouring villages, had assembled at the cross-roads, there held revolutionary speeches, and was even now marching toward the castle still shouting and singing and brandishing a miscellaneous collection of weapons chiefly consisting of scythes and axes.

"The guard is under arms, I imagine," was M. le duc's comment on this not altogether unforeseen piece of news.

"Everything is in perfect order," replied the head-bailiff cooly, "for the defence of M. le duc and his property—and of Mademoiselle."

M. le duc, who had been lounging in one of the big armchairs in the stately hall of Kernogan, jumped to his feet at these words: his cheeks suddenly pallid, and a look of deadly fear in his eyes.

"Mademoiselle," he said hurriedly, "by G—d, Labrunière, I had forgotten—momentarily——"

"M. le duc?" stammered the bailiff in anxious inquiry.

"Mademoiselle de Kernogan is on her way home—even now— she spent the day with Mme. le Marquise d'Herbignac—she was to return at about eight o'clock. . . . If those devils meet her carriage on the road. . . . "

"There is no cause for anxiety, M. le duc," broke in Labrunière hurriedly. "I will see that half a dozen men get to horse at once and go and meet Mademoiselle and escort her home. . . . "

"Yes . . . yes . . . Labrunière," murmured the duc, who seemed very much overcome with terror now that his daughter's safety was in jeopardy, "see to it at once. Quick! quick! I shall wax crazy with anxiety."

While Labrunière ran to make the necessary arrangements for an efficient escort for Mademoiselle de Kernogan and gave the sergeant in charge of the posse the necessary directions, M. le duc remained motionless, huddled up in the capacious armchair, his head buried in his hand, shivering in front of the huge fire which burned in the monumental hearth, himself the prey of nameless, overwhelming terror.

He knew—none better—the appalling hatred wherewith he and all his family and belongings were regarded by the local peasantry. Astride upon his manifold rights—feudal, territorial, seignorial rights— he had all his life ridden roughshod over the prejudices, the miseries, the undoubted rights of the poor people, who were little better than serfs in the possession of the high and mighty duc de Kernogan. He also knew—none better—that gradually, very gradually it is true, but with unerring certainty, those same downtrodden, ignorant, miserable and half-starved peasants were turning against their oppressors, that riots and outrages had occurred in many rural districts in the North and that the insidious poison of social revolution was gradually creeping toward the South and West, and had already infected the villages and small townships which were situated quite unpleasantly close to Nantes and to Kernogan.

For this reason he had kept a company of artillery at his own expense inside the precincts of his château, and with the aristocrat's open contempt for this peasantry which it had not yet learned to fear, he had disdained to take further measures for the repression of local gatherings, and would not pay the village rabble the compliment of being afraid of them in any way.

But with his daughter Yvonne in the open roadway on the very night when an assembly of that same rabble was obviously bent on mischief, matters became very serious. Insult, outrage or worse might befall the proud aristocrat's only child, and knowing that from these people, whom she had been taught to look upon as little better than beasts, she could expect neither mercy nor chivalry, the duc de Kernogan within his unassailable castle felt for his daughter'ssafety the most abject, the most deadly fear which hath ever unnerved any man.

Labrunière a few minutes later did his best to reassure his master.

"I have ordered the men to take the best horses out of the stables, M. le duc," he said, "and to cut across the fields toward la Gramoire so as to intercept Mademoiselle's coach ere it reach the cross-roads. I feel confident that there is no cause for alarm," he added emphatically.

"Pray God you are right, Labrunière," murmured the duc feebly. "Do you know how strong the rabble crowd is?"

"No, Monseigneur, not exactly. Camille the under-bailiff, who brought me the news, was riding homewards across the meadows about an hour ago when he saw a huge conflagration which seemed to come from the back of Adet's mill: the whole sky has been lit up by a lurid light for the past hour, and I fancied myself that Adet's straw must be on fire. But Camille pushed his horse up the rising ground which culminates at Adet's farmery. It seems that he heard a great deal of shouting which did not seem to be accompanied by any attempt at putting out the fire. So he dismounted and led his horse round the hillock skirting Adet's farm buildings so that he should not be seen. Under cover of darkness he heard and saw the old miller with his son Pierre engaged in distributing scythes, poles and axes to a crowd of youngsters and haranguing them wildly all the time. He also heard Pierre Adet speak of the conflagration as a preconcerted signal, and say that he and his mates would meet the lads of the neighbouring villages at the cross-roads . . . and that four hundred of them would then march on Kernogan and pillage the castle."

"Bah!" quoth M. le duc in a voice hoarse with execration and contempt, "a lot of oafs who will give the hangman plenty of trouble to-morrow. As for that Adet and his son, they shall suffer for this . . . I can promise them that. . . . If only Mademoiselle were home!" he added with a heartrending sigh.

## V

Indeed, had M. le duc de Kernogan been gifted with second sight, the agony of mind which he was enduring would have been aggravated an hundredfold. At the very moment when the head-bailiff was doing his best to reassure his liege-lord as to the safety of Mlle. de Kernogan, her coach was speeding along from the château of Herbignac toward those same cross-roads where a couple of hundred hot-headed peasant lads were planning as much mischief as their unimaginative minds could conceive.

The fury of the gale had in no way abated, and now a heavy rain was falling—a drenching, sopping rain which in the space of half an hour had added five centimetres to the depth of the mud on the roads, and had in that same space of time considerably damped the enthusiasm of some of the poor lads. Three score or so had assembled from Goulaine, two score from les Sorinières, some three dozen from Doulon: they had rallied to the signal in hot haste, gathered their scythes and spades, very eager and excited, and had reached the cross-roads which were much nearer to their respective villages than to Jean Adet's farm and the mill, even while the old man was admonishing his son and the lads of Vertou on the summit of the blazing hillock. Here they had spent half an hour in cooling their heels and their tempers under the drenching rain—wet to the skin—fuming and fretting at the delay.

But even so—damped in ardour and chilled to the marrow—they were still a dangerous crowd and prudence ought to have dictated to Mademoiselle de Kernogan the wiser course of ordering her coachman Jean-Marie to head his horses back toward Herbignac the moment that the outrider reported that a mob, armed with scythes, spades and axes, held the cross-roads, and that it would be dangerous for the coach to advance any further.

Already for the past few minutes the sound of loud shouting had been heard even above the tramp of the horses and the clatter of the coach. Jean-Marie had pulled up and sent one of the outriders on ahead to see what was amiss: the man returned with very unpleasant tidings—in his opinion it certainly would be dangerous to go any further. The mob appeared bent on mischief: he had heard threats and curses all levelled against M. le duc de Kernogan—the conflagration up at Vertou was evidently a signal which would bring along a crowd of malcontents from all the neighbouring villages. He was for turning back forthwith. But Mademoiselle put her head out of the window just then and asked what was amiss. On hearing that Jean-Marie and the postilion and outriders were inclined to be afraid of a mob of peasant lads who had assembled at the cross-roads, and were apparently threatening to do mischief, she chided them for their cowardice.

"Jean-Marie," she called scornfully to the old coachman, who had been in her father's service for close on half a century, "do you really mean to tell me that you are afraid of that rabble!"

"Why no! Mademoiselle, so please you," replied the old man, nettled in his pride by the taunt, "but the temper of the peasantry round here has been ugly of late, and 'tis your safety I have got to guard."

"'Tis my commands you have got to obey," retorted Mademoiselle with a gay little laugh which mitigated the peremptoriness of her tone. "If my father should hear that there's trouble on the road he will die of anxiety if I do not return: so whip up the horses, Jean-Marie. No one will dare to attack the coach."

"But Mademoiselle——" remonstrated the old man.

"*Ah çà!*" she broke in more impatiently, "am I to be openly disobeyed? Best join that rabble, Jean-Marie, if you have no respect for my commands."

Thus twitted by Mademoiselle's sharp tongue, Jean-Marie could not help but obey. He tried to peer into the distance through the veil of blinding rain which beat against his face and stung the horses to restlessness. But the light from the coach lanthorns prevented his seeing clearly into the darkness beyond. Still it seemed to him that on ahead a dense and solid mass was moving toward the coach, also that the sound of shouting and of excited humanity was considerably nearer than it had been before. No doubt the mob had perceived the lights of the coach, and was even now making towards it, with what intent Jean-Marie divined all too accurately.

But he had his orders, and, though he was an old and trusted servant, disobedience these days was not even to be thought of. So he did as he was bid. He whipped up his horses, which were high-spirited and answered to the lash with a bound and a plunge forward. Mlle. de Kernogan leaned back on the cushions of the coach. She was satisfied that Jean-Marie had done as he was told, and she was not in the least afraid.

But less than five minutes later she had a rude awakening. The coach gave a terrific lurch. The horses reared and plunged, there was a deafening clamour all around: men were shouting and cursing: there was the clash of wood and iron and the cracking of whips: the tramp of horses' hoofs in the soft ground, and the dull thud of human bodies falling in the mud, followed by loud cries of pain. There was the sudden crash of broken glass, the coach lanthorns had been seized and broken: it seemed to Yvonne de Kernogan that out of the darkness faces distorted with fury were peering at her through the window-panes. But through all the confusion, the coach kept moving on. Jean-Marie stuck to his post, as did also the postilion and the four outriders, and with whip and tongue they urged their horses to break through the crowd regardless of human lives, knocking and trampling down men and lads heedless of curses and blasphemies which were hurled on them and on the occupants of the coach, whoever they might be.

The next moment, however, the coach came to a sudden halt, and a wild cry of triumph drowned the groans of the injured and the dying.

"Kernogan! Kernogan!" was shouted from every side.

"Adet! Adet!"

"You limbs of Satan," cried Jean-Marie, "you'll rue this night's work and weep tears of blood for the rest of your lives. Let me tell you that! Mademoiselle is in the coach. When M. le duc hears of this, there will be work for the hangman. . . . "

"Mademoiselle in the coach," broke in a hoarse voice with a rough tone of command. "Let's look at her. . . . "

"Aye! Aye! let's have a look at Mademoiselle," came with a volley of objurgations and curses from the crowd.

"You devils—you would dare?" protested Jean-Marie.

Within the coach Yvonne de Kernogan hardly dared to breathe. She sat bolt upright, her cape held tightly round her shoulders: her eyes dilated now with excitement, if not with fear, were fixed upon the darkness beyond the window-panes. She could see nothing, but she felt the presence of that hostile crowd who had succeeded in over-powering Jean-Marie and were intent on doing her harm.

But she belonged to a caste which never reckoned cowardice amongst its many faults. During these few moments when she knew that her life hung on the merest thread of chance, she neither screamed nor fainted but sat rigidly still, her heart beating in unison with the agonising seconds which went so fatefully by. And even now, when the carriage door was torn violently open and even through the darkness she discerned vaguely the forms of these avowed enemies close beside her, and anon felt a rough hand seize her wrist, she did not move, but said quite calmly, with hardly a tremor in her voice:

"Who are you? and what do you want?"

An outburst of harsh and ironical laughter came in response.

"Who are we, my fine lady?" said the foremost man in the crowd, he who had seized her wrist and was half in and half out of the coach at this moment, "we are the men who throughout our lives have toiled and starved whilst you and such as you travel in fine coaches and eat your fill. What we want? Why, just the spectacle of such a fine lady as you are being knocked down into the mud just as our wives and daughters are if they happen to be in the way when your coach is passing. Isn't that it, *mes amis?*"

"Aye! aye!" they replied, shouting lustily. "Into the mud with the fine lady. Out with her, Adet. Let's have a look at Mademoiselle how she will look with her face in the mud. Out with her, quick!"

But the man who was still half in and half out of the coach, and who had hold of Mademoiselle's wrist did not obey his mates immediately. He drew her nearer to him and suddenly threw his rough, begrimed arms round her, and with one hand pulled back her hood, then placing two fingers under her chin, he jerked it up till her face was level with his own.

Yvonne de Kernogan was certainly no coward, but at the loathsome contact of this infuriated and vengeful creature, she was overcome with such a hideous sense of fear that for the moment consciousness almost left her: not completely alas! for though she could not distinguish his face she could feel his hot breath upon her cheeks, she could smell the nauseating odour of his damp clothes, and she could hear his hoarse mutterings as for the space of a few seconds he held her thus close to him in an embrace which to her was far more awesome than that of death.

"And just to punish you, my fine lady," he said in a whisper which sent a shudder of horror right through her, "to punish you for what you are, the brood of tyrants, proud, disdainful, a budding tyrant yourself, to punish you for every misery my mother and sister have had to endure, for every luxury which you have enjoyed, I will kiss you on the lips and the cheeks and just between your white throat and chin and never as long as you live if you die this night or live to be an hundred will you be able to wash off those kisses showered upon you by one who hates and loathes you—a miserable peasant whom you despise and who in your sight is lower far than your dogs."

Yvonne, with eyes closed, hardly breathed, but through the veil of semi-consciousness which mercifully wrapped her senses, she could still hear those awful words, and feel the pollution of those loathsome kisses with which—true to his threat—this creature—half man, wholly devil, whom she could not see, but whom she hated and feared as she would Satan himself—now covered her face and throat.

After that she remembered nothing more. Consciousness mercifully forsook her altogether. When she recovered her senses, she was within the precincts of the castle: a confused murmur of voices reached her ears, and her father's arms were round her. Gradually she distinguished what was being said: she gathered the threads of the story which Jean-Marie and the postilion and outriders were hastily unravelling in response to M. le duc's commands.

These men of course knew nothing of the poignant little drama which had been enacted inside the coach. All they knew was that they had been surrounded by a rough crowd—a hundred or so strong—who brandished scythes and spades, that they had made valiant efforts to break through the crowd by whipping up their horses, but that suddenly some of those devils more plucky than the others seized the horses by their bits and rendered poor Jean-Marie quite helpless. He thought then that all would be up with the lot of them and was thinking of scrambling down from his box in order to protect Mademoiselle with his body, and the pistols which he had in the boot, when happily for every one concerned, he heard in the distance—above the clatter which that abominable rabble was making, the hurried tramp of horses. At once he jumped to the conclusion that these could be none other than a company of soldiers sent by M. le duc. This spurred him to a fresh effort, and gave him a new idea. To Carmail the postilion who had a pistol in his holster he gave the peremptory order to fire a shot into the air or into the crowd, Jean-Marie cared not which. This Carmail did, and at once the horses, already maddened by the crowd, plunged and reared wildly, shaking themselves free. Jean-Marie, however, had them well in hand, and from far away there came the cries of encouragement from the advancing horsemen who were bearing down on them full tilt. The next moment there was a general mêlée. Jean-Marie saw nothing save his horses' heads, but the outriders declared that men were trampled down like flies all around, while others vanished into the night.

What happened after that none of the men knew or cared. Jean-Marie galloped his horses all the way to the castle and never drew rein until the precincts were reached.

VI

Had M. de Kernogan had his way and a free hand to mete out retributive justice in the proportion that he desired, there is no doubt that the hangman of Nantes would have been kept exceedingly busy. As it was a number of arrests were effected the following day—half the manhood of the countryside was implicated in the aborted Jacquerie and the city prison was not large enough to hold it all.

A court of justice presided over by M. le duc, and composed of half a dozen men who were directly or indirectly in his employ, pronounced summary sentences on the rioters which were to have been carried out as soon as the necessary arrangements for such wholesale executions could be made. Nantes was turned into a city of wailing; peasant-women—mothers, sisters, daughters, wives of the condemned, trooped from their villages into the city, loudly calling on M. le duc for mercy, besieging the improvised court-house, the prison gates, the town residence of M. le duc, the palace of the bishop: they pushed their way into the courtyards and the very corridors of those buildings— flunkeys could not cope with them—they fought with fists and elbows for the right to make a direct appeal to the liege-lord who had power of life and death over their men.

The municipality of Nantes held aloof from this distressful state of things, and the town councillors, the city functionaries and their families shut themselves up in their houses in order to avoid being a witness to the heartrending scenes which took place uninterruptedly round the court-house and the prison. The mayor himself was powerless to interfere, but it is averred that he sent a secret courier to Paris to M. de Mirabeau, who was known to be a personal friend of his, with a detailed account of the Jacquerie and of the terrible measures of reprisal contemplated by M. le duc de Kernogan, together with an earnest request that pressure from the highest possible quarters be brought to bear upon His Grace so that he should abate something of his vengeful rigours.

Poor King Louis, who in these days was being terrorised by the National Assembly and swept off his feet by the eloquence of M. de Mirabeau, was only too ready to make concessions to the democratic spirit of the day. He also desired his noblesse to be equally ready with such concessions. He sent a personal letter to M. le duc, not only asking him, but commanding him, to show grace and mercy to a lot of misguided peasant lads whose loyalty and adherence—he urged—might be won by a gracious and unexpected act of clemency.

The King's commands could not in the nature of things be disobeyed: the same stroke of the pen which was about to send half a hundred young countrymen to the gallows granted them M. le duc's gracious pardon and their liberty: the only exception to this general amnesty being Pierre Adet, the son of the miller. M. le duc's servants had deposed to seeing him pull open the door of the coach and stand for some time half in and half out of the carriage, obviously trying to terrorise Mademoiselle. Mademoiselle refused either to corroborate or to deny this statement, but she had arrived fainting at the gate of the château, and she had been very ill ever since. She had sustained a serious shock to her nerves, so the doctor hastily summoned from Paris had averred, and it was supposed that she had lost all recollection of the terrible incidents of that night But M. le duc was satisfied that it was Pierre Adet's presence inside the coach which had brought about his daughter's mysterious illness and that heartrending look of nameless horror which had dwelt in her eyes ever since. Therefore with regard to that man M. le duc remained implacable and as a concession to a father's outraged feelings both the mayor of Nantes and the city functionaries accepted Adet's condemnation without a murmur of dissent.

The sentence of death finally passed upon Pierre, the son of Jean Adet, miller of Vertou, could not, however, be executed, for the simple reason that Pierre had disappeared and that the most rigorous search instituted in the neighbourhood and for miles around failed to bring him to justice.

One of the outriders who had been in attendance on Mademoiselle on that fateful night declared that when Jean-Marie finally whipped up his horses at the approach of the party of soldiers, Adet fell backwards from the step of the carriage and was run over by the hind wheels and instantly killed. But his body was never found among the score or so which were left lying there in the mud of the road until the women and old men came to seek their loved ones among the dead.

Pierre Adet had disappeared. But M. le duc's vengeance had need of a prey. The outrage which he was quite convinced had been perpetrated against his daughter must be punished by death—if not by the death of the chief offender, then by that of the one who stood nearest to him.

Thus was Jean Adet the miller dragged from his home and cast into prison. Was he not implicated himself in the riots? Camille the bailiff had seen and heard him among the insurgents on the hillock that night. At first it was stated that he would be held as hostage for the reappearance of his son. But Pierre Adet had evidently fled the countryside: he was obviously ignorant of the terrible fate which his own folly had brought upon his father.

Many thought that he had gone to seek his fortune in Paris where his talents and erudition would ensure him a good place in the present mad rush for equality amongst all men. Certain it is that he did not return and that with merciless hate and vengeful relentlessness M. le duc de Kernogan had Jean Adet hanged for a supposed crime said to be committed by his son.

Jean Adet died protesting his innocence. But the outburst of indignation and revolt aroused by this crying injustice was swamped by the torrent of the revolution which, gathering force by these very acts of tyranny and of injustice, soon swept innocent and guilty alike into a vast whirlpool of blood and shame and tears.

# BOOK I: BATH, 1793
## CHAPTER 1: THE MOOR

### I

Silence. Loneliness. Desolation.

And the darkness of late afternoon in November, when the fog from the Bristol Channel has laid its pall upon moor and valley and hill: the last grey glimmer of a wintry sunset has faded in the west: earth and sky are wrapped in the gloomy veils of oncoming night. Some little way ahead a tiny light flickers feebly.

"Surely we cannot be far now."

"A little more patience, Mounzeer. Twenty minutes and we be there."

"Twenty minutes, *mordieu*. And I have ridden since the morning. And you tell me it was not far."

"Not far, Mounzeer. But we be not 'orzemen either of us. We doan't travel very fast."

"How can I ride fast on this heavy beast? And in this *satané* mud. My horse is up to his knees in it. And I am wet—ah! wet to my skin in this *sacré* fog of yours."

The other made no reply. Indeed he seemed little inclined for conversation: his whole attention appeared to be riveted on the business of keeping in his saddle, and holding his horse's head turned in the direction in which he wished it to go: he was riding a yard or two ahead of his companion, and it did not need any assurance on his part that he was no horseman: he sat very loosely in his saddle, his broad shoulders bent, his head thrust forward, his knees turned out, his hands clinging alternately to the reins and to the pommel with that ludicrous inconsequent gesture peculiar to those who are wholly unaccustomed to horse exercise.

His attitude, in fact, as well as the promiscuous set of clothes which he wore—a labourer's smock, a battered high hat, threadbare corduroys and fisherman's boots—at once suggested the loafer, the do-nothing who hangs round the yards of half-way houses and posting inns on the chance of earning a few coppers by an easy job which does not entail too much exertion on his part and which will not take him too far from his favourite haunts. When he spoke—which was not often —the soft burr in the pronunciation of the sibilants betrayed the Westcountryman.

His companion, on the other hand, was obviously a stranger:

high of stature, and broadly built, his wide shoulders and large hands and feet, his square head set upon a short thick neck, all bespoke the physique of a labouring man, whilst his town-made clothes—his heavy caped coat, admirably tailored, his buckskin breeches and boots of fine leather—suggested, if not absolutely the gentleman, at any rate one belonging to the well-to-do classes. Though obviously not quite so inexperienced in the saddle as the other man appeared to be, he did not look very much at home in the saddle either: he held himself very rigid and upright and squared his shoulders with a visible effort at seeming at ease, like a townsman out for a constitutional on the fashionable promenade of his own city, or a cavalry subaltern but lately emerged from a riding school. He spoke English quite fluently, even colloquially at times, but with a marked Gallic accent.

## II

The road along which the two cavaliers were riding was unspeakably lonely and desolate—an offshoot from the main Bath to Weston road. It had been quite a good secondary road once. The accounts of the county administration under date 1725 go to prove that it was completed in that year at considerable expense and with stone brought over for the purpose all the way from Draycott quarries, and for twenty years after that a coach used to ply along it between Chelwood and Redhill as well as two or three carriers, and of course there was all the traffic in connexion with the Stanton markets and the Norton Fairs. But that was nigh on fifty years ago now, and somehow— once the mail-coach was discontinued—it had never seemed worth while to keep the road in decent repair. It had gone from bad to worse since then, and travelling on it these days either ahorse or afoot had become very unpleasant. It was full of ruts and crevasses and knee-deep in mud, as the stranger had very appositely remarked, and the stone parapet which bordered it on either side, and which had once given it such an air of solidity and of value, was broken down in very many places and threatened soon to disappear altogether.

The country round was as lonely and desolate as the road. And that sense of desolation seemed to pervade the very atmosphere right through the darkness which had descended on upland and valley and hill. Though nothing now could be seen through the gloom and the mist, the senses were conscious that even in broad daylight there would be nothing to see. Loneliness dwelt in the air as well as upon the moor. There were no homesteads for miles around, no cattle grazing, no pastures, no hedges, nothing—just arid wasteland with here and there a group of stunted trees or an isolated yew, and tracts of rough, coarse grass not nearly good enough for cattle to eat.

There are vast stretches of upland equally desolate in many

parts of Europe—notably in Northern Spain—but in England, where they are rare, they seem to gain an additional air of loneliness through the very life which pulsates in their vicinity. This bit of Somersetshire was one of them in this year of grace 1793. Despite the proximity of Bath and its fashionable life, its gaieties and vitality, distant only a little over twenty miles, and of Bristol distant less than thirty, it had remained wild and forlorn, almost savage in its grim isolation, primitive in the grandeur of its solitude.

## III

The road at the point now reached by the travellers begins to slope in a gentle gradient down to the level of the Chew, a couple of miles further on: it was midway down this slope that the only sign of living humanity could be perceived in that tiny light which glimmered persistently. The air itself under its mantle of fog had become very still, only the water of some tiny moorland stream murmured feebly in its stony bed ere it lost its entity in the bosom of the river far away.

"Five more minutes and we be at th' Bottom Inn," quoth the man who was ahead in response to another impatient ejaculation from his companion.

"If we don't break our necks meanwhile in this confounded darkness," retorted the other, for his horse had just stumbled and the inexperienced rider had been very nearly pitched over into the mud.

"I be as anxious to arrive as you are, Mounzeer," observed the countryman laconically.

"I thought you knew the way," muttered the stranger.

"'Ave I not brought you safely through the darkness?" retorted the other; "you was pretty well ztranded at Chelwood, Mounzeer, or I be much mistaken. Who else would 'ave brought you out 'ere at this time o' night, I'd like to know—and in this weather too? You wanted to get to th' Bottom Inn and didn't know 'ow to zet about it: none o' the gaffers up to Chelwood 'peared eager to 'elp you when I come along. Well, I've brought you to th' Bottom Inn and. . . . Whoa! Whoa! my beauty! Whoa, confound you! Whoa!"

And for the next moment or two the whole of his attention had perforce to be concentrated on the business of sticking to his saddle whilst he brought his fagged-out, ill-conditioned nag to a standstill.

The little glimmer of light had suddenly revealed itself in the shape of a lanthorn hung inside the wooden porch of a small house which had loomed out of the darkness and the fog. It stood at an angle of the road where a narrow lane had its beginnings ere it plunged into the moor beyond and was swallowed up by the all-enveloping gloom. The house was small and ugly; square like a box and built of grey stone, its front flush with the road, its rear flanked by several small outbuildings. Above the porch hung a plain sign-board bearing the legend: "The Bottom Inn" in white letters upon a black ground: to right and left of the porch there was a window with closed shutters, and on the floor above two more windows—also shuttered—completed the architectural features of the Bottom Inn.

It was uncompromisingly ugly and uninviting, for beyond the faint glimmer of the lanthorn only one or two narrow streaks of light filtrated through the chinks of the shutters.

## IV

The travellers, after some difference of opinion with their respective horses, contrived to pull up and to dismount without any untoward accident. The stranger looked about him, peering into the darkness. The place indeed appeared dismal and inhospitable enough: its solitary aspect suggested footpads and the abode of cut-throats. The silence of the moor, the pall of mist and gloom that hung over upland and valley sent a shiver through his spine.

"You are sure this is the place?" he queried.

"Can't ye zee the zign?" retorted the other gruffly.

"Can you hold the horses while I go in?"

I doan't know as 'ow I can, Mounzeer. I've never 'eld two 'orzes all at once. Suppose they was to start kickin' or thought o' runnin' away?"

"Running away, you fool!" muttered the stranger, whose temper had evidently suffered grievously during the weary, cold journey from Chelwood. "I'll break your *satané* head if anything happens to the beasts. How can I get back to Bath save the way I came? Do you think I want to spend the night in this God-forsaken hole?"

Without waiting to hear any further protests from the lout, he turned into the porch and with his riding whip gave three consecutive raps against the door of the inn, followed by two more. The next moment there was the sound of a rattling of bolts and chains, the door was cautiously opened and a timid voice queried:

"Is it Mounzeer?"

*Pardieu!* Who else?" growled the stranger. "Open the door, woman. I am perished with cold."

With an unceremonious kick he pushed the door further open and strode in. A woman was standing in the dimly lighted passage. As the stranger walked in she bobbed him a respectful curtsey.

"It is all right, Mounzeer," she said; "the Captain's in the coffee-room. He came over from Bristol early this afternoon."

"No one else here, I hope," he queried curtly.

"No one, zir. It ain't their hour not yet. You'll 'ave the 'ouse to yourself till after midnight. After that there'll be a bustle, I reckon. Two shiploads come into Watchet last night—brandy and cloth, Mounzeer, so the Captain says, and worth a mint o' money. The pack 'orzes will be through yere in the small hours."

"That's all right, then. Send me in a bite and a mug of hot ale."

"I'll see to it, Mounzeer."

"And stay—have you some sort of stabling where the man can put the two horses up for an hour's rest?"

"Aye, aye, zir."

"Very well then, see to that too: and see that the horses get a feed and a drink and give the man something to eat."

"Very good, Mounzeer. This way, zir. I'll see the man presently. Straight down the passage, zir. The coffee-room is on the right. The Captain's there, waiting for ye."

She closed the front door carefully, then followed the stranger to the door of the coffee-room. Outside an anxious voice was heard muttering a string of inconsequent and wholly superfluous "Whoa's!" Of a truth the two wearied nags were only too anxious for a little rest.

# Chapter 2: The Bottom Inn

I

A man was sitting, huddled up in the ingle-nook of the small coffee-room, sipping hot ale from a tankard which he had in his hand.

Anything less suggestive of a rough sea-faring life than his appearance it would be difficult to conceive; and how he came by the appellation "the Captain" must for ever remain a mystery. He was small and spare, with thin delicate face and slender hands: though dressed in very rough garments, he was obviously ill at ease in them; his narrow shoulders scarcely appeared able to bear the weight of the coarsely made coat, and his thin legs did not begin to fill the big fisherman's boots which reached midway up his lean thighs. His hair was lank and plentifully sprinkled with grey: he wore it tied at the nape of the neck with a silk bow which certainly did not harmonise with the rest of his clothing. A wide-brimmed felt hat something the shape of a sailor's, but with higher crown—of the shape worn by the peasantry in Brittany—lay on the bench beside him.

When the stranger entered he had greeted him curtly, speaking in French.

The room was inexpressibly stuffy, and reeked of the fumes of stale tobacco, stale victuals and stale beer; but it was warm, and the stranger, stiff to the marrow and wet to the skin, uttered an exclamation of well-being as he turned to the hearth, wherein a bright fire burned cheerily. He had put his hat down when first he entered and had divested himself of his big coat: now he held one foot and then the other to the blaze and tried to infuse new life into his numbed hands.

"The Captain" took scant notice of his comings and goings. He did not attempt to help him off with his coat, nor did he make an effort to add another log to the fire. He sat silent and practically motionless, save when from time to time he took a sip out of his mug of ale. But whenever the new-comer came within his immediate circle of vision he shot a glance at the latter's elegant attire—the well-cut coat, the striped waistcoat, the boots of fine leather—the glance was quick and comprehensive and full of scorn, a flash that lasted only an instant and was at once veiled again by the droop of the flaccid lids which hid the pale, keen eyes.

"When the woman has brought me something to eat and drink," the stranger said after a while, "we can talk. I have a good hour to spare, as those miserable nags must have some rest."

He too spoke in French and with an air of authority, not to say arrogance, which caused "the Captain's" glance of scorn to light up with an added gleam of hate and almost of cruelty. But he made no remark and continued to sip his ale in silence, and for the next half-hour the two men took no more notice of one another, just as if they had never travelled all those miles and come to this desolate spot for the sole purpose of speaking with one another. During the course of that half-hour the woman brought in a dish of mutton stew, a chunk of bread, a piece of cheese and a jug of spiced ale, and placed them on the table: all of these good things the stranger consumed with an obviously keen appetite. When he had eaten and drunk his fill, he rose from the table, drew a bench into the ingle-nook and sat down so that his profile only was visible to his friend "the Captain."

"Now, citizen Chauvelin," he said with at attempt at ease and familiarity not unmixed with condescension, "I am ready for your news."

## II

Chauvelin had winced perceptibly both at the condescension and the familiarity. It was such a very little while ago that men had trembled at a look, a word from him: his silence had been wont to strike terror in quaking hearts. It was such a very little while ago that he had been president of the Committee of Public Safety, all powerful, the right hand of citizen Robespierre, the master sleuth-hound who could track an unfortunate "suspect" down to his most hidden lair, before whose keen, pale eyes the innermost secrets of a soul stood revealed, who guessed at treason ere it was wholly born, who scented treachery ere it was formulated. A year ago he had with a word sent scores of men, women and children to the guillotine—he had with a sign brought the whole machinery of the ruthless Committee to work against innocent or guilty alike on mere suspicion, or to gratify his own hatred against all those whom he considered to be the enemies of that bloody revolution which he had helped to make. Now his presence, his silence, had not even the power to ruffle the self-assurance of an upstart.

But in the hard school both of success and of failure through which he had passed during the last decade, there was one lesson which Armand once Marquis de Chauvelin had learned to the last letter, and that was the lesson of self-control. He had winced at the other's familiarity, but neither by word nor gesture did he betray what he felt.

"I can tell you," he merely said quite curtly, "all I have to say in far less time than it has taken you to eat and drink, citizen Adet. . . . "

But suddenly, at sound of that name, the other had put a warning hand on Chauvelin's arm, even as he cast a rapid, anxious look all round the narrow room.

"Hush, man!" he murmured hurriedly, "you know quite well

that that name must never be pronounced here in England. I am Martin-Roget now," he added, as he shook off his momentary fright with equal suddenness, and once more resumed his tone of easy condescension, "and try not to forget it."

Chauvelin without any haste quietly freed his arm from the other's grasp. His pale face was quite expressionless, only the thin lips were drawn tightly over the teeth now, and a curious hissing sound escaped faintly from them as he said:

"I'll try and remember, citizen, that here in England you are an *aristo*, the same as all these confounded English whom may the devil sweep into a bottomless sea."

Martin-Roget gave a short, complacent laugh.

"Ah," he said lightly, "no wonder you hate them, citizen Chauvelin. You too were an *aristo* here in England once—not so very long ago, I am thinking—special envoy to His Majesty King George, what?—until failure to bring one of these *satané* Britishers to book made you ... er ... well, made you what you are now."

He drew up his tall, broad figure as he spoke and squared his massive shoulders as he looked down with a fatuous smile and no small measure of scorn on the hunched-up little figure beside him. It had seemed to him that something in the nature of a threat had crept into Chauvelin's attitude, and he, still flushed with his own importance, his immeasurable belief in himself, at once chose to measure his strength against this man who was the personification of failure and disgrace— this man whom so many people had feared for so long and whom it might not be wise to defy even now.

"No offence meant, citizen Chauvelin," he added with an air of patronage which once more made the other wince. "I had no wish to wound your susceptibilities. I only desired to give you timely warning that what I do here is no one's concern, and that I will brook interference and criticism from no man."

And Chauvelin, who in the past had oft with a nod sent a man to the guillotine, made no reply to this arrogant taunt. His small figure seemed to shrink still further within itself: and anon he passed his thin, claw-like hand over his face as if to obliterate from its surface any expression which might war with the utter humility wherewith he now spoke.

"Nor was there any offence meant on my part, citizen Martin-Roget," he said suavely. "Do we not both labour for the same end? The glory of the Republic and the destruction of her foes?"

Martin-Roget gave a sigh of satisfaction. The battle had been won: he felt himself strong again—stronger than before through that very act of deference paid to him by the once all-powerful Chauvelin. Now he was quite prepared to be condescending and jovial once again:

"Of course, of course," he said pleasantly, as he once more bent his tall figure to the fire. "We are both servants of the Republic, and I may yet help you to retrieve your past failures, citizen, by giving you an active part in the work I have in hand. And now," he added in a calm, business-like manner, the manner of a master addressing a servant who has been found at fault and is taken into favour again, "let me hear your news."

"I have made all the arrangements about the ship," said Chauvelin quietly.

"Ah! that is good news indeed. What is she?"

"She is a Dutch ship. Her master and crew are all Dutch. . . . "

"That's a pity. A Danish master and crew would have been safer."

"I could not come across any Danish ship willing to take the risks," said Chauvelin dryly.

"Well! And what about this Dutch ship then?"

"She is called the Hollandia and is habitually engaged in the sugar trade: but her master does a lot of contraband—more that than fair trading, I imagine: anyway, he is willing for the sum you originally named to take every risk and incidentally to hold his tongue about the whole business."

"For two thousand francs?"

"Yes."

"And he will run the Hollandia into Le Croisic?"

"When you command."

"And there is suitable accommodation on board her for a lady and her woman?"

"I don't know what you call suitable," said Chauvelin with a sarcastic tone, which the other failed or was unwilling to note, "and I don't know what you call a lady. The accommodation available on board the Hollandia will be sufficient for two men and two women."

"And her master's name?" queried Martin-Roget.

"Some outlandish Dutch name," replied Chauvelin. "It is spelt K U Y P E R. The devil only knows how it is pronounced."

"Well! And does Captain K U Y P E R understand exactly what I want?"

"He says he does. The Hollandia will put into Portishead on the last day of this month. You and your guests can get aboard her any day after that you choose. She will be there at your disposal, and can start within an hour of your getting aboard. Her master will have all his papers ready. He will have a cargo of West Indian sugar on board—destination Amsterdam, consignee Mynheer van Smeer—everything perfectly straight and square. French *aristos*, *émigrés* on board on their way to join the army of the Princes. There will be no difficulty in England."

"And none in Le Croisic. The man is running no risks."

"He thinks he is. France does not make Dutch ships and Dutch crews exactly welcome just now, does she?"

"Certainly not. But in Le Croisic and with citizen Adet on board. . . . "

"I thought that name was not to be mentioned here," retorted Chauvelin dryly.

"You are right, citizen," whispered the other, "it escaped me and. . . . "

Already he had jumped to his feet, his face suddenly pale, his whole manner changed from easy, arrogant self-assurance to uncertainty and obvious dread. He moved to the window, trying to subdue the sound of his footsteps upon the uneven floor.

## III

"Are you afraid of eavesdroppers, citizen Roget?" queried Chauvelin with a shrug of his narrow shoulders.

"No. There is no one there. Only a lout from Chelwood who brought me here. The people of the house are safe enough. They have plenty of secrets of their own to keep."

He was obviously saying all this in order to reassure himself, for there was no doubt that his fears were on the alert. With a febrile gesture he unfastened the shutters, and pushed them open, peering out into the night.

"Hallo!" he called.

But he received no answer.

"It has started to rain," he said more calmly. "I imagine that lout has found shelter in an outhouse with the horses."

"Very likely," commented Chauvelin laconically.

"Then if you have nothing more to tell me," quoth Martin-Roget, "I may as well think about getting back. Rain or no rain, I want to be in Bath before midnight."

"Ball or supper-party at one of your duchesses?" queried the other with a sneer. "I know them."

To this Martin-Roget vouchsafed no reply.

"How are things at Nantes?" he asked.

"Splendid! Carrier is like a wild beast let loose. The prisons are over-full: the surplus of accused, condemned and suspect fills the cellars and warehouses along the wharf. Priests and suchlike trash are kept on disused galliots up stream. The guillotine is never idle, and friend Carrier fearing that she might give out—get tired, what?—or break down—has invented a wonderful way of getting rid of shoals of undesirable people at one magnificent swoop. You have heard tell of it no doubt."

"Yes. I have heard of it," remarked the other curtly.

"He began with a load of priests. Requisitioned an old barge. Ordered Baudet the shipbuilder to construct half a dozen portholes in her bottom. Baudet demurred: he could not understand what the order could possibly mean. But Foucaud and Lamberty—Carrier's agents—you know them—explained that the barge would be towed down the Loire and then up one of the smaller navigable streams which it was feared the royalists were preparing to use as a way for making a descent upon Nantes, and that the idea was to sink the barge in midstream in order to obstruct the passage of their army. Baudet, satisfied, put five of his men to the task. Everything was ready on the 16th of last month. I know the woman Pichot, who keeps a small tavern opposite La Sécherie. She saw the barge glide up the river toward the galliot where twenty-five priests of the diocese of Nantes had been living for the past two months in the company of rats and other vermin as noxious as themselves. Most lovely moonlight there was that night. The Loire looked like a living ribbon of silver. Foucaud and Lamberty directed operations, and Carrier had given them full instructions. They tied the calotins up two and two and transferred them from the galliot to the barge. It seems they were quite pleased to go. Had enough of the rats, I presume. The only thing they didn't like was being searched. Some had managed to secrete silver ornaments about their person when they were arrested. Crucifixes and such like. They didn't like to part with these, it seems. But Foucaud and Lamberty relieved them of everything but the necessary clothing, and they didn't want much of that, seeing whither they were going. Foucaud made a good pile, so they say. Self-seeking, avaricious brute! He'll learn the way to one of Carrier's barges too one day, I'll bet."

He rose and with quick footsteps moved to the table. There was some ale left in the jug which the woman had brought for Martin-Roget a while ago. Chauvelin poured the contents of it down his throat. He had talked uninterruptedly, in short, jerky sentences, without the slightest expression of horror at the atrocities which he recounted. His whole appearance had become transfigured while he spoke. Gone was the urbane manner which he had learnt at courts long ago, gone was the last instinct of the gentleman sunk to proletarianism through stress of circumstances, or financial straits or even political convictions. The erstwhile Marquis de Chauvelin—envoy of the Republic at the Court of St. James'—had become citizen Chauvelin in deed and in fact, a part of that rabble which he had elected to serve, one of that vile crowd of bloodthirsty revolutionaries who had sullied the pure robes of Liberty and of Fraternity by spattering them with blood. Now he smacked his lips, wiped his mouth with his sleeve, and burying his hands in the pockets of his breeches he stood with legs wide apart and a look of savage satisfaction settled upon his pale face. Martin-Roget had made no comment upon the narrative. He had resumed his seat by the fire and was listening attentively. Now while the other drank and paused, he showed no sign of impatience, but there was something in the look of the bent shoulders, in the rigidity of the attitude, in the large, square hands tightly clasped together which suggested the deepest interest and an intentness that was almost painful.

"I was at the woman Pichot's tavern that night," resumed Chauvelin after a while. "I saw the barge—a moving coffin, what?— gliding down stream towed by the galliot and escorted by a small boat. The floating battery at La Samaritaine challenged her as she passed, for Carrier had prohibited all navigation up or down the Loire until further notice. Foucaud, Lamberty, Fouquet and O'Sullivan the armourer were in the boat: they rowed up to the pontoon and Vailly the chief gunner of the battery challenged them once more. However, they had some sort of written authorisation from Carrier, for they were allowed to pass. Vailly remained on guard. He saw the barge glide further down stream. It seems that the moon on that time was hidden by a cloud. But the night was not dark and Vailly watched the barge till she was out of sight. She was towed past Trentemoult and Chantenay into the wide reach of the river just below Cheviré where, as you know, the Loire is nearly two thousand feet wide."

Once more he paused, looking down with grim amusement on the bent shoulders of the other man.

"Well?"

Chauvelin laughed. The query sounded choked and hoarse, whether through horror, excitement or mere impatient curiosity it were impossible to say.

"Well!" he retorted with a careless shrug of the shoulders. "I was too far up stream to see anything and Vailly saw nothing either. But he heard. So did others who happened to be on the shore close by."

"What did they hear?"

"The hammering," replied Chauvelin curtly, "when the portholes were knocked open to let in the flood of water. And the screams and yells of five and twenty drowning priests."

"Not one of them escaped, I suppose?"

"Not one."

Once more Chauvelin laughed. He had a way of laughing—just like that—in a peculiar mirthless, derisive manner, as if with joy at another man's discomfiture, at another's material or moral downfall. There is only one language in the world which has a word to express that type of mirth; the word is Schadenfreude.

It was Chauvelin's turn to triumph now. He had distinctly perceived the signs of an inward shudder which had gone right through Martin-Roget's spine: he had also perceived through the man's bent shoulders, his silence, his rigidity that his soul was filled with horror at the story of that abominable crime which he—Chauvelin—had so blandly retailed and that he was afraid to show the horror which he felt. And the man who is afraid can never climb the ladder of success above the man who is fearless.

IV

There was silence in the low raftered room for awhile: silence only broken by the crackling and sizzling of damp logs in the hearth, and the tap-tapping of a loosely fastened shutter which sounded weird and ghoulish like the knocking of ghosts against the window-frame. Martin-Roget bending still closer to the fire knew that Chauvelin was watching him and that Chauvelin had triumphed, for—despite failure, despite humiliation and disgrace—that man's heart and will had never softened: he had remained as merciless, as fanatical, as before and still looked upon every sign of pity and humanity for a victim of that bloody revolution—which was his child, the thing of his creation, yet worshipped by him, its creator—as a crime against patriotism and against the Republic.

And Martin-Roget fought within himself lest something he might say or do, a look, a gesture should give the other man an indication that the horrible account of a hideous crime perpetrated against twenty-five defenceless men had roused a feeling of unspeakable horror in his heart. That was the punishment of these callous makers of a ruthless revolution—that was their hell upon earth, that they were doomed to hate and to fear one another; every man feeling that the other's hand was up against him as it had been against law and order, against the guilty and the innocent, the rebel and the defenceless; every man knowing that the other was always there on the alert, ready to pounce like a beast of prey upon any victim—friend, comrade, brother—who came within reach of his hand.

Like many men stronger than himself, Pierre Adet—or Martin-Roget as he now called himself—had been drawn into the vortex of bloodshed and of tyranny out of which now he no longer had the power to extricate himself. Nor had he any wish to extricate himself. He had too many past wrongs to avenge, too much injustice on the part of Fate and Circumstance to make good, to wish to draw back now that a newly-found power had been placed in the hands of men such as he through the revolt of an entire people. The sickening sense of horror which a moment ago had caused him to shudder and to turn away in loathing from Chauvelin was only like the feeble flicker of a light before it wholly dies down—the light of something purer, early lessons of childhood, former ideals, earlier aspirations, now smothered beneath the passions of revenge and of hate.

And he would not give Chauvelin the satisfaction of seeing him wince. He was himself ashamed of his own weakness. He had

THE SCARLET PIMPERNEL ANTHOLOGY VOLUME II    319

deliberately thrown in his lot with these men and he was determined not to fall a victim to their denunciations and to their jealousies. So now he made a great effort to pull himself together, to bring back before his mind those memory-pictures of past tyranny and oppression which had effectually killed all sense of pity in his heart, and it was in a tone of perfect indifference which gave no loophole to Chauvelin's sneers that he asked after awhile:

"And was citizen Carrier altogether pleased with the result of his patriotic efforts?"

"Oh, quite!" replied the other. "He has no one's orders to take. He is proconsul—virtual dictator in Nantes: and he has vowed that he will purge the city from all save its most deserving citizens. The cargo of priests was followed by one of malefactors, night-birds, cut-throats and such like. That is where Carrier's patriotism shines out in all its glory. It is not only priests and *aristos*, you see—other miscreants are treated with equal fairness."

"Yes! I see he is quite impartial," remarked Martin-Roget coolly.

"Quite," retorted Chauvelin, as he once more sat down in the ingle-nook. And, leaning his elbows upon his knees he looked straight and deliberately into the other man's face, and added slowly: "You will have no cause to complain of Carrier's want of patriotism when you hand over your bag of birds to him."

This time Martin-Roget had obviously winced, and Chauvelin had the satisfaction of seeing that his thrust had gone home: though Martin-Roget's face was in shadow, there was something now in his whole attitude, in the clasping and unclasping of his large, square hands which indicated that the man was labouring under the stress of a violent emotion. In spite of this he managed to say quite coolly: "What do you mean exactly by that, citizen Chauvelin?"

"Oh!" replied the other, "you know well enough what I mean—I am no fool, what? . . . or the Revolution would have no use for me. If after my many failures she still commands my services and employs me to keep my eyes and ears open, it is because she knows that she can count on me. I do keep my eyes and ears open, citizen Adet or Martin-Roget, whatever you like to call yourself, and also my mind—and I have a way of putting two and two together to make four. There are few people in Nantes who do not know that old Jean Adet, the miller, was hanged four years ago, because his son Pierre had taken part in some kind of open revolt against the tyranny of the *ci-devant* duc de Kernogan, and was not there to take his punishment himself. I knew old Jean Adet. . . . I was on the Place du Bouffay at Nantes when he was hanged. . . . "

But already Martin-Roget had jumped to his feet with a muttered blasphemy.

"Have done, man," he said roughly, "have done!" And he started pacing up and down the narrow room like a caged panther, snarling and showing his teeth, whilst his rough, toil-worn hands quivered with the desire to clutch an unseen enemy by the throat and to squeeze the life out of him. "Think you," he added hoarsely, "that I need reminding of that?"

"No. I do not think that, citizen," replied Chauvelin calmly, "I only desired to warn you."

"Warn me? Of what?"

Nervous, agitated, restless, Martin-Roget had once more gone back to his seat: his hands were trembling as he held them up mechanically to the blaze and his face was the colour of lead. In contrast with his restlessness Chauvelin appeared the more calm and bland.

"Why should you wish to warn me?" asked the other querulously, but with an attempt at his former over-bearing manner. "What are my affairs to you—what do you know about them?"

"Oh, nothing, nothing, citizen Martin-Roget," replied Chauvelin pleasantly, "I was only indulging the fancy I spoke to you about just now of putting two and two together in order to make four. The chartering of a smuggler's craft—*aristos* on board her—her ostensible destination Holland—her real objective Le Croisic. . . . Le Croisic is now the port for Nantes and we don't bring *aristos* into Nantes these days for the object of providing them with a feather-bed and a competence, what?"

"And," retorted Martin-Roget quietly, "if your surmises are correct, citizen Chauvelin, what then?"

"Oh, nothing!" replied the other indifferently. "Only . . . take care, citizen . . . that is all."

"Take care of what?"

"Of the man who brought me, Chauvelin, to ruin and disgrace."

"Oh! I have heard of that legend before now," said Martin-Roget with a contemptuous shrug of the shoulders. "The man they call the Scarlet Pimpernel you mean?"

"Why, yes!"

"What have I to do with him?"

"I don't know. But remember that I myself have twice been after that man here in England; that twice he slipped through my fingers when I thought I held him so tightly that he could not possibly escape and that twice in consequence I was brought to humiliation and to shame. I am a marked man now—the guillotine will soon claim me for her future use. Your affairs, citizen, are no concern of mine, but I have marked that Scarlet Pimpernel for mine own. I won't have any blunderings on your part give him yet another triumph over us all."

Once more Martin-Roget swore one of his favourite oaths.

"By Satan and all his brood, man," he cried in a passion of fury, "have done with this interference. Have done, I say. I have nothing to do, I tell you, with your *satané* Scarlet Pimpernel. My concern is with. . . . "

"With the duc de Kernogan," broke in Chauvelin calmly, "and with his daughter; I know that well enough. You want to be even with them over the murder of your father. I know that too. All that is your affair. But beware, I tell you. To begin with, the secrecy of your identity is absolutely essential to the success of your plan. What?"

"Of course it is. But. . . . "

"But nevertheless, your identity is known to the most astute, the keenest enemy of the Republic."

"Impossible," asserted Martin-Roget hotly.

"The duc de Kernogan. . . . "

"Bah! He had never the slightest suspicion of me. Think you his High and Mightiness in those far-off days ever looked twice at a village lad so that he would know him again four years later? I came into this country as an émigré stowed away in a smuggler's ship like a bundle of contraband goods. I have papers to prove that my name is Martin-Roget and that I am a banker from Brest. The worthy bishop of Brest— denounced to the Committee of Public Safety for treason against the Republic—was given his life and a safe conduct into Spain on the condition that he gave me—Martin-Roget—letters of personal introduction to various high-born émigrés in Holland, in Germany and in England. Armed with these I am invulnerable. I have been presented to His Royal Highness the Regent, and to the élite of English society in Bath. I am the friend of M. le duc de Kernogan now and the accredited suitor for his daughter's hand."

"His daughter!" broke in Chauvelin with a sneer, and his pale, keen eyes had in them a spark of malicious mockery.

Martin-Roget made no immediate retort to the sneer. A curious hot flush had spread over his forehead and his ears, leaving his cheeks wan and livid.

"What about the daughter?" reiterated Chauvelin.

"Yvonne de Kernogan has never seen Pierre Adet the miller's son," replied the other curtly. "She is now the affianced wife of Martin-Roget the millionaire banker of Brest. To-night I shall persuade M. le duc to allow my marriage with his daughter to take place within the week. I shall plead pressing business in Holland and my desire that my wife shall accompany me thither. The duke will consent and Yvonne de Kernogan will not be consulted. The day after my wedding I shall be on board the Hollandia with my wife and father-in-law, and together we will be on our way to Nantes where Carrier will deal with them both."

"You are quite satisfied that this plan of yours is known to no one, that no one at the present moment is aware of the fact that Pierre

Adet, the miller's son, and Martin-Roget, banker of Brest, are one and the same?"

"Quite satisfied," replied Martin-Roget emphatically.

"Very well, then, let me tell you this, citizen," rejoined Chauvelin slowly and deliberately, "that in spite of what you say I am as convinced as that I am here, alive, that your real identity will be known —if it is not known already—to a gentleman who is at this present moment in Bath, and who is known to you, to me, to the whole of France as the Scarlet Pimpernel."

Martin-Roget laughed and shrugged his shoulders.

"Impossible!" he retorted. "Pierre Adet no longer exists . . . he never existed . . . much. . . . Anyhow, he ceased to be on that stormy day in September, 1789. Unless your pet enemy is a wizard he cannot know."

"There is nothing that my pet enemy—as you call him—cannot ferret out if he has a mind to. Beware of him, citizen Martin-Roget. Beware, I tell you."

"How can I," laughed the other contemptuously, "if I don't know who he is?"

"If you did," retorted Chauvelin, "it wouldn't help you . . . much. But beware of every man you don't know; beware of every stranger you meet; trust no one; above all, follow no one. He is there where you least expect him under a disguise you would scarcely dream of."

"Tell me who he is then—since you know him—so that I may duly beware of him."

"No," rejoined Chauvelin with the same slow deliberation, "I will not tell you who he is. Knowledge in this case would be a very dangerous thing."

"Dangerous? To whom?"

"To yourself probably. To me and to the Republic most undoubtedly. No! I will not tell you who the Scarlet Pimpernel is. But take my advice, citizen Martin-Roget," he added emphatically, "go back to Paris or to Nantes and strive there to serve your country rather than run your head into a noose by meddling with things here in England, and running after your own schemes of revenge."

"My own schemes of revenge!" exclaimed Martin-Roget with a hoarse cry that was like a snarl. . . . It seemed as if he wanted to say something more, but that the words choked him even before they reached his lips. The hot flush died down from his forehead and his face was once more the colour of lead. He took up a log from the corner of the hearth and threw it with a savage, defiant gesture into the fire.

Somewhere in the house a clock struck nine.

V

Martin-Roget waited until the last echo of the gong had died away, then he said very slowly and very quietly:

"Forgo my own schemes of revenge? Can you even remotely guess, citizen Chauvelin, what it would mean to a man of my temperament and of my calibre to give up that for which I have toiled and striven for the past four years? Think of what I was on that day when a conglomeration of adverse circumstances turned our proposed expedition against the château de Kernogan into a disaster for our village lads, and a triumph for the duc. I was knocked down and crushed all but to death by the wheels of Mlle. de Kernogan's coach. I managed to crawl in the mud and the cold and the rain, on my hands and knees, hurt, bleeding, half dead, as far as the presbytery of Vertou where the curé kept me hidden at risk of his own life for two days until I was able to crawl farther away out of sight. The curé did not know, I did not know then of the devilish revenge which the duc de Kernogan meant to wreak against my father. The news reached me when it was all over and I had worked my way to Paris with the few sous in my pocket which that good curé had given me, earning bed and bread as I went along. I was an ignorant lout when I arrived in Paris. I had been one of the *ci-devant* Kernogan's labourers—his chattel, what?—little better or somewhat worse off than a slave. There I heard that my father had been foully murdered—hung for a crime which I was supposed to have committed, for which I had not even been tried. Then the change in me began. For four years I starved in a garret, toiling like a galley-slave with my hands and muscles by day and at my books by night. And what am I now? I have worked at books, at philosophy, at science: I am a man of education. I can talk and discuss with the best of those d——d *aristos* who flaunt their caprices and their mincing manners in the face of the outraged democracy of two continents. I speak English—almost like a native—and Danish and German too. I can quote English poets and criticise M. de Voltaire. I am an *aristo*, what? For this I have worked, citizen Chauvelin—day and night—oh! those nights! how I have slaved to make myself what I now am! And all for the one object— the sole object without which existence would have been absolutely unendurable. That object guided me, helped me to bear and to toil, it cheered and comforted me! To be even one day with the duc de Kernogan and with his daughter! to be their master! to hold them at my mercy! . . . to destroy or pardon as I choose! . . . to be the arbiter of their fate! . . . I have worked for four years: now my goal is in sight, and you talk glibly of forgoing my own schemes of revenge! Believe me, citizen Chauvelin," he concluded, "it would be easier for me to hold my right hand into those flames until it hath burned to a cinder than to forgo the hope of that vengeance which has eaten into my soul. It would hurt much less."

He had spoken thus at great length, but with extraordinary restraint. Never once did he raise his voice or indulge in gesture. He spoke in even, monotonous tones, like one who is reciting a lesson; and he sat straight in front of the fire, his elbow on his knee, his chin resting in his hand and his eyes fixed upon the flames.

Chauvelin had listened in perfect silence. The scorn, the resentful anger, the ill-concealed envy of the fallen man for the successful upstart had died out of his glance. Martin-Roget's story, the intensity of feeling betrayed in that absolute, outward calm had caused a chord of sympathy to vibrate in the other's atrophied heart. How well he understood that vibrant passion of hate, that longing to exact an eye for an eye, an outrage for an outrage! Was not his own life given over now to just such a longing?—a mad aching desire to be even once with that hated enemy, that maddening, mocking, elusive Scarlet Pimpernel who had fooled and baffled him so often?

## VI

Some few moments had gone by since Martin-Roget's harsh, monotonous voice had ceased to echo through the low raftered room: silence had fallen between the two men—there was indeed nothing more to say; the one had unburthened his over-full heart and the other had understood. They were of a truth made to understand one another, and the silence between them betokened sympathy.

Around them all was still, the stillness of a mist-laden night; in the house no one stirred: the shutter even had ceased to creak; only the crackling of the wood fire broke that silence which soon became oppressive.

Martin-Roget was the first to rouse himself from this trance-like state wherein memory was holding such ruthless sway: he brought his hands sharply down on his knees, turned to look for a moment on his companion, gave a short laugh and finally rose, saying briskly the while:

"And now, citizen, I shall have to bid you adieu and make my way back to Bath. The nags have had the rest they needed and I cannot spend the night here."

He went to the door and opening it called a loud "Hallo, there!"

The same woman who had waited on him on his arrival came slowly down the stairs in response.

"The man with the horses," commanded Martin-Roget peremptorily. "Tell him I'll be ready in two minutes."

He returned to the room and proceeded to struggle into his heavy coat, Chauvelin as before making no attempt to help him. He sat once more huddled up in the ingle-nook hugging his elbows with his thin white hands. There was a smile half scornful, but not wholly dissatisfied around his bloodless lips. When Martin-Roget was ready to go he called out quietly after him:

"The Hollandia remember! At Portishead on the last day of the month. Captain K U Y P E R."

"Quite right," replied Martin-Roget laconically. "I'm not like to forget."

He then picked up his hat and riding whip and went out.

## VII

Outside in the porch he found the woman bending over the recumbent figure of his guide.

"He be azleep, Mounzeer," she said placidly, "fast azleep, I do believe."

"Asleep?" cried Martin-Roget roughly, "we'll soon see about waking him up."

He gave the man a violent kick with the toe of his boot. The man groaned, stretched himself, turned over and rubbed his eyes. The light of the swinging lanthorn showed him the wrathful face of his employer. He struggled to his feet very quickly after that.

"Stir yourself, man," cried Martin-Roget savagely, as he gripped the fellow by the shoulder and gave him a vigorous shaking. "Bring the horses along now, and don't keep me waiting, or there'll be trouble."

"All right, Mounzeer, all right," muttered the man placidly, as he shook himself free from the uncomfortable clutch on his shoulder and leisurely made his way out of the porch.

"Haven't you got a boy or a man who can give that lout a hand with those *sacré* horses?" queried Martin-Roget impatiently. "He hardly knows a horse's head from its tail."

"No, zir, I've no one to-night," replied the woman gently. "My man and my son they be gone down to Watchet to 'elp with the cargo and the pack-'orzes. They won't be 'ere neither till after midnight. But," she added more cheerfully, "I can straighten a saddle if you want it."

"That's all right then—but. . . . "

He paused suddenly, for a loud cry of "Hallo! Well! I'm . . . " rang through the night from the direction of the rear of the house. The cry expressed both surprise and dismay.

"What the —— is it?" called Martin-Roget loudly in response.

"The 'orzes!"

"What about them?"

To this there was no reply, and with a savage oath and calling to the woman to show him the way Martin-Roget ran out in the direction whence had come the cry of dismay. He fell straight into the arms of his guide, who promptly set up another cry, more dismal, more expressive of bewilderment than the first.

"They be gone," he shouted excitedly.

"Who have gone?" queried the Frenchman.

"The 'orzes!"

"The horses? What in —— do you mean?"

"The 'orzes have gone, Mounzeer. There was no door to the ztables and they be gone."

"You're a fool," growled Martin-Roget, who of a truth had not taken in as yet the full significance of the man's jerky sentences. "Horses don't walk out of the stables like that. They can't have done if you tied them up properly."

"I didn't tie them up," protested the man. "I didn't know 'ow to tie the beastly nags up, and there was no one to 'elp me. I didn't think they'd walk out like that."

"Well! if they're gone you'll have to go and get them back somehow, that's all," said Martin-Roget, whose temper by now was beyond his control, and who was quite ready to give the lout a furious thrashing.

"Get them back, Mounzeer," wailed the man, "'ow can I? In the dark, too. Besides, if I did come nose to nose wi' 'em I shouldn't know 'ow to get 'em. Would you, Mounzeer?" he added with bland impertinence.

"I shall know how to lay you out, you *satané* idiot," growled Martin-Roget, "if I have to spend the night in this hole."

He strode on in the darkness in the direction where a little glimmer of light showed the entrance to a wide barn which obviously was used as a rough stabling. He stumbled through a yard and over a miscellaneous lot of rubbish. It was hardly possible to see one's hands before one's eyes in the darkness and the fog. The woman followed him, offering consolation in the shape of a seat in the coffee-room whereon to pass the night, for indeed she had no bed to spare, and the man from Chelwood brought up the rear—still ejaculating cries of astonishment rather than distress.

"You are that careless, man!" the woman admonished him placidly, "and I give you a lanthorn and all for to look after your 'orzes properly."

"But you didn't give me a 'and for to tie 'em up in their stalls, and give 'em their feed. Drat 'em! I 'ate 'orzes and all to do with 'em."

"Didn't you give 'em the feed I give you for 'em then?"

"No, I didn't. Think you I'd go into one o' them narrow stalls and get kicked for my pains."

"Then they was 'ungry, pore things," she concluded, "and went out after the 'ay what's just outside. I don't know 'ow you'll ever get 'em back in this fog." ˙

There was indeed no doubt that the nags had made their way

out of the stables, in that irresponsible fashion peculiar to animals, and that they had gone astray in the dark. There certainly was no sound in the night to denote their presence anywhere near.

"We'll get 'em all right in the morning," remarked the woman with her exasperating placidity.

"To-morrow morning!" exclaimed Martin-Roget in a passion of fury. "And what the d——l am I going to do in the meanwhile?"

The woman reiterated her offers of a seat by the fire in the coffee-room.

"The men won't mind ye, zir," she said, "heaps of 'em are Frenchies like yourself, and I'll tell 'em you ain't a spying on 'em."

"It's no more than five mile to Chelwood," said the man blandly, "and maybe you get a better shakedown there."

"A five-mile tramp," growled Martin-Roget, whose wrath seemed to have spent itself before the hopelessness of his situation, "in this fog and gloom, and knee-deep in mud. . . . There'll be a sovereign for you, woman," he added curtly, "if you can give me a clean bed for the night."

The woman hesitated for a second or two.

"Well! a zovereign is tempting, zir," she said at last. "You shall 'ave my son's bed. I know 'e'd rather 'ave the zovereign if 'e was ever zo tired. This way, zir," she added, as she once more turned toward the house, "mind them 'urdles there."

"And where am I goin' to zleep?" called the man from Chelwood after the two retreating figures.

"I'll look after the man for you, zir," said the woman; "for a matter of a shillin' 'e can sleep in the coffee-room, and I'll give 'im 'is breakfast too."

"Not one farthing will I pay for the idiot," retorted Martin-Roget savagely. "Let him look after himself."

He had once more reached the porch. Without another word, and not heeding the protests and curses of the unfortunate man whom he had left standing shelterless in the middle of the yard, he pushed open the front door of the house and once more found himself in the passage outside the coffee-room.

But the woman had turned back a little before she followed her guest into the house, and she called out to the man in the darkness:

"You may zleep in any of them outhouses and welcome, and zure there'll be a bit o' porridge for ye in the mornin'!"

"Think ye I'll stop," came in a furious growl out of the gloom, "and conduct that d——d frogeater back to Chelwood? No fear. Five miles ain't nothin' to me, and 'e can keep the miserable shillin' 'e'd 'ave give me for my pains. Let 'im get 'is 'orzes back 'izelf and get to Chelwood as best 'e can. I'm off, and you can tell 'im zo from me. It'll make 'im sleep all the better, I reckon."

The woman was obviously not of a disposition that would ever argue a matter of this sort out. She had done her best, she reckoned, both for master and man, and if they chose to quarrel between themselves that was their business and not hers.

So she quietly went into the house again; barred and bolted the door, and finding the stranger still waiting for her in the passage she conducted him to a tiny room on the floor above.

"My son's room, Mounzeer," she said; "I 'ope as 'ow ye'll be comfortable."

"It will do all right," assented Martin-Roget. "Is 'the Captain' sleeping in the house to-night?" he added as with an afterthought.

"Only in the coffee-room, Mounzeer. I couldn't give 'im a bed. 'The Captain' will be leaving with the pack 'orzes a couple of hours before dawn. Shall I tell 'im you be 'ere."

"No, no," he replied promptly. "Don't tell him anything. I don't want to see him again: and he'll be gone before I'm awake, I reckon."

"That 'e will, zir, most like. Good-night, zir."

"Good-night. And—mind—that lout gets the two horses back again for my use in the morning. I shall have to make my way to Chelwood as early as may be."

"Aye, aye, zir," assented the woman placidly. It were no use, she thought, to upset the Mounzeer's temper once more by telling him that his guide had decamped. Time enough in the morning, when she would be less busy.

"And my John can see 'im as far as Chelwood," she thought to herself as she finally closed the door on the stranger and made her way slowly down the creaking stairs.

# CHAPTER 3: THE ASSEMBLY ROOMS

## I

The sigh of satisfaction was quite unmistakable.

It could be heard from end to end, from corner to corner of the building. It sounded above the din of the orchestra who had just attacked with vigour the opening bars of a schottische, above the brouhaha of moving dancers and the frou-frou of skirts: it travelled from the small octagon hall, through the central salon to the tea-room, the ball-room and the card-room: it reverberated from the gallery in the ball-room to the maids' gallery: it distracted the ladies from their gossip and the gentlemen from their cards.

It was a universal, heartfelt "Ah!" of intense and pleasurable satisfaction.

Sir Percy Blakeney and his lady had just arrived. It was close on midnight, and the ball had positively languished. What was a ball without the presence of Sir Percy? His Royal Highness too had been expected earlier than this. But it was not thought that he would come at all, despite his promise, if the spoilt pet of Bath society remained unaccountably absent; and the Assembly Rooms had worn an air of woe even in the face of the gaily dressed throng which filled every vast room in its remotest angle.

But now Sir Percy Blakeney had arrived, just before the clocks had struck midnight, and exactly one minute before His Royal Highness drove up himself from the Royal Apartments. Lady Blakeney was looking more radiant and beautiful than ever before, so everyone remarked, when a few moments later she appeared in the crowded ball-room on the arm of His Royal Highness and closely followed by my lord Anthony Dewhurst and by Sir Percy himself, who had the young Duchess of Flintshire on his arm.

"What do you mean, you incorrigible rogue," her Grace was saying with playful severity to her cavalier, "by coming so late to the ball? Another two minutes and you would have arrived after His Royal Highness himself: and how would you have justified such solecism, I would like to know."

"By swearing that thoughts of your Grace had completely addled my poor brain," he retorted gaily, "and that in the mental contemplation of such charms I forgot time, place, social duties, everything."

"Even the homage due to truth," she laughed. "Cannot you for once in your life be serious, Sir Percy?"

"Impossible, dear lady, whilst your dainty hand rests upon

mine arm."

## II

It was not often that His Royal Highness graced Bath with his presence, and the occasion was made the excuse for quite exceptional gaiety and brilliancy. The new fashions of this memorable year of 1793 had defied the declaration of war and filtrated through from Paris: London milliners had not been backward in taking the hint, and though most of the more starchy dowagers obstinately adhered to the pre-war fashions—the huge hooped skirts, stiff stomachers, pointed waists, voluminous panniers and monumental head erections—the young and smart matrons were everywhere to be seen in the new gracefully flowing skirts innocent of steel constructions, the high waist line, the pouter pigeon-like draperies over their pretty bosoms.

Her Grace of Flintshire looked ravishing with her curly fair hair entirely free from powder, and Lady Betty Draitune's waist seemed to be nestling under her arm-pits. Of course Lady Blakeney wore the very latest thing in striped silks and gossamer-like muslin and lace, and it was hard to enumerate all the pretty *débutantes* and young brides who fluttered about the Assembly Rooms this night.

And gliding through that motley throng, bright-plumaged like a swarm of butterflies, there were a few figures dressed in sober blacks and greys—the *émigrés* over from France—men, women, young girls and gilded youth from out that seething cauldron of revolutionary France—who had shaken the dust of that rampant demagogism from off their buckled shoes, taking away with them little else but their lives. Mostly chary of speech, grave in their demeanour, bearing upon their wan faces traces of that horror which had seized them when they saw all the traditions of their past tottering around them, the proletariat whom they had despised turning against them with all the fury of caged beasts let loose, their kindred and friends massacred, their King and Queen murdered. The shelter and security which hospitable England had extended to them, had not altogether removed from their hearts the awful sense of terror and of gloom.

Many of them had come to Bath because the more genial climate of the West of England consoled them for the inclemencies of London's fogs. Received with open arms and with that lavish hospitality which the refugees and the oppressed had already learned to look for in England, they had gradually allowed themselves to be drawn into the fashionable life of the gay little city. The Comtesse de Tournai was here and her daughter, Lady Ffoulkes, Sir Andrew's charming and happy bride, and M. Paul Déroulède and his wife—beautiful Juliette Déroulède with the strange, haunted look in her large eyes, as of one who has looked closely on death; and M. le duc de

Kernogan with his exquisite daughter, whose pretty air of seriousness and of repose sat so quaintly upon her young face. But every one remarked as soon as M. le duc entered the rooms that M. Martin-Roget was not in attendance upon Mademoiselle, which was quite against the order of things; also that M. le duc appeared to keep a more sharp eye than usual upon his daughter in consequence, and that he asked somewhat anxiously if milor Anthony Dewhurst was in the room, and looked obviously relieved when the reply was in the negative.

At which trifling incident every one who was in the know smiled and whispered, for M. le duc made it no secret that he favoured his own compatriot's suit for Mademoiselle Yvonne's hand rather than that of my lord Tony—which—as old Euclid has it—is absurd.

### III

But with the arrival of the royal party M. de Kernogan's troubles began. To begin with, though M. Martin-Roget had not arrived, my lord Tony undoubtedly had. He had come in, in the wake of Lady Blakeney, but very soon he began wandering round the room obviously in search of some one. Immediately there appeared to be quite a conspiracy among the young folk in the ball-room to keep both Lord Tony's and Mlle. Yvonne's movements hidden from the prying eyes of M. le duc: and anon His Royal Highness, after a comprehensive survey of the ball-room and a few gracious words to his more intimate circle, wandered away to the card-room, and as luck would have it he claimed M. le duc de Kernogan for a partner at faro.

Now M. le duc was a courtier of the old régime: to have disobeyed the royal summons would in his eyes have been nothing short of a crime. He followed the royal party to the card-room, and on his way thither had one gleam of comfort in that he saw Lady Blakeney sitting on a sofa in the octagon hall engaged in conversation with his daughter, whilst Lord Anthony Dewhurst was nowhere in sight.

However, the gleam of comfort was very brief, for less than a quarter of an hour after he had sat down at His Highness' table, Lady Blakeney came into the card-room and stood thereafter for some little while close beside the Prince's chair. The next hour after that was one of special martyrdom for the anxious father, for he knew that his daughter was in all probability sitting out in a specially secluded corner in the company of my lord Tony.

If only Martin-Roget were here!

### IV

Martin-Roget with the eagle eyes and the airs of an accredited suitor would surely have intervened when my lord Tony in the face of the whole brilliant assembly in the ball-room, drew Mlle. de Kernogan into the seclusion of the recess underneath the gallery.

My lord Tony was never very glib of tongue. That peculiar dignified shyness which is one of the chief characteristics of well-bred Englishmen caused him to be tongue-tied when he had most to say. It was just with gesture and an appealing pressure of his hand upon her arm that he persuaded Yvonne de Kernogan to sit down beside him on the sofa in the remotest and darkest corner of the recess, and there she remained beside him silent and grave for a moment or two, and stole timid glances from time to time through the veil of her lashes at the finely-chiselled, expressive face of her young English lover.

He was pining to put a question to her, and so great was his excitement that his tongue refused him service, and she, knowing what was hovering on his lips, would not help him out, but a humorous twinkle in her dark eyes, and a faint smile round her lips lit up the habitual seriousness of her young face.

"Mademoiselle . . ." he managed to stammer at last. "Mademoiselle Yvonne . . . you have seen Lady Blakeney?"

"Yes," she replied demurely, "I have seen Lady Blakeney."

"And . . . and . . . she told you?"

"Yes. Lady Blakeney told me many things."

"She told you that . . . that. . . . In God's name, Mademoiselle Yvonne," he added desperately, "do help me out—it is cruel to tease me! Can't you see that I'm nearly crazy with anxiety?"

Then she looked up at him, her dark eyes glowing and brilliant, her face shining with the light of a great tenderness.

"Nay, milor," she said earnestly, "I had no wish to tease you. But you will own 'tis a grave and serious step which Lady Blakeney suggested that I should take. I have had no time to think . . . as yet."

"But there is no time for thinking, Mademoiselle Yvonne," he said *naïvely*. "If you will consent. . . . Oh! you will consent, will you not?" he pleaded.

She made no immediate reply, but gradually her hand which rested upon the sofa stole nearer and then nearer to his; and with a quiver of exquisite happiness his hand closed upon hers. The tips of his fingers touched the smooth warm palm and poor Lord Tony had to close his eyes for a moment as his sense of superlative ecstasy threatened to make him faint. Slowly he lifted that soft white hand to his lips.

"Upon my word, Yvonne," he said with quiet fervour, "you will never have cause to regret that you have trusted me."

"I know that well, milor," she replied demurely.

She settled down a shade or two closer to him still.

They were now like two birds in a cosy nest—secluded from the rest of the assembly, who appeared to them like dream-figures flitting in some other world that had nothing to do with their happiness. The strains of the orchestra who had struck the measure of the first figure of a contredanse sounded like fairy-music, distant, unreal in their ears. Only their love was real, their joy in one another's company, their hands clasped closely together!

"Tell me," she said after awhile, "how it all came about. It is all so terribly sudden . . . so exquisitely sudden. I was prepared of course . . . but not so soon . . . and certainly not to-night. Tell me just how it happened."

She spoke English quite fluently, with just a charming slight accent, which he thought the most adorable thing he had ever heard.

"You see, dear heart," he replied, and there was a quiver of intense feeling in his voice as he spoke, "there is a man who not only is the friend whom I love best in all the world, but is also the one whom I trust absolutely, more than myself. Two hours ago he sent for me and told me that grave danger threatened you—threatened our love and our happiness, and he begged me to urge you to consent to a secret marriage . . . at once . . . to-night."

"And you think this . . . this friend knew?"

"I know," he replied earnestly, "that he knew, or he would not have spoken to me as he did. He knows that my whole life is in your exquisite hands—he knows that our happiness is somehow threatened by that man Martin-Roget. How he obtained that information I could not guess . . . he had not the time or the inclination to tell me. I flew to make all arrangements for our marriage to-night and prayed to God— as I have never prayed in my life before—that you, dear heart, would deign to consent."

"How could I refuse when Lady Blakeney advised? She is the kindest and dearest friend I possess. She and your friend ought to know one another. Will you not tell me who he is?"

"I will present him to you, dear heart, as soon as we are married," he replied with awkward evasiveness. Then suddenly he exclaimed with boyish enthusiasm: "I can't believe it! I can't believe it! It is the most extraordinary thing in the world. . . . "

"What is that, milor?" she asked.

"That you should have cared for me at all. For of course you must care, or you wouldn't be sitting here with me now . . . you would not have consented . . . would you?"

"You know that I do care, milor," she said in her grave quiet way. "How could it be otherwise?"

"But I am so stupid and so slow," he said *naïvely*. "Why! look at me now. My heart is simply bursting with all that I want to say to you, but I just can't find the words, and I do nothing but talk rubbish and feel how you must despise me."

Once more that humorous little smile played for a moment

round Yvonne de Kernogan's serious mouth. She didn't say anything just then, but her delicate fingers gave his hand an expressive squeeze.

"You are not frightened?" he asked abruptly.

"Frightened? Of what?" she rejoined.

"At the step you are going to take?"

"Would I take it," she retorted gently, "if I had any misgivings?"

"Oh! if you had. . . . Do you know that even now . . . " he continued clumsily and haltingly, "now that I have realised just what it will mean to have you . . . and just what it would mean to me, God help me—if I were to lose you . . . well! . . . that even now I would rather go through that hell than that you should feel the least bit doubtful or unhappy about it all."

Again she smiled, gently, tenderly up into his eager, boyish face.

"The only unhappiness," she said gravely, "that could ever overtake me in the future would be parting from you, milor."

"Oh! God bless you for that, my dear! God bless you for that! But for pity's sake turn your dear eyes away from me or I vow I shall go crazy with joy. Men do go crazy with joy sometimes, you know, and I feel that in another moment I shall stand up and shout at the top of my voice to all the people in the room that within the next few hours the loveliest girl in all the world is going to be my wife."

"She certainly won't be that, if you do shout it at the top of your voice, milor, for father would hear you and there would be an end to our beautiful adventure."

"It will be a beautiful adventure, won't it?" he sighed with unconcealed ecstasy.

"So beautiful, my dear lord," she replied with gentle earnestness, "so perfect, in fact, that I am almost afraid something must happen presently to upset it all."

"Nothing can happen," he assured her. "M. Martin-Roget is not here, and His Royal Highness is even now monopolising M. le duc de Kernogan so that he cannot get away."

"Your friend must be very clever to manipulate so many strings on our behalf!"

"It is long past midnight now, sweetheart," he said with sudden irrelevance.

"Yes, I know. I have been watching the time: and I have already thought everything out for the best. I very often go home from balls and routs in the company of Lady Ffoulkes and sleep in her house those nights. Father is always quite satisfied, when I do that, and to-night he will be doubly satisfied feeling that I shall be taken away from your society. Lady Ffoulkes is in the secret, of course, so Lady Blakeney told me, and she will be ready for me in a few minutes now: she'll take me home with her and there I will change my dress and rest for awhile, waiting for the happy hour. She will come to the church with me and then . . . oh then! Oh! my dear milor!" she added suddenly with a deep sigh whilst her whole face became irradiated with a light of intense happiness, "as you say it is the most wonderful thing in all the world— this—our beautiful adventure together."

"The parson will be ready at half-past six, dear heart, it was the earliest hour that I could secure . . . after that we go at once to your church and the priest will tie up any loose threads which our English parson failed to make tight. After those two ceremonies we shall be very much married, shan't we?. . . and nothing can come between us, dear heart, can it?" he queried with a look of intense anxiety on his young face.

"Nothing," she replied. Then she added with a short sigh: "Poor father!"

"Dear heart, he will only fret for a little while. I don't believe he can really want you to marry that man Martin-Roget. It is just obstinacy on his part. He can't have anything against me really . . . save of course that I am not clever and that I shall never do anything very big in the world . . . except to love you, Yvonne, with my whole heart and soul and with every fibre and muscle in me. . . . Oh! I'll do that," he added with boyish enthusiasm, "better than anyone else in all the world could do! And your father will, I'll be bound, forgive me for stealing you, when he sees that you are happy, and contented, and have everything you want and . . . and. . . . "

As usual Lord Tony's eloquence was not equal to all that it should have expressed. He blushed furiously and with a quaint, shy gesture, passed his large, well-shaped hand over his smooth, brown hair. "I am not much, I know," he continued with a winning air of self-deprecation, "and you are far above me as the stars—you are so wonderful, so clever, so accomplished and I am nothing at all . . . but . . . but I have plenty of high-born connexions, and I have plenty of money and influential friends . . . and . . . and Sir Percy Blakeney, who is the most accomplished and finest gentleman in England, calls me his friend."

She smiled at his eagerness. She loved him for his clumsy little ways, his halting speech, that big loving heart of his which was too full of fine and noble feelings to find vent in mere words.

"Have you ever met a finer man in all the world?" he added enthusiastically.

Yvonne de Kernogan smiled once more. Her recollections of Sir Percy Blakeney showed her an elegant man of the world, whose mind seemed chiefly occupied on the devising and the wearing of exquisite clothes, in the uttering of lively witticisms for the entertainment of his royal friend and the ladies of his entourage: it showed her a man of great wealth and vast possessions who seemed willing to spend both in the mere pursuit of pleasures. She liked Sir Percy Blakeney well enough, but she could not understand clever and charming Marguerite Blakeney's adoration for her inane and foppish husband, nor the whole-hearted admiration openly lavished upon him by men like Sir Andrew Ffoulkes, my lord Hastings, and others. She would gladly have seen her own dear milor choose a more sober and intellectual friend. But then she loved him for his marvellous power of whole-hearted friendship, for his loyalty to those he cared for, for everything in fact that made up the sum total of his winning personality, and she pinned her faith on that other mysterious friend whose individuality vastly intrigued her.

"I am more interested in your anonymous friend," she said quaintly, "than in Sir Percy Blakeney. But he too is kindness itself and Lady Blakeney is an angel. I like to think that the happiest days of my life—our honeymoon, my dear lord—will be spent in their house."

"Blakeney has lent me Combwich Hall for as long as we like to stay there. We'll drive thither directly after the service, dear heart, and then we'll send a courier to your father and ask for his blessing and his forgiveness."

"Poor father!" sighed Yvonne again. But evidently compassion for the father whom she had elected to deceive did not weigh over heavily in the balance of her happiness. Her little hand once more stole like a timid and confiding bird into the shelter of his firm grasp.

V

In the card-room at His Highness' table Sir Percy Blakeney was holding the bank and seemingly luck was dead against him. Around the various tables the ladies stood about, chattering and hindering the players. Nothing appeared serious to-night, not even the capricious chances of hazard.

His Royal Highness was in rare good humour, for he was winning prodigiously.

Her Grace of Flintshire placed her perfumed and beringed hand upon Sir Percy Blakeney's shoulder; she stood behind his chair, chattering incessantly in a high flutey treble just like a canary. Blakeney vowed that she was so ravishing that she had put Dame Fortune to flight.

"You have not yet told us, Sir Percy," she said roguishly, "how you came to arrive so late at the ball."

"Alas, madam," he sighed dolefully, "'twas the fault of my cravat."

"Your cravat?"

"Aye indeed! You see I spent the whole of to-day in perfecting my new method for tying a butterfly bow, so as to give the neck an appearance of utmost elegance with a minimum of discomfort. Lady

Blakeney will bear me out when I say that I set my whole mind to my task. Was I not busy all day m'dear?" he added, making a formal appeal to Marguerite, who stood immediately behind His Highness' chair, and with her luminous eyes, full of merriment and shining with happiness fixed upon her husband.

"You certainly spent a considerable time in front of the looking-glass," she said gaily, "with two valets in attendance and my lord Tony an interested spectator in the proceedings."

"There now!" rejoined Sir Percy triumphantly, "her ladyship's testimony thoroughly bears me out. And now you shall see what Tony says on the matter. Tony! Where's Tony!" he added as his lazy grey eyes sought the brilliant crowd in the card-room. "Tony, where the devil are you?"

There was no reply, and anon Sir Percy's merry gaze encountered that of M. le duc de Kernogan who, dressed in sober black, looked strangely conspicuous in the midst of this throng of bright-coloured butterflies, and whose grave eyes, as they rested on the gorgeous figure of the English exquisite, held a world of contempt in their glance.

"Ah! M. le duc," continued Blakeney, returning that scornful look with his habitual good-humoured one, "I had not noticed that mademoiselle Yvonne was not with you, else I had not thought of inquiring so loudly for my friend Tony."

"My lord Antoine is dancing with my daughter, Sir Percy," said the other man gravely, in excellent if somewhat laboured English, "he had my permission to ask her."

"And is a thrice happy man in consequence," retorted Blakeney lightly, "though I fear me M. Martin-Roget's wrath will descend upon my poor Tony's head with unexampled vigour in consequence."

"M. Martin-Roget is not here this evening," broke in the Duchess, "and methought," she added in a discreet whisper, "that my lord Tony was all the happier for his absence. The two young people have spent a considerable time together under the shadow of the gallery in the ball-room, and, if I mistake not, Lord Tony is making the most of his time."

She talked very volubly and with a slight North-country brogue which no doubt made it a little difficult for the stranger to catch her every word. But evidently M. le duc had understood the drift of what she said, for now he rejoined with some acerbity:

"Mlle. de Kernogan is too well educated, I hope, to allow the attentions of any gentleman, against her father's will."

"Come, come, M. de Kernogan," here interposed His Royal Highness with easy familiarity, "Lord Anthony Dewhurst is the son of my old friend the Marquis of Atiltone: one of our most distinguished families in this country, who have helped to make English history. He has moreover inherited a large fortune from his mother, who was a Cruche of Crewkerne and one of the richest heiresses in the land. He is a splendid fellow—a fine sportsman, a loyal gentleman. His attentions to any young lady, however high-born, can be but flattering—and I should say welcome to those who have her future welfare at heart."

But in response to this gracious tirade, M. le duc de Kernogan bowed gravely, and his stern features did not relax as he said coldly:

"Your Royal Highness is pleased to take an interest in the affairs of my daughter. I am deeply grateful."

There was a second's awkward pause, for every one felt that despite his obvious respect and deference M. le duc de Kernogan had endeavoured to inflict a snub upon the royal personage, and one or two hot-headed young fops in the immediate entourage even muttered the word: "Impertinence!" inaudibly through their teeth. Only His Royal Highness appeared not to notice anything unusual or disrespectful in M. le duc's attitude. It seemed as if he was determined to remain good-humoured and pleasant. At any rate he chose to ignore the remark which had offended the ears of his entourage. Only those who stood opposite to His Highness, on the other side of the card table, declared afterwards that the Prince had frowned and that a haughty rejoinder undoubtedly hovered on his lips.

Be that as it may, he certainly did not show the slightest sign of ill-humour: quite gaily and unconcernedly he scooped up his winnings which Sir Percy Blakeney, who held the Bank, was at this moment pushing towards him.

"Don't go yet, M. de Kernogan," he said as the Frenchman made a movement to work his way out of the crowd, feeling no doubt that the atmosphere round him had become somewhat frigid if not exactly inimical, "don't go yet, I beg of you. *Pardi!* Can't you see that you have been bringing me luck? As a rule Blakeney, who can so well afford to lose, has the devil's own good fortune, but to-night I have succeeded in getting some of my own back from him. Do not, I entreat you, break the run of my luck by going."

"Oh, Monseigneur," rejoined the old courtier suavely, "how can my poor presence influence the gods, who of a surety always preside over your Highness' fortunes?"

"Don't attempt to explain it, my dear sir," quoth the Prince gaily. "I only know that if you go now, my luck may go with you and I shall blame you for my losses."

"Oh! in that case, Monseigneur...."

"And with all that, Blakeney," continued His Highness, once more taking up the cards and turning to his friend, "remember that we still await your explanation as to your coming so late to the ball."

"An omission, your Royal Highness," rejoined Blakeney, "an absence of mind brought about by your severity, and that of Her Grace.

The trouble was that all my calculations with regard to the exact adjustment of the butterfly bow were upset when I realised that the set of the present day waistcoat would not harmonise with it. Less than two hours before I was due to appear at this ball my mind had to make a complete volte-face in the matter of cravats. I became bewildered, lost, utterly confused. I have only just recovered, and one word of criticism on my final efforts would plunge me now into the depths of despair."

"Blakeney, you are absolutely incorrigible," retorted His Highness with a laugh. "M. le duc," he added, once more turning to the grave Frenchman with his wonted graciousness, "I pray you do not form your judgment on the gilded youth of England by the example of my friend Blakeney. Some of us can be serious when occasion demands, you know."

"Your Highness is pleased to jest," said M. de Kernogan stiffly. "What greater occasion for seriousness can there be than the present one. True, England has never suffered as France is suffering now, but she has engaged in a conflict against the most powerful democracy the world has ever known, she has thrown down the gauntlet to a set of human beasts of prey who are as determined as they are ferocious. England will not emerge victorious from this conflict, Monseigneur, if her sons do not realise that war is not mere sport and that victory can only be attained by the sacrifice of levity and of pleasure."

He had dropped into French in response to His Highness' remark, in order to express his thoughts more accurately. The Prince—a little bored no doubt—seemed disinclined to pursue the subject. Nevertheless, it seemed as if once again he made a decided effort not to show ill-humour. He even gave a knowing wink—a wink!—in the direction of his friend Blakeney and of Her Grace as if to beg them to set the ball of conversation rolling once more along a smoother—a less boring—path. He was obviously quite determined not to release M. de Kernogan from attendance near his royal person.

VI

As usual Sir Percy threw himself in the breach, filling the sudden pause with his infectious laugh:

"La!" he said gaily, "how beautifully M. le duc does talk. Ffoulkes," he added, addressing Sir Andrew, who was standing close by, "I'll wager you ten pounds to a pinch of snuff that you couldn't deliver yourself of such splendid sentiments, even in your own native lingo."

"I won't take you, Blakeney," retorted Sir Andrew with a laugh. "I'm no good at peroration."

"You should hear our distinguished guest M. Martin-Roget on

the same subject," continued Sir Percy with mock gravity. "By Gad! can't he talk? I feel a d——d worm when he talks about our national levity, our insane worship of sport, our . . . our . . . M. le duc," he added with becoming seriousness and in atrocious French, "I appeal to you. Does not M. Martin-Roget talk beautifully?"

"M. Martin-Roget," replied the duc gravely, "is a man of marvellous eloquence, fired by overwhelming patriotism. He is a man who must command respect wherever he goes."

"You have known him long, M. le duc?" queried His Royal Highness graciously.

"Indeed not very long, Monseigneur. He came over as an émigré from Brest some three months ago, hidden in a smuggler's ship. He had been denounced as an aristocrat who was furthering the cause of the royalists in Brittany by helping them plentifully with money, but he succeeded in escaping, not only with his life, but also with the bulk of his fortune."

"Ah! M. Martin-Roget is rich?"

"He is sole owner of a rich banking business in Brest, Monseigneur, which has an important branch in America and correspondents all over Europe. Monseigneur the Bishop of Brest recommended him specially to my notice in a very warm letter of introduction, wherein he speaks of M. Martin-Roget as a gentleman of the highest patriotism and integrity. Were I not quite satisfied as to M. Martin-Roget's antecedents and present connexions I would not have ventured to present him to your Highness."

"Nor would you have accepted him as a suitor for your daughter, M. le duc, c'est entendu!" concluded His Highness urbanely. "M. Martin-Roget's wealth will no doubt cover his lack of birth."

"There are plenty of high-born gentlemen devoted to the royalist cause, Monseigneur," rejoined the duc in his grave, formal manner. "But the most just and purest of causes must at times be helped with money. The Vendéens in Brittany, the Princes at Coblentz are all sorely in need of funds. . . . "

"And M. Martin-Roget son-in-law of M. le duc de Kernogan is more likely to feed those funds than M. Martin-Roget the plain business man who has no aristocratic connexions," concluded His Royal Highness dryly. "But even so, M. le duc," he added more gravely, "surely you cannot be so absolutely certain as you would wish that M. Martin-Roget's antecedents are just as he has told you. Monseigneur the Bishop of Brest may have acted in perfect good faith. . . . "

"Monseigneur the Bishop of Brest, your Highness, is a man who has our cause, the cause of our King and of our Faith, as much at heart as I have myself. He would know that on his recommendation I would trust any man absolutely. He was not like to make careless use of such knowledge."

"And you are quite satisfied that the worthy Bishop did not act under some dire pressure . . . ?"

"Quite satisfied, Monseigneur," replied the duc firmly. "What pressure could there be that would influence a prelate of such high integrity as Monseigneur the Bishop of Brest?"

## VII

There was silence for a moment or two, during which the heavy bracket clock over the door struck the first hour after midnight. His Royal Highness looked round at Lady Blakeney, and she gave him a smile and an almost imperceptible nod. Sir Andrew Ffoulkes had in the meanwhile quietly slipped away.

"I understand," said His Royal Highness quite gravely, turning back to M. le duc, "and I must crave your pardon, sir, for what must have seemed to you an indiscretion. You have given me a very clear exposé of the situation. I confess that until to-night it had seemed to me—and to all your friends, Monsieur, a trifle obscure. In fact, it had been my intention to intercede with you in favour of my young friend Lord Anthony Dewhurst, who of a truth is deeply enamoured of your daughter."

"Though your Highness' wishes are tantamount to a command, yet would I humbly assert that my wishes with regard to my daughter are based upon my loyalty and my duty to my Sovereign King Louis XVII, whom may God guard and protect, and that therefore it is beyond my power now to modify them."

"May God trounce you for an obstinate fool," murmured His Highness in English, and turning his head away so that the other should not hear him. But aloud and with studied graciousness he said:

"M. le duc, will you not take a hand at hazard? My luck is turning, and I have faith in yours. We must fleece Blakeney to-night. He has had Satan's own luck these past few weeks. Such good fortune becomes positively revolting."

There was no more talk of Mlle. de Kernogan after that. Indeed her father felt that her future had already been discussed far too freely by all these well-wishers who of a truth were not a little indiscreet. He thought that the manners and customs of good society were very peculiar here in this fog-ridden England. What business was it of all these high-born ladies and gentlemen—of His Royal Highness himself for that matter—what plans he had made for Yvonne's future? Martin-Roget was bourgeois by birth, but he was vastly rich and had promised to pour a couple of millions into the coffers of the royalist army if Mlle. de Kernogan became his wife. A couple of millions with more to follow, no doubt, and a loyal adherence to the royalist cause was worth these days all the blue blood that flowed in my lord Anthony Dewhurst's veins.

So at any rate thought M. le duc this night, while His Royal Highness kept him at cards until the late hours of the morning.

# CHAPTER 4: THE FATHER

## I

It was close on ten o'clock now in the morning on the following day, and M. le duc de Kernogan was at breakfast in his lodgings in Laura Place, when a courier was announced who was the bearer of a letter for M. le duc.

He thought the man must have been sent by Martin-Roget, who mayhap was sick, seeing that he had not been present at the Assembly Rooms last night, and the duc took the letter and opened it without misgivings. He read the address on the top of the letter: "Combwich Hall"—a place unknown to him, and the first words of the letter: "Dear father!" And even then he had no misgivings.

In fact he had to read the letter through three times before the full meaning of its contents had penetrated into his brain. Whilst he read, he sat quite still, and even the hand which held the paper had not the slightest tremor. When he had finished he spoke quite quietly to his valet:

"Give the courier a glass of ale, Frédérick," he said, "and tell him he can go; there is no answer. And—stay," he added, "I want you to go round at once to M. Martin-Roget's lodgings and ask him to come and speak with me as early as possible."

The valet left the room, and M. le duc deliberately read through the letter from end to end for the fourth time. There was no doubt, no possible misapprehension. His daughter Yvonne de Kernogan had eloped clandestinely with my lord Anthony Dewhurst and had been secretly married to him in the small hours of the morning in the Protestant church of St. James, and subsequently before a priest of her own religion in the Priory Church of St. John the Evangelist.

She apprised her father of this fact in a few sentences which purported to be dictated by profound affection and filial respect, but in which M. de Kernogan failed to detect the slightest trace of contrition. Yvonne! his Yvonne! the sole representative now of the old race— eloped like a kitchen-wench! Yvonne! his daughter! his asset for the future! his thing! his fortune! that which he meant with perfect egoism to sacrifice on the altar of his own beliefs and his own loyalty to the kingship of France! Yvonne had taken her future in her own hands! She knew that her hand, her person, were the purchase price of so many millions to be poured into the coffers of the royalist cause, and she had disposed of both, in direct defiance of her father's will and of her duty to her King and to his cause!

Yvonne de Kernogan was false to her traditions, false to her father! false to her King and country! In the years to come when the chroniclers of the time came to write the histories of the great families that had rallied round their King in the hour of his deadly peril, the name of Kernogan would be erased from those glorious pages. The Kernogans will have failed in their duty, failed in their loyalty! Oh! the shame of it all! The shame!!

The duc was far too proud a gentleman to allow his valet to see him under the stress of violent emotion, but now that he was alone his thin, hard face—with that air of gravity which he had transmitted to his daughter—became distorted with the passion of unbridled fury; he tore the letter up into a thousand little pieces and threw the fragments into the fire. On the bureau beside him there stood a miniature of Yvonne de Kernogan painted by Hall three years ago, and framed in a circlet of brilliants. M. le duc's eyes casually fell upon it; he picked it up and with a violent gesture of rage threw it on the floor and stamped upon it with his heel, destroying in this paroxysm of silent fury a work of art worth many hundred pounds.

His daughter had deceived him. She had also upset all his plans whereby the army of M. le Prince de Condé would have been enriched by a couple of million francs. In addition to the shame upon her father, she had also brought disgrace upon herself and her good name, for she was a minor and this clandestine marriage, contracted without her father's consent, was illegal in France, illegal everywhere: save perhaps in England—of this M. de Kernogan was not quite sure, but he certainly didn't care. And in this solemn moment he registered a vow that never as long as he lived would he be reconciled to that English nincompoop who had dared to filch his daughter from him, and never—as long as he lived—would he by his consent render the marriage legal, and the children born of that wedlock legitimate in the eyes of his country's laws.

A calm akin to apathy had followed his first outbreak of fury. He sat down in front of the fire, and buried his chin in his hand. Something of course must be done to get his daughter back. If only Martin-Roget were here, he would know better how to act. Would Martin-Roget stick to his bargain and accept the girl for wife, now that her fame and honour had been irretrievably tarnished? There was the question which the next half-hour would decide. M. de Kernogan cast a feverish, anxious look on the clock. Half an hour had gone by since Frédérick went to seek Martin-Roget, and the latter had not yet appeared.

Until he had seen Martin-Roget and spoken with Martin-Roget M. de Kernogan could decide nothing. For one brief, mad moment, the project had formed itself in his disordered brain to rush down to Combwich Hall and provoke that impudent Englishman who had stolen his daughter: to kill him or be killed by him; in either case

Yvonne would then be parted from him for ever. But even then, the thought of Martin-Roget brought more sober reflection. Martin-Roget would see to it. Martin-Roget would know what to do. After all, the outrage had hit the accredited lover just as hard as the father.

But why in the name of —— did Martin-Roget not come?

## II

It was past midday when at last Martin-Roget knocked at the door of M. le duc's lodgings in Laura Place. The older man had in the meanwhile gone through every phase of overwhelming emotions. The outbreak of unreasoning fury—when like a maddened beast that bites and tears he had broken his daughter's miniature and trampled it under foot—had been followed by a kind of dull apathy, when for close upon an hour he had sat staring into the flames, trying to grapple with an awful reality which seemed to elude him all the time. He could not believe that this thing had really happened: that Yvonne, his well-bred dutiful daughter, who had shown such marvellous courage and presence of mind when the necessity of flight and of exile had first presented itself in the wake of the awful massacres and wholesale executions of her own friends and kindred, that she should have eloped —like some flirtatious wench—and outraged her father in this monstrous fashion, by a clandestine marriage with a man of alien race and of a heretical religion! M. de Kernogan could not realise it. It passed the bounds of possibility. The very flames in the hearth seemed to dance and to mock the bare suggestion of such an atrocious transgression.

To this gloomy numbing of the senses had succeeded the inevitable morbid restlessness: the pacing up and down the narrow room, the furtive glances at the clock, the frequent orders to Frédérick to go out and see if M. Martin-Roget was not yet home. For Frédérick had come back after his first errand with the astounding news that M. Martin-Roget had left his lodgings the previous day at about four o'clock, and had not been seen or heard of since. In fact his landlady was very anxious about him and was sorely tempted to see the town-crier on the subject.

Four times did Frédérick have to go from Laura Place to the Bear Inn in Union Street, where M. Martin-Roget lodged, and three times he returned with the news that nothing had been heard of Mounzeer yet. The fourth time—it was then close on midday—he came back running—thankful to bring back the good tidings, since he was tired of that walk from Laura Place to the Bear Inn. M. Martin-Roget had come home. He appeared very tired and in rare ill-humour: but Frédérick had delivered the message from M. le duc, whereupon M. Martin-Roget had become most affable and promised that he would come round immediately. In fact he was even then treading hard on Frédérick's heels.

## III

"My daughter has gone! She left the ball clandestinely last night, and was married to Lord Anthony Dewhurst in the small hours of the morning. She is now at a place called Combwich Hall—with him!"

M. le duc de Kernogan literally threw these words in Martin-Roget's face, the moment the latter had entered the room, and Frédérick had discreetly closed the door.

"What? What?" stammered the other vaguely. "I don't understand. What do you mean?" he added, bewildered at the duc's violence, tired after his night's adventure and the long ride in the early morning, irritable with want of sleep and decent food. He stared, uncomprehending, at the duc, who had once more started pacing up and down the room, like a caged beast, with hands tightly clenched behind his back, his eyes glowering both at the new-comer and at the imaginary presence of his most bitter enemy—the man who had dared to come between him and his projects for his daughter.

Martin-Roget passed his hand across his brow like a man who is not yet fully awake.

"What do you mean?" he reiterated hazily.

"Just what I say," retorted the other roughly. "Yvonne has eloped with that nincompoop Lord Anthony Dewhurst. They have gone through some sort of marriage ceremony together. And she writes me a letter this morning to tell me that she is quite happy and contented and spending her honeymoon at a place called Combwich Hall. Honeymoon!" he repeated savagely, as if to lash his fury up anew, "Tsha!"

Martin-Roget on the other hand was not the man to allow himself to fall into a state of frenzy, which would necessarily interfere with calm consideration.

He had taken the fact in now. Yvonne's elopement with his English rival, the clandestine marriage, everything. But he was not going to allow his inward rage to obscure his vision of the future. He did not spend the next precious seconds—as men of his race are wont to do—in smashing things around him, in raving and fuming and gesticulating. No. That was not the temper M. Martin-Roget was in at this moment when Fate and a girl's folly were ranging themselves against his plans. His friend, citizen Chauvelin, would have envied him his calm in the face of this disaster.

Whilst M. le duc still stormed and raved, Martin-Roget sat down quietly in front of the fire, rested his chin in his hand and waited for a lull in the other man's paroxysm ere he spoke.

"From your attitude, M. le duc," he then said quietly, hiding obvious sarcasm behind a veil of studied deference, "from your attitude I gather that your wishes with regard to Mlle. de Kernogan have undergone no modification. You would still honour me by desiring that she should become my wife?"

"I am not in the habit of changing my mind," said M. le duc gruffly. He desired the marriage, he coveted Martin-Roget's millions for the royalist cause, but he had no love for the man. All the pride of the Kernogans, their long line of ancestry, rebelled against the thought of a fair descendant of this glorious race being allied to a roturier—a bourgeois—a tradesman, what? and the cause of King and country counted few greater martyrdoms than that of the duc de Kernogan whenever he met the banker Martin-Roget on an equal social footing.

"Then there is not much harm done," rejoined the latter coolly; "the marriage is not a legal one. It need not even be dissolved— Mademoiselle de Kernogan is still Mademoiselle de Kernogan and I her humble and faithful adorer."

M. le duc paused in his restless walk.

"You would . . . " he stammered, then checked himself, turning abruptly away. He had some difficulty in hiding the scorn wherewith he regarded the other's coolness. Bourgeois blood was not to be gainsaid. The tradesman—or banker, whatever he was—who hankered after an alliance with Mademoiselle de Kernogan, and was ready to lay down a couple of millions for the privilege—was not to be deterred from his purpose by any considerations of pride or of honour. M. le duc was satisfied and re-assured, but he despised the man for his leniency for all that.

"The marriage is no marriage at all according to the laws of France," reiterated Martin-Roget calmly.

"No, it is not," assented the Duke roughly.

For a while there was silence: Martin-Roget seemed immersed in his own thoughts and not to notice the febrile comings and goings of the other man.

"What we have to do, M. le duc," he said after a while; "is to induce Mlle. de Kernogan to return here immediately."

"How are you going to accomplish that?" sneered the Duke.

"Oh! I was not suggesting that I should appear in the matter at all," rejoined Martin-Roget with a shrug of the shoulders.

"Then how can I . . . ?"

"Surely . . . " argued the younger man tentatively.

"You mean . . . ?"

Martin-Roget nodded. Despite these ambiguous half-spoken sentences the two men had understood one another.

"We must get her back, of course," assented the Duke, who had suddenly become as calm as the other man.

"There is no harm done," reiterated Martin-Roget with slow and earnest emphasis.

Whereupon the Duke, completely pacified, drew a chair close to the hearth and sat down, leaning his elbows on his knees and holding his fine, aristocratic hands to the blaze.

Frédérick came in half an hour later to ask if M. le duc would have his luncheon. He found the two gentlemen sitting quite close together over the dying embers of a fire that had not been fed for close upon an hour: and that prince of valets was glad to note that M. le duc's temper had quite cooled down and that he was talking calmly and very affably to M. Martin-Roget.

# Chapter 5: The Nest

There are lovely days in England sometimes in November or December, days when the departing year strives to make us forget that winter is nigh, and autumn smiles, gentle and benignant, caressing with a still tender kiss the last leaves of the scarlet oak which linger on the boughs, and touching up with a vivid brush the evergreen verdure of bay trees, of ilex and of yew. The sky is of that pale, translucent blue which dwellers in the South never see, with the soft transparency of an aquamarine as it fades into the misty horizon at midday. And at dusk the thrushes sing: "Kiss me quick! kiss me quick! kiss me quick" in the naked branches of old acacias and chestnuts, and the robins don their crimson waistcoats and dart in and out among the coppice and through the feathery arms of larch and pine. And the sun which tips the prickly points of holly leaves with gold, joins in this merry make-believe that winter is still a very, very long way off, and that mayhap he has lost his way altogether, and is never coming to this balmy beautiful land again.

Just such a day was the penultimate one of November, 1793, when Lady Anthony Dewhurst sat at a desk in the wide bay window of the drawing-room in Combwich Hall, trying to put into a letter to Lady Blakeney all that her heart would have wished to express of love and gratitude and happiness.

Three whole days had gone by since that exciting night, when before break of day in the dimly-lighted old church, in the presence of two or three faithful friends, she had plighted her troth to Lord Anthony: even whilst other kind friends—including His Royal Highness —formed part of the little conspiracy which kept her father occupied and, if necessary, would have kept M. Martin-Roget out of the way. Since then her life had been one continuous dream of perfect bliss. From the moment when after the second religious ceremony in the Roman Catholic church she found herself alone in the carriage with milor, and felt his arms—so strong and yet so tender—closing round her and his lips pressed to hers in the first masterful kiss of complete possession, until this hour when she saw his tall, elegant figure hurrying across the garden toward the gate and suddenly turning toward the window whence he knew that she was watching him, every hour and every minute had been nothing but unalloyed happiness.

Even there where she had looked for sorrow and difficulty her path had been made smooth for her. Her father, who she had feared would prove hard and irreconcilable, had been tender and forgiving to such an extent that tears almost of shame would gather in her eyes whenever she thought of him.

As soon as she arrived at Combwich Hall she had written a long and deeply affectionate letter to her father, imploring his forgiveness for the deception and unfilial conduct which on her part must so deeply have grieved him. She pleaded for her right to happiness in words of impassioned eloquence, she pleaded for her right to love and to be loved, for her right to a home, which a husband's devotion would make a paradise for her.

This letter she had sent by special courier to her father and the very next day she had his reply. She had opened the letter with trembling fingers, fearful lest her father's harshness should mar the perfect serenity of her life. She was afraid of what he would say, for she knew her father well: knew his faults as well as his qualities, his pride, his obstinacy, his unswerving determination and his loyalty to the King's cause—all of which must have been deeply outraged by his daughter's high-handed action. But as she began to read, astonishment, amazement at once filled her soul: she could hardly trust her comprehension, hardly believe that what she read could indeed be reality, and not just the continuance of the happy dream wherein she was dwelling these days.

Her father—gently reproachful—had not one single harsh word to utter. He would not, he said, at the close of his life, after so many bitter disappointments, stand in the way of his daughter's happiness: "You should have trusted me, my child," he wrote: and indeed Yvonne could not believe her eyes. "I had no idea that your happiness was at stake in this marriage, or I should never have pressed the claims of my own wishes in the matter. I have only you in the world left, now that misery and exile are to be my portion! Is it likely that I would allow any personal desires to weigh against my love for you?"

Happy as she was Yvonne cried—cried bitterly with remorse and shame when she read that letter. How could she have been so blind, so senseless as to misjudge her father so? Her young husband found her in tears, and had much ado to console her: he too read the letter and was deeply touched by the kind reference to himself contained therein: "My lord Anthony is a gallant gentleman," wrote M. le duc de Kernogan, "he will make you happy, my child, and your old father will be more than satisfied. All that grieves me is that you did not trust me sooner. A clandestine marriage is not worthy of a daughter of the Kernogans."

"I did speak most earnestly to M. le duc," said Lord Tony reflectively, "when I begged him to allow me to pay my addresses to you. But then," he added cheerfully, "I am such a clumsy lout when I have to talk at any length—and especially clumsy when I have to plead my own cause. I suppose I put my case so badly before your father, m'dear, that he thought me three parts an idiot and would not listen to me."

"I too begged and entreated him, dear," she said with a smile, "but he was very determined then and vowed that I should marry M. Martin-Roget despite my tears and protestations. Dear father! I suppose he didn't realise that I was in earnest."

"He has certainly accepted the inevitable very gracefully," was my lord Tony's final comment.

## II

Then they read the letter through once more, sitting close together, he with one arm round her shoulder, she nestling against his chest, her hair brushing against his lips and with the letter in her hands which she could scarcely read for the tears of joy which filled her eyes.

"I don't feel very well to-day," the letter concluded; "the dampness and the cold have got into my bones: moreover you two young love birds will not desire company just yet, but to-morrow if the weather is more genial I will drive over to Combwich in the afternoon, and perhaps you will give me supper and a bed for the night. Send me word by the courier who will forthwith return to Bath if this will be agreeable to you both."

Could anything be more adorable, more delightful? It was just the last drop that filled Yvonne's cup of happiness right up to the brim.

## III

The next afternoon she sat at her desk in order to tell Lady Blakeney all about it. She made out a copy of her father's letter and put that in with her own, and begged dear Lady Blakeney to see Lady Ffoulkes forthwith and tell her all that had happened. She herself was expecting her father every minute and milor Tony had gone as far as the gate to see if the barouche was in sight.

Half an hour later M. de Kernogan had arrived and his daughter lay in his arms, happy, beyond the dreams of men. He looked rather tired and wan and still complained that the cold had got into his bones: evidently he was not very well and Yvonne after the excitement of the meeting felt not a little anxious about him. As the evening wore on he became more and more silent; he hardly would eat anything and soon after eight o'clock he announced his desire to retire to bed.

"I am not ill," he said as he kissed his daughter and bade her a fond "Good-night," "only a little wearied . . . with emotion no doubt. I shall be better after a night's rest."

He had been quite cordial with my lord Tony, though not effusive, which was only natural—he was at all times a very reserved man, and—unlike those of his race—never demonstrative in his manner: but with his daughter he had been singularly tender, with a wistful affection which almost suggested remorse, even though it was she who, on his arrival, had knelt down before him and had begged for his blessing and his forgiveness.

IV

But the following morning he appeared to be really ill: his cheeks looked sunken, almost livid, his eyes dim and hollow. Nevertheless he would not hear of staying on another day or so.

"No, no," he declared emphatically, "I shall be better in Bath. It is more sheltered there, here the north winds would drive me to my bed very quickly. I shall take a course of baths at once. They did me a great deal of good before, you remember, Yvonne—in September, when I caught a chill . . . they soon put me right. That is all that ails me now. . . . I've caught a chill."

He did his best to reassure his daughter, but she was far from satisfied: more especially as he hardly would touch the cup of chocolate which she had prepared for him with her own hands.

"I shall be quite myself again in Bath," he declared, "and in a day or two when you can spare the time—or when milor can spare you—perhaps you will drive over to see how the old father is getting on, eh?"

"Indeed," she said firmly, "I shall not allow you to go to Bath alone. If you will go, I shall accompany you."

"Nay!" he protested, "that is foolishness, my child. The barouche will take me back quite comfortably. It is less than two hours' drive and I shall be quite safe and comfortable."

"You will be quite safe and comfortable in my company," she retorted with a tender, anxious glance at his pale face and the nervous tremor of his hands. "I have consulted with my dear husband and he has given his consent that I should accompany you."

"But you can't leave milor like that, my child," he protested once more. "He will be lonely and miserable without you."

"Yes. I think he will," she said wistfully. "But he will be all the happier when you are well again, and I can return to Combwich satisfied."

Whereupon M. le duc yielded. He kissed and thanked his daughter and seemed even relieved at the prospect of her company. The barouche was ordered for eleven o'clock, and a quarter of an hour before that time Lord Tony had his young wife in his arms, bidding her a sad farewell.

"I hate your going from me, sweetheart," he said as he kissed her eyes, her hair, her lips. "I cannot bear you out of my sight even for an hour . . . let alone a couple of days."

"Yet I must go, dear heart," she retorted, looking up with that sweet, grave smile of hers into his eager young face. "I could not let him travel alone . . . could I?"

"No, no," he assented somewhat dubiously, "but remember, dear heart, that you are infinitely precious and that I shall scarce live for sheer anxiety until I have you here, safe, once more in my arms."

"I'll send you a courier this evening," she rejoined, as she extricated herself gently from his embrace, "and if I can come back to-morrow. . . ."

"I'll ride over to Bath in any case in the morning so that I may escort you back if you really can come."

"I will come if I am reassured about father. Oh, my dear lord," she added with a wistful little sigh, "I knew yesterday morning that I was too happy, and that something would happen to mar the perfect felicity of these last few days."

"You are not seriously anxious about M. le duc's health, dear heart?"

"No, not seriously anxious. Farewell, milor. It is *au revoir* . . . a few hours and we'll resume our dream."

## V

There was nothing in all that to arouse my lord Tony's suspicions. All day he was miserable and forlorn because Yvonne was not there—but he was not suspicious.

Fate had a blow in store for him, from which he was destined never wholly to recover, but she gave him no warning, no premonition. He spent the day in making up arrears of correspondence, for he had a large private fortune to administer—trust funds on behalf of brothers and sisters who were minors—and he always did it conscientiously and to the best of his ability. The last few days he had lived in a dream and there was an accumulation of business to go through. In the evening he expected the promised courier, who did not arrive: but his was not the sort of disposition that would fret and fume because of a contretemps which might be attributable to the weather—it had rained heavily since afternoon—or to sundry trifling causes which he at Combwich, ten or a dozen miles from Bath, could not estimate. He had no suspicions even then. How could he have? How could he guess? Nevertheless when he ultimately went to bed, it was with the firm resolve that he would in any case go over to Bath in the morning and remain there until Yvonne was able to come back with him.

Combwich without her was anyhow unendurable.

## VI

He started for Bath at nine o'clock in the morning. It was still raining hard. It had rained all night and the roads were very muddy. He started out without a groom. A little after half-past ten, he drew rein outside his house in Chandos Buildings, and having changed his clothes he started to walk to Laura Place. The rain had momentarily left off, and a pale wintry sun peeped out through rolling banks of grey clouds. He went round by way of Saw Close and the Upper Borough Walls, as he wanted to avoid the fashionable throng that crowded the neighbourhood of the Pump Room and the Baths. His intention was to seek out the Blakeneys at their residence in the Circus after he had seen Yvonne and obtained news of M. le duc.

He had no suspicions. Why should he have?

The Abbey clock struck a quarter-past eleven when finally he knocked at the house in Laura Place. Long afterwards he remembered how just at that moment a dense grey mist descended into the valley. He had not noticed it before, now he saw that it had enveloped this part of the city so that he could not even see clearly across the Place.

A woman came to open the door. Lord Tony then thought this strange considering how particular M. le duc always was about everything pertaining to the management of his household: "The house of a poor exile," he was wont to say, "but nevertheless that of a gentleman."

"Can I go straight up?" he asked the woman, who he thought was standing ostentatiously in the hall as if to bar his way. "I desire to see M. le duc."

"Ye can walk upstairs, zir," said the woman, speaking with a broad Somersetshire accent, "but I doubt me if ye'll see 'is Grace the Duke. 'Es been gone these two days."

Tony had paid no heed to her at first; he had walked across the narrow hall to the oak staircase, and was half-way up the first flight when her last words struck upon his ear . . . quite without meaning for the moment . . . but nevertheless he paused, one foot on one tread, and the other two treads below . . . and he turned round to look at the woman, a swift frown across his smooth forehead.

"Gone these two days," he repeated mechanically; "what do you mean?"

"Well! 'Is Grace left the day afore yesterday—Thursday it was. . . . 'Is man went yesterday afternoon with luggage and sich . . . 'e went by coach 'e did. . . . Leave off," she cried suddenly; "what are ye doin'? Ye're 'urtin' me."

For Lord Tony had rushed down the stairs again and was across the hall, gripping the unoffending woman by the wrist and glaring into her expressionless face until she screamed with fright.

"I beg your pardon," he said humbly as he released her wrist: all the instincts of the courteous gentleman arrayed against his loss of control. "I . . . I forgot myself for the moment," he stammered; "would you mind telling me again . . . what . . . what you said just now?"

The woman was prepared to put on the airs of outraged dignity, she even glanced up at the malapert with scorn expressed in her small beady eyes. But at sight of his face her anger and her fears both fell away from her. Lord Tony was white to the lips, his cheeks were the colour of dead ashes, his mouth trembled, his eyes alone glowed with ill-repressed anxiety.

"'Is Grace," she said with slow emphasis, for of a truth she thought that the young gentleman was either sick or daft, "'Is Grace left this 'ouse the day afore yesterday in a hired barouche. 'Is man—Frederick—went yesterday afternoon with the liggage. 'E caught the Bristol coach at two o'clock. I was 'Is Grace's 'ousekeeper and I am to look after the 'ouse and the zervants until I 'ear from 'Is Grace again. Them's my orders. I know no more than I'm tellin' ye."

"But His Grace returned here yesterday forenoon," argued Lord Tony calmly, mechanically, as one who would wish to convince an obstinate child. "And my lady . . . Mademoiselle Yvonne, you know . . . was with him."

"*Noa! Noa!*" said the woman placidly. "'Is Grace 'asn't been near this 'ouse come Thursday afternoon, and 'is man left yesterday wi' th' liggage. Why!" she added confidentially, "'e ain't gone far. It was all zettled that zuddint I didn't know nothing about it myzelf till I zeed Mr. Frederick start off wi' th' liggage. Not much liggage neither it wasn't. Sure but 'Is Grace'll be 'ome zoon. 'E can't 'ave gone far. Not wi' that bit o' liggage. Zure."

"But my lady . . . Mademoiselle Yvonne. . . . "

"Lor, zir, didn't ye know? Why 'twas all over th' town o' Tuesday as 'ow Mademozell 'ad eloped with my lord Anthony Dew'urst, and. . . . "

"Yes! yes! But you have seen my lady since?"

"Not clapped eyes on 'er, zir, since she went to the ball come Monday evenin'. An' a picture she looked in 'er white gown. . . . "

"And . . . did His Grace leave no message . . . for . . . for anyone? . . . no letter?"

"Ah, yes, now you come to mention it, zir. Mr. Frederick 'e give me a letter yesterday. "Is Grace,' sez 'e, 'left this yere letter on 'is desk. I just found it,' sez 'e. 'If my lord Anthony Dew'urst calls,' sez 'e, 'give it to 'im.' I've got the letter zomewhere, zir. What may your name be?"

"I am Lord Anthony Dewhurst," replied the young man mechanically.

"Your pardon, my lord, I'll go fetch th' letter."

## VII

Lord Tony never moved while the woman shuffled across the

passage and down the back stairs. He was like a man who has received a knock-out blow and has not yet had time to recover his scattered senses. At first when the woman spoke, his mind had jumped to fears of some awful accident . . . runaway horses . . . a broken barouche . . . or a sudden aggravation of the duc's ill-health. But soon he was forced to reject what now would have seemed a consoling thought: had there been an accident, he would have heard—a rumour would have reached him—Yvonne would have sent a courier. He did not know yet what to think, his mind was like a slate over which a clumsy hand had passed a wet sponge—impressions, recollections, above all a hideous, nameless fear, were all blurred and confused within his brain.

The woman came back carrying a letter which was crumpled and greasy from a prolonged sojourn in the pocket of her apron. Lord Tony took the letter and broke its heavy seal. The woman watched him, curiously, pityingly now, for he was good to look on, and she scented the significance of the tragedy which she had been the means of revealing to him. But he had become quite unconscious of her presence, of everything in fact save those few sentences, written in French, in a cramped hand, and which seemed to dance a wild saraband before his eyes:

"Milor,—

"You tried to steal my daughter from me, but I have taken her from you now. By the time this reaches you we shall be on the high seas on our way to Holland, thence to Coblentz, where Mademoiselle de Kernogan will in accordance with my wishes be united in lawful marriage to M. Martin-Roget whom I have chosen to be her husband. She is not and never was your wife. As far as one may look into the future, I can assure you that you will never in life see her again."

And to this monstrous document of appalling callousness and cold-blooded cruelty there was appended the signature of André Dieudonné Duc de Kernogan.

But unlike the writer thereof Lord Anthony Dewhurst neither stormed nor raged: he did not even tear the execrable letter into an hundred fragments. His firm hand closed over it with one convulsive clutch, and that was all. Then he slipped the crumpled paper into his pocket. Quite deliberately he took out some money and gave a piece of silver to the woman.

"I thank you very much," he said somewhat haltingly. "I quite understand everything now."

The woman curtseyed and thanked him; tears were in her eyes, for it seemed to her that never had she seen such grief depicted upon any human face. She preceded him to the hall door and held it open for him, while he passed out. After the brief gleam of sunshine it had started to rain again, but he didn't seem to care. The woman suggested fetching a hackney coach, but he refused quite politely, quite gently: he even lifted his hat as he went out. Obviously he did not know what he was doing. Then he went out into the rain and strode slowly across the Place.

# CHAPTER 6: THE SCARLET PIMPERNEL

## I

Instinct kept him away from the more frequented streets—and instinct after awhile drew him in the direction of his friend's house at the comer of The Circus. Sir Percy Blakeney had not gone out fortunately: the lacquey who opened the door to my lord Tony stared astonished and almost paralysed for the moment at the extraordinary appearance of his lordship. Rain dropped down from the brim of his hat on to his shoulders: his boots were muddy to the knees, his clothes wringing wet. His eyes were wild and hazy and there was a curious tremor round his mouth.

The lacquey declared with a knowing wink afterwards that his lordship must 'ave been drinkin'!

But at the moment his sense of duty urged him to show my lord —who was his master's friend—into the library, whatever condition he was in. He took his dripping coat and hat from him and marshalled him across the large, square hall.

Sir Percy Blakeney was sitting at his desk, writing, when Lord Tony was shown in. He looked up and at once rose and went to his friend.

"Sit down, Tony," he said quietly, "while I get you some brandy."

He forced the young man down gently into a chair in front of the fire and threw another log into the blaze. Then from a cupboard he fetched a flask of brandy and a glass, poured some out and held it to Tony's lips. The latter drank—unresisting—like a child. Then as some warmth penetrated into his bones, he leaned forward, resting his elbows on his knees and buried his face in his hands. Blakeney waited quietly, sitting down opposite to him, until his friend should be able to speak.

"And after all that you told me on Monday night!" were the first words which came from Tony's quivering lips, "and the letter you sent me over on Tuesday! Oh! I was prepared to mistrust Martin-Roget. Why! I never allowed her out of my sight! . . . But her father! . . . How could I guess?"

"Can you tell me exactly what happened?"
Lord Tony drew himself up, and staring vacantly into the fire told his friend the events of the past four days. On Wednesday the courier with M. de Kernogan's letter, breathing kindness and forgiveness. On Thursday his arrival and seeming ill-health, on Friday his departure with Yvonne. Tony spoke quite calmly. He had never been anything but

calm since first, in the house in Laura Place, he had received that awful blow.

"I ought to have known," he concluded dully, "I ought to have guessed. Especially since you warned me."

"I warned you that Martin-Roget was not the man he pretended to be," said Blakeney gently, "I warned you against him. But I too failed to suspect the duc de Kernogan. We are Britishers, you and I, my dear Tony," he added with a quaint little laugh, "our minds will never be quite equal to the tortuous ways of these Latin races. But we are not going to waste time now talking about the past. We have got to find your wife before those brutes have time to wreak their devilries against her."

"On the high seas . . . on the way to Holland . . . thence to Coblentz . . . " murmured Tony, "I have not yet shown you the duc's letter to me."

He drew from his pocket the crumpled, damp piece of paper on which the ink had run into patches and blotches, and which had become almost undecipherable now. Sir Percy took it from him and read it through:

"The duc de Kernogan and Lady Anthony Dewhurst are not on their way to Holland and to Coblentz," he said quietly as he handed the letter back to Lord Tony.

"Not on their way to Holland?" queried the young man with a puzzled frown. "What do you mean?"

Blakeney drew his chair closer to his friend: a marvellous and subtle change had suddenly taken place in his individuality. Only a few moments ago he was the polished, elegant man of the world, then the kindly and understanding friend—self-contained, reserved, with a perfect manner redolent of sympathy and dignity. Suddenly all that was changed. His manner was still perfect and outwardly calm, his gestures scarce, his speech deliberate, but the compelling power of the leader—which is the birth-right of such men—glowed and sparkled now in his deep-set eyes: the spirit of adventure and reckless daring was awake—insistent and rampant—and subtle effluvia of enthusiasm and audacity emanated from his entire personality.

Sir Percy Blakeney had sunk his individuality in that of the Scarlet Pimpernel.

"I mean," he said, returning his friend's anxious look with one that was inspiring in its unshakable confidence, "I mean that on Monday last, the night before your wedding—when I urged you to obtain Yvonne de Kernogan's consent to an immediate marriage—I had followed Martin-Roget to a place called "The Bottom Inn" on Goblin Combe—a place well known to every smuggler in the county."

"You, Percy!" exclaimed Tony in amazement.

"Yes, I," laughed the other lightly. "Why not? I had had my

suspicions of him for some time. As luck would have it he started off on the Monday afternoon by hired coach to Chelwood. I followed. From Chelwood he wanted to go on to Redhill: but the roads were axle deep in mud, and evening was gathering in very fast. Nobody would take him. He wanted a horse and a guide. I was on the spot—as disreputable a bar-loafer as you ever saw in your life. I offered to take him. He had no choice. He had to take me. No one else had offered. I took him to the Bottom Inn. There he met our esteemed friend M. Chauvelin. . . . "

"Chauvelin!" cried Tony, suddenly roused from the dull apathy of his immeasurable grief, at sound of that name which recalled so many exciting adventures, such mad, wild, hair-breadth escapes. "Chauvelin! What in the world is he doing here in England?"

"Brewing mischief, of course," replied Blakeney dryly. "In disgrace, discredited, a marked man—what you will—my friend M. Chauvelin has still an infinite capacity for mischief. Through the interstices of a badly fastened shutter I heard two blackguards devising infinite devilry. That is why, Tony," he added, "I urged an immediate marriage as the only real protection for Yvonne de Kernogan against those blackguards."

"Would to God you had been more explicit!" exclaimed Tony with a bitter sigh.

"Would to God I had," rejoined the other, "but there was so little time, with licences and what not all to arrange for, and less than an hour to do it in. And would you have suspected the Duc himself of such execrable duplicity even if you had known, as I did then, that the so-called Martin-Roget hath name Adet, and that he matures thoughts of deadly revenge against the duc de Kernogan and his daughter?"

"Martin-Roget? the banker—the exiled royalist who. . . . "

"He may be a banker now . . . but he certainly is no royalist—he is the son of a peasant who was unjustly put to death four years ago by the duc de Kernogan."

"Ye gods!"

"He came over to England plentifully supplied with money—I could not gather if the money is his or if it has been entrusted to him by the revolutionary government for purposes of spying and corruption— but he came to England in order to ingratiate himself with the duc de Kernogan and his daughter, and then to lure them back to France, for what purpose you may well imagine."

"Good God, man . . . you can't mean . . . ?"

"He has chartered a smuggler's craft—or rather Chauvelin has done it for him. Her name is the Hollandia, her master hath name Kuyper. She was to be in Portishead harbour on the last day of November: all her papers in order. Cargo of West India sugar, destination Amsterdam, consignee some Mynheer over there. But Martin-Roget, or whatever his name may be, and no doubt our friend

Chauvelin too, were to be aboard her, and also M. le duc de Kernogan and his daughter. And the Hollandia is to put into Le Croisic for Nantes, whose revolutionary proconsul, that infamous Carrier, is of course Chauvelin's bosom friend."

Sir Percy Blakeney finished speaking. Lord Tony had listened to him quietly and in silence: now he rose and turned resolutely to his friend. There was no longer any trace in him of that stunned apathy which had been the primary result of the terrible blow. His young face was still almost unrecognisable from the lines of grief and horror which marred its habitual fresh, boyish look. He looked twenty years older than he had done a few hours ago, but there was also in his whole attitude now the virility of more mature manhood, its determination and unswerving purpose.

"And what can I do now?" he asked simply, knowing that he could trust his friend and leader with what he held dearest in all the world. "Without you, Blakeney, I am of course impotent and lost. I haven't the head to think. I haven't sufficient brains to pit against those cunning devils. But if you will help me. . . . "

Then he checked himself abruptly, and the look of hopeless despair once more crept into his eyes.

"I am mad, Percy," he said with a self-deprecating shrug of the shoulders, "gone crazy with grief, I suppose, or I shouldn't talk of asking your help, of risking your life in my cause."

"Tony, if you talk that rubbish, I shall be forced to punch your head," retorted Blakeney with his light laugh. "Why man," he added gaily, "can't you see that I am aching to have at my old friend Chauvelin again?"

And indeed the zest of adventure, the zest to fight, never dormant, was glowing with compelling vigour now in those lazy eyes of his which were resting with such kindliness upon his stricken friend. "Go home, Tony!" he added, "go, you rascal, and collect what things you want, while I send for Hastings and Ffoulkes, and see that four good horses are ready for us within the hour. To-night we sleep at Portishead, Tony. The Day-Dream is lying off there, ready to sail at any hour of the day or night. The Hollandia has twenty-four hour's start of us, alas! and we cannot overtake her now: but we'll be in Nantes ere those devils can do much mischief: and once in Nantes! . . . Why, Tony man! think of the glorious escapes we've had together, you and I! Think of the gay, mad rides across the north of France, with half-fainting women and swooning children across our saddle-bows! Think of the day when we smuggled the de Tournais out of Calais harbour, the day we snatched Juliette Déroulède and her Paul out of the tumbril and tore across Paris with that howling mob at our heels! Think! think, Tony! of all the happiest, merriest moments of your life and they will seem dull and lifeless beside what is in store for you, when with your dear wife's arms clinging round your neck, we'll fly along the quays of Nantes on the road to liberty! Ah, Tony lad! were it not for the anxiety which I know is gnawing at your heart, I would count this one of the happiest hours of my happy life!"

He was so full of enthusiasm, so full of vitality, that life itself seemed to emanate from him and to communicate itself to the very atmosphere around. Hope lit up my lord Tony's wan face: he believed in his friend as mediæval ascetics believed in the saints whom they adored. Enthusiasm had crept into his veins, dull despair fell away from him like a mantle.

"God bless you, Percy," he exclaimed as his firm and loyal hand grasped that of the leader whom he revered.

"Nay!" retorted Blakeney with sudden gravity. "He hath done that already. Pray for His help to-day, lad, as you have never prayed before."

# Chapter 7: Marguerite

I

Lord Tony had gone, and for the space of five minutes Sir Percy Blakeney stood in front of the hearth staring into the fire. Something lay before him, something had to be done now, which represented the heavy price that had to be paid for those mad and happy adventures, for that reckless daring, aye for that selfless supreme sacrifice which was as the very breath of life to the Scarlet Pimpernel.

And in the dancing flames he could see Marguerite's blue eyes, her ardent hair, her tender smile all pleading with him not to go. She had so much to give him—so much happiness, such an infinity of love, and he was all that she had in the world! It seemed to him as if he could feel her arms around him even now, as if he could hear her voice whispering appealingly: "Do not go! Am I nothing to you that thoughts of others should triumph over my pleading? that the need of others should outweigh mine own most pressing need? I want you, Percy! aye! even I! You have done so much for others—it is my turn now."

But even as in a kind of trance those words seemed to reach his strained senses, he knew that he must go, that he must tear himself away once more from the clinging embrace of her dear arms and shut his eyes to the tears which anon would fill her own. Destiny demanded that he should go. He had chosen his path in life himself, at first only in a spirit of wild recklessness, a mad tossing of his life into the scales of Fate. But now that same destiny which he had chosen had become his master: he no longer could draw back. What he had done once, twenty times, an hundred times, that he must do again, all the while that the weak and the defenceless called mutely to him from across the seas, all the while that innocent women suffered and orphaned children cried.

And to-day it was his friend, his comrade, who had come to him in his distress: the young wife whom he idolised was in the most dire peril that could possibly threaten any woman: she was at the mercy of a man who, driven by the passion of revenge, meant to show her no mercy, and the devil alone knew these days to what lengths of infamy a man so driven would go.

The minutes sped on. Blakeney's eyes grew hot and wearied from staring into the fire. He closed them for a moment and then quietly turned to go.

II

All those who knew Marguerite Blakeney these days marvelled

if she was ever unhappy. Lady Ffoulkes, who was her most trusted friend, vowed that she was not. She had moments—days—sometimes weeks of intense anxiety, which amounted to acute agony. Whenever she saw her husband start on one of those expeditions to France wherein every minute, every hour, he risked his life and more in order to snatch yet another threatened victim from the awful clutches of those merciless Terrorists, she endured soul-torture such as few women could have withstood who had not her splendid courage and her boundless faith. But against such crushing sorrow she had to set off the happiness of those reunions with the man whom she loved so passionately—happiness which was so great, that it overrode and conquered the very memory of past anxieties.

Marguerite Blakeney suffered terribly at times—at others she was overwhelmingly happy—the measure of her life was made up of the bitter dregs of sorrow and the sparkling wine of joy! No! she was not altogether unhappy: and gradually that enthusiasm which irradiated from the whole personality of the valiant Scarlet Pimpernel, which dominated his every action, entered into Marguerite Blakeney's blood too. His vitality was so compelling, those impulses which carried him headlong into unknown dangers were so generous and were actuated by such pure selflessness, that the noble-hearted woman whose very soul was wrapped up in the idolised husband, allowed herself to ride by his side on the buoyant waves of his enthusiasm and of his desires: she smothered every expression of anxiety, she swallowed her tears, she learned to say the word "Good-bye" and forgot the word "Stay!"

## III

It was half an hour after midday when Percy knocked at the door of her boudoir. She had just come in from a walk in the meadows round the town and along the bank of the river: the rain had overtaken her and she had come in very wet, but none the less exhilarated by the movement and the keen, damp, salt-laden air which came straight over the hills from the Channel. She had taken off her hat and her mantle and was laughing gaily with her maid who was shaking the wet out of a feather. She looked round at her husband when he entered, and with a quick gesture ordered the maid out of the room.

She had learned to read every line on Percy's face, every expression of his lazy, heavy-lidded eyes. She saw that he was dressed with more than his usual fastidiousness, but in dark clothes and travelling mantle. She knew, moreover, by that subtle instinct which had become a second nature and which warned her whenever he meant to go.

Nor did he announce his departure to her in so many words. As soon as the maid had gone, he took his beloved in his arms.

"They have stolen Tony's wife from him," he said with that light, quaint laugh of his. "I told you that the man Martin-Roget had planned some devilish mischief—well! he has succeeded so far, thanks to that unspeakable fool the duc de Kernogan."

He told her briefly the history of the past few days.

"Tony did not take my warning seriously enough," he concluded with a sigh; "he ought never to have allowed his wife out of his sight."

Marguerite had not interrupted him while he spoke. At first she just lay in his arms, quiescent and listening, nerving herself by a supreme effort not to utter one sigh of misery or one word of appeal. Then, as her knees shook under her, she sank back into a chair by the hearth and he knelt beside her with his arms clasped tightly round her shoulders, his cheek pressed against hers. He had no need to tell her that duty and friendship called, that the call of honour was once again —as it so often has been in the world—louder than that of love.

She understood and she knew, and he, with that supersensitive instinct of his, understood the heroic effort which she made.

"Your love, dear heart," he whispered, "will draw me back safely home as it hath so often done before. You believe that, do you not?"

And she had the supreme courage to murmur: "Yes!"

# CHAPTER 8: THE ROAD TO PORTISHEAD

It was not until Bath had very obviously been left behind that Yvonne de Kernogan—Lady Anthony Dewhurst—realised that she had been trapped.

During the first half-hour of the journey her father had lain back against the cushions of the carriage with eyes closed, his face pale and wan as if with great suffering. Yvonne, her mind a prey to the gravest anxiety, sat beside him, holding his limp cold hand in hers. Once or twice she ventured on a timid question as to his health and he invariably murmured a feeble assurance that he felt well, only very tired and disinclined to talk. Anon she suggested—diffidently, for she did not mean to disturb him—that the driver did not appear to know his way into Bath, he had turned into a side road which she felt sure was not the right one. M. le duc then roused himself for a moment from his lethargy. He leaned forward and gazed out of the window.

"The man is quite right, Yvonne," he said quietly, "he knows his way. He brought me along this road yesterday. He gets into Bath by a slight détour but it is pleasanter driving."

This reply satisfied her. She was a stranger in the land, and knew little or nothing of the environs of Bath. True, last Monday morning after the ceremony of her marriage she had driven out to Combwich, but dawn was only just breaking then, and she had lain for the most part—wearied and happy—in her young husband's arms. She had taken scant note of roads and signposts.

A few minutes later the coach came to a halt and Yvonne, looking through the window, saw a man who was muffled up to the chin and enveloped in a huge travelling cape, mount swiftly up beside the driver.

"Who is that man?" she queried sharply.

"Some friend of the coachman's, no doubt," murmured her father in reply, "to whom he is giving a lift as far as Bath."

The barouche had moved on again.

Yvonne could not have told you why, but at her father's last words she had felt a sudden cold grip at her heart—the first since she started. It was neither fear nor yet suspicion, but a chill seemed to go right through her. She gazed anxiously through the window, and then looked at her father with eyes that challenged and that doubted. But M. le duc would not meet her gaze. He had once more closed his eyes and sat quite still, pale and haggard, like a man who is suffering acutely.

II

"Father we are going back to Bath, are we not?"

The query came out trenchant and hard from her throat which now felt hoarse and choked. Her whole being was suddenly pervaded by a vast and nameless fear. Time had gone on, and there was no sign in the distance of the great city. M. de Kernogan made no reply, but he opened his eyes and a curious glance shot from them at the terror-stricken face of his daughter.

Then she knew—knew that she had been tricked and trapped—that her father had played a hideous and complicated *rôle* of hypocrisy and duplicity in order to take her away from the husband whom she idolised.

Fear and her love for the man of her choice gave her initiative and strength. Before M. de Kernogan could realise what she was doing, before he could make a movement to stop her, she had seized the handle of the carriage door, wrenched the door open and jumped out into the road. She fell on her face in the mud, but the next moment she picked herself up again and started to run—down the road which the carriage had just traversed, on and on as fast as she could go. She ran on blindly, unreasoningly, impelled by a purely physical instinct to escape, not thinking how childish, how futile such an attempt was bound to be.

Already after the first few minutes of this swift career over the muddy road, she heard quick, heavy footsteps behind her. Her father could not run like that—the coachman could not have thus left his horses—but still she could hear those footsteps at a run—a quicker run than hers—and they were gaining on her—every minute, every second. The next, she felt two powerful arms suddenly seizing her by the shoulders. She stumbled and would once more have fallen, but for those same strong arms which held her close.

"Let me go! Let me go!" she cried, panting.

But she was held and could no longer move. She looked up into the face of Martin-Roget, who without any hesitation or compunction lifted her up as if she had been a bale of light goods and carried her back toward the coach. She had forgotten the man who had been picked up on the road awhile ago, and had been sitting beside the coachman since.

He deposited her in the barouche beside her father, then quietly closed the door and once more mounted to his seat on the box. The carriage moved on again. M. de Kernogan was no longer lethargic, he looked down on his daughter's inert form beside him, and not one look of tenderness or compassion softened the hard callousness of his face.

"Any resistance, my child," he said coldly, "will as you see be useless as well as undignified. I deplore this necessary violence, but I should be forced once more to requisition M. Martin-Roget's help if you attempted such foolish tricks again. When you are a little more calm, we will talk openly together."

For the moment she was lying back against the cushions of the carriage; her nerves having momentarily given way before this appalling catastrophe which had overtaken her and the hideous outrage to which she was being subjected by her own father. She was sobbing convulsively. But in the face of his abominable callousness, she made a great effort to regain her self-control. Her pride, her dignity came to the rescue. She had had time in those few seconds to realise that she was indeed more helpless than any bird in a fowler's net, and that only absolute calm and presence of mind could possibly save her now.

If indeed there was the slightest hope of salvation.

She drew herself up and resolutely dried her eyes and readjusted her hair and her hood and mantle.

"We can talk openly at once, sir," she said coldly. "I am ready to hear what explanation you can offer for this monstrous outrage."

"I owe you no explanation, my child," he retorted calmly. "Presently when you are restored to your own sense of dignity and of self-respect you will remember that a lady of the house of Kernogan does not elope in the night with a stranger and a heretic like some kitchen-wench. Having so far forgotten herself my daughter must, alas! take the consequences, which I deplore, of her own sins and lack of honour."

"And no doubt, father," she retorted, stung to the quick by his insults, "that you too will anon be restored to your own sense of self-respect and remember that hitherto no gentleman of the house of Kernogan has acted the part of a liar and of a hypocrite!"

"Silence!" he commanded sternly.

"Yes!" she reiterated wildly, "it was the *rôle* of a liar and of a hypocrite that you played from the moment when you sat down to pen that letter full of protestations of affection and forgiveness, until like a veritable Judas you betrayed your own daughter with a kiss. Shame on you, father!" she cried. "Shame!"

"Enough!" he said, as he seized her wrist so roughly that the cry of pain which involuntarily escaped her effectually checked the words in her mouth. "You are mad, beside yourself, a thoughtless, senseless creature whom I shall have to coerce more effectually if you do not cease your ravings. Do not force me to have recourse once again to M. Martin-Roget's assistance to keep your undignified outburst in check."

The name of the man whom she had learned to hate and fear more than any other human being in the world was sufficient to restore to her that measure of self-control which had again threatened to leave her.

"Enough indeed," she said more calmly; "the brain that could devise and carry out such infamy in cold blood is not like to be influenced by a defenceless woman's tears. Will you at least tell me whither you are taking me?"

"We go to a place on the coast now," he replied coldly, "the outlandish name of which has escaped me. There we embark for Holland, from whence we shall join their Royal Highnesses at Coblentz. It is at Coblentz that your marriage with M. Martin-Roget will take place, and. . . . "

"Stay, father," she broke in, speaking quite as calmly as he did, "ere you go any further. Understand me clearly, for I mean every word that I say. In the sight of God—if not in that of the laws of France—I am the wife of Lord Anthony Dewhurst. By everything that I hold most sacred and most dear I swear to you that I will never become Martin-Roget's wife. I would die first," she added with burning but resolutely suppressed passion.

He shrugged his shoulders.

"Pshaw, my child," he said quietly, "many a time since the world began have women registered such solemn and sacred vows, only to break them when force of circumstance and their own good sense made them ashamed of their own folly."

"How little you know me, father," was all that she said in reply.


## III


Indeed, Yvonne de Kernogan—Yvonne Dewhurst as she was now in sight of God and men—had far too much innate dignity and self-respect to continue this discussion, seeing that in any case she was physically the weaker, and that she was absolutely helpless and defenceless in the hands of two men, one of whom—her own father—who should have been her protector, was leagued with her bitterest enemy against her.

That Martin-Roget was her enemy—aye and her father's too—she had absolutely no doubt. Some obscure yet keen instinct was working in her heart, urging her to mistrust him even more wholly than she had done before. Just now, when he laid ruthless hands on her and carried her, inert and half-swooning, back into the coach, and she lay with closed eyes, her very soul in revolt against this contact with him, against the feel of his arms around her, a vague memory surcharged with horror and with dread stirred within her brain: and over the vista of the past few years she looked back upon an evening in the autumn—a rough night with the wind from the Atlantic blowing across the lowlands of Poitou and soughing in the willow trees that bordered the

Loire—she seemed to hear the tumultuous cries of enraged human creatures dominating the sound of the gale, she felt the crowd of evil-intentioned men around the closed carriage wherein she sat, calm and unafraid. Darkness then was all around her. She could not see. She could only hear and feel. And she heard the carriage door being wrenched open, and she felt the cold breath of the wind upon her cheek, and also the hot breath of a man in a passion of fury and of hate.

She had seen nothing then, and mercifully semi-unconsciousness had dulled her aching senses, but even now her soul shrunk with horror at the vague remembrance of that ghostlike form—the spirit of hate and of revenge—of its rough arms encircling her shoulders, its fingers under her chin—and then that awful, loathsome, contaminating kiss which she thought then would have smirched her for ever. It had taken all the pure, sweet kisses of a brave and loyal man whom she loved and revered, to make her forget that hideous, indelible stain: and in the arms of her dear milor she had forgotten that one terrible moment, when she had felt that the embrace of death must be more endurable than that of this unknown and hated man.

It was the memory of that awful night which had come back to her as in a flash while she lay passive and broken in Martin-Roget's arms. Of course for the moment she had no thought of connecting the rich banker from Brest, the enthusiastic royalist and émigré, with one of those turbulent, uneducated peasant lads who had attacked her carriage that night: all that she was conscious of was that she was outraged by his presence, just as she had been outraged then, and that the contact of his hands, of his arms, was absolutely unendurable.

To fight against the physical power which held her a helpless prisoner in the hands of the enemy was sheer impossibility. She knew that, and was too proud to make feeble and futile efforts which could only end in defeat and further humiliation. She felt hideously wretched and lonely—thoughts of her husband, who at this hour was still serenely unconscious of the terrible catastrophe which had befallen him, brought tears of acute misery to her eyes. What would he do when —to-morrow, perhaps—he realised that his bride had been stolen from him, that he had been fooled and duped as she had been too. What could he do when he knew?

She tried to solace her own soul-agony by thinking of his influential friends who, of course, would help him as soon as they knew. There was that mysterious and potent friend of whom he spoke so little, who already had warned him of coming danger and urged on the secret marriage which should have proved a protection. There was Sir Percy Blakeney, of whom he spoke much, who was enormously rich, independent, the most intimate friend of the Regent himself. There was. . . .

But what was the use of clinging even for one instant to those feeble cords of Hope's broken lyre? By the time her dear lord knew that she was gone, she would be on the high seas, far out of his reach.

And she had not even the solace of tears—heart-broken sobs rose in her throat, but she resolutely kept them back. Her father's cold, impassive face, the callous glitter in his eyes told her that every tear would be in vain, her most earnest appeal an object for his sneers.

## IV

As to how long the journey in the coach lasted after that Yvonne Dewhurst could not have said. It may have been a few hours, it may have been a cycle of years. She had been young—a happy bride, a dutiful daughter—when she left Combwich Hall. She was an old woman now, a supremely unhappy one, parted from the man she loved without hope of ever seeing him again in life, and feeling nothing but hatred and contempt for the father who had planned such infamy against her.

She offered no resistance whatever to any of her father's commands. After the first outburst of revolt and indignation she had not even spoken to him.

There was a halt somewhere on the way, when in the low-raftered room of a posting-inn, she had to sit at table with the two men who had compassed her misery. She was thirsty, feverish and weak: she drank some milk in silence. She felt ill physically as well as mentally, and the constant effort not to break down had helped to shatter her nerves. As she had stepped out of the barouche without a word, so she stepped into it again when it stood outside, ready with a fresh relay of horses to take her further, still further, away from the cosy little nest where even now her young husband was waiting longingly for her return. The people of the inn—a kindly-looking woman, a portly middle-aged man, one or two young ostlers and serving-maids were standing about in the yard when her father led her to the coach. For a moment the wild idea rushed to her mind to run to these people and demand their protection, to proclaim at the top of her voice the infamous act which was dragging her away from her husband and her home, and lead her a helpless prisoner to a fate that was infinitely worse than death. She even ran to the woman who looked so benevolent and so kind, she placed her small quivering hand on the other's rough toil-worn one and in hurried, appealing words begged for her help and the shelter of a home till she could communicate with her husband.

The woman listened with a look of kindly pity upon her homely face, she patted the small, trembling hand and stroked it gently, tears of compassion gathered in her eyes:

"Yes, yes, my dear," she said soothingly, speaking as she would to a sick woman or to a child, "I quite understand. I wouldna' fret if I was you. I would jess go quietly with your pore father: 'e knows what's best for you, that 'e do. You come 'long wi' me," she added as she drew Yvonne's hands through her arm, "I'll see ye're comfortable in the coach."

Yvonne, bewildered, could not at first understand either the woman's sympathy or her obvious indifference to the pitiable tale, until —Oh! the shame of it!—she saw the two young serving-maids looking on her with equal pity expressed in their round eyes, and heard one of them whispering to the other:

"Pore lady! so zad ain't it? I'm that zorry for the pore father!"

And the girl with a significant gesture indicated her own forehead and glanced knowingly at her companion. Yvonne felt a hot flush rise to the very roots of her hair. So her father and Martin-Roget had thought of everything, and had taken every precaution to cut the ground from under her feet. Wherever a halt was necessary, wherever the party might come in contact with the curious or the indifferent, it would be given out that the poor young lady was crazed, that she talked wildly, and had to be kept under restraint.

Yvonne as she turned away from that last faint glimmer of hope, encountered Martin-Roget's glance of triumph and saw the sneer which curled his full lips. Her father came up to her just then and took her over from the kindly hostess, with the ostentatious manner of one who has charge of a sick person, and must take every precaution for her welfare.

"Another loss of dignity, my child," he said to her in French, so that none but Martin-Roget could catch what he said. "I guessed that you would commit some indiscretion, you see, so M. Martin-Roget and myself warned all the people at the inn the moment we arrived. We told them that I was travelling with a sick daughter who had become crazed through the death of her lover, and believed herself—like most crazed persons do—to be persecuted and oppressed. You have seen the result. They pitied you. Even the serving-maids smiled. It would have been wiser to remain silent."

Whereupon he handed her into the barouche with loving care, a crowd of sympathetic onlookers gazing with obvious compassion on the poor crazed lady and her sorely tried father.

After this episode Yvonne gave up the struggle.

No one but God could help her, if He chose to perform a miracle.

V

The rest of the journey was accomplished in silence. Yvonne gazed, unseeing, through the carriage window as the barouche rattled on the cobble-stones of the streets of Bristol. She marvelled at the number of people who went gaily by along the streets, unheeding, unknowing that the greatest depths of misery to which any human being could sink had been probed by the unfortunate young girl who wide-eyed, mute and broken-hearted gazed out upon the busy world without.

Portishead was reached just when the grey light of day turned to a gloomy twilight. Yvonne unresisting, insentient, went whither she was bidden to go. Better that, than to feel Martin-Roget's coercive grip on her arm, or to hear her father's curt words of command.

She walked along the pier and anon stepped into a boat, hardly knowing what she was doing: the twilight was welcome to her, for it hid much from her view and her eyes—hot with unshed tears—ached for the restful gloom. She realised that the boat was being rowed along for some little way down the stream, that Frédérick, who had come she knew not how or whence, was in the boat too with some luggage which she recognised as being familiar: that another woman was there whom she did not know, but who appeared to look after her comforts, wrapped a shawl closer round her knees and drew the hood of her mantle closer round her neck. But it was all like an ugly dream: the voices of her father and of Martin-Roget, who were talking in monosyllables, the sound of the oars as they struck the water, or creaked in their rowlocks, came to her as from an ever-receding distance.

A couple of hours later she came back to complete consciousness. She was in a narrow place, which at first appeared to her like a cupboard: the atmosphere was both cold and stuffy and reeked of tar and of oil. She was lying on a hard bed with her mantle and a shawl wrapped round her. It was very dark save where the feeble glimmer of a lamp threw a circle of light around. Above her head there was a constant and heavy tramping of feet, and the sound of incessant and varied creakings and groanings of wood, cordage and metal filled the night air with their weird and dismal sounds. A slow feeling of movement coupled with a gentle oscillation confirmed the unfortunate girl's first waking impression that she was on board a ship. How she had got there she did not know. She must ultimately have fainted in the small boat and been carried aboard. She raised herself slightly on her elbow and peered round her into the dark corners of the cabin: opposite to her upon a bench, also wrapped up in shawl and mantle, lay the woman who had been in attendance on her in the boat.

The woman's heavy breathing indicated that she was fast asleep.

Loneliness! Misery! Desolation encompassed the happy bride of yesterday. With a moan of exquisite soul-agony she fell back against the hard cushions, and for the first time this day a convulsive flow of tears eased the superacuteness of her misery.

# CHAPTER 9: THE COAST OF FRANCE

## I

The whole of that wretched mournful day Yvonne Dewhurst spent upon the deck of the ship which was bearing her away every hour, every minute, further and still further from home and happiness. She seldom spoke: she ate and drank when food was brought to her: she was conscious neither of cold nor of wet, of well-being or ill. She sat upon a pile of cordages in the stern of the ship leaning against the taffrail and in imagination seeing the coast of England fade into illimitable space.

Part of the time it rained, and then she sat huddled up in the shawls and tarpaulins which the woman placed about her: then, when the sun came out, she still sat huddled up, closing her eyes against the glare.

When daylight faded into dusk, and then twilight into night she gazed into nothingness as she had gazed on water and sky before, thinking, thinking, thinking! This could not be the end—it could not. So much happiness, such pure love, such perfect companionship as she had had with the young husband whom she idolised could not all be wrenched from her like that, without previous foreboding and without some warning from Fate. This miserable, sordid, wretched journey to an unknown land could not be the epilogue to the exquisite romance which had suddenly changed the dreary monotony of her life into one long, glowing dream of joy and of happiness! This could not be the end!

And gazing into the immensity of the far horizon she thought and thought and racked her memory for every word, every look which she had had from her dear milor. And upon the grey background of sea and sky she seemed to perceive the vague and dim outline of that mysterious friend—the man who knew everything—who foresaw everything, even and above all the dangers that threatened those whom he loved. He had foreseen this awful danger too! Oh! if only milor and she herself had realised its full extent! But now surely! surely! he would help, he would know what to do. Milor was wont to speak of him as being omniscient and having marvellous powers.

Once or twice during the day M. le duc de Kernogan came to sit beside his daughter and tried to speak a few words of comfort and of sympathy. Of a truth—here on the open sea—far both from home and kindred and from the new friends he had found in hospitable England —his heart smote him for all the wrong he had done to his only child. He dared not think of the gentle and patient wife who lay at rest in the churchyard of Kernogan, for he feared that with his thoughts he would conjure up her pale, avenging ghost who would demand an account of what he had done with her child.

Cold and exposure—the discomfort of the long sea-journey in this rough trading ship had somewhat damped M. de Kernogan's pride and obstinacy: his loyalty to the cause of his King had paled before the demands of a father's duty toward his helpless daughter.

## II

It was close on six o'clock and the night, after the turbulent and capricious alternations of rain and sunshine, promised to be beautifully clear, though very cold. The pale crescent of the moon had just emerged from behind the thick veil of cloud and mist which still hung threateningly upon the horizon: a fitful sheen of silver danced upon the waves.

M. le duc stood beside his daughter. He had inquired after her health and well-being and received her monosyllabic reply with an impatient sigh. M. Martin-Roget was pacing up and down the deck with restless and vigorous strides: he had just gone by and made a loud and cheery comment on the weather and the beauty of the night.

Could Yvonne Dewhurst have seen her father's face now, or had she cared to study it, she would have perceived that he was gazing out to sea in the direction to which the schooner was heading with an intent look of puzzlement, and that there was a deep furrow between his brows. Half an hour went by and he still stood there, silent and absorbed: then suddenly a curious exclamation escaped his lips: he stooped and seized his daughter by the wrist.

"Yvonne!" he said excitedly, "tell me! am I dreaming, or am I crazed?"

"What is it?" she asked coldly.

"Out there! Look! Just tell me what you see?"

He appeared so excited and his pressure on her wrist was so insistent that she dragged herself to her feet and looked out to sea in the direction to which he was pointing.

"Tell me what you see," he reiterated with ever-growing excitement, and she felt that the hand which held her wrist trembled violently.

"The light from a lighthouse, I think," she said.

"And besides that?"

"Another light—a much smaller one—considerably higher up. It must be perched up on some cliffs."

"Anything else?"

"Yes. There are lights dotted about here and there. Some village on the coast."

"On the coast?" he murmured hoarsely, "and we are heading towards it."

"So it appears," she said indifferently. What cared she to what shore she was being taken: every land save England was exile to her now.

Just at this moment M. Martin-Roget in his restless wanderings once more passed by.

"M. Martin-Roget!" called the duc.

And vaguely Yvonne wondered why his voice trembled so.

"At your service, M. le duc," replied the other as he came to a halt, and then stood with legs wide apart firmly planted upon the deck, his hands buried in the pockets of his heavy mantle, his head thrown back, as if defiantly, his whole attitude that of a master condescending to talk with slaves.

"What are those lights over there, ahead of us?" asked M. le duc quietly.

"The lighthouse of Le Croisic, M. le duc," replied Martin-Roget dryly, "and of the guard-house above and the harbour below. All at your service," he added, with a sneer.

"Monsieur. . . . " exclaimed the duc.

"Eh? what?" queried the other blandly.

"What does this mean?"

In the vague, dim light of the moon Yvonne could just distinguish the two men as they stood confronting one another. Martin-Roget, tall, massive, with arms now folded across his breast, shrugging his broad shoulders at the duc's impassioned query—and her father who suddenly appeared to have shrunk within himself, who raised one trembling hand to his forehead and with the other sought with pathetic entreaty the support of his daughter's arm.

"What does this mean?" he murmured again.

"Only," replied Martin-Roget with a laugh, "that we are close to the coast of France and that with this unpleasant but useful north-westerly wind we shall be in Nantes two hours before midnight."

"In Nantes?" queried the duc vaguely, not understanding, speaking tonelessly like a somnambulist or a man in a trance. He was leaning heavily now on his daughter's arm, and she with that motherly instinct which is ever present in a good woman's heart even in the presence of her most cruel enemy, drew him tenderly towards her, gave him the support he needed, not quite understanding herself yet what it was that had befallen them both.

"Yes, in Nantes, M. le duc," reiterated Martin-Roget with a sneer.

"But 'twas to Holland we were going."

"To Nantes, M. le duc," retorted the other with a ringing note of triumph in his voice, "to Nantes, from which you fled like a coward when you realised that the vengeance of an outraged people had at last overtaken you and your kind."

"I do not understand," stammered the duc, and mechanically now—instinctively—father and daughter clung to one another as if each was striving to protect the other from the raving fury of this madman. Never for a moment did they believe that he was sane. Excitement, they thought, had turned his brain: he was acting and speaking like one possessed.

"I dare say it would take far longer than the next four hours while we glide gently along the Loire, to make such as you understand that your arrogance and your pride are destined to be humbled at last and that you are now in the power of those men who awhile ago you did not deem worthy to lick your boots. I dare say," he continued calmly, "you think that I am crazed. Well! perhaps I am, but sane enough anyhow, M. le duc, to enjoy the full flavour of revenge."

"Revenge?. . . what have we done?. . . what has my daughter done? . . . " stammered the duc incoherently. "You swore you loved her . . . desired to make her your wife . . . I consented . . . she. . . . "

Martin-Roget's harsh laugh broke in on his vague murmurings.

"And like an arrogant fool you fell into the trap," he said with calm irony, "and you were too blind to see in Martin-Roget, suitor for your daughter's hand, Pierre Adet, the son of the victim of your execrable tyranny, the innocent man murdered at your bidding."

"Pierre Adet . . . I don't understand."

"'Tis but little meseems that you do understand, M. le duc," sneered the other. "But turn your memory back, I pray you, to the night four years ago when a few hot-headed peasant lads planned to give you a fright in your castle of Kernogan . . . the plan failed and Pierre Adet, the leader of that unfortunate band, managed to fly the country, whilst you, like a crazed and blind tyrant, administered punishment right and left for the fright which you had had. Just think of it! those boors! those louts! that swinish herd of human cattle had dared to raise a cry of revolt against you! To death with them all! to death! Where is Pierre Adet, the leader of those hogs? to him an exemplary punishment must be meted! a deterrent against any other attempt at revolt. Well, M. le duc, do you remember what happened then? Pierre Adet, severely injured in the mêlée, had managed to crawl away into safety. While he lay betwixt life and death, first in the presbytery of Vertou, then in various ditches on his way to Paris, he knew nothing of what happened at Nantes. When he returned to consciousness and to active life he heard that his father, Jean Adet the miller, who was innocent of any share in the revolt, had been hanged by order of M. le duc de Kernogan."

He paused awhile and a curious laugh—half-convulsive and not unmixed with sobs—shook his broad shoulders. Neither the duc nor Yvonne made any comment on what they heard: the duc felt like a fly caught in a death-dealing web. He was dazed with the horror of his

position, dazed above all with the rush of bitter remorse which had
surged up in his heart and mind, when he realised that it was his own
folly, his obstinacy—aye! and his heartlessness which had brought this
awful fate upon his daughter. And Yvonne felt that whatever she might
endure of misery and hopelessness was nothing in comparison with
what her father must feel with the addition of bitter self-reproach.

"Are you beginning to understand the position better now, M. le
duc?" queried Martin-Roget after awhile.

The duc sank back nerveless upon the pile of cordages close by.
Yvonne was leaning with her back against the taffrail, her two arms
outstretched, the north-west wind blowing her soft brown hair about
her face whilst her eyes sought through the gloom to read the lines of
cruelty and hatred which must be distorting Martin-Roget's face now.

"And," she said quietly after awhile, "you have waited all these
years, Monsieur, nursing thoughts of revenge and of hate against us.
Ah! believe me," she added earnestly, "though God knows my heart is
full of misery at this moment, and though I know that at your bidding
death will so soon claim me and my father as his own, yet would I not
change my wretchedness for yours."

"And I, citizeness," he said roughly, addressing her for the first
time in the manner prescribed by the revolutionary government,
"would not change places with any king or other tyrant on earth. Yes,"
he added as he came a step or two closer to her, "I have waited all these
years. For four years I have thought and striven and planned, planned
to be even with your father and with you one day. You had fled the
country—like cowards, bah!—ready to lend your arms to the foreigner
against your own country in order to re-establish a tyrant upon the
throne whom the whole of the people of France loathed and detested.
You had fled, but soon I learned whither you had gone. Then I set to
work to gain access to you. . . . I learned English. . . . I too went to
England . . . under an assumed name . . . with the necessary
introductions so as to gain a footing in the circles in which you moved.
I won your father's condescension—almost his friendship! . . . The rich
banker from Brest should be fleeced in order to provide funds for the
armies that were to devastate France—and the rich banker of Brest
refused to be fleeced unless he was lured by the promise of Mlle. de
Kernogan's hand in marriage."

"You need not, Monsieur," rejoined Yvonne coldly, while
Martin-Roget paused in order to draw breath, "you need not, believe
me, take the trouble to recount all the machinations which you carried
through in order to gain your ends. Enough that my father was so
foolish as to trust you, and that we are now completely in your power,
but. . . ."

"There is no 'but,'" he broke in gruffly, "you are in my power
and will be made to learn the law of the talion which demands an eye

for an eye, a life for a life: that is the law which the people are applying to that herd of *aristos* who were arrogant tyrants once and are shrinking, cowering slaves now. Oh! you were very proud that night, Mademoiselle Yvonne de Kernogan, when a few peasant lads told you some home truths while you sat disdainful and callous in your carriage, but there is one fact that you can never efface from your memory, strive how you may, and that is that for a few minutes I held you in my arms and that I kissed you, my fine lady, aye! kissed you like I would any pert kitchen wench, even I, Pierre Adet, the miller's son."

He drew nearer and nearer to her as he spoke; she, leaning against the taffrail, could not retreat any further from him. He laughed.

"If you fall over into the water, I shall not complain," he said, "it will save our proconsul the trouble, and the guillotine some work. But you need not fear. I am not trying to kiss you again. You are nothing to me, you and your father, less than nothing. Your death in misery and wretchedness is all I want, whether you find a dishonoured grave in the Loire or by suicide I care less than nothing. But let me tell you this," he added, and his voice came now like a hissing sound through his set teeth, "that there is no intention on my part to make glorious martyrs of you both. I dare say you have heard some pretty stories over in England of *aristos* climbing the steps of the guillotine with an ecstatic look of martyrdom upon their face: and tales of the tumbrils of Paris laden with men and women going to their death and shouting "God save the King" all the way. That is not the sort of paltry revenge which would satisfy me. My father was hanged by yours as a malefactor— hanged, I say, like a common thief! he, a man who had never wronged a single soul in the whole course of his life, who had been an example of fine living, of hard work, of noble courage through many adversities. My mother was left a widow—not the honoured widow of an honourable man—but a pariah, the relict of a malefactor who had died of the hangman's rope—my sister was left an orphan—dishonoured— without hope of gaining the love of a respectable man. All that I and my family owe to *ci-devant* M. le duc de Kernogan, and therefore I tell you, that both he and his daughter shall not die like martyrs but like malefactors too—shamed—dishonoured—loathed and execrated even by their own kindred! Take note of that, M. le duc de Kernogan! You have sown shame, shame shall you reap! and the name of which you are so proud will be dragged in the mire until it has become a by-word in the land for all that is despicable and base."

Perhaps at no time of his life had Martin-Roget, erstwhile Pierre Adet, spoken with such an intensity of passion, even though he was at all times turbulent and a ready prey to his own emotions. But all that he had kept hidden in the inmost recesses of his heart, ever since as a young stripling he had chafed at the social conditions of his country, now welled forth in that wild harangue. For the first time in his life he felt that he was really master of those who had once despised and oppressed him. He held them and was the arbiter of their fate. The sense of possession and of power had gone to his head like wine: he was intoxicated with his own feeling of triumphant revenge, and this impassioned rhetoric flowed from his mouth like the insentient babble of a drunken man.

The duc de Kernogan, sitting on the coil of cordages with his elbows on his knees and his head buried in his hands, had no thought of breaking in on the other man's ravings. The bitterness of remorse paralysed his thinking faculties. Martin-Roget's savage words struck upon his senses like blows from a sledge-hammer. He knew that nothing but his own folly was the cause of Yvonne's and his own misfortune. Yvonne had been safe from all evil fortune under the protection of her fine young English husband; he—the father who should have been her chief protector—had dragged her by brute force away from that husband's care and had landed her . . . where? . . . A shudder like acute ague went through the unfortunate man's whole body as he thought of the future.

Nor did Yvonne Dewhurst attempt to make reply to her enemy's delirious talk. She would not give him even the paltry satisfaction of feeling that he had stung her into a retort. She did not fear him—she hated him too much for that—but like her father she had no illusions as to his power over them both. While he stormed and raved she kept her eyes steadily fixed upon him. She could only just barely distinguish him in the gloom, and he no doubt failed to see the expression of lofty indifference wherewith she contrived to regard him: but he felt her contempt, and but for the presence of the sailors on the deck he probably would have struck her.

As it was when, from sheer lack of breath, he had to pause, he gave one last look of hate on the huddled figure of the duc, and the proud, upstanding one of Yvonne, then with a laugh which sounded like that of a fiend—so cruel, so callous was it, he turned on his heel, and as he strode away towards the bow his tall figure was soon absorbed in the surrounding gloom.

III

The duc de Kernogan and his daughter saw little or nothing of Martin-Roget after that. For awhile longer they caught sight of him from time to time as he walked up and down the deck with ceaseless restlessness and in the company of another man, who was much shorter and slimmer than himself and whom they had not noticed hitherto. Martin-Roget talked most of the time in a loud and excited voice, the other appearing to listen to him with a certain air of deference. Whether the conversation between these two was actually intended for the ears of the two unfortunates, or whether it was merely chance which brought certain phrases to their ears when the two men passed closely by, it were impossible to say. Certain it is that from such chance phrases they gathered that the barque would not put into Nantes, as the navigation of the Loire was suspended for the nonce by order of Proconsul Carrier. He had need of the river for his awesome and nefarious deeds. Yvonne's ears were regaled with tales—told with loud ostentation—of the terrible noyades, the wholesale drowning of men, women and children, malefactors and traitors, so as to ease the burden of the guillotine.

After three bells it got so bitterly cold that Yvonne, fearing that her father would become seriously ill, suggested their going down to their stuffy cabins together. After all, even the foul and shut-up atmosphere of these close, airless cupboards was preferable to the propinquity of those two human fiends up on deck and the tales of horror and brutality which they loved to tell.

And for two hours after that, father and daughter sat in the narrow cell-like place, locked in each other's arms. She had everything to forgive, and he everything to atone for: but Yvonne suffered so acutely, her misery was so great that she found it in her heart to pity the father whose misery must have been even greater than hers. The supreme solace of bestowing love and forgiveness and of easing the racking paroxysms of remorse which brought the unfortunate man to the verge of dementia, warmed her heart towards him and brought surcease to her own sorrow.

# Book II: Nantes, December, 1793
## Chapter 1: The Tiger's Lair

I

Nantes is in the grip of the tiger.

Representative Carrier—with powers as of a proconsul—has been sent down to stamp out the lingering remnants of the counter-revolution. La Vendée is temporarily subdued; the army of the royalists driven back across the Loire; but traitors still abound—this the National Convention in Paris hath decreed—there are traitors everywhere. They were not all massacred at Cholet and Savenay. Disbanded, yes! but not exterminated, and wolves must not be allowed to run loose, lest they band again, and try to devour the flocks.

Therefore extermination is the order of the day. Every traitor or would-be traitor—every son and daughter and father and mother of traitors must be destroyed ere they do more mischief. And Carrier—Carrier the coward who turned tail and bolted at Cholet—is sent to Nantes to carry on the work of destruction. Wolves and wolflings all! Let none survive. Give them fair trial, of course. As traitors they have deserved death—have they not taken up arms against the Republic and against the Will and the Reign of the People? But let a court of justice sit in Nantes town; let the whole nation know how traitors are dealt with: let the nation see that her rulers are both wise and just. Let wolves and wolflings be brought up for trial, and set up the guillotine on Place du Bouffay with four executioners appointed to do her work. There would be too much work for two, or even three. Let there be four —and let the work of extermination be complete.

And Carrier—with powers as of a proconsul—arrives in Nantes town and sets to work to organise his household. Civil and military— with pomp and circumstance—for the son of a small farmer, destined originally for the Church and for obscurity is now virtual autocrat in one of the great cities of France. He has power of life and death over thousands of citizens—under the direction of justice, of course! So now he has citizens of the bedchamber, and citizens of the household, he has a guard of honour and a company of citizens of the guard. And above all he has a crowd of spies around him—servants of the Committee of Public Safety so they are called—they style themselves "*La Compagnie Marat*" in honour of the great patriot who was foully murdered by a female wolfling.

So la Compagnie Marat is formed—they wear red bonnets on their heads—no stockings on their feet—short breeches to display their

bare shins: their captain, Fleury, has access at all times to the person of
the proconsul, to make report on the raids which his company effect at
all hours of the day or night. Their powers are supreme too. In and out
of houses—however private—up and down the streets—through shops,
taverns and warehouses, along the quays and the yards—everywhere
they go. Everywhere they have the right to go! to ferret and to spy, to
listen, to search, to interrogate—the red-capped Company is paid for
what it can find. Piece-work, what? Work for the guillotine!

And they it is who keep the guillotine busy. Too busy in fact.
And the court of justice sitting in the Hôtel du Département is
overworked too. Carrier gets impatient. Why waste the time of patriots
by so much paraphernalia of justice? Wolves and wolflings can be
exterminated so much more quickly, more easily than that. It only
needs a stroke of genius, one stroke, and Carrier has it.

He invents the Noyades!

The Drownages we may call them!

They are so simple! An old flat-bottomed barge. The work of
two or three ship's carpenters! Portholes below the water-line and
made to open at a given moment. All so very, very simple. Then a
journey downstream as far as Belle Isle or la Maréchale, and "sentence
of deportation" executed without any trouble on a whole crowd of
traitors—"vertical deportation" Carrier calls it facetiously and is
mightily proud of his invention and of his witticism too.

The first attempt was highly successful. Ninety priests, and not
one escaped. Think of the work it would have entailed on the guillotine
—and on the friends of Carrier who sit in justice in the Hôtel du
Département! Ninety heads! Bah! That old flat-bottomed barge is the
most wonderful labour-saving machine.

After that the "Drownages" become the order of the day. The
red-capped Company recruits victims for the hecatomb, and over
Nantes Town there hangs a pall of unspeakable horror. The prisons are
not vast enough to hold all the victims, so the huge *entrepôt*, the
bonded warehouse on the quay, is converted: instead of chests of coffee
it is now encumbered with human freight: into it pell-mell are thrown
all those who are destined to assuage Carrier's passion for killing: ten
thousand of them: men, women, and young children, counter-
revolutionists, innocent tradesmen, thieves, aristocrats, criminals and
women of evil fame—they are herded together like cattle, without straw
whereon to lie, without water, without fire, with barely food enough to
keep up the last attenuated thread of a miserable existence.

And when the warehouse gets over full, to the Loire with them!
—a hundred or two at a time! Pestilence, dysentery decimates their
numbers. Under pretence of hygienic requirements two hundred are
flung into the river on the 14th day of December. Two hundred—many
of them women—crowds of children and a batch of parish priests.

Some there are among Carrier's colleagues—those up in Paris—who protest! Such wholesale butchery will not redound to the credit of any revolutionary government—it even savours of treachery—it is unpatriotic! There are the emissaries of the National Convention, deputed from Paris to supervise and control—they protest as much as they dare—but such men are swept off their feet by the torrent of Carrier's gluttony for blood. Carrier's mission is to "purge the political body of every evil that infests it." Vague and yet precise! He reckons that he has full powers and thinks he can flaunt those powers in the face of those sent to control him. He does it too for three whole months ere he in his turn meets his doom. But for the moment he is omnipotent. He has to make report every week to the Committee of Public Safety, and he sends brief, garbled versions of his doings. "He is pacifying La Vendée! he is stamping out the remnants of the rebellion! he is purging the political body of every evil that infests it." Anon he succeeds in getting the emissaries of the National Convention recalled. He is impatient of control. "They are weak, pusillanimous, unpatriotic! He must have freedom to act for the best."

After that he remains virtual dictator, with none but obsequious, terrified myrmidons around him: these are too weak to oppose him in any way. And the municipality dare not protest either—nor the district council—nor the departmental. They are merely sheep who watch others of their flock being sent to the slaughter.

After that from within his lair the man tiger decides that it is a pity to waste good barges on the cattle: "Fling them out!" he cries. "Fling them out! Tie two and two together. Man and woman! criminal and *aristo!* the thief with the *ci-devant* duke's daughter! the *ci-devant* marquis with the slut from the streets! Fling them all out together into the Loire and pour a hail of grape shot above them until the last struggler has disappeared!" "Equality!" he cries, "Equality for all! Fraternity! Unity in death!"

His friends call this new invention of his: "Marriage Républicain!" and he is pleased with the mot.

And Republican marriages become the order of the day.

## II

Nantes itself now is akin to a desert—a desert wherein the air is filled with weird sounds of cries and of moans, of furtive footsteps scurrying away into dark and secluded byways, of musketry and confused noises, of sorrow and of lamentations.

Nantes is a city of the dead—a city of sleepers. Only Carrier is awake—thinking and devising and planning shorter ways and swifter, for the extermination of traitors.

In the Hôtel de la Villestreux the tiger has built his lair: at the apex of the island of Feydeau, with the windows of the hotel facing straight down the Loire. From here there is a magnificent view downstream upon the quays which are now deserted and upon the once prosperous port of Nantes.

The staircase of the hotel which leads up to the apartments of the proconsul is crowded every day and all day with suppliants and with petitioners, with the citizens of the household and the members of the Compagnie Marat.

But no one has access to the person of the dictator. He stands aloof, apart, hidden from the eyes of the world, a mysterious personality whose word sends hundreds to their death, whose arbitrary will has reduced a once flourishing city to abject poverty and squalor. No tyrant has ever surrounded himself with a greater paraphernalia of pomp and circumstance—no *aristo* has ever dwelt in greater luxury: the spoils of churches and chateaux fill the Hôtel de la Villestreux from attic to cellar, gold and silver plate adorn his table, priceless works of art hang upon his walls, he lolls on couches and chairs which have been the resting-place of kings. The wholesale spoliation of the entire country-side has filled the demagogue's abode with all that is most sumptuous in the land.

And he himself is far more inaccessible than was le Roi Soleil in the days of his most towering arrogance, than were the Popes in the glorious days of mediæval Rome. Jean Baptiste Carrier, the son of a small farmer, the obscure deputy for Cantal in the National Convention, dwells in the Hôtel de la Villestreux as in a stronghold. No one is allowed near him save a few—a very few—intimates: his valet, two or three women, Fleury the commander of the Marats, and that strange and abominable youngster, Jacques Lalouët, about whom the chroniclers of that tragic epoch can tell us so little—a cynical young braggart, said to be a cousin of Robespierre and the son of a midwife of Nantes, beardless, handsome and vicious: the only human being—so we are told—who had any influence over the sinister proconsul: mere hanger-on of Carrier or spy of the National Convention, no one can say —a malignant personality which has remained an enigma and a mystery to this hour.

None but these few are ever allowed now inside the inner sanctuary wherein dwells and schemes the dictator. Even Lamberty, Fouquet and the others of the staff are kept at arm's length. Martin-Roget, Chauvelin and other strangers are only allowed as far as the ante-room. The door of the inner chamber is left open and they hear the proconsul's voice and see his silhouette pass and repass in front of them, but that is all.

Fear of assassination—the inevitable destiny of the tyrant— haunts the man-tiger even within the fastnesses of his lair. Day and night a carriage with four horses stands in readiness on La Petite

Hollande, the great, open, tree-bordered Place at the extreme end of the Isle Feydeau and on which give the windows of the Hôtel de la Villestreux. Day and night the carriage is ready—with coachman on the box and postillion in the saddle, who are relieved every two hours lest they get sleepy or slack—with luggage in the boot and provisions always kept fresh inside the coach; everything always ready lest something—a warning from a friend or a threat from an enemy, or merely a sudden access of unreasoning terror, the haunting memory of a bloody act— should decide the tyrant at a moment's notice to fly from the scenes of his brutalities.

### III

Carrier in the small room which he has fitted up for himself as a sumptuous boudoir, paces up and down just like a wild beast in its cage: and he rubs his large bony hands together with the excitement engendered by his own cruelties, by the success of this wholesale butchery which he has invented and carried through.

There never was an uglier man than Carrier, with that long hatchet-face of his, those abnormally high cheekbones, that stiff, lanky hair, that drooping, flaccid mouth and protruding underlip. Nature seemed to have set herself the task of making the face a true mirror of the soul—the dark and hideous soul on which of a surety Satan had already set his stamp. But he is dressed with scrupulous care—not to say elegance—and with a display of jewelry the provenance of which is as unjustifiable as that of the works of art which fill his private sanctum in every nook and cranny.

In front of the tall window, heavy curtains of crimson damask are drawn closely together, in order to shut out the light of day: the room is in all but total darkness: for that is the proconsul's latest caprice: that no one shall see him save in semi-obscurity.

Captain Fleury has stumbled into the room, swearing lustily as he barks his shins against the angle of a priceless Louis XV bureau. He has to make report on the work done by the Compagnie Marat. Fifty-three priests from the department of Anjou who have refused to take the new oath of obedience to the government of the Republic. The red-capped Company who tracked them down and arrested them, vow that all these calotins have precious objects—money, jewelry, gold plate— concealed about their persons. What is to be done about these things? Are the calotins to be allowed to keep them or to dispose of them for their own profit?

Carrier is highly delighted. What a haul!

"Confiscate everything," he cries, "then ship the whole crowd of that pestilential rabble, and don't let me hear another word about them."

Fleury goes. And that same night fifty-three priests are "shipped" in accordance with the orders of the proconsul, and Carrier, still rubbing his large bony hands contentedly together, exclaims with glee:

"What a torrent, eh! What a torrent! What a revolution!"

And he sends a letter to Robespierre. And to the Committee of Public Safety he makes report:

"Public spirit in Nantes," he writes, "is magnificent: it has risen to the most sublime heights of revolutionary ideals."

## IV

After the departure of Fleury, Carrier suddenly turned to a slender youth, who was standing close by the window, gazing out through the folds of the curtain on the fine vista of the Loire and the quays which stretched out before him.

"Introduce citizen Martin-Roget into the ante-room now, Lalouët," he said loftily. "I will hear what he has to say, and citizen Chauvelin may present himself at the same time."

Young Lalouët lolled across the room, smothering a yawn.

"Why should you trouble about all that rabble?" he said roughly, "it is nearly dinner-time and you know that the chef hates the soup to be kept waiting."

"I shall not trouble about them very long," replied Carrier, who had just started picking his teeth with a tiny gold tool. "Open the door, boy, and let the two men come."

Lalouët did as he was told. The door through which he passed he left wide open, he then crossed the ante-room to a further door, threw it open and called in a loud voice:

"Citizen Chauvelin! Citizen Martin-Roget!"

For all the world like the ceremonious audiences at Versailles in the days of the great Louis.

There was sound of eager whisperings, of shuffling of feet, of chairs dragged across the polished floor. Young Lalouët had already and quite unconcernedly turned his back on the two men who, at his call, had entered the room.

Two chairs were placed in front of the door which led to the private sanctuary—still wrapped in religious obscurity—where Carrier sat enthroned. The youth curtly pointed to the two chairs, then went back to the inner room. The two men advanced. The full light of midday fell upon them from the tall window on their right—the pale, grey, colourless light of December. They bowed slightly in the direction of the audience chamber where the vague silhouette of the proconsul was alone visible.

The whole thing was a farce. Martin-Roget held his lips tightly closed together lest a curse or a sneer escaped them. Chauvelin's face was impenetrable—but it is worthy of note that just one year later when the half-demented tyrant was in his turn brought before the bar of the Convention and sentenced to the guillotine, it was citizen Chauvelin's testimony which weighed most heavily against him.

There was silence for a time: Martin-Roget and Chauvelin were waiting for the dictator's word. He sat at his desk with the scanty light, which filtrated between the curtains, immediately behind him, his ungainly form with the high shoulders and mop-like, shaggy hair half swallowed up by the surrounding gloom. He was deliberately keeping the other two men waiting and busied himself with turning over desultorily the papers and writing tools upon his desk, in the intervals of picking at his teeth and muttering to himself all the time as was his wont. Young Lalouët had resumed his post beside the curtained window and he was giving sundry signs of his growing impatience.

At last Carrier spoke:

"And now, citizen Martin-Roget," he said in tones of that lofty condescension which he loved to affect, "I am prepared to hear what you have to tell me with regard to the cattle which you brought into our city the other day. Where are the *aristos* now? and why have they not been handed over to commandant Fleury?"

"The girl," replied Martin-Roget, who had much ado to keep his vehement temper in check, and who chose for the moment to ignore the second of Carrier's peremptory queries, "the girl is in lodgings in the Carrefour de la Poissonnerie. The house is kept by my sister, whose lover was hanged four years ago by the *ci-devant* duc de Kernogan for trapping two pigeons. A dozen or so lads from our old village—men who worked with my father and others who were my friends—lodge in my sister's house. They keep a watchful eye over the wench for the sake of the past, for my sake and for the sake of my sister Louise. The *ci-devant* Kernogan woman is well-guarded. I am satisfied as to that."

"And where is the *ci-devant duc*?"

"In the house next door—a tavern at the sign of the Rat Mort—a place which is none too reputable, but the landlord—Lemoine—is a good patriot and he is keeping a close eye on the *aristo* for me."

"And now will you tell me, citizen," rejoined Carrier with that unctuous suavity which always veiled a threat, "will you tell me how it comes that you are keeping a couple of traitors alive all this while at the country's expense?"

"At mine," broke in Martin-Roget curtly.

"At the country's expense," reiterated the proconsul inflexibly. "Bread is scarce in Nantes. What traitors eat is stolen from good patriots. If you can afford to fill two mouths at your expense, I can supply you with some that have never done aught but proclaim their adherence to the Republic. You have had those two *aristos* inside the city nearly a week and——"

"Only three days," interposed Martin-Roget, "and you must have patience with me, citizen Carrier. Remember I have done well by you, by bringing such high game to your bag——"

"Your high game will be no use to me," retorted the other with a harsh laugh, "if I am not to have the cooking of it. You have talked of disgrace for the rabble and of your own desire for vengeance over them, but——"

"Wait, citizen," broke in Martin-Roget firmly, "let us understand one another. Before I embarked on this business you gave me your promise that no one—not even you—would interfere between me and my booty."

"And no one has done so hitherto to my knowledge, citizen," rejoined Carrier blandly. "The Kernogan rabble has been yours to do with what you like—er—so far," he added significantly. "I said that I would not interfere and I have not done so up to now, even though the pestilential crowd stinks in the nostrils of every good patriot in Nantes. But I don't deny that it was a bargain that you should have a free hand with them . . . for a time, and Jean Baptiste Carrier has never yet gone back on a given word."

Martin-Roget made no comment on this peroration. He shrugged his broad shoulders and suddenly fell to contemplating the distant landscape. He had turned his head away in order to hide the sneer which curled his lips at the recollection of that "bargain" struck with the imperious proconsul. It was a matter of five thousand francs which had passed from one pocket to the other and had bound Carrier down to a definite promise.

After a brief while Carrier resumed: "At the same time," he said, "my promise was conditional, remember. I want that cattle out of Nantes—I want the bread they eat—I want the room they occupy. I can't allow you to play fast and loose with them indefinitely—a week is quite long enough——"

"Three days," corrected Martin-Roget once more.

"Well! three days or eight," rejoined the other roughly. "Too long in any case. I must be rid of them out of this city or I shall have all the spies of the Convention about mine ears. I am beset with spies, citizen Martin-Roget, yes, even I—Jean Baptiste Carrier—the most selfless the most devoted patriot the Republic has ever known! Mine enemies up in Paris send spies to dog my footsteps, to watch mine every action. They are ready to pounce upon me at the slightest slip, to denounce me, to drag me to their bar—they have already whetted the knife of the guillotine which is to lay low the head of the finest patriot in France——"

"Hold on! hold on, Jean Baptiste my friend," here broke in young Lalouët with a sneer, "we don't want protestations of your patriotism just now. It is nearly dinner time."

Carrier had been carried away by his own eloquence. At Lalouët's mocking words he pulled himself together: murmured: "You young viper!" in tones of tigerish affection, and then turned back to Martin-Roget and resumed more calmly:

"They'll be saying that I harbour *aristos* in Nantes if I keep that Kernogan rabble here any longer. So I must be rid of them, citizen Martin-Roget . . . say within the next four-and-twenty hours. . . . " He paused for a moment or two, then added drily: "That is my last word, and you must see to it. What is it you do want to do with them enfin?"

"I want their death," replied Martin-Roget with a curse, and he brought his heavy fist crashing down upon the arm of his chair, "but not a martyr's death, understand? I don't want the pathetic figure of Yvonne Kernogan and her father to remain as a picture of patient resignation in the hearts and minds of every other *aristo* in the land. I don't want it to excite pity or admiration. Death is nothing for such as they! they glory in it! they are proud to die. The guillotine is their final triumph! What I want for them is shame . . . degradation . . . a sensational trial that will cover them with dishonour. . . . I want their name dragged in the mire—themselves an object of derision or of loathing. I want articles in the Moniteur giving account of the trial of the *ci-devant* duc de Kernogan and his daughter for something that is ignominious and base. I want shame and mud slung at them—noise and beating of drums to proclaim their dishonour. Noise! noise! that will reach every corner of the land, aye that will reach Coblentz and Germany and England. It is that which they would resent—the shame of it—the disgrace to their name!"

"Tshaw!" exclaimed Carrier. "Why don't you marry the wench, citizen Martin-Roget? That would be disgrace enough for her, I'll warrant," he added with a loud laugh, enchanted at his witticism.

"I would to-morrow," replied the other, who chose to ignore the coarse insult, "if she would consent. That is why I have kept her at my sister's house these three days."

"Bah! you have no need of a traitor's consent. My consent is sufficient. . . . I'll give it if you like. The laws of the Republic permit, nay desire every good patriot to ally himself with an *aristo*, if he have a mind. And the Kernogan wench face to face with the guillotine—or worse—would surely prefer your embraces, citizen, what?"

A deep frown settled between Martin-Roget's glowering eyes, and gave his face a sinister expression.

"I wonder . . . " he muttered between his teeth.

"Then cease wondering, citizen," retorted Carrier cynically, "and try our Republican marriage on your Kernogans . . . thief linked to *aristo*, cut-throat to a proud wench . . . and then the Loire! Shame? Dishonour? Fal lal I say! Death, swift and sure and unerring. Nothing better has yet been invented for traitors."

Martin-Roget shrugged his shoulders.

"You have never known," he said quietly, "what it is to hate."

Carrier uttered an exclamation of impatience.

"Bah!" he said, "that is all talk and nonsense. Theories, what? Citizen Chauvelin is a living example of the futility of all that rubbish. He too has an enemy it seems whom he hates more thoroughly than any good patriot has ever hated the enemies of the Republic. And hath this deadly hatred availed him, forsooth? He too wanted the disgrace and dishonour of that confounded Englishman whom I would simply have tossed into the Loire long ago, without further process. What is the result? The Englishman is over in England, safe and sound, making long noses at citizen Chauvelin, who has much ado to keep his own head out of the guillotine."

Martin-Roget once more was silent: a look of sullen obstinacy had settled upon his face.

"You may be right, citizen Carrier," he muttered after awhile.

"I am always right," broke in Carrier curtly.

"Exactly . . . but I have your promise."

"And I'll keep it, as I have said, for another four and twenty hours. Curse you for a mulish fool," added the proconsul with a snarl, "what in the d——l's name do you want to do? You have talked a vast deal of rubbish but you have told me nothing of your plans. Have you any . . . that are worthy of my attention?"

## V

Martin-Roget rose from his seat and began pacing up and down the narrow room. His nerves were obviously on edge. It was difficult for any man—let alone one of his temperament and half-tutored disposition—to remain calm and deferential in face of the overbearance of this brutal Jack-in-office, Martin-Roget—himself an upstart— loathed the offensive self-assertion of that uneducated and bestial parvenu, who had become all-powerful through the sole might of his savagery, and it cost him a mighty effort to keep a violent retort from escaping his lips—a retort which probably would have cost him his head.

Chauvelin, on the other hand, appeared perfectly unconcerned. He possessed the art of outward placidity to a masterly degree. Throughout all this while he had taken no part in the discussion. He sat silent and all but motionless, facing the darkened room in front of him, as if he had done nothing else in all his life but interview great dictators who chose to keep their sacred persons in the dark. Only from time to time did his slender fingers drum a tattoo on the arm of his chair.

Carrier had resumed his interesting occupation of picking his teeth: his long, thin legs were stretched out before him; from beneath his flaccid lids he shot swift glances upwards, whenever Martin-Roget in his restless pacing crossed and recrossed in front of the open door. But anon, when the latter came to a halt under the lintel and with his foot almost across the threshold, young Lalouët was upon him in an instant, barring the way to the inner sanctum.

"Keep your distance, citizen," he said drily, "no one is allowed to enter here."

Instinctively Martin-Roget had drawn back—suddenly awed despite himself by the air of mystery which hung over that darkened room, and by the dim silhouette of the sinister tyrant who at his approach had with equal suddenness cowered in his lair, drawing his limbs together and thrusting his head forward, low down over the desk, like a leopard crouching for a spring. But this spell of awe only lasted a few seconds, during which Martin-Roget's unsteady gaze encountered the half-mocking, wholly supercilious glance of young Lalouët.

The next, he had recovered his presence of mind. But this crowning act of audacious insolence broke the barrier of his self-restraint. An angry oath escaped him.

"Are we," he exclaimed roughly, "back in the days of Capet, the tyrant, and of Versailles, that patriots and citizens are treated like menials and obtrusive slaves? *Pardieu*, citizen Carrier, let me tell you this. . . . "

"*Pardieu*, citizen Martin-Roget," retorted Carrier with a growl like that of a savage dog, "let me tell you that for less than two pins I'll throw you into the next barge that will float with open portholes down the Loire. Get out of my presence, you swine, ere I call Fleury to throw you out."

Martin-Roget at the insult and the threat had become as pale as the linen at his throat: a cold sweat broke out upon his forehead and he passed his hand two or three times across his brow like a man dazed with a sudden and violent blow. His nerves, already overstrained and very much on edge, gave way completely. He staggered and would have measured his length across the floor, but that his hand encountered the back of his chair and he just contrived to sink into it, sick and faint, horror-struck and pallid.

A low cackle—something like a laugh—broke from Chauvelin's thin lips. As usual he had witnessed the scene quite unmoved.

"My friend Martin-Roget forgot himself for the moment, citizen Carrier," he said suavely, "already he is ready to make amends."

Jacques Lalouët looked down for a moment with infinite scorn expressed in his fine eyes, on the presumptuous creature who had dared to defy the omnipotent representative of the People. Then he turned on his heel, but he did not go far this time: he remained standing close beside the door—the terrier guarding his master.

Carrier laughed loud and long. It was a hideous, strident laugh which had not a tone of merriment in it.

"Wake up, friend Martin-Roget," he said harshly, "I bear no malice: I am a good dog when I am treated the right way. But if anyone pulls my tail or treads on my paws, why! I snarl and growl of course. If the offence is repeated . . . I bite . . . remember that; and now let us resume our discourse, though I confess I am getting tired of your Kernogan rabble."

While the great man spoke, Martin-Roget had succeeded in pulling himself together. His throat felt parched, his hands hot and moist: he was like a man who had been stumbling along a road in the dark and been suddenly pulled up on the edge of a yawning abyss into which he had all but fallen. With a few harsh words, with a monstrous insult Carrier had made him feel the gigantic power which could hurl any man from the heights of self-assurance and of ambition to the lowest depths of degradation: he had shown him the glint of steel upon the guillotine.

He had been hit as with a sledge-hammer—the blow hurt terribly, for it had knocked all his self-esteem into nothingness and pulverised his self-conceit. It had in one moment turned him into a humble and cringing sycophant.

"I had no mind," he began tentatively, "to give offence. My thoughts were bent on the Kernogans. They are a fine haul for us both, citizen Carrier, and I worked hard and long to obtain their confidence over in England and to induce them to come with me to Nantes."

"No one denies that you have done well," retorted Carrier gruffly and not yet wholly pacified. "If the haul had not been worth having you would have received no help from me."

"I have shown my gratitude for your help, citizen Carrier. I would show it again . . . more substantially if you desire. . . . "

He spoke slowly and quite deferentially but the suggestion was obvious. Carrier looked up into his face: the light of measureless cupidity—the cupidity of the coarse-grained, enriched peasant—glittered in his pale eyes. It was by a great effort of will that he succeeded in concealing his eagerness beneath his habitual air of lofty condescension:

"Eh? What?" he queried airily.

"If another five thousand francs is of any use to you. . . . "

"You seem passing rich, citizen Martin-Roget," sneered Carrier.

"I have slaved and saved for four years. What I have amassed I will sacrifice for the completion of my revenge."

"Well!" rejoined Carrier with an expressive wave of the hand, "it certainly is not good for a pure-minded republican to own too much wealth. Have we not fought," he continued with a grandiloquent gesture, "for equality of fortune as well as of privileges. . . . "

A sardonic laugh from young Lalouët broke in on the proconsul's eloquent effusion.

Carrier swore as was his wont, but after a second or two he began again more quietly:

"I will accept a further six thousand francs from you, citizen Martin-Roget, in the name of the Republic and all her needs. The Republic of France is up in arms against the entire world. She hath need of men, of arms, of. . . . "

"Oh! cut that," interposed young Lalouët roughly.

But the over-vain, high and mighty despot who was ready to lash out with unbridled fury against the slightest show of disrespect on the part of any other man, only laughed at the boy's impudence.

"Curse you, you young viper," he said with that rude familiarity which he seemed to reserve for the boy, "you presume too much on my forbearance. These children you know, citizen. . . . Name of a dog!" he added roughly, "we are wasting time! What was I saying . . . ?"

"That you would take six thousand francs," replied Martin-Roget curtly, "in return for further help in the matter of the Kernogans."

"Why, yes!" rejoined Carrier blandly, "I was forgetting. But I'll show you what a good dog I am. I'll help you with those Kernogans . . . but you mistook my words, citizen: 'tis ten thousand francs you must pour into the coffers of the Republic, for her servants will have to be placed at the disposal of your private schemes of vengeance."

"Ten thousand francs is a large sum," said Martin-Roget. "Let me hear what you will do for me for that."

He had regained something of his former complacency. The man who buys—be it goods, consciences or services—is always for the moment master of the man who sells. Carrier, despite his dictatorial ways, felt this disadvantage, no doubt, for his tone was more bland, his manner less curt. Only young Jacques Lalouët stood by—like a snarling terrier—still arrogant and still disdainful—the master of the situation— seeing that neither schemes of vengeance nor those of corruption had ruffled his self-assurance. He remained beside the door, ready to pounce on either of the two intruders if they showed the slightest sign of forgetting the majesty of the great proconsul.

## VI

"I told you just now, citizen Martin-Roget," resumed Carrier after a brief pause, "and I suppose you knew it already, that I am surrounded with spies."

"Spies, citizen?" murmured Martin-Roget, somewhat taken aback by this sudden irrelevance. "I didn't know . . . I imagine. . . . Any one in your position. . . . "

"That's just it," broke in Carrier roughly. "My position is envied by those who are less competent, less patriotic than I am. Nantes is swarming with spies. Mine enemies in Paris are working against me. They want to undermine the confidence which the National Convention reposes in her accredited representative."

"Preposterous," ejaculated young Lalouët solemnly.

"Well!" rejoined Carrier with a savage oath, "you would have thought that the Convention would be only too thankful to get a strong man at the head of affairs in this hotbed of treason and of rebellion. You would have thought that it was no one's affair to interfere with the manner in which I administer the powers that have been given me. I command in Nantes, what? Yet some busybodies up in Paris, some fools, seem to think that we are going too fast in Nantes. They have become weaklings over there since Marat has gone. It seems that they have heard rumours of our flat-bottomed barges and of our fine Republican marriages: apparently they disapprove of both. They don't realise that we have to purge an entire city of every kind of rabble— traitors as well as criminals. They don't understand my aspirations, my ideals," he added loftily and with a wide, sweeping gesture of his arm, "which is to make Nantes a model city, to free her from the taint of crime and of treachery, and. . . . "

An impatient exclamation from young Lalouët once again broke in on Carrier's rhetoric, and Martin-Roget was able to slip in the query which had been hovering on his lips:

"And is this relevant, citizen Carrier," he asked, "to the subject which we have been discussing?"

"It is," replied Carrier drily, "as you will see in a moment. Learn then, that it has been my purpose for some time to silence mine enemies by sending to the National Convention a tangible reply to all the accusations which have been levelled against me. It is my purpose to explain to the Assembly my reasons for mine actions in Nantes, my Drownages, my Republican marriages, all the coercive measures which I have been forced to take in order to purge the city from all that is undesirable."

"And think you, citizen Carrier," queried Martin-Roget without the slightest trace of a sneer, "that up in Paris they will understand your explanations?"

"Yes! they will—they must when they realise that everything that I have done has been necessitated by the exigencies of public safety."

"They will be slow to realise that," mused the other. "The National Convention to-day is not what the Constitutional Assembly was in '92. It has become soft and sentimental. Many there are who will disapprove of your doings. . . . Robespierre talks loftily of the dignity of the Republic . . . her impartial justice. . . . The Girondins. . . . "

Carrier interposed with a coarse imprecation. He suddenly leaned forward, sprawling right across the desk. A shaft of light from between the damask curtains caught the end of his nose and the tip of his protruding chin, distorting his face and making it seem grotesque as well as hideous in the dim light. He appeared excited and inflated with vanity. He always gloried in the atrocities which he committed, and though he professed to look with contempt on every one of his colleagues, he was always glad of an opportunity to display his inventive powers before them, and to obtain their fulsome eulogy.

"I know well enough what they talk about in Paris," he said, "but I have an answer—a substantial, definite answer for all their rubbish. Dignity of the Republic? Bah! Impartial justice? 'Tis force, strength, Spartan vigour that we want . . . and I'll show them. . . . Listen to my plan, citizen Martin-Roget, and see how it will work in with yours. My idea is to collect together all the most disreputable and notorious evil-doers of this city . . . there are plenty in the entrepôt at the present moment, and there are plenty more still at large in the streets of Nantes—thieves, malefactors, forgers of State bonds, assassins and women of evil fame . . . and to send them in a batch to Paris to appear before the Committee of Public Safety, whilst I will send to my colleagues there a letter couched in terms of gentle reproach: 'See!' I shall say, 'what I have to contend with in Nantes. See! the moral pestilence that infests the city. These evil-doers are but a few among the hundreds and thousands of whom I am vainly trying to purge this city which you have entrusted to my care!' They won't know how to deal with the rabble," he continued with his harsh strident laugh. "They may send them to the guillotine wholesale or deport them to Cayenne, and they will have to give them some semblance of a trial in any case. But they will have to admit that my severe measures are justified, and in future, I imagine, they will leave me more severely alone."

"If as you say," urged Martin-Roget, "the National Convention give your crowd a trial, you will have to produce some witnesses."

"So I will," retorted Carrier cynically. "So I will. Have I not said that I will round up all the most noted evil-doers in the town? There are plenty of them I assure you. Lately, my Company Marat have not greatly troubled about them. After Savenay there was such a crowd of rebels to deal with, there was no room in our prisons for malefactors as well. But we can easily lay our hands on a couple of hundred or so, and members of the municipality or of the district council, or tradespeople of substance in the city will only be too glad to be rid of them, and will testify against those that were actually caught red-handed. Not one but has suffered from the pestilential rabble that has infested the streets at night, and lately I have been pestered with complaints of all these night-birds—men and women and. . . . "

Suddenly he paused. He had caught Martin-Roget's feverish gaze fixed excitedly upon him. Whereupon he leaned back in his chair, threw his head back and broke into loud and immoderate laughter.

"By the devil and all his myrmidons, citizen!" he said, as soon as he had recovered his breath, "meseems you have tumbled to my meaning as a pig into a heap of garbage. Is not ten thousand francs far too small a sum to pay for such a perfect realisation of all your dreams? We'll send the Kernogan girl and her father to Paris with the herd, what?... I promise you that such filth and mud will be thrown on them and on their precious name that no one will care to bear it for centuries to come."

Martin-Roget of a truth had much ado to control his own excitement. As the proconsul unfolded his infamous plan, he had at once seen as in a vision the realisation of all his hopes. What more awful humiliation, what more dire disgrace could be devised for proud Kernogan and his daughter than being herded together with the vilest scum that could be gathered together among the flotsam and jetsam of the population of a seaport town? What more perfect retaliation could there be for the ignominious death of Jean Adet the miller?

Martin-Roget leaned forward in his chair. The hideous figure of Carrier was no longer hideous to him. He saw in that misshapen, gawky form the very embodiment of the god of vengeance, the wielder of the flail of retributive justice which was about to strike the guilty at last.

"You are right, citizen Carrier," he said, and his voice was thick and hoarse with excitement. He rested his elbow on his knee and his chin in his hand. He hammered his nails against his teeth. "That was exactly in my mind while you spoke."

"I am always right," retorted Carrier loftily. "No one knows better than I do how to deal with traitors."

"And how is the whole thing to be accomplished? The wench is in my sister's house at present ... the father is in the Rat Mort...."

"And the Rat Mort is an excellent place. . . . I know of none better. It is one of the worst-famed houses in the whole of Nantes ... the meeting-place of all the vagabonds, the thieves and the cut-throats of the city."

"Yes! I know that to my cost. My sister's house is next door to it. At night the street is not safe for decent females to be abroad: and though there is a platoon of Marats on guard at Le Bouffay close by, they do nothing to free the neighbourhood of that pest."

"Bah!" retorted Carrier with cynical indifference, "they have more important quarry to net. Rebels and traitors swarm in Nantes, what? Commandant Fleury has had no time hitherto to waste on mere cut-throats, although I had thoughts before now of razing the place to the ground. Citizen Lamberty has his lodgings on the other side and he does nothing but complain of the brawls that go on there o' nights. Sure it is that while a stone of the Rat Mort remains standing all the night-hawks of Nantes will congregate around it and brew mischief there which is no good to me and no good to the Republic."

"Yes! I know all about the Rat Mort. I found a night's shelter there four years ago when. . . . "

"When the *ci-devant* duc de Kernogan was busy hanging your father—the miller—for a crime which he never committed. Well then, citizen Martin-Roget," continued Carrier with one of his hideous leers, "since you know the Rat Mort so well what say you to your fair and stately Yvonne de Kernogan and her father being captured there in the company of the lowest scum of the population of Nantes?"

"You mean . . . ?" murmured Martin-Roget, who had become livid with excitement.

"I mean that my Marats have orders to raid some of the haunts of our Nantese cut-throats, and that they may as well begin to-night and with the Rat Mort. They will make a descent on the house and a thorough perquisition, and every person—man, woman and child—found on the premises will be arrested and sent with a batch of malefactors to Paris, there to be tried as felons and criminals and deported to Cayenne where they will, I trust, rot as convicts in that pestilential climate. Think you," concluded the odious creature with a sneer, "that when put face to face with the alternative, your Kernogan wench will still refuse to become the wife of a fine patriot like yourself?"

"I don't know," murmured Martin-Roget. "I . . . I. . . . "

"But I do know," broke in Carrier roughly, "that ten thousand francs is far too little to pay for so brilliant a realisation of all one's hopes. Ten thousand francs? 'Tis a hundred thousand you should give to show your gratitude."

Martin-Roget rose and stretched his large, heavy figure to its full height. He was at great pains to conceal the utter contempt which he felt for the abominable wretch before whom he was forced to cringe.

"You shall have ten thousand francs, citizen Carrier," he said slowly; "it is all that I possess in the world now—the last remaining fragment of a sum of twenty-five thousand francs which I earned and scraped together for the past four years. You have had five thousand francs already. And you shall have the other ten. I do not grudge it. If twenty years of my life were any use to you, I would give you that, in exchange for the help you are giving me in what means far more than life to me."

The proconsul laughed and shrugged his shoulders—of a truth he thought citizen Martin-Roget an awful fool.

"Very well then," he said, "we will call the matter settled. I confess that it amuses me, although remember that I have warned you. With all these *aristos*, I believe in the potency of my barges rather than in your elaborate schemes. Still! it shall never be said that Jean Baptiste Carrier has left a friend in the lurch."

"I am grateful for your help, citizen Carrier," said Martin-Roget coldly. Then he added slowly, as if reviewing the situation in his own mind: "To-night, you say?"

"Yes. To-night. My Marats under the command of citizen Fleury will make a descent upon the Rat Mort. Those shall be my orders. The place will be swept clean of every man, woman and child who is inside. If your two Kernogans are there . . . well!" he said with a cynical laugh and a shrug of his shoulders, "they can be sent up to Paris with the rest of the herd."

"The dinner bell has gone long ago," here interposed young Lalouët drily, "the soup will be stone-cold and the chef red-hot with anger."

"You are right, citizen Lalouët," said Carrier as he leaned back in his chair once more and stretched out his long legs at his ease. "We have wasted far too much time already over the affairs of a couple of *aristos*, who ought to have been at the bottom of the Loire a week ago. The audience is ended," he added airily, and he made a gesture of overweening condescension, for all the world like the one wherewith the Grand Monarque was wont to dismiss his courtiers.

Chauvelin rose too and quietly turned to the door. He had not spoken a word for the past half-hour, ever since in fact he had put in a conciliatory word on behalf of his impetuous colleague. Whether he had taken an active interest in the conversation or not it were impossible to say. But now, just as he was ready to go, and young Lalouët prepared to close the doors of the audience chamber, something seemed suddenly to occur to him and he called somewhat peremptorily to the young man.

"One moment, citizen," he said.

"What is it now?" queried the youth insolently, and from his fine eyes there shot a glance of contempt on the meagre figure of the once powerful Terrorist.

"About the Kernogan wench," continued Chauvelin. "She will have to be conveyed some time before night to the tavern next door. There may be agencies at work on her behalf. . . . "

"Agencies?" broke in the boy gruffly. "What agencies?"

"Oh!" said Chauvelin vaguely, "we all know that *aristos* have powerful friends these days. It will not be over safe to take the girl across after dark from one house to another . . . the alley is badly lighted: the wench will not go willingly. She might scream and create a disturbance and draw . . . er . . . those same unknown agencies to her rescue. I think a body of Marats should be told off to convey her to the Rat Mort. . . . "

Young Lalouët shrugged his shoulders.

"That's your affair," he said curtly. "Eh, Carrier?" And he glanced over his shoulder at the proconsul, who at once assented.

Martin-Roget—struck by his colleague's argument—would have interposed, but Carrier broke in with one of his uncontrolled outbursts of fury.

"Ah *ça*," he exclaimed, "enough of this now. Citizen Lalouët is right and I have done enough for you already. If you want the Kernogan wench to be at the Rat Mort, you must see to getting her there yourself. She is next door, what? I won't have anything to do with it and I won't have my Marats implicated in the affair either. Name of a dog! have I not told you that I am beset with spies? It would of a truth be a climax if I was denounced as having dragged *aristos* to a house of ill-fame and then had them arrested there as malefactors! Now out with you! I have had enough of this! If your rabble is at the Rat Mort to-night, they shall be arrested with all the other cut-throats. That is my last word. The rest is your affair. Lalouët! the door!"

And without another word, and without listening to further protests from Martin-Roget or Chauvelin, Jacques Lalouët closed the doors of the audience chamber in their face.

VII

Outside on the landing, Martin-Roget swore a violent, all comprehensive oath.

"To think that we are under the heel of that skunk!" he said.

"And that in the pursuit of our own ends we have need of his help!" added Chauvelin with a sigh.

"If it were not for that. . . . And even now," continued Martin-Roget moodily, "I doubt what I can do. Yvonne de Kernogan will not follow me willingly either to the Rat Mort or elsewhere, and if I am not to have her conveyed by the guard. . . ."

He paused and swore again. His companion's silence appeared to irritate him.

"What do you advise me to do, citizen Chauvelin?" he asked.

"For the moment," replied Chauvelin imperturbably, "I should advise you to join me in a walk along the quay as far as Le Bouffay. I have work to see to inside the building and the north-westerly wind is sure to be of good counsel."

An angry retort hovered on Martin-Roget's lips, but after a second or two he succeeded in holding his irascible temper in check. He gave a quick sigh of impatience.

"Very well," he said curtly. "Let us to Le Bouffay by all means. I have much to think on, and as you say the north-westerly wind may blow away the cobwebs which for the nonce do o'ercloud my brain."

And the two men wrapped their mantles closely round their

shoulders, for the air was keen. Then they descended the staircase of the hotel and went out into the street.

# Chapter 2: Le Bouffay

In the centre of the Place the guillotine stood idle—the paint had worn off her sides—she looked weatherbeaten and forlorn—stern and forbidding still, but in a kind of sullen loneliness, with the ugly stains of crimson on her, turned to rust and grime.

The Place itself was deserted, in strange contrast to the bustle and the movement which characterised it in the days when the death of men, women and children was a daily spectacle here for the crowd. Then a constant stream of traffic, of carts and of tumbrils, of soldiers and gaffers encumbered it in every corner, now a few tumble-down booths set up against the frontage of the grim edifice—once the stronghold of the Dukes of Brittany, now little else but a huge prison—a few vendors and still fewer purchasers of the scanty wares displayed under their ragged awnings, one or two idlers loafing against the mud-stained walls, one or two urchins playing in the gutters were the only signs of life. Martin-Roget with his colleague Chauvelin turned into the Place from the quay—they walked rapidly and kept their mantles closely wrapped under their chin, for the afternoon had turned bitterly cold. It was then close upon five o'clock—a dark, moonless, starless night had set in with only a suspicion of frost in the damp air; but a blustering north-westerly wind blowing down the river and tearing round the narrow streets and the open Place, caused passers-by to muffle themselves, shivering, yet tighter in their cloaks.

Martin-Roget was talking volubly and excitedly, his tall, broad figure towering above the slender form of his companion. From time to time he tossed his mantle aside with an impatient, febrile gesture and then paused in the middle of the Place, with one hand on the other man's shoulder, marking a point in his discourse or emphasising his argument with short staccato sentences and brief, emphatic words. Chauvelin—placid and impenetrable as usual—listened much and talked little. He was ready to stand still or to walk along just as his colleague's mood demanded; in the darkness, and with the collar of a large mantle pulled tightly up to his ears, it was impossible to guess by any sign in his face what was going on in his mind.

They were a strange contrast these two men—temperamentally as well as physically—even though they had so much in common and were both the direct products of that same social upheaval which was shaking the archaic dominion of France to its very foundations. Martin-Roget, tall, broad-shouldered, bull-necked, the typical self-educated peasant, with square jaw and flat head, with wide bony hands and spatulated fingers: and Chauvelin—the aristocrat turned demagogue, thin and frail-looking, bland of manner and suave of speech, with delicate hands and pale, almost ascetic face.

The one represented all that was most brutish and sensual in this fight of one caste against the other, the thirst for the other's blood, the human beast that has been brought to bay through wrongs perpetrated against it by others and has turned upon its oppressors, lashing out right and left with blind and lustful fury at the crowd of tyrants that had kept him in subjection for so long. Whilst Chauvelin was the personification of the spiritual side of this bloody Revolution— the spirit of cool and calculating reprisals that would demand an eye for an eye and see that it got two. The idealist who dreams of the righteousness of his own cause and the destruction of its enemies, but who leaves to others the accomplishment of all the carnage and the bloodshed which his idealism has demanded, and which his reason has appraised as necessary for the triumph of which he dreams. Chauvelin was the man of thought and Martin-Roget the man of action. With the one, revenge and reprisals were selfish desires, the avenging of wrongs done to himself or to his caste, hatred for those who had injured him or his kindred. The other had no personal feelings of hatred: he had no personal wrongs to avenge: his enemies were the enemies of his party, the erstwhile tyrants who in the past had oppressed an entire people. Every man, woman or child who was not satisfied with the present Reign of Terror, who plotted or planned for its overthrow, who was not ready to see husband, father, wife or child sacrificed for the ultimate triumph of the Revolution was in Chauvelin's sight a noxious creature, fit only to be trodden under heel and ground into subjection or annihilation as a danger to the State.

Martin-Roget was the personification of sans-culottism, of rough manners and foul speech—he chafed against the conventions which forced him to wear decent clothes and boots on his feet—he would gladly have seen every one go about the streets half-naked, unwashed, a living sign of that downward levelling of castes which he and his friends stood for, and for which they had fought and striven and committed every crime which human passions let loose could invent. Chauvelin, on the other hand, was one of those who wore fine linen and buckled shoes and whose hands were delicately washed and perfumed whilst they signed decrees which sent hundreds of women and children to a violent and cruel death.

The one trod in the paths of Danton: the other followed in the footsteps of Robespierre.

## II

Together the two men mounted the outside staircase which

leads up past the lodge of the concierge and through the clerk's office to the interior of the stronghold. Outside the monumental doors they had to wait a moment or two while the clerk examined their permits to enter.

"Will you come into my office with me?" asked Chauvelin of his companion; "I have a word or two to add to my report for the Paris courier to-night. I won't be long."

"You are still in touch with the Committee of Public Safety then?" asked Martin-Roget.

"Always," replied the other curtly.

Martin-Roget threw a quick, suspicious glance on his companion. Darkness and the broad brim of his sugar-loaf hat effectually concealed even the outlines of Chauvelin's face, and Martin-Roget fell to musing over one or two things which Carrier had blurted out awhile ago. The whole of France was overrun with spies these days —every one was under suspicion, every one had to be on his guard.

Every word was overheard, every glance seen, every sign noted. What was this man Chauvelin doing here in Nantes? What reports did he send up to Paris by special courier? He, the miserable failure who had ceased to count was nevertheless in constant touch with that awful Committee of Public Safety which was wont to strike at all times and unexpectedly in the dark. Martin-Roget shivered beneath his mantle. For the first time since his schemes of vengeance had wholly absorbed his mind he regretted the freedom and safety which he had enjoyed in England, and he marvelled if the miserable game which he was playing would be worth the winning in the end. Nevertheless he had followed Chauvelin without comment. The man appeared to exercise a fascination over him—a kind of subtle power, which emanated from his small shrunken figure, from his pale keen eyes and his well-modulated, suave mode of speech.

### III

The clerk had handed the two men their permits back. They were allowed to pass through the gates.

In the hall some half-dozen men were nominally on guard— nominally, because discipline was not over strict these days, and the men sat or lolled about the place; two of them were intent on a game of dominoes, another was watching them, whilst the other three were settling some sort of quarrel among themselves which necessitated vigorous and emphatic gestures and the copious use of expletives. One man, who appeared to be in command, divided his time impartially between the domino-players and those who were quarrelling.

The vast place was insufficiently lighted by a chandelier which hung from the ceiling and a couple of small oil-lamps placed in the circular niches in the wall opposite the front door.

No one took any notice of Martin-Roget or of Chauvelin as they crossed the hall, and presently the latter pushed open a door on the left of the main gates and held it open for his colleague to pass through.

"You are sure that I shall not be disturbing you?" queried Martin-Roget.

"Quite sure," replied the other curtly. "And there is something which I must say to you . . . where I know that I shall not be overheard."

Then he followed Martin-Roget into the room and closed the door behind him. The room was scantily furnished with a square deal table in the centre, two or three chairs, a broken-down bureau leaning against one wall and an iron stove wherein a meagre fire sent a stream of malodorous smoke through sundry cracks in its chimney-pipe. From the ceiling there hung an oil-lamp the light of which was thrown down upon the table, by a large green shade made of cardboard.

Chauvelin drew a chair to the bureau and sat down; he pointed to another and Martin-Roget took a seat beside the table. He felt restless and excited—his nerves all on the jar: his colleague's calm, sardonic glance acted as a further irritant to his temper.

"What is it that you wished to say to me, citizen Chauvelin?" he asked at last.

"Just a word, citizen," replied the other in his quiet urbane manner. "I have accompanied you faithfully on your journey to England: I have placed my feeble powers at your disposal: awhile ago I stood between you and the proconsul's wrath. This, I think, has earned me the right of asking what you intend to do."

"I don't know about the right," retorted Martin-Roget gruffly, "but I don't mind telling you. As you remarked awhile ago the North-West wind is wont to be of good counsel. I have thought the matter over whilst I walked with you along the quay and I have decided to act on Carrier's suggestion. Our eminent proconsul said just now that it was the duty of every true patriot to marry an *aristo*, an he be free and Chance puts a comely wench in his way. I mean," he added with a cynical laugh, "to act on that advice and marry Yvonne de Kernogan . . . if I can."

"She has refused you up to now?"

"Yes . . . up to now."

"You have threatened her—and her father?"

"Yes—both. Not only with death but with shame."

"And still she refuses?"

"Apparently," said Martin-Roget with ever-growing irritation.

"It is often difficult," rejoined Chauvelin meditatively, "to compel these *aristos*. They are obstinate. . . . "

"Oh! don't forget that I am in a position now to bring additional pressure on the wench. That lout Carrier has splendid ideas—a brute, what? but clever and full of resource. That suggestion of his about the Rat Mort is splendid. . . . "

"You mean to try and act on it?"

"Of course I do," said Martin-Roget roughly. "I am going over presently to my sister's house to see the Kernogan wench again, and to have another talk with her. Then if she still refuses, if she still chooses to scorn the honourable position which I offer her, I shall act on Carrier's suggestion. It will be at the Rat Mort to-night that she and I will have our final interview, and there when I dangle the prospect of Cayenne and the convict's brand before her, she may not prove so obdurate as she has been up to now."

"H'm! That is as may be," was Chauvelin's dry comment. "Personally I am inclined to agree with Carrier. Death, swift and sure—the Loire or the guillotine—is the best that has yet been invented for traitors and *aristos*. But we won't discuss that again. I know your feelings in the matter and in a measure I respect them. But if you will allow me I would like to be present at your interview with the soi-disant Lady Anthony Dewhurst. I won't disturb you and I won't say a word . . . but there is something I would like to make sure of. . . . "

"What is that?"

"Whether the wench has any hopes . . . " said Chauvelin slowly, "whether she has received a message or has any premonition . . . whether in short she thinks that outside agencies are at work on her behalf."

"Tshaw!" exclaimed Martin-Roget impatiently, "you are still harping on that Scarlet Pimpernel idea."

"I am," retorted the other drily.

"As you please. But understand, citizen Chauvelin, that I will not allow you to interfere with my plans, whilst you go off on one of those wild-goose chases which have already twice brought you into disrepute."

"I will not interfere with your plans, citizen," rejoined Chauvelin with unwonted gentleness, "but let me in my turn impress one thing upon you, and that is that unless you are as wary as the serpent, as cunning as the fox, all your precious plans will be upset by that interfering Englishman whom you choose to disregard."

"What do you mean?"

"I mean that I know him—to my cost—and you do not. But you will, an I am not gravely mistaken, make acquaintance with him ere your great adventure with these Kernogan people is successfully at an end. Believe me, citizen Martin-Roget," he added impressively, "you would have been far wiser to accept Carrier's suggestion and let him fling that rabble into the Loire for you."

"Pshaw! you are not childish enough to imagine, citizen Chauvelin, that your Englishman can spirit away that wench from under my sister's eyes? Do you know what my sister suffered at the hands of the Kernogans? Do you think that she is like to forget my father's ignominious death any more than I am? And she mourns a lover as well as a father—she mourns her youth, her happiness, the mother whom she worshipped. Think you a better gaoler could be found anywhere? And there are friends of mine—lads of our own village, men who hate the Kernogans as bitterly as I do myself—who are only too ready to lend Louise a hand in case of violence. And after that —suppose your magnificent Scarlet Pimpernel succeeded in hoodwinking my sister and in evading the vigilance of a score of determined village lads, who would sooner die one by one than see the Kernogan escape—suppose all that, I say, there would still be the guard at every city gate to challenge. No! no! it couldn't be done, citizen Chauvelin," he added with a complacent laugh. "Your Englishman would need the help of a legion of angels, what? to get the wench out of Nantes this time."

Chauvelin made no comment on his colleague's impassioned harangue. Memory had taken him back to that one day in September in Boulogne when he too had set one prisoner to guard a precious hostage: it brought back to his mind a vision of a strangely picturesque figure as it appeared to him in the window-embrasure of the old castle-hall:[1] it brought back to his ears the echo of that quaint, irresponsible laughter, of that lazy, drawling speech, of all that had acted as an irritant on his nerves ere he found himself baffled, foiled, eating out his heart with vain reproach at his own folly.

"I see you are unconvinced, citizen Martin-Roget," he said quietly, "and I know that it is the fashion nowadays among young politicians to sneer at Chauvelin—the living embodiment of failure. But let me just add this. When you and I talked matters over together at the Bottom Inn, in the wilds of Somersetshire, I warned you that not only was your identity known to the man who calls himself the Scarlet Pimpernel, but also that he knew every one of your plans with regard to the Kernogan wench and her father. You laughed at me then . . . do you remember? . . . you shrugged your shoulders and jeered at what you call my far-fetched ideas . . . just as you do now. Well! will you let me remind you of what happened within four-and-twenty hours of that warning which you chose to disregard? . . . Yvonne de Kernogan was married to Lord Anthony Dewhurst and. . . . "

"I know all that, man," broke in Martin-Roget impatiently. "It was all a mere coincidence . . . the marriage must have been planned long before that . . . your Scarlet Pimpernel could not possibly have had anything to do with it."

"Perhaps not," rejoined Chauvelin drily. "But mark what has happened since. Just now when we crossed the Place I saw in the distance a figure flitting past—the gorgeous figure of an exquisite who of a surety is a stranger in Nantes: and carried upon the wings of the north-westerly wind there came to me the sound of a voice which, of late, I have only heard in my dreams. On my soul, citizen Martin-Roget," he added with earnest emphasis, "I assure you that the Scarlet Pimpernel is in Nantes at the present moment, that he is scheming, plotting, planning to rescue the Kernogan wench out of your clutches. He will not leave her in your power, on this I would stake my life; she is the wife of one of his dearest friends: he will not abandon her, not while he keeps that resourceful head of his on his shoulders. Unless you are desperately careful he will outwit you; of that I am as convinced as that I am alive."

"Bah! you have been dreaming, citizen Chauvelin," rejoined Martin-Roget with a laugh and shrugging his broad shoulders; "your mysterious Englishman in Nantes? Why man! the navigation of the Loire has been totally prohibited these last fourteen days—no carriage, van or vehicle of any kind is allowed to enter the city—no man, woman or child to pass the barriers without special permit signed either by the proconsul himself or by Fleury the captain of the Marats. Why! even I, when I brought the Kernogans in overland from Le Croisic, I was detained two hours outside Nantes while my papers were sent in to Carrier for inspection. You know that, you were with me."

"I know it," replied Chauvelin drily, "and yet. . . . "

He paused, with one claw-like finger held erect to demand attention. The door of the small room in which they sat gave on the big hall where the half-dozen Marats were stationed, the single window at right angles to the door looked out upon the Place below. It was from there that suddenly there came the sound of a loud peal of laughter—quaint and merry—somewhat inane and affected, and at the sound Chauvelin's pale face took on the hue of ashes and even Martin-Roget felt a strange sensation of cold creeping down his spine.

For a few seconds the two men remained quite still, as if a spell had been cast over them through that light-hearted peal of rippling laughter. Then equally suddenly the younger man shook himself free of the spell; with a few long strides he was already at the door and out in the vast hall; Chauvelin following closely on his heels.

IV

The clock in the tower of the edifice was even then striking five. The Marats in the hall looked up with lazy indifference at the two men who had come rushing out in such an abrupt and excited manner.

"Any stranger been through here?" queried Chauvelin peremptorily of the sergeant in command.

"No," replied the latter curtly. "How could they, without a permit?"

He shrugged his shoulders and the men resumed their game and their argument. Martin-Roget would have parleyed with them but Chauvelin had already crossed the hall and was striding past the clerk's office and the lodge of the concierge out toward the open. Martin-Roget, after a moment's hesitation, followed him.

The Place was wrapped in gloom. From the platform of the guillotine an oil-lamp hoisted on a post threw a small circle of light around. Small pieces of tallow candle, set in pewter sconces, glimmered feebly under the awnings of the booths, and there was a street-lamp affixed to the wall of the old château immediately below the parapet of the staircase, and others at the angles of the Rue de la Monnaye and the narrow Ruelle des Jacobins.

Chauvelin's keen eyes tried to pierce the surrounding darkness. He leaned over the parapet and peered into the remote angles of the building and round the booths below him.

There were a few people on the Place, some walking rapidly across from one end to the other, intent on business, others pausing in order to make purchases at the booths. Up and down the steps of the guillotine a group of street urchins were playing hide-and-seek. Round the angles of the narrow streets the vague figures of passers-by flitted to and fro, now easily discernible in the light of the street lanthorns, anon swallowed up again in the darkness beyond. Whilst immediately below the parapet two or three men of the Company Marat were lounging against the walls. Their red bonnets showed up clearly in the flickering light of the street lamps, as did their bare shins and the polished points of their sabots. But of an elegant, picturesque figure such as Chauvelin had described awhile ago there was not a sign.

Martin-Roget leaned over the parapet and called peremptorily:

"Hey there! citizens of the Company Marat!"

One of the red-capped men looked up leisurely.

"Your desire, citizen?" he queried with insolent deliberation, for they were mighty men, this bodyguard of the great proconsul, his spies and tools in the awesome work of frightfulness which he carried on so ruthlessly.

"Is that you Paul Friche?" queried Martin-Roget in response.

"At your service, citizen," came the glib reply, delivered not without mock deference.

"Then come up here. I wish to speak with you."

"I can't leave my post, nor can my mates," retorted the man who had answered to the name of Paul Friche. "Come down, citizen, an you desire to speak with us."

Martin-Roget swore lustily.

"The insolence of that rabble . . . " he murmured.

"Hush! I'll go," interposed Chauvelin quickly. "Do you know that man Friche? Is he trustworthy?"

"Yes, I know him. As for being trustworthy . . . " added Martin-Roget with a shrug of the shoulders. "He is a corporal in the Marats and high in favour with commandant Fleury."

Every second was of value, and Chauvelin was not the man to waste time in useless parleyings. He ran down the stairs at the foot of which one of the red-capped gentry deigned to speak with him.

"Have you seen any strangers across the Place just now?" he queried in a whisper.

"Yes," replied the man Friche. "Two!"

Then he spat upon the ground and added spitefully: "*Aristos*, what? In fine clothes—like yourself, citizen. . . . "

"Which way did they go?"

"Down the Ruelle des Jacobins."

"When?"

"Two minutes ago."

"Why did you not follow them?. . . *Aristos* and. . . . "

"I would have followed," retorted Paul Friche with studied insolence; "'twas you called me away from my duty."

"After them then!" urged Chauvelin peremptorily. "They cannot have gone far. They are English spies, and remember, citizen, that there's a reward for their apprehension."

The man grunted an eager assent. The word "reward" had fired his zeal. In a trice he had called to his mates and the three Marats soon sped across the Place and down the Ruelle des Jacobins where the surrounding gloom quickly swallowed them up.

Chauvelin watched them till they were out of sight, then he rejoined his colleague on the landing at the top of the stairs. For a second or two longer the click of the men's sabots upon the stones resounded on the adjoining streets and across the Place, and suddenly that same quaint, merry, somewhat inane laugh woke the echoes of the grim buildings around and caused many a head to turn inquiringly, marvelling who it could be that had the heart to laugh these days in the streets of Nantes.

V

Five minutes or so later the three Marats could vaguely be seen recrossing the Place and making their way back to Le Bouffay, where Martin-Roget and Chauvelin still stood on the top of the stairs excited and expectant. At sight of the men Chauvelin ran down the steps to meet them.

"Well?" he queried in an eager whisper.

"We never saw them," replied Paul Friche gruffly, "though we could hear them clearly enough, talking, laughing and walking very rapidly toward the quay. Then suddenly the earth or the river swallowed them up. We saw and heard nothing more."

Chauvelin swore and a curious hissing sound escaped his thin lips.

"Don't be too disappointed, citizen," added the man with a coarse laugh, "my mate picked this up at the corner of the Ruelle, when, I fancy, we were pressing the *aristos* pretty closely."

He held out a small bundle of papers tied together with a piece of red ribbon: the bundle had evidently rolled in the mud, for the papers were covered with grime. Chauvelin's thin, claw-like fingers had at once closed over them.

"You must give me back those papers, citizen," said the man, "they are my booty. I can only give them up to citizen-captain Fleury."

"I'll give them to the citizen-captain myself," retorted Chauvelin. "For the moment you had best not leave your post of duty," he added more peremptorily, seeing that the man made as he would follow him.

"I take orders from no one except . . . " protested the man gruffly.

"You will take them from me now," broke in Chauvelin with a sudden assumption of command and authority which sat with weird strangeness upon his thin shrunken figure. "Go back to your post at once, ere I lodge a complaint against you for neglect of duty, with the citizen proconsul."

He turned on his heel and, without paying further heed to the man and his mutterings, he remounted the stone stairs.

"No success, I suppose?" queried Martin-Roget.

"None," replied Chauvelin curtly.

He had the packet of papers tightly clasped in his hand. He was debating in his mind whether he would speak of them to his colleague or not.

"What did Friche say?" asked the latter impatiently.

"Oh! very little. He and his mates caught sight of the strangers and followed them as far as the quays. But they were walking very fast and suddenly the Marats lost their trace in the darkness. It seemed, according to Paul Friche, as if the earth or the night had swallowed them up."

"And was that all?"

"Yes. That was all."

"I wonder," added Martin-Roget with a light laugh and a careless shrug of his wide shoulders, "I wonder if you and I, citizen Chauvelin—and Paul Friche too for that matter—have been the victims of our nerves."

"I wonder," assented Chauvelin drily. And—quite quietly—he slipped the packet of papers in the pocket of his coat.

"Then we may as well adjourn. There is nothing else you wish to say to me about that enigmatic Scarlet Pimpernel of yours?"

"No—nothing."

"And you still would like to hear what the Kernogan wench will say and see how she will look when I put my final proposal before her?"

"If you will allow me."

"Then come," said Martin-Roget. "My sister's house is close by."

# CHAPTER 3: THE FOWLERS

## I

In order to reach the Carrefour de la Poissonnerie the two men had to skirt the whole edifice of Le Bouffay, walk a little along the quay and turn up the narrow alley opposite the bridge. They walked on in silence, each absorbed in his own thoughts.

The house occupied by the citizeness Adet lay back a little from the others in the street. It was one of an irregular row of mean, squalid, tumble-down houses, some of them little more than lean-to sheds built into the walls of Le Bouffay. Most of them had overhanging roofs which stretched out like awnings more than half way across the road, and even at midday shut out any little ray of sunshine which might have a tendency to peep into the street below.

In this year II of the Republic the Carrefour de la Poissonnerie was unpaved, dark and evil-smelling. For two thirds of the year it was ankle-deep in mud: the rest of the time the mud was baked into cakes and emitted clouds of sticky dust under the shuffling feet of the passers-by. At night it was dimly lighted by one or two broken-down lanthorns which were hung on transverse chains overhead from house to house. These lanthorns only made a very small circle of light immediately below them: the rest of the street was left in darkness, save for the faint glimmer which filtrated through an occasional ill-fitting doorway or through the chinks of some insecurely fastened shutter.

The Carrefour de la Poissonnerie was practically deserted in the daytime; only a few children—miserable little atoms of humanity showing their meagre, emaciated bodies through the scanty rags which failed to cover their nakedness—played weird, mirthless games in the mud and filth of the street. But at night it became strangely peopled with vague and furtive forms that were wont to glide swiftly by, beneath the hanging lanthorns, in order to lose themselves again in the welcome obscurity beyond: men and women—ill-clothed and unshod, with hands buried in pockets or beneath scanty shawls—their feet, oft-times bare, making no sound as they went squishing through the mud. A perpetual silence used to reign in this kingdom of squalor and of darkness, where night-hawks alone fluttered their wings; only from time to time a joyless greeting of boon-companions, or the hoarse cough of some wretched consumptive would wake the dormant echoes that lingered in the gloom.

## II

Martin-Roget knew his way about the murky street well enough. He went up to the house which lay a little back from the others. It appeared even more squalid than the rest, not a sound came from within—hardly a light—only a narrow glimmer found its way through the chink of a shutter on the floor above. To right and left of it the houses were tall, with walls that reeked of damp and of filth: from one of these—the one on the left—an iron sign dangled and creaked dismally as it swung in the wind. Just above the sign there was a window with partially closed shutters: through it came the sound of two husky voices raised in heated argument.

In the open space in front of Louise Adet's house vague forms standing about or lounging against the walls of the neighbouring houses were vaguely discernible in the gloom. Martin-Roget and Chauvelin as they approached were challenged by a raucous voice which came to them out of the inky blackness around.

"Halt! who goes there?"

"Friends!" replied Martin-Roget promptly. "Is citizeness Adet within?"

"Yes! she is!" retorted the man bluntly; "excuse me, friend Adet —I did not know you in this confounded darkness."

"No harm done," said Martin-Roget. "And it is I who am grateful to you all for your vigilance."

"Oh!" said the other with a laugh, "there's not much fear of your bird getting out of its cage. Have no fear, friend Adet! That Kernogan rabble is well looked after."

The small group dispersed in the darkness and Martin-Roget rapped against the door of his sister's house with his knuckles.

"That is the Rat Mort," he said, indicating the building on his left with a nod of the head. "A very unpleasant neighbourhood for my sister, and she has oft complained of it—but name of a dog! won't it prove useful this night?"

Chauvelin had as usual followed his colleague in silence, but his keen eyes had not failed to note the presence of the village lads of whom Martin-Roget had spoken. There are no eyes so watchful as those of hate, nor is there aught so incorruptible. Every one of these men here had an old wrong to avenge, an old score to settle with those ci-devant Kernogans who had once been their masters and who were so completely in their power now. Louise Adet had gathered round her a far more efficient bodyguard than even the proconsul could hope to have.

A moment or two later the door was opened, softly and cautiously, and Martin-Roget asked: "Is that you, Louise?" for of a truth the darkness was almost deeper within than without, and he could not see who it was that was standing by the door.

"Yes! it is," replied a weary and querulous voice. "Enter quickly. The wind is cruel, and I can't keep myself warm. Who is with you, Pierre?"

"A friend," said Martin-Roget drily. "We want to see the *aristo*."

The woman without further comment closed the door behind the new-comers. The place now was as dark as pitch, but she seemed to know her way about like a cat, for her shuffling footsteps were heard moving about unerringly. A moment or two later she opened another door opposite the front entrance, revealing an inner room—a sort of kitchen—which was lighted by a small lamp.

"You can go straight up," she called curtly to the two men.

The narrow, winding staircase was divided from this kitchen by a wooden partition. Martin-Roget, closely followed by Chauvelin, went up the stairs. On the top of these there was a tiny landing with a door on either side of it. Martin-Roget without any ceremony pushed open the door on his right with his foot.

A tallow candle fixed in a bottle and placed in the centre of a table in the middle of the room flickered in the draught as the door flew open. It was bare of everything save a table and a chair, and a bundle of straw in one corner. The tiny window at right angles to the door was innocent of glass, and the north-westerly wind came in an icy stream through the aperture. On the table, in addition to the candle, there was a broken pitcher half-filled with water, and a small chunk of brown bread blotched with stains of mould.

On the chair beside the table and immediately facing the door sat Yvonne Lady Dewhurst. On the wall above her head a hand unused to calligraphy had traced in clumsy characters the words: "*Liberté! Fraternité! Egalité!*" and below that "*ou la Mort.*"

## III

The men entered the narrow room and Chauvelin carefully closed the door behind him. He at once withdrew into a remote corner of the room and stood there quite still, wrapped in his mantle, a small, silent, mysterious figure on which Yvonne fixed dark, inquiring eyes.

Martin-Roget, restless and excited, paced up and down the small space like a wild animal in a cage. From time to time exclamations of impatience escaped him and he struck one fist repeatedly against his open palm. Yvonne followed his movements with a quiet, uninterested glance, but Chauvelin paid no heed whatever to him.

He was watching Yvonne ceaselessly, and closely.

Three days' incarceration in this wind-swept attic, the lack of decent food and of warmth, the want of sleep and the horror of her present position all following upon the soul-agony which she had endured when she was forcibly torn away from her dear milor, had left their mark on Yvonne Dewhurst's fresh young face. The look of gravity which had always sat so quaintly on her piquant features had now changed to one of deep and abiding sorrow; her large dark eyes were circled and sunk; they had in them the unnatural glow of fever, as well as the settled look of horror and of pathetic resignation. Her soft brown hair had lost its lustre; her cheeks were drawn and absolutely colourless.

Martin-Roget paused in his restless walk. For a moment he stood silent and absorbed, contemplating by the flickering light of the candle all the havoc which his brutality had wrought upon Yvonne's dainty face.

But Yvonne after a while ceased to look at him—she appeared to be unconscious of the gaze of these two men, each of whom was at this moment only thinking of the evil which he meant to inflict upon her— each of whom only thought of her as a helpless bird whom he had at last ensnared and whom he could crush to death as soon as he felt so inclined.

She kept her lips tightly closed and her head averted. She was gazing across at the unglazed window into the obscurity beyond, marvelling in what direction lay the sea and the shores of England.

Martin-Roget crossed his arms over his broad chest and clutched his elbows with his hands with an obvious effort to keep control over his movements and his temper in check. The quiet, almost indifferent attitude of the girl was exasperating to his over-strung nerves.

"Look here, my girl," he said at last, roughly and peremptorily, "I had an interview with the proconsul this afternoon. He chides me for my leniency toward you. Three days he thinks is far too long to keep traitors eating the bread of honest citizens and taking up valuable space in our city. Yesterday I made a proposal to you. Have you thought on it?"

Yvonne made no reply. She was still gazing out into nothingness and just at that moment she was very far away from the narrow, squalid room and the company of these two inhuman brutes. She was thinking of her dear milor and of that lovely home at Combwich wherein she had spent three such unforgettable days. She was remembering how beautiful had been the colour of the bare twigs in the chestnut coppice when the wintry sun danced through and in between them and drew fantastic patterns of living gold upon the carpet of dead leaves; and she remembered too how exquisite were the tints of russet and blue on the distant hills, and how quaintly the thrushes had called: "Kiss me quick!" She saw again those trembling leaves of a delicious faintly crimson hue which still hung upon the branches of the scarlet oak, and the early flowering heath which clothed the moors with a gorgeous mantle of rosy amethyst.

Martin-Roget's harsh voice brought her abruptly back to the hideous reality of the moment.

"Your obstinacy will avail you nothing," he said, speaking quietly, even though a note of intense irritation was distinctly perceptible in his voice. "The proconsul has given me a further delay wherein to deal leniently with you and with your father if I am so minded. You know what I have proposed to you: Life with me as my wife—in which case your father will be free to return to England or to go to the devil as he pleases—or the death of a malefactor for you both in the company of all the thieves and evil-doers who are mouldering in the prisons of Nantes at this moment. Another delay wherein to choose between an honourable life and a shameful death. The proconsul waits. But to-night he must have his answer."

Then Yvonne turned her head slowly and looked calmly on her enemy.

"The tyrant who murders innocent men, women and children," she said, "can have his answer now. I choose death which is inevitable in preference to a life of shame."

"You seem," he retorted, "to have lost sight of the fact that the law gives me the right to take by force that which you so obstinately refuse."

"Have I not said," she replied, "that death is my choice? Life with you would be a life of shame."

"I can get a priest to marry us without your consent: and your religion forbids you to take your own life," he said with a sneer.

To this she made no reply, but he knew that he had his answer. Smothering a curse, he resumed after a while:

"So you prefer to drag your father to death with you? Yet he has begged you to consider your decision and to listen to reason. He has given his consent to our marriage."

"Let me see my father," she retorted firmly, "and hear him say that with his own lips.

"Ah!" she added quickly, for at her words Martin-Roget had turned his head away and shrugged his shoulders with well-assumed indifference, "you cannot and dare not let me see him. For three days now you have kept us apart and no doubt fed us both up with your lies. My father is duc de Kernogan, Marquis de Trentemoult," she added proudly, "he would far rather die side by side with his daughter than see her wedded to a criminal."

"And you, my girl," rejoined Martin-Roget coldly, "would you see your father branded as a malefactor, linked to a thief and sent to perish in the Loire?"

"My father," she retorted, "will die as he has lived, a brave and honourable gentleman. The brand of a malefactor cannot cling to his name. Sorrow we are ready to endure—death is less than nothing to us —we will but follow in the footsteps of our King and of our Queen and of many whom we care for and whom you and your proconsul and your colleagues have brutally murdered. Shame cannot touch us, and our honour and our pride are so far beyond your reach that your impious and blood-stained hands can never sully them."

She had spoken very slowly and very quietly. There were no heroics about her attitude. Even Martin-Roget—callous brute though he was—felt that she had only spoken just as she felt, and that nothing that he might say, no plea that he might urge, would ever shake her determination.

"Then it seems to me," he said, "that I am only wasting my time by trying to make you see reason and common-sense. You look upon me as a brute. Well! perhaps I am. At any rate I am that which your father and you have made me. Four years ago, when you had power over me and over mine, you brutalised us. To-day we—the people—are your masters and we make you suffer, not for all—that were impossible —but for part of what you made us suffer. That, after all, is only bare justice. By making you my wife I would have saved you from death— not from humiliation, for that you must endure, and at my hands in a full measure—but I would have made you my wife because I still have pleasant recollections of that kiss which I snatched from you on that never-to-be-forgotten night and in the darkness—a kiss for which you would gladly have seen me hang then, if you could have laid hands on me."

He paused, trying to read what was going on behind those fine eyes of hers, with their vacant, far-seeing gaze which seemed like another barrier between her and him. At this rough allusion to that moment of horror and of shame, she had not moved a muscle, nor did her gaze lose its fixity.

He laughed.

"It is an unpleasant recollection, eh, my proud lady? The first kiss of passion was not implanted on your exquisite lips by that fine gentleman whom you deemed worthy of your hand and your love, but by Pierre Adet, the miller's son, what? a creature not quite so human as your horse or your pet dog. Neither you nor I are like to forget that methinks. . . . "

Yvonne vouchsafed no reply to the taunt, and for a moment there was silence in the room, until Chauvelin's thin, suave voice broke in quite gently:

"Do not lose your patience with the wench, citizen Martin-Roget. Your time is too precious to be wasted in useless recriminations."

"I have finished with her," retorted the other sullenly. "She shall be dealt with now as I think best. I agree with citizen Carrier. He is right after all. To the Loire with the lot of that foul brood!"

"Nay!" here rejoined Chauvelin with placid urbanity, "are you not a little harsh, citizen, with our fair Yvonne? Remember! Women have moods and megrims. What they indignantly refuse to yield to us one day, they will grant with a smile the next. Our beautiful Yvonne is no exception to this rule, I'll warrant."

Even while he spoke he threw a glance of warning on his colleague. There was something enigmatic in his manner at this moment, in the strange suavity wherewith he spoke these words of conciliation and of gentleness. Martin-Roget was as usual ready with an impatient retort. He was in a mood to bully and to brutalise, to heap threat upon threat, to win by frightfulness that which he could not gain by persuasion. Perhaps that at this moment he desired Yvonne de Kernogan for wife, more even than he desired her death. At any rate his headstrong temper was ready to chafe against any warning or advice. But once again Chauvelin's stronger mentality dominated over his less resolute colleague. Martin-Roget—the fowler—was in his turn caught in the net of a keener snarer than himself, and whilst—with the obstinacy of the weak—he was making mental resolutions to rebuke Chauvelin for his interference later on, he had already fallen in with the latter's attitude.

"The wench has had three whole days wherein to alter her present mood," he said more quietly, "and you know yourself, citizen, that the proconsul will not wait after to-day."

"The day is young yet," rejoined Chauvelin. "It still hath six hours to its credit. . . . Six hours. . . . Three hundred and sixty minutes!" he continued with a pleasant little laugh; "time enough for a woman to change her mind three hundred and sixty times. Let me advise you, citizen, to leave the wench to her own meditations for the present, and I trust that she will accept the advice of a man who has a sincere regard for her beauty and her charms and who is old enough to be her father, and seriously think the situation over in a conciliatory spirit. M. le duc de Kernogan will be grateful to her, for of a truth he is not over happy either at the moment . . . and will be still less happy in the *dépôt* to-morrow: it is over-crowded, and typhus, I fear me, is rampant among the prisoners. He has, I am convinced—in spite of what the citizeness says to the contrary—a rooted objection to being hurled into the Loire, or to be arraigned before the bar of the Convention, not as an aristocrat and a traitor but as an unit of an undesirable herd of criminals sent up to Paris for trial, by an anxious and harried proconsul. There! there!" he added benignly, "we will not worry our fair Yvonne any longer, will we, citizen? I think she has grasped the alternative and will soon realise that marriage with an honourable patriot is not such an untoward fate after all."

"And now, citizen Martin-Roget," he concluded, "I pray you allow me to take my leave of the fair lady and to give you the wise recommendation to do likewise. She will be far better alone for awhile. Night brings good counsel, so they say."

He watched the girl keenly while he spoke. Her impassivity had not deserted her for a single moment: but whether her calmness was of hope or of despair he was unable to decide. On the whole he thought it must be the latter: hope would have kindled a spark in those dark, purple-rimmed eyes, it would have brought moisture to the lips, a tremor to the hand.

The Scarlet Pimpernel was in Nantes—that fact was established beyond a doubt—but Chauvelin had come to the conclusion that so far as Yvonne Dewhurst herself was concerned, she knew nothing of the mysterious agencies that were working on her behalf.

Chauvelin's hand closed with a nervous contraction over the packet of papers in his pocket. Something of the secret of that enigmatic English adventurer lay revealed within its folds. Chauvelin had not yet had the opportunity of examining them: the interview with Yvonne had been the most important business for the moment.

From somewhere in the distance a city clock struck six. The afternoon was wearing on. The keenest brain in Europe was on the watch to drag one woman and one man from the deadly trap which had been so successfully set for them. A few hours more and Chauvelin in his turn would be pitting his wits against the resources of that intricate brain, and he felt like a war-horse scenting blood and battle. He was aching to get to work—aching to form his plans—to lay his snares—to dispose his trap so that the noble English quarry should not fail to be caught within its meshes.

He gave a last look to Yvonne, who was still sitting quite impassive, gazing through the squalid walls into some beautiful distance, the reflection of which gave to her pale, wan face an added beauty.

"Let us go, citizen Martin-Roget," he said peremptorily. "There is nothing else that we can do here."

And Martin-Roget, the weaker morally of the two, yielded to the stronger personality of his colleague. He would have liked to stay on for awhile, to gloat for a few moments longer over the helplessness of the woman who to him represented the root of every evil which had ever befallen him and his family. But Chauvelin commanded and he felt impelled to obey. He gave one long, last look on Yvonne—a look that was as full of triumph as of mockery—he looked round the four dank walls, the unglazed window, the broken pitcher, the mouldy bread. Revenge was of a truth the sweetest emotion of the human heart. Pierre Adet—son of the miller who had been hanged by orders of the Duc de Kernogan for a crime which he had never committed—would not at this moment have changed places with Fortune's Benjamin.

## IV

Downstairs in Louise Adet's kitchen, Martin-Roget seized his colleague by the arm.

"Sit down a moment, citizen," he said persuasively, "and tell me what you think of it all."

Chauvelin sat down at the other's invitation. All his movements were slow, deliberate, perfectly calm.

"I think," he said drily, "as far as your marriage with the wench is concerned, that you are beaten, my friend."

"Tshaw!" The exclamation, raucous and surcharged with hate came from Louise Adet. She, too, like Pierre—more so than Pierre mayhap—had cause to hate the Kernogans. She, too, like Pierre had lived the last three days in the full enjoyment of the thought that Fate and Chance were about to level things at last between herself and those detested *aristos*. Silent and sullen she was shuffling about in the room, among her pots and pans, but she kept an eye upon her brother's movements and an ear on what he said. Men were apt to lose grit where a pretty wench was concerned. It takes a woman's rancour and a woman's determination to carry a scheme of vengeance against another to a successful end.

Martin-Roget rejoined more calmly:

"I knew that she would still be obstinate," he said. "If I forced her into a marriage, which I have the right to do, she might take her own life and make me look a fool. So I don't want to do that. I believe in the persuasiveness of the Rat Mort to-night," he added with a cynical laugh, "and if that fails. . . . Well! I was never really in love with the fair Yvonne, and now she has even ceased to be desirable. . . . If the Rat Mort fails to act on her sensibilities as I would wish, I can easily console myself by following Carrier's herd to Paris. Louise shall come with me—eh, little sister?—and we'll give ourselves the satisfaction of seeing M. le duc de Kernogan and his exquisite daughter stand in the felon's dock—tried for malpractices and for evil living. We'll see them branded as convicts and packed off like so much cattle to Cayenne. That will be a sight," he concluded with a deep sigh of satisfaction, "which will bring rest to my soul."

He paused: his face looked sullen and evil under the domination of that passion which tortured him.

Louise Adet had shuffled up close to her brother. In one hand she held the wooden spoon wherewith she had been stirring the soup: with the other she brushed away the dark, lank hair which hung in strands over her high, pale forehead. In appearance she was a woman immeasurably older than her years. Her face had the colour of yellow

parchment, her skin was stretched tightly over her high cheekbones—
her lips were colourless and her eyes large, wide-open, were pale in hue
and circled with red. Just now a deep frown of puzzlement between her
brows added a sinister expression to her cadaverous face:

"The Rat Mort?" she queried in that tired voice of hers,
"Cayenne? What is all that about?"

"A splendid scheme of Carrier's, my Louise," replied Martin-
Roget airily. "We convey the Kernogan woman to the Rat Mort. To-
night a descent will be made on that tavern of ill-fame by a company of
Marats and every man, woman and child within it will be arrested and
sent to Paris as undesirable inhabitants of this most moral city: in Paris
they will be tried as malefactors or evil-doers—cut throats, thieves,
what? and deported as convicts to Cayenne, or else sent to the
guillotine. The Kernogans among that herd! What sayest thou to that,
little sister? Thy father, thy lover, hung as thieves! M. le Duc and
Mademoiselle branded as convicts! 'Tis pleasant to think on, eh?"

Louise made no reply. She stood looking at her brother, her
pale, red-rimmed eyes seemed to drink in every word that he uttered,
while her bony hand wandered mechanically across and across her
forehead as if in a pathetic endeavour to clear the brain from
everything save of the satisfying thoughts which this prospect of
revenge had engendered.

Chauvelin's gentle voice broke in on her meditations.

"In the meanwhile," he said placidly, "remember my warning,
citizen Martin-Roget. There are passing clever and mighty agencies at
work, even at this hour, to wrest your prey from you. How will you
convey the wench to the Rat Mort? Carrier has warned you of spies—
but I have warned you against a crowd of English adventurers far more
dangerous than an army of spies. Three pairs of eyes—probably more,
and one pair the keenest in Europe—will be on the watch to seize upon
the woman and to carry her off under your very nose."

Martin-Roget uttered a savage oath.

"That brute Carrier has left me in the lurch," he said roughly. "I
don't believe in your nightmares and your English adventurers, still it
would have been better if I could have had the woman conveyed to the
tavern under armed escort."

"Armed escort has been denied you, and anyway it would not be
much use. You and I, citizen Martin-Roget, must act independently of
Carrier. Your friends down there," he added, indicating the street with
a jerk of the head, "must redouble their watchfulness. The village lads
of Vertou are of a truth no match intellectually with our English
adventurers, but they have vigorous fists in case there is an attack on
the wench while she walks across to the Rat Mort."

"It would be simpler," here interposed Louise roughly, "if we
were to knock the wench on the head and then let the lads carry her

across."

"It would not be simpler," retorted Chauvelin drily, "for Carrier might at any moment turn against us. Commandant Fleury with half a company of Marats will be posted round the Rat Mort, remember. They may interfere with the lads and arrest them and snatch the wench from us, when all our plans may fall to the ground . . . one never knows what double game Carrier may be playing. No! no! the girl must not be dragged or carried to the Rat Mort. She must walk into the trap of her own free will."

"But name of a dog! how is it to be done?" ejaculated Martin-Roget, and he brought his clenched fist crashing down upon the table. "The woman will not follow me—or Louise either—anywhere willingly."

"She must follow a stranger then—or one whom she thinks a stranger—some one who will have gained her confidence. . . . "

"Impossible."

"Oh! nothing is impossible, citizen," rejoined Chauvelin blandly.

"Do you know a way then?" queried the other with a sneer.

"I think I do. If you will trust me that is——"

"I don't know that I do. Your mind is so intent on those English adventurers, you are like as not to let the *aristos* slip through your fingers."

"Well, citizen," retorted Chauvelin imperturbably, "will you take the risk of conveying the fair Yvonne to the Rat Mort by twelve o'clock to-night? I have very many things to see to, I confess that I should be glad if you will ease me from that responsibility."

"I have already told you that I see no way," retorted Martin-Roget with a snarl.

"Then why not let me act?"

"What are you going to do?"

"For the moment I am going for a walk on the quay and once more will commune with the North-West wind."

"Tshaw!" ejaculated Martin-Roget savagely.

"Nay, citizen," resumed Chauvelin blandly, "the winds of heaven are excellent counsellors. I told you so just now and you agreed with me. They blow away the cobwebs of the mind and clear the brain for serious thinking. You want the Kernogan girl to be arrested inside the Rat Mort and you see no way of conveying her thither save by the use of violence, which for obvious reasons is to be deprecated: Carrier, for equally obvious reasons, will not have her taken to the place by force. On the other hand you admit that the wench would not follow you willingly——Well, citizen, we must find a way out of that impasse, for it is too unimportant an one to stand in the way of our plans: for this I must hold a consultation with the North-West wind."

"I won't allow you to do anything without consulting me."

"Am I likely to do that? To begin with I shall have need of your co-operation and that of the citizeness."

"In that case . . . " muttered Martin-Roget grudgingly. "But remember," he added with a return to his usual self-assured manner, "remember that Yvonne and her father belong to me and not to you. I brought them into Nantes for mine own purposes—not for yours. I will not have my revenge jeopardised so that your schemes may be furthered."

"Who spoke of my schemes, citizen Martin-Roget?" broke in Chauvelin with perfect urbanity. "Surely not I? What am I but an humble tool in the service of the Republic? . . . a tool that has proved useless—a failure, what? My only desire is to help you to the best of my abilities. Your enemies are the enemies of the Republic: my ambition is to help you in destroying them."

For a moment longer Martin-Roget hesitated: he abominated this suggestion of becoming a mere instrument in the hands of this man whom he still would have affected to despise—had he dared. But here came the difficulty: he no longer dared to despise Chauvelin. He felt the strength of the man—the clearness of his intellect, and though he—Martin-Roget—still chose to disregard every warning in connexion with the English spies, he could not wholly divest his mind from the possibility of their presence in Nantes. Carrier's scheme was so magnificent, so satisfying, that the ex-miller's son was ready to humble his pride and set his arrogance aside in order to see it carried through successfully.

So after a moment or two, despite the fact that he positively ached to shut Chauvelin out of the whole business, Martin-Roget gave a grudging assent to his proposal.

"Very well!" he said, "you see to it. So long as it does not interfere with my plans. . . . "

"It can but help them," rejoined Chauvelin suavely. "If you will act as I shall direct I pledge you my word that the wench will walk to the Rat Mort of her free will and at the hour when you want her. What else is there to say?"

"When and where shall we meet again?"

"Within the hour I will return here and explain to you and to the citizeness what I want you to do. We will get the *aristos* inside the Rat Mort, never fear; and after that I think that we may safely leave Carrier to do the rest, what?"

He picked up his hat and wrapped his mantle round him. He took no further heed of Martin-Roget or of Louise, for suddenly he had felt the crackling of crisp paper inside the breast-pocket of his coat and in a moment the spirit of the man had gone a-roaming out of the narrow confines of this squalid abode. It had crossed the English Channel and wandered once more into a brilliantly-lighted ball-room where an exquisitely dressed dandy declaimed inanities and doggrel rhymes for the delectation of a flippant assembly: it heard once more the lazy, drawling speech, the inane, affected laugh, it caught the glance of a pair of lazy, grey eyes fixed mockingly upon him. Chauvelin's thin claw-like hand went back to his pocket: it felt that packet of papers, it closed over it like a vulture's talon does upon a prey. He no longer heard Martin-Roget's obstinate murmurings, he no longer felt himself to be the disgraced, humiliated servant of the State: rather did he feel once more the master, the leader, the successful weaver of an hundred clever intrigues. The enemy who had baffled him so often had chosen once more to throw down the glove of mocking defiance. So be it! The battle would be fought this night—a decisive one—and long live the Republic and the power of the people!

With a curt nod of the head Chauvelin turned on his heel and without waiting for Martin-Roget to follow him, or for Louise to light him on his way, he strode from the room, and out of the house, and had soon disappeared in the darkness in the direction of the quay.

V

Once more free from the encumbering companionship of Martin-Roget, Chauvelin felt free to breathe and to think. He, the obscure and impassive servant of the Republic, the cold-blooded Terrorist who had gone through every phrase of an exciting career without moving a muscle of his grave countenance, felt as if every one of his arteries was on fire. He strode along the quay in the teeth of the north-westerly wind, grateful for the cold blast which lashed his face and cooled his throbbing temples.

The packet of papers inside his coat seemed to sear his breast.

Before turning to go along the quay he paused, hesitating for a moment what he would do. His very humble lodgings were at the far end of the town, and every minute of time was precious. Inside Le Bouffay, where he had a small room allotted to him as a minor representative in Nantes of the Committee of Public Safety, there was the ever present danger of prying eyes.

On the whole—since time was so precious—he decided on returning to Le Bouffay. The concierge and the clerk fortunately let him through without those official delays which he—Chauvelin—was wont to find so galling ever since his disgrace had put a bar against the opening of every door at the bare mention of his name or the display of his tricolour scarf.

He strode rapidly across the hall: the men on guard eyed him with lazy indifference as he passed. Once inside his own sanctum he looked carefully around him; he drew the curtain closer across the window and dragged the table and a chair well away from the range which might be covered by an eye at the keyhole. It was only when he had thoroughly assured himself that no searching eye or inquisitive ear could possibly be watching over him that he at last drew the precious packet of papers from his pocket. He undid the red ribbon which held it together and spread the papers out on the table before him. Then he examined them carefully one by one.

As he did so an exclamation of wrath or of impatience escaped him from time to time, once he laughed—involuntarily—aloud.

The examination of the papers took him some time. When he had finished he gathered them all together again, retied the bit of ribbon round them and slipped the packet back into the pocket of his coat. There was a look of grim determination on his face, even though a bitter sigh escaped his set lips.

"Oh! for the power," he muttered to himself, "which I had a year ago! for the power to deal with mine enemy myself. So you have come to Nantes, my valiant Sir Percy Blakeney?" he added while a short, sardonic laugh escaped his thin, set lips: "and you are determined that I shall know how and why you came! Do you reckon, I wonder, that I have no longer the power to deal with you? Well! . . . "

He sighed again but with more satisfaction this time.

"Well! . . . " he reiterated with obvious complacency. "Unless that oaf Carrier is a bigger fool than I imagine him to be I think I have you this time, my elusive Scarlet Pimpernel."

# Chapter 4: The Net

## I

It was not an easy thing to obtain an audience of the great proconsul at this hour of the night, nor was Chauvelin, the disgraced servant of the Committee of Public Safety, a man to be considered. Carrier, with his love of ostentation and of tyranny, found great delight in keeping his colleagues waiting upon his pleasure, and he knew that he could trust young Jacques Lalouët to be as insolent as any tyrant's flunkey of yore.

"I must speak with the proconsul at once," had been Chauvelin's urgent request of Fleury, the commandant of the great man's bodyguard.

"The proconsul dines at this hour," had been Fleury's curt reply.

"'Tis a matter which concerns the welfare and the safety of the State!"

"The proconsul's health is the concern of the State too, and he dines at this hour and must not be disturbed."

"Commandant Fleury!" urged Chauvelin, "you risk being implicated in a disaster. Danger and disgrace threaten the proconsul and all his adherents. I must speak with citizen Carrier at once."

Fortunately for Chauvelin there were two keys which, when all else failed, were apt to open the doors of Carrier's stronghold: the key of fear and that of cupidity. He tried both and succeeded. He bribed and he threatened: he endured Fleury's brutality and Lalouët's impertinence but he got his way. After an hour's weary waiting and ceaseless parleyings he was once more ushered into the antechamber where he had sat earlier in the day. The doors leading to the inner sanctuary were open. Young Jacques Lalouët stood by them on guard. Carrier, fuming and raging at having been disturbed, vented his spleen and ill-temper on Chauvelin.

"If the news that you bring me is not worth my consideration," he cried savagely, "I'll send you to moulder in Le Bouffay or to drink the waters of the Loire."

Chauvelin silent, self-effaced, allowed the flood of the great man's wrath to spend itself in threats. Then he said quietly:

"Citizen proconsul I have come to tell you that the English spy, who is called the Scarlet Pimpernel, is now in Nantes. There is a reward of twenty thousand francs for his capture and I want your help to lay him by the heels."

Carrier suddenly paused in his ravings. He sank into a chair and a livid hue spread over his face.

"It's not true!" he murmured hoarsely.

"I saw him—not an hour ago. . . . "

"What proof have you?"

"I'll show them to you—but not across this threshold. Let me enter, citizen proconsul, and close your sanctuary doors behind me rather than before. What I have come hither to tell you, can only be said between four walls."

"I'll make you tell me," broke in Carrier in a raucous voice, which excitement and fear caused almost to choke in his throat. "I'll make you . . . curse you for the traitor that you are. . . . Curse you!" he cried more vigorously, "I'll make you speak. Will you shield a spy by your silence, you miserable traitor? If you do I'll send you to rot in the mud of the Loire with other traitors less accursed than yourself."

"If you only knew," was Chauvelin's calm rejoinder to the other's ravings, "how little I care for life. I only live to be even one day with an enemy whom I hate. That enemy is now in Nantes, but I am like a bird of prey whose wings have been clipped. If you do not help me mine enemy will again go free—and death in that case matters little or nothing to me."

For a moment longer Carrier hesitated. Fear had gripped him by the throat. Chauvelin's earnestness seemed to vouch for the truth of his assertion, and if this were so—if those English spies were indeed in Nantes—then his own life was in deadly danger. He—like every one of those bloodthirsty tyrants who had misused the sacred names of Fraternity and of Equality—had learned to dread the machinations of those mysterious Englishmen and of their unconquerable leader. Popular superstition had it that they were spies of the English Government and that they were not only bent on saving traitors from well-merited punishment but that they were hired assassins paid by Mr. Pitt to murder every faithful servant of the Republic. The name of the Scarlet Pimpernel, so significantly uttered by Chauvelin, had turned Carrier's sallow cheeks to a livid hue. Sick with terror now he called Lalouët to him. He clung to the boy with both arms as to the one being in this world whom he trusted.

"What shall we do, Jacques?" he murmured hoarsely, "shall we let him in?"

The boy roughly shook himself free from the embrace of the great proconsul.

"If you want twenty thousand francs," he said with a dry laugh, "I should listen quietly to what citizen Chauvelin has to say."

Terror and rapacity were ranged on one side against inordinate vanity. The thought of twenty thousand francs made Carrier's ugly mouth water. Money was ever scarce these days: also the fear of assassination was a spectre which haunted him at all hours of the day and night. On the other hand he positively worshipped the mystery wherewith he surrounded himself. It had been his boast for some time now that no one save the chosen few had crossed the threshold of his private chamber: and he was miserably afraid not only of Chauvelin's possible evil intentions, but also that this despicable ex-*aristo* and equally despicable failure would boast in the future of an ascendancy over him.

He thought the matter over for fully five minutes, during which there was dead silence in the two rooms—silence only broken by the stertorous breathing of that wretched coward, and the measured ticking of the fine Buhl clock behind him. Chauvelin's pale eyes were fixed upon the darkness, through which he could vaguely discern the uncouth figure of the proconsul, sprawling over his desk. Which way would his passions sway him? Chauvelin as he watched and waited felt that his habitual self-control was perhaps more severely taxed at this moment than it had ever been before. Upon the swaying of those passions, the passions of a man infinitely craven and infinitely base, depended all his—Chauvelin's—hopes of getting even at last with a daring and resourceful foe. Terror and rapacity were the counsellors which ranged themselves on the side of his schemes, but mere vanity and caprice fought a hard battle too.

In the end it was rapacity that gained the victory. An impatient exclamation from young Lalouët roused Carrier from his sombre brooding and hastened on a decision which was destined to have such momentous consequences for the future of both these men.

"Introduce citizen Chauvelin in here, Lalouët," said the proconsul grudgingly. "I will listen to what he has to say."

## II

Chauvelin crossed the threshold of the tyrant's sanctuary, in no way awed by the majesty of that dreaded presence or confused by the air of mystery which hung about the room.

He did not even bestow a glance on the multitudinous objects of art and the priceless furniture which littered the tiger's lair. His pale face remained quite expressionless as he bowed solemnly before Carrier and then took the chair which was indicated to him. Young Lalouët fetched a candelabra from the ante-room and carried it into the audience chamber: then he closed the communicating doors. The candelabra he placed on a console-table immediately behind Carrier's desk and chair, so that the latter's face remained in complete shadow, whilst the light fell full upon Chauvelin.

"Well! what is it?" queried the proconsul roughly. "What is this story of English spies inside Nantes? How did they get here? Who is responsible for keeping such rabble out of our city? Name of a dog, but some one has been careless of duty! and carelessness these days is closely allied to treason."

He talked loudly and volubly—his inordinate terror causing the words to come tumbling, almost incoherently, out of his mouth. Finally he turned on Chauvelin with a snarl like an angry cat:

"And how comes it, citizen," he added savagely, "that you alone here in Nantes are acquainted with the whereabouts of those dangerous spies?"

"I caught sight of them," rejoined Chauvelin calmly, "this afternoon after I left you. I knew we should have them here, the moment citizen Martin-Roget brought the Kernogans into the city. The woman is the wife of one of them."

"Curse that blundering fool Martin-Roget for bringing that rabble about our ears, and those assassins inside our gates."

"Nay! Why should you complain, citizen proconsul," rejoined Chauvelin in his blandest manner. "Surely you are not going to let the English spies escape this time? And if you succeed in laying them by the heels—there where every one else has failed—you will have earned twenty thousand francs and the thanks of the entire Committee of Public Safety."

He paused: and young Lalouët interposed with his impudent laugh:

"Go on, citizen Chauvelin," he said, "if there is twenty thousand francs to be made out of this game, I'll warrant that the proconsul will take a hand in it—eh, Carrier?"

And with the insolent familiarity of a terrier teasing a grizzly he tweaked the great man's ear.

Chauvelin in the meanwhile had drawn the packet of papers from his pocket and untied the ribbon that held them together. He now spread the papers out on the desk.

"What are these?" queried Carrier.

"A few papers," replied Chauvelin, "which one of your Marats, Paul Friche by name, picked up in the wake of the Englishmen. I caught sight of them in the far distance, and sent the Marats after them. For awhile Paul Friche kept on their track, but after that they disappeared in the darkness."

"Who were the senseless louts," growled Carrier, "who allowed a pack of foreign assassins to escape? I'll soon make them disappear . . . in the Loire."

"You will do what you like about that, citizen Carrier," retorted Chauvelin drily; "in the meanwhile you would do well to examine these papers."

He sorted these out, examined them one by one, then passed them across to Carrier. Lalouët, impudent and inquisitive, sat on the corner of the desk, dangling his legs. With scant ceremony he snatched one paper after another out of Carrier's hands and examined them curiously.

"Can you understand all this gibberish?" he asked airily. "Jean Baptiste, my friend, how much English do you know?"

"Not much," replied the proconsul, "but enough to recognise that abominable doggrel rhyme which has gone the round of the Committees of Public Safety throughout the country."

"I know it by heart," rejoined young Lalouët. "I was in Paris once, when citizen Robespierre received a copy of it. Name of a dog!" added the youngster with a coarse laugh, "how he cursed!"

It is doubtful however if citizen Robespierre did on that occasion curse quite so volubly as Carrier did now.

"If I only knew why that *satané* Englishman throws so much calligraphy about," he said, "I would be easier in my mind. Now this senseless rhyme . . . I don't see. . . . "

"Its importance?" broke in Chauvelin quietly. "I dare say not. On the face of it, it appears foolish and childish: but it is intended as a taunt and is really a poor attempt at humour. They are a queer people these English. If you knew them as I do, you would not be surprised to see a man scribbling off a cheap joke before embarking on an enterprise which may cost him his head."

"And this inane rubbish is of that sort," concluded young Lalouët. And in his thin high treble he began reciting:
"We seek him here;
We seek him there!
Those Frenchies seek him everywhere.
Is he in heaven?
Is he in h——ll?
That demmed elusive Pimpernel?"

"Pointless and offensive," he said as he tossed the paper back on the table.

"A cursed *aristo* that Englishman of yours," growled Carrier. "Oh! when I get him. . . . "

He made an expressive gesture which made Lalouët laugh.

"What else have we got in the way of documents, citizen Chauvelin?" he asked.

"There is a letter," replied the latter.

"Read it," commanded Carrier. "Or rather translate it as you read. I don't understand the whole of the gibberish."

And Chauvelin, taking up a sheet of paper which was covered with neat, minute writing, began to read aloud, translating the English into French as he went along:

"'Here we are at last, my dear Tony! Didn't I tell you that we can get in anywhere despite all precautions taken against us!'"

"The impudent devils!" broke in Carrier.

—"'Did you really think that they could keep us out of Nantes while Lady Anthony Dewhurst is a prisoner in their hands?'"

"Who is that?"

"The Kernogan woman. As I told you just now, she is married to an Englishman who is named Dewhurst and who is one of the members of that thrice cursed League."

Then he continued to read:

"'And did you really suppose that they would spot half a dozen English gentlemen in the guise of peat-gatherers, returning at dusk and covered with grime from their work? Not like, friend Tony! Not like! If you happen to meet mine engaging friend M. Chambertin before I have that privilege myself, tell him I pray you, with my regards, that I am looking forward to the pleasure of making a long nose at him once more. Calais, Boulogne, Paris—now Nantes—the scenes of his triumphs multiply exceedingly.'"

"What in the devil's name does all this mean?" queried Carrier with an oath.

"You don't understand it?" rejoined Chauvelin quietly.

"No. I do not."

"Yet I translated quite clearly."

"It is not the language that puzzles me. The contents seem to me such drivel. The man wants secrecy, what? He is supposed to be astute, resourceful, above all mysterious and enigmatic. Yet he writes to his friend—matter of no importance between them, recollections of the past, known to them both—and threats for the future, equally futile and senseless. I cannot reconcile it all. It puzzles me."

"And it would puzzle me," rejoined Chauvelin, while the ghost of a smile curled his thin lips, "did I not know the man. Futile? Senseless, you say? Well, he does futile and senseless things one moment and amazing deeds of personal bravery and of astuteness the next. He is three parts a braggart too. He wanted you, me—all of us to know how he and his followers succeeded in eluding our vigilance and entered our closely-guarded city in the guise of grimy peat-gatherers. Now I come to think of it, it was easy enough for them to do that. Those peat-gatherers who live inside the city boundaries return from their work as the night falls in. Those cursed English adventurers are passing clever at disguise—they are born mountebanks the lot of them. Money and impudence they have in plenty. They could easily borrow or purchase some filthy rags from the cottages on the dunes, then mix with the crowd on its return to the city. I dare say it was cleverly done. That Scarlet Pimpernel is just a clever adventurer and nothing more. So far his marvellous good luck has carried him through. Now we shall see."

Carrier had listened in silence. Something of his colleague's calm had by this time communicated itself to him too. He was no longer raving like an infuriated bull—his terror no longer made a half-cringing, wholly savage brute of him. He was sprawling across the desk

—his arms folded, his deep-set eyes studying closely the well-nigh inscrutable face of Chauvelin. Young Lalouët too had lost something of his impudence. That mysterious spell which seemed to emanate from the elusive personality of the bold English adventurer had been cast over these two callous, bestial natures, humbling their arrogance and making them feel that here was no ordinary situation to be dealt with by smashing, senseless hitting and the spilling of innocent blood. Both felt instinctively too that this man Chauvelin, however wholly he may have failed in the past, was nevertheless still the only man who might grapple successfully with the elusive and adventurous foe.

"Are you assuming, citizen Chauvelin," queried Carrier after awhile, "that this packet of papers was dropped purposely by the Englishman, so that it might get into our hands?"

"There is always such a possibility," replied Chauvelin drily. "With that type of man one must be prepared to meet the unexpected."

"Then go on, citizen Chauvelin. What else is there among those *satané* papers?"

"Nothing further of importance. There is a map of Nantes, and one of the coast and of Le Croisic. There is a cutting from Le Moniteur dated last September, and one from the London Gazette dated three years ago. The Moniteur makes reference to the production of Athalie at the Théâtre Molière, and the London Gazette to the sale of fat cattle at an Agricultural Show. There is a receipted account from a London tailor for two hundred pounds worth of clothes supplied, and one from a Lyons mercer for an hundred francs worth of silk cravats. Then there is the one letter which alone amidst all this rubbish appears to be of any consequence. . . . "

He took up the last paper; his hand was still quite steady.

"Read the letter," said Carrier.

"It is addressed in the English fashion to Lady Anthony Dewhurst," continued Chauvelin slowly, "the Kernogan woman, you know, citizen. It says:

"'Keep up your courage. Your friends are inside the city and on the watch. Try the door of your prison every evening at one hour before midnight. Once you will find it yield. Slip out and creep noiselessly down the stairs. At the bottom a friendly hand will be stretched out to you. Take it with confidence—it will lead you to safety and to freedom. Courage and  secrecy.'"

Lalouët had been looking over his shoulder while he read: now he pointed to the bottom of the letter.

"And there is the device," he said, "we have heard so much about of late—a five-petalled flower drawn in red ink . . . the Scarlet Pimpernel, I presume."

"Aye! the Scarlet Pimpernel," murmured Chauvelin, "as you say! Braggadocio on his part or accident, his letters are certainly in our hands now and will prove—must prove, the tool whereby we can be even with him once and for all."

"And you, citizen Chauvelin," interposed Carrier with a sneer, "are mighty lucky to have me to help you this time. I am not going to be fooled, as Candeille and you were fooled last September, as you were fooled in Calais and Héron in Paris. I shall be seeing this time to the capture of those English adventurers."

"And that capture should not be difficult," added Lalouët with a complacent laugh. "Your famous adventurer's luck hath deserted him this time: an all-powerful proconsul is pitted against him and the loss of his papers hath destroyed the anonymity on which he reckons."

Chauvelin paid no heed to the fatuous remarks.

How little did this flippant young braggart and this coarse-grained bully understand the subtle workings of that same adventurer's brain! He himself—one of the most astute men of the day—found it difficult. Even now—the losing of those letters in the open streets of Nantes—it was part of a plan. Chauvelin could have staked his head on that—a part of a plan for the liberation of Lady Anthony Dewhurst—but what plan?—what plan?

He took up the letter which his colleague had thrown down: he fingered it, handled it, letting the paper crackle through his fingers, as if he expected it to yield up the secret which it contained. The time had come—of that he felt no doubt—when he could at last be even with his enemy. He had endured more bitter humiliation at the hands of this elusive Pimpernel than he would have thought himself capable of bearing a couple of years ago. But the time had come at last—if only he kept his every faculty on the alert, if Fate helped him and his own nerves stood the strain. Above all if this blundering, self-satisfied Carrier could be reckoned on! . . .

There lay the one great source of trouble! He—Chauvelin—had no power: he was disgraced—a failure—a nonentity to be sneered at. He might protest, entreat, wring his hands, weep tears of blood and not one man would stir a finger to help him: this brute who sprawled here across his desk would not lend him half a dozen men to enable him to lay by the heels the most powerful enemy the Government of the Terror had ever known. Chauvelin inwardly ground his teeth with rage at his own impotence, at his own dependence on this clumsy lout, who was at this moment possessed of powers which he himself would give half his life to obtain.

But on the other hand he did possess a power which no one could take from him—the power to use others for the furtherance of his own aims—to efface himself while others danced as puppets to his piping. Carrier had the power: he had spies, Marats, prison-guards at his disposal. He was greedy for the reward, and cupidity and fear would make of him a willing instrument. All that Chauvelin need do was to use that instrument for his own ends. One would be the head to direct, the other—a mere insentient tool.

From this moment onwards every minute, every second and every fraction of a second would be full of portent, full of possibilities. Sir Percy Blakeney was in Nantes with at least three or four members of his League: he was at this very moment taxing every fibre of his resourceful brain in order to devise a means whereby he could rescue his friend's wife from the fate which was awaiting her: to gain this end he would dare everything, risk everything—risk and dare a great deal more than he had ever dared and risked before.

Chauvelin was finding a grim pleasure in reviewing the situation, in envisaging the danger of failure which he knew lay in wait for him, unless he too was able to call to his aid all the astuteness, all the daring, all the resource of his own fertile brain. He studied his colleague's face keenly—that sullen, savage expression in it, the arrogance, the blundering vanity. It was terrible to have to humour and fawn to a creature of that stamp when all one's hopes, all one's future, one's ideals and the welfare of one's country were at stake.

But this additional difficulty only served to whet the man's appetite for action. He drew in a long breath of delight, like a captive who first after many days and months of weary anguish scents freedom and ozone. He straightened out his shoulders. A gleam of triumph and of hope shot out of his keen pale eyes. He studied Carrier and he studied Lalouët and he felt that he could master them both—quietly, diplomatically, with subtle skill that would not alarm the proconsul's rampant self-esteem: and whilst this coarse-fibred brute gloated in anticipatory pleasure over the handling of a few thousand francs, and whilst Martin-Roget dreamed of a clumsy revenge against one woman and one man who had wronged him four years ago, he—Chauvelin— would pursue his work of striking at the enemy of the Revolution—of bringing to his knees the man who spent life and fortune in combating its ideals and in frustrating its aims. The destruction of such a foe was worthy a patriot's ambition.

On the other hand some of Carrier's bullying arrogance had gone. He was terrified to the very depths of his cowardly heart, and for once he was turning away from his favourite Jacques Lalouët and inclined to lean on Chauvelin for advice. Robespierre had been known to tremble at sight of that small scarlet device, how much more had he —Carrier—cause to be afraid. He knew his own limitations and he was terrified of the assassin's dagger. As Marat had perished, so he too might end his days, and the English spies were credited with murderous intentions and superhuman power. In his innermost self Carrier knew that despite countless failures Chauvelin was mentally his superior, and though he never would own to this and at this moment did not attempt to shed his over-bearing manner, he was watching the other keenly and anxiously, ready to follow the guidance of an intellect stronger than his own.

### III

At last Carrier elected to speak.

"And now, citizen Chauvelin," he said, "we know how we stand. We know that the English assassins are in Nantes. The question is how are we going to lay them by the heels."

Chauvelin gave him no direct reply. He was busy collecting his precious papers together and thrusting them back into the pocket of his coat. Then he said quietly:

"It is through the Kernogan woman that we can get hold of him."

"How?"

"Where she is, there will the Englishmen be. They are in Nantes for the sole purpose of getting the woman and her father out of your clutches. . . . "

"Then it will be a fine haul inside the Rat Mort," ejaculated Carrier with a chuckle. "Eh, Jacques, you young scamp? You and I must go and see that, what? You have been complaining that life was getting monotonous. Drownages—Republican marriages! They have all palled in their turn on your jaded appetite. . . . But the capture of the English assassins, eh? . . . of that League of the Scarlet Pimpernel which has even caused citizen Robespierre much uneasiness—that will stir up your sluggish blood, you lazy young vermin! . . . Go on, go on, citizen Chauvelin, I am vastly interested!"

He rubbed his dry, bony hands together and cackled with glee. Chauvelin interposed quietly:

"Inside the Rat Mort, eh, citizen?" he queried.

"Why, yes. Citizen Martin-Roget means to convey the Kernogan woman to the Rat Mort, doesn't he?"

"He does."

"And you say that where the Kernogan woman is there the Englishmen will be. . . . "

"The inference is obvious."

"Which means ten thousand francs from that fool Martin-Roget for having the wench and her father arrested inside the Rat Mort! and twenty thousand for the capture of the English spies. . . . Have you forgotten, citizen Chauvelin," he added with a raucous cry of triumph, "that commandant Fleury has my orders to make a raid on the Rat Mort this night with half a company of my Marats, and to arrest every one whom they find inside?"

"The Kernogan wench is not at the Rat Mort yet," quoth Chauvelin drily, "and you have refused to lend a hand in having her conveyed thither."

"I can't do it, my little Chauvelin," rejoined Carrier, somewhat sobered by this reminder. "I can't do it . . . you understand . . . my Marats taking an *aristo* to a house of ill-fame where presently I have her arrested . . . it won't do . . . it won't do . . . you don't know how I am spied upon just now. . . . It really would not do. . . . I can't be mixed up in that part of the affair. The wench must go to the Rat Mort of her own free will, or the whole plan falls to the ground. . . . That fool Martin-Roget must think of a way . . . it's his affair, after all. He must see to it. . . . Or you can think of a way," he added, assuming the coaxing ways of a tiger-cat; "you are so clever, my little Chauvelin."

"Yes," replied Chauvelin quietly, "I can think of a way. The Kernogan wench shall leave the house of citizeness Adet and walk into the tavern of the Rat Mort of her own free will. Your reputation, citizen Carrier," he added without the slightest apparent trace of a sneer, "your reputation shall be safeguarded in this matter. But supposing that in the interval of going from the one house to the other the English adventurer succeeds in kidnapping her. . . . "

"Pah! is that likely?" quoth Carrier with a shrug of the shoulders.

"Exceedingly likely, citizen; and you would not doubt it if you knew this Scarlet Pimpernel as I do. I have seen him at his nefarious work. I know what he can do. There is nothing that he would not venture . . . there are few ventures in which he does not succeed. He is as strong as an ox, as agile as a cat. He can see in the dark and he can always vanish in a crowd. Here, there and everywhere, you never know where he will appear. He is a past master in the art of disguise and he is a born mountebank. Believe me, citizen, we shall want all the resources of our joint intellects to frustrate the machinations of such a foe."

Carrier mused for a moment in silence.

"H'm!" he said after awhile, and with a sardonic laugh. "You may be right, citizen Chauvelin. You have had experience with the rascal . . . you ought to know him. We won't leave anything to chance—don't be afraid of that. My Marats will be keen on the capture. We'll promise commandant Fleury a thousand francs for himself and another thousand to be distributed among his men if we lay hands on the English assassins to-night. We'll leave nothing to chance," he reiterated with an oath.

"In which case, citizen Carrier, you must on your side agree to two things," rejoined Chauvelin firmly.

"What are they?"

"You must order Commandant Fleury to place himself and half a company of his Marats at my disposal."

"What else?"

"You must allow them to lend a hand if there is an attempt to kidnap the Kernogan wench while she is being conveyed to the Rat Mort. . . . "

Carrier hesitated for a second or two, but only for form's sake: it was his nature whenever he was forced to yield to do so grudgingly.

"Very well!" he said at last. "I'll order Fleury to be on the watch and to interfere if there is any street-brawling outside or near the Rat Mort. Will that suit you?"

"Perfectly. I shall be on the watch too—somewhere close by. . . . I'll warn commandant Fleury if I suspect that the English are making ready for a coup outside the tavern. Personally I think it unlikely—because the duc de Kernogan will be inside the Rat Mort all the time, and he too will be the object of the Englishmen's attacks on his behalf. Citizen Martin-Roget too has about a score or so of his friends posted outside his sister's house: they are lads from his village who hate the Kernogans as much as he does himself. Still! I shall feel easier in my mind now that I am certain of commandant Fleury's co-operation."

"Then it seems to me that we have arranged everything satisfactorily, what?"

"Everything, except the exact moment when Commandant Fleury shall advance with his men to the door of the tavern and demand admittance in the name of the Republic."

"Yes, he will have to make quite sure that the whole of our quarry is inside the net, eh? . . . before he draws the strings . . . or all our pretty plans fall to nought."

"As you say," rejoined Chauvelin, "we must make sure. Supposing therefore that we get the wench safely into the tavern, that we have her there with her father, what we shall want will be some one in observation—some one who can help us to draw our birds into the snare just when we are ready for them. Now there is a man whom I have in my mind: he hath name Paul Friche and is one of your Marats —a surly, ill-conditioned giant . . . he was on guard outside Le Bouffay this afternoon. . . . I spoke to him . . . he would suit our purpose admirably."

"What do you want him to do?"

"Only to make himself look as like a Nantese cut-throat as he can. . . . "

"He looks like one already," broke in Jacques Lalouët with a laugh.

"So much the better. He'll excite no suspicion in that case in the minds of the frequenters of the Rat Mort. Then I'll instruct him to start a brawl—a fracas—soon after the arrival of the Kernogan wench. The row will inevitably draw the English adventurers hot-haste to the spot, either in the hope of getting the Kernogans away during the mêlée or with a view to protecting them. As soon as they have appeared upon the scene, the half company of the Marats will descend on the house and arrest every one inside it."

"It all sounds remarkably simple," rejoined Carrier, and with a leer of satisfaction he turned to Jacques Lalouët.

"What think you of it, citizen?" he asked.

"That it sounds so remarkably simple," replied young Lalouët, "that personally I should be half afraid. . . . "

"Of what?" queried Chauvelin blandly.

"If you fail, citizen Chauvelin. . . . "

"Impossible!"

"If the Englishmen do not appear?"

"Even so the citizen proconsul will have lost nothing. He will merely have failed to gain the twenty thousand francs. But the Kernogans will still be in his power and citizen Martin-Roget's ten thousand francs are in any case assured."

"Friend Jean-Baptiste," concluded Lalouët with his habitual insolent familiarity, "you had better do what citizen Chauvelin wants. Ten thousand francs are good . . . and thirty better still. Our privy purse has been empty far too long, and I for one would like the handling of a few brisk notes."

"It will only be twenty-eight, citizen Lalouët," interposed Chauvelin blandly, "for commandant Fleury will want one thousand francs and his men another thousand to stimulate their zeal. Still! I imagine that these hard times twenty-eight thousand francs are worth fighting for."

"You seem to be fighting and planning and scheming for nothing, citizen Chauvelin," retorted young Lalouët with a sneer. "What are you going to gain, I should like to know, by the capture of that dare-devil Englishman?"

"Oh!" replied Chauvelin suavely, "I shall gain the citizen proconsul's regard, I hope—and yours too, citizen Lalouët. I want nothing more except the success of my plan."

Young Lalouët jumped down to his feet. He shrugged his shoulders and through his fine eyes shot a glance of mockery and scorn on the thin, shrunken figure of the Terrorist.

"How you do hate that Englishman, citizen Chauvelin," he said with a light laugh.

## IV

Carrier having fully realised that he in any case stood to make a vast sum of money out of the capture of the band of English spies, gave his support generously to Chauvelin's scheme. Fleury, summoned into his presence, was ordered to place himself and half a company of Marats at the disposal of citizen Chauvelin. He demurred and growled like a bear with a sore head at being placed under the orders of a civilian, but it was not easy to run counter to the proconsul's will. A good deal of swearing, one or two overt threats and the citizen commandant was reduced to submission.

The promise of a thousand francs, when the reward for the capture of the English spies was paid out by a grateful Government, overcame his last objections.

"I think you should rid yourself of that obstinate oaf," was young Lalouët's cynical comment, when Fleury had finally left the audience chamber; "he is too argumentative for my taste."

Chauvelin smiled quietly to himself. He cared little what became of every one of these Nantese louts once his great object had been attained.

"I need not trouble you further, citizen Carrier," he said as he finally rose to take his leave. "I shall have my hands full until I myself lay that meddlesome Englishman bound and gagged at your feet."

The phrase delighted Carrier's insensate vanity. He was overgracious to Chauvelin now.

"You shall do that at the Rat Mort, citizen Chauvelin," he said with marked affability, "and I myself will commend you for your zeal to the Committee of Public Safety."

"Always supposing," interposed Jacques Lalouët with his cynical laugh, "that citizen Chauvelin does not let the whole rabble slip through his fingers."

"If I do," concluded Chauvelin drily, "you may drag the Loire for my body to-morrow."

"Oh!" laughed Carrier, "we won't trouble to do that. *Au revoir*, citizen Chauvelin," he added with one of his grandiloquent gestures of dismissal, "I wish you luck at the Rat Mort to-night."

Jacques Lalouët ushered Chauvelin out. When he was finally left standing alone at the head of the stairs and young Lalouët's footsteps had ceased to resound across the floors of the rooms beyond, he remained quite still for awhile, his eyes fixed into vacancy, his face set and expressionless; and through his lips there came a long-drawn-out sigh of intense satisfaction.

"And now, my fine Scarlet Pimpernel," he murmured softly, "once more à nous deux."

Then he ran swiftly down the stairs and a moment later was once more speeding toward Le Bouffay.

# CHAPTER 5: THE MESSAGE OF HOPE

## I

After Martin-Roget and Chauvelin had left her, Yvonne had sat for a long time motionless, almost unconscious. It seemed as if gradually, hour by hour, minute by minute, her every feeling of courage and of hope were deserting her. Three days now she had been separated from her father—three days she had been under the constant supervision of a woman who had not a single thought of compassion or of mercy for the "aristocrat" whom she hated so bitterly.

At night, curled up on a small bundle of dank straw Yvonne had made vain efforts to snatch a little sleep. Ever since the day when she had been ruthlessly torn away from the protection of her dear milor, she had persistently clung to the belief that he would find the means to come to her, to wrest her from the cruel fate which her pitiless enemies had devised for her. She had clung to that hope throughout that dreary journey from dear England to this abominable city. She had clung to it even whilst her father knelt at her feet in an agony of remorse. She had clung to hope while Martin-Roget alternately coaxed and terrorised her, while her father was dragged away from her, while she endured untold misery, starvation, humiliation at the hands of Louise Adet: but now—quite unaccountably—that hope seemed suddenly to have fled from her, leaving her lonely and inexpressibly desolate. That small, shrunken figure which, wrapped in a dark mantle, had stood in the corner of the room watching her like a serpent watches its prey, had seemed like the forerunner of the fate with which Martin-Roget, gloating over her helplessness, had already threatened her.

She knew, of course, that neither from him, nor from the callous brute who governed Nantes, could she expect the slightest justice or mercy. She had been brought here by Martin-Roget not only to die, but to suffer grievously at his hands in return for a crime for which she personally was in no way responsible. To hope for mercy from him at the eleventh hour were worse than futile. Her already overburdened heart ached at thought of her father: he suffered all that she suffered, and in addition he must be tortured with anxiety for her and with remorse. Sometimes she was afraid that under the stress of desperate soul-agony he might perhaps have been led to suicide. She knew nothing of what had happened to him, where he was, nor whether privations and lack of food or sleep, together with Martin-Roget's threats, had by now weakened his morale and turned his pride into humiliating submission.

## II

A distant tower-clock struck the evening hours one after the other. Yvonne for the past three days had only been vaguely conscious of time. Martin-Roget had spoken of a few hours' respite only, of the proconsul's desire to be soon rid of her. Well! this meant no doubt that the morrow would see the end of it all—the end of her life which such a brief while ago seemed so full of delight, of love and of happiness.

The end of her life! She had hardly begun to live and her dear milor had whispered to her such sweet promises of endless vistas of bliss.

Yvonne shivered beneath her thin gown. The north-westerly blast came in cruel gusts through the unglazed window and a vague instinct of self-preservation caused Yvonne to seek shelter in the one corner of the room where the icy draught did not penetrate quite so freely.

Eight, nine and ten struck from the tower-clock far away: she heard these sounds as in a dream. Tired, cold and hungry her vitality at that moment was at its lowest ebb—and, with her back resting against the wall she fell presently into a torpor-like sleep.

Suddenly something roused her, and in an instant she sat up— wide-awake and wide-eyed, every one of her senses conscious and on the alert. Something had roused her—at first she could not say what it was—or remember. Then presently individual sounds detached themselves from the buzzing in her ears. Hitherto the house had always been so still; except on the isolated occasions when Martin-Roget had come to visit her and his heavy tread had caused every loose board in the tumble-down house to creak, it was only Louise Adet's shuffling footsteps which had roused the dormant echoes, when she crept upstairs either to her own room, or to throw a piece of stale bread to her prisoner.

But now—it was neither Martin-Roget's heavy footfall nor the shuffling gait of Louise Adet which had roused Yvonne from her trance-like sleep. It was a gentle, soft, creeping step which was slowly, cautiously mounting the stairs. Yvonne crouching against the wall could count every tread—now and then a board creaked—now and then the footsteps halted.

Yvonne, wide-eyed, her heart stirred by a nameless terror was watching the door.

The piece of tallow-candle flickered in the draught. Its feeble light just touched the remote corner of the room. And Yvonne heard those soft, creeping footsteps as they reached the landing and came to a halt outside the door.

Every drop of blood in her seemed to be frozen by terror: her knees shook: her heart almost stopped its beating.

Under the door something small and white had just been introduced—a scrap of paper; and there it remained—white against the darkness of the unwashed boards—a mysterious message left here by an unknown hand, whilst the unknown footsteps softly crept down the stairs again.

For awhile longer Yvonne remained as she was—cowering against the wall—like a timid little animal, fearful lest that innocent-looking object hid some unthought-of danger. Then at last she gathered courage. Trembling with excitement she raised herself to her knees and then on hands and knees—for she was very weak and faint—she crawled up to that mysterious piece of paper and picked it up.

Her trembling hand closed over it. With wide staring terror-filled eyes she looked all round the narrow room, ere she dared cast one more glance on that mysterious scrap of paper. Then she struggled to her feet and tottered up to the table. She sat down and with fingers numbed with cold she smoothed out the paper and held it close to the light, trying to read what was written on it.

Her sight was blurred. She had to pull herself resolutely together, for suddenly she felt ashamed of her weakness and her overwhelming terror yielded to feverish excitement.

The scrap of paper contained a message—a message addressed to her in that name of which she was so proud—the name which she thought she would never be allowed to bear again: Lady Anthony Dewhurst. She reiterated the words several times, her lips clinging lovingly to them—and just below them there was a small device, drawn in red ink . . . a tiny flower with five petals. . . .
Yvonne frowned and murmured, vaguely puzzled—no longer frightened now: "A flower . . . drawn in red . . . what can it mean?"

And as a vague memory struggled for expression in her troubled mind she added half aloud: "Oh! if it should be . . . !"

But now suddenly all her fears fell away from her. Hope was once more knocking at the gates of her heart—vague memories had taken definite shape . . . the mysterious letter . . . the message of hope . . . the red flower . . . all were gaining significance. She stooped low to read the letter by the feeble light of the flickering candle. She read it through with her eyes first—then with her lips in a soft murmur, while her mind gradually took in all that it meant for her.

"Keep up your courage. Your friends are inside the city and on the watch. Try the door of your prison every evening at one hour before midnight. Once you will find it yield. Slip out and creep noiselessly down the stairs. At the bottom a friendly hand will be stretched out for you. Take it with confidence—it will lead you to safety and to freedom. Courage and secrecy."

When she had finished reading, her eyes were swimming in tears. There was no longer any doubt in her mind about the message

now, for her dear milor had so often spoken to her about the brave
Scarlet Pimpernel who had risked his precious life many a time ere this,
in order to render service to the innocent and the oppressed. And now,
of a surety, this message came from him: from her dear milor and from
his gallant chief. There was the small device—the little red flower which
had so often brought hope to despairing hearts. And it was more than
hope that it brought to Yvonne. It brought certitude and happiness, and
a sweet, tender remorse that she should ever have doubted. She ought
to have known all along that everything would be for the best: she had
no right ever to have given way to despair. In her heart she prayed for
forgiveness from her dear absent milor.

How could she ever doubt him? Was it likely that he would
abandon her?—he and that brave friend of his whose powers were
indeed magical. Why! she ought to have done her best to keep up her
physical as well as her mental faculties—who knows? But perhaps
physical strength might be of inestimable value both to herself and to
her gallant rescuers presently.

She took up the stale brown bread and ate it resolutely. She
drank some water and then stamped round the room to get some
warmth into her limbs.

A distant clock had struck ten awhile ago—and if possible she
ought to get an hour's rest before the time came for her to be strong
and to act: so she shook up her meagre straw *paillasse* and lay down,
determined if possible to get a little sleep—for indeed she felt that that
was just what her dear milor would have wished her to do.

Thus time went by—waking or dreaming, Yvonne could never
afterwards have said in what state she waited during that one long hour
which separated her from the great, blissful moment. The bit of candle
burnt low and presently died out. After that Yvonne remained quite
still upon the straw, in total darkness: no light came in through the tiny
window, only the cold north-westerly wind blew in in gusts. But of a
surety the prisoner who was within sight of freedom felt neither cold
nor fatigue now.

The tower-clock in the distance struck the quarters with dreary
monotony.

### III

The last stroke of eleven ceased to vibrate through the stillness
of the winter's night.

Yvonne roused herself from the torpor-like state into which she
had fallen. She tried to struggle to her feet, but intensity of excitement
had caused a strange numbness to invade her limbs. She could hardly
move. A second or two ago it had seemed to her that she heard a gentle
scraping noise at the door—a drawing of bolts—the grating of a key in

the lock—then again, soft, shuffling footsteps that came and went and that were not those of Louise Adet.

At last Yvonne contrived to stand on her feet; but she had to close her eyes and to remain quite still for awhile after that, for her ears were buzzing and her head swimming: she thought that she must fall if she moved and mayhap lose consciousness.

But this state of weakness only lasted a few seconds: the next she had groped her way to the door and her hand had found the iron latch. It yielded. Then she waited, calling up all her strength—for the hour had come wherein she must not only think and act for herself, but think of every possibility which might occur, and act as she imagined her dear lord would require it of her.

She pressed the clumsy iron latch further: it yielded again, and anon she was able to push open the door.

Excited yet confident she tip-toed out of the room. The darkness—like unto pitch—was terribly disconcerting. With the exception of her narrow prison Yvonne had only once seen the interior of the house and that was when, half fainting, she had been dragged across its threshold and up the stairs. She had therefore only a very vague idea as to where the stairs lay and how she was to get about without stumbling.

Slowly and cautiously she crept a few paces forward, then she turned and carefully closed the door behind her. There was not a sound inside the house: everything was silent around her: neither footfall nor whisperings reached her straining ears. She felt about her with her hands, she crouched down on her knees: anon she discovered the head of the stairs.

Then suddenly she drew back, like a frightened hare conscious of danger. All the blood rushed back to her heart, making it beat so violently that she once more felt sick and faint. A sound—gentle as a breath—had broken that absolute and dead silence which up to now had given her confidence. She felt suddenly that she was no longer alone in the darkness—that somewhere close by there was some one—friend or foe—who was lying in watch for her—that somewhere in the darkness something moved and breathed.

The crackling of the paper inside her kerchief served to remind her that her dear milor was on the watch and that the blessed message had spoken of a friendly hand which would be stretched out to her and which she was enjoined to take with confidence. Reassured she crept on again, and anon a softly murmured: "Hush—sh!—sh!—" reached her ear. It seemed to come from down below—not very far—and Yvonne, having once more located the head of the stairs with her hands, began slowly to creep downstairs—softly as a mouse—step by step—but every time that a board creaked she paused, terrified, listening for Louise Adet's heavy footstep, for a sound that would mean the near approach of danger.

"Hush—sh—sh" came again as a gentle murmur from below and the something that moved and breathed in the darkness seemed to draw nearer to Yvonne.

A few more seconds of soul-racking suspense, a few more steps down the creaking stairs and she felt a strong hand laid upon her wrist and heard a muffled voice whisper in English:

"All is well! Trust me! Follow me!"

She did not recognise the voice, even though there was something vaguely familiar in its intonation. Yvonne did not pause to conjecture: she had been made happy by the very sound of the language which stood to her for every word of love she had ever heard: it restored her courage and her confidence in their fullest measure.

Obeying the whispered command, Yvonne was content now to follow her mysterious guide who had hold of her hand. The stairs were steep and winding—at a turn she perceived a feeble light at their foot down below. Up against this feeble light the form of her guide was silhouetted in a broad, dark mass. Yvonne could see nothing of him beyond the square outline of his shoulders and that of his sugar-loaf hat. Her mind now was thrilled with excitement and her fingers closed almost convulsively round his hand. He led her across Louise Adet's back kitchen. It was from here that the feeble light came—from a small oil lamp which stood on the centre table. It helped to guide Yvonne and her mysterious friend to the bottom of the stairs, then across the kitchen to the front door, where again complete darkness reigned. But soon Yvonne—who was following blindly whithersoever she was led— heard the click of a latch and the grating of a door upon its hinges: a cold current of air caught her straight in the face. She could see nothing, for it seemed to be as dark out of doors as in: but she had the sensation of that open door, of a threshold to cross, of freedom and happiness beckoning to her straight out of the gloom. Within the next second or two she would be out of this terrible place, its squalid and dank walls would be behind her. On ahead in that thrice welcome obscurity her dear milor and his powerful friend were beckoning to her to come boldly on—their protecting arms were already stretched out for her; it seemed to her excited fancy as if the cold night-wind brought to her ears the echo of their endearing words.

She filled her lungs with the keen winter air: hope, happiness, excitement thrilled her every nerve.

"A short walk, my lady," whispered the guide, still speaking in English; "you are not cold?"

"No, no, I am not cold," she whispered in reply. "I am conscious of nothing save that I am free."

"And you are not afraid?"

"Indeed, indeed I am not afraid," she murmured fervently.

"May God reward you, sir, for what you do."

Again there had been that certain something—vaguely familiar —in the way the man spoke which for the moment piqued Yvonne's curiosity. She did not, of a truth, know English well enough to detect the very obvious foreign intonation; she only felt that sometime in the dim and happy past she had heard this man speak. But even this vague sense of puzzlement she dismissed very quickly from her mind. Was she not taking everything on trust? Indeed hope and confidence had a very firm hold on her at last.

# Chapter 6: The Rat Mort

The guide had stepped out of the house into the street, Yvonne following closely on his heels. The night was very dark and the narrow little Carrefour de la Poissonnerie very sparsely lighted. Somewhere overhead on the right, something groaned and creaked persistently in the wind. A little further on a street lanthorn was swinging aloft, throwing a small circle of dim, yellowish light on the unpaved street below. By its fitful glimmer Yvonne could vaguely perceive the tall figure of her guide as he stepped out with noiseless yet firm tread, his shoulder brushing against the side of the nearest house as he kept closely within the shadow of its high wall. The sight of his broad back thrilled her. She had fallen to imagining whether this was not perchance that gallant and all-powerful Scarlet Pimpernel himself: the mysterious friend of whom her dear milor so often spoke with an admiration that was akin to worship. He too was probably tall and broad—for English gentlemen were usually built that way; and Yvonne's over-excited mind went galloping on the wings of fancy, and in her heart she felt that she was glad that she had suffered so much, and then lived through such a glorious moment as this.

Now from the narrow unpaved yard in front of the house the guide turned sharply to the right. Yvonne could only distinguish outlines. The streets of Nantes were familiar to her, and she knew pretty well where she was. The lanthorn inside the clock tower of Le Bouffay guided her—it was now on her right—the house wherein she had been kept a prisoner these past three days was built against the walls of the great prison house. She knew that she was in the Carrefour de la Poissonnerie.

She felt neither fatigue nor cold, for she was wildly excited. The keen north-westerly wind searched all the weak places in her worn clothing and her thin shoes were wet through. But her courage up to this point had never once forsaken her. Hope and the feeling of freedom gave her marvellous strength, and when her guide paused a moment ere he turned the angle of the high wall and whispered hurriedly: "You have courage, my lady?" she was able to answer serenely: "In plenty, sir."

She tried to peer into the darkness in order to realise whither she was being led. The guide had come to a halt in front of the house which was next to that of Louise Adet: it projected several feet in front of the latter: the thing that had creaked so weirdly in the wind turned out to be a painted sign, which swung out from an iron bracket fixed into the wall. Yvonne could not read the writing on the sign, but she noticed that just above it there was a small window dimly lighted from within.

What sort of a house it was Yvonne could not, of course, see. The frontage was dark save for narrow streaks of light which peeped through the interstices of the door and through the chinks of ill-fastened shutters on either side. Not a sound came from within, but now that the guide had come to a halt it seemed to Yvonne—whose nerves and senses had become preternaturally acute—that the whole air around her was filled with muffled sounds, and when she stood still and strained her ears to listen she was conscious right through the inky blackness of vague forms—shapeless and silent—that glided past her in the gloom.

## II

"Your friends will meet you here," the guide whispered as he pointed to the door of the house in front of him. "The door is on the latch. Push it open and walk in boldly. Then gather up all your courage, for you will find yourself in the company of poor people, whose manners are somewhat rougher than those to which you have been accustomed. But though the people are uncouth, you will find them kind. Above all you will find that they will pay no heed to you. So I entreat you do not be afraid. Your friends would have arranged for a more refined place wherein to come and find you, but as you may well imagine they had no choice."

"I quite understand, sir," said Yvonne quietly, "and I am not afraid."

"Ah! that's brave!" he rejoined. "Then do as I tell you. I give you my word that inside that house you will be perfectly safe until such time as your friends are able to get to you. You may have to wait an hour, or even two; you must have patience. Find a quiet place in one of the comers of the room and sit there quietly, taking no notice of what goes on around you. You will be quite safe, and the arrival of your friends is only a question of time."

"My friends, sir?" she said earnestly, and her voice shook slightly as she spoke, "are you not one of the most devoted friends I can ever hope to have? I cannot find the words now wherewith to thank you, but. . . . "

"I pray you do not thank me," he broke in gruffly, "and do not waste time in parleying. The open street is none too safe a place for you just now. The house is."

His hand was on the latch and he was about to push open the door, when Yvonne stopped him with a word.

"My father?" she whispered with passionate entreaty. "Will you help him too?"

"M. le duc de Kernogan is as safe as you are, my lady," he replied. "He will join you anon. I pray you have no fears for him. Your friends are caring for him in the same way as they care for you."

"Then I shall see him . . . soon?"

"Very soon. And in the meanwhile," he added, "I pray you to sit quite still and to wait events . . . despite anything you may see or hear. Your father's safety and your own—not to speak of that of your friends —hangs on your quiescence, your silence, your obedience."

"I will remember, sir," rejoined Yvonne quietly. "I in my turn entreat you to have no fears for me."

Even while she said this, the man pushed the door open.

## III

Yvonne had meant to be brave. Above all she had meant to be obedient. But even so, she could not help recoiling at sight of the place where she had just been told she must wait patiently and silently for an hour, or even two.

The room into which her guide now gently urged her forward was large and low, only dimly lighted by an oil-lamp which hung from the ceiling and emitted a thin stream of black smoke and evil smell. Such air as there was, was foul and reeked of the fumes of alcohol and charcoal, of the smoking lamp and of rancid grease. The walls had no doubt been whitewashed once, now they were of a dull greyish tint, with here and there hideous stains of red or the marks of a set of greasy fingers. The plaster was hanging in strips and lumps from the ceiling; it had fallen away in patches from the walls where it displayed the skeleton laths beneath. There were two doors in the wall immediately facing the front entrance, and on each side of the latter there was a small window, both insecurely shuttered. To Yvonne the whole place appeared unspeakably squalid and noisome. Even as she entered her ears caught the sound of hideous muttered blasphemy, followed by quickly suppressed hoarse and mirthless laughter and the piteous cry of an infant at the breast.

There were perhaps sixteen to twenty people in the room— amongst them a goodly number of women, some of whom had tiny, miserable atoms of humanity clinging to their ragged skirts. A group of men in tattered shirts, bare shins and sabots stood in the centre of the room and had apparently been in conclave when the entrance of Yvonne and her guide caused them to turn quickly to the door and to scan the new-comers with a furtive, suspicious look which would have been pathetic had it not been so full of evil intent. The muttered blasphemy had come from this group; one or two of the men spat upon the ground in the direction of the door, where Yvonne instinctively had remained rooted to the spot.

As for the women, they only betrayed their sex by the ragged clothes which they wore: there was not a face here which had on it a single line of softness or of gentleness: they might have been old women or young: their hair was of a uniform, nondescript colour, lank and unkempt, hanging in thin strands over their brows; their eyes were sunken, their cheeks either flaccid or haggard—there was no individuality amongst them—just one uniform sisterhood of wretchedness which had already gone hand in hand with crime.

Across one angle of the room there was a high wooden counter like a bar, on which stood a number of jugs and bottles, some chunks of bread and pieces of cheese, and a collection of pewter mugs. An old man and a fat, coarse-featured, middle-aged woman stood behind it and dispensed various noxious-looking liquors. Above their heads upon the grimy, tumble-down wall the Republican device "Liberté! Egalité! Fraternité!" was scrawled in charcoal in huge characters, and below it was scribbled the hideous doggrel which an impious mind had fashioned last autumn on the subject of the martyred Queen.

## IV

Yvonne had closed her eyes for a moment as she entered; now she turned appealingly toward her guide.

"Must it be in here?" she asked.

"I am afraid it must," he replied with a sigh. "You told me that you would be brave."

She pulled herself together resolutely. "I will be brave," she said quietly.

"Ah! that's better," he rejoined. "I give you my word that you will be absolutely safe in here until such time as your friends can get to you. I entreat you to gather up your courage. I assure you that these wretched people are not unkind: misery—not unlike that which you yourself have endured—has made them what they are. No doubt we should have arranged for a better place for you wherein to await your friends if we had the choice. But you will understand that your safety and our own had to be our paramount consideration, and we had no choice."

"I quite understand, sir," said Yvonne valiantly, "and am already ashamed of my fears."

And without another word of protest she stepped boldly into the room.

For a moment or two the guide remained standing on the threshold, watching Yvonne's progress. She had already perceived an empty bench in the furthest angle of the room, up against the door opposite, where she hoped or believed that she could remain

452    BARONESS EMMUSKA ORCZY

unmolested while she waited patiently and in silence as she had been ordered to do. She skirted the groups of men in the centre of the room as she went, but even so she felt more than she heard that muttered insults accompanied the furtive and glowering looks wherewith she was regarded. More than one wretch spat upon her skirts on the way.

But now she was in no sense frightened, only wildly excited; even her feeling of horror she contrived to conquer. The knowledge that her own attitude, and above all her obedience, would help her gallant rescuers in their work gave her enduring strength. She felt quite confident that within an hour or two she would be in the arms of her dear milor who had risked his life in order to come to her. It was indeed well worth while to have suffered as she had done, to endure all that she might yet have to endure, for the sake of the happiness which was in store for her.

She turned to give a last look at her guide—a look which was intended to reassure him completely as to her courage and her obedience: but already he had gone and had closed the door behind him, and quite against her will the sudden sense of loneliness and helplessness clutched at her heart with a grip that made it ache. She wished that she had succeeded in catching sight of the face of so valiant a friend: the fact that she was safely out of Louise Adet's vengeful clutches was due to the man who had just disappeared behind that door. It would be thanks to him presently if she saw her father again. Yvonne felt more convinced than ever that he was the Scarlet Pimpernel—milor's friend—who kept his valiant personality a mystery, even to those who owed their lives to him. She had seen the outline of his broad figure, she had felt the touch of his hand. Would she recognise these again when she met him in England in the happy days that were to come? In any case she thought that she would recognise the voice and the manner of speaking, so unlike that of any English gentleman she had known.

V

The man who had so mysteriously led Yvonne de Kernogan from the house of Louise Adet to the Rat Mort, turned away from the door of the tavern as soon as it had closed on the young girl, and started to go back the way he came.

At the angle formed by the high wall of the tavern he paused; a moving form had detached itself from the surrounding gloom and hailed him with a cautious whisper.

"Hist! citizen Martin-Roget, is that you?"

"Yes."

"Everything just as we anticipated?"

"Everything."

"And the wench safely inside?"

"Quite safely."

The other gave a low cackle, which might have been intended for a laugh.

"The simplest means," he said, "are always the best."

"She never suspected me. It was all perfectly simple. You are a magician, citizen Chauvelin," added Martin-Roget grudgingly. "I never would have thought of such a clever ruse."

"You see," rejoined Chauvelin drily, "I graduated in the school of a master of all ruses—a master of daring and a past master in the art of mimicry. And hope was our great ally—the hope that never forsakes a prisoner—that of getting free. Your fair Yvonne had boundless faith in the power of her English friends, therefore she fell into our trap like a bird."

"And like a bird she shall struggle in vain after this," said Martin-Roget slowly. "Oh! that I could hasten the flight of time—the next few minutes will hang on me like hours. And I wish too it were not so bitterly cold," he added with a curse; "this north-westerly wind has got into my bones."

"On to your nerves, I imagine, citizen," retorted Chauvelin with a laugh; "for my part I feel as warm and comfortable as on a lovely day in June."

"Hark! Who goes there?" broke in the other man abruptly, as a solitary moving form detached itself from the surrounding inky blackness and the sound of measured footsteps broke the silence of the night.

"Quite in order, citizen!" was the prompt reply.

The shadowy form came a step or two further forward.

"Is it you, citizen Fleury?" queried Chauvelin.

"Himself, citizen," replied the other.

The men had spoken in a whisper. Fleury now placed his hand on Chauvelin's arm.

"We had best not stand so close to the tavern," he said, "the night hawks are already about and we don't want to scare them."

He led the others up the yard, then into a very narrow passage which lay between Louise Adet's house and the Rat Mort and was bordered by the high walls of the houses on either side.

"This is a blind alley," he whispered. "We have the wall of Le Bouffay in front of us: the wall of the Rat Mort is on one side and the house of the citizeness Adet on the other. We can talk here undisturbed."

Overhead there was a tiny window dimly lighted from within. Chauvelin pointed up to it.

"What is that?" he asked.

"An aperture too small for any human being to pass through," replied Fleury drily. "It gives on a small landing at the foot of the stairs. I told Friche to try and manœuvre so that the wench and her father are pushed in there out of the way while the worst of the fracas is going on. That was your suggestion, citizen Chauvelin."

"It was. I was afraid the two *aristos* might get spirited away while your men were tackling the crowd in the tap-room. I wanted them put away in a safe place."

"The staircase is safe enough," rejoined Fleury; "it has no egress save that on the tap-room and only leads to the upper story and the attic. The house has no back entrance—it is built against the wall of Le Bouffay."

"And what about your Marats, citizen commandant?"

"Oh! I have them all along the street—entirely under cover but closely on the watch—half a company and all keen after the game. The thousand francs you promised them has stimulated their zeal most marvellously, and as soon as Paul Friche in there has whipped up the tempers of the frequenters of the Rat Mort, we shall be ready to rush the place and I assure you, citizen Chauvelin, that only a disembodied ghost—if there be one in the place—will succeed in evading arrest."

"Is Paul Friche already at his post then?"

"And at work—or I'm much mistaken," replied Fleury as he suddenly gripped Chauvelin by the arm.

For just at this moment the silence of the winter's night was broken by loud cries which came from the interior of the Rat Mort— voices were raised to hoarse and raucous cries—men and women all appeared to be shrieking together, and presently there was a loud crash as of overturned furniture and broken glass.

"A few minutes longer, citizen Fleury," said Chauvelin, as the commandant of the Marats turned on his heel and started to go back to the Carrefour de la Poissonnerie.

"Oh yes!" whispered the latter, "we'll wait awhile longer to give the Englishmen time to arrive on the scene. The coast is clear for them —my Marats are hidden from sight behind the doorways and shop-fronts of the houses opposite. In about three minutes from now I'll send them forward."

"And good luck to your hunting, citizen," whispered Chauvelin in response.

Fleury very quickly disappeared in the darkness and the other two men followed in his wake. They hugged the wall of the Rat Mort as they went along and its shadow enveloped them completely: their shoes made no sound on the unpaved ground. Chauvelin's nostrils quivered as he drew the keen, cold air into his lungs and faced the north-westerly blast which at this moment also lashed the face of his enemy. His keen eyes tried to pierce the gloom, his ears were strained to hear that merry peal of laughter which in the unforgettable past had been wont to proclaim the presence of the reckless adventurer. He knew—he felt—as certainly as he felt the air which he breathed, that the man whom he hated beyond everything on earth was somewhere close by, wrapped in the murkiness of the night—thinking, planning, intriguing, pitting his sharp wits, his indomitable pluck, his impudent dare-devilry against the sure and patient trap which had been set for him.

Half a company of Marats in front—the walls of Le Bouffay in the rear! Chauvelin rubbed his thin hands together!

"You are not a disembodied ghost, my fine Scarlet Pimpernel," he murmured, "and this time I really think——"

# CHAPTER 7: THE FRACAS IN THE TAVERN

Yvonne had settled herself in a corner of the tap-room on a bench and had tried to lose consciousness of her surroundings.

It was not easy! Glances charged with rancour were levelled at her dainty appearance—dainty and refined despite the look of starvation and of weariness on her face and the miserable state of her clothing—and not a few muttered insults waited on those glances.

As soon as she was seated Yvonne noticed that the old man and the coarse, fat woman behind the bar started an animated conversation together, of which she was very obviously the object, for the two heads —the lean and the round—were jerked more than once in her direction. Presently the man—it was George Lemoine, the proprietor of the Rat Mort—came up to where she was sitting: his lank figure was bent so that his lean back formed the best part of an arc, and an expression of mock deference further distorted his ugly face.

He came up quite close to Yvonne and she found it passing difficult not to draw away from him, for the leer on his face was appalling: his eyes, which were set very near to his hooked nose, had a horrible squint, his lips were thick and moist, and his breath reeked of alcohol.

"What will the noble lady deign to drink?" he now asked in an oily, suave voice.

And Yvonne, remembering the guide's admonitions, contrived to smile unconcernedly into the hideous face.

"I would very much like some wine," she said cheerfully, "but I am afraid that I have no money wherewith to pay you for it."

The creature with a gesture of abject humility rubbed his greasy hands together.

"And may I respectfully ask," he queried blandly, "what are the intentions of the noble lady in coming to this humble abode, if she hath no desire to partake of refreshments?"

"I am expecting friends," replied Yvonne bravely; "they will be here very soon, and will gladly repay you lavishly for all the kindness which you may be inclined to show to me the while."

She was very brave indeed and looked this awful misshapen specimen of a man quite boldly in the face: she even contrived to smile, though she was well aware that a number of men and women—perhaps a dozen altogether—had congregated in front of her in a compact group around the landlord, that they were nudging one another and pointing derisively—malevolently—at her. It was impossible, despite all attempts at valour, to mistake the hostile attitude of these people. Some of the most obscene words, coined during these last horrible days of the Revolution, were freely hurled at her, and one woman suddenly cried out in a shrill treble:

"Throw her out, citizen Lemoine! We don't want spies in here!"

"Indeed, indeed," said Yvonne as quietly as she could, "I am no spy. I am poor and wreched like yourselves! and desperately lonely, save for the kind friends who will meet me here anon."

"*Aristos* like yourself!" growled one of the men. "This is no place for you or for them."

"No! No! This is no place for *aristos*," cried one of the women in a voice which many excesses and many vices had rendered hoarse and rough. "Spy or not, we don't want you in here. Do we?" she added as with arms akimbo she turned to face those of her own sex, who behind the men had come up in order to see what was going on.

"Throw her out, Lemoine," reiterated a man who appeared to be an oracle amongst the others.

"Please! please let me stop here!" pleaded Yvonne; "if you turn me out I shall not know what to do: I shall not know where to meet my friends. . . . "

"Pretty story about those friends," broke in Lemoine roughly. "How do I know if you're lying or not?"

From the opposite angle of the room, the woman behind the bar had been watching the little scene with eyes that glistened with cupidity. Now she emerged from behind her stronghold of bottles and mugs and slowly waddled across the room. She pushed her way unceremoniously past her customers, elbowing men, women and children vigorously aside with a deft play of her large, muscular arms. Having reached the forefront of the little group she came to a standstill immediately in front of Yvonne, and crossing her mighty arms over her ponderous chest she eyed the "*aristo*" with unconcealed malignity.

"We do know that the slut is lying—that is where you make the mistake, Lemoine. A slut, that's what she is—and the friend whom she's going to meet . . . ? Well!" she added, turning with an ugly leer toward the other women, "we all know what sort of friend that one is likely to be, eh, mesdames? Bringing evil fame on this house, that's what the wench is after . . . so as to bring the police about our ears . . . I wouldn't trust her, not another minute. Out with you and at once—do you hear?. . . this instant . . . Lemoine has parleyed quite long enough with you already!"

Despite all her resolutions Yvonne was terribly frightened. While the hideous old hag talked and screamed and waved her coarse, red arms about, the unfortunate young girl with a great effort of will, kept repeating to herself: "I am not frightened—I must not be frightened. He assured me that these people would do me no harm. . . . "

But now when the woman had ceased speaking there was a general murmur of:

"Throw her out! Spy or *aristo* we don't want her here!" whilst some of the men added significantly: "I am sure that she is one of Carrier's spies and in league with his Marats! We shall have those devils in here in a moment if we don't look out! Throw her out before she can signal to the Marats!"

Ugly faces charged with hatred and virulence were thrust threateningly forward—one or two of the women were obviously looking forward to joining in the scramble, when this "stuck-up wench" would presently be hurled out into the street.

"Now then, my girl, out you get," concluded the woman Lemoine, as with an expressive gesture she proceeded to roll her sleeves higher up her arm. She was about to lay her dirty hands on Yvonne, and the poor girl was nearly sick with horror, when one of the men—a huge, coarse giant, whose muscular torso, covered with grease and grime showed almost naked through a ragged shirt which hung from his shoulders in strips—seized the woman Lemoine by the arm and dragged her back a step or two away from Yvonne.

"Don't be a fool, *petite mère*," he said, accompanying this admonition with a blasphemous oath. "Slut or no, the wench may as well pay you something for the privilege of staying here. Look at that cloak she's wearing—the shoe-leather on her feet. Aren't they worth a bottle of your sour wine?"

"What's that to you, Paul Friche?" retorted the woman roughly, as with a vigorous gesture she freed her arm from the man's grasp. "Is this my house or yours?"

"Yours, of course," replied the man with a coarse laugh and a still coarser jest, "but this won't be the first time that I have saved you from impulsive folly. Yesterday you were for harbouring a couple of rogues who were Marats in disguise: if I hadn't given you warning, you would now have swallowed more water from the Loire than you would care to hold. But for me two days ago you would have received the goods pinched by Ferté out of Balaze's shop, and been thrown to the fishes in consequence for the entertainment of the proconsul and his friends. You must admit that I've been a good friend to you before now."

"And if you have, Paul Friche," retorted the hag obstinately, "I paid you well for your friendship, both yesterday and the day before, didn't I?"

"You did," assented Friche imperturbably. "That's why I want to serve you again to-night."

"Don't listen to him, *petite mère*," interposed one of two out of the crowd. "He is a white-livered skunk to talk to you like that."

"Very well! Very well!" quoth Paul Friche, and he spat

THE SCARLET PIMPERNEL ANTHOLOGY VOLUME II 459

vigorously on the ground in token that henceforth he divested himself from any responsibility in this matter, "don't listen to me. Lose a benefit of twenty, perhaps forty francs for the sake of a bit of fun. Very well! Very well!" he continued as he turned and slouched out of the group to the further end of the room, where he sat down on a barrel. He drew the stump of a clay pipe out of the pocket of his breeches, stuffed it into his mouth, stretched his long legs out before him and sucked away at his pipe with complacent detachment. "I didn't know," he added with biting sarcasm by way of a parting shot, "that you and Lemoine had come into a fortune recently and that forty or fifty francs are nothing to you now."

"Forty or fifty? Come! come!" protested Lemoine feebly.

## II

Yvonne's fate was hanging in the balance. The attitude of the small crowd was no less threatening than before, but immediate action was withheld while the Lemoines obviously debated in their minds what was best to be done. The instinct to "have at" an *aristo* with all the accumulated hatred of many generations was warring with the innate rapacity of the Breton peasant.

"Forty or fifty?" reiterated Paul Friche emphatically. "Can't you see that the wench is an *aristo* escaped out of Le Bouffay or the entrepôt?" he added contemptuously.

"I know that she is an *aristo*," said the woman, "that's why I want to throw her out."

"And get nothing for your pains," retorted Friche roughly. "If you wait for her friends we may all of us get as much as twenty francs each to hold our tongues."

"Twenty francs each. . . . " The murmur was repeated with many a sigh of savage gluttony, by every one in the room—and repeated again and again—especially by the women.

"You are a fool, Paul Friche . . . " commented Lemoine.

"A fool am I?" retorted the giant. "Then let me tell you, that 'tis you who are a fool and worse. I happen to know," he added, as he once more rose and rejoined the group in the centre of the room, "I happen to know that you and every one here is heading straight for a trap arranged by the Committee of Public Safety, whose chief emissary came into Nantes awhile ago and is named Chauvelin. It is a trap which will land you all in the criminal dock first and on the way to Cayenne or the guillotine afterwards. This place is surrounded with Marats, and orders have been issued to them to make a descent on this place, as soon as papa Lemoine's customers are assembled. There are two members of the accursed company amongst us at the present moment. . . . "

He was standing right in the middle of the room, immediately beneath the hanging lamp. At his words—spoken with such firm confidence, as one who knows and is therefore empowered to speak—a sudden change came over the spirit of the whole assembly. Everything was forgotten in the face of this new danger—two Marats, the sleuth-hounds of the proconsul—here present, as spies and as informants! Every face became more haggard—every cheek more livid. There was a quick and furtive scurrying toward the front door.

"Two Marats here?" shouted one man, who was bolder than the rest. "Where are they?"

Paul Friche, who towered above his friends, stood at this moment quite close to a small man, dressed like the others in ragged breeches and shirt, and wearing the broad-brimmed hat usually affected by the Breton peasantry.

"Two Marats? Two spies?" screeched a woman. "Where are they?"

"Here is one," replied Paul Friche with a loud laugh: and with his large grimy hand he lifted the hat from his neighbour's head and threw it on the ground; "and there," he added as with long, bony finger he pointed to the front door, where another man—a square-built youngster with tow-coloured hair somewhat resembling a shaggy dog—was endeavouring to effect a surreptitious exit, "there is the other; and he is on the point of slipping quietly away in order to report to his captain what he has seen and heard at the Rat Mort. One moment, citizen," he added, and with a couple of giant strides he too had reached the door; his large rough hand had come down heavily on the shoulder of the youth with the tow-coloured hair, and had forced him to veer round and to face the angry, gesticulating crowd.

"Two Marats! Two spies!" shouted the men. "Now we'll soon settle their little business for them!"

"Marat yourself," cried the small man who had first been denounced by Friche. "I am no Marat, as a good many of you here know. *Maman* Lemoine," he added pleading, "you know me. Am I a Marat?"

But the Lemoines—man and wife—at the first suggestion of police had turned a deaf ear to all their customers. Their own safety being in jeopardy they cared little what happened to anybody else. They had retired behind their counter and were in close consultation together, no doubt as to the best means of escape if indeed the man Paul Friche spoke the truth.

"I know nothing about him," the woman was saying, "but he certainly was right last night about those two men who came ferreting in here—and last week too. . . . "

"Am I a Marat, *maman* Lemoine?" shouted the small man as he hammered his fists upon the counter. "For ten years and more I have been a customer in this place and. . . . "

"Am I a Marat?" shouted the youth with the tow-coloured hair addressing the assembly indiscriminately. "Some of you here know me well enough. Jean Paul, you know—Ledouble, you too. . . . "

"Of course! Of course I know you well enough, Jacques Leroux," came with a loud laugh from one of the crowd. "Who said you were a Marat?"

"Am I a Marat, *maman* Lemoine?" reiterated the small man at the counter.

"Oh! leave me alone with your quarrels," shouted the woman Lemoine in reply. "Settle them among yourselves."

"Then if Jacques Leroux is not a Marat," now came in a bibulous voice from a distant comer of the room, "and this compeer here is known to *maman* Lemoine, where are the real Marats who according to this fellow Friche, whom we none of us know, are spying upon us?"

"Yes! where are they?" suggested another. "Show 'em to us, Paul Friche, or whatever your accursed name happens to be."

"Tell us where you come from yourself," screamed the woman with the shrill treble, "it seems to me quite possible that you're a Marat yourself."

This suggestion was at once taken up.

"Marat yourself!" shouted the crowd, and the two men who a moment ago had been accused of being spies in disguise shouted louder than the rest: "Marat yourself!"

### III

After that, pandemonium reigned.

The words "police" and "Marats" had aroused the terror of all these night-hawks, who were wont to think themselves immune inside their lair: and terror is at all times an evil counsellor. In the space of a few seconds confusion held undisputed sway. Every one screamed, waved arms, stamped feet, struck out with heavy bare fists at his nearest neighbour. Every one's hand was against every one else.

"Spy! Marat! Informer!" were the three words that detached themselves most clearly from out the babel of vituperations freely hurled from end to end of the room.

The children screamed, the women's shrill or hoarse treble mingled with the cries and imprecations of the men.

Paul Friche had noted that the turn of the tide was against him, long before the first naked fist had been brandished in his face. Agile as a monkey he had pushed his way through to the bar, and placing his two hands upon it, with a swift leap he had taken up a sitting position in the very middle of the table amongst the jugs and bottles, which he promptly seized and used as missiles and weapons, whilst with his dangling feet encased in heavy sabots he kicked out vigorously and unceasingly against the shins of his foremost assailants.

He had the advantage of position and used it cleverly. In his right hand he held a pewter mug by the handle and used it as a swivel against his aggressors with great effect.

"The Loire for you—you blackmailer! liar! traitor!" shouted some of the women who, bolder than the men, thrust shaking fists at Paul Friche as closely as that pewter mug would allow.

"Break his jaw before he can yell for the police," admonished one of the men from the rear, "before he can save his own skin."

But those who shouted loudest had only their fists by way of weapon and Paul Friche had mugs and bottles, and those sabots of his kicked out with uncomfortable agility.

"Break my jaw, will you," he shouted every time that a blow from the mug went home, "a spy am I? Very well then, here's for you, Jacques Leroux; go and nurse your cracked skull at home. You want a row," he added hitting at a youth who brandished a heavy fist in his face, "well! you shall have it and as much of it as you like! as much of it as will bring the patrols of police comfortably about your ears."

Bang! went the pewter mug crashing against a man's hard skull! Bang went Paul Friche's naked fist against the chest of another. He was a hard hitter and swift.

The Lemoines from behind their bar shouted louder than the rest, doing as much as their lungs would allow them in the way of admonishing, entreating, protesting—cursing every one for a set of fools who were playing straight into the hands of the police.

"Now then! Now then, children, stop that bellowing, will you? There are no spies here. Paul Friche was only having his little joke! We all know one another, what?"

"Camels!" added Lemoine more forcibly. "They'll bring the patrols about our ears for sure."

Paul Friche was not by any means the only man who was being vigorously attacked. After the first two or three minutes of this kingdom of pandemonium, it was difficult to say who was quarrelling with whom. Old grudges were revived, old feuds taken up there, where they had previously been interrupted. Accusations of spying were followed by abuse for some past wrong of black-legging or cheating a confrère. The temperature of the room became suffocating. All these violent passions seething within these four walls seemed to become tangible and to mingle with the atmosphere already surcharged with the fumes of alcohol, of tobacco and of perspiring humanity. There was many a black-eye already, many a contusion: more than one knife— surreptitiously drawn—was already stained with red.

IV

There was also a stampede for the door. One man gave the signal. Seeing that his mates were wasting precious time by venting their wrath against Paul Friche and then quarrelling among themselves, he hoped to effect an escape ere the police came to stop the noise. No one believed in the place being surrounded. Why should it be? The Marats were far too busy hunting up rebels and *aristos* to trouble much about the Rat Mort and its customers, but it was quite possible that a brawl would bring a patrol along, and then 'ware the police correctionnelle and the possibility of deportation or worse. Retreat was undoubtedly safer while there was time. One man first: then one or two more on his heels, and those among the women who had children in their arms or clinging to their skirts: they turned stealthily to the door—almost ashamed of their cowardice, ashamed lest they were seen abandoning the field of combat.

It was while confusion reigned unchecked that Yvonne—who was cowering, frankly terrified at last, in the corner of the room, became aware that the door close beside her—the door situated immediately opposite the front entrance—was surreptitiously opened. She turned quickly to look—for she was like a terror-stricken little animal now—one that scents and feels and fears danger from every quarter round. The door was being pushed open very slowly by what was still to Yvonne an unseen hand. Somehow that opening door fascinated her: for the moment she forgot the noise and the confusion around her.

Then suddenly with a great effort of will she checked the scream which had forced itself up to her throat.

"Father!" was all that she contrived to say in a hoarse and passionate murmur.

Fortunately as he peered cautiously round the room, M. le duc caught sight of his daughter. She was staring at him—wide-eyed, her lips bloodless, her cheeks the colour of ashes. He looked but the ghost now of that proud aristocrat who little more than a week ago was the centre of a group of courtiers round the person of the heir to the English throne. Starved, emaciated, livid, he was the shadow of his former self, and there was a haunted look in his purple-rimmed eyes which spoke with pathetic eloquence of sleepless nights and of a soul tortured with remorse.

Just for the moment no one took any notice of him—every one was shrieking, every one was quarrelling, and M. le duc, placing a finger to his lips, stole cautiously round to his daughter. The next instant they were clinging to one another, these two, who had endured so much together—he the father who had wrought such an unspeakable wrong, and she the child who was so lonely, so forlorn and almost happy in finding some one who belonged to her, some one to whom she could cling.

"Father, dear! what shall we do?" Yvonne murmured, for she felt the last shred of her fictitious courage oozing out of her, in face of this awful lawlessness which literally paralysed her thinking faculties.

"Sh! dear!" whispered M. le duc in reply. "We must get out of this loathsome place while this hideous row is going on. I heard it all from the filthy garret up above, where those devils have kept me these three days. The door was not locked. . . . I crept downstairs. . . . No one is paying heed to us. . . . We can creep out. Come."

But at the suggestion, Yvonne's spirits, which had been stunned by the events of the past few moments, revived with truly mercurial rapidity.

"No! no! dear," she urged. "We must stay here. . . . You don't know. . . . I have had a message—from my own dear milor—my husband . . . he sent a friend to take me out of the hideous prison where that awful Pierre Adet was keeping me—a friend who assured me that my dear milor was watching over me . . . he brought me to this place— and begged me not to be frightened . . . but to wait patiently . . . and I must wait, dear . . . I must wait!"

She spoke rapidly in whispers and in short jerky sentences. M. le duc listened to her wide-eyed, a deep line of puzzlement between his brows. Sorrow, remorse, starvation, misery had in a measure numbed his mind. The thought of help, of hope, of friends could not penetrate into his brain.

"A message," he murmured inanely, "a message. No! no! my girl, you must trust no one. . . . Pierre Adet. . . . Pierre Adet is full of evil tricks—he will trap you . . . he means to destroy us both . . . he has brought you here so that you should be murdered by these ferocious devils."

"Impossible, father dear," she said, still striving to speak bravely. "We have both of us been all this while in the power of Pierre Adet; he could have had no object in bringing me here to-night."

But the father who had been an insentient tool in the schemes of that miserable intriguer, who had been the means of bringing his only child to this terrible and deadly pass—the man who had listened to the lying counsels and proposals of his own most bitter enemy, could only groan now in terror and in doubt.

"Who can probe the depths of that abominable villain's plans?" he murmured vaguely.

In the meanwhile the little group who had thought prudence the better part of valour had reached the door. The foremost man amongst them opened it and peered cautiously out into the darkness. He turned back to those behind him, put a finger to his lip and beckoned to them to follow him in silence.

"Yvonne, let us go!" whispered the duc, who had seized his daughter by the hand.

"But father. . . . "

"Let us go!" he reiterated pitiably. "I shall die if we stay here!"

"It won't be for long, father dear," she entreated; "if milor should come with his friend, and find us gone, we should be endangering his life as well as our own."

"I don't believe it," he rejoined with the obstinacy of weakness. "I don't believe in your message . . . how could milor or anyone come to your rescue, my child?. . . No one knows that you are here, in this hell in Nantes."

Yvonne clung to him with the strength of despair. She too was as terrified as any human creature could be and live, but terror had not altogether swept away her belief in that mysterious message, in that tall guide who had led her hither, in that scarlet device—the five-petalled flower which stood for everything that was most gallant and most brave.

She desired with all her might to remain here—despite everything, despite the awful brawl that was raging round her and which sickened her, despite the horror of the whole thing—to remain here and to wait. She put her arms round her father: she dragged him back every time that he tried to move. But a sort of unnatural strength seemed to have conquered his former debility. His attempts to get away became more and more determined and more and more febrile.

"Come, Yvonne! we must go!" he continued to murmur intermittently and with ever-growing obstinacy. "No one will notice us. . . . I heard the noise from my garret upstairs. . . . I crept down. . . . I knew no one would notice me. . . . Come—we must go . . . now is our time."

"Father, dear, whither could we go? Once in the streets of Nantes what would happen to us?"

"We can find our way to the Loire!" he retorted almost brutally. He shook himself free from her restraining arms and gripped her firmly by the hand. He tried to drag her toward the door, whilst she still struggled to keep him back. He had just caught sight of the group of men and women at the front door: their leader was standing upon the threshold and was still peering out into the darkness.

But the next moment they all came to a halt: what their leader had perceived through the darkness did not evidently quite satisfy him: he turned and held a whispered consultation with the others. M. le duc strove with all his might to join in with that group. He felt that in its wake would lie the road to freedom. He would have struck Yvonne for standing in the way of her own safety.

"Father dear," she contrived finally to say to him, "if you go hence, you will go alone. Nothing will move me from here, because I know that milor will come."

"Curse you for your obstinacy," retorted the duc, "you jeopardise my life and yours."

Then suddenly from the angle of the room where wrangling and fighting were at their fiercest, there came a loud call:

"Look out, *père* Lemoine, your *aristos* are running away. You are losing your last chance of those fifty francs."

It was Paul Friche who had shouted. His position on the table was giving him a commanding view over the heads of the threatening, shouting, perspiring crowd, and he had just caught sight of M. le duc dragging his daughter by force toward the door.

"The authors of all this pother," he added with an oath, "and they will get away whilst we have the police about our ears."

"Name of a name of a dog," swore Lemoine from behind his bar, "that shall not be. Come along, *maman*, let us bring those *aristos* along here. Quick now."

It was all done in a second. Lemoine and his wife, with the weight and authority of the masters of the establishment, contrived to elbow their way through the crowd. The next moment Yvonne felt herself forcibly dragged away from her father.

"This way, my girl, and no screaming," a bibulous voice said in her ear, "no screaming, or I'll smash some of those front teeth of yours. You said some rich friends were coming along for you presently. Well then! come and wait for them out of the crowd!"

Indeed Yvonne had no desire to struggle or to scream. Salvation she thought had come to her and to her father in this rough guise. In another moment mayhap he would have forced her to follow him, to leave milor in the lurch, to jeopardise for ever every chance of safety.

"It is all for the best, father dear," she managed to cry out over her shoulder, for she had just caught sight of him being seized round the shoulders by Lemoine and heard him protesting loudly:

"I'll not go! I'll not go! Let me go!" he shouted hoarsely. "My daughter! Yvonne! Let me go! You devil!"

But Lemoine had twice the vigour of the duc de Kernogan, nor did he care one jot about the other's protests. He hated all this row inside his house, but there had been rows in it before and he was beginning to hope that nothing serious would come of it. On the other hand, Paul Friche might be right about these *aristos*; there might be forty or fifty francs to be made out of them, and in any case they had one or two things upon their persons which might be worth a few francs—and who knows? they might even have something in their pockets worth taking.

This hope and thought gave Lemoine additional strength, and seeing that the *aristo* struggled so desperately, he thought to silence him by bringing his heavy fist with a crash upon the old man's head.

"Yvonne! *A moi!*" shouted M. le duc ere he fell back senseless.

That awful cry, Yvonne heard it as she was being dragged through the noisome crowd. It mingled in her ear with the other awful sounds—the oaths and blasphemies which filled the air with their hideousness. It died away just as a formidable crash against the entrance door suddenly silenced every cry within.

"All hands up!" came with a peremptory word of command from the doorway.

"Mercy on us!" murmured the woman Lemoine, who still had Yvonne by the hand, "we are undone this time."

There was a clatter and grounding of arms—a scurrying of bare feet and sabots upon the floor, the mingled sounds of men trying to fly and being caught in the act and hurled back: screams of terror from the women, one or two pitiable calls, a few shrill cries from frightened children, a few dull thuds as of human bodies falling. . . . It was all so confused, so unspeakably horrible. Yvonne was hardly conscious. Near her some one whispered hurriedly:

"Put the *aristos* away somewhere, *maman* Lemoine . . . the whole thing may only be a scare . . . he Marats may only be here about the *aristos* . . . they will probably leave you alone if you give them up . . . perhaps you'll get a reward. . . . Put them away till some of this row subsides . . . I'll talk to commandant Fleury if I can."

Yvonne felt her knees giving way under her. There was nothing more to hope for now—nothing. She felt herself lifted from the ground —she was too sick and faint to realise what was happening: through the din which filled her ears she vainly tried to distinguish her father's voice again.

V

A moment or two later she found herself squatting somewhere on the ground. How she got here she did not know—where she was she knew still less. She was in total darkness. A fusty, close smell of food and wine gave her a wretched feeling of nausea—her head ached intolerably, her eyes were hot, her throat dry: there was a constant buzzing in her ears.

The terrible sounds of fighting and screaming and cursing, the crash of broken glass and overturned benches came to her as through a partition—close by but muffled.

In the immediate nearness all was silence and darkness.

# CHAPTER 8: THE ENGLISH ADVENTURERS

## I

It was with that muffled din still ringing in her ear and with the conception of all that was going on, on the other side of the partition, standing like an awesome spectre of evil before her mind, that Yvonne woke to the consciousness that her father was dead.

He lay along the last half-dozen steps of a narrow wooden staircase which had its base in the narrow, cupboard-like landing on to which the Lemoines had just thrust them both. Through a small heart-shaped hole cut in the door of the partition-wall, a shaft of feeble light struck straight across to the foot of the stairs: it lit up the recumbent figure of the last of the ducs de Kernogan, killed in a brawl in a house of evil fame.

Weakened by starvation, by the hardships of the past few days, his constitution undermined by privations and mayhap too by gnawing remorse, he had succumbed to the stunning blow dealt to him by a half drunken brute. His cry: "Yvonne! *A moi!*" was the last despairing call of a soul racked with remorse to the daughter whom he had so cruelly wronged.

When first that feeble shaft of light had revealed to her the presence of that inert form upon the steps, she had struggled to her feet and—dazed—had tottered up to it. Even before she had touched the face, the hands, before she had bent her ear to the half-closed mouth and failed to catch the slightest breath, she knew the full extent of her misery. The look in the wide-open eyes did not terrify her, but they told her the truth, and since then she had cowered beside her dead father on the bottom step of the narrow stairs, her fingers tightly closed over that one hand which never would be raised against her.

An unspeakable sense of horror filled her soul. The thought that he—the proud father, the haughty aristocrat, should lie like this and in such a spot, dragged in and thrown down—no doubt by Lemoine—like a parcel of rubbish and left here to be dragged away again and thrown again like a dog into some unhallowed ground—that thought was so horrible, so monstrous, that at first it dominated even sorrow. Then came the heartrending sense of loneliness. Yvonne Dewhurst had endured so much these past few days that awhile ago she would have affirmed that nothing could appal her in the future. But this was indeed the awful and overwhelming climax to what had already been a surfeit of misery.

This! she, Yvonne, cowering beside her dead father, with no one to stand between her and any insult, any outrage which might be put upon her, with nothing now but a few laths between her and that yelling, screeching mob outside.

Oh! the loneliness! the utter, utter loneliness!

She kissed the inert hand, the pale forehead: with gentle, reverent fingers she tried to smooth out those lines of horror and of fear which gave such a pitiful expression to the face. Of all the wrongs which her father had done her she never thought for a moment. It was he who had brought her to this terrible pass: he who had betrayed her into the hands of her deadliest enemy: he who had torn her from the protecting arms of her dear milor and flung her and himself at the mercy of a set of inhuman wretches who knew neither compunction nor pity.

But all this she forgot, as she knelt beside the lifeless form—the last thing on earth that belonged to her—the last protection to which she might have clung.

II

Out of the confusion of sounds which came—deadened by the intervening partition—to her ear, it was impossible to distinguish anything very clearly. All that Yvonne could do, as soon as she had in a measure collected her scattered senses, was to try and piece together the events of the last few minutes—minutes which indeed seemed like days and even years to her.

Instinctively she gave to the inert hand which she held an additional tender touch. At any rate her father was out of it all. He was at rest and at peace. As for the rest, it was in God's hands. Having only herself to think of now, she ceased to care what became of her. He was out of it all: and those wretches after all could not do more than kill her. A complete numbness of senses and of mind had succeeded the feverish excitement of the past few hours: whether hope still survived at this moment in Yvonne Dewhurst's mind it were impossible to say. Certain it is that it lay dormant—buried beneath the overwhelming misery of her loneliness.

She took the fichu from her shoulders and laid it reverently over the dead man's face: she folded the hands across the breast. She could not cry: she could only pray, and that quite mechanically.

The thought of her dear milor, of his clever friend, of the message which she had received in prison, of the guide who had led her to this awful place, was relegated—almost as a memory—in the furthermost cell of her brain.

III

But after awhile outraged nature, still full of vitality and of youth, re-asserted itself. She felt numb and cold and struggled to her feet. From somewhere close to her a continuous current of air indicated the presence of some sort of window. Yvonne, faint with the close and sickly smell, which even that current failed to disperse, felt her way all round the walls of the narrow landing.

The window was in the wall between the partition and the staircase, it was small and quite low down. It was crossed with heavy iron bars. Yvonne leaned up against it, grateful for the breath of pure air.

For awhile yet she remained unconscious of everything save the confused din which still went on inside the tavern, and at first the sounds which came through the grated window mingled with those on the other side of the partition. But gradually as she contrived to fill her lungs with the cold breath of heaven, it seemed as if a curtain was being slowly drawn away from her atrophied senses.

Just below the window two men were speaking. She could hear them quite distinctly now—and soon one of the voices—clearer than the other—struck her ear with unmistakable familiarity.

"I told Paul Friche to come out here and speak to me," Yvonne heard that same voice say.

"Then he should be here," replied the other, "and if I am not mistaken. . . . "

There was a pause, and then the first voice was raised again.

"Halt! Is that Paul Friche?"

"At your service, citizen," came in reply.

"Well! Is everything working smoothly inside?"

"Quite smoothly; but your Englishmen are not there."

"How do you know?"

"Bah! I know most of the faces that are to be found inside the Rat Mort at this hour: there are no strangers among them."

The voice that had sounded so familiar to Yvonne was raised now in loud and coarse laughter.

"Name of a dog! I never for a moment thought that there were any Englishmen about. Citizen Chauvelin was suffering from nightmare."

"It is early yet," came in response from a gentle bland voice, "you must have patience, citizen."

"Patience? Bah!" ejaculated the other roughly. "As I told you before 'tis but little I care about your English spies. 'Tis the Kernogans I am interested in. What have you done with them, citizen?"

"I got that blundering fool Lemoine to lock them up on the landing at the bottom of the stairs."

"Is that safe?"

"Absolutely. It has no egress save into the tap-room and up the stairs, to the rooms above. Your English spies if they came now would have to fly in and out of those top windows ere they could get to the *aristos*."

"Then in Satan's name keep them there awhile," urged the more gentle, insinuating voice, "until we can make sure of the English spies."

"Tshaw! What foolery!" interjected the other, who appeared to be in a towering passion. "Bring them out at once, citizen Friche . . . bring them out . . . right into the middle of the rabble in the tap-room.. . . Commandant Fleury is directing the perquisition—he is taking down the names of all that cattle which he is arresting inside the premises— let the *ci-devant* duc de Kernogan and his exquisite daughter figure among the vilest cut-throats of Nantes."

"Citizen, let me urge on you once more . . . " came in earnest persuasive accents from that gentle voice.

"Nothing!" broke in the other savagely. "To h——ll with your English spies. It is the Kernogans that I want."

Yvonne, half-crazed with horror, had heard the whole of this abominable conversation wherein she had not failed to recognise the voice of Martin-Roget or Pierre-Adet, as she now knew him to be. Who the other two men were she could easily conjecture. The soft bland voice she had heard twice during these past few days, which had been so full of misery, of terror and of surprise: once she had heard it on board the ship which had taken her away from England and once again a few hours since, inside the narrow room which had been her prison. The third man who had subsequently arrived on the scene was that coarse and grimy creature who had seemed to be the moving evil spirit of that awful brawl in the tavern.

What the conversation meant to her she could not fail to guess. Pierre Adet had by what he said made the whole of his abominable intrigue against her palpably clear. Her father had been right, after all. It was Pierre Adet who through some clever trickery had lured her to this place of evil. How it was all done she could not guess. The message . . . the device . . . her walk across the street . . . the silence . . . the mysterious guide . . . which of these had been the trickery?. . . which had been concocted by her enemy? . . . which devised by her dear milor?

Enough that the whole thing was a trap, a trap all the more hideous as she, Yvonne, who would have given her heart's blood for her beloved, was obviously the bait wherewith these friends meant to capture him and his noble chief. They knew evidently of the presence of the gallant Scarlet Pimpernel and his band of heroes here in Nantes— they seemed to expect their appearance at this abominable place to-night. She, Yvonne, was to be the decoy which was to lure to this hideous lair those noble eagles who were still out of reach.

And if that was so—if indeed her beloved and his valiant friends had followed her hither, then some part of the message of hope must have come from them or from their chief . . . and milor and his friend must even now be somewhere close by, watching their opportunity to come to her rescue . . . heedless of the awful danger which lay in wait for them . . . ignorant mayhap of the abominable trap which had been so cunningly set for them by these astute and ferocious brutes.

Yvonne a prisoner in this narrow space, clinging to the bars of what was perhaps the most cruel prison in which she had yet been confined, bruised her hands and arms against those bars in a wild desire to get out. She longed with all her might to utter one long, loud and piercing cry of warning to her dear milor not to come nigh her now, to fly, to run while there was yet time; and all the while she knew that if she did utter such a cry he would hurry hot-haste to her side. One moment she would have had him near—another she wished him an hundred miles away.

IV

In the tap-room a more ordered medley of sounds had followed on the wild pandemonium of awhile ago. Brief, peremptory words of command, steady tramping of feet, loud harsh questions and subdued answers, occasionally a moan or a few words of protest quickly suppressed, came through the partition to Yvonne's straining ears.

"Your name?"

"Where do you live?"

"Your occupation?"

"That's enough. Silence. The next."

"Your name?"

"Where do you live?"

Men, women and even children were being questioned, classified, packed off, God knew whither. Sometimes a child would cry, a man utter an oath, a woman shriek: then would come harsh orders delivered in a gruff voice, more swearing, the grounding of arms and more often than not a dull, flat sound like a blow struck against human flesh, followed by a volley of curses, or a cry of pain.

"Your name?"

"George Amédé Lemoine."

"Where do you live?"

"In this house."

"Your occupation?"

"I am the proprietor of the tavern, citizen. I am an honest man and a patriot. The Republic. . . . "

"That's enough."

"But I protest."

"Silence. The next."

All with dreary, ceaseless monotony: and Yvonne like a trapped bird was bruising her wings against the bars of her cage. Outside the window Chauvelin and Martin-Roget were still speaking in whispers: the fowlers were still watching for their prey. The third man had apparently gone away. What went on beyond the range of her prison window—out in the darkness of the night which Yvonne's aching eyes could not pierce—she, the miserable watcher, the bait set here to catch the noble game, could not even conjecture. The window was small and her vision was further obstructed by heavy bars. She could see nothing —hear nothing save those two men talking in whispers. Now and again she caught a few words:

"A little while longer, citizen . . . you lose nothing by waiting. Your Kernogans are safe enough. Paul Friche has assured you that the landing where they are now has no egress save through the tap-room, and to the floor above. Wait at least until commandant Fleury has got the crowd together, after which he will send his Marats to search the house. It won't be too late then to lay hands on your *aristos*, if in the meanwhile. . . . "

"'Tis futile to wait," here interrupted Martin-Roget roughly, "and you are a fool, citizen, if you think that those Englishmen exist elsewhere than in your imagination."

"Hark!" broke in the gentle voice abruptly and with forceful command.

And as Yvonne too in instinctive response to that peremptory call was further straining her every sense in order to listen, there came from somewhere, not very far away, right through the stillness of the night, a sound which caused her pulses to still their beating and her throat to choke with the cry which rose from her breast.

It was only the sound of a quaint and drawly voice saying loudly and in English:

"Egad, Tony! ain't you getting demmed sleepy?"

Just for the space of two or three seconds Yvonne had remained quite still while this unexpected sound sent its dulcet echo on the wings of the north-westerly blast. The next—stumbling in the dark—she had run to the stairs even while she heard Martin-Roget calling loudly and excitedly to Paul Friche.

One reverent pause beside her dead father, one mute prayer commending his soul to the mercy of his Maker, one agonised entreaty to God to protect her beloved and his friend, and then she ran swiftly up the winding steps.

At the top of the stairs, immediately in front of her, a door— slightly ajar—showed a feeble light through its aperture. Yvonne pushed the door further open and slipped into the room beyond. She did not pause to look round but went straight to the window and throwing open the ricketty sash she peeped out. For the moment she felt that she would gladly have bartered away twenty years of her life to know exactly whence had come that quaint and drawling voice. She leaned far out of the window trying to see. It gave on the side of the Rat Mort over against Louise Adet's house—the space below seemed to her to be swarming with men: there were hurried and whispered calls— orders were given to stand at close attention, whilst Martin-Roget had apparently been questioning Paul Friche, for Yvonne heard the latter declare emphatically:

"I am certain that it came either from inside the house or from the roof. And with your permission, citizen, I would like to make assurance doubly sure."

Then one of the men must suddenly have caught sight of the vague silhouette leaning out of the window, for Martin-Roget and Friche uttered a simultaneous cry, whilst Chauvelin said hurriedly:

"You are right, citizen, something is going on inside the house."

"What can we do?" queried Martin-Roget excitedly.

"Nothing for the moment but wait. The Englishmen are caught sure enough like rats in their holes."

"Wait!" ejaculated Martin-Roget with a savage oath, "wait! always wait! while the quarry slips through one's fingers."

"It shall not slip through mine," retorted Paul Friche. "I was a steeple-jack by trade in my day: it won't be the first time that I have climbed the side of a house by the gutter-pipe. A moi Jean-Pierre," he added, "and may I be drowned in the Loire if between us two we do not lay those cursed English spies low."

"An hundred francs for each of you," called Chauvelin lustily, "if you succeed."

Yvonne did not think to close the window again. Vigorous shouting and laughter from below testified that that hideous creature Friche and his mate had put their project in immediate execution; she turned and ran down the stairs—feeling now like an animal at bay; by the time that she had reached the bottom, she heard a prolonged, hoarse cry of triumph from below and guessed that Paul Friche and his mate had reached the window-sill: the next moment there was a crash overhead of broken window-glass and of furniture kicked from one end of the room to the other, immediately followed by the sound of heavy footsteps running helter-skelter down the stairs.

Yvonne, half-crazed with terror, faint and sick, fell unconscious over the body of her father.

V

Inside the tap-room commandant Fleury was still at work.

"Your name?"

"Where do you live?"

"Your occupation?"

The low room was filled to suffocation: the walls lined with Marats, the doors and windows which were wide open were closely guarded, whilst in the corner of the room, huddled together like bales of rubbish, was the human cattle that had been driven together, preparatory to being sent for a trial to Paris in vindication of Carrier's brutalities against the city.

Fleury for form's sake made entries in a notebook—the whole thing was a mere farce—these wretched people were not likely to get a fair trial—what did the whole thing matter? Still! the commandant of the Marats went solemnly through the farce which Carrier had invented with a view to his own justification.

Lemoine and his wife had protested and been silenced: men had struggled and women had fought—some of them like wild cats—in trying to get away. Now there were only half a dozen or so more to docket. Fleury swore, for he was tired and hot.

"This place is like a pest-house," he said.

Just then came the sound of that lusty cry of triumph from outside, followed by all the clatter and the breaking of window glass.

"What's that?" queried Fleury.

The heavy footsteps running down the stairs caused him to look up from his work and to call briefly to a sergeant of the Marats who stood beside his chair:

"Go and see what that sacré row is about," he commanded. "In there," he added as he indicated the door of the landing with a jerk of the head.

But before the man could reach the door, it was thrown open from within with a vigorous kick from the point of a sabot, and Paul Friche appeared under the lintel with the *aristo* wench thrown over his shoulder like a sack of potatoes, his thick, muscular arms encircling her knees. His scarlet bonnet was cocked over one eye, his face was smeared with dirt, his breeches were torn at the knees, his shirt hung in strips from his powerful shoulders. Behind him his mate—who had climbed up the gutter-pipe into the house in his wake—was tottering under the load of the *ci-devant* duc de Kernogan's body which he had slung across his back and was holding on to by the wrists.

Fleury jumped to his feet—the appearance of these two men, each with his burden, caused him to frown with anger and to demand peremptorily: "What is the meaning of this?"

"The *aristos*," said Paul Friche curtly; "they were trying to escape."

He strode into the room, carrying the unconscious form of the girl as if it were a load of feathers. He was a huge, massive-looking giant: the girl's shoulders nearly touched the low ceiling as he swung forward facing the angry commandant.

"How did you get into the house? and by whose orders?"

demanded Fleury roughly.

"Climbed in by the window, *pardi*," retorted the man, "and by the orders of citizen Martin-Roget."

"A corporal of the Company Marat takes orders only from me; you should know that, citizen Friche."

"Nay!" interposed the sergeant quickly, "this man is not a corporal of the Company Marat, citizen commandant. As for Corporal Friche, why! he was taken to the infirmary some hours ago with a cracked skull, he. . . . "

"Not Corporal Friche," exclaimed Fleury with an oath, "then who in the devil's name is this man?"

"The Scarlet Pimpernel, at your service, citizen commandant," came loudly and with a merry laugh from the pseudo Friche.

And before either Fleury or the sergeant or any of the Marats could even begin to realise what was happening, he had literally bounded across the room, and as he did so he knocked against the hanging lamp which fell with a crash to the floor, scattering oil and broken glass in every direction and by its fall plunging the place into total darkness. At once there arose a confusion and medley of terrified screams, of piercing shrieks from the women and the children, and of loud imprecations from the men. These mingled with the hasty words of command, with quick orders from Fleury and the sergeant, with the grounding of arms and the tramping of many feet, and with the fall of human bodies that happened to be in the way of the reckless adventurer and his flight.

"He is through the door," cried the men who had been there on guard.

"After him then!" shouted Fleury. "Curse you all for cowards and for fools."

The order had no need to be repeated. The confusion, though great, had only been momentary. Within a second or less, Fleury and his sergeant had fought their way through to the door, urging the men to follow.

"After him . . . quick! . . . he is heavily loaded . . . he cannot have got far . . . " commanded Fleury as soon as he had crossed the threshold. "Sergeant, keep order within, and on your life see that no one else escapes."

# CHAPTER 9: THE PROCONSUL

## I

From round the angle of the house Martin-Roget and Chauvelin were already speeding along at a rapid pace.

"What does it all mean?" queried the latter hastily.

"The Englishman—with the wench on his back? have you seen him?"

"Malediction! what do you mean?"

"Have you seen him?" reiterated Fleury hoarsely.

"No."

"He couldn't have passed you?"

"Impossible."

"Then unless some of us here have eyes like cats that limb of Satan will get away. On to him, my men," he called once more. "Can you see him?"

The darkness outside was intense. The north-westerly wind was whistling down the narrow street, drowning the sound of every distant footfall: it tore mercilessly round the men's heads, snatching the bonnets from off their heads, dragging at their loose shirts and breeches, adding to the confusion which already reigned.

"He went this way . . . " shouted one.

"No! that!" cried another.

"There he is!" came finally in chorus from several lusty throats. "Just crossing the bridge."

"After him," cried Fleury, "an hundred francs to the man who first lays hands on that devil."

Then the chase began. The Englishman on ahead was unmistakable with that burden on his shoulder. He had just reached the foot of the bridge where a street lanthorn fixed on a tall bracket on the corner stone had suddenly thrown him into bold relief. He had less than an hundred metres start of his pursuers and with a wild cry of excitement they started in his wake.

He was now in the middle of the bridge—an unmistakable figure of a giant vaguely silhouetted against the light from the lanthorns on the further end of the bridge—seeming preternaturally tall and misshapen with that hump upon his back.

From right and left, from under the doorways of the houses in the Carrefour de la Poissonnerie the Marats who had been left on guard in the street now joined in the chase. Overhead windows were thrown open—the good burghers of Nantes, awakened from their sleep, forgetful for the nonce of all their anxieties, their squalor and their miseries, leaned out to see what this new kind of din might mean. From everywhere—it almost seemed as if some sprang out of the earth—men, either of the town-guard or Marats on patrol duty, or merely idlers and night hawks who happened to be about, yielded to that primeval instinct of brutality which causes men as well as beasts to join in a pursuit against a fellow creature.

Fleury was in the rear of his posse. Martin-Roget and Chauvelin, walking as rapidly as they could by his side, tried to glean some information out of the commandant's breathless and scrappy narrative:

"What happened exactly?"

"It was the man Paul Friche . . . with the *aristo* wench on his back . . . and another man carrying the *ci-devant aristo* . . . they were the English spies . . . in disguise . . . they knocked over the lamp . . . and got away. . . . "

"Name of a. . . . "

"No use swearing, citizen Martin-Roget," retorted Fleury as hotly as his agitated movements would allow. "You and citizen Chauvelin are responsible for the affair. It was you, citizen Chauvelin, who placed Paul Friche inside that tavern in observation—you told him what to do. . . . "

"Well?"

"Paul Friche—the real Paul Friche—was taken to the infirmary some hours ago . . . with a cracked skull, dealt him by your Englishman, I've no doubt. . . . "

"Impossible," reiterated Chauvelin with a curse.

"Impossible? why impossible?"

"The man I spoke to outside Le Bouffay. . . . "

"Was not Paul Friche."

"He was on guard in the Place with two other Marats."

"He was not Paul Friche—the others were not Marats."

"Then the man who was inside the tavern? . . . "

"Was not Paul Friche."

" . . . who climbed the gutter pipe . . . ?"

"Malediction!"

And the chase continued—waxing hotter every minute. The hare had gained slightly on the hounds—there were more than a hundred hot on the trail by now—having crossed the bridge he was on the Isle Feydeau, and without hesitating a moment he plunged at once into the network of narrow streets which cover the island in the rear of La Petite Hollande and the Hôtel de le Villestreux, where lodged Carrier, the representative of the people. The hounds after him had lost some ground by halting—if only for a second or two—first at the head of the bridge, then at the corners of the various streets, while they peered into the darkness to see which way had gone that fleet-footed hare.

"Down this way!"

"No! That!"

"There he goes!"

It always took a few seconds to decide, during which the man on ahead with his burden on his shoulder had time mayhap to reach the end of a street and to turn a corner and once again to plunge into darkness and out of sight. The street lanthorns were few in this squalid corner of the city, and it was only when perforce the running hare had to cross a circle of light that the hounds were able to keep hot on the trail.

"To the bridges for your lives!" now shouted Fleury to the men nearest to him. "Leave him to wander on the island. He cannot come off it, unless he jumps into the Loire."

The Marats—intelligent and ferociously keen on the chase—had already grasped the importance of this order: with the bridges guarded that fleet-footed Englishman might run as much as he liked, he was bound to be run to earth like a fox in his burrow. In a moment they had dispersed along the quays, some to one bridge-head, some to another—the Englishman could not double back now, and if he had already crossed to the Isle Gloriette, which was not joined to the left bank of the river by any bridge, he would be equally caught like a rat in a trap.

"Unless he jumps into the Loire," reiterated Fleury triumphantly.

"The proconsul will have more excitement than he hoped for," he added with a laugh. "He was looking forward to the capture of the English spy, and in deadly terror lest he escaped. But now meseems that we shall run our fox down in sight of the very gates of la Villestreux."

Martin-Roget's thoughts ran on Yvonne and the duc.

"You will remember, citizen commandant," he contrived to say to Fleury, "that the *ci-devant* Kernogans were found inside the Rat Mort."

Fleury uttered an exclamation of rough impatience. What did he, what did anyone care at this moment for a couple of *aristos* more or less when the noblest game that had ever fallen to the bag of any Terrorist was so near being run to earth? But Chauvelin said nothing. He walked on at a brisk pace, keeping close to commandant Fleury's side, in the immediate wake of the pursuit. His lips were pressed tightly together and a hissing breath came through his wide-open nostrils. His pale eyes were fixed into the darkness and beyond it, where the most bitter enemy of the cause which he loved was fighting his last battle against Fate.

## II

"He cannot get off the island!" Fleury had said awhile ago. Well! there was of a truth little or nothing now between the hunted hare and capture. The bridges were well guarded: the island swarming with hounds, the Marats at their posts and the Loire an impassable barrier all round.

And Chauvelin, the most tenacious enemy man ever had, Fleury keen on a reward and Martin-Roget with a private grudge to pay off, all within two hundred yards behind him.

True for the moment the Englishman had disappeared. Burden and all, the gloom appeared to have swallowed him up. But there was nowhere he could go; mayhap he had taken refuge under a doorway in one of the narrow streets and hoped perhaps under cover of the darkness to allow his pursuers to slip past him and then to double back.

Fleury was laughing in the best of humours. He was gradually collecting all the Marats together and sending them to the bridge-heads under the command of their various sergeants. Let the Englishman spend the night on the islands if he had a mind. There was a full company of Marats here to account for him as soon as he attempted to come out in the open.

The idlers and night hawks as well as the municipal town guard continued to run excitedly up and down the streets—sometimes there would come a lusty cry from a knot of pursuers who thought they spied the Englishman through the darkness, at others there would be a call of halt, and feverish consultation held at a street corner as to the best policy to adopt.

The town guard, jealous of the Marats, were pining to lay hands on the English spy for the sake of the reward. Fleury, coming across their provost, called him a fool for his pains.

"My Marats will deal with the English spies, citizen," he said roughly, "he is no concern of yours."

The provost demurred: an altercation might have ensued when Chauvelin's suave voice poured oil on the troubled waters.

"Why not," he said, "let the town guard continue their search on the island, citizen commandant? The men may succeed in digging our rat out of his hole and forcing him out into the open all the sooner. Your Marats will have him quickly enough after that."

To this suggestion the provost gave a grudging assent. The reward when the English spy was caught could be fought for later on. For the nonce he turned unceremoniously on his heel, and left Fleury cursing him for a meddlesome busybody.

"So long as he and his rabble does not interfere with my Marats," growled the commandant.

"Will you see your sergeants, citizen?" queried Chauvelin

tentatively. "They will have to keep very much on the alert, and will require constant prodding to their vigilance. If I can be of any service. . . . "

"No," retorted Fleury curtly, "you and citizen Martin-Roget had best try and see the proconsul and tell him what we have done."

"He'll be half wild with terror when he hears that the English spy is at large upon the island."

"You must pacify him as best you can. Tell him I have a score of Marats at every bridge head and that I am looking personally to every arrangement. There is no escape for the devil possible save by drowning himself and the wench in the Loire."

## III

Chauvelin and Martin-Roget turned from the quay on to the Petite Hollande—the great open ground with its converging row of trees which ends at the very apex of the Isle of Feydeau. Opposite to them at the further corner of the Place was the Hôtel de la Villestreux. One or two of the windows in the hotel were lighted from within. No doubt the proconsul was awake, trembling in the remotest angle of his lair, with the spectre of assassination rampant before him—aroused by the continued disturbance of the night, by the feverishness of this man-hunt carried on almost at his gates.

Even through the darkness it was easy to perceive groups of people either rushing backwards and forwards on the Place or congregating in groups under the trees. Excitement was in the air. It could be felt and heard right through the soughing of the north-westerly wind which caused the bare branches of the trees to groan and to crackle, and the dead leaves, which still hung on the twigs, to fly wildly through the night.

In the centre of the Place, two small lights, gleaming like eyes in the midst of the gloom, betrayed the presence of the proconsul's coach, which stood there as always, ready to take him away to a place of safety —away from this city where he was mortally hated and dreaded— whenever the spectre of terror became more insistent than usual, and drove him hence out of his stronghold. The horses were pawing the frozen ground and champing their bits—the steam from their nostrils caught the rays of the carriage lamps, which also lit up with a feeble flicker the vague outline of the coachman on his box and of the postilion rigid in his saddle.

The citizens of Nantes were never tired of gaping at the carriage —a huge C-springed barouche—at the coachman's fine caped coat of bottle-green cloth and at the horses with their handsome harness set off with heavy brass bosses: they never tired of bandying words with the successive coachmen as they mounted their box and gathered up the reins, or with the postilions who loved to crack their whips and to appear smart and well-groomed, in the midst of the squalor which reigned in the terror-stricken city. They were the guardians of the mighty proconsul: on their skill, quickness and presence of mind might depend his precious life.

Even when the shadow of death hangs over an entire community, there will be some who will stand and gape and crack jokes at an uncommon sight.

And now when the pall of night hung over the abode of the man-tiger and his lair, and wrapped in its embrace the hunted and the hunters, there still was a knot of people standing round the carriage—between it and the hotel—gazing with lack-lustre eyes on the costly appurtenances wherewith the representative of a wretched people loved to surround himself. They could only see the solid mass of the carriage and of the horses, but they could hear the coachman clicking with his tongue and the postilion cracking his whip, and these sights broke the absolute dreary monotony of their lives.

It was from behind this knot of gaffers that there rose gradually a tumult as of a man calling out in wrath and lashing himself into a fury. Chauvelin and Martin-Roget were just then crossing La Petite Hollande from one bank of the river to the other: they were walking rapidly towards the hotel, when they heard the tumult which presently culminated in a hoarse cry and a volley of oaths.

"My coach! my coach at once. . . . Lalouët, don't leave me. . . . Curse you all for a set of cowardly oafs. . . . My coach I say. . . . "

"The proconsul," murmured Chauvelin as he hastened forward, Martin-Roget following closely on his heels.

By the time that they had come near enough to the coach to distinguish vaguely in the gloom what was going on, people came rushing to the same spot from end to end of the Place. In a moment there was quite a crowd round the carriage, and the two men had much ado to push their way through by a vigorous play of their elbows.

"Citizen Carrier!" cried Chauvelin at the top of his voice, trying to dominate the hubbub, "one minute . . . I have excellent news for you. . . . The English spy. . . . "

"Curse you for a set of blundering fools," came with a husky cry from out the darkness, "you have let that English devil escape . . . I knew it . . . I knew it . . . the assassin is at large . . . the murderer . . . my coach at once . . . my coach. . . . Lalouët—do not leave me."

Chauvelin had by this time succeeded in pushing his way to the forefront of the crowd: Martin-Roget, tall and powerful, had effectually made a way for him. Through the dense gloom he could see the misshapen form of the proconsul, wildly gesticulating with one arm and with the other clinging convulsively to young Lalouët who already had his hand on the handle of the carriage door.

With a quick, resolute gesture Chauvelin stepped between the door and the advancing proconsul.

"Citizen Carrier," he said with calm determination, "on my oath there is no cause for alarm. Your life is absolutely safe. . . . I entreat you to return to your lodgings. . . . "

To emphasise his words he had stretched out a hand and firmly grasped the proconsul's coat sleeve. This gesture, however, instead of pacifying the apparently terror-stricken maniac, seemed to have the effect of further exasperating his insensate fear. With a loud oath he tore himself free from Chauvelin's grasp.

"Ten thousand devils," he cried hoarsely, "who is this fool who dares to interfere with me? Stand aside man . . . stand aside or. . . . "

And before Chauvelin could utter another word or Martin-Roget come to his colleague's rescue, there came the sudden sharp report of a pistol; the horses reared, the crowd was scattered in every direction, Chauvelin was knocked over by a smart blow on the head whilst a vigorous drag on his shoulder alone saved him from falling under the wheels of the coach.

Whilst confusion was at its highest, the carriage door was closed to with a bang and there was a loud, commanding cry hurled through the window at the coachman on his box.

"*En avant*, citizen coachman! Drive for your life! through the Savenay gate. The English assassins are on our heels."

The postilion cracked his whip. The horses, maddened by the report, by the pushing, jostling crowd and the confused cries and screams around, plunged forward, wild with excitement. Their hoofs clattered on the hard road. Some of the crowd ran after the coach across the Place, shouting lustily: "The proconsul! the proconsul!"

Chauvelin—dazed and bruised—was picked up by Martin-Roget.

"The cowardly brute!" was all that he said between his teeth, "he shall rue this outrage as soon as I can give my mind to his affairs. In the meanwhile. . . . "

The clatter of the horses' hoofs was already dying away in the distance. For a few seconds longer the rattle of the coach was still accompanied by cries of "The proconsul! the proconsul!" Fleury at the bridge head, seeing and hearing its approach, had only just time to order his Marats to stand at attention. A salvo should have been fired when the representative of the people, the high and mighty proconsul, was abroad, but there was no time for that, and the coach clattered over the bridge at breakneck speed, whilst Carrier with his head out of the window was hurling anathemas and insults at Fleury for having allowed the paid spies of that cursed British Government to threaten the life of a representative of the people.

"I go to Savenay," he shouted just at the last, "until that

assassin has been thrown in the Loire. But when I return . . . look to yourself commandant Fleury."

Then the carriage turned down the Quai de la Fosse and a few minutes later was swallowed up by the gloom.

## IV

Chauvelin, supported by Martin-Roget, was hobbling back across the Place. The crowd was still standing about, vaguely wondering why it had got so excited over the departure of the proconsul and the rattle of a coach and pair across the bridge, when on the island there was still an assassin at large—an English spy, the capture of whom would be one of the great events in the chronicles of the city of Nantes.

"I think," said Martin-Roget, "that we may as well go to bed now, and leave the rest to commandant Fleury. The Englishman may not be captured for some hours, and I for one am over-fatigued."

"Then go to bed if you desire, citizen Martin-Roget," retorted Chauvelin drily, "I for one will stay here until I see the Englishman in the hands of commandant Fleury."

"Hark," interposed Martin-Roget abruptly. "What was that?"

Chauvelin had paused even before Martin-Roget's restraining hand had rested on his arm. He stood still in the middle of the Place and his knees shook under him so that he nearly fell prone to the ground.

"What is it?" reiterated Martin-Roget with vague puzzlement. "It sounds like young Lalouët's voice."

Chauvelin said nothing. He had forgotten his bruises: he no longer hobbled—he ran across the Place to the front of the hotel whence the voice had come which was so like that of young Lalouët.

The youngster—it was undoubtedly he—was standing at the angle of the hotel: above him a lanthorn threw a dim circle of light on his bare head with its mass of dark curls, and on a small knot of idlers with two or three of the town guard amongst them. The first words spoken by him which Chauvelin distinguished quite clearly were:

"You are all mad . . . or else drunk. . . . The citizen proconsul is upstairs in his room. . . . He has just sent me down to hear what news there is of the English spies. . . . "

## V

No one made reply. It seemed as if some giant and spectral hand had passed over this mass of people and with its magic touch had stilled their turbulent passions, silenced their imprecations and cooled their ardour—and left naught but a vague fear, a subtle sense of awe as when something unexplainable and supernatural has manifested itself before the eyes of men.

From far away the roll of coach wheels rapidly disappearing in the distance alone broke the silence of the night.

"Is there no one here who will explain what all this means?" queried young Lalouët, who alone had remained self-assured and calm, for he alone knew nothing of what had happened. "Citizen Fleury, are you there?"

Then as once again he received no reply, he added peremptorily:

"Hey! some one there! Are you all louts and oafs that not one of you can speak?"

A timid voice from the rear ventured on explanation.

"The citizen proconsul was here a moment ago. . . . We all saw him, and you citizen Lalouët were with him. . . . "

An imprecation from young Lalouët silenced the timid voice for the nonce . . . and then another resumed the halting narrative.

"We all could have sworn that we saw you, citizen Lalouët, also the citizen proconsul. . . . He got into his coach with you . . . you . . . that is . . . they have driven off. . . . "

"This is some awful and treacherous hoax," cried the youngster now in a towering passion; "the citizen proconsul is upstairs in bed, I tell you . . . and I have only just come out of the hotel . . . ! Name of a name of a dog! am I standing here or am I not?"

Then suddenly he bethought himself of the many events of the day which had culminated in this gigantic feat of leger-de-main.

"Chauvelin!" he exclaimed. "Where in the name of h——ll is citizen Chauvelin?"

But Chauvelin for the moment could nowhere be found. Dazed, half-unconscious, wholly distraught, he had fled from the scene of his discomfiture as fast as his trembling knees would allow. Carrier searched the city for him high and low, and for days afterwards the soldiers of the Compagnie Marat gave *aristos* and rebels a rest: they were on the look-out for a small, wizened figure of a man—the man with the pale, keen eyes who had failed to recognise in the pseudo-Paul Friche, in the dirty, out-at-elbows sans-culotte—the most exquisite dandy that had ever graced the salons of Bath and of London: they were searching for the man with the acute and sensitive brain who had failed to scent in the pseudo-Carrier and the pseudo-Lalouët his old and arch enemy Sir Percy Blakeney and the charming wife of my lord Anthony Dewhurst.

# CHAPTER 10: LORD TONY

## I

A quarter of an hour later citizen-commandant Fleury was at last ushered into the presence of the proconsul and received upon his truly innocent head the full torrent of the despot's wrath. But Martin-Roget had listened to the counsels of prudence: for obvious reasons he desired to avoid any personal contact for the moment with Carrier, whom fear of the English spies had made into a more abject and more craven tyrant than ever before. At the same time he thought it wisest to try and pacify the brute by sending him the ten thousand francs—the bribe agreed upon for his help in the undertaking which had culminated in such a disastrous failure.

At the self-same hour whilst Carrier—fuming and swearing— was for the hundredth time uttering that furious "How?" which for the hundredth time had remained unanswered, two men were taking leave of one another at the small postern gate which gives on the cemetery of St. Anne. The taller and younger one of the two had just dropped a heavy purse into the hand of the other. The latter stooped and kissed the kindly hand.

"Milor," he said, "I swear to you most solemnly that M. le duc de Kernogan will rest in peace in hallowed ground. M. le curé de Vertou —ah! he is a saint and a brave man, milor—comes over whenever he can prudently do so and reads the offices for the dead—over those who have died as Christians, and there is a piece of consecrated ground out here in the open which those fiends of Terrorists have not discovered yet."

"And you will bury M. le duc immediately," admonished the younger man, "and apprise M. le curé of what has happened."

"Aye! aye! I'll do that, milor, within the hour. Though M. le duc was never a very kind master to me in the past, I cannot forget that I served him and his family for over thirty years as coachman. I drove Mlle. Yvonne in the first pony-cart she ever possessed. I drove her—ah! that was a bitter day!—her and M. le duc when they left Kernogan never to return. I drove Mlle. Yvonne on that memorable night when a crowd of miserable peasants attacked her coach, and that brute Pierre Adet started to lead a rabble against the château. That was the beginning of things, milor. God alone knows what has happened to Pierre Adet. His father Jean was hanged by order of M. le duc. Now M. le duc is destined to lie in a forgotten grave. I serve this abominable Republic by digging graves for her victims. I would be happier, I think, if I knew what had become of Mlle. Yvonne."

"Mlle. Yvonne is my wife, old friend," said the younger man softly. "Please God she has years of happiness before her, if I succeed in making her forget all that she has suffered."

"Amen to that, milor!" rejoined the man fervently. "Then I pray you tell the noble lady to rest assured. Jean-Marie—her old coachman whom she used to trust implicitly in the past—will see that M. le duc de Kernogan is buried as a gentleman and a Christian should be."

"You are not running too great a risk by this, I hope, my good Jean-Marie," quoth Lord Tony gently.

"No greater risk, milor," replied Jean-Marie earnestly, "than the one which you ran by carrying my old master's dead body on your shoulders through the streets of Nantes."

"Bah! that was simple enough," said the younger man, "the hue and cry is after higher quarry to-night. Pray God the hounds have not run the noble game to earth."

Even as he spoke there came from far away through the darkness the sound of a fast trotting pair of horses and the rumble of coach-wheels on the unpaved road.

"There they are, thank God!" exclaimed Lord Tony, and the tremor in his voice alone betrayed the torturing anxiety which he had been enduring, ever since he had seen the last both of his adored young wife and of his gallant chief in the squalid tap-room of the Rat Mort.

With the dead body of Yvonne's father on his back he had quietly worked his way out of the tavern in the wake of his chief. He had his orders, and for the members of that gallant League of the Scarlet Pimpernel there was no such word as "disobedience" and no such word as "fail." Through the darkness and through the tortuous streets of Nantes Lord Anthony Dewhurst—the young and wealthy exquisite, the hero of an hundred fêtes and galas in Bath, in London—staggered under the weight of a burden imposed upon him only by his loyalty and a noble sense of self-prescribed discipline—and that burden the dead body of the man who had done him an unforgivable wrong. Without a thought of revolt he had obeyed—and risked his life and worse in the obedience.

The darkness of the night was his faithful handmaiden, and the excitement of the chase after the other quarry had fortunately drawn every possible enemy from his track. He had set his teeth and accomplished his task, and even the deathly anxiety for the wife whom he idolised had been crushed, under the iron heel of a grim resolve. Now his work was done, and from far away he heard the rattle of the coach wheels which were bringing his beloved nearer and nearer to him.

Five minutes longer and the coach came to a halt. A cheery voice called out gaily:

"Tony! are you there?"

"Percy!" exclaimed the young man.

Already he knew that all was well. The gallant leader, the loyal and loving friend, had taxed every resource of a boundlessly fertile brain in order to win yet another wreath of immortal laurels for the League which he commanded, and the very tone of his merry voice proclaimed the triumph which had crowned his daring scheme.

The next moment Yvonne lay in the arms of her dear milor. He had stepped into the carriage, even while Sir Percy climbed nimbly on the box and took the reins from the bewildered coachman's hands.

"Citizen proconsul . . . " murmured the latter, who of a truth thought that he was dreaming.

"Get off the box, you old noodle," quoth the pseudo-proconsul peremptorily. "Thou and thy friend the postilion will remain here in the road, and on the morrow you'll explain to whomsoever it may concern that the English spy made a murderous attack on you both and left you half dead outside the postern gate of the cemetery of Ste. Anne. Here," he added as he threw a purse down to the two men—who half-dazed and overcome by superstitious fear had indeed scrambled down, one from his box, the other from his horse—"there's a hundred francs for each of you in there, and mind you drink to the health of the English spy and the confusion of your brutish proconsul."

There was no time to lose: the horses—still very fresh—were fretting to start.

"Where do we pick up Hastings and Ffoulkes?" asked Sir Percy Blakeney finally as he turned toward the interior of the barouche, the hood of which hid its occupants from view.

"At the comer of the rue de Gigan," came the quick answer. "It is only two hundred metres from the city gate. They are on the look out for you."

"Ffoulkes shall be postilion," rejoined Sir Percy with a laugh, "and Hastings sit beside me on the box. And you will see how at the city gate and all along the route soldiers of the guard will salute the equipage of the all-powerful proconsul of Nantes. By Gad!" he added under his breath, "I've never had a merrier time in all my life—not even when. . . . "

He clicked his tongue and gave the horses their heads—and soon the coachman and the postilion and Jean-Marie the gravedigger of the cemetery of Ste. Anne were left gaping out into the night in the direction where the barouche had so quickly disappeared.

"Now for Le Croisic and the Day-Dream," sighed the daring adventurer contentedly, " . . . and for Marguerite!" he added wistfully.

## II

Under the hood of the barouche Yvonne, wearied but

immeasurably happy, was doing her best to answer all her dear milor's impassioned questions and to give him a fairly clear account of that terrible chase and flight through the streets of the Isle Feydeau.

"Ah, milor, how can I tell you what I felt when I realised that I was being carried along in the arms of the valiant Scarlet Pimpernel? A word from him and I understood. After that I tried to be both resourceful and brave. When the chase after us was at its hottest we slipped into a ruined and deserted house. In a room at the back there were several bundles of what looked like old clothes. 'This is my storehouse,' milor said to me; 'now that we have reached it we can just make long noses at the whole pack of bloodhounds.' He made me slip into some boy's clothes which he gave me, and whilst I donned these he disappeared. When he returned I truly did not recognise him. He looked horrible, and his voice . . . ! After a moment or two he laughed, and then I knew him. He explained to me the *rôle* which I was to play, and I did my best to obey him in everything. But oh! I hardly lived while we once more emerged into the open street and then turned into the great Place which was full—oh full!—of people. I felt that at every moment we might be suspected. Figure to yourself, my dear milor. . . . "

What Yvonne Dewhurst was about to say next will never be recorded. My lord Tony had closed her lips with a kiss.

# THE LEAGUE OF THE
# SCARLET PIMPERNEL

BARONESS EMMUSKA ORCZY

# Sir Percy Explains

It was not, Heaven help us all! a very uncommon occurrence these days: a woman almost unsexed by misery, starvation, and the abnormal excitement engendered by daily spectacles of revenge and of cruelty. They were to be met with every day, round every street corner, these harridans, more terrible far than were the men.

This one was still comparatively young, thirty at most; would have been good-looking too, for the features were really delicate, the nose chiselled, the brow straight, the chin round and small. But the mouth! Heavens, what a mouth! Hard and cruel and thin-lipped; and those eyes! sunken and rimmed with purple; eyes that told tales of sorrow and, yes! of degradation. The crowd stood round her, sullen and apathetic; poor, miserable wretches like herself, staring at her antics with lack-lustre eyes and an ever-recurrent contemptuous shrug of the shoulders.

The woman was dancing, contorting her body in the small circle of light formed by a flickering lanthorn which was hung across the street from house to house, striking the muddy pavement with her shoeless feet, all to the sound of a be-ribboned tambourine which she struck now and again with her small, grimy hand. From time to time she paused, held out the tambourine at arm's length, and went the round of the spectators, asking for alms. But at her approach the crowd at once seemed to disintegrate, to melt into the humid evening air; it was but rarely that a greasy token fell into the outstretched tambourine. Then as the woman started again to dance the crowd gradually reassembled, and stood, hands in pockets, lips still sullen and contemptuous, but eyes watchful of the spectacle. There were such few spectacles these days, other than the monotonous processions of tumbrils with their load of aristocrats for the guillotine!

So the crowd watched, and the woman danced. The lanthorn overhead threw a weird light on red caps and tricolour cockades, on the sullen faces of the men and the shoulders of the women, on the dancer's weird antics and her flying, tattered skirts. She was obviously tired, as a poor, performing cur might be, or a bear prodded along to uncongenial buffoonery. Every time that she paused and solicited alms with her tambourine the crowd dispersed, and some of them laughed because she insisted.

"*Voyons,*" she said with a weird attempt at gaiety, "a couple of sous for the entertainment, citizen! You have stood here half an hour. You can't have it all for nothing, what?"

The man—young, square-shouldered, thick-lipped, with the look of a bully about his well-clad person—retorted with a coarse insult, which the woman resented. There were high words; the crowd for the most part ranged itself on the side of the bully. The woman backed against the wall nearest to her, held feeble, emaciated hands up to her ears in a vain endeavour to shut out the hideous jeers and ribald jokes which were the natural weapons of this untamed crowd.

Soon blows began to rain; not a few fell upon the unfortunate woman. She screamed, and the more she screamed the louder did the crowd jeer, the uglier became its temper. Then suddenly it was all over. How it happened the woman could not tell. She had closed her eyes, feeling sick and dizzy; but she had heard a loud call, words spoken in English (a language which she understood), a pleasant laugh, and a brief but violent scuffle. After that the hurrying retreat of many feet, the click of sabots on the uneven pavement and patter of shoeless feet, and then silence.

She had fallen on her knees and was cowering against the wall, had lost consciousness probably for a minute or two. Then she heard that pleasant laugh again and the soft drawl of the English tongue.

"I love to see those beggars scuttling off, like so many rats to their burrows, don't you, Ffoulkes?"

"They didn't put up much fight, the cowards!" came from another voice, also in English. "A dozen of them against this wretched woman. What had best be done with her?"

"I'll see to her," rejoined the first speaker. "You and Tony had best find the others. Tell them I shall be round directly."

It all seemed like a dream. The woman dared not open her eyes lest reality—hideous and brutal—once more confronted her. Then all at once she felt that her poor, weak body, encircled by strong arms, was lifted off the ground, and that she was being carried down the street, away from the light projected by the lanthorn overhead, into the sheltering darkness of a yawning *porte cochere*. But she was not then fully conscious.

## II

When she reopened her eyes she was in what appeared to be the lodge of a concierge. She was lying on a horsehair sofa. There was a sense of warmth and of security around her. No wonder that it still seemed like a dream. Before her stood a man, tall and straight, surely a being from another world—or so he appeared to the poor wretch who, since uncountable time, had set eyes on none but the most miserable dregs of struggling humanity, who had seen little else but rags, and faces either cruel or wretched. This man was clad in a huge caped coat, which made his powerful figure seem preternaturally large. His hair was fair and slightly curly above his low, square brow; the eyes beneath their heavy lids looked down on her with unmistakable kindness.

The poor woman struggled to her feet. With a quick and pathetically humble gesture she drew her ragged, muddy skirts over her ankles and her tattered kerchief across her breast.

"I had best go now, Monsieur . . . citizen," she murmured, while a hot flush rose to the roots of her unkempt hair. "I must not stop here. . . . I-"

"You are not going, Madame," he broke in, speaking now in perfect French and with a great air of authority, as one who is accustomed to being implicitly obeyed, "until you have told me how, a lady of culture and of refinement, comes to be masquerading as a street-dancer. The game is a dangerous one, as you have experienced to-night."

"It is no game, Monsieur . . . citizen," she stammered; "nor yet a masquerade. I have been a street-dancer all my life, and—"

By way of an answer he took her hand, always with that air of authority which she never thought to resent.

"This is not a street-dancer's hand; Madame," he said quietly. "Nor is your speech that of the people."

She drew her hand away quickly, and the flush on her haggard face deepened.

"If you will honour me with your confidence, Madame," he insisted.

The kindly words, the courtesy of the man, went to the poor creature's heart. She fell back upon the sofa and with her face buried in her arms she sobbed out her heart for a minute or two. The man waited quite patiently. He had seen many women weep these days, and had dried many a tear through deeds of valour and of self-sacrifice, which were for ever recorded in the hearts of those whom he had succoured.

When this poor woman had succeeded in recovering some semblance of self-control, she turned her wan, tear-stained face to him and said simply:

"My name is Madeleine Lannoy, Monsieur. My husband was killed during the emeutes at Versailles, whilst defending the persons of the Queen and of the royal children against the fury of the mob. When I was a girl I had the misfortune to attract the attentions of a young doctor named Jean Paul Marat. You have heard of him, Monsieur?"

The other nodded.

"You know him, perhaps," she continued, "for what he is: the most cruel and revengeful of men. A few years ago he threw up his lucrative appointment as Court physician to Monseigneur le Comte d'Artois, and gave up the profession of medicine for that of journalist and politician. Politician! Heaven help him! He belongs to the most bloodthirsty section of revolutionary brigands. His creed is pillage, murder, and revenge; and he chooses to declare that it is I who, by rejecting his love, drove him to these foul extremities. May God forgive him that abominable lie! The evil we do, Monsieur, is within us; it does not come from circumstance. I, in the meanwhile, was a happy wife. My husband, M. de Lannoy, who was an officer in the army, idolised me. We had one child, a boy—"

She paused, with another catch in her throat. Then she resumed, with calmness that, in view of the tale she told, sounded strangely weird:

"In June last year my child was stolen from me—stolen by Marat in hideous revenge for the supposed wrong which I had done him. The details of that execrable outrage are of no importance. I was decoyed from home one day through the agency of a forged message purporting to come from a very dear friend whom I knew to be in grave trouble at the time. Oh! the whole thing was thoroughly well thought out, I can assure you!" she continued, with a harsh laugh which ended in a heartrending sob. "The forged message, the suborned servant, the threats of terrible reprisals if anyone in the village gave me the slightest warning or clue. When the whole miserable business was accomplished, I was just like a trapped animal inside a cage, held captive by immovable bars of obstinate silence and cruel indifference. No one would help me. No one ostensibly knew anything; no one had seen anything, heard anything. The child was gone! My servants, the people in the village—some of whom I could have sworn were true and sympathetic—only shrugged their shoulders. 'Que voulez-vous, Madame? Children of bourgeois as well as of aristos were often taken up by the State to be brought up as true patriots and no longer pampered like so many lap-dogs.'

"Three days later I received a letter from that inhuman monster, Jean Paul Marat. He told me that he had taken my child away from me, not from any idea of revenge for my disdain in the past, but from a spirit of pure patriotism. My boy, he said, should not be brought up with the same ideas of bourgeois effeteness and love of luxury which had disgraced the nation for centuries. No! he should be reared amongst men who had realised the true value of fraternity and equality and the ideal of complete liberty for the individual to lead his own life, unfettered by senseless prejudices of education and refinement. Which means, Monsieur," the poor woman went on with passionate misery, "that my child is to be reared up in the company of all that is most vile and most degraded in the disease-haunted slums of indigent Paris; that, with the connivance of that execrable fiend Marat, my only son will, mayhap, come back to me one day a potential thief, a criminal probably, a drink-sodden reprobate at best. Such things are done every day in this glorious Revolution of ours—done in the sacred name of France and of Liberty. And the moral murder of my child is to be my punishment for daring to turn a deaf ear to the indign passion of a brute!"

Once more she paused, and when the melancholy echo of her broken voice had died away in the narrow room, not another murmur broke the stillness of this far-away corner of the great city.

The man did not move. He stood looking down upon the poor woman before him, a world of pity expressed in his deep-set eyes. Through the absolute silence around there came the sound as of a gentle flutter, the current of cold air, mayhap, sighing through the ill-fitting shutters, or the soft, weird soughing made by unseen things. The man's heart was full of pity, and it seemed as if the Angel of Compassion had come at his bidding and enfolded the sorrowing woman with his wings.

A moment or two later she was able to finish her pathetic narrative.

"Do you marvel, Monsieur," she said, "that I am still sane—still alive? But I only live to find my child. I try and keep my reason in order to fight the devilish cunning of a brute on his own ground. Up to now all my inquiries have been in vain. At first I squandered money, tried judicial means, set an army of sleuth-hounds on the track. I tried bribery, corruption. I went to the wretch himself and abased myself in the dust before him. He only laughed at me and told me that his love for me had died long ago; he now was lavishing its treasures upon the faithful friend and companion—that awful woman, Simonne Evrard—who had stood by him in the darkest hours of his misfortunes. Then it was that I decided to adopt different tactics. Since my child was to be reared in the midst of murderers and thieves, I, too, would haunt their abodes. I became a street-singer, dancer, what you will. I wear rags now and solicit alms. I haunt the most disreputable cabarets in the lowest slums of Paris. I listen and I spy; I question every man, woman, and child who might afford some clue, give me some indication. There is hardly a house in these parts that I have not visited and whence I have not been kicked out as an importunate beggar or worse. Gradually I am narrowing the circle of my investigations. Presently I shall get a clue. I shall! I know I shall! God cannot allow this monstrous thing to go on!"

Again there was silence. The poor woman had completely broken down. Shame, humiliation, passionate grief, had made of her a mere miserable wreckage of humanity.

The man waited awhile until she was composed, then he said simply:

"You have suffered terribly, Madame; but chiefly, I think, because you have been alone in your grief. You have brooded over it until it has threatened your reason. Now, if you will allow me to act as your friend, I will pledge you my word that I will find your son for you. Will you trust me sufficiently to give up your present methods and place yourself entirely in my hands? There are more than a dozen gallant gentlemen, who are my friends, and who will help me in my search. But for this I must have a free hand, and only help from you when I require it. I can find you lodgings where you will be quite safe under the protection of my wife, who is as like an angel as any man or woman I have ever met on this earth. When your son is once more in your arms, you will, I hope, accompany us to England, where so many of your friends have already found a refuge. If this meets with your approval, Madame, you may command me, for with your permission I mean to be your most devoted servant."

Dante, in his wild imaginations of hell and of purgatory and fleeting glimpses of paradise, never put before us the picture of a soul that was lost and found heaven, after a cycle of despair. Nor could Madeleine Lannoy ever explain her feelings at that moment, even to herself. To begin with, she could not quite grasp the reality of this ray of hope, which came to her at the darkest hour of her misery. She stared at the man before her as she would on an ethereal vision; she fell on her knees and buried her face in her hands.

What happened afterwards she hardly knew; she was in a state of semi-consciousness. When she once more woke to reality, she was in comfortable lodgings; she moved and talked and ate and lived like a human being. She was no longer a pariah, an outcast, a poor, half-demented creature, insentient save for an infinite capacity for suffering. She suffered still, but she no longer despaired. There had been such marvellous power and confidence in that man's voice when he said: "I pledge you my word." Madeleine Lannoy lived now in hope and a sweet sense of perfect mental and bodily security. Around her there was an influence, too, a presence which she did not often see, but always felt to be there: a woman, tall and graceful and sympathetic, who was always ready to cheer, to comfort, and to help. Her name was Marguerite. Madame Lannoy never knew her by any other. The man had spoken of her as being as like an angel as could be met on this earth, and poor Madeleine Lannoy fully agreed with him.

III

Even that bloodthirsty tiger, Jean Paul Marat, has had his apologists. His friends have called him a martyr, a selfless and incorruptible exponent of social and political ideals. We may take it that Simonne Evrard loved him, for a more impassioned obituary speech was, mayhap, never spoken than the one which she delivered before the National Assembly in honour of that sinister demagogue, whose writings and activities will for ever sully some of the really fine pages of that revolutionary era.

But with those apologists we have naught to do. History has talked its fill of the inhuman monster. With the more intimate biographists alone has this true chronicle any concern. It is one of these who tells us that on or about the eighteenth day of Messidor, in the year I of the Republic (a date which corresponds with the sixth of July, 1793, of our own calendar), Jean Paul Marat took an additional man into his service, at the instance of Jeannette Marechal, his cook and maid-of-all-work. Marat was at this time a martyr to an unpleasant form of skin disease, brought on by the terrible privations which he had endured during the few years preceding his association with Simonne Evrard, the faithful friend and housekeeper, whose small fortune subsequently provided him with some degree of comfort.

The man whom Jeannette Marechal, the cook, introduced into the household of No. 30, Rue des Cordeliers, that worthy woman had literally picked one day out of the gutter where he was grabbing for scraps of food like some wretched starving cur. He appeared to be known to the police of the section, his identity book proclaiming him to be one Paul Mole, who had served his time in gaol for larceny. He professed himself willing to do any work required of him, for the merest pittance and some kind of roof over his head. Simonne Evrard allowed Jeannette to take him in, partly out of compassion and partly with a view to easing the woman's own burden, the only other domestic in the house—a man named Bas—being more interested in politics and the meetings of the Club des Jacobins than he was in his master's ailments. The man Mole, moreover, appeared to know something of medicine and of herbs and how to prepare the warm baths which alone eased the unfortunate Marat from pain. He was powerfully built, too, and though he muttered and grumbled a great deal, and indulged in prolonged fits of sulkiness, when he would not open his mouth to anyone, he was, on the whole, helpful and good-tempered.

There must also have been something about his whole wretched personality which made a strong appeal to the "Friend of the People," for it is quite evident that within a few days Paul Mole had won no small measure of his master's confidence.

Marat, sick, fretful, and worried, had taken an unreasoning dislike to his servant Bas. He was thankful to have a stranger about him, a man who was as miserable as he himself had been a very little while ago; who, like himself, had lived in cellars and in underground burrows, and lived on the scraps of food which even street-curs had disdained.

On the seventh day following Mole's entry into the household, and while the latter was preparing his employer's bath, Marat said abruptly to him:

"You'll go as far as the Chemin de Pantin to-day for me, citizen. You know your way?"

"I can find it, what?" muttered Mole, who appeared to be in one of his surly moods.

"You will have to go very circumspectly," Marat went on, in his cracked and feeble voice. "And see to it that no one spies upon your movements. I have many enemies, citizen . . . one especially . . . a woman. . . . She is always prying and spying on me. . . . So beware of any woman you see lurking about at your heels."

Mole gave a half-audible grunt in reply.

"You had best go after dark," the other rejoined after awhile. "Come back to me after nine o'clock. It is not far to the Chemin de Pantin—just where it intersects the Route de Meaux. You can get there and back before midnight. The people will admit you. I will give you a ring—the only thing I possess. . . . It has little or no value," he added with a harsh, grating laugh. "It will not be worth your while to steal it. You will have to see a brat and report to me on his condition—his appearance, what? . . . Talk to him a bit. . . . See what he says and let me know. It is not difficult."

"No, citizen."

Mole helped the suffering wretch into his bath. Not a movement, not a quiver of the eyelid betrayed one single emotion which he may have felt—neither loathing nor sympathy, only placid indifference. He was just a half-starved menial, thankful to accomplish any task for the sake of satisfying a craving stomach. Marat stretched out his shrunken limbs in the herbal water with a sigh of well-being.

"And the ring, citizen?" Mole suggested presently.

The demagogue held up his left hand—it was emaciated and disfigured by disease. A cheap-looking metal ring, set with a false stone, glistened upon the fourth finger.

"Take it off," he said curtly.

The ring must have all along been too small for the bony hand of the once famous Court physician. Even now it appeared embedded in the flabby skin and refused to slide over the knuckle.

"The water will loosen it," remarked Mole quietly.

Marat dipped his hand back into the water, and the other stood beside him, silent and stolid, his broad shoulders bent, his face naught but a mask, void and expressionless beneath its coating of grime.

One or two seconds went by. The air was heavy with steam and a medley of evil-smelling fumes, which hung in the close atmosphere of the narrow room. The sick man appeared to be drowsy, his head rolled over to one side, his eyes closed. He had evidently forgotten all about the ring.

A woman's voice, shrill and peremptory, broke the silence which had become oppressive:

"Here, citizen Mole, I want you! There's not a bit of wood chopped up for my fire, and how am I to make the coffee without firing, I should like to know?"

"The ring, citizen," Mole urged gruffly.

Marat had been roused by the woman's sharp voice. He cursed her for a noisy harridan; then he said fretfully:

"It will do presently—when you are ready to start. I said nine o'clock . . . it is only four now. I am tired. Tell citizeness Evrard to bring me some hot coffee in an hour's time . . . You can go and fetch me the Moniteur now, and take back these proofs to citizen Dufour. You will find him at the 'Cordeliers,' or else at the printing works. . . . Come back at nine o'clock. . . . I am tired now . . . too tired to tell you where to find the house which is off the Chemin de Pantin. Presently will do . . . "

Even while he spoke he appeared to drop into a fitful sleep. His two hands were hidden under the sheet which covered the bath. Mole watched him in silence for a moment or two, then he turned on his heel and shuffled off through the ante-room into the kitchen beyond, where presently he sat down, squatting in an angle by the stove, and started with his usual stolidness to chop wood for the citizeness' fire.

When this task was done, and he had received a chunk of sour bread for his reward from Jeannette Marechal, the cook, he shuffled out of the place and into the street, to do his employer's errands.

## IV

Paul Mole had been to the offices of the Moniteur and to the printing works of L'Ami du Peuple. He had seen the citizen Dufour at the Club and, presumably, had spent the rest of his time wandering idly about the streets of the quartier, for he did not return to the rue des Cordeliers until nearly nine o'clock.

As soon as he came to the top of the street, he fell in with the crowd which had collected outside No. 30. With his habitual slouchy gait and the steady pressure of his powerful elbows, he pushed his way to the door, whilst gleaning whisperings and rumours on his way.

"The citizen Marat has been assassinated."

"By a woman."

"A mere girl."

"A wench from Caen. Her name is Corday."

"The people nearly tore her to pieces awhile ago."

"She is as much as guillotined already."

The latter remark went off with a loud guffaw and many a ribald joke.

Mole, despite his great height, succeeded in getting through unperceived. He was of no account, and he knew his way inside the house. It was full of people: journalists, gaffers, women and men—the usual crowd that come to gape. The citizen Marat was a great personage. The Friend of the People. An Incorruptible, if ever there was one. Just look at the simplicity, almost the poverty, in which he lived! Only the *aristos* hated him, and the fat bourgeois who battened on the

502 BARONESS EMMUSKA ORCZY

people. Citizen Marat had sent hundreds of them to the guillotine with a stroke of his pen or a denunciation from his fearless tongue.

Mole did not pause to listen to these comments. He pushed his way through the throng up the stairs, to his late employer's lodgings on the first floor.

The anteroom was crowded, so were the other rooms; but the greatest pressure was around the door immediately facing him, the one which gave on the bathroom. In the kitchen on his right, where awhile ago he had been chopping wood under a flood of abuse from Jeannette Marechal, he caught sight of this woman, cowering by the hearth, her filthy apron thrown over her head, and crying—yes! crying for the loathsome creature, who had expiated some of his abominable crimes at the hands of a poor, misguided girl, whom an infuriated mob was even now threatening to tear to pieces in its rage.

The parlour and even Simonne's room were also filled with people: men, most of whom Mole knew by sight; friends or enemies of the ranting demagogue who lay murdered in the very bath which his casual servant had prepared for him. Every one was discussing the details of the murder, the punishment of the youthful assassin. Simonne Evrard was being loudly blamed for having admitted the girl into citizen Marat's room. But the wench had looked so simple, so innocent, and she said she was the bearer of a message from Caen. She had called twice during the day, and in the evening the citizen himself said that he would see her. Simonne had been for sending her away. But the citizen was peremptory. And he was so helpless . . . in his bath . . . name of a name, the pitiable affair!

No one paid much attention to Mole. He listened for a while to Simonne's impassioned voice, giving her version of the affair; then he worked his way stolidly into the bathroom.

It was some time before he succeeded in reaching the side of that awful bath wherein lay the dead body of Jean Paul Marat. The small room was densely packed—not with friends, for there was not a man or woman living, except Simonne Evrard and her sisters, whom the bloodthirsty demagogue would have called "friend"; but his powerful personality had been a menace to many, and now they came in crowds to see that he was really dead, that a girl's feeble hand had actually done the deed which they themselves had only contemplated. They stood about whispering, their heads averted from the ghastly spectacle of this miserable creature, to whom even death had failed to lend his usual attribute of tranquil dignity.

The tiny room was inexpressibly hot and stuffy. Hardly a breath of outside air came in through the narrow window, which only gave on the bedroom beyond. An evil-smelling oil-lamp swung from the low ceiling and shed its feeble light on the upturned face of the murdered man.

Mole stood for a moment or two, silent and pensive, beside that hideous form. There was the bath, just as he had prepared it: the board spread over with a sheet and laid across the bath, above which only the head and shoulders emerged, livid and stained. One hand, the left, grasped the edge of the board with the last convulsive clutch of supreme agony.

On the fourth finger of that hand glistened the shoddy ring which Marat had said was not worth stealing. Yet, apparently, it roused the cupidity of the poor wretch who had served him faithfully for these last few days, and who now would once more be thrown, starving and friendless, upon the streets of Paris.

Mole threw a quick, furtive glance around him. The crowd which had come to gloat over the murdered Terrorist stood about whispering, with heads averted, engrossed in their own affairs. He slid his hand surreptitiously over that of the dead man. With dexterous manipulation he lifted the finger round which glistened the metal ring. Death appeared to have shrivelled the flesh still more upon the bones, to have contracted the knuckles and shrunk the tendons. The ring slid off quite easily. Mole had it in his hand, when suddenly a rough blow struck him on the shoulder.

"Trying to rob the dead?" a stern voice shouted in his ear. "Are you a disguised *aristo*, or what?"

At once the whispering ceased. A wave of excitement went round the room. Some people shouted, others pressed forward to gaze on the abandoned wretch who had been caught in the act of committing a gruesome deed.

"Robbing the dead!"

They were experts in evil, most of these men here. Their hands were indelibly stained with some of the foulest crimes ever recorded in history. But there was something ghoulish in this attempt to plunder that awful thing lying there, helpless, in the water. There was also a great relief to nerve-tension in shouting Horror and Anathema with self-righteous indignation; and additional excitement in the suggested "*Aristo* in disguise."

Mole struggled vigorously. He was powerful and his fists were heavy. But he was soon surrounded, held fast by both arms, whilst half a dozen hands tore at his tattered clothes, searched him to his very skin, for the booty which he was thought to have taken from the dead.

"Leave me alone, curse you!" he shouted, louder than his aggressors. "My name is Paul Mole, I tell you. Ask the citizeness Evrard. I waited on citizen Marat. I prepared his bath. I was the only friend who did not turn away from him in his sickness and his poverty. Leave me alone, I say! Why," he added, with a hoarse laugh, "Jean Paul in his bath was as naked as on the day he was born!"

"'Tis true," said one of those who had been most active in

rummaging through Mole's grimy rags. "There's nothing to be found on him."

But suspicion once aroused was not easily allayed. Mole's protestations became more and more vigorous and emphatic. His papers were all in order, he vowed. He had them on him: his own identity papers, clear for anyone to see. Someone had dragged them out of his pocket; they were dank and covered with splashes of mud— hardly legible. They were handed over to a man who stood in the immediate circle of light projected by the lamp. He seized them and examined them carefully. This man was short and slight, was dressed in well-made cloth clothes; his hair was held in at the nape of the next in a modish manner with a black taffeta bow. His hands were clean, slender, and claw-like, and he wore the tricolour scarf of office round his waist which proclaimed him to be a member of one of the numerous Committees which tyrannised over the people.

The papers appeared to be in order, and proclaimed the bearer to be Paul Mole, a native of Besancon, a carpenter by trade. The identity book had recently been signed by Jean Paul Marat, the man's latest employer, and been counter-signed by the Commissary of the section.

The man in the tricolour scarf turned with some acerbity on the crowd who was still pressing round the prisoner.

"Which of you here," he queried roughly, "levelled an unjust accusation against an honest citizen?"

But, as usual in such cases, no one replied directly to the charge. It was not safe these days to come into conflict with men like Mole. The Committees were all on their side, against the bourgeois as well as against the *aristos*. This was the reign of the proletariat, and the sans-culotte always emerged triumphant in a conflict against the well-to-do. Nor was it good to rouse the ire of citizen Chauvelin, one of the most powerful, as he was the most pitiless members of the Committee of Public Safety. Quiet, sarcastic rather than aggressive, something of the *aristo*, too, in his clean linen and well-cut clothes, he had not even yielded to the defunct Marat in cruelty and relentless persecution of aristocrats.

Evidently his sympathies now were all with Mole, the out-at-elbows, miserable servant of an equally miserable master. His pale-coloured, deep-set eyes challenged the crowd, which gave way before him, slunk back into the corners, away from his coldly threatening glance. Thus he found himself suddenly face to face with Mole, somewhat isolated from the rest, and close to the tin bath with its grim contents. Chauvelin had the papers in his hand.

"Take these, citizen," he said curtly to the other. "They are all in order."

He looked up at Mole as he said this, for the latter, though his shoulders were bent, was unusually tall, and Mole took the papers from him. Thus for the space of a few seconds the two men looked into one another's face, eyes to eyes—and suddenly Chauvelin felt an icy sweat coursing down his spine. The eyes into which he gazed had a strange, ironical twinkle in them, a kind of good-humoured arrogance, whilst through the firm, clear-cut lips, half hidden by a dirty and ill-kempt beard, there came the sound—oh! a mere echo—of a quaint and inane laugh.

The whole thing—it seemed like a vision—was over in a second. Chauvelin, sick and faint with the sudden rush of blood to his head, closed his eyes for one brief instant. The next, the crowd had closed round him; anxious inquiries reached his re-awakened senses.

But he uttered one quick, hoarse cry:

"Hebert! *A moi!* Are you there?"

"Present, citizen!" came in immediate response. And a tall figure in the tattered uniform affected by the revolutionary guard stepped briskly out of the crowd. Chauvelin's claw-like hand was shaking visibly.

"The man Mole," he called in a voice husky with excitement. "Seize him at once! And, name of a dog! do not allow a living soul in or out of the house!"

Hebert turned on his heel. The next moment his harsh voice was heard above the din and the general hubbub around:

"Quite safe, citizen!" he called to his chief. "We have the rogue right enough!"

There was much shouting and much cursing, a great deal of bustle and confusion, as the men of the Surete closed the doors of the defunct demagogue's lodgings. Some two score men, a dozen or so women, were locked in, inside the few rooms which reeked of dirt and of disease. They jostled and pushed, screamed and protested. For two or three minutes the din was quite deafening. Simonne Evrard pushed her way up to the forefront of the crowd.

"What is this I hear?" she queried peremptorily. "Who is accusing citizen Mole? And of what, I should like to know? I am responsible for everyone inside these apartments . . . and if citizen Marat were still alive - "

Chauvelin appeared unaware of all the confusion and of the woman's protestations. He pushed his way through the crowd to the corner of the anteroom where Mole stood, crouching and hunched up, his grimy hands idly fingering the papers which Chauvelin had returned to him a moment ago. Otherwise he did not move.

He stood, silent and sullen; and when Chauvelin, who had succeeded in mastering his emotion, gave the peremptory command: "Take this man to the depot at once. And do not allow him one instant out of your sight!" he made no attempt at escape.

He allowed Hebert and the men to seize him, to lead him away. He followed without a word, without a struggle. His massive figure was hunched up like that of an old man; his hands, which still clung to his identity papers, trembled slightly like those of a man who is very frightened and very helpless. The men of the Surete handled him very roughly, but he made no protest. The woman Evrard did all the protesting, vowing that the people would not long tolerate such tyranny. She even forced her way up to Hebert. With a gesture of fury she tried to strike him in the face, and continued, with a loud voice, her insults and objurgations, until, with a movement of his bayonet, he pushed her roughly out of the way.

After that Paul Mole, surrounded by the guard, was led without ceremony out of the house. Chauvelin gazed after him as if he had been brought face to face with a ghoul.

## V

Chauvelin hurried to the depot. After those few seconds wherein he had felt dazed, incredulous, almost under a spell, he had quickly regained the mastery of his nerves, and regained, too, that intense joy which anticipated triumph is wont to give.

In the out-at-elbows, half-starved servant of the murdered Terrorist, citizen Chauvelin, of the Committee of Public Safety, had recognised his arch enemy, that meddlesome and adventurous Englishman who chose to hide his identity under the pseudonym of the Scarlet Pimpernel. He knew that he could reckon on Hebert; his orders not to allow the prisoner one moment out of sight would of a certainty be strictly obeyed.

Hebert, indeed, a few moments later, greeted his chief outside the doors of the depot with the welcome news that Paul Mole was safely under lock and key.

"You had no trouble with him?" Chauvelin queried, with ill-concealed eagerness.

"No, no! citizen, no trouble," was Hebert's quick reply. "He seems to be a well-known rogue in these parts," he continued with a complacent guffaw; "and some of his friends tried to hustle us at the corner of the Rue de Tourraine; no doubt with a view to getting the prisoner away. But we were too strong for them, and Paul Mole is now sulking in his cell and still protesting that his arrest is an outrage against the liberty of the people."

Chauvelin made no further remark. He was obviously too excited to speak. Pushing past Hebert and the men of the Surete who stood about the dark and narrow passages of the depot, he sought the Commissary of the Section in the latter's office.

It was now close upon ten o'clock. The citizen Commissary

Cuisinier had finished his work for the day and was preparing to go home and to bed. He was a family man, had been a respectable bourgeois in his day, and though he was a rank opportunist and had sacrificed not only his political convictions but also his conscience to the exigencies of the time, he still nourished in his innermost heart a secret contempt for the revolutionary brigands who ruled over France at this hour.

To any other man than citizen Chauvelin, the citizen Commissary would, no doubt, have given a curt refusal to a request to see a prisoner at this late hour of the evening. But Chauvelin was not a man to be denied, and whilst muttering various objections in his ill-kempt beard, Cuisinier, nevertheless, gave orders that the citizen was to be conducted at once to the cells.

Paul Mole had in truth turned sulky. The turnkey vowed that the prisoner had hardly stirred since first he had been locked up in the common cell. He sat in a corner at the end of the bench, with his face turned to the wall, and paid no heed either to his fellow-prisoners or to the facetious remarks of the warder.

Chauvelin went up to him, made some curt remark. Mole kept an obstinate shoulder turned towards him—a grimy shoulder, which showed naked through a wide rent in his blouse. This portion of the cell was well-nigh in total darkness; the feeble shaft of light which came through the open door hardly penetrated to this remote angle of the squalid burrow. The same sense of mystery and unreality overcame Chauvelin again as he looked on the miserable creature in whom, an hour ago, he had recognised the super-exquisite Sir Percy Blakeney. Now he could only see a vague outline in the gloom: the stooping shoulders, the long limbs, that naked piece of shoulder which caught a feeble reflex from the distant light. Nor did any amount of none too gentle prodding on the part of the warder induce him to change his position.

"Leave him alone," said Chauvelin curly at last. "I have seen all that I wished to see."

The cell was insufferably hot and stuffy. Chauvelin, finical and queasy, turned away with a shudder of disgust. There was nothing to be got now out of a prolonged interview with his captured foe. He had seen him: that was sufficient. He had seen the super-exquisite Sir Percy Blakeney locked up in a common cell with some of the most scrubby and abject rogues which the slums of indigent Paris could yield, having apparently failed in some undertaking which had demanded for its fulfilment not only tattered clothes and grimy hands, but menial service with a beggarly and disease-ridden employer, whose very propinquity must have been positive torture to the fastidious dandy.

Of a truth this was sufficient for the gratification of any revenge. Chauvelin felt that he could now go contentedly to rest after an evening's work excellently done.

He gave order that Mole should be put in a separate cell, denied all intercourse with anyone outside or in the depot, and that he should be guarded on sight day and night. After that he went his way.

VI

The following morning citizen Chauvelin, of the Committee of Public Safety, gave due notice to citizen Fouquier-Tinville, the Public Prosecutor, that the dangerous English spy, known to the world as the Scarlet Pimpernel, was now safely under lock and key, and that he must be transferred to the Abbaye prison forthwith and to the guillotine as quickly as might be. No one was to take any risks this time; there must be no question either of discrediting his famous League or of obtaining other more valuable information out of him. Such methods had proved disastrous in the past.

There were no safe Englishmen these days, except the dead ones, and it would not take citizen Fouquier-Tinville much thought or time to frame an indictment against the notorious Scarlet Pimpernel, which would do away with the necessity of a prolonged trial. The revolutionary government was at war with England now, and short work could be made of all poisonous spies.

By order, therefore, of the Committee of Public Safety, the prisoner, Paul Mole, was taken out of the cells of the depot and conveyed in a closed carriage to the Abbaye prison. Chauvelin had the pleasure of watching this gratifying spectacle from the windows of the Commissariat. When he saw the closed carriage drive away, with Hebert and two men inside and two others on the box, he turned to citizen Commissary Cuisinier with a sigh of intense satisfaction.

"There goes the most dangerous enemy our glorious revolution has had," he said, with an accent of triumph which he did not attempt to disguise.

Cuisinier shrugged his shoulders.

"Possibly," he retorted curtly. "He did not seem to me to be very dangerous and his papers were quite in order."

To this assertion Chauvelin made no reply. Indeed, how could he explain to this stolid official the subtle workings of an intriguing brain? Had he himself not had many a proof of how little the forging of identity papers or of passports troubled the members of that accursed League? Had he not seen the Scarlet Pimpernel, that exquisite Sir Percy Blakeney, under disguises that were so grimy and so loathsome that they would have repelled the most abject, suborned spy?

Indeed, all that was wanted now was the assurance that Hebert —who himself had a deadly and personal grudge against the Scarlet Pimpernel—would not allow him for one moment out of his sight.

Fortunately as to this, there was no fear. One hint to Hebert and the man was as keen, as determined, as Chauvelin himself.

"Set your mind at rest, citizen," he said with a rough oath. "I guessed how matters stood the moment you gave me the order. I knew you would not take all that trouble for a real Paul Mole. But have no fear! That accursed Englishman has not been one second out of my sight, from the moment I arrested him in the late citizen Marat's lodgings, and by Satan! he shall not be either, until I have seen his impudent head fall under the guillotine."

He himself, he added, had seen to the arrangements for the disposal of the prisoner in the Abbaye: an inner cell, partially partitioned off in one of the guard-rooms, with no egress of its own, and only a tiny grated air-hole high up in the wall, which gave on an outside corridor, and through which not even a cat could manage to slip. Oh! the prisoner was well guarded! The citizen Representative need, of a truth, have no fear! Three or four men—of the best and most trustworthy—had not left the guard-room since the morning. He himself (Hebert) had kept the accursed Englishman in sight all night, had personally conveyed him to the Abbaye, and had only left the guard-room a moment ago in order to speak with the citizen Representative. He was going back now at once, and would not move until the order came for the prisoner to be conveyed to the Court of Justice and thence to summary execution.

For the nonce, Hebert concluded with a complacent chuckle, the Englishman was still crouching dejectedly in a corner of his new cell, with little of him visible save that naked shoulder through his torn shirt, which, in the process of transference from one prison to another, had become a shade more grimy than before.

Chauvelin nodded, well satisfied. He commended Hebert for his zeal, rejoiced with him over the inevitable triumph. It would be well to avenge that awful humiliation at Calais last September. Nevertheless, he felt anxious and nervy; he could not comprehend the apathy assumed by the factitious Mole. That the apathy was assumed Chauvelin was keen enough to guess. What it portended he could not conjecture. But that the Englishman would make a desperate attempt at escape was, of course, a foregone conclusion. It rested with Hebert and a guard that could neither be bribed nor fooled into treachery, to see that such an attempt remained abortive.

What, however, had puzzled citizen Chauvelin all along was the motive which had induced Sir Percy Blakeney to play the role of menial to Jean Paul Marat. Behind it there lay, undoubtedly, one of those subtle intrigues for which that insolent Scarlet Pimpernel was famous; and with it was associated an attempt at theft upon the murdered body of the demagogue . . . an attempt which had failed, seeing that the supposititious Paul Mole had been searched and nothing suspicious been found upon his person.

Nevertheless, thoughts of that attempted theft disturbed Chauvelin's equanimity. The old legend of the crumpled roseleaf was applicable in his case. Something of his intense satisfaction would pale if this final enterprise of the audacious adventurer were to be brought to a triumphant close in the end.

## VII

That same forenoon, on his return from the Abbaye and the depot, Chauvelin found that a visitor was waiting for him. A woman, who gave her name as Jeannette Marechal, desired to speak with the citizen Representative. Chauvelin knew the woman as his colleague Marat's maid-of-all-work, and he gave orders that she should be admitted at once.

Jeannette Marechal, tearful and not a little frightened, assured the citizen Representative that her errand was urgent. Her late employer had so few friends; she did not know to whom to turn until she bethought herself of citizen Chauvelin. It took him some little time to disentangle the tangible facts out of the woman's voluble narrative. At first the words: "Child . . . Chemin de Pantin . . . Leridan," were only a medley of sounds which conveyed no meaning to his ear. But when occasion demanded, citizen Chauvelin was capable of infinite patience. Gradually he understood what the woman was driving at.

"The child, citizen!" she reiterated excitedly. "What's to be done about him? I know that citizen Marat would have wished - "

"Never mind now what citizen Marat would have wished," Chauvelin broke in quietly. "Tell me first who this child is."

"I do not know, citizen," she replied.

"How do you mean, you do not know? Then I pray you, citizeness, what is all this pother about?"

"About the child, citizen," reiterated Jeannette obstinately.

"What child?"

"The child whom citizen Marat adopted last year and kept at that awful house on the Chemin de Pantin."

"I did not know citizen Marat had adopted a child," remarked Chauvelin thoughtfully.

"No one knew," she rejoined. "Not even citizeness Evrard. I was the only one who knew. I had to go and see the child once every month. It was a wretched, miserable brat," the woman went on, her shrivelled old breast vaguely stirred, mayhap, by some atrophied feeling of motherhood. "More than half-starved . . . and the look in its eyes, citizen! It was enough to make you cry! I could see by his poor little emaciated body and his nice little hands and feet that he ought never to have been put in that awful house, where - "

She paused, and that quick look of furtive terror, which was so often to be met with in the eyes of the timid these days, crept into her wrinkled face.

"Well, citizeness," Chauvelin rejoined quietly, "why don't you proceed? That awful house, you were saying. Where and what is that awful house of which you speak?"

"The place kept by citizen Leridan, just by Bassin de l'Ourcq," the woman murmured. "You know it, citizen."

Chauvelin nodded. He was beginning to understand.

"Well, now, tell me," he said, with that bland patience which had so oft served him in good stead in his unavowable profession. "Tell me. Last year citizen Marat adopted—we'll say adopted—a child, whom he placed in the Leridans' house on the Pantin road. Is that correct?"

"That is just how it is, citizen. And I - "

"One moment," he broke in somewhat more sternly, as the woman's garrulity was getting on his nerves. "As you say, I know the Leridans' house. I have had cause to send children there myself. Children of *aristos* or of fat bourgeois, whom it was our duty to turn into good citizens. They are not pampered there, I imagine," he went on drily; "and if citizen Marat sent his—er—adopted son there, it was not with a view to having him brought up as an *aristo*, what?"

"The child was not to be brought up at all," the woman said gruffly. "I have often heard citizen Marat say that he hoped the brat would prove a thief when he grew up, and would take to alcoholism like a duck takes to water."

"And you know nothing of the child's parents?"

"Nothing, citizen. I had to go to Pantin once a month and have a look at him and report to citizen Marat. But I always had the same tale to tell. The child was looking more and more like a young reprobate every time I saw him."

"Did citizen Marat pay the Leridans for keeping the child?"

"Oh, no, citizen! The Leridans make a trade of the children by sending them out to beg. But this one was not to be allowed out yet. Citizen Marat's orders were very stern, and he was wont to terrify the Leridans with awful threats of the guillotine if they ever allowed the child out of their sight."

Chauvelin sat silent for a while. A ray of light had traversed the dark and tortuous ways of his subtle brain. While he mused the woman became impatient. She continued to talk on with the volubility peculiar to her kind. He paid no heed to her, until one phrase struck his ear.

"So now," Jeannette Marechal was saying, "I don't know what to do. The ring has disappeared, and the Leridans are suspicious."

"The ring?" queried Chauvelin curtly. "What ring?"

"As I was telling you, citizen," she replied querulously, "when I went to see the child, the citizen Marat always gave me this ring to show to the Leridans. Without I brought the ring they would not admit me inside their door. They were so terrified with all the citizen's threats of the guillotine."

"And now you say the ring has disappeared. Since when?"

"Well, citizen," replied Jeannette blandly, "since you took poor Paul Mole into custody."

"What do you mean?" Chauvelin riposted. "What had Paul Mole to do with the child and the ring?"

"Only this, citizen, that he was to have gone to Pantin last night instead of me. And thankful I was not to have to go. Citizen Marat gave the ring to Mole, I suppose. I know he intended to give it to him. He spoke to me about it just before that execrable woman came and murdered him. Anyway, the ring has gone and Mole too. So I imagine that Mole has the ring and - "

"That's enough!" Chauvelin broke in roughly. "You can go!"

"But, citizen - "

"You can go, I said," he reiterated sharply. "The matter of the child and the Leridans and the ring no longer concerns you. You understand?"

"Y—y—yes, citizen," murmured Jeannette, vaguely terrified.

And of a truth the change in citizen Chauvelin's demeanour was enough to scare any timid creature. Not that he raved or ranted or screamed. Those were not his ways. He still sat beside his desk as he had done before, and his slender hand, so like the talons of a vulture, was clenched upon the arm of his chair. But there was such a look of inward fury and of triumph in his pale, deep-set eyes, such lines of cruelty around his thin, closed lips, that Jeannette Marechal, even with the picture before her mind of Jean Paul Marat in his maddest moods, fled, with the unreasoning terror of her kind, before the sternly controlled, fierce passion of this man.

Chauvelin never noticed that she went. He sat for a long time, silent and immovable. Now he understood. Thank all the Powers of Hate and Revenge, no thought of disappointment was destined to embitter the overflowing cup of his triumph. He had not only brought his arch-enemy to his knees, but had foiled one of his audacious ventures. How clear the whole thing was! The false Paul Mole, the newly acquired menial in the household of Marat, had wormed himself into the confidence of his employer in order to wrest from him the secret of the *aristo's* child. Bravo! bravo! my gallant Scarlet Pimpernel! Chauvelin now could see it all. Tragedies such as that which had placed an *aristo's* child in the power of a cunning demon like Marat were not rare these days, and Chauvelin had been fitted by nature and by temperament to understand and appreciate an execrable monster of the type of Jean Paul Marat.

And Paul Mole, the grimy, degraded servant of the indigent

demagogue, the loathsome mask which hid the fastidious personality of Sir Percy Blakeney, had made a final and desperate effort to possess himself of the ring which would deliver the child into his power. Now, having failed in his machinations, he was safe under lock and key—guarded on sight. The next twenty-four hours would see him unmasked, awaiting his trial and condemnation under the scathing indictment prepared by Fouquier-Tinville, the unerring Public Prosecutor. The day after that, the tumbril and the guillotine for that execrable English spy, and the boundless sense of satisfaction that his last intrigue had aborted in such a signal and miserable manner.

Of a truth Chauvelin at this hour had every cause to be thankful, and it was with a light heart that he set out to interview the Leridans.

## VIII

The Leridans, anxious, obsequious, terrified, were only too ready to obey the citizen Representative in all things.

They explained with much complacency that, even though they were personally acquainted with Jeannette Marechal, when the citizeness presented herself this very morning without the ring they had refused her permission to see the brat.

Chauvelin, who in his own mind had already reconstructed the whole tragedy of the stolen child, was satisfied that Marat could not have chosen more efficient tools for the execution of his satanic revenge than these two hideous products of revolutionary Paris.

Grasping, cowardly, and avaricious, the Leridans would lend themselves to any abomination for a sufficiency of money; but no money on earth would induce them to risk their own necks in the process. Marat had obviously held them by threats of the guillotine. They knew the power of the "Friend of the People," and feared him accordingly. Chauvelin's scarf of office, his curt, authoritative manner, had an equally awe-inspiring effect upon the two miserable creatures. They became absolutely abject, cringing, maudlin in their protestations of good-will and loyalty. No one, they vowed, should as much as see the child—ring or no ring—save the citizen Representative himself. Chauvelin, however, had no wish to see the child. He was satisfied that its name was Lannoy—for the child had remembered it when first he had been brought to the Leridans. Since then he had apparently forgotten it, even though he often cried after his *"Maman!"*

Chauvelin listened to all these explanations with some impatience. The child was nothing to him, but the Scarlet Pimpernel had desired to rescue it from out of the clutches of the Leridans; had risked his all—and lost it—in order to effect that rescue! That in itself was a sufficient inducement for Chauvelin to interest himself in the execution of Marat's vengeance, whatever its original mainspring may have been.

At any rate, now he felt satisfied that the child was safe, and that the Leridans were impervious to threats or bribes which might land them on the guillotine.

All that they would own to was to being afraid.

"Afraid of what?" queried Chauvelin sharply.

That the brat may be kidnapped . . . stolen. Oh! he could not be decoyed . . . they were too watchful for that! But apparently there were mysterious agencies at work. . . .

"Mysterious agencies!" Chauvelin laughed aloud at the suggestion. The "mysterious agency" was even now rotting in an obscure cell at the Abbaye. What other powers could be at work on behalf of the brat?

Well, the Leridans had had a warning!

What warning?

"A letter," the man said gruffly. "But as neither my wife nor I can read - "

"Why did you not speak of this before?" broke in Chauvelin roughly. "Let me see the letter."

The woman produced a soiled and dank scrap of paper from beneath her apron. Of a truth she could not read its contents, for they were writ in English in the form of a doggerel rhyme which caused Chauvelin to utter a savage oath.

"When did this come?" he asked. "And how?"

"This morning, citizen," the woman mumbled in reply. "I found it outside the door, with a stone on it to prevent the wind from blowing it away. What does it mean, citizen?" she went on, her voice shaking with terror, for of a truth the citizen Representative looked as if he had seen some weird and unearthly apparition.

He gave no reply for a moment or two, and the two catiffs had no conception of the tremendous effort at self-control which was hidden behind the pale, rigid mask of the redoubtable man.

"It probably means nothing that you need fear," Chauvelin said quietly at last. "But I will see the Commissary of the Section myself, and tell him to send a dozen men of the Surete along to watch your house and be at your beck and call if need be. Then you will feel quite safe, I hope."

"Oh, yes! quite safe, citizen!" the woman replied with a sigh of genuine relief. Then only did Chauvelin turn on his heel and go his way.

IX

But that crumpled and soiled scrap of paper given to him by the woman Leridan still lay in his clenched hand as he strode back rapidly citywards. It seemed to scorch his palm. Even before he had glanced at the contents he knew what they were. That atrocious English doggerel, the signature—a five-petalled flower traced in crimson! How well he knew them!

"We seek him here, we seek him there!"

The most humiliating moments in Chauvelin's career were associated with that silly rhyme, and now here it was, mocking him even when he knew that his bitter enemy lay fettered and helpless, caught in a trap, out of which there was no escape possible; even though he knew for a positive certainty that the mocking voice which had spoken those rhymes on that far-off day last September would soon be stilled for ever.

No doubt one of that army of abominable English spies had placed this warning outside the Leridans' door. No doubt they had done that with a view to throwing dust in the eyes of the Public Prosecutor and causing a confusion in his mind with regard to the identity of the prisoner at the Abbaye, all to the advantage of their chief.

The thought that such a confusion might exist, that Fouquier-Tinville might be deluded into doubting the real personality of Paul Mole, brought an icy sweat all down Chauvelin's spine. He hurried along the interminably long Chemin de Pantin, only paused at the Barriere du Combat in order to interview the Commissary of the Section on the matter of sending men to watch over the Leridans' house. Then, when he felt satisfied that this would be effectively and quickly done, an unconquerable feeling of restlessness prompted him to hurry round to the lodgings of the Public Prosecutor in the Rue Blanche—just to see him, to speak with him, to make quite sure.

Oh! he must be sure that no doubts, no pusillanimity on the part of any official would be allowed to stand in the way of the consummation of all his most cherished dreams. Papers or no papers, testimony or no testimony, the incarcerated Paul Mole was the Scarlet Pimpernel—of this Chauvelin was as certain as that he was alive. His every sense had testified to it when he stood in the narrow room of the Rue des Cordeliers, face to face—eyes gazing into eyes—with his sworn enemy.

Unluckily, however, he found the Public Prosecutor in a surly and obstinate mood, following on an interview which he had just had with citizen Commissary Cuisinier on the matter of the prisoner Paul Mole.

"His papers are all in order, I tell you," he said impatiently, in answer to Chauvelin's insistence. "It is as much as my head is worth to demand a summary execution."

"But I tell you that, those papers of his are forged," urged Chauvelin forcefully.

"They are not," retorted the other. "The Commissary swears to his own signature on the identity book. The concierge at the Abbaye swears that he knows Mole, so do all the men of the Surete who have seen him. The Commissary has known him as an indigent, good-for-nothing lubbard who has begged his way in the streets of Paris ever since he was released from gaol some months ago, after he had served a term for larceny. Even your own man Hebert admits to feeling doubtful on the point. You have had the nightmare, citizen," concluded Fouquier-Tinville with a harsh laugh.

"But, name of a dog!" broke in Chauvelin savagely. "You are not proposing to let the man go?"

"What else can I do?" the other rejoined fretfully. "We shall get into terrible trouble if we interfere with a man like Paul Mole. You know yourself how it is these days. We should have the whole of the rabble of Paris clamouring for our blood. If, after we have guillotined him, he is proved to be a good patriot, it will be my turn next. No! I thank you!"

"I tell you, man," retorted Chauvelin desperately, "that the man is not Paul Mole—that he is the English spy whom we all know as the Scarlet Pimpernel."

"*Eh Bien!*" riposted Fouquier-Tinville. "Bring me more tangible proof that our prisoner is not Paul Mole and I'll deal with him quickly enough, never fear. But if by to-morrow morning you do not satisfy me on the point . . . I must let him go his way."

A savage oath rose to Chauvelin's lips. He felt like a man who has been running, panting to reach a goal, who sees that goal within easy distance of him, and is then suddenly captured, caught in invisible meshes which hold him tightly, and against which he is powerless to struggle. For the moment he hated Fouquier-Tinville with a deadly hatred, would have tortured and threatened him until he wrung a consent, an admission, out of him.

Name of a name! when that damnable English spy was actually in his power, the man was a pusillanimous fool to allow the rich prize to slip from his grasp! Chauvelin felt as if he were choking; his slender fingers worked nervily around his cravat; beads of perspiration trickled unheeded down his pallid forehead.

Then suddenly he had an inspiration—nothing less! It almost seemed as if Satan, his friend, had whispered insinuating words into his ear. That scrap of paper! He had thrust it awhile ago into the breast pocket of his coat. It was still there, and the Public Prosecutor wanted a tangible proof . . . Then, why not . . . ?

Slowly, his thoughts still in the process of gradual coordination, Chauvelin drew that soiled scrap of paper out of his pocket. Fouquier-Tinville, surly and ill-humoured, had his back half-turned towards him, was moodily picking at his teeth. Chauvelin had all the leisure which he required. He smoothed out the creases in the paper and spread it out carefully upon the desk close to the other man's elbow. Fouquier-Tinville looked down on it, over his shoulder.

"What is that?" he queried.

"As you see, citizen," was Chauvelin's bland reply. "A message, such as you yourself have oft received, methinks, from our mutual enemy, the Scarlet Pimpernel."

But already the Public Prosecutor had seized upon the paper, and of a truth Chauvelin had no longer cause to complain of his colleague's indifference. That doggerel rhyme, no less than the signature, had the power to rouse Fouquier-Tinville's ire, as it had that of disturbing Chauvelin's well-studied calm.

"What is it?" reiterated the Public Prosecutor, white now to the lips.

"I have told you, citizen," rejoined Chauvelin imperturbably. "A message from that English spy. It is also the proof which you have demanded of me—the tangible proof that the prisoner, Paul Mole, is none other than the Scarlet Pimpernel."

"But," ejaculated the other hoarsely, "where did you get this?"

"It was found in the cell which Paul Mole occupied in the depot of the Rue de Tourraine, where he was first incarcerated. I picked it up there after he was removed . . . the ink was scarcely dry upon it."

The lie came quite glibly to Chauvelin's tongue. Was not every method good, every device allowable, which would lead to so glorious an end?

"Why did you not tell me of this before?" queried Fouquier-Tinville, with a sudden gleam of suspicion in his deep-set eyes.

"You had not asked me for a tangible proof before," replied Chauvelin blandly. "I myself was so firmly convinced of what I averred that I had well-nigh forgotten the existence of this damning scrap of paper."

Damning indeed! Fouquier-Tinville had seen such scraps of paper before. He had learnt the doggerel rhyme by heart, even though the English tongue was quite unfamiliar to him. He loathed the English —the entire nation—with all that deadly hatred which a divergence of political aims will arouse in times of acute crises. He hated the English government, Pitt and Burke and even Fox, the happy-go-lucky apologist of the young Revolution. But, above all, he hated that League of English spies—as he was pleased to call them—whose courage, resourcefulness, as well as reckless daring, had more than once baffled his own hideous schemes of murder, of pillage, and of rape.

Thank Beelzebub and his horde of evil spirits, citizen Chauvelin had been clear-sighted enough to detect that elusive Pimpernel under the disguise of Paul Mole.

"You have deserved well of your country," said Tinville with lusty fervour, and gave Chauvelin a vigorous slap on the shoulder. "But for you I should have allowed that abominable spy to slip through our fingers."

"I have succeeded in convincing you, citizen?" Chauvelin retorted dryly.

"Absolutely!" rejoined the other. "You may now leave the matter to me. And 'twill be friend Mole who will be surprised to-morrow," he added with a harsh guffaw, "when he finds himself face to face with me, before a Court of Justice."

He was all eagerness, of course. Such a triumph for him! The indictment of the notorious Scarlet Pimpernel on a charge of espionage would be the crowning glory of his career! Let other men look to their laurels! Those who brought that dangerous enemy of revolution to the guillotine would for ever be proclaimed as the saviours of France.

"A short indictment," he said, when Chauvelin, after a lengthy discussion on various points, finally rose to take his leave, "but a scathing one! I tell you, citizen Chauvelin, that to-morrow you will be the first to congratulate me on an unprecedented triumph."

He had been arguing in favour of a sensational trial and no less sensational execution. Chauvelin, with his memory harking back on many mysterious abductions at the very foot of the guillotine, would have liked to see his elusive enemy quietly put to death amongst a batch of traitors, who would help to mask his personality until after the guillotine had fallen, when the whole of Paris should ring with the triumph of this final punishment of the hated spy.

In the end, the two friends agreed upon a compromise, and parted well pleased with the turn of events which a kind Fate had ordered for their own special benefit.

X

Thus satisfied, Chauvelin returned to the Abbaye. Hebert was safe and trustworthy, but Hebert, too, had been assailed with the same doubts which had well-nigh wrecked Chauvelin's triumph, and with such doubts in his mind he might slacken his vigilance.

Name of a name! every man in charge of that damnable Scarlet Pimpernel should have three pairs of eyes wherewith to watch his movements. He should have the alert brain of a Robespierre, the physical strength of a Danton, the relentlessness of a Marat. He should be a giant in sheer brute force, a tiger in caution, an elephant in weight, and a mouse in stealthiness!

Name of a name! but 'twas only hate that could give such powers to any man!

Hebert, in the guard-room, owned to his doubts. His comrades, too, admitted that after twenty-four hours spent on the watch, their minds were in a whirl. The Citizen Commissary had been so sure—so was the chief concierge of the Abbaye even now; and the men of the Surete! . . . they themselves had seen the real Mole more than once . . . and this man in the cell . . . Well, would the citizen Representative have a final good look at him?

"You seem to forget Calais, citizen Hebert," Chauvelin said sharply, "and the deadly humiliation you suffered then at the hands of this man who is now your prisoner. Surely your eyes should have been, at least, as keen as mine own."

Anxious, irritable, his nerves well-nigh on the rack, he nevertheless crossed the guard-room with a firm step and entered the cell where the prisoner was still lying upon the palliasse, as he had been all along, and still presenting that naked piece of shoulder through the hole in his shirt.

"He has been like this the best part of the day," Hebert said with a shrug of the shoulders. "We put his bread and water right under his nose. He ate and he drank, and I suppose he slept. But except for a good deal of swearing, he has not spoken to any of us."

He had followed his chief into the cell, and now stood beside the palliasse, holding a small dark lantern in his hand. At a sign from Chauvelin he flashed the light upon the prisoner's averted head.

Mole cursed for awhile, and muttered something about "good patriots" and about "retribution." Then, worried by the light, he turned slowly round, and with fish-like, bleary eyes looked upon his visitor.

The words of stinging irony and triumphant sarcasm, all fully prepared, froze on Chauvelin's lips. He gazed upon the prisoner, and a weird sense of something unfathomable and mysterious came over him as he gazed. He himself could not have defined that feeling: the very next moment he was prepared to ridicule his own cowardice—yes, cowardice! because for a second or two he had felt positively afraid.

Afraid of what, forsooth? The man who crouched here in the cell was his arch-enemy, the Scarlet Pimpernel—the man whom he hated most bitterly in all the world, the man whose death he desired more than that of any other living creature. He had been apprehended by the very side of the murdered man whose confidence he had all but gained. He himself (Chauvelin) had at that fateful moment looked into the factitious Mole's eyes, had seen the mockery in them, the lazy insouciance which was the chief attribute of Sir Percy Blakeney. He had heard a faint echo of that inane laugh which grated upon his nerves. Hebert had then laid hands upon this very same man; agents of the Surete had barred every ingress and egress to the house, had conducted their prisoner straightway to the depot and thence to the Abbaye, had since that moment guarded him on sight, by day and by night. Hebert and the other men as well as the chief warder, all swore to that!

No, no! There could be no doubt! There was no doubt! The days of magic were over! A man could not assume a personality other than his own; he could not fly out of that personality like a bird out of its cage. There on the palliasse in the miserable cell were the same long limbs, the broad shoulders, the grimy face with the three days' growth of stubbly beard—the whole wretched personality of Paul Mole, in fact, which hid the exquisite one of Sir Percy Blakeney, Bart. And yet! . . .

A cold sweat ran down Chauvelin's spine as he gazed, mute and immovable, into those fish-like, bleary eyes, which were not—no! they were not those of the real Scarlet Pimpernel.

The whole situation became dreamlike, almost absurd. Chauvelin was not the man for such a mock-heroic, melodramatic situation. Commonsense, reason, his own cool powers of deliberation, would soon reassert themselves. But for the moment he was dazed. He had worked too hard, no doubt; had yielded too much to excitement, to triumph, and to hate. He turned to Hebert, who was standing stolidly by, gave him a few curt orders in a clear and well-pitched voice. Then he walked out of the cell, without bestowing another look on the prisoner.

Mole had once more turned over on his palliasse and, apparently, had gone to sleep. Hebert, with a strange and puzzled laugh, followed his chief out of the cell.

## XI

At first Chauvelin had the wish to go back and see the Public Prosecutor—to speak with him—to tell him—what? Yes, what? That he, Chauvelin, had all of a sudden been assailed with the same doubts which already had worried Hebert and the others?—that he had told a deliberate lie when he stated that the incriminating doggerel rhyme had been found in Mole's cell? No, no! Such an admission would not only be foolish, it would be dangerous now, whilst he himself was scarce prepared to trust to his own senses. After all, Fouquier-Tinville was in the right frame of mind for the moment. Paul Mole, whoever he was, was safely under lock and key.

The only danger lay in the direction of the house on the Chemin de Pantin. At the thought Chauvelin felt giddy and faint. But he would allow himself no rest. Indeed, he could not have rested until something approaching certainty had once more taken possession of his soul. He could not—would not—believe that he had been deceived. He was still prepared to stake his very life on the identity of the prisoner at the Abbaye. Tricks of light, the flash of the lantern, the perfection of the disguise, had caused a momentary illusion—nothing more.

Nevertheless, that awful feeling of restlessness which had possessed him during the last twenty-four hours once more drove him to activity. And although commonsense and reason both pulled one way, an eerie sense of superstition whispered in his ear the ominous words, "If, after all!"

At any rate, he would see the Leridans, and once more make sure of them; and, late as was the hour, he set out for the lonely house on the Pantin Road.

Just inside the Barriere du Combat was the Poste de Section, where Commissary Burban was under orders to provide a dozen men of the Surete, who were to be on the watch round and about the house of the Leridans. Chauvelin called in on the Commissary, who assured him that the men were at their post.

Thus satisfied, he crossed the Barriere and started at a brisk walk down the long stretch of the Chemin de Pantin. The night was dark. The rolling clouds overhead hid the face of the moon and presaged the storm. On the right, the irregular heights of the Buttes Chaumont loomed out dense and dark against the heavy sky, whilst to the left, on ahead, a faintly glimmering, greyish streak of reflected light revealed the proximity of the canal.

Close to the spot where the main Route de Meux intersects the Chemin de Pantin, Chauvelin slackened his pace. The house of the Leridans now lay immediately on his left; from it a small, feeble ray of light, finding its way no doubt through an ill-closed shutter, pierced the surrounding gloom. Chauvelin, without hesitation, turned up a narrow track which led up to the house across a field of stubble. The next moment a peremptory challenge brought him to a halt.

"Who goes there?"

"Public Safety," replied Chauvelin. "Who are you?"

"Of the Surete," was the counter reply. "There are a dozen of us about here."

"When did you arrive?"

"Some two hours ago. We marched out directly after you left the orders at the Commissariat."

"You are prepared to remain on the watch all night?"

"Those are our orders, citizen," replied the man.

"You had best close up round the house, then. And, name of a dog!" he added, with a threatening ring in his voice. "Let there be no slackening of vigilance this night. No one to go in or out of that house, no one to approach it under any circumstances whatever. Is that understood?"

"Those were our orders from the first, citizen," said the man simply.

"And all has been well up to now?"

"We have seen no one, citizen."

The little party closed in around their chief and together they marched up to the house. Chauvelin, on tenterhooks, walked quicker than the others. He was the first to reach the door. Unable to find the bell-pull in the dark, he knocked vigorously.

The house appeared silent and wrapped in sleep. No light showed from within save that one tiny speck through the cracks of an ill-fitting shutter, in a room immediately overhead.

In response to Chauvelin's repeated summons, there came anon the sound of someone moving in one of the upstairs rooms, and presently the light overhead disappeared, whilst a door above was heard to open and to close and shuffling footsteps to come slowly down the creaking stairs.

A moment or two later the bolts and bars of the front door were unfastened, a key grated in the rusty lock, a chain rattled in its socket, and then the door was opened slowly and cautiously.

The woman Leridan appeared in the doorway. She held a guttering tallow candle high above her head. Its flickering light illumined Chauvelin's slender figure.

"Ah! the citizen Representative!" the woman ejaculated, as soon as she recognised him. "We did not expect you again to-day, and at this late hour, too. I'll tell my man—"

"Never mind your man," broke in Chauvelin impatiently, and pushed without ceremony past the woman inside the house. "The child? Is it safe?"

He could scarcely control his excitement. There was a buzzing, as of an angry sea, in his ears. The next second, until the woman spoke, seemed like a cycle of years.

"Quite safe, citizen," she said placidly. "Everything is quite safe. We were so thankful for those men of the Surete. We had been afraid before, as I told the citizen Representative, and my man and I could not rest for anxiety. It was only after they came that we dared go to bed."

A deep sigh of intense relief came from the depths of Chauvelin's heart. He had not realised himself until this moment how desperately anxious he had been. The woman's reassuring words appeared to lift a crushing weight from his mind. He turned to the man behind him.

"You did not tell me," he said, "that some of you had been here already."

"We have not been here before," the sergeant in charge of the little platoon said in reply. "I do not know what the woman means."

"Some of your men came about three hours ago," the woman retorted; "less than an hour after the citizen Representative was here. I remember that my man and I marvelled how quickly they did come, but they said that they had been on duty at the Barriere du Combat when the citizen arrived, and that he had dispatched them off at once. They said they had run all the way. But even so, we thought it was quick work - "

The words were smothered in her throat in a cry of pain, for, with an almost brutal gesture, Chauvelin had seized her by the shoulders.

"Where are those men?" he queried hoarsely. "Answer!"

"In there, and in there," the woman stammered, well-nigh faint with terror as she pointed to two doors, one on each side of the passage. "Three in each room. They are asleep now, I should say, as they seem so quiet. But they were an immense comfort to us, citizen . . . we were so thankful to have them in the house. . . . "

But Chauvelin had snatched the candle from her hand. Holding it high above his head, he strode to the door on the right of the passage. It was ajar. He pushed it open with a vicious kick. The room beyond was in total darkness.

"Is anyone here?" he queried sharply.

Nothing but silence answered him. For a moment he remained there on the threshold, silent and immovable as a figure carved in stone. He had just a sufficiency of presence of mind and of will power not to drop the candle, to stand there motionless, with his back turned to the woman and to the men who had crowded in, in his wake. He would not let them see the despair, the rage and grave superstitious fear, which distorted every line of his pallid face.

He did not ask about the child. He would not trust himself to speak, for he had realised already how completely he had been baffled. Those abominable English spies had watched their opportunity, had worked on the credulity and the fears of the Leridans and, playing the game at which they and their audacious chief were such unconquerable experts, they had made their way into the house under a clever ruse.

The men of the Surete, not quite understanding the situation, were questioning the Leridans. The man, too, corroborated his wife's story. Their anxiety had been worked upon at the moment that it was most acute. After the citizen Representative left them, earlier in the evening, they had received another mysterious message which they had been unable to read, but which had greatly increased their alarm. Then, when the men of the Surete came . . . Ah! they had no cause to doubt that they were men of the Surete! . . . their clothes, their speech, their appearance . . . figure to yourself, even their uniforms! They spoke so nicely, so reassuringly. The Leridans were so thankful to see them! Then they made themselves happy in the two rooms below, and for additional safety the Lannoy child was brought down from its attic and put to sleep in the one room with the men of the Surete.

After that the Leridans went to bed. Name of a dog! how were they to blame? Those men and the child had disappeared, but they (the Leridans) would go to the guillotine swearing that they were not to blame.

Whether Chauvelin heard all these jeremiads, he could not afterwards have told you. But he did not need to be told how it had all been done. It had all been so simple, so ingenious, so like the methods usually adopted by that astute Scarlet Pimpernel! He saw it all so clearly before him. Nobody was to blame really, save he himself—he, who alone knew and understood the adversary with whom he had to deal.

But these people here should not have the gratuitous spectacle of a man enduring the torments of disappointment and of baffled revenge. Whatever Chauvelin was suffering now would for ever remain the secret of his own soul. Anon, when the Leridans' rasping voices died away in one of the more distant portions of the house and the men of the Sureté were busy accepting refreshment and gratuity from the two terrified wretches, he had put down the candle with a steady hand and then walked with a firm step out of the house.

Soon the slender figure was swallowed up in the gloom as he strode back rapidly towards the city.

XII

Citizen Fouquier-Tinville had returned home from the Palais at a very late hour that same evening. His household in his simple lodgings in the Place Dauphine was already abed: his wife and the twins were asleep. He himself had sat down for a moment in the living-room, in dressing-gown and slippers, and with the late edition of the Moniteur in his hand, too tired to read.

It was half-past ten when there came a ring at the front door bell. Fouquier-Tinville, half expecting citizen Chauvelin to pay him a final visit, shuffled to the door and opened it.

A visitor, tall, well-dressed, exceedingly polite and urbane, requested a few minutes' conversation with citizen Fouquier-Tinville.

Before the Public Prosecutor had made up his mind whether to introduce such a late-comer into his rooms, the latter had pushed his way through the door into the ante-chamber, and with a movement as swift as it was unexpected, had thrown a scarf round Fouquier-Tinville's neck and wound it round his mouth, so that the unfortunate man's call for help was smothered in his throat.

So dexterously and so rapidly indeed had the miscreant acted, that his victim had hardly realised the assault before he found himself securely gagged and bound to a chair in his own ante-room, whilst that dare-devil stood before him, perfectly at his ease, his hands buried in the capacious pockets of his huge caped coat, and murmuring a few casual words of apology.

"I entreat you to forgive, citizen," he was saying in an even and pleasant voice, "this necessary violence on my part towards you. But my errand is urgent, and I could not allow your neighbours or your household to disturb the few minutes' conversation which I am obliged to have with you. My friend Paul Mole," he went on, after a slight pause, "is in grave danger of his life owing to a hallucination on the part of our mutual friend citizen Chauvelin; and I feel confident that you yourself are too deeply enamoured of your own neck to risk it wilfully by sending an innocent and honest patriot to the guillotine."

Once more he paused and looked down upon his unwilling interlocutor, who, with muscles straining against the cords that held him, and with eyes nearly starting out of their sockets in an access of fear and of rage, was indeed presenting a pitiful spectacle.

"I dare say that by now, citizen," the brigand continued imperturbably, "you will have guessed who I am. You and I have oft crossed invisible swords before; but this, methinks, is the first time that we have met face to face. I pray you, tell my dear friend M. Chauvelin that you have seen me. Also that there were two facts which he left entirely out of his calculations, perfect though these were. The one fact was that there were two Paul Moles—one real and one factitious. Tell him that, I pray you. It was the factitious Paul Mole who stole the ring and who stood for one moment gazing into clever citizen Chauvelin's eyes. But that same factitious Paul Mole had disappeared in the crowd even before your colleague had recovered his presence of mind. Tell him, I pray you, that the elusive Pimpernel whom he knows so well never assumes a fanciful disguise. He discovered the real Paul Mole first, studied him, learned his personality, until his own became a perfect replica of the miserable caitiff. It was the false Paul Mole who induced Jeannette Marechal to introduce him originally into the household of citizen Marat. It was he who gained the confidence of his employer; he, for a consideration, borrowed the identity papers of his real prototype. He again who for a few francs induced the real Paul Mole to follow him into the house of the murdered demagogue and to mingle there with the throng. He who thrust the identity papers back into the hands of their rightful owner whilst he himself was swallowed up by the crowd. But it was the real Paul Mole who was finally arrested and who is now lingering in the Abbaye prison, whence you, citizen Fouquier-Tinville, must free him on the instant, on pain of suffering yourself for the nightmares of your friend."

"The second fact," he went on with the same good-humoured pleasantry, "which our friend citizen Chauvelin had forgotten was that, though I happen to have aroused his unconquerable ire, I am but one man amongst a league of gallant English gentlemen. Their chief, I am proud to say; but without them, I should be powerless. Without one of them near me, by the side of the murdered Marat, I could not have rid myself of the ring in time, before other rough hands searched me to my skin. Without them, I could not have taken Madeleine Lannoy's child from out that terrible hell, to which a miscreant's lustful revenge had condemned the poor innocent. But while citizen Chauvelin, racked with triumph as well as with anxiety, was rushing from the Leridans' house to yours, and thence to the Abbaye prison, to gloat over his captive enemy, the League of the Scarlet Pimpernel carefully laid and carried out its plans at leisure. Disguised as men of the Surete, we took advantage of the Leridans' terror to obtain access into the house. Frightened to death by our warnings, as well as by citizen Chauvelin's threats, they not only admitted us into their house, but actually placed Madeleine Lannoy's child in our charge. Then they went contentedly to bed, and we, before the real men of the Surete arrived upon the scene, were already safely out of the way. My gallant English friends are some way out of Paris by now, escorting Madeleine Lannoy and her child into safety. They will return to Paris, citizen," continued the audacious adventurer, with a laugh full of joy and of unconquerable vitality, "and be my henchmen as before in many an adventure which will cause you and citizen Chauvelin to gnash your teeth with rage. But I myself will remain in Paris," he concluded lightly. "Yes, in Paris; under your very nose, and entirely at your service!"

The next second he was gone, and Fouquier-Tinville was left to marvel if the whole apparition had not been a hideous dream. Only there was no doubt that he was gagged and tied to a chair with cords: and here his wife found him, an hour later, when she woke from her first sleep, anxious because he had not yet come to bed.

# A QUESTION OF PASSPORTS

Bibot was very sure of himself. There never was, never had been, there never would be again another such patriotic citizen of the Republic as was citizen Bibot of the Town Guard.

And because his patriotism was so well known among the members of the Committee of Public Safety, and his uncompromising hatred of the aristocrats so highly appreciated, citizen Bibot had been given the most important military post within the city of Paris.

He was in command of the Porte Montmartre, which goes to prove how highly he was esteemed, for, believe me, more treachery had been going on inside and out of the Porte Montmartre than in any other quarter of Paris. The last commandant there, citizen Ferney, was guillotined for having allowed a whole batch of aristocrats—traitors to the Republic, all of them—to slip through the Porte Montmartre and to find safety outside the walls of Paris. Ferney pleaded in his defence that these traitors had been spirited away from under his very nose by the devil's agency, for surely that meddlesome Englishman who spent his time in rescuing aristocrats—traitors, all of them—from the clutches of Madame la Guillotine must be either the devil himself, or at any rate one of his most powerful agents.

"*Nom de Dieu!* just think of his name! The Scarlet Pimpernel they call him! No one knows him by any other name! and he is preternaturally tall and strong and superhumanly cunning! And the power which he has of being transmuted into various personalities—rendering himself quite unrecognisable to the eyes of the most sharp-seeing patriot of France, must of a surety be a gift of Satan!"

But the Committee of Public Safety refused to listen to Ferney's explanations. The Scarlet Pimpernel was only an ordinary mortal—an exceedingly cunning and meddlesome personage it is true, and endowed with a superfluity of wealth which enabled him to break the thin crust of patriotism that overlay the natural cupidity of many Captains of the Town Guard—but still an ordinary man for all that! and no true lover of the Republic should allow either superstitious terror or greed to interfere with the discharge of his duties which at the Porte Montmartre consisted in detaining any and every person—aristocrat, foreigner, or otherwise traitor to the Republic—who could not give a satisfactory reason for desiring to leave Paris. Having detained such persons, the patriot's next duty was to hand them over to the Committee of Public Safety, who would then decide whether Madame la Guillotine would have the last word over them or not.

And the guillotine did nearly always have the last word to say,

528 BARONESS EMMUSKA ORCZY

unless the Scarlet Pimpernel interfered.

The trouble was, that that same accursed Englishman interfered at times in a manner which was positively terrifying. His impudence, certes, passed all belief. Stories of his daring and of his impudence were abroad which literally made the lank and greasy hair of every patriot curl with wonder. 'Twas even whispered—not too loudly, forsooth—that certain members of the Committee of Public Safety had measured their skill and valour against that of the Englishman and emerged from the conflict beaten and humiliated, vowing vengeance which, of a truth, was still slow in coming.

Citizen Chauvelin, one of the most implacable and unyielding members of the Committee, was known to have suffered overwhelming shame at the hands of that daring gang, of whom the so-called Scarlet Pimpernel was the accredited chief. Some there were who said that citizen Chauvelin had for ever forfeited his prestige, and even endangered his head by measuring his well-known astuteness against that mysterious League of spies.

But then Bibot was different!

He feared neither the devil, nor any Englishman. Had the latter the strength of giants and the protection of every power of evil, Bibot was ready for him. Nay! he was aching for a tussle, and haunted the purlieus of the Committees to obtain some post which would enable him to come to grips with the Scarlet Pimpernel and his League.

Bibot's zeal and perseverance were duly rewarded, and anon he was appointed to the command of the guard at the Porte Montmartre.

A post of vast importance as aforesaid; so much so, in fact, that no less a person than citizen Jean Paul Marat himself came to speak with Bibot on that third day of Nivose in the year I of the Republic, with a view to impressing upon him the necessity of keeping his eyes open, and of suspecting every man, woman, and child indiscriminately until they had proved themselves to be true patriots.

"Let no one slip through your fingers, citizen Bibot," Marat admonished with grim earnestness. "That accursed Englishman is cunning and resourceful, and his impudence surpasses that of the devil himself."

"He'd better try some of his impudence on me!" commented Bibot with a sneer, "he'll soon find out that he no longer has a Ferney to deal with. Take it from me, citizen Marat, that if a batch of aristocrats escape out of Paris within the next few days, under the guidance of the d—d Englishman, they will have to find some other way than the Porte Montmartre."

"Well said, citizen!" commented Marat. "But be watchful to-night . . . to-night especially. The Scarlet Pimpernel is rampant in Paris just now."

"How so?"

"The *ci-devant* Duc and Duchesse de Montreux and the whole of their brood—sisters, brothers, two or three children, a priest, and several servants—a round dozen in all, have been condemned to death. The guillotine for them to-morrow at daybreak! Would it could have been to-night," added Marat, whilst a demoniacal leer contorted his face which already exuded lust for blood from every pore. "Would it could have been to-night. But the guillotine has been busy; over four hundred executions to-day . . . and the tumbrils are full—the seats bespoken in advance—and still they come. . . . But to-morrow morning at daybreak Madame la Guillotine will have a word to say to the whole of the Montreux crowd!"

"But they are in the Conciergerie prison surely, citizen! out of the reach of that accursed Englishman?"

"They are on their way, an I mistake not, to the prison at this moment. I came straight on here after the condemnation, to which I listened with true joy. Ah, citizen Bibot! the blood of these hated aristocrats is good to behold when it drips from the blade of the guillotine. Have a care, citizen Bibot, do not let the Montreux crowd escape!"

"Have no fear, citizen Marat! But surely there is no danger! They have been tried and condemned! They are, as you say, even now on their way—well guarded, I presume—to the Conciergerie prison!—to-morrow at daybreak, the guillotine! What is there to fear?"

"Well! well!" said Marat, with a slight tone of hesitation, "it is best, citizen Bibot, to be over-careful these times."

Even whilst Marat spoke his face, usually so cunning and so vengeful, had suddenly lost its look of devilish cruelty which was almost superhuman in the excess of its infamy, and a greyish hue—suggestive of terror—had spread over the sunken cheeks. He clutched Bibot's arm, and leaning over the table he whispered in his ear:

"The Public Prosecutor had scarce finished his speech to-day, judgment was being pronounced, the spectators were expectant and still, only the Montreux woman and some of the females and children were blubbering and moaning, when suddenly, it seemed from nowhere, a small piece of paper fluttered from out the assembly and alighted on the desk in front of the Public Prosecutor. He took the paper up and glanced at its contents. I saw that his cheeks had paled, and that his hand trembled as he handed the paper over to me."

"And what did that paper contain, citizen Marat?" asked Bibot, also speaking in a whisper, for an access of superstitious terror was gripping him by the throat.

"Just the well-known accursed device, citizen, the small scarlet flower, drawn in red ink, and the few words: 'To-night the innocent men and women now condemned by this infamous tribunal will be beyond your reach!'"

"And no sign of a messenger?"

"None."

"And when did-"

"Hush!" said Marat peremptorily, "no more of that now. To your post, citizen, and remember—all are suspect! let none escape!"

The two men had been sitting outside a small tavern, opposite the Porte Montmartre, with a bottle of wine between them, their elbows resting on the grimy top of a rough wooden table. They had talked in whispers, for even the walls of the tumble-down cabaret might have had ears.

Opposite them the city wall—broken here by the great gate of Montmartre—loomed threateningly in the fast-gathering dusk of this winter's afternoon. Men in ragged red shirts, their unkempt heads crowned with Phrygian caps adorned with a tricolour cockade, lounged against the wall, or sat in groups on the top of piles of refuse that littered the street, with a rough deal plank between them and a greasy pack of cards in their grimy fingers. Guns and bayonets were propped against the wall. The gate itself had three means of egress; each of these was guarded by two men with fixed bayonets at their shoulders, but otherwise dressed like the others, in rags—with bare legs that looked blue and numb in the cold—the sans-culottes of revolutionary Paris.

Bibot rose from his seat, nodding to Marat, and joined his men.

From afar, but gradually drawing nearer, came the sound of a ribald song, with chorus accompaniment sung by throats obviously surfeited with liquor.

For a moment—as the sound approached—Bibot turned back once more to the Friend of the People.

"Am I to understand, citizen," he said, "that my orders are not to let anyone pass through these gates to-night?"

"No, no, citizen," replied Marat, "we dare not do that. There are a number of good patriots in the city still. We cannot interfere with their liberty or—"

And the look of fear of the demagogue—himself afraid of the human whirlpool which he has let loose—stole into Marat's cruel, piercing eyes.

"No, no," he reiterated more emphatically, "we cannot disregard the passports issued by the Committee of Public Safety. But examine each passport carefully, citizen Bibot! If you have any reasonable ground for suspicion, detain the holder, and if you have not-"

The sound of singing was quite near now. With another wink and a final leer, Marat drew back under the shadow of the cabaret, and Bibot swaggered up to the main entrance of the gate.

"*Qui va la?*" he thundered in stentorian tones as a group of some half-dozen people lurched towards him out of the gloom, still shouting hoarsely their ribald drinking song.

The foremost man in the group paused opposite citizen Bibot, and with arms akimbo, and legs planted well apart tried to assume a rigidity of attitude which apparently was somewhat foreign to him at this moment.

"Good patriots, citizen," he said in a thick voice which he vainly tried to render steady.

"What do you want?" queried Bibot.

"To be allowed to go on our way unmolested."

"What is your way?"

"Through the Porte Montmartre to the village of Barency."

"What is your business there?"

This query delivered in Bibot's most pompous manner seemed vastly to amuse the rowdy crowd. He who was the spokesman turned to his friends and shouted hilariously:

"Hark at him, citizens! He asks me what is our business. Oh, citizen Bibot, since when have you become blind? A dolt you've always been, else you had not asked the question."

But Bibot, undeterred by the man's drunken insolence, retorted gruffly:

"Your business, I want to know."

"Bibot! my little Bibot!" cooed the bibulous orator now in dulcet tones, "dost not know us, my good Bibot? Yet we all know thee, citizen —Captain Bibot of the Town Guard, eh, citizens! Three cheers for the citizen captain!"

When the noisy shouts and cheers from half a dozen hoarse throats had died down, Bibot, without more ado, turned to his own men at the gate.

"Drive these drunken louts away!" he commanded; "no one is allowed to loiter here."

Loud protest on the part of the hilarious crowd followed, then a slight scuffle with the bayonets of the Town Guard. Finally the spokesman, somewhat sobered, once more appealed to Bibot.

"Citizen Bibot! you must be blind not to know me and my mates! And let me tell you that you are doing yourself a deal of harm by interfering with the citizens of the Republic in the proper discharge of their duties, and by disregarding their rights of egress through this gate, a right confirmed by passports signed by two members of the Committee of Public Safety."

He had spoken now fairly clearly and very pompously. Bibot, somewhat impressed and remembering Marat's admonitions, said very civilly:

"Tell me your business then, citizen, and show me your passports. If everything is in order you may go your way."

"But you know me, citizen Bibot?" queried the other.

"Yes, I know you—unofficially, citizen Durand."

"You know that I and the citizens here are the carriers for citizen Legrand, the market gardener of Barency?"

"Yes, I know that," said Bibot guardedly, "unofficially."

"Then, unofficially, let me tell you, citizen, that unless we get to Barency this evening, Paris will have to do without cabbages and potatoes to-morrow. So now you know that you are acting at your own risk and peril, citizen, by detaining us."

"Your passports, all of you," commanded Bibot.

He had just caught sight of Marat still sitting outside the tavern opposite, and was glad enough, in this instance, to shelve his responsibility on the shoulders of the popular "Friend of the People." There was general searching in ragged pockets for grimy papers with official seals thereon, and whilst Bibot ordered one of his men to take the six passports across the road to citizen Marat for his inspection, he himself, by the last rays of the setting winter sun, made close examination of the six men who desired to pass through the Porte Montmartre.

As the spokesman had averred, he—Bibot—knew every one of these men. They were the carriers to citizen Legrand, the Barency market gardener. Bibot knew every face. They passed with a load of fruit and vegetables in and out of Paris every day. There was really and absolutely no cause for suspicion, and when citizen Marat returned the six passports, pronouncing them to be genuine, and recognising his own signature at the bottom of each, Bibot was at last satisfied, and the six bibulous carriers were allowed to pass through the gate, which they did, arm in arm, singing a wild curmagnole, and vociferously cheering as they emerged out into the open.

But Bibot passed an unsteady hand over his brow. It was cold, yet he was in a perspiration. That sort of thing tells on a man's nerves. He rejoined Marat, at the table outside the drinking booth, and ordered a fresh bottle of wine.

The sun had set now, and with the gathering dusk a damp mist descended on Montmartre. From the wall opposite, where the men sat playing cards, came occasional volleys of blasphemous oaths. Bibot was feeling much more like himself. He had half forgotten the incident of the six carriers, which had occurred nearly half an hour ago.

Two or three other people had, in the meanwhile, tried to pass through the gates, but Bibot had been suspicious and had detained them all.

Marat having commended him for his zeal took final leave of him. Just as the demagogue's slouchy, grimy figure was disappearing down a side street there was the loud clatter of hoofs from that same direction, and the next moment a detachment of the mounted Town Guard, headed by an officer in uniform, galloped down the ill-paved street.

Even before the troopers had drawn rein the officer had hailed Bibot.

"Citizen," he shouted, and his voice was breathless, for he had evidently ridden hard and fast, "this message to you from the citizen Chief Commissary of the Section. Six men are wanted by the Committee of Public Safety. They are disguised as carriers in the employ of a market gardener, and have passports for Barency!... The passports are stolen: the men are traitors—escaped aristocrats—and their spokesman is that d—d Englishman, the Scarlet Pimpernel."

Bibot tried to speak; he tugged at the collar of his ragged shirt; an awful curse escaped him.

"Ten thousand devils!" he roared.

"On no account allow these people to go through," continued the officer.

"Keep their passports. Detain them! . . . Understand?"

Bibot was still gasping for breath even whilst the officer, ordering a quick "Turn!" reeled his horse round, ready to gallop away as far as he had come.

"I am for the St. Denis Gate—Grosjean is on guard there!" he shouted.

"Same orders all round the city. No one to leave the gates! . . . Understand?"

His troopers fell in. The next moment he would be gone, and those cursed aristocrats well in safety's way.

"Citizen Captain!"

The hoarse shout at last contrived to escape Bibot's parched throat. As if involuntarily, the officer drew rein once more.

"What is it? Quick!—I've no time. That confounded Englishman may be at the St. Denis Gate even now!"

"Citizen Captain," gasped Bibot, his breath coming and going like that of a man fighting for his life. "Here! . . . at this gate! . . . not half an hour ago . . . six men . . . carriers . . . market gardeners . . . I seemed to know their faces. . . ."

"Yes! yes! market gardener's carriers," exclaimed the officer gleefully, "aristocrats all of them . . . and that d—d Scarlet Pimpernel. You've got them? You've detained them? . . . Where are they? . . . Speak, man, in the name of hell! . . ."

"Gone!" gasped Bibot. His legs would no longer bear him. He fell backwards on to a heap of street debris and refuse, from which lowly vantage ground he contrived to give away the whole miserable tale.

"Gone! half an hour ago. Their passports were in order! . . . I seemed to know their faces! Citizen Marat was here. . . . He, too-"

In a moment the officer had once more swung his horse round, so that the animal reared, with wild forefeet pawing the air, with champing of bit, and white foam scattered around.

"A thousand million curses!" he exclaimed. "Citizen Bibot, your head will pay for this treachery. Which way did they go?"

A dozen hands were ready to point in the direction where the merry party of carriers had disappeared half an hour ago; a dozen tongues gave rapid, confused explanations.

"Into it, my men!" shouted the officer; "they were on foot! They can't have gone far. Remember the Republic has offered ten thousand francs for the capture of the Scarlet Pimpernel."

Already the heavy gates had been swung open, and the officer's voice once more rang out clear through a perfect thunder-clap of fast galloping hoofs:

"*Ventre a terre!* Remember!—ten thousand francs to him who first sights the Scarlet Pimpernel!"

The thunder-clap died away in the distance, the dust of four score hoofs was merged in the fog and in the darkness; the voice of the captain was raised again through the mist-laden air. One shout . . . a shout of triumph . . . then silence once again.

Bibot had fainted on the heap of debris.

His comrades brought him wine to drink. He gradually revived. Hope came back to his heart; his nerves soon steadied themselves as the heavy beverage filtrated through into his blood.

"Bah!" he ejaculated as he pulled himself together, "the troopers were well-mounted . . . the officer was enthusiastic; those carriers could not have walked very far. And, in any case, I am free from blame. Citoyen Marat himself was here and let them pass!"

A shudder of superstitious terror ran through him as he recollected the whole scene: for surely he knew all the faces of the six men who had gone through the gate. The devil indeed must have given the mysterious Englishman power to transmute himself and his gang wholly into the bodies of other people.

More than an hour went by. Bibot was quite himself again, bullying, commanding, detaining everybody now.

At that time there appeared to be a slight altercation going on, on the farther side of the gate. Bibot thought it his duty to go and see what the noise was about. Someone wanting to get into Paris instead of out of it at this hour of the night was a strange occurrence.

Bibot heard his name spoken by a raucous voice. Accompanied by two of his men he crossed the wide gates in order to see what was happening. One of the men held a lanthorn, which he was swinging high above his head. Bibot saw standing there before him, arguing with the guard by the gate, the bibulous spokesman of the band of carriers.

He was explaining to the sentry that he had a message to deliver to the citizen commanding at the Porte Montmartre.

"It is a note," he said, "which an officer of the mounted guard gave me. He and twenty troopers were galloping down the great North Road not far from Barency. When they overtook the six of us they drew rein, and the officer gave me this note for citizen Bibot and fifty francs if I would deliver it tonight."

"Give me the note!" said Bibot calmly.

But his hand shook as he took the paper; his face was livid with fear and rage.

The paper had no writing on it, only the outline of a small scarlet flower done in red—the device of the cursed Englishman, the Scarlet Pimpernel.

"Which way did the officer and the twenty troopers go," he stammered, "after they gave you this note?"

"On the way to Calais," replied the other, "but they had magnificent horses, and didn't spare them either. They are a league and more away by now!"

All the blood in Bibot's body seemed to rush up to his head, a wild buzzing was in his ears . . .

And that was how the Duc and Duchesse de Montreux, with their servants and family, escaped from Paris on that third day of Nivose in the year I of the Republic.

# Two Good Patriots

Being the deposition of citizeness Fanny Roussell, who was brought up, together with her husband, before the Tribunal of the Revolution on a charge of treason—both being subsequently acquitted.

My name is Fanny Roussell, and I am a respectable married woman, and as good a patriot as any of you sitting there.

Aye, and I'll say it with my dying breath, though you may send me to the guillotine . . . as you probably will, for you are all thieves and murderers, every one of you, and you have already made up your minds that I and my man are guilty of having sheltered that accursed Englishman whom they call the Scarlet Pimpernel . . . and of having helped him to escape.

But I'll tell you how it all happened, because, though you call me a traitor to the people of France, yet am I a true patriot and will prove it to you by telling you exactly how everything occurred, so that you may be on your guard against the cleverness of that man, who, I do believe, is a friend and confederate of the devil . . . else how could he have escaped that time?

Well! it was three days ago, and as bitterly cold as anything that my man and I can remember. We had no travellers staying in the house, for we are a good three leagues out of Calais, and too far for the folk who have business in or about the harbour. Only at midday the coffee-room would get full sometimes with people on their way to or from the port.

But in the evenings the place was quite deserted, and so lonely that at times we fancied that we could hear the wolves howling in the forest of St. Pierre.

It was close on eight o'clock, and my man was putting up the shutters, when suddenly we heard the tramp of feet on the road outside, and then the quick word, "Halt!"

The next moment there was a peremptory knock at the door. My man opened it, and there stood four men in the uniform of the 9th Regiment of the Line . . . the same that is quartered at Calais. The uniform, of course, I knew well, though I did not know the men by sight.

"In the name of the People and by the order of the Committee of Public Safety!" said one of the men, who stood in the forefront, and who, I noticed, had a corporal's stripe on his left sleeve.

He held out a paper, which was covered with seals and with writing, but as neither my man nor I can read, it was no use our looking at it.

Hercule—that is my husband's name, citizens—asked the corporal what the Committee of Public Safety wanted with us poor hoteliers of a wayside inn.

"Only food and shelter for to-night for me and my men," replied the corporal, quite civilly.

"You can rest here," said Hercule, and he pointed to the benches in the coffee-room, "and if there is any soup left in the stockpot, you are welcome to it."

Hercule, you see, is a good patriot, and he had been a soldier in his day . . . No! No . . . do not interrupt me, any of you . . .you would only be saying that I ought to have known . . . but listen to the end.

"The soup we'll gladly eat," said the corporal very pleasantly. "As for shelter . . . well! I am afraid that this nice warm coffee-room will not exactly serve our purpose. We want a place where we can lie hidden, and at the same time keep a watch on the road. I noticed an outhouse as we came. By your leave we will sleep in there."

"As you please," said my man curtly.

He frowned as he said this, and it suddenly seemed as if some vague suspicion had crept into Hercule's mind.

The corporal, however, appeared unaware of this, for he went on quite cheerfully:

"Ah! that is excellent! Entre nous, citizen, my men and I have a desperate customer to deal with. I'll not mention his name, for I see you have guessed it already. A small red flower, what? . . . Well, we know that he must be making straight for the port of Calais, for he has been traced through St. Omer and Ardres. But he cannot possibly enter Calais city to-night, for we are on the watch for him. He must seek shelter somewhere for himself and any other aristocrat he may have with him, and, bar this house, there is no other place between Ardres and Calais where he can get it. The night is bitterly cold, with a snow blizzard raging round. I and my men have been detailed to watch this road, other patrols are guarding those that lead toward Boulogne and to Gravelines; but I have an idea, citizen, that our fox is making for Calais, and that to me will fall the honour of handing that tiresome scarlet flower to the Public Prosecutor en route for Madame la Guillotine."

Now I could not really tell you, citizens, what suspicions had by this time entered Hercule's head or mine; certainly what suspicions we did have were still very vague.

I prepared the soup for the men and they ate it heartily, after which my husband led the way to the outhouse where we sometimes stabled a traveller's horse when the need arose.

It is nice and dry, and always filled with warm, fresh straw. The entrance into it immediately faces the road; the corporal declared that nothing would suit him and his men better.

They retired to rest apparently, but we noticed that two men remained on the watch just inside the entrance, whilst the two others curled up in the straw.

Hercule put out the lights in the coffee-room, and then he and I went upstairs—not to bed, mind you—but to have a quiet talk together over the events of the past half-hour.

The result of our talk was that ten minutes later my man quietly stole downstairs and out of the house. He did not, however, go out by the front door, but through a back way which, leading through a cabbage-patch and then across a field, cuts into the main road some two hundred metres higher up.

Hercule and I had decided that he would walk the three leagues into Calais, despite the cold, which was intense, and the blizzard, which was nearly blinding, and that he would call at the post of gendarmerie at the city gates, and there see the officer in command and tell him the exact state of the case. It would then be for that officer to decide what was to be done; our responsibility as loyal citizens would be completely covered.

Hercule, you must know, had just emerged from our cabbage-patch on to the field when he was suddenly challenged:

"*Qui va la?*"

He gave his name. His certificate of citizenship was in his pocket; he had nothing to fear. Through the darkness and the veil of snow he had discerned a small group of men wearing the uniform of the 9th Regiment of the Line.

"Four men," said the foremost of these, speaking quickly and commandingly, "wearing the same uniform that I and my men are wearing . . . have you seen them?"

"Yes," said Hercule hurriedly.

"Where are they?"

"In the outhouse close by."

The other suppressed a cry of triumph.

"At them, my men!" he said in a whisper, "and you, citizen, thank your stars that we have not come too late."

"These men . . . " whispered Hercule. "I had my suspicions."

"Aristocrats, citizen," rejoined the commander of the little party, "and one of them is that cursed Englishman—the Scarlet Pimpernel."

Already the soldiers, closely followed by Hercule, had made their way through our cabbage-patch back to the house.

The next moment they had made a bold dash for the barn. There was a great deal of shouting, a great deal of swearing and some firing, whilst Hercule and I, not a little frightened, remained in the coffee-room, anxiously awaiting events.

Presently the group of soldiers returned, not the ones who had first come, but the others. I noticed their leader, who seemed to be exceptionally tall.

He looked very cheerful, and laughed loudly as he entered the coffee-room. From the moment that I looked at his face I knew, somehow, that Hercule and I had been fooled, and that now, indeed, we stood eye to eye with that mysterious personage who is called the Scarlet Pimpernel.

I screamed, and Hercule made a dash for the door; but what could two humble and peaceful citizens do against this band of desperate men, who held their lives in their own hands? They were four and we were two, and I do believe that their leader has supernatural strength and power.

He treated us quite kindly, even though he ordered his followers to bind us down to our bed upstairs, and to tie a cloth round our mouths so that our cries could not be distinctly heard.

Neither my man nor I closed an eye all night, of course, but we heard the miscreants moving about in the coffee-room below. But they did no mischief, nor did they steal any of the food or wines.

At daybreak we heard them going out by the front door, and their footsteps disappearing toward Calais. We found their discarded uniforms lying in the coffee-room. They must have entered Calais by daylight, when the gates were opened—just like other peaceable citizens. No doubt they had forged passports, just as they had stolen uniforms.

Our maid-of-all-work released us from our terrible position in the course of the morning, and we released the soldiers of the 9th Regiment of the Line, whom we found bound and gagged, some of them wounded, in the outhouse.

That same afternoon we were arrested, and here we are, ready to die if we must, but I swear that I have told you the truth, and I ask you, in the name of justice, if we have done anything wrong, and if we did not act like loyal and true citizens, even though we were pitted against an emissary of the devil?

# THE OLD SCARECROW

Nobody in the quartier could quite recollect when it was that the new Public Letter-Writer first set up in business at the angle formed by the Quai des Augustins and the Rue Dauphine, immediately facing the Pont Neuf; but there he certainly was on the 28th day of February, 1793, when Agnes, with eyes swollen with tears, a market basket on her arm, and a look of dreary despair on her young face, turned that selfsame angle on her way to the Pont Neuf, and nearly fell over the rickety construction which sheltered him and his stock-in-trade.

"Oh, *mon Dieu!* citizen Lepine, I had no idea you were here," she exclaimed as soon as she had recovered her balance.

"Nor I, citizeness, that I should have the pleasure of seeing you this morning," he retorted.

"But you were always at the other corner of the Pont Neuf," she argued.

"So I was," he replied, "so I was. But I thought I would like a change. The Faubourg St. Michel appealed to me; most of my clients came to me from this side of the river—all those on the other side seem to know how to read and write."

"I was just going over to see you," she remarked.

"You, citizeness," he exclaimed in unfeigned surprise, "what should procure a poor public writer the honour of - "

"Hush, in God's name!" broke in the young girl quickly as she cast a rapid, furtive glance up and down the *quai* and the narrow streets which converged at this angle.

She was dressed in the humblest and poorest of clothes, her skimpy shawl round her shoulders could scarce protect her against the cold of this cruel winter's morning; her hair was entirely hidden beneath a frilled and starched cap, and her feet were encased in coarse worsted stockings and sabots, but her hands were delicate and fine, and her face had that nobility of feature and look of patient resignation in the midst of overwhelming sorrow which proclaimed a lofty refinement both of soul and of mind.

The old Letter-Writer was surveying the pathetic young figure before him through his huge horn-rimmed spectacles, and she smiled on him through her fast-gathering tears. He used to have his pitch at the angle of the Pont Neuf, and whenever Agnes had walked past it, she had nodded to him and bidden him "Good morrow!" He had at times done little commissions for her and gone on errands when she needed a messenger; to-day, in the midst of her despair, she had suddenly thought of him and that rumour credited him with certain knowledge which she would give her all to possess.

She had sallied forth this morning with the express purpose of speaking with him; but now suddenly she felt afraid, and stood looking at him for a moment or two, hesitating, wondering if she dared tell him —one never knew these days into what terrible pitfall an ill-considered word might lead one.

A scarecrow he was, that old Public Letter-Writer, more like a great, gaunt bird than a human being, with those spectacles of his, and his long, very sparse and very lanky fringe of a beard which fell from his cheeks and chin and down his chest for all the world like a crumpled grey bib. He was wrapped from head to foot in a caped coat which had once been green in colour, but was now of many hues not usually seen in rainbows. He wore his coat all buttoned down the front, like a dressing-gown, and below the hem there peeped out a pair of very large feet encased in boots which had never been a pair. He sat upon a rickety, straw-bottomed chair under an improvised awning which was made up of four poles and a bit of sacking. He had a table in front of him—a table partially and very insecurely propped up by a bundle of old papers and books, since no two of its four legs were completely whole—and on the table there was a neckless bottle half-filled with ink, a few sheets of paper and a couple of quill pens.

The young girl's hesitation had indeed not lasted more than a few seconds.

Furtively, like a young creature terrified of lurking enemies, she once more glanced to right and left of her and down the two streets and the river bank, for Paris was full of spies these days—human bloodhounds ready for a few sous to sell their fellow-creatures' lives. It was middle morning now, and a few passers-by were hurrying along wrapped to the nose in mufflers, for the weather was bitterly cold.

Agnes waited until there was no one in sight, then she leaned forward over the table and whispered under her breath:

"They say, citizen, that you alone in Paris know the whereabouts of the English milor'—of him who is called the Scarlet Pimpernel . . ."

"Hush-sh-sh!" said the old man quickly, for just at that moment two men had gone by, in ragged coats and torn breeches, who had leered at Agnes and her neat cap and skirt as they passed. Now they had turned the angle of the street and the old man, too, sank his voice to a whisper.

"I know nothing of any Englishman," he muttered.

"Yes, you do," she rejoined insistently. "When poor Antoine Carre was somewhere in hiding and threatened with arrest, and his mother dared not write to him lest her letter be intercepted, she spoke to you about the English milor', and the English milor' found Antoine Carre and took him and his mother safely out of France. Mme. Carre is my godmother. . . . I saw her the very night when she went to meet the English milor' at his commands. I know all that happened then.... I know that you were the intermediary."

"And if I was," he muttered sullenly as he fiddled with his pen and paper, "maybe I've had cause to regret it. For a week after that Carre episode I dared not show my face in the streets of Paris; for nigh on a fortnight I dared not ply my trade ... I have only just ventured again to set up in business. I am not going to risk my old neck again in a hurry . . ."

"It is a matter of life and death," urged Agnes, as once more the tears rushed to her pleading eyes and the look of misery settled again upon her face.

"Your life, citizeness?" queried the old man, "or that of citizen-deputy Fabrice?"

"Hush!" she broke in again, as a look of real terror now overspread her face. Then she added under her breath: "You know?"

"I know that Mademoiselle Agnes de Lucines is fiancee to the citizen-deputy Arnould Fabrice," rejoined the old man quietly, "and that it is Mademoiselle Agnes de Lucines who is speaking with me now."

"You have known that all along?"

"Ever since mademoiselle first tripped past me at the angle of the Pont Neuf dressed in winsey kirtle and wearing sabots on her feet . . ."

"But how?" she murmured, puzzled, not a little frightened, for his knowledge might prove dangerous to her. She was of gentle birth, and as such an object of suspicion to the Government of the Republic and of the Terror; her mother was a hopeless cripple, unable to move: this together with her love for Arnould Fabrice had kept Agnes de Lucines in France these days, even though she was in hourly peril of arrest.

"Tell me what has happened," the old man said, unheeding her last anxious query. "Perhaps I can help . . ."

"Oh! you cannot—the English milor' can and will if only we could know where he is. I thought of him the moment I received that awful man's letter—and then I thought of you . . ."

"Tell me about the letter—quickly," he interrupted her with some impatience. "I'll be writing something—but talk away, I shall hear every word. But for God's sake be as brief as you can."

He drew some paper nearer to him and dipped his pen in the ink. He appeared to be writing under her dictation. Thin, flaky snow had begun to fall and settled in a smooth white carpet upon the frozen ground, and the footsteps of the passers-by sounded muffled as they hurried along. Only the lapping of the water of the sluggish river close by broke the absolute stillness of the air.

Agnes de Lucines' pale face looked ethereal in this framework of white which covered her shoulders and the shawl crossed over her bosom: only her eyes, dark, appealing, filled with a glow of immeasurable despair, appeared tensely human and alive.

"I had a letter this morning," she whispered, speaking very rapidly, "from citizen Heriot—that awful man—you know him?"

"Yes, yes!"

"He used to be valet in the service of deputy Fabrice. Now he, too, is a member of the National Assembly . . . he is arrogant and cruel and vile. He hates Arnould Fabrice and he professes himself passionately in love with me."

"Yes, yes!" murmured the old man, "but the letter?"

"It came this morning. In it he says that he has in his possession a number of old letters, documents and manuscripts which are quite enough to send deputy Fabrice to the guillotine. He threatens to place all those papers before the Committee of Public Safety unless . . . unless I . . ."

She paused, and a deep blush, partly of shame, partly of wrath, suffused her pale cheeks.

"Unless you accept his grimy hand in marriage," concluded the man dryly.

Her eyes gave him answer. With pathetic insistence she tried now to glean a ray of hope from the old scarecrow's inscrutable face. But he was bending over his writing: his fingers were blue with cold, his great shoulders were stooping to his task.

"Citizen," she pleaded.

"Hush!" he muttered, "no more now. The very snowflakes are made up of whispers that may reach those bloodhounds yet. The English milor' shall know of this. He will send you a message if he thinks fit."

"Citizen-"

"Not another word, in God's name! Pay me five sous for this letter and pray Heaven that you have not been watched."

She shivered and drew her shawl closer round her shoulders, then she counted out five sous with elaborate care and laid them out upon the table. The old man took up the coins. He blew into his fingers, which looked paralysed with the cold. The snow lay over everything now; the rough awning had not protected him or his wares.

Agnes turned to go. The last she saw of him, as she went up the rue Dauphine, was one broad shoulder still bending over the table, and clad in the shabby, caped coat all covered with snow like an old Santa Claus.

## II

It was half-an-hour before noon, and citizen-deputy Heriot was preparing to go out to the small tavern round the corner where he habitually took his dejeuner. Citizen Rondeau, who for the consideration of ten sous a day looked after Heriot's paltry creature-comforts, was busy tidying up the squalid apartment which the latter occupied on the top floor of a lodging-house in the Rue Cocatrice. This apartment consisted of three rooms leading out of one another; firstly there was a dark and narrow antichambre wherein slept the aforesaid citizen-servant; then came a sitting-room sparsely furnished with a few chairs, a centre table and an iron stove, and finally there was the bedroom wherein the most conspicuous object was a large oak chest clamped with wide iron hinges and a massive writing-desk; the bed and a very primitive washstand were in an alcove at the farther end of the room and partially hidden by a tapestry curtain.

At exactly half-past seven that morning there came a peremptory knock at the door of the antichambre, and as Rondeau was busy in the bedroom, Heriot went himself to see who his unexpected visitor might be. On the landing outside stood an extraordinary-looking individual—more like a tall and animated scarecrow than a man—who in a tremulous voice asked if he might speak with the citizen Heriot.

"That is my name," said the deputy gruffly, "what do you want?"

He would have liked to slam the door in the old scarecrow's face, but the latter, with the boldness which sometimes besets the timid, had already stepped into the anti-chambre and was now quietly sauntering through to the next room into the one beyond. Heriot, being a representative of the people and a social democrat of the most advanced type, was supposed to be accessible to every one who desired speech with him. Though muttering sundry curses, he thought it best not to go against his usual practice, and after a moment's hesitation he followed his unwelcome visitor.

The latter was in the sitting-room by this time; he had drawn a chair close to the table and sat down with the air of one who has a perfect right to be where he is; as soon as Heriot entered he said placidly:

"I would desire to speak alone with the citizen-deputy."

And Heriot, after another slight hesitation, ordered Rondeau to close the bedroom door.

"Keep your ears open in case I call," he added significantly.

"You are cautious, citizen," merely remarked the visitor with a smile.

To this Heriot vouchsafed no reply. He, too, drew a chair forward and sat opposite his visitor, then he asked abruptly: "Your name and quality?"

"My name is Lepine at your service," said the old man, "and by profession I write letters at the rate of five sous or so, according to length, for those who are not able to do it for themselves."

"Your business with me?" queried Heriot curtly.

"To offer you two thousand francs for the letters which you stole from deputy Fabrice when you were his valet," replied Lepine with perfect calm.

In a moment Heriot was on his feet, jumping up as if he had been stung; his pale, short-sighted eyes narrowed till they were mere slits, and through them he darted a quick, suspicious glance at the extraordinary out-at-elbows figure before him. Then he threw back his head and laughed till the tears streamed down his cheeks and his sides began to ache.

"This is a farce, I presume, citizen," he said when he had recovered something of his composure.

"No farce, citizen," replied Lepine calmly. "The money is at your disposal whenever you care to bring the letters to my pitch at the angle of the Rue Dauphine and the Quai des Augustins, where I carry on my business."

"Whose money is it? Agnes de Lucines' or did that fool Fabrice send you?"

"No one sent me, citizen. The money is mine—a few savings I possess—I honour citizen Fabrice—I would wish to do him service by purchasing certain letters from you."

Then as Heriot, moody and sullen, remained silent and began pacing up and down the long, bare floor of the room, Lepine added persuasively, "Well! what do you say? Two thousand francs for a packet of letters—not a bad bargain these hard times."

"Get out of this room," was Heriot's fierce and sudden reply.

"You refuse?"

"Get out of this room!"

"As you please," said Lepine as he, too, rose from his chair. "But before I go, citizen Heriot," he added, speaking very quietly, "let me tell you one thing. Mademoiselle Agnes de Lucines would far sooner cut off her right hand than let yours touch it even for one instant. Neither she nor deputy Fabrice would ever purchase their lives at such a price."

"And who are you—you mangy old scarecrow?" retorted Heriot, who was getting beside himself with rage, "that you should assert these things? What are those people to you, or you to them, that you should interfere in their affairs?"

"Your question is beside the point, citizen," said Lepine blandly; "I am here to propose a bargain. Had you not better agree to it?"

"Never!" reiterated Heriot emphatically.

"Two thousand francs," reiterated the old man imperturbably.

"Not if you offered me two hundred thousand," retorted the

other fiercely. "Go and tell that, to those who sent you. Tell them that I —Heriot—would look upon a fortune as mere dross against the delight of seeing that man Fabrice, whom I hate beyond everything in earth or hell, mount up the steps to the guillotine. Tell them that I know that Agnes de Lucines loathes me, that I know that she loves him. I know that I cannot win her save by threatening him. But you are wrong, citizen Lepine," he continued, speaking more and more calmly as his passions of hatred and of love seemed more and more to hold him in their grip; "you are wrong if you think that she will not strike a bargain with me in order to save the life of Fabrice, whom she loves. Agnes de Lucines will be my wife within the month, or Arnould Fabrice's head will fall under the guillotine, and you, my interfering friend, may go to the devil, if you please."

"That would be but a tame proceeding, citizen, after my visit to you," said the old man, with unruffled *sang-froid*. "But let me, in my turn, assure you of this, citizen Heriot," he added, "that Mlle. de Lucines will never be your wife, that Arnould Fabrice will not end his valuable life under the guillotine—and that you will never be allowed to use against him the cowardly and stolen weapon which you possess."

Heriot laughed—a low, cynical laugh and shrugged his thin shoulders:

"And who will prevent me, I pray you?" he asked sarcastically. The old man made no immediate reply, but he came just a step or two closer to the citizen-deputy and, suddenly drawing himself up to his full height, he looked for one brief moment down upon the mean and sordid figure of the ex-valet. To Heriot it seemed as if the whole man had become transfigured; the shabby old scarecrow looked all of a sudden like a brilliant and powerful personality; from his eyes there flashed down a look of supreme contempt and of supreme pride, and Heriot—unable to understand this metamorphosis which was more apparent to his inner consciousness than to his outward sight, felt his knees shake under him and all the blood rush back to his heart in an agony of superstitious terror.

From somewhere there came to his ear the sound of two words: "I will!" in reply to his own defiant query. Surely those words uttered by a man conscious of power and of strength could never have been spoken by the dilapidated old scarecrow who earned a precarious living by writing letters for ignorant folk.

But before he could recover some semblance of presence of mind citizen Lepine had gone, and only a loud and merry laugh seemed to echo through the squalid room.

Heriot shook off the remnant of his own senseless terror; he tore open the door of the bedroom and shouted to Rondeau, who truly was thinking that the citizen-deputy had gone mad:

"After him!—after him! Quick! curse you!" he cried.

"After whom?" gasped the man.

"The man who was here just now—an *aristo*."

"I saw no one—but the Public Letter-Writer, old Lepine—I know him well—-"

"Curse you for a fool!" shouted Heriot savagely, "the man who was here was that cursed Englishman—the one whom they call the Scarlet Pimpernel. Run after him—stop him, I say!"

"Too late, citizen," said the other placidly; "whoever was here before is certainly half-way down the street by now."

## III

"No use, Ffoulkes," said Sir Percy Blakeney to his friend half-an-hour later, "the man's passions of hatred and desire are greater than his greed."

The two men were sitting together in one of Sir Percy Blakeney's many lodgings—the one in the Rue des Petits Peres—and Sir Percy had just put Sir Andrew Ffoulkes au fait with the whole sad story of Arnould Fabrice's danger and Agnes de Lucines' despair.

"You could do nothing with the brute, then?" queried Sir Andrew.

"Nothing," replied Blakeney. "He refused all bribes, and violence would not have helped me, for what I wanted was not to knock him down, but to get hold of the letters."

"Well, after all, he might have sold you the letters and then denounced Fabrice just the same."

"No, without actual proofs he could not do that. Arnould Fabrice is not a man against whom a mere denunciation would suffice. He has the grudging respect of every faction in the National Assembly. Nothing but irrefutable proof would prevail against him—and bring him to the guillotine."

"Why not get Fabrice and Mlle. de Lucines safely over to England?"

"Fabrice would not come. He is not of the stuff that emigres are made of. He is not an aristocrat; he is a republican by conviction, and a demmed honest one at that. He would scorn to run away, and Agnes de Lucines would not go without him."

"Then what can we do?"

"Filch those letters from that brute Heriot," said Blakeney calmly.

"House-breaking, you mean!" commented Sir Andrew Ffoulkes dryly.

"Petty theft, shall we say?" retorted Sir Percy. "I can bribe the lout who has charge of Heriot's rooms to introduce us into his master's sanctum this evening when the National Assembly is sitting and the citizen-deputy safely out of the way."

And the two men—one of whom was the most intimate friend of
the Prince of Wales and the acknowledged darling of London society—
thereupon fell to discussing plans for surreptitiously entering a man's
room and committing larceny, which in normal times would entail, if
discovered, a long term of imprisonment, but which, in these days, in
Paris, and perpetrated against a member of the National Assembly,
would certainly be punished by death.

## IV

Citizen Rondeau, whose business it was to look after the
creature comforts of deputy Heriot, was standing in the antichambre
facing the two visitors whom he had just introduced into his master's
apartments, and idly turning a couple of gold coins over and over
between his grimy fingers.

"And mind, you are to see nothing and hear nothing of what
goes on in the next room," said the taller of the two strangers; "and
when we go there'll be another couple of louis for you. Is that
understood?"

"Yes! it's understood," grunted Rondeau sullenly; "but I am
running great risks. The citizen-deputy sometimes returns at ten
o'clock, but sometimes at nine. . . . I never know."

"It is now seven," rejoined the other; "we'll be gone long before
nine."

"Well," said Rondeau surlily, "I go out now for my supper. I'll
return in half an hour, but at half-past eight you must clear out."

Then he added with a sneer:

"Citizens Legros and Desgas usually come back with deputy
Heriot of nights, and citizens Jeanniot and Bompard come in from next
door for a game of cards. You wouldn't stand much chance if you were
caught here."

"Not with you to back up so formidable a quintette of
stalwarts," assented the tall visitor gaily. "But we won't trouble about
that just now. We have a couple of hours before us in which to do all
that we want. So *au revoir*, friend Rondeau . . . two more louis for your
complaisance, remember, when we have accomplished our purpose."

Rondeau muttered something more, but the two strangers paid
no further heed to him; they had already walked to the next room,
leaving Rondeau in the antichambre.

Sir Percy Blakeney did not pause in the sitting-room where an
oil lamp suspended from the ceiling threw a feeble circle of light above
the centre table. He went straight through to the bedroom. Here, too, a
small lamp was burning which only lit up a small portion of the room—
the writing-desk and the oak chest—leaving the corners and the alcove,

with its partially drawn curtains, in complete shadow.

Blakeney pointed to the oak chest and to the desk.

"You tackle the chest, Ffoulkes, and I will go for the desk," he said quietly, as soon as he had taken a rapid survey of the room. "You have your tools?"

Ffoulkes nodded, and anon in this squalid room, ill-lit, ill-ventilated, barely furnished, was presented one of the most curious spectacles of these strange and troublous times: two English gentlemen, the acknowledged dandies of London drawing-rooms, busy picking locks and filing hinges like any common house-thieves.

Neither of them spoke, and a strange hush fell over the room—a hush only broken by the click of metal against metal, and the deep breathing of the two men bending to their task. Sir Andrew Ffoulkes was working with a file on the padlocks of the oak chest, and Sir Percy Blakeney, with a bunch of skeleton keys, was opening the drawers of the writing-desk. These, when finally opened, revealed nothing of any importance; but when anon Sir Andrew was able to lift the lid of the oak chest, he disclosed an innumerable quantity of papers and documents tied up in neat bundles, docketed and piled up in rows and tiers to the very top of the chest.

"Quick to work, Ffoulkes," said Blakeney, as in response to his friend's call he drew a chair forward and, seating himself beside the chest, started on the task of looking through the hundreds of bundles which lay before him. "It will take us all our time to look through these."

Together now the two men set to work—methodically and quietly—piling up on the floor beside them the bundles of papers which they had already examined, and delving into the oak chest for others. No sound was heard save the crackling of crisp paper and an occasional ejaculation from either of them when they came upon some proof or other of Heriot's propensity for blackmail.

"Agnes de Lucines is not the only one whom this brute is terrorising," murmured Blakeney once between his teeth; "I marvel that the man ever feels safe, alone in these lodgings, with no one but that weak-kneed Rondeau to protect him. He must have scores of enemies in this city who would gladly put a dagger in his heart or a bullet through his back."

They had been at work for close on half an hour when an exclamation of triumph, quickly smothered, escaped Sir Percy's lips.

"By Gad, Ffoulkes!" he said, "I believe I have got what we want!"

With quick, capable hands he turned over a bundle which he had just extracted from the chest. Rapidly he glanced through them. "I have them, Ffoulkes," he reiterated more emphatically as he put the bundle into his pocket; "now everything back in its place and—"

Suddenly he paused, his slender hand up to his lips, his head turned toward the door, an expression of tense expectancy in every line of his face.

"Quick, Ffoulkes," he whispered, "everything back into the chest, and the lid down."

"What ears you have," murmured Ffoulkes as he obeyed rapidly and without question. "I heard nothing."

Blakeney went to the door and bent his head to listen.

"Three men coming up the stairs," he said; "they are on the landing now."

"Have we time to rush them?"

"No chance! They are at the door. Two more men have joined them, and I can distinguish Rondeau's voice, too."

"The quintette," murmured Sir Andrew. "We are caught like two rats in a trap."

Even as he spoke the opening of the outside door could be distinctly heard, then the confused murmur of many voices. Already Blakeney and Ffoulkes had with perfect presence of mind put the finishing touches to the tidying of the room—put the chairs straight, shut down the lid of the oak chest, closed all the drawers of the desk.

"Nothing but good luck can save us now," whispered Blakeney as he lowered the wick of the lamp. "Quick now," he added, "behind that tapestry in the alcove and trust to our stars."

Securely hidden for the moment behind the curtains in the dark recess of the alcove the two men waited. The door leading into the sitting-room was ajar, and they could hear Heriot and his friends making merry irruption into the place. From out the confusion of general conversation they soon gathered that the debates in the Chamber had been so dull and uninteresting that, at a given signal, the little party had decided to adjourn to Heriot's rooms for their habitual game of cards. They could also hear Heriot calling to Rondeau to bring bottles and glasses, and vaguely they marvelled what Rondeau's attitude might be like at this moment. Was he brazening out the situation, or was he sick with terror?

Suddenly Heriot's voice came out more distinctly.

"Make yourselves at home, friends," he was saying; "here are cards, dominoes, and wine. I must leave you to yourselves for ten minutes whilst I write an important letter."

"All right, but don't be long," came in merry response.

"Not longer than I can help," rejoined Heriot. "I want my revenge against Bompard, remember. He did fleece me last night."

"Hurry on, then," said one of the men. "I'll play Desgas that return game of dominoes until then."

"Ten minutes and I'll be back," concluded Heriot.

He pushed open the bedroom door. The light within was very

dim. The two men hidden behind the tapestry could hear him moving about the room muttering curses to himself. Presently the light of the lamp was shifted from one end of the room to the other. Through the opening between the two curtains Blakeney could just see Heriot's back as he placed the lamp at a convenient angle upon his desk, divested himself of his overcoat and muffler, then sat down and drew pen and paper closer to him. He was leaning forward, his elbow resting upon the table, his fingers fidgeting with his long, lank hair. He had closed the door when he entered, and from the other room now the voices of his friends sounded confused and muffled. Now and then an exclamation: "Double!" "*Je . . . tiens!*" "*Cinq-deux!*" an oath, a laugh, the click of glasses and bottles came out more clearly; but the rest of the time these sounds were more like a droning accompaniment to the scraping of Heriot's pen upon the paper when he finally began to write his letter.

Two minutes went by and then two more. The scratching of Heriot's pen became more rapid as he appeared to be more completely immersed in his work. Behind the curtain the two men had been waiting: Blakeney ready to act, Ffoulkes equally ready to interpret the slightest signal from his chief.

The next minute Blakeney had stolen out of the alcove, and his two hands—so slender and elegant looking, and yet with a grip of steel —had fastened themselves upon Heriot's mouth, smothering within the space of a second the cry that had been half-uttered. Ffoulkes was ready to complete the work of rendering the man helpless: one handkerchief made an efficient gag, another tied the ankles securely. Heriot's own coat-sleeves supplied the handcuffs, and the blankets off the bed tied around his legs rendered him powerless to move. Then the two men lifted this inert mass on to the bed and Ffoulkes whispered anxiously: "Now, what next?"

Heriot's overcoat, hat, and muffler lay upon a chair. Sir Percy, placing a warning finger upon his lips, quickly divested himself of his own coat, slipped that of Heriot on, twisted the muffler round his neck, hunched up his shoulders, and murmuring: "Now for a bit of luck!" once more lowered the light of the lamp and then went to the door.

"Rondeau!" he called. "Hey, Rondeau!" And Sir Percy himself was surprised at the marvellous way in which he had caught the very inflection of Heriot's voice.

"Hey, Rondeau!" came from one of the players at the table, "the citizen-deputy is calling you!"

They were all sitting round the table: two men intent upon their game of dominoes, the other two watching with equal intentness. Rondeau came shuffling out of the antichambre. His face, by the dim light of the oil lamp, looked jaundiced with fear.

"Rondeau, you fool, where are you?" called Blakeney once

again.

The next moment Rondeau had entered the room. No need for a signal or an order this time. Ffoulkes knew by instinct what his chief's bold scheme would mean to them both if it succeeded. He retired into the darkest corner of the room as Rondeau shuffled across to the writing-desk. It was all done in a moment. In less time than it had taken to bind and gag Heriot, his henchman was laid out on the floor, his coat had been taken off him, and he was tied into a mummy-like bundle with Sir Andrew Ffoulkes' elegant coat fastened securely round his arms and chest. It had all been done in silence. The men in the next room were noisy and intent on their game; the slight scuffle, the quickly smothered cries had remained unheeded.

"Now, what next?" queried Sir Andrew Ffoulkes once more.

"The impudence of the d—- l, my good Ffoulkes," replied Blakeney in a whisper, "and may our stars not play us false. Now let me make you look as like Rondeau as possible—there! Slip on his coat— now your hair over your forehead—your coat-collar up—your knees bent—that's better!" he added as he surveyed the transformation which a few deft strokes had made in Sir Andrew Ffoulkes' appearance. "Now all you have to do is to shuffle across the room—here's your prototype's handkerchief—of dubious cleanliness, it is true, but it will serve—blow your nose as you cross the room, it will hide your face. They'll not heed you—keep in the shadows and God guard you—I'll follow in a moment or two . . . but don't wait for me."

He opened the door, and before Sir Andrew could protest his chief had pushed him out into the room where the four men were still intent on their game. Through the open door Sir Percy now watched his friend who, keeping well within the shadows, shuffled quietly across the room. The next moment Sir Andrew was through and in the antichambre. Blakeney's acutely sensitive ears caught the sound of the opening of the outer door. He waited for a while, then he drew out of his pocket the bundle of letters which he had risked so much to obtain. There they were neatly docketed and marked: "The affairs of Arnould Fabrice."

Well! if he got away to-night Agnes de Lucines would be happy and free from the importunities of that brute Heriot; after that he must persuade her and Fabrice to go to England and to freedom.
For the moment his own safety was terribly in jeopardy; one false move —one look from those players round the table . . . Bah! even then—!

With an inward laugh he pushed open the door once more and stepped into the room. For the moment no one noticed him; the game was at its most palpitating stage; four shaggy heads met beneath the lamp and four pairs of eyes were gazing with rapt attention upon the intricate maze of the dominoes.

Blakeney walked quietly across the room; he was just midway

and on a level with the centre table when a voice was suddenly raised from that tense group beneath the lamp: "Is it thou, friend Heriot?"

Then one of the men looked up and stared, and another did likewise and exclaimed: "It is not Heriot!"

In a moment all was confusion, but confusion was the very essence of those hair-breadth escapes and desperate adventures which were as the breath of his nostrils to the Scarlet Pimpernel. Before those four men had had time to jump to their feet, or to realise that something was wrong with their friend Heriot, he had run across the room, his hand was on the knob of the door—the door that led to the antichambre and to freedom.

Bompard, Desgas, Jeanniot, Legros were at his heels, but he tore open the door, bounded across the threshold, and slammed it to with such a vigorous bang that those on the other side were brought to a momentary halt. That moment meant life and liberty to Blakeney; already he had crossed the antichambre. Quite coolly and quietly now he took out the key from the inner side of the main door and slipped it to the outside. The next second—even as the four men rushed helter-skelter into the antichambre he was out on the landing and had turned the key in the door.

His prisoners were safely locked in—in Heriot's apartments—and Sir Percy Blakeney, calmly and without haste, was descending the stairs of the house in the Rue Cocatrice.

The next morning Agnes de Lucines received, through an anonymous messenger, the packet of letters which would so gravely have compromised Arnould Fabrice. Though the weather was more inclement than ever, she ran out into the streets, determined to seek out the old Public Letter-Writer and thank him for his mediation with the English milor, who surely had done this noble action.

But the old scarecrow had disappeared.

# A Fine Bit Of Work

"Sh! . . . sh! . . . It's the Englishman. I'd know his footstep anywhere – "

"God bless him!" murmured *petite maman* fervently.

Pere Lenegre went to the door; he stepped cautiously and with that stealthy foot-tread which speaks in eloquent silence of daily, hourly danger, of anguish and anxiety for lives that are dear.

The door was low and narrow—up on the fifth floor of one of the huge tenement houses in the Rue Jolivet in the Montmartre quarter of Paris. A narrow stone passage led to it—pitch-dark at all times, but dirty, and evil-smelling when the concierge—a free citizen of the new democracy—took a week's holiday from his work in order to spend whole afternoons either at the wineshop round the corner, or on the Place du Carrousel to watch the guillotine getting rid of some twenty aristocrats an hour for the glorification of the will of the people.

But inside the small apartment everything was scrupulously neat and clean. *Petite maman* was such an excellent manager, and Rosette was busy all the day tidying and cleaning the poor little home, which Pere Lenegre contrived to keep up for wife and daughter by working fourteen hours a day in the government saddlery.

When Pere Lenegre opened the narrow door, the entire framework of it was filled by the broad, magnificent figure of a man in heavy caped coat and high leather boots, with dainty frills of lace at throat and wrist, and elegant *chapeau-bras* held in the hand.

Pere Lenegre at sight of him, put a quick finger to his own quivering lips.

"Anything wrong, *vieux papa?*" asked the newcomer lightly.

The other closed the door cautiously before he made reply. But *petite maman* could not restrain her anxiety.

"My little Pierre, milor?" she asked as she clasped her wrinkled hands together, and turned on the stranger her tear- dimmed restless eyes.

"Pierre is safe and well, little mother," he replied cheerily. "We got him out of Paris early this morning in a coal cart, carefully hidden among the sacks. When he emerged he was black but safe. I drove the cart myself as far as Courbevoie, and there handed over your Pierre and those whom we got out of Paris with him to those of my friends who were going straight to England. There's nothing more to be afraid of, *petite maman*," he added as he took the old woman's wrinkled hands in both his own; "your son is now under the care of men who would die rather than see him captured. So make your mind at ease, Pierre will be in England, safe and well, within a week."

*Petite maman* couldn't say anything just then because tears were choking her, but in her turn she clasped those two strong and slender hands—the hands of the brave Englishman who had just risked his life in order to save Pierre from the guillotine—and she kissed them as fervently as she kissed the feet of the Madonna when she knelt before her shrine in prayer.

Pierre had been a footman in the household of unhappy Marie Antoinette. His crime had been that he remained loyal to her in words as well as in thought. A hot-headed but nobly outspoken harangue on behalf of the unfortunate queen, delivered in a public place, had at once marked him out to the spies of the Terrorists as suspect of intrigue against the safety of the Republic. He was denounced to the Committee of Public Safety, and his arrest and condemnation to the guillotine would have inevitably followed had not the gallant band of Englishmen, known as the League of the Scarlet Pimpernel, succeeded in effecting his escape.

What wonder that *petite maman* could not speak for tears when she clasped the hands of the noble leader of that splendid little band of heroes? What wonder that Pere Lenegre, when he heard that his son was safe murmured a fervent: "God bless you, milor, and your friends!" and that Rosette surreptitiously raised the fine caped coat to her lips, for Pierre was her twin-brother, and she loved him very dearly.

But already Sir Percy Blakeney had, with one of his characteristic cheery words, dissipated the atmosphere of tearful emotion which oppressed these kindly folk.

"Now, Papa Lenegre," he said lightly, "tell me why you wore such a solemn air when you let me in just now."

"Because, milor," replied the old man quietly, "that d——d concierge, Jean Baptiste, is a black-hearted traitor."

Sir Percy laughed, his merry, infectious laugh.

"You mean that while he has been pocketing bribes from me, he has denounced me to the Committee."

Pere Lenegre nodded: "I only heard it this morning," he said, "from one or two threatening words the treacherous brute let fall. He knows that you lodge in the Place des Trois Maries, and that you come here frequently. I would have given my life to warn you then and there," continued the old man with touching earnestness, "but I didn't know where to find you. All I knew was that you were looking after Pierre."

Even while the man spoke there darted from beneath the Englishman's heavy lids a quick look like a flash of sudden and brilliant light out of the lazy depths of his merry blue eyes; it was one of those glances of pure delight and exultation which light up the eyes of the true soldier when there is serious fighting to be done.

"La, man," he said gaily, "there was no cause to worry. Pierre is safe, remember that! As for me," he added with that wonderful insouciance which caused him to risk his life a hundred times a day with a shrug of his broad shoulders and a smile upon his lips; "as for me, I'll look after myself, never fear."

He paused awhile, then added gravely: "So long as you are safe, my good Lenegre, and , and Rosette."

Whereupon the old man was silent,  murmured a short prayer, and Rosette began to cry. The hero of a thousand gallant rescues had received his answer.

"You, too, are on the black list, Pere Lenegre?" he asked quietly.

The old man nodded.

"How do you know?" queried the Englishman.

"Through Jean Baptiste, milor."

"Still that demmed concierge," muttered Sir Percy.

"He frightened *petite maman* with it all this morning, saying that he knew my name was down on the Sectional Committee's list as a 'suspect.' That's when he let fall a word or two about you, milor. He said it is known that Pierre has escaped from justice, and that you helped him to it.

"I am sure that we shall get a domiciliary visit presently," continued Pere Lenegre, after a slight pause. "The gendarmes have not yet been, but I fancy that already this morning early I saw one or two of the Committee's spies hanging about the house, and when I went to the workshop I was followed all the time."

The Englishman looked grave: "And tell me," he said, "have you got anything in this place that may prove compromising to any of you?"

"No, milor. But, as Jean Baptiste said, the Sectional Committee know about Pierre. It is because of my son that I am suspect."

The old man spoke quite quietly, very simply, like a philosopher who has long ago learned to put behind him the fear of death. Nor did *petite maman* cry or lament. Her thoughts were for the brave milor who had saved her boy; but her fears for her old man left her dry-eyed and dumb with grief.

There was silence in the little room for one moment while the angel of sorrow and anguish hovered round these faithful and brave souls, then the Englishman's cheery voice, so full of spirit and merriment, rang out once more—he had risen to his full, towering height, and now placed a kindly hand on the old man's shoulder:

"It seems to me, my good Lenegre," he said, "that you and I haven't many moments to spare if we mean to cheat those devils by saving your neck. Now, *petite maman*," he added, turning to the old woman, "are you going to be brave?"

"I will do anything, milor," she replied quietly, "to help my old man."

"Well, then," said Sir Percy Blakeney in that optimistic, light-hearted yet supremely authoritative tone of which he held the secret, "you and Rosette remain here and wait for the gendarmes. When they come, say nothing; behave with absolute meekness, and let them search your place from end to end. If they ask you about your husband say that you believe him to be at his workshop. Is that clear?"

"Quite clear, milor," replied *petite maman*.

"And you, Pere Lenegre," continued the Englishman, speaking now with slow and careful deliberation, "listen very attentively to the instructions I am going to give you, for on your implicit obedience to them depends not only your own life but that of these two dear women. Go at once, now, to the Rue Ste. Anne, round the corner, the second house on your right, which is numbered thirty-seven. The *porte cochere* stands open, go boldly through, past the concierge's box, and up the stairs to apartment number twelve, second floor. Here is the key of the apartment," he added, producing one from his coat pocket and handing it over to the old man. "The rooms are nominally occupied by a certain Maitre Turandot, maker of violins, and not even the concierge of the place knows that the hunchbacked and snuffy violin-maker and the meddlesome Scarlet Pimpernel, whom the Committee of Public Safety would so love to lay by the heels, are one and the same person. The apartment, then, is mine; one of the many which I occupy in Paris at different times," he went on. "Let yourself in quietly with this key, walk straight across the first room to a wardrobe, which you will see in front of you. Open it. It is hung full of shabby clothes; put these aside, and you will notice that the panels at the back do not fit very closely, as if the wardrobe was old or had been badly put together. Insert your fingers in the tiny aperture between the two middle panels. These slide back easily: there is a recess immediately behind them. Get in there; pull the doors of the wardrobe together first, then slide the back panels into their place. You will be perfectly safe there, as the house is not under suspicion at present, and even if the revolutionary guard, under some meddle-some sergeant or other, chooses to pay it a surprise visit, your hiding-place will be perfectly secure. Now is all that quite understood?"

"Absolutely, milor," replied Lenegre, even as he made ready to obey Sir Percy's orders, "but what about you? You cannot get out of this house, milor," he urged; "it is watched, I tell you."

"La!" broke in Blakeney, in his light-hearted way, "and do you think I didn't know that? I had to come and tell you about Pierre, and now I must give those worthy gendarmes the slip somehow. I have my rooms downstairs on the ground floor, as you know, and I must make certain arrangements so that we can all get out of Paris comfortably this evening. The demmed place is no longer safe either for you, my good Lenegre, or for *petite maman* and Rosette. But wherever I may be, meanwhile, don't worry about me. As soon as the gendarmes have been and gone, I'll go over to the Rue Ste. Anne and let you know what arrangements I've been able to make. So do as I tell you now, and in Heaven's name let me look after myself."

Whereupon, with scant ceremony, he hustled the old man out of the room.

Pere Lenegre had contrived to kiss *petite maman* and Rosette before he went. It was touching to see the perfect confidence with which these simple-hearted folk obeyed the commands of milor. Had he not saved Pierre in his wonderful, brave, resourceful way? Of a truth he would know how to save Pere Lenegre also. But, nevertheless, anguish gripped the women's hearts; anguish doubly keen since the saviour of Pierre was also in danger now.

When Pere Lenegre's shuffling footsteps had died away along the flagged corridor, the stranger once more turned to the two women.

"And now, *petite maman*," he said cheerily, as he kissed the old woman on both her furrowed cheeks, "keep up a good heart, and say your prayers with Rosette. Your old man and I will both have need of them."

He did not wait to say good-bye, and anon it was his firm footstep that echoed down the corridor. He went off singing a song, at the top of his voice, for the whole house to hear, and for that traitor, Jean Baptiste, to come rushing out of his room marvelling at the impudence of the man, and cursing the Committee of Public Safety who were so slow in sending the soldiers of the Republic to lay this impertinent Englishman by the heels.

## II

A quarter of an hour later half dozen men of the Republican Guard, with corporal and sergeant in command, were in the small apartment on the fifth floor of the tenement house in the Rue Jolivet. They had demanded an entry in the name of the Republic, had roughly hustled *petite maman* and Rosette, questioned them to Lenegre's whereabouts, and not satisfied with the reply which they received, had turned the tidy little home topsy-turvy, ransacked every cupboard, dislocated every bed, table or sofa which might presumably have afforded a hiding place for a man.

Satisfied now that the "suspect" whom they were searching for was not on the premises, the sergeant stationed four of his men with the corporal outside the door, and two within, and himself sitting down in the centre of the room ordered the two women to stand before him and to answer his questions clearly on pain of being dragged away forthwith to the St. Lazare house of detention.

*Petite maman* smoothed out her apron, crossed her arms before her, and looked the sergeant quite straight in the face. Rosette's eyes were full of tears, but she showed no signs of fear either, although her shoulder—where one of the gendarmes had seized it so roughly—was terribly painful.

"Your husband, citizeness," asked the sergeant peremptorily, "where is he?"

"I am not sure, citizen," replied *petite maman*. "At this hour he is generally at the government works in the Quai des Messageries."

"He is not there now," asserted the sergeant. "We have knowledge that he did not go back to his work since dinner-time."

*Petite maman* was silent.

"Answer," ordered the sergeant.

"I cannot tell you more, citizen sergeant," she said firmly. "I do not know."

"You do yourself no good, woman, by this obstinacy," he continued roughly. "My belief is that your husband is inside this house, hidden away somewhere. If necessary I can get orders to have every apartment searched until he is found: but in that case it will go much harder with you and with your daughter, and much harder too with your husband than if he gave us no trouble and followed us quietly."

But with sublime confidence in the man who had saved Pierre and who had given her explicit orders as to what she should do, *petite maman*, backed by Rosette, reiterated quietly:

"I cannot tell you more, citizen sergeant, I do not know."

"And what about the Englishman?" queried the sergeant more roughly, "the man they call the Scarlet Pimpernel, what do you know of him?"

"Nothing, citizen," replied *petite maman*, "what should we poor folk know of an English milor?"

"You know at any rate this much, citizeness, that the English milor helped your son Pierre to escape from justice."

"If that is so," said *petite maman* quietly, "it cannot be wrong for a mother to pray to God to bless her son's preserver."

"It behooves every good citizen," retorted the sergeant firmly, "to denounce all traitors to the Republic."

"But since I know nothing about the Englishman, citizen sergeant—?"

And *petite maman* shrugged her thin shoulders as if the matter had ceased to interest her.

"Think again, citizeness," admonished the sergeant, "it is your husband's neck as well as your daughter's and your own that you are risking by so much obstinacy."

He waited a moment or two as if willing to give the old woman time to speak: then, when he saw that she kept her thin, quivering lips resolutely glued together he called his corporal to him.

"Go to the citizen Commissary of the Section," he commanded, "and ask for a general order to search every apartment in No. 24 Rue Jolivet. Leave two of our men posted on the first and third landings of this house and leave two outside this door. Be as quick as you can. You can be back here with the order in half an hour, or perhaps the committee will send me an extra squad; tell the citizen Commissary that this is a big house, with many corridors. You can go."

The corporal saluted and went.

*Petite maman* and Rosette the while were still standing quietly in the middle of the room, their arms folded underneath their aprons, their wide-open, anxious eyes fixed into space. Rosette's tears were falling slowly, one by one down her cheeks, but *petite maman* was dry-eyed. She was thinking, and thinking as she had never had occasion to think before.

She was thinking of the brave and gallant Englishman who had saved Pierre's life only yesterday. The sergeant, who sat there before her, had asked for orders from the citizen Commissary to search this big house from attic to cellar. That is what made *petite maman* think and think.

The brave Englishman was in this house at the present moment: the house would be searched from attic to cellar and he would be found, taken, and brought to the guillotine.

The man who yesterday had risked his life to save her boy was in imminent and deadly danger, and she—*petite maman*—could do nothing to save him.

Every moment now she thought to hear milor's firm tread resounding on stairs or corridor, every moment she thought to hear snatches of an English song, sung by a fresh and powerful voice, never after to-day to be heard in gaiety again.

The old clock upon the shelf ticked away these seconds and minutes while *petite maman* thought and thought, while men set traps to catch a fellow-being in a deathly snare, and human carnivorous beasts lay lurking for their prey.

### III

Another quarter of an hour went by. *Petite maman* and Rosette had hardly moved. The shadows of evening were creeping into the narrow room, blurring the outlines of the pieces of furniture and wrapping all the corners in gloom.

The sergeant had ordered Rosette to bring in a lamp. This she had done, placing it upon the table so that the feeble light glinted upon the belt and buckles of the sergeant and upon the tricolour cockade which was pinned to his hat. *Petite maman* had thought and thought until she could think no more.

Anon there was much commotion on the stairs; heavy footsteps were heard ascending from below, then crossing the corridors on the various landings. The silence which reigned otherwise in the house, and which had fallen as usual on the squalid little street, void of traffic at this hour, caused those footsteps to echo with ominous power.

*Petite maman* felt her heart beating so vigorously that she could hardly breathe. She pressed her wrinkled hands tightly against her bosom.

There were the quick words of command, alas! so familiar in France just now, the cruel, peremptory words that invariably preceded an arrest, preliminaries to the dragging of some wretched—often wholly harmless—creature before a tribunal that knew neither pardon nor mercy.

The sergeant, who had become drowsy in the close atmosphere of the tiny room, roused himself at the sound and jumped to his feet. The door was thrown open by the men stationed outside even before the authoritative words, "Open! in the name of the Republic!" had echoed along the narrow corridor.

The sergeant stood at attention and quickly lifted his hand to his forehead in salute. A fresh squad of some half-dozen men of the Republican Guard stood in the doorway; they were under the command of an officer of high rank, a rough, uncouth, almost bestial-looking creature, with lank hair worn the fashionable length under his greasy *chapeau-bras*, and unkempt beard round an ill-washed and bloated face. But he wore the tricolour sash and badge which proclaimed him one of the military members of the Sectional Committee of Public Safety, and the sergeant, who had been so overbearing with the women just now, had assumed a very humble and even obsequious manner.

"You sent for a general order to the sectional Committee," said the new-comer, turning abruptly to the sergeant after he had cast a quick, searching glance round the room, hardly condescending to look on *petite maman* and Rosette, whose very souls were now gazing out of their anguish-filled eyes.

"I did, citizen commandant," replied the sergeant.

"I am not a commandant," said the other curtly. "My name is Rouget, member of the Convention and of the Committee of Public Safety. The sectional Committee to whom you sent for a general order of search thought that you had blundered somehow, so they sent me to put things right."

"I am not aware that I committed any blunder, citizen," stammered the sergeant dolefully. "I could not take the responsibility of making a domiciliary search all through the house. So I begged for fuller orders."

"And wasted the Committee's time and mine by such

nonsense," retorted Rouget harshly. "Every citizen of the Republic worthy of the name should know how to act on his own initiative when the safety of the nation demands it."

"I did not know—I did not dare—" murmured the sergeant, obviously cowed by this reproof, which had been delivered in the rough, overbearing tones peculiar to these men who, one and all, had risen from the gutter to places of importance and responsibility in the newly-modelled State.

"Silence!" commanded the other peremptorily. "Don't waste any more of my time with your lame excuses. You have failed in zeal and initiative. That's enough. What else have you done? Have you got the man Lenegre?"

"No, citizen. He is not in hiding here, and his wife and daughter will not give us any information about him."

"That is their look-out," retorted Rouget with a harsh laugh. "If they give up Lenegre of their own free will the law will deal leniently with them, and even perhaps with him. But if we have to search the house for him, then it means the guillotine for the lot of them."

He had spoken these callous words without even looking on the two unfortunate women; nor did he ask them any further questions just then, but continued speaking to the sergeant:

"And what about the Englishman? The sectional Committee sent down some spies this morning to be on the look-out for him on or about this house. Have you got him?"

"Not yet, citizen. But—"

"Ah ca, citizen sergeant," broke in the other brusquely, "meseems that your zeal has been even more at fault than I had supposed. Have you done anything at all, then, in the matter of Lenegre or the Englishman?"

"I have told you, citizen," retorted the sergeant sullenly, "that I believe Lenegre to be still in this house. At any rate, he had not gone out of it an hour ago—that's all I know. And I wanted to search the whole of this house, as I am sure we should have found him in one of the other apartments. These people are all friends together, and will always help each other to evade justice. But the Englishman was no concern of mine. The spies of the Committee were ordered to watch for him, and when they reported to me I was to proceed with the arrest. I was not set to do any of the spying work. I am a soldier, and obey my orders when I get them."

"Very well, then, you'd better obey them now, citizen sergeant," was Rouget's dry comment on the other man's surly explanation, "for you seem to have properly blundered from first to last, and will be hard put to it to redeem your character. The Republic, remember, has no use for fools."

The sergeant, after this covert threat, thought it best,

apparently, to keep his tongue, whilst Rouget continued, in the same aggressive, peremptory tone:

"Get on with your domiciliary visits at once. Take your own men with you, and leave me the others. Begin on this floor, and leave your sentry at the front door outside. Now let me see your zeal atoning for your past slackness. Right turn! Quick march!"

Then it was that *petite maman* spoke out. She had thought and thought, and now she knew what she ought to do; she knew that that cruel, inhuman wretch would presently begin his tramp up and down corridors and stairs, demanding admittance at every door, entering every apartment. She knew that the man who had saved her Pierre's life was in hiding somewhere in the house—that he would be found and dragged to the guillotine, for she knew that the whole governing body of this abominable Revolution was determined not to allow that hated Englishman to escape again.

She was old and feeble, small and thin—that's why everyone called her *petite maman*—but once she knew what she ought to do, then her spirit overpowered the weakness of her wizened body.

Now she knew, and even while that arrogant member of an execrated murdering Committee was giving final instructions to the sergeant, *petite maman* said, in a calm, piping voice:

"No need, citizen sergeant, to go and disturb all my friends and neighbours. I'll tell you where my husband is."

In a moment Rouget had swung round on his heel, a hideous gleam of satisfaction spread over his grimy face, and he said, with an ugly sneer:

"So! you have thought better of it, have you? Well, out with it! You'd better be quick about it if you want to do yourselves any good."

"I have my daughter to think of," said *petite maman* in a feeble, querulous way, "and I won't have all my neighbours in this house made unhappy because of me. They have all been kind neighbours. Will you promise not to molest them and to clear the house of soldiers if I tell you where Lenegre is?"

"The Republic makes no promises," replied Rouget gruffly. "Her citizens must do their duty without hope of a reward. If they fail in it, they are punished. But privately I will tell you, woman, that if you save us the troublesome and probably unprofitable task of searching this rabbit-warren through and through, it shall go very leniently with you and with your daughter, and perhaps—I won't promise, remember—perhaps with your husband also."

"Very good, citizen," said *petite maman* calmly. "I am ready."

"Ready for what?" he demanded.

"To take you to where my husband is in hiding."

"Oho! He is not in the house, then?"

"No."

"Where is he, then?"

"In the Rue Ste. Anne. I will take you there."

Rouget cast a quick, suspicious glance on the old woman, and exchanged one of understanding with the sergeant.

"Very well," he said after a slight pause. "But your daughter must come along too. Sergeant," he added, "I'll take three of your men with me; I have half a dozen, but it's better to be on the safe side. Post your fellows round the outer door, and on my way to the rue Ste. Anne I will leave word at the gendarmerie that a small reinforcement be sent on to you at once. These can be here in five minutes; until then you are quite safe."

Then he added under his breath, so that the women should not hear: "The Englishman may still be in the house. In which case, hearing us depart, he may think us all gone and try to give us the slip. You'll know what to do?" he queried significantly.

"Of course, citizen," replied the sergeant.

"Now, then, citizeness—hurry up."

Once more there was tramping of heavy feet on stone stairs and corridors. A squad of soldiers of the Republican Guard, with two women in their midst, and followed by a member of the Committee of Public Safety, a sergeant, corporal and two or three more men, excited much anxious curiosity as they descended the steep flights of steps from the fifth floor.

Pale, frightened faces peeped shyly through the doorways at sound of the noisy tramp from above, but quickly disappeared again at sight of the grimy scarlet facings and tricolour cockades.

The sergeant and three soldiers remained stationed at the foot of the stairs inside the house. Then citizen Rouget roughly gave the order to proceed. It seemed strange that it should require close on a dozen men to guard two women and to apprehend one old man, but as the member of the Committee of Public Safety whispered to the sergeant before he finally went out of the house: "The whole thing may be a trap, and one can't be too careful. The Englishman is said to be very powerful; I'll get the gendarmerie to send you another half-dozen men, and mind you guard the house until my return."

IV

Five minutes later the soldiers, directed by *petite maman*, had reached No. 37 Rue Ste. Anne. The big outside door stood wide open, and the whole party turned immediately into the house.

The concierge, terrified and obsequious, rushed—trembling—out of his box.

"What was the pleasure of the citizen soldiers?" he asked.

"Tell him, citizeness," commanded Rouget curtly.

"We are going to apartment No. 12 on the second floor," said *petite maman* to the concierge.

"Have you a key of the apartment?" queried Rouget.

"No, citizen," stammered the concierge, "but—"

"Well, what is it?" queried the other peremptorily.

"Papa Turandot is a poor, harmless maker of volins," said the concierge. "I know him well, though he is not often at home. He lives with a daughter somewhere Passy way, and only uses this place as a workshop. I am sure he is no traitor."

"We'll soon see about that," remarked Rouget dryly.

*Petite maman* held her shawl tightly crossed over her bosom: her hands felt clammy and cold as ice. She was looking straight out before her, quite dry-eyed and calm, and never once glanced on Rosette, who was not allowed to come anywhere near her mother.

As there was no duplicate key to apartment No. 12, citizen Rouget ordered his men to break in the door. It did not take very long: the house was old and ramshackle and the doors rickety. The next moment the party stood in the room which a while ago the Englishman had so accurately described to pere Lenegre in *petite maman*'s hearing.

There was the wardrobe. *Petite maman*, closely surrounded by the soldiers, went boldly up to it; she opened it just as milor had directed, and pushed aside the row of shabby clothes that hung there. Then she pointed to the panels that did not fit quite tightly together at the back. *Petite maman* passed her tongue over her dry lips before she spoke.

"There's a recess behind those panels," she said at last. "They slide back quite easily. My old man is there."

"And God bless you for a brave, loyal soul," came in merry, ringing accent from the other end of the room. "And God save the Scarlet Pimpernel!"

These last words, spoken in English, completed the blank amazement which literally paralysed the only three genuine Republican soldiers there—those, namely, whom Rouget had borrowed from the sergeant. As for the others, they knew what to do. In less than a minute they had overpowered and gagged the three bewildered soldiers.

Rosette had screamed, terror-stricken, from sheer astonishment, but *petite maman* stood quite still, her pale, tear-dimmed eyes fixed upon the man whose gay "God bless you!" had so suddenly turned her despair into hope.

How was it that in the hideous, unkempt and grimy Rouget she had not at once recognised the handsome and gallant milor who had saved her Pierre's life? Well, of a truth he had been unrecognisable, but now that he tore the ugly wig and beard from his face, stretched out his fine figure to its full height, and presently turned his lazy, merry eyes on her, she could have screamed for very joy.

The next moment he had her by the shoulders and had imprinted two sounding kisses upon her cheeks.

"Now, *petite maman*," he said gaily, "let us liberate the old man."

Pere Lenegre, from his hiding-place, had heard all that had been going on in the room for the last few moments. True, he had known exactly what to expect, for no sooner had he taken possession of the recess behind the wardrobe than milor also entered the apartment and then and there told him of his plans not only for pere's own safety, but for that of *petite maman* and Rosette who would be in grave danger if the old man followed in the wake of Pierre.

Milor told him in his usual light-hearted way that he had given the Committee's spies the slip.

"I do that very easily, you know," he explained. "I just slip into my rooms in the Rue Jolivet, change myself into a snuffy and hunchback violin-maker, and walk out of the house under the noses of the spies. In the nearest wine-shop my English friends, in various disguises, are all ready to my hand: half a dozen of them are never far from where I am in case they may be wanted."

These half-dozen brave Englishmen soon arrived one by one: one looked like a coal-heaver, another like a seedy musician, a third like a coach-driver. But they all walked boldly into the house and were soon all congregated in apartment No. 12. Here fresh disguises were assumed, and soon a squad of Republican Guards looked as like the real thing as possible.

Pere Lenegre admitted himself that though he actually saw milor transforming himself into citizen Rouget, he could hardly believe his eyes, so complete was the change.

"I am deeply grieved to have frightened and upset you so, *petite maman*," now concluded milor kindly, "but I saw no other way of getting you and Rosette out of the house and leaving that stupid sergeant and some of his men behind. I did not want to arouse in him even the faintest breath of suspicion, and of course if he had asked me for the written orders which he was actually waiting for, or if his corporal had returned sooner than I anticipated, there might have been trouble. But even then," he added with his usual careless insouciance, "I should have thought of some way of baffling those brutes."

"And now," he concluded more authoritatively, "it is a case of getting out of Paris before the gates close. Pere Lenegre, take your wife and daughter with you and walk boldly out of this house. The sergeant and his men have not vacated their post in the Rue Jolivet, and no one else can molest you. Go straight to the Porte de Neuilly, and on the other side wait quietly in the little cafe at the corner of the Avenue until I come. Your old passes for the barriers still hold good; you were only placed on the 'suspect' list this morning, and there has not been a hue and cry yet about you. In any case some of us will be close by to help you if needs be."

"But you, milor," stammered pere Lenegre, "and your friends —?"

"La, man," retorted Blakeney lightly, "have I not told you before never to worry about me and my friends? We have more ways than one of giving the slip to this demmed government of yours. All you've got to think of is your wife and your daughter. I am afraid that *petite maman* cannot take more with her than she has on, but we'll do all we can for her comfort until we have you all in perfect safety—in England—with Pierre."

Neither pere Lenegre, nor *petite maman*, nor Rosette could speak just then, for tears were choking them, but anon when milor stood nearer, *petite maman* knelt down, and, imprisoning his slender hand in her brown, wrinkled ones, she kissed it reverently.

He laughed and chided her for this.

"'Tis I should kneel to you in gratitude, *petite maman*," he said earnestly, "you were ready to sacrifice your old man for me."

"You have saved Pierre, milor," said the mother simply.

A minute later pere Lenegre and the two women were ready to go. Already milor and his gallant English friends were busy once more transforming themselves into grimy workmen or seedy middle-class professionals.

As soon as the door of apartment No. 12 finally closed behind the three good folk, my lord Tony asked of his chief:

"What about these three wretched soldiers, Blakeney?"

"Oh! they'll be all right for twenty-four hours. They can't starve till then, and by that time the concierge will have realised that there's something wrong with the door of No. 12 and will come in to investigate the matter. Are they securely bound, though?"

"And gagged! Rather!" ejaculated one of the others. "Odds life, Blakeney!" he added enthusiastically, "that was a fine bit of work!"

# How Jean Pierre Met The

# Scarlet Pimpernel As Told By Himself

I

Ah, monsieur! the pity of it, the pity! Surely there are sins which *le bon Dieu* Himself will condone. And if not—well, I had to risk His displeasure anyhow. Could I see them both starve, monsieur? I ask you! and M. le Vicomte had become so thin, so thin, his tiny, delicate bones were almost through his skin. And Mme. la Marquise! an angel, monsieur! Why, in the happy olden days, before all these traitors and assassins ruled in France, M. and Mme. la Marquise lived only for the child, and then to see him dying—yes, dying, there was no shutting one's eyes to that awful fact—M. le Vicomte de Mortain was dying of starvation and of disease.

There we were all herded together in a couple of attics—one of which little more than a cupboard—at the top of a dilapidated half-ruined house in the Rue des Pipots—Mme. la Marquise, M. le Vicomte and I—just think of that, monsieur! M. le Marquis had his chateau, as no doubt you know, on the outskirts of Lyons. A loyal high-born gentleman; was it likely, I ask you, that he would submit passively to the rule of those execrable revolutionaries who had murdered their King, outraged their Queen and Royal family, and, God help them! had already perpetrated every crime and every abomination for which of a truth there could be no pardon either on earth or in Heaven? He joined that plucky but, alas! small and ill-equipped army of royalists who, unable to save their King, were at least determined to avenge him.

Well, you know well enough what happened. The counter-revolution failed; the revolutionary army brought Lyons down to her knees after a siege of two months. She was then marked down as a rebel city, and after the abominable decree of October 9th had deprived her of her very name, and Couthon had exacted bloody reprisals from the entire population for its loyalty to the King, the infamous Laporte was sent down in order finally to stamp out the lingering remnants of the rebellion. By that time, monsieur, half the city had been burned down, and one-tenth and more of the inhabitants—men, women, and children—had been massacred in cold blood, whilst most of the others had fled in terror from the appalling scene of ruin and desolation. Laporte completed the execrable work so ably begun by Couthon. He was a very celebrated and skilful doctor at the Faculty of Medicine, now turned into a human hyena in the name of Liberty and Fraternity.

M. le Marquis contrived to escape with the scattered remnant of the Royalist army into Switzerland. But Mme la Marquise throughout all these strenuous times had stuck to her post at the chateau like the valiant creature that she was. When Couthon entered Lyons at the head of the revolutionary army, the whole of her household fled, and I was left alone to look after her and M. le Vicomte.

Then one day when I had gone into Lyons for provisions, I suddenly chanced to hear outside an eating-house that which nearly froze the marrow in my old bones. A captain belonging to the Revolutionary Guard was transmitting to his sergeant certain orders, which he had apparently just received.

The orders were to make a perquisition at ten o'clock this same evening in the chateau of Mortaine as the Marquis was supposed to be in hiding there, and in any event to arrest every man, woman, and child who was found within its walls.

"Citizen Laporte," the captain concluded, "knows for a certainty that the *ci-devant* Marquise and her brat are still there, even if the Marquis has fled like the traitor that he is. Those cursed English spies who call themselves the League of the Scarlet Pimpernel have been very active in Lyons of late, and citizen Laporte is afraid that they might cheat the guillotine of the carcase of those *aristos*, as they have already succeeded in doing in the case of a large number of traitors."

I did not, of course, wait to hear any more of that abominable talk. I sped home as fast as my old legs would carry me. That self-same evening, as soon as it was dark, Mme. la Marquise, carrying M. le Vicomte in her arms and I carrying a pack with a few necessaries on my back, left the ancestral home of the Mortaines never to return to it again: for within an hour of our flight a detachment of the revolutionary army made a descent upon the chateau; they ransacked it from attic to cellar, and finding nothing there to satisfy their lust of hate, they burned the stately mansion down to the ground.

We were obliged to take refuge in Lyons, at any rate for a time. Great as was the danger inside the city, it was infinitely greater on the high roads, unless we could arrange for some vehicle to take us a considerable part of the way to the frontier, and above all for some sort of passports—forged or otherwise—to enable us to pass the various toll-gates on the road, where vigilance was very strict. So we wandered through the ruined and deserted streets of the city in search of shelter, but found every charred and derelict house full of miserable tramps and destitutes like ourselves. Half dead with fatigue, Mme. la Marquise was at last obliged to take refuge in one of these houses which was situated in the Rue des Pipots. Every room was full to overflowing with a miserable wreckage of humanity thrown hither by the tide of anarchy and of bloodshed. But at the top of the house we found an attic. It was empty save for a couple of chairs, a table and a broken-down bedstead on which were a ragged mattress and pillow.

Here, monsieur, we spent over three weeks, at the end of which time M. le Vicomte fell ill, and then there followed days, monsieur, through which I would not like my worst enemy to pass.

Mme. la Marquise had only been able to carry away in her flight what ready money she happened to have in the house at the time. Securities, property, money belonging to aristocrats had been ruthlessly confiscated by the revolutionary government in Lyons. Our scanty resources rapidly became exhausted, and what was left had to be kept for milk and delicacies for M. le Vicomte. I tramped through the streets in search of a doctor, but most of them had been arrested on some paltry charge or other of rebellion, whilst others had fled from the city. There was only that infamous Laporte—a vastly clever doctor, I knew—but as soon take a lamb to a hungry lion as the Vicomte de Mortaine to that bloodthirsty cut-throat.

Then one day our last franc went and we had nothing left. Mme. la Marquise had not touched food for two days. I had stood at the corner of the street, begging all the day until I was driven off by the gendarmes. I had only obtained three sous from the passers-by. I bought some milk and took it home for M. le Vicomte. The following morning when I entered the larger attic I found that Mme. la Marquise had fainted from inanition.

I spent the whole of the day begging in the streets and dodging the guard, and even so I only collected four sous. I could have got more perhaps, only that at about midday the smell of food from an eating-house turned me sick and faint, and when I regained consciousness I found myself huddled up under a doorway and evening gathering in fast around me. If Mme. la Marquise could go two days without food I ought to go four. I struggled to my feet; fortunately I had retained possession of my four sous, else of a truth I would not have had the courage to go back to the miserable attic which was the only home I knew.

I was wending my way along as fast as I could—for I knew that Mme. la Marquise would be getting terribly anxious—when, just as I turned into the Rue Blanche, I spied two gentlemen—obviously strangers, for they were dressed with a luxury and care with which we had long ceased to be familiar in Lyons—walking rapidly towards me. A moment or two later they came to a halt, not far from where I was standing, and I heard the taller one of the two say to the other in English—a language with which I am vaguely conversant: "All right again this time, what, Tony?"

Both laughed merrily like a couple of schoolboys playing truant, and then they disappeared under the doorway of a dilapidated house, whilst I was left wondering how two such elegant gentlemen dared be abroad in Lyons these days, seeing that every man, woman and child who was dressed in anything but threadbare clothes was sure to be insulted in the streets for an aristocrat, and as often as not summarily arrested as a traitor.

However, I had other things to think about, and had already dismissed the little incident from my mind, when at the bottom of the Rue Blanche I came upon a knot of gaffers, men and women, who were talking and gesticulating very excitedly outside the door of a cook-shop. At first I did not take much notice of what was said: my eyes were glued to the front of the shop, on which were displayed sundry delicacies of the kind which makes a wretched, starved beggar's mouth water as he goes by; a roast capon especially attracted my attention, together with a bottle of red wine; these looked just the sort of luscious food which Mme. la Marquise would relish.

Well, sir, the law of God says: "Thou shalt not covet!" and no doubt that I committed a grievous sin when my hungry eyes fastened upon that roast capon and that bottle of Burgundy. We also know the stories of Judas Iscariot and of Jacob's children who sold their own brother Joseph into slavery—such a crime, monsieur, I took upon my conscience then; for just as the vision of Mme. la Marquise eating that roast capon and drinking that Burgundy rose before my eyes, my ears caught some fragments of the excited conversation which was going on all around me.

"He went this way!" someone said.

"No; that!" protested another.

"There's no sign of him now, anyway."

The owner of the shop was standing on his own doorstep, his legs wide apart, one arm on his wide hip, the other still brandishing the knife wherewith he had been carving for his customers.

"He can't have gone far," he said, as he smacked his thick lips.

"The impudent rascal, flaunting such fine clothes—like the *aristo* that he is."

"Bah! these cursed English! They are *aristos* all of them! And this one with his followers is no better than a spy!"

"Paid by that damned English Government to murder all our patriots and to rob the guillotine of her just dues."

"They say he had a hand in the escape of the *ci-devant* Duc de Sermeuse and all his brats from the very tumbril which was taking them to execution."

A cry of loathing and execration followed this statement. There was vigorous shaking of clenched fists and then a groan of baffled rage.

"We almost had him this time. If it had not been for these confounded, ill-lighted streets—"

"I would give something," concluded the shopkeeper, "if we could lay him by the heels."

"What would you give, citizen Dompierre?" queried a woman in the crowd, with a ribald laugh, "one of your roast capons?"

"Aye, little mother," he replied jovially, "and a bottle of my best Burgundy to boot, to drink confusion to that meddlesome Englishman and his crowd and a speedy promenade up the steps of the guillotine."

Monsieur, I assure you that at that moment my heart absolutely stood still. The tempter stood at my elbow and whispered, and I deliberately smothered the call of my conscience. I did what Joseph's brethren did, what brought Judas Iscariot to hopeless remorse. There was no doubt that the hue and cry was after the two elegantly dressed gentlemen whom I had seen enter the dilapidated house in the Rue Blanche. For a second or two I closed my eyes and deliberately conjured up the vision of Mme. la Marquise fainting for lack of food, and of M. le Vicomte dying for want of sustenance; then I worked my way to the door of the shop and accosted the burly proprietor with as much boldness as I could muster.

"The two Englishmen passed by me at the top of the Rue Blanche," I said to him. "They went into a house . . . I can show you which it is—"

In a moment I was surrounded by a screeching, gesticulating crowd. I told my story as best I could; there was no turning back now from the path of cowardice and of crime. I saw that brute Dompierre pick up the largest roast capon from the front of his shop, together with a bottle of that wine which I had coveted; then he thrust both these treasures into my trembling hands and said:

"*En avant!*"

And we all started to run up the street, shouting: "Death to the English spies!" I was the hero of the expedition. Dompierre and another man carried me, for I was too weak to go as fast as they wished. I was hugging the capon and the bottle of wine to my heart; I had need to do that, so as to still the insistent call of my conscience, for I felt a coward—a mean, treacherous, abominable coward!

When we reached the house and I pointed it out to Dompierre, the crowd behind us gave a cry of triumph. In the topmost storey a window was thrown open, two heads appeared silhouetted against the light within, and the cry of triumph below was answered by a merry, prolonged laugh from above.

I was too dazed to realise very clearly what happened after that. Dompierre, I know, kicked open the door of the house, and the crowd rushed in, in his wake. I managed to keep my feet and to work my way gradually out of the crowd. I must have gone on mechanically, almost unconsciously, for the next thing that I remember with any distinctness was that I found myself once more speeding down the Rue Blanche, with all the yelling and shouting some little way behind me.

With blind instinct, too, I had clung to the capon and the wine, the price of my infamy. I was terribly weak and felt sick and faint, but I struggled on for a while, until my knees refused me service and I came down on my two hands, whilst the capon rolled away into the gutter, and the bottle of Burgundy fell with a crash against the pavement, scattering its precious contents in every direction.

There I lay, wretched, despairing, hardly able to move, when suddenly I heard rapid and firm footsteps immediately behind me, and the next moment two firm hands had me under the arms, and I heard a voice saying:

"Steady, old friend. Can you get up? There! Is that better?"

The same firm hands raised me to my feet. At first I was too dazed to see anything, but after a moment or two I was able to look around me, and, by the light of a street lanthorn immediately overhead, I recognised the tall, elegantly dressed Englishman and his friend, whom I had just betrayed to the fury of Dompierre and a savage mob.

I thought that I was dreaming, and I suppose that my eyes betrayed the horror which I felt, for the stranger looked at me scrutinisingly for a moment or two, then he gave the quaintest laugh I had ever heard in all my life, and said something to his friend in English, which this time I failed to understand.

Then he turned to me:

"By my faith," he said in perfect French—so that I began to doubt if he was an English spy after all—"I verily believe that you are the clever rogue, eh? who obtained a roast capon and a bottle of wine from that fool Dompierre. He and his boon companions are venting their wrath on you, old compeer; they are calling you liar and traitor and cheat, in the intervals of wrecking what is left of the house, out of which my friend and I have long since escaped by climbing up the neighbouring gutter-pipes and scrambling over the adjoining roofs."

Monsieur, will you believe me when I say that he was actually saying all this in order to comfort me? I could have sworn to that because of the wonderful kindliness which shone out of his eyes, even through the good-humoured mockery wherewith he obviously regarded me. Do you know what I did then, monsieur? I just fell on my knees and loudly thanked God that he was safe; at which both he and his friend once again began to laugh, for all the world like two schoolboys who had escaped a whipping, rather than two men who were still threatened with death.

"Then it *was* you!" said the taller stranger, who was still laughing so heartily that he had to wipe his eyes with his exquisite lace handkerchief.

"May God forgive me," I replied.

The next moment his arm was again round me. I clung to him as to a rock, for of a truth I had never felt a grasp so steady and withal so gentle and kindly, as was his around my shoulders. I tried to murmur words of thanks, but again that wretched feeling of sickness and faintness overcame me, and for a second or two it seemed to me as if I were slipping into another world. The stranger's voice came to my ear, as it were through cotton-wool.

"The man is starving," he said. "Shall we take him over to your lodgings, Tony? They are safer than mine. He may be able to walk in a minute or two, if not I can carry him."

My senses at this partly returned to me, and I was able to protest feebly:

"No, no! I must go back—I must—kind sirs," I murmured. "Mme. La Marquise will be getting so anxious."

No sooner were these foolish words out of my mouth than I could have bitten my tongue out for having uttered them; and yet, somehow, it seemed as if it was the stranger's magnetic personality, his magic voice and kindly act towards me, who had so basely sold him to his enemies, which had drawn them out of me. He gave a low, prolonged whistle.

"Mme. la Marquise?" he queried, dropping his voice to a whisper.

Now to have uttered Mme. la Marquise de Mortaine's name here in Lyons, where every aristocrat was termed a traitor and sent without trial to the guillotine, was in itself an act of criminal folly, and yet—you may believe me, monsieur, or not—there was something within me just at that moment that literally compelled me to open my heart out to this stranger, whom I had so basely betrayed, and who requited my abominable crime with such gentleness and mercy. Before I fully realised what I was doing, monsieur, I had blurted out the whole history of Mme. la Marquise's flight and of M. le Vicomte's sickness to him. He drew me under the cover of an open doorway, and he and his friend listened to me without speaking a word until I had told them my pitiable tale to the end.

When I had finished he said quietly:

"Take me to see Mme. la Marquise, old friend. Who knows? perhaps I may be able to help."

Then he turned to his friend.

"Will you wait for me at my lodgings, Tony," he said, "and let Ffoulkes and Hastings know that I may wish to speak with them on my return?"

He spoke like one who had been accustomed all his life to give command, and I marvelled how his friend immediately obeyed him. Then when the latter had disappeared down the dark street, the stranger once more turned to me.

"Lean on my arm, good old friend," he said, "and we must try and walk as quickly as we can. The sooner we allay the anxieties of Mme. la Marquise the better."

I was still hugging the roast capon with one arm, with the other

I clung to him as together we walked in the direction of the Rue des Pipots. On the way we halted at a respectable eating-house, where my protector gave me some money wherewith to buy a bottle of good wine and sundry provisions and delicacies which we carried home with us.

## II

Never shall I forget the look of horror which came in Mme. la Marquise's eyes when she saw me entering our miserable attic in the company of a stranger. The last of the little bit of tallow candle flickered in its socket. Madame threw her emaciated arms over her child, just like some poor hunted animal defending its young. I could almost hear the cry of terror which died down in her throat ere it reached her lips. But then, monsieur, to see the light of hope gradually illuminating her pale, wan face as the stranger took her hand and spoke to her—oh! so gently and so kindly—was a sight which filled my poor, half-broken heart with joy.

"The little invalid must be seen by a doctor at once," he said, "after that only can we think of your ultimate safety."

Mme. la Marquise, who herself was terribly weak and ill, burst out crying. "Would I not have taken him to a doctor ere now?" she murmured through her tears. "But there is no doctor in Lyons. Those who have not been arrested as traitors have fled from this stricken city. And my little Jose is dying for want of medical care."

"Your pardon, madame," he rejoined gently, "one of the ablest doctors in France is at present in Lyons—"

"That infamous Laporte," she broke in, horrified. "He would snatch my sick child from my arms and throw him to the guillotine."

"He would save your boy from disease," said the stranger earnestly, "his own professional pride or professional honour, whatever he might choose to call it, would compel him to do that. But the moment the doctor's work was done, that of the executioner would commence."

"You see, milor," moaned Madame in pitiable agony, "that there is no hope for us."

"Indeed there is," he replied. "We must get M. le Vicomte well first—after that we shall see."

"But you are not proposing to bring that infamous Laporte to my child's bedside!" she cried in horror.

"Would you have your child die here before your eyes," retorted the stranger, "as he undoubtedly will this night?"

This sounded horribly cruel, and the tone in which it was said was commanding. There was no denying its truth. M. le Vicomte was dying. I could see that. For a moment or two madame remained quite still, with her great eyes, circled with pain and sorrow, fixed upon the stranger. He returned her gaze steadily and kindly, and gradually that frozen look of horror in her pale face gave place to one of deep puzzlement, and through her bloodless lips there came the words, faintly murmured: "Who are you?"

He gave no direct reply, but from his little finger he detached a ring and held it out for her to see. I saw it too, for I was standing close by Mme. la Marquise, and the flickering light of the tallow candle fell full upon the ring. It was of gold, and upon it there was an exquisitely modelled, five-petalled little flower in vivid red enamel.

Madame la Marquise looked at the ring, then once again up into his face. He nodded assent, and my heart seemed even then to stop its beating as I gazed upon his face. Had we not—all of us—heard of the gallant Scarlet Pimpernel? And did I not know—far better than Mme. la Marquise herself—the full extent of his gallantry and his self-sacrifice? The hue and cry was after him. Human bloodhounds were even now on his track, and he spoke calmly of walking out again in the streets of Lyons and of affronting that infamous Laporte, who would find glory in sending him to death. I think he guessed what was passing in my mind, for he put a finger up to his lip and pointed significantly to M. le Vicomte.

But it was beautiful to see how completely Mme. la Marquise now trusted him. At his bidding she even ate a little of the food and drank some wine—and I was forced to do likewise. And even when anon he declared his intention of fetching Laporte immediately, she did not flinch. She kissed M. le Vicomte with passionate fervour, and then gave the stranger her solemn promise that the moment he returned she would take refuge in the next room and never move out of it until after Laporte had departed.

When he went I followed him to the top of the stairs. I was speechless with gratitude and also with fears for him. But he took my hand and said, with that same quaint, somewhat inane laugh which was so characteristic of him:

"Be of good cheer, old fellow! Those confounded murderers will not get me this time."

### III

Less than half an hour later, monsieur, citizen Laporte, one of the most skilful doctors in France and one of the most bloodthirsty tyrants this execrable Revolution has known, was sitting at the bedside of M. le Vicomte de Mortaine, using all the skill, all the knowledge he possessed in order to combat the dread disease of which the child was dying, ere he came to save him—as he cynically remarked in my hearing—for the guillotine.

I heard afterwards how it all came about.

Laporte, it seems, was in the habit of seeing patients in his own house every evening after he had settled all his business for the day. What a strange contradiction in the human heart, eh, monsieur? The tiger turned lamb for the space of one hour in every twenty-four—the butcher turned healer. How well the English milor had gauged the strange personality of that redoubtable man! Professional pride—interest in intricate cases—call it what you will—was the only redeeming feature in Laporte's abominable character. Everything else in him, every thought, every action was ignoble, cruel and vengeful.

Milor that night mingled with the crowd who waited on the human hyena to be cured of their hurts. It was a motley crowd that filled the dreaded pro-consul's ante-chamber—men, women and children—all of them too much preoccupied with their own troubles to bestow more than a cursory glance on the stranger who, wrapped in a dark mantle, quietly awaited his turn. One or two muttered curses were flung at the *aristo*, one or two spat in his direction to express hatred and contempt, then the door which gave on the inner chamber would be flung open—a number called—one patient would walk out, another walk in—and in the ever-recurring incident the stranger for the nonce was forgotten.

His turn came—his number being called—it was the last on the list, and the ante-chamber was now quite empty save for him. He walked into the presence of the pro-consul. Claude Lemoine, who was on guard in the room at the time, told me that just for the space of two seconds the two men looked at one another. Then the stranger threw back his head and said quietly:

"There's a child dying of pleurisy, or worse, in an attic in the Rue des Pipots. There's not a doctor left in Lyons to attend on him, and the child will die for want of medical skill. Will you come to him, citizen doctor?"

It seems that for a moment or two Laporte hesitated.

"You look to me uncommonly like an *aristo*, and therefore a traitor," he said, "and I've half a mind—"

"To call your guard and order my immediate arrest," broke in milor with a whimsical smile, "but in that case a citizen of France will die for want of a doctor's care. Let me take you to the child's bedside, citizen doctor, you can always have me arrested afterwards."

But Laporte still hesitated.

"How do I know that you are not one of those English spies?" he began.

"Take it that I am," rejoined milor imperturbably, "and come and see the patient."

Never had a situation been carried off with so bold a hand. Claude Lemoine declared that Laporte's mouth literally opened for the call which would have summoned the sergeant of the guard into the room and ordered the summary arrest of this impudent stranger. During the veriest fraction of a second life and death hung in the balance for the gallant English milor. In the heart of Laporte every evil passion fought the one noble fibre within him. But the instinct of the skilful healer won the battle, and the next moment he had hastily collected what medicaments and appliances he might require, and the two men were soon speeding along the streets in the direction of the Rue des Pipots.

* * * * *

During the whole of that night, milor and Laporte sat together by the bedside of M. le Vicomte. Laporte only went out once in order to fetch what further medicaments he required. Mme. la Marquise took the opportunity of running out of her hiding-place in order to catch a glimpse of her child. I saw her take milor's hand and press it against her heart in silent gratitude. On her knees she begged him to go away and leave her and the boy to their fate. Was it likely that he would go? But she was so insistent that at last he said:

"Madame, let me assure you that even if I were prepared to play the coward's part which you would assign to me, it is not in my power to do so at this moment. Citizen Laporte came to this house under the escort of six picked men of his guard. He has left these men stationed on the landing outside this door."

Madame la Marquise gave a cry of terror, and once more that pathetic look of horror came into her face. Milor took her hand and then pointed to the sick child.

"Madame," he said, "M. le Vicomte is already slightly better. Thanks to medical skill and a child's vigorous hold on life, he will live. The rest is in the hands of God."

Already the heavy footsteps of Laporte were heard upon the creaking stairs. Mme. la Marquise was forced to return to her hiding-place.

Soon after dawn he went. M. le Vicomte was then visibly easier. Laporte had all along paid no heed to me, but I noticed that once or twice during his long vigil by the sick-bed his dark eyes beneath their overhanging brows shot a quick suspicious look at the door behind which cowered Mme. la Marquise. I had absolutely no doubt in my mind then that he knew quite well who his patient was.

He gave certain directions to milor—there were certain fresh medicaments to be got during the day. While he spoke there was a sinister glint in his eyes—half cynical, wholly menacing—as he looked up into the calm, impassive face of milor.

"It is essential for the welfare of the patient that these medicaments be got for him during the day," he said dryly, "and the guard have orders to allow you to pass in and out. But you need have no fear," he added significantly, "I will leave an escort outside the house to accompany you on your way."

He gave a mocking, cruel laugh, the meaning of which was unmistakable. His well-drilled human bloodhounds would be on the track of the English spy, whenever the latter dared to venture out into the streets.

Mme. la Marquise and I were prisoners for the day. We spent it in watching alternately beside M. le Vicomte. But milor came and went as freely as if he had not been carrying his precious life in his hands every time that he ventured outside the house.

In the evening Laporte returned to see his patient, and again the following morning, and the next evening. M. le Vicomte was making rapid progress towards recovery.

The third day in the morning Laporte pronounced his patient to be out of danger, but said that he would nevertheless come again to see him at the usual hour in the evening. Directly he had gone, milor went out in order to bring in certain delicacies of which the invalid was now allowed to partake. I persuaded Madame to lie down and have a couple of hours' good sleep in the inner attic, while I stayed to watch over the child.

To my horror, hardly had I taken up my stand at the foot of the bed when Laporte returned; he muttered something as he entered about having left some important appliance behind, but I was quite convinced that he had been on the watch until milor was out of sight, and then slipped back in order to find me and Madame here alone.

He gave a glance at the child and another at the door of the inner attic, then he said in a loud voice:

"Yes, another twenty-four hours and my duties as doctor will cease and those of patriot will re-commence. But Mme. la Marquise de Mortaine need no longer be in any anxiety about her son's health, nor will Mme. la Guillotine be cheated of a pack of rebels."

He laughed, and was on the point of turning on his heel when the door which gave on the smaller attic was opened and Mme. la Marquise appeared upon the threshold.

Monsieur, I had never seen her look more beautiful than she did now in her overwhelming grief. Her face was as pale as death, her eyes, large and dilated, were fixed upon the human monster who had found it in his heart to speak such cruel words. Clad in a miserable, threadbare gown, her rich brown hair brought to the top of her head like a crown, she looked more regal than any queen.

But proud as she was, monsieur, she yet knelt at the feet of that wretch. Yes, knelt, and embraced his knees and pleaded in such pitiable accents as would have melted the heart of a stone. She pleaded, monsieur—ah, not for herself. She pleaded for her child and for me, her faithful servant, and she pleaded for the gallant gentleman who had risked his life for the sake of the child, who was nothing to him.

"Take me!" she said. "I come of a race that have always known how to die! But what harm has that innocent child done in this world? What harm has poor old Jean-Pierre done, and, oh . . . is the world so full of brave and noble men that the bravest of them all be so unjustly sent to death?"

Ah, monsieur, any man, save one of those abject products of that hideous Revolution, would have listened to such heartrending accents. But this man only laughed and turned on his heel without a word.

\* \* \* \* \*

Shall I ever forget the day that went by? Mme. la Marquise was well-nigh prostrate with terror, and it was heartrending to watch the noble efforts which she made to amuse M. le Vicomte. The only gleams of sunshine which came to us out of our darkness were the brief appearances of milor. Outside we could hear the measured tramp of the guard that had been set there to keep us close prisoners. They were relieved every six hours, and, in fact, we were as much under arrest as if we were already incarcerated in one of the prisons of Lyons.

At about four o'clock in the afternoon milor came back to us after a brief absence. He stayed for a little while playing with M. le Vicomte. Just before leaving he took Madame's hand in his and said very earnestly, and sinking his voice to the merest whisper:

"To-night! Fear nothing! Be ready for anything! Remember that the League of the Scarlet Pimpernel have never failed to succour, and that I hereby pledge you mine honour that you and those you care for will be out of Lyons this night."

He was gone, leaving us to marvel at his strange words. Mme. la Marquise after that was just like a person in a dream. She hardly spoke to me, and the only sound that passed her lips was a quaint little lullaby which she sang to M. le Vicomte ere he dropped off to sleep.

The hours went by leaden-footed. At every sound on the stairs Madame started like a frightened bird. That infamous Laporte usually paid his visits at about eight o'clock in the evening, and after it became quite dark, Madame sat at the tiny window, and I felt that she was counting the minutes which still lay between her and the dreaded presence of that awful man.

At a quarter before eight o'clock we heard the usual heavy footfall on the stairs. Madame started up as if she had been struck. She ran to the bed—almost like one demented, and wrapping the one poor blanket round M. le Vicomte, she seized him in her arms. Outside we could hear Laporte's raucous voice speaking to the guard. His usual query: "Is all well?" was answered by the brief: "All well, citizen." Then he asked if the English spy were within, and the sentinel replied: "No, citizen, he went out at about five o'clock and has not come back since."

"Not come back since five o'clock?" said Laporte with a loud curse.

"*Pardi!* I trust that that fool Caudy has not allowed him to escape."

"I saw Caudy about an hour ago, citizen," said the man.

"Did he say anything about the Englishman then?"

It seemed to us, who were listening to this conversation with bated breath, that the man hesitated a moment ere he replied; then he spoke with obvious nervousness.

"As a matter of fact, citizen," he said, "Caudy thought then that the Englishman was inside the house, whilst I was equally sure that I had seen him go downstairs an hour before."

"A thousand devils!" cried Laporte with a savage oath, "if I find that you, citizen sergeant, or Caudy have blundered there will be trouble for you."

To the accompaniment of a great deal more swearing he suddenly kicked open the door of our attic with his boot, and then came to a standstill on the threshold with his hands in the pockets of his breeches and his legs planted wide apart, face to face with Mme. la Marquise, who confronted him now, herself like a veritable tigress who is defending her young.

He gave a loud, mocking laugh.

"Ah, the *aristos!*" he cried, "waiting for that cursed Englishman, what? to drag you and your brat out of the claws of the human tiger. . . . Not so, my fine *ci-devant* Marquise. The brat is no longer sick—he is well enough, anyhow, to breathe the air of the prisons of Lyons for a few days pending a final rest in the arms of Mme. la Guillotine. Citizen sergeant," he called over his shoulder, "escort these *aristos* to my carriage downstairs. When the Englishman returns, tell him he will find his friends under the tender care of Doctor Laporte. *En avant*, little mother," he added, as he gripped Mme. la Marquise tightly by the arm, "and you, old scarecrow," he concluded, speaking to me over his shoulder, "follow the citizen sergeant, or-"

Mme. la Marquise made no resistance. As I told you, she had been, since dusk, like a person in a dream; so what could I do but follow her noble example? Indeed, I was too dazed to do otherwise.

We all went stumbling down the dark, rickety staircase, Laporte leading the way with Mme. la Marquise, who had M. le Vicomte tightly clasped in her arms. I followed with the sergeant, whose hand was on my shoulder; I believe that two soldiers walked behind, but of that I cannot be sure.

At the bottom of the stairs through the open door of the house I caught sight of the vague outline of a large barouche, the lanthorns of which threw a feeble light upon the cruppers of two horses and of a couple of men sitting on the box.

Mme. la Marquise stepped quietly into the carriage. Laporte followed her, and I was bundled in in his wake by the rough hands of the soldiery. Just before the order was given to start, Laporte put his head out of the window and shouted to the sergeant:

"When you see Caudy tell him to report himself to me at once. I will be back here in half an hour; keep strict guard as before until then, citizen sergeant."

The next moment the coachman cracked his whip, Laporte called loudly, "*En avant!*" and the heavy barouche went rattling along the ill-paved streets.

Inside the carriage all was silence. I could hear Mme. la Marquise softly whispering to M. le Vicomte, and I marvelled how wondrously calm—nay, cheerful, she could be. Then suddenly I heard a sound which of a truth did make my heart stop its beating. It was a quaint and prolonged laugh which I once thought I would never hear again on this earth. It came from the corner of the barouche next to where Mme. la Marquise was so tenderly and gaily crooning to her child. And a kindly voice said merrily:

"In half an hour we shall be outside Lyons. To-morrow we'll be across the Swiss frontier. We've cheated that old tiger after all. What say you, Mme. la Marquise?"

It was milor's voice, and he was as merry as a school-boy.

"I told you, old Jean-Pierre," he added, as he placed that firm hand which I loved so well upon my knee, "I told you that those confounded murderers would not get me this time."

And to think that I did not know him, as he stood less than a quarter of an hour ago upon the threshold of our attic in the hideous guise of that abominable Laporte. He had spent two days in collecting old clothes that resembled those of that infamous wretch, and in taking possession of one of the derelict rooms in the house in the Rue des Pipots. Then while we were expecting every moment that Laporte would order our arrest, milor assumed the personality of the monster, hoodwinked the sergeant on the dark staircase, and by that wonderfully audacious coup saved Mme. la Marquise, M. le Vicomte and my humble self from the guillotine.

Money, of which he had plenty, secured us immunity on the way, and we were in safety over the Swiss frontier, leaving Laporte to eat out his tigerish heart with baffled rage.

# OUT OF THE JAWS OF DEATH

*Being a fragment from the diary of Valentine Lemercier, in the possession of her great-granddaughter.*

We were such a happy family before this terrible Revolution broke out; we lived rather simply, but very comfortably, in our dear old home just on the borders of the forest of Compiegne. Jean and Andre were the twins; just fifteen years old they were when King Louis was deposed from the throne of France which God had given him, and sent to prison like a common criminal, with our beautiful Queen Marie Antoinette and the Royal children, and Madame Elizabeth, who was so beloved by the poor!

Ah! that seems very, very long ago now. No doubt you know better than I do all that happened in our beautiful land of France and in lovely Paris about that time: goods and property confiscated, innocent men, women, and children condemned to death for acts of treason which they had never committed.

It was in August last year that they came to "Mon Repos" and arrested papa, and *maman,* and us four young ones and dragged us to Paris, where we were imprisoned in a narrow and horribly dank vault in the Abbaye, where all day and night through the humid stone walls we heard cries and sobs and moans from poor people, who no doubt were suffering the same sorrows and the same indignities as we were.

I had just passed my nineteenth birthday, and Marguerite was only thirteen. *Maman* was a perfect angel during that terrible time; she kept up our courage and our faith in God in a way that no one else could have done. Every night and morning we knelt round her knee and papa sat close beside her, and we prayed to God for deliverance from our own afflictions, and for the poor people who were crying and moaning all the day.

But of what went on outside our prison walls we had not an idea, though sometimes poor papa would brave the warder's brutalities and ask him questions of what was happening in Paris every day.

"They are hanging all the *aristos* to the street-lamps of the city," the man would reply with a cruel laugh, "and it will be your turn next."

We had been in prison for about a fortnight, when one day—oh! shall I ever forget it?—we heard in the distance a noise like the rumbling of thunder; nearer and nearer it came, and soon the sound became less confused, cries and shrieks could be heard above that rumbling din; but so weird and menacing did those cries seem that instinctively—though none of us knew what they meant—we all felt a nameless terror grip our hearts.

Oh! I am not going to attempt the awful task of describing to you all the horrors of that never-to-be-forgotten day. People, who to-day cannot speak without a shudder of the September massacres, have not the remotest conception of what really happened on that awful second day of that month.

We are all at peace and happy now, but whenever my thoughts fly back to that morning, whenever the ears of memory recall those hideous yells of fury and of hate, coupled with the equally horrible cries for pity, which pierced through the walls behind which the six of us were crouching, trembling, and praying, whenever I think of it all my heart still beats violently with that same nameless dread which held it in its deathly grip then.

Hundreds of men, women, and children were massacred in the prisons of that day—it was a St. Bartholomew even more hideous than the last.

*Maman* was trying in vain to keep our thoughts fixed upon God —papa sat on the stone bench, his elbows resting on his knees, his head buried in his hands; but *maman* was kneeling on the floor, with her dear arms encircling us all and her trembling lips moving in continuous prayer.

We felt that we were facing death—and what a death, O my God!

Suddenly the small grated window—high up in the dank wall— became obscured. I was the first to look up, but the cry of terror which rose from my heart was choked ere it reached my throat.

Jean and Andre looked up, too, and they shrieked, and so did Marguerite, and papa jumped up and ran to us and stood suddenly between us and the window like a tiger defending its young.

But we were all of us quite silent now. The children did not even cry; they stared, wide-eyed, paralysed with fear.

Only *maman* continued to pray, and we could hear papa's rapid and stertorous breathing as he watched what was going on at that window above.

Heavy blows were falling against the masonry round the grating, and we could hear the nerve-racking sound of a file working on the iron bars; and farther away, below the window, those awful yells of human beings transformed by hate and fury into savage beasts.

How long this horrible suspense lasted I cannot now tell you; the next thing I remember clearly is a number of men in horrible ragged clothing pouring into our vault-like prison from the window above; the next moment they rushed at us simultaneously—or so it seemed to me, for I was just then recommending my soul to God, so certain was I that in that same second I would cease to live.

It was all like a dream, for instead of the horrible shriek of satisfied hate which we were all expecting to hear, a whispering voice, commanding and low, struck our ears and dragged us, as it were, from out the abyss of despair into the sudden light of hope.

"If you will trust us," the voice whispered, "and not be afraid, you will be safely out of Paris within an hour."

Papa was the first to realise what was happening; he had never lost his presence of mind even during the darkest moment of this terrible time, and he said quite calmly and steadily now:

"What must we do?"

"Persuade the little ones not to be afraid, not to cry, to be as still and silent as may be," continued the voice, which I felt must be that of one of God's own angels, so exquisitely kind did it sound to my ear.

"They will be quiet and still without persuasion," said papa; "eh, children?"

And Jean, Andre, and Marguerite murmured: "Yes!" whilst *maman* and I drew them closer to us and said everything we could think of to make them still more brave.

And the whispering, commanding voice went on after awhile:

"Now will you allow yourselves to be muffled and bound, and, after that, will you swear that whatever happens, whatever you may see or hear, you will neither move nor speak? Not only your own lives, but those of many brave men will depend upon your fulfilment of this oath."

Papa made no reply save to raise his hand and eyes up to where God surely was watching over us all. *Maman* said in her gentle, even voice:

"For myself and my children, I swear to do all that you tell us."

A great feeling of confidence had entered into her heart, just as it had done into mine. We looked at one another and knew that we were both thinking of the same thing: we were thinking of the brave Englishman and his gallant little band of heroes, about whom we had heard many wonderful tales—how they had rescued a number of innocent people who were unjustly threatened with the guillotine; and we all knew that the tall figure, disguised in horrible rags, who spoke to us with such a gentle yet commanding voice, was the man whom rumour credited with supernatural powers, and who was known by the mysterious name of "The Scarlet Pimpernel."

Hardly had we sworn to do his bidding than his friends most unceremoniously threw great pieces of sacking over our heads, and then proceeded to tie ropes round our bodies. At least, I know that that is what one of them was doing to me, and from one or two whispered words of command which reached my ear I concluded that papa and *maman* and the children were being dealt with in the same summary way.

I felt hot and stifled under that rough bit of sacking, but I would not have moved or even sighed for worlds. Strangely enough, as soon as my eyes and ears were shut off from the sounds and sights immediately round me, I once more became conscious of the horrible and awful din which was going on, not only on the other side of our prison walls, but inside the whole of the Abbaye building and in the street beyond.

Once more I heard those terrible howls of rage and of satisfied hatred, uttered by the assassins who were being paid by the government of our beautiful country to butcher helpless prisoners in their hundreds.

Suddenly I felt myself hoisted up off my feet and slung up on to a pair of shoulders that must have been very powerful indeed, for I am no light weight, and once more I heard the voice, the very sound of which was delight, quite close to my ear this time, giving a brief and comprehensive command:

"All ready!—remember your part—*en avant!*"

Then it added in English. "Here, Tony, you start kicking against the door whilst we begin to shout!"

I loved those few words of English, and hoped that *maman* had heard them too, for it would confirm her—as it did me—in the happy knowledge that God and a brave man had taken our rescue in hand.

But from that moment we might have all been in the very ante-chamber of hell. I could hear the violent kicks against the heavy door of our prison, and our brave rescuers seemed suddenly to be transformed into a cageful of wild beasts. Their shouts and yells were as horrible as any that came to us from the outside, and I must say that the gentle, firm voice which I had learnt to love was as execrable as any I could hear.

Apparently the door would not yield, as the blows against it became more and more violent, and presently from somewhere above my head—the window presumably—there came a rough call, and a raucous laugh:

"Why? what in the name of—— is happening here?"

And the voice near me answered back equally roughly: "A quarry of six—but we are caught in this confounded trap—get the door open for us, citizen—we want to get rid of this booty and go in search for more."

A horrible laugh was the reply from above, and the next instant I heard a terrific crash; the door had at last been burst open, either from within or without, I could not tell which, and suddenly all the din, the cries, the groans, the hideous laughter and bibulous songs which had sounded muffled up to now burst upon us with all their hideousness.

That was, I think, the most awful moment of that truly fearful hour. I could not have moved then, even had I wished or been able to do so; but I knew that between us all and a horrible, yelling, murdering mob there was now nothing—except the hand of God and the heroism of a band of English gentlemen.

Together they gave a cry—as loud, as terrifying as any that were uttered by the butchering crowd in the building, and with a wild rush they seemed to plunge with us right into the thick of the awful melee.

At least, that is what it all felt like to me, and afterwards I heard from our gallant rescuer himself that that is exactly what he and his friends did. There were eight of them altogether, and we four young ones had each been hoisted on a pair of devoted shoulders, whilst *maman* and papa were each carried by two men.

I was lying across the finest pair of shoulders in the world, and close to me was beating the bravest heart on God's earth.

Thus burdened, these eight noble English gentlemen charged right through an army of butchering, howling brutes, they themselves howling with the fiercest of them.

All around me I heard weird and terrific cries: "What ho! citizens—what have you there?"

"Six *aristos!*" shouted my hero boldly as he rushed on, forging his way through the crowd.

"What are you doing with them?" yelled a raucous voice.

"Food for the starving fish in the river," was the ready response. "Stand aside, citizen," he added, with a round curse; "I have my orders from citizen Danton himself about these six *aristos*. You hinder me at your peril."

He was challenged over and over again in the same way, and so were his friends who were carrying papa and *maman* and the children; but they were always ready with a reply, ready with an invective or a curse; with eyes that could not see, one could imagine them as hideous, as vengeful, as cruel as the rest of the crowd.

I think that soon I must have fainted from sheer excitement and terror, for I remember nothing more till I felt myself deposited on a hard floor, propped against the wall, and the stifling piece of sacking taken off my head and face.

I looked around me, dazed and bewildered; gradually the horrors of the past hour came back to me, and I had to close my eyes again, for I felt sick and giddy with the sheer memory of it all.

But presently I felt stronger and looked around me again. Jean and Andre were squatting in a corner close by, gazing wide-eyed at the group of men in filthy, ragged clothing, who sat round a deal table in the centre of a small, ill-furnished room.

*Maman* was lying on a horsehair sofa at the other end of the room, with Marguerite beside her, and papa sat in a low chair by her side, holding her hand.

The voice I loved was speaking in its quaint, somewhat drawly cadence:

"You are quite safe now, my dear Monsieur Lemercier," it said;

"after Madame and the young people have had a rest, some of my friends will find you suitable disguises, and they will escort you out of Paris, as they have some really genuine passports in their possessions, which we obtain from time to time through the agency of a personage highly placed in this murdering government, and with the help of English banknotes. Those passports are not always unchallenged, I must confess," added my hero with a quaint laugh; "but to-night everyone is busy murdering in one part of Paris, so the other parts are comparatively safe."

Then he turned to one of his friends and spoke to him in English:

"You had better see this through, Tony," he said, "with Hastings and Mackenzie. Three of you will be enough; I shall have need of the others."

No one seemed to question his orders. He had spoken, and the others made ready to obey. Just then papa spoke up:

"How are we going to thank you, sir?" he asked, speaking broken English, but with his habitual dignity of manner.

"By leaving your welfare in our hands, Monsieur," replied our gallant rescuer quietly.

Papa tried to speak again, but the Englishman put up his hand to stop any further talk.

"There is no time now, Monsieur," he said with gentle courtesy. "I must leave you, as I have much work yet to do."

"Where are you going, Blakeney?" asked one of the others.

"Back to the Abbaye prison," he said; "there are other women and children to be rescued there!"

# THE TRAITOR

Not one of them had really trusted him for some time now. Heaven and his conscience alone knew what had changed my Lord Kulmsted from a loyal friend and keen sportsman into a surly and dissatisfied adherent —adherent only in name.

Some say that lack of money had embittered him. He was a confirmed gambler, and had been losing over-heavily of late; and the League of the Scarlet Pimpernel demanded sacrifices of money at times from its members, as well as of life if the need arose. Others averred that jealousy against the chief had outweighed Kulmsted's honesty. Certain it is that his oath of fealty to the League had long ago been broken in the spirit. Treachery hovered in the air.

But the Scarlet Pimpernel himself, with that indomitable optimism of his, and almost maddening insouciance, either did not believe in Kulmsted's disloyalty or chose not to heed it.

He even asked him to join the present expedition—one of the most dangerous undertaken by the League for some time, and which had for its object the rescue of some women of the late unfortunate Marie Antoinette's household: maids and faithful servants, ruthlessly condemned to die for their tender adherence to a martyred queen. And yet eighteen pairs of faithful lips had murmured words of warning.

It was towards the end of November, 1793. The rain was beating down in a monotonous drip, drip, drip on to the roof of a derelict house in the Rue Berthier. The wan light of a cold winter's morning peeped in through the curtainless window and touched with its weird grey brush the pallid face of a young girl—a mere child—who sat in a dejected attitude on a rickety chair, with elbows leaning on the rough deal table before her, and thin, grimy fingers wandering with pathetic futility to her tearful eyes.

In the farther angle of the room a tall figure in dark clothes was made one, by the still lingering gloom, with the dense shadows beyond.

"We have starved," said the girl, with rebellious tears. "Father and I and the boys are miserable enough, God knows; but we have always been honest."

From out the shadows in that dark corner of the room there came the sound of an oath quickly suppressed.

"Honest!" exclaimed the man, with a harsh, mocking laugh, which made the girl wince as if with physical pain. "Is it honest to harbour the enemies of your country? Is it honest—"

But quickly he checked himself, biting his lips with vexation, feeling that his present tactics were not like to gain the day.

He came out of the gloom and approached the girl with every

outward sign of eagerness. He knelt on the dusty floor beside her, his arms stole round her meagre shoulders, and his harsh voice was subdued to tones of gentleness.

"I was only thinking of your happiness, Yvonne," he said tenderly; "of poor blind papa and the two boys to whom you have been such a devoted little mother. My only desire is that you should earn the gratitude of your country by denouncing her most bitter enemy—an act of patriotism which will place you and those for whom you care for ever beyond the reach of sorrow or of want."

The voice, the appeal, the look of love, was more than the poor, simple girl could resist. Milor was so handsome, so kind, so good.

It had all been so strange: these English aristocrats coming here, she knew not whence, and who seemed fugitives even though they had plenty of money to spend. Two days ago they had sought shelter like malefactors escaped from justice—in this same tumbledown, derelict house where she, Yvonne, with her blind father and two little brothers, crept in of nights, or when the weather was too rough for them all to stand and beg in the streets of Paris.

There were five of them altogether, and one seemed to be the chief. He was very tall, and had deep blue eyes, and a merry voice that went echoing along the worm-eaten old rafters. But milor—the one whose arms were encircling her even now—was the handsomest among them all. He had sought Yvonne out on the very first night when she had crawled shivering to that corner of the room where she usually slept.

The English aristocrats had frightened her at first, and she was for flying from the derelict house with her family and seeking shelter elsewhere; but he who appeared to be the chief had quickly reassured her. He seemed so kind and good, and talked so gently to blind papa, and made such merry jests with Francois and Clovis that she herself could scarce refrain from laughing through her tears.

But later on in the night, milor—her milor, as she soon got to call him—came and talked so beautifully that she, poor girl, felt as if no music could ever sound quite so sweetly in her ear.

That was two days ago, and since then milor had often talked to her in the lonely, abandoned house, and Yvonne had felt as if she dwelt in Heaven. She still took blind papa and the boys out to beg in the streets, but in the morning she prepared some hot coffee for the English aristocrats, and in the evening she cooked them some broth. Oh! they gave her money lavishly; but she quite understood that they were in hiding, though what they had to fear, being English, she could not understand.

And now milor—her milor—was telling her that these Englishmen, her friends, were spies and traitors, and that it was her duty to tell citizen Robespierre and the Committee of Public Safety all about them and their mysterious doings. And poor Yvonne was greatly puzzled and deeply distressed, because, of course, whatever milor said, that was the truth; and yet her conscience cried out within her poor little bosom, and the thought of betraying those kind Englishmen was horrible to her.

"Yvonne," whispered milor in that endearing voice of his, which was like the loveliest music in her ear, "my little Yvonne, you do trust me, do you not?"

"With all my heart, milor," she murmured fervently.

"Then, would you believe it of me that I would betray a real friend?"

"I believe, milor, that whatever you do is right and good."

A sigh of infinite relief escaped his lips.

"Come, that's better!" he said, patting her cheek kindly with his hand. "Now, listen to me, little one. He who is the chief among us here is the most unscrupulous and daring rascal whom the world has ever known. He it is who is called the 'Scarlet Pimpernel!'"

"The Scarlet Pimpernel!" murmured Yvonne, her eyes dilated with superstitious awe, for she too had heard of the mysterious Englishman and of his followers, who rescued aristocrats and traitors from the death to which the tribunal of the people had justly condemned them, and on whom the mighty hand of the Committee of Public Safety had never yet been able to fall.

"This Scarlet Pimpernel," said milor earnestly after a while, "is also mine own most relentless enemy. With lies and promises he induced me to join him in his work of spying and of treachery, forcing me to do this work against which my whole soul rebels. You can save me from this hated bondage, little one. You can make me free to live again, make me free to love and place my love at your feet."

His voice had become exquisitely tender, and his lips, as he whispered the heavenly words, were quite close to her ear. He, a great gentleman, loved the miserable little waif whose kindred consisted of a blind father and two half-starved little brothers, and whose only home was this miserable hovel, whence milor's graciousness and bounty would soon take her.

Do you think that Yvonne's sense of right and wrong, of honesty and treachery, should have been keener than that primeval instinct of a simple-hearted woman to throw herself trustingly into the arms of the man who has succeeded in winning her love?

Yvonne, subdued, enchanted, murmured still through her tears: "What would milor have me do?"

Lord Kulmsted rose from his knees satisfied.

"Listen to me, Yvonne," he said. "You are acquainted with the Englishman's plans, are you not?"

"Of course," she replied simply. "He has had to trust me."

"Then you know that at sundown this afternoon I and the three others are to leave for Courbevoie on foot, where we are to obtain what horses we can whilst awaiting the chief."

"I did not know whither you and the other three gentlemen were going, milor," she replied; "but I did know that some of you were to make a start at four o'clock, whilst I was to wait here for your leader and prepare some supper against his coming."

"At what time did he tell you that he would come?"

"He did not say; but he did tell me that when he returns he will have friends with him—a lady and two little children. They will be hungry and cold. I believe that they are in great danger now, and that the brave English gentleman means to take them away from this awful Paris to a place of safety."

"The brave English gentleman, my dear," retorted milor, with a sneer, "is bent on some horrible work of spying. The lady and the two children are, no doubt, innocent tools in his hands, just as I am, and when he no longer needs them he will deliver them over to the Committee of Public Safety, who will, of a surety, condemn them to death. That will also be my fate, Yvonne, unless you help me now."

"Oh, no, no!" she exclaimed fervently. "Tell me what to do, milor, and I will do it."

"At sundown," he said, sinking his voice so low that even she could scarcely hear, "when I and the three others have started on our way, go straight to the house I spoke to you about in the Rue Dauphine —you know where it is?"

"Oh, yes, milor."

"You will know the house by its tumbledown portico and the tattered red flag that surmounts it. Once there, push the door open and walk in boldly. Then ask to speak with citizen Robespierre."

"Robespierre?" exclaimed the child in terror.

"You must not be afraid, Yvonne," he said earnestly; "you must think of me and of what you are doing for me. My word on it— Robespierre will listen to you most kindly."

"What shall I tell him?" she murmured.

"That a mysterious party of Englishmen are in hiding in this house—that their chief is known among them as the Scarlet Pimpernel. The rest leave to Robespierre's discretion. You see how simple it is?"

It was indeed very simple! Nor did the child recoil any longer from the ugly task which milor, with suave speech and tender voice, was so ardently seeking to impose on her.

A few more words of love, which cost him nothing, a few kisses which cost him still less, since the wench loved him, and since she was young and pretty, and Yvonne was as wax in the hands of the traitor.

## II

Silence reigned in the low-raftered room on the ground floor of the house in the Rue Dauphine.

Citizen Robespierre, chairman of the Cordeliers Club, the most bloodthirsty, most Evolutionary club of France, had just re-entered the room.

He walked up to the centre table, and through the close atmosphere, thick with tobacco smoke, he looked round on his assembled friends.

"We have got him," he said at last curtly.

"Got him! Whom?" came in hoarse cries from every corner of the room.

"That Englishman," replied the demagogue, "the Scarlet Pimpernel!"

A prolonged shout rose in response—a shout not unlike that of a caged herd of hungry wild beasts to whom a succulent morsel of flesh has unexpectedly been thrown.

"Where is he?" "Where did you get him?" "Alive or dead?" And many more questions such as these were hurled at the speaker from every side.

Robespierre, calm, impassive, immaculately neat in his tightly fitting coat, his smart breeches, and his lace cravat, waited awhile until the din had somewhat subsided. Then he said calmly:

"The Scarlet Pimpernel is in hiding in one of the derelict houses in the Rue Berthier."

Snarls of derision as vigorous as the former shouts of triumph drowned the rest of his speech.

"Bah! How often has that cursed Scarlet Pimpernel been said to be alone in a lonely house? Citizen Chauvelin has had him at his mercy several times in lonely houses."

And the speaker, a short, thick-set man with sparse black hair plastered over a greasy forehead, his shirt open at the neck, revealing a powerful chest and rough, hairy skin, spat in ostentatious contempt upon the floor.

"Therefore will we not boast of his capture yet, citizen Roger," resumed Robespierre imperturbably. "I tell you where the Englishman is. Do you look to it that he does not escape."

The heat in the room had become intolerable. From the grimy ceiling an oil-lamp, flickering low, threw lurid, ruddy lights on tricolour cockades, on hands that seemed red with the blood of innocent victims of lust and hate, and on faces glowing with desire and with anticipated savage triumph.

"Who is the informer?" asked Roger at last.

"A girl," replied Robespierre curtly. "Yvonne Lebeau, by name;

she and her family live by begging. There are a blind father and two boys; they herd together at night in the derelict house in the Rue Berthier. Five Englishmen have been in hiding there these past few days. One of them is their leader. The girl believes him to be the Scarlet Pimpernel."

"Why has she not spoken of this before?" muttered one of the crowd, with some skepticism.

"Frightened, I suppose. Or the Englishman paid her to hold her tongue."

"Where is the girl now?"

"I am sending her straight home, a little ahead of us. Her presence should reassure the Englishman whilst we make ready to surround the house. In the meanwhile, I have sent special messengers to every gate of Paris with strict orders to the guard not to allow anyone out of the city until further orders from the Committee of Public Safety. And now," he added, throwing back his head with a gesture of proud challenge, "citizens, which of you will go man-hunting to-night?"

This time the strident roar of savage exultation was loud and deep enough to shake the flickering lamp upon its chain.

A brief discussion of plans followed, and Roger—he with the broad, hairy chest and that gleam of hatred for ever lurking in his deep-set, shifty eyes—was chosen the leader of the party.

Thirty determined and well-armed patriots set out against one man, who mayhap had supernatural powers. There would, no doubt, be some aristocrats, too, in hiding in the derelict house—the girl Lebeau, it seems, had spoken of a woman and two children. Bah! These would not count. It would be thirty to one, so let the Scarlet Pimpernel look to himself.

From the towers of Notre Dame the big bell struck the hour of six, as thirty men in ragged shirts and torn breeches, shivering beneath a cold November drizzle, began slowly to wend their way towards the Rue Berthier.

They walked on in silence, not heeding the cold or the rain, but with eyes fixed in the direction of their goal, and nostrils quivering in the evening air with the distant scent of blood.

### III

At the top of the Rue Berthier the party halted. On ahead— some two hundred metres farther—Yvonne Lebeau's little figure, with her ragged skirt pulled over her head and her bare feet pattering in the mud, was seen crossing one of those intermittent patches of light formed by occasional flickering street lamps, and then was swallowed up once more by the inky blackness beyond.

The Rue Berthier is a long, narrow, ill-paved and ill-lighted street, composed of low and irregular houses, which abut on the line of fortifications at the back, and are therefore absolutely inaccessible save from the front.

Midway down the street a derelict house rears ghostly debris of roofs and chimney-stacks upward to the sky. A tiny square of yellow light, blinking like a giant eye through a curtainless window, pierced the wall of the house. Roger pointed to that light.

"That," he said, "is the quarry where our fox has run to earth."

No one said anything; but the dank night air seemed suddenly alive with all the passions of hate let loose by thirty beating hearts.

The Scarlet Pimpernel, who had tricked them, mocked them, fooled them so often, was there, not two hundred metres away; and they were thirty to one, and all determined and desperate.

The darkness was intense.

Silently now the party approached the house, then again they halted, within sixty metres of it.

"Hist!"

The whisper could scarce be heard, so low was it, like the sighing of the wind through a misty veil.

"Who is it?" came in quick challenge from Roger.

"I—Yvonne Lebeau!"

"Is he there?" was the eager whispered query.

"Not yet. But he may come at any moment. If he saw a crowd round the house, mayhap he would not come."

"He cannot see a crowd. The night is as dark as pitch."

"He can see in the darkest night," and the girl's voice sank to an awed whisper, "and he can hear through a stone wall."

Instinctively, Roger shuddered. The superstitious fear which the mysterious personality of the Scarlet Pimpernel evoked in the heart of every Terrorist had suddenly seized this man in its grip.

Try as he would, he did not feel as valiant as he had done when first he emerged at the head of his party from under the portico of the Cordeliers Club, and it was with none too steady a voice that he ordered the girl roughly back to the house. Then he turned once more to his men.

The plan of action had been decided on in the Club, under the presidency of Robespierre; it only remained to carry the plans through with success.

From the side of the fortifications there was, of course, nothing to fear. In accordance with military regulations, the walls of the houses there rose sheer from the ground without doors or windows, whilst the broken-down parapets and dilapidated roofs towered forty feet above the ground.

The derelict itself was one of a row of houses, some inhabited, others quite abandoned. It was the front of that row of houses, therefore, that had to be kept in view. Marshalled by Roger, the men flattened their meagre bodies against the walls of the houses opposite, and after that there was nothing to do but wait.

To wait in the darkness of the night, with a thin, icy rain soaking through ragged shirts and tattered breeches, with bare feet frozen by the mud of the road—to wait in silence while turbulent hearts beat well-nigh to bursting—to wait for food whilst hunger gnaws the bowels—to wait for drink whilst the parched tongue cleaves to the roof of the mouth—to wait for revenge whilst the hours roll slowly by and the cries of the darkened city are stilled one by one!

Once—when a distant bell tolled the hour of ten—a loud prolonged laugh, almost impudent in its suggestion of merry insouciance, echoed through the weird silence of the night.

Roger felt that the man nearest to him shivered at that sound, and he heard a volley or two of muttered oaths.

"The fox seems somewhere near," he whispered. "Come within. We'll wait for him inside his hole."

He led the way across the street, some of the men following him.

The door of the derelict house had been left on the latch. Roger pushed it open.

Silence and gloom here reigned supreme; utter darkness, too, save for a narrow streak of light which edged the framework of a door on the right. Not a sound stirred the quietude of this miserable hovel, only the creaking of boards beneath the men's feet as they entered.

Roger crossed the passage and opened the door on the right. His friends pressed closely round to him and peeped over his shoulder into the room beyond.

A guttering piece of tallow candle, fixed to an old tin pot, stood in the middle of the floor, and its feeble, flickering light only served to accentuate the darkness that lay beyond its range. One or two rickety chairs and a rough deal table showed vaguely in the gloom, and in the far corner of the room there lay a bundle of what looked like heaped-up rags, but from which there now emerged the sound of heavy breathing and also a little cry of fear.

"Yvonne," came in feeble, querulous accents from that same bundle of wretchedness, "are these the English milors come back at last?"

"No, no, father," was the quick whispered reply.

Roger swore a loud oath, and two puny voices began to whimper piteously.

"It strikes me the wench has been fooling us," muttered one of the men savagely.

The girl had struggled to her feet. She crouched in the darkness, and two little boys, half-naked and shivering, were clinging to her skirts. The rest of the human bundle seemed to consist of an oldish man, with long, gaunt legs and arms blue with the cold. He turned vague, wide-open eyes in the direction whence had come the harsh voices.

"Are they friends, Yvonne?" he asked anxiously.

The girl did her best to reassure him.

"Yes, yes, father," she whispered close to his ear, her voice scarce above her breath; "they are good citizens who hoped to find the English milor here. They are disappointed that he has not yet come."

"Ah! but he will come, of a surety," said the old man in that querulous voice of his. "He left his beautiful clothes here this morning, and surely he will come to fetch them." And his long, thin hand pointed towards a distant corner of the room.

Roger and his friends, looking to where he was pointing, saw a parcel of clothes, neatly folded, lying on one of the chairs. Like so many wild cats snarling at sight of prey, they threw themselves upon those clothes, tearing them out from one another's hands, turning them over and over as if to force the cloth and satin to yield up the secret that lay within their folds.

In the skirmish a scrap of paper fluttered to the ground. Roger seized it with avidity, and, crouching on the floor, smoothed the paper out against his knee.

It contained a few hastily scrawled words, and by the feeble light of the fast-dying candle Roger spelt them out laboriously:

"If the finder of these clothes will take them to the cross-roads opposite the foot-bridge which leads straight to Courbevoie, and will do so before the clock of Courbevoie Church has struck the hour of midnight, he will be rewarded with the sum of five hundred francs."

"There is something more, citizen Roger," said a raucous voice close to his ear.

"Look! Look, citizen—in the bottom corner of the paper!"

"The signature."

"A scrawl done in red," said Roger, trying to decipher it.

"It looks like a small flower."

"That accursed Scarlet Pimpernel!"

And even as he spoke the guttering tallow candle, swaying in its socket, suddenly went out with a loud splutter and a sizzle that echoed through the desolate room like the mocking laugh of ghouls.

## IV

Once more the tramp through the dark and deserted streets, with the drizzle—turned now to sleet—beating on thinly clad shoulders. Fifteen men only on this tramp. The others remained behind to watch the house. Fifteen men, led by Roger, and with a blind old man, a young girl carrying a bundle of clothes, and two half-naked children dragged as camp-followers in the rear.

Their destination now was the sign-post which stands at the cross-roads, past the footbridge that leads to Courbevoie.

The guard at the Maillot Gate would have stopped the party, but Roger, member of the Committee of Public Safety, armed with his papers and his tricolour scarf, overruled Robespierre's former orders, and the party mached out of the gate.

They pressed on in silence, instinctively walking shoulder to shoulder, vaguely longing for the touch of another human hand, the sound of a voice that would not ring weirdly in the mysterious night.

There was something terrifying in this absolute silence, in such intense darkness, in this constant wandering towards a goal that seemed for ever distant, and in all this weary, weary fruitless waiting; and these men, who lived their life through, drunken with blood, deafened by the cries of their victims, satiated with the moans of the helpless and the innocent, hardly dared to look around them, lest they should see ghoulish forms flitting through the gloom.

Soon they reached the cross-roads, and in the dense blackness of the night the gaunt arms of the sign-post pointed ghostlike towards the north.

The men hung back, wrapped in the darkness as in a pall, while Roger advanced alone.

"*Hola!* Is anyone there?" he called softly.

Then, as no reply came, he added more loudly:

"*Hola!* A friend—with some clothes found in the Rue Berthier. Is anyone here? *Hola!* A friend!"

But only from the gently murmuring river far away the melancholy call of a waterfowl seemed to echo mockingly:

"A friend!"

Just then the clock of Courbevoie Church struck the midnight hour.

"It is too late," whispered the men.

They did not swear, nor did they curse their leader. Somehow it seemed as if they had expected all along that the Englishman would evade their vengeance yet again, that he would lure them out into the cold and into the darkness, and then that he would mock them, fool them, and finally disappear into the night.

It seemed futile to wait any longer. They were so sure that they had failed again.

"Who goes there?"

The sound of naked feet and of wooden sabots pattering on the distant footbridge had caused Roger to utter the quick challenge.

"*Hola! Hola!* Are you there?" was the loud, breathless response.

The next moment the darkness became alive with men moving

quickly forward, and raucous shouts of "Where are they?" "Have you got them?" "Don't let them go!" filled the air.

"Got whom?" "Who are they?" "What is it?" were the wild counter-cries.

"The man! The girl! The children! Where are they?"

"What? Which? The Lebeau family? They are here with us."

"Where?"

Where, indeed? To a call to them from Roger there came no answer, nor did a hasty search result in finding them—the old man, the two boys, and the girl carrying the bundle of clothes had vanished into the night.

"In the name of—-, what does this mean?" cried hoarse voices in the crowd.

The new-comers, breathless, terrified, shaking with superstitious fear, tried to explain.

"The Lebeau family—the old man, the girl, the two boys—we discovered after your departure, locked up in the cellar of the house—prisoners."

"But, then—the others?" they gasped.

"The girl and the children whom you saw must have been some aristocrats in disguise. The old man who spoke to you was that cursed Englishman—the Scarlet Pimpernel!"

And as if in mocking confirmation of these words there suddenly rang, echoing from afar, a long and merry laugh.

"The Scarlet Pimpernel!" cried Roger. "In rags and barefooted! At him, citizens; he cannot have got far!"

"Hush! Listen!" whispered one of the men, suddenly gripping him by the arm.

And from the distance—though Heaven only knew from what direction—came the sound of horses' hoofs pawing the soft ground; the next moment they were heard galloping away at breakneck speed.

The men turned to run in every direction, blindly, aimlessly, in the dark, like bloodhounds that have lost the trail.

One man, as he ran, stumbled against a dark mass prone upon the ground.

With a curse on his lips, he recovered his balance.

"Hold! What is this?" he cried.

Some of his comrades gathered round him. No one could see anything, but the dark mass appeared to have human shape, and it was bound round and round with cords. And now feeble moans escaped from obviously human lips.

"What is it? Who is it?" asked the men.

"An Englishman," came in weak accents from the ground.

"Your name?"

"I am called Kulmsted."

"Bah! An aristocrat!"

"No! An enemy of the Scarlet Pimpernel, like yourselves. I would have delivered him into your hands. But you let him escape you. As for me, he would have been wiser if he had killed me."

They picked him up and undid the cords from round his body, and later on took him with them back into Paris.

But there, in the darkness of the night, in the mud of the road, and beneath the icy rain, knees were shaking that had long ago forgotten how to bend, and hasty prayers were muttered by lips that were far more accustomed to blaspheme.

# The Cabaret De La Liberte

## I

"Eight!"

"Twelve!"

"Four!"

A loud curse accompanied this last throw, and shouts of ribald laughter greeted it.

"No luck, Guidal!"

"Always at the tail end of the cart, eh, citizen?"

"Do not despair yet, good old Guidal! Bad beginnings oft make splendid ends!"

Then once again the dice rattled in the boxes; those who stood around pressed closer round the gamesters; hot, avid faces, covered with sweat and grime, peered eagerly down upon the table.

"Eight and eleven—nineteen!"

"Twelve and zero! By Satan! Curse him! Just my luck!"

"Four and nine—thirteen! Unlucky number!"

"Now then—once more! I'll back Merri! Ten assignats of the most worthless kind! Who'll take me that Merri gets the wench in the end?"

This from one of the lookers-on, a tall, cadaverous-looking creature, with sunken eyes and broad, hunched-up shoulders, which were perpetually shaken by a dry, rasping cough that proclaimed the ravages of some mortal disease, left him trembling as with ague and brought beads of perspiration to the roots of his lank hair. A recrudescence of excitement went the round of the spectators. The gamblers sitting round a narrow deal table, on which past libations had left marks of sticky rings, had scarce room to move their elbows.

"Nineteen and four—twenty-three!"

"You are out of it, Desmonts!"

"Not yet!"

"Twelve and twelve!"

"There! What did I tell you?"

"Wait! wait! Now, Merri! Now! Remember I have backed you for ten assignats, which I propose to steal from the nearest Jew this very night."

"Thirteen and twelve! Twenty-five, by all the demons and the ghouls!" came with a triumphant shout from the last thrower.

"Merri has it! *Vive* Merri!" was the unanimous and clamorous response.

Merri was evidently the most popular amongst the three

gamblers.

Now he sprawled upon the bench, leaning his back against the table, and surveyed the assembled company with the air of an Achilles having vanquished his Hector.

Good luck to you and to your *aristo!*" began his backer lustily— would, no doubt, have continued his song of praise had not a violent fit of coughing smothered the words in his throat. The hand which he had raised in order to slap his friend genially on the back now went with a convulsive clutch to his own chest.

His obvious distress did not apparently disturb the equanimity of Merri, or arouse even passing interest in the lookers-on.

"May she have as much money as rumour avers," said one of the men sententiously.

Merri gave a careless wave of his grubby hand.

"More, citizen; more!" he said loftily.

Only the two losers appeared inclined to scepticism.

"Bah!" one of them said—it was Desmonts. "The whole matter of the woman's money may be a tissue of lies!"

"And England is a far cry!" added Guidal.

But Merri was not likely to be depressed by these dismal croakings.

"'Tis simple enough," he said philosophically, "to disparage the goods if you are not able to buy."

Then a lusty voice broke in from the far corner of the room:

"And now, citizen Merri, 'tis time you remembered that the evening is hot and your friends thirsty!"

The man who spoke was a short, broad-shouldered creature, with crimson face surrounded by a shock of white hair, like a ripe tomato wrapped in cotton wool.

"And let me tell you," he added complacently, "that I have a cask of rum down below, which came straight from that accursed country, England, and is said to be the nectar whereon feeds that confounded Scarlet Pimpernel. It gives him the strength, so 'tis said, to intrigue successfully against the representatives of the people."

"Then by all means, citizen," concluded Merri's backer, still hoarse and spent after his fit of coughing, "let us have some of your nectar. My friend, citizen Merri, will need strength and wits too, I'll warrant, for, after he has married the *aristo*, he will have to journey to England to pluck the rich dowry which is said to lie hidden there."

"Cast no doubt upon that dowry, citizen Rateau, curse you!" broke in Merri, with a spiteful glance directed against his former rivals, "or Guidal and Desmonts will cease to look glum, and half my joy in the *aristo* will have gone."

Which, the conversation drifted to general subjects, became hilarious and ribald, while the celebrated rum from England filled the close atmosphere of the narrow room with its heady fumes.

## II

Open to the street in front, the locality known under the pretentious title of "Cabaret de la Liberte" was a favoured one among the flotsam and jetsam of the population of this corner of old Paris; men and sometimes women, with nothing particular to do, no special means of livelihood save the battening on the countless miseries and sorrows which this Revolution, which was to have been so glorious, was bringing in its train; idlers and loafers, who would crawl desultorily down the few worn and grimy steps which led into the cabaret from the level of the street. There was always good brandy or eau de vie to be had there, and no questions asked, no scares from the revolutionary guards or the secret agents of the Committee of Public Safety, who knew better than to interfere with the citizen host and his dubious clientele. There was also good Rhine wine or rum to be had, smuggled across from England or Germany, and no interference from the spies of some of those countless Committees, more autocratic than any *ci-devant* despot. It was, in fact, an ideal place wherein to conduct those shady transactions which are unavoidable corollaries of an unfettered democracy. Projects of burglary, pillage, rapine, even murder, were hatched within this underground burrow, where, as soon as evening drew in, a solitary, smoky oil-lamp alone cast a dim light upon faces that liked to court the darkness, and whence no sound that was not meant for prying ears found its way to the street above. The walls were thick with grime and smoke, the floor mildewed and cracked; dirt vied with squalor to make the place a fitting abode for thieves and cut-throats, for some of those sinister night-birds, more vile even than those who shrieked with satisfied lust at sight of the tumbril, with its daily load of unfortunates for the guillotine.

On this occasion the project that was being hatched was one of the most abject. A young girl, known by some to be possessed of a fortune, was the stake for which these workers of iniquity gambled across one of mine host's greasy tables. The latest decree of the Convention, encouraging, nay, commanding, the union of aristocrats with so-called patriots, had fired the imagination of this nest of jail-birds with thoughts of glorious possibilities. Some of them had collected the necessary information; and the report had been encouraging.

That self-indulgent *aristo*, the *ci-devant* banker Amede Vincent, who had expiated his villainies upon the guillotine, was known to have been successful in abstracting the bulk of his ill-gotten wealth and concealing it somewhere—it was not exactly known where, but thought to be in England—out of the reach, at any rate, of deserving patriots.

Some three or four years ago, before the glorious principles of Liberty, Equality, and Fraternity had made short shrift of all such pestilential aristocrats, the *ci-devant* banker, then a widower with an only daughter, Esther, had journeyed to England. He soon returned to Paris, however, and went on living there with his little girl in comparative retirement, until his many crimes found him out at last and he was made to suffer the punishment which he so justly deserved. Those crimes consisted for the most part in humiliating the aforesaid deserving patriots with his benevolence, shaming them with many kindnesses, and the simplicity of his home-life, and, above all, in flouting the decrees of the Revolutionary Government, which made every connection with *ci-devant* churches and priests a penal offence against the security of the State.

Amede Vincent was sent to the guillotine, and the representatives of the people confiscated his house and all his property on which they could lay their hands; but they never found the millions which he was supposed to have concealed. Certainly his daughter Esther—a young girl, not yet nineteen—had not found them either, for after her father's death she went to live in one of the poorer quarters of Paris, alone with an old and faithful servant named Lucienne. And while the Committee of Public Safety was deliberating whether it would be worth while to send Esther to the guillotine, to follow in her father's footsteps, a certain number of astute jail-birds plotted to obtain possession of her wealth.

The wealth existed, over in England; of that they were ready to take their oath, and the project which they had formed was as ingenious as it was diabolic: to feign a denunciation, to enact a pretended arrest, to place before the unfortunate girl the alternative of death or marriage with one of the gang, were the chief incidents of this inquitous project, and it was in the Cabaret de la Liberte that lots were thrown as to which among the herd of miscreants should be the favoured one to play the chief role in the sinister drama.

The lot fell to Merri; but the whole gang was to have a share in the putative fortune—even Rateau, the wretched creature with the hacking cough, who looked as if he had one foot in the grave, and shivered as if he were stricken with ague, put in a word now and again to remind his good friend Merri that he, too, was looking forward to his share of the spoils. Merri, however, was inclined to repudiate him altogether.

"Why should I share with you?" he said roughly, when, a few hours later, he and Rateau parted in the street outside the Cabaret de la Liberte. "Who are you, I would like to know, to try and poke your ugly nose into my affairs? How do I know where you come from, and whether you are not some crapulent spy of one of those pestilential committees?"

From which eloquent flow of language we may infer that the friendship between these two worthies was not of very old duration. Rateau would, no doubt, have protested loudly, but the fresh outer air had evidently caught his wheezy lungs, and for a minute or two he could do nothing but cough and splutter and groan, and cling to his unresponsive comrade for support. Then at last, when he had succeeded in recovering his breath, he said dolefully and with a ludicrous attempt at dignified reproach:

"Do not force me to remind you, citizen Merri, that if it had not been for my suggestion that we should all draw lots, and then play hazard as as to who shall be the chosen one to woo the *ci-devant* millionairess, there would soon have been a free fight inside the cabaret, a number of broken heads, and no decision whatever arrived at; whilst you, who were never much of a fighter, would probably be lying now helpless, with a broken nose, and deprived of some of your teeth, and with no chance of entering the lists for the heiress. Instead of which, here you are, the victor by a stroke of good fortune, which you should at least have the good grace to ascribe to me."

Whether the poor wretch's argument had any weight with citizen Merri, or whether that worthy patriot merely thought that procrastination would, for the nonce, prove the best policy, it were impossible to say. Certain it is that in response to his companion's tirade he contented himself with a dubious grunt, and without another word turned on his heel and went slouching down the street.

## III

For the persistent and optimistic romanticist, there were still one or two idylls to be discovered flourishing under the shadow of the grim and relentless Revolution. One such was that which had Esther Vincent and Jack Kennard for hero and heroine. Esther, the orphaned daughter of one of the richest bankers of pre-Revolution days, now a daily governess and household drudge at ten francs a week in the house of a retired butcher in the Rue Richelieu, and Jack Kennard, formerly the representative of a big English firm of woollen manufacturers, who had thrown up his employment and prospects in England in order to watch over the girl whom he loved. He, himself an alien enemy, an Englishman, in deadly danger of his life every hour that he remained in France; and she, unwilling at the time to leave the horrors of revolutionary Paris while her father was lingering at the Conciergerie awaiting condemnation, as such forbidden to leave the city. So Kennard stayed on, unable to tear himself away from her, and obtained an unlucrative post as accountant in a small wine shop over by Montmartre. His life, like hers, was hanging by a thread; any day, any hour now, some malevolent denunciation might, in the sight of the Committee of Public Safety, turn the eighteen years old "suspect" into a living peril to the State, or the alien enemy into a dangerous spy.

Some of the happiest hours these two spent in one another's company were embittered by that ever-present dread of the peremptory knock at the door, the portentous: "Open, in the name of the Law!" the perquisition, the arrest, to which the only issue, these days, was the guillotine.

But the girl was only just eighteen, and he not many years older, and at that age, in spite of misery, sorrow, and dread, life always has its compensations. Youth cries out to happiness so insistently that happiness is forced to hear, and for a few moments, at the least, drives care and even the bitterest anxiety away.

For Esther Vincent and her English lover there were moments when they believed themselves to be almost happy. It was in the evenings mostly, when she came home from her work and he was free to spend an hour or two with her. Then old Lucienne, who had been Esther's nurse in the happy, olden days, and was an unpaid maid-of-all-work and a loved and trusted friend now, would bring in the lamp and pull the well-darned curtains over the windows. She would spread a clean cloth upon the table and bring in a meagre supper of coffee and black bread, perhaps a little butter or a tiny square of cheese. And the two young people would talk of the future, of the time when they would settle down in Kennard's old home, over in England, where his mother and sister even now were eating out their hearts with anxiety for him.

"Tell me all about the South Downs," Esther was very fond of saying; "and your village, and your house, and the rambler roses and the clematis arbour."

She never tired of hearing, or he of telling. The old Manor House, bought with his father's savings; the garden which was his mother's hobby; the cricket pitch on the village green. Oh, the cricket! She thought that so funny—the men in high, sugar-loaf hats, grown-up men, spending hours and hours, day after day, in banging at a ball with a wooden bat!

"Oh, Jack! The English are a funny, nice, dear, kind lot of people. I remember—"

She remembered so well that happy summer which she had spent with her father in England four years ago. It was after the Bastille had been stormed and taken, and the banker had journeyed to England with his daughter in something of a hurry. Then her father had talked of returning to France and leaving her behind with friends in England. But Esther would not be left. Oh, no! Even now she glowed with pride at the thought of her firmness in the matter. If she had remained in England she would never have seen her dear father again. Here remembrances grew bitter and sad, until Jack's hand reached soothingly, consolingly out to her, and she brushed away her tears, so as not to sadden him still more.

Then she would ask more questions about his home and his garden, about his mother and the dogs and the flowers; and once more they would forget that hatred and envy and death were already stalking their door.

IV

"Open, in the name of the Law!"

It had come at last. A bolt from out the serene blue of their happiness. A rough, dirty, angry, cursing crowd, who burst through the heavy door even before they had time to open it. Lucienne collapsed into a chair, weeping and lamenting, with her apron thrown over her head. But Esther and Kennard stood quite still and calm, holding one another by the hand, just to give one another courage.

Some half dozen men stalked into the little room. Men? They looked like ravenous beasts, and were unspeakably dirty, wore soiled tricolour scarves above their tattered breeches in token of their official status. Two of them fell on the remnants of the meagre supper and devoured everything that remained on the table—bread, cheese, a piece of home-made sausage. The others ransacked the two attic-rooms which had been home for Esther and Lucienne: the little living-room under the sloping roof, with the small hearth on which very scanty meals were wont to be cooked, and the bare, narrow room beyond, with the iron bedstead, and the palliasse on the floor for Lucienne.

The men poked about everywhere, struck great, spiked sticks through the poor bits of bedding, and ripped up the palliasse. They tore open the drawers of the rickety chest and of the broken-down wardrobe, and did not spare the unfortunate young girl a single humiliation or a single indignity.

Kennard, burning with wrath, tried to protest.

"Hold that cub!" commanded the leader of the party, almost as soon as the young Englishman's hot, indignant words had resounded above the din of overturned furniture. "And if he opens his mouth again throw him into the street!" And Kennard, terrified lest he should be parted from Esther, thought it wiser to hold his peace.

They looked at one another, like two young trapped beasts—not despairing, but trying to infuse courage one into the other by a look of confidence and of love. Esther, in fact, kept her eyes fixed on her good-looking English lover, firmly keeping down the shudder of loathing which went right through her when she saw those awful men coming nigh her. There was one especially whom she abominated worse than the others, a bandy-legged ruffian, who regarded her with a leer that caused her an almost physical nausea. He did not take part in the perquisition, but sat down in the centre of the room and sprawled over the table with the air of one who was in authority. The others addressed him as "citizen Merri," and alternately ridiculed and deferred to him. And there was another, equally hateful, a horrible, cadaverous creature, with huge bare feet thrust into sabots, and lank hair, thick with grime.

He did most of the talking, even though his loquacity occasionally broke down in a racking cough, which literally seemed to tear at his chest, and left him panting, hoarse, and with beads of moisture upon his low, pallid forehead.

Of course, the men found nothing that could even remotely be termed compromising. Esther had been very prudent in deference to Kennard's advice; she also had very few possessions. Nevertheless, when the wretches had turned every article of furniture inside out, one of them asked curtly:

"What do we do next, citizen Merri?"

"Do?" broke in the cadaverous creature, even before Merri had time to reply. "Do? Why, take the wench to—to—"

He got no further, became helpless with coughing. Esther, quite instinctively, pushed the carafe of water towards him.

"Nothing of the sort!" riposted Merri sententiously. "The wench stays here!"

Both Esther and Jack had much ado to suppress an involuntary cry of relief, which at this unexpected pronouncement had risen to their lips.

The man with the cough tried to protest.

"But—" he began hoarsely.

"I said, the wench stays here!" broke in Merri peremptorily. "Ah ca!" he added, with a savage imprecation. "Do you command here, citizen Rateau, or do I?"

The other at once became humble, even cringing.

"You, of course, citizen," he rejoined in his hollow voice. "I would only remark-"

"Remark nothing," retorted the other curtly. "See to it that the cub is out of the house. And after that put a sentry outside the wench's door. No one to go in and out of here under any pretext whatever. Understand?"

Kennard this time uttered a cry of protest. The helplessness of his position exasperated him almost to madness. Two men were holding him tightly by his sinewy arms. With an Englishman's instinct for a fight, he would not only have tried, but also succeeded in knocking these two down, and taken the other four on after that, with quite a reasonable chance of success. That tuberculous creature, now! And that bandy-legged ruffian! Jack Kennard had been an amateur middle-weight champion in his day, and these brutes had no more science than an enraged bull! But even as he fought against that instinct he realised the futility of a struggle. The danger of it, too—not for himself, but for her. After all, they were not going to take her away to one of those awful places from which the only egress was the way to the guillotine; and if there was that amount of freedom there was bound to be some hope. At twenty there is always hope!

So when, in obedience to Merri's orders, the two ruffians began to drag him towards the door, he said firmly:

"Leave me alone. I'll go without this unnecessary struggling."

Then, before the wretches realised his intention, he had jerked himself free from them and run to Esther.

"Have no fear," he said to her in English, and in a rapid whisper. "I'll watch over you. The house opposite. I know the people. I'll manage it somehow. Be on the look-out."

They would not let him say more, and she only had the chance of responding firmly: "I am not afraid, and I'll be on the look-out." The next moment Merri's compeers seized him from behind—four of them this time.

Then, of course, prudence went to the winds. He hit out to the right and left. Knocked two of those recreants down, and already was prepared to seize Esther in his arms, make a wild dash for the door, and run with her, whither only God knew, when Rateau, that awful consumptive reprobate, crept slyly up behind him and dealt him a swift and heavy blow on the skull with his weighted stick. Kennard staggered, and the bandits closed upon him. Those on the floor had time to regain their feet. To make assurance doubly sure, one of them emulated Rateau's tactics, and hit the Englishman once more on the head from behind. After that, Kennard became inert; he had partly lost consciousness. His head ached furiously. Esther, numb with horror, saw him bundled out of the room. Rateau, coughing and spluttering, finally closed the door upon the unfortunate and the four brigands who had hold of him.

Only Merri and that awful Rateau had remained in the room. The latter, gasping for breath now, poured himself out a mugful of water and drank it down at one draught. Then he swore, because he wanted rum, or brandy, or even wine. Esther watched him and Merri, fascinated. Poor old Lucienne was quietly weeping behind her apron.

"Now then, my wench," Merri began abruptly, "suppose you sit down here and listen to what I have to say."

He pulled a chair close to him and, with one of those hideous leers which had already caused her to shudder, he beckoned her to sit. Esther obeyed as if in a dream. Her eyes were dilated like those of one in a waking trance. She moved mechanically, like a bird attracted by a serpent, terrified, yet unresisting. She felt utterly helpless between these two villainous brutes, and anxiety for her English lover seemed further to numb her senses. When she was sitting she turned her gaze, with an involuntary appeal for pity, upon the bandy-legged ruffian beside her. He laughed.

"No! I am not going to hurt you," he said with smooth condescension, which was far more loathsome to Esther's ears than his comrades' savage oaths had been. "You are pretty and you have pleased me. 'Tis no small matter, forsooth!" he added, with loud-voiced bombast, "to have earned the good-will of citizen Merri. You, my wench, are in luck's way. You realise what has occurred just now. You are amenable to the law which has decreed you to be suspect. I hold an order for your arrest. I can have you seized at once by my men, dragged to the Conciergerie, and from thence nothing can save you—neither your good looks nor the protection of citizen Merri. It means the guillotine. You understand that, don't you?"

She sat quite still; only her hands were clutched convulsively together.

But she contrived to say quite firmly:

"I do, and I am not afraid."

Merri waved a huge and very dirty hand with a careless gesture.

"I know," he said with a harsh laugh. "They all say that, don't they, citizen Rateau?"

"Until the time comes," assented that worthy dryly.

"Until the time comes," reiterated the other. "Now, my wench," he added, once more turning to Esther, "I don't want that time to come. I don't want your pretty head to go rolling down into the basket, and to receive the slap on the face which the citizen executioner has of late taken to bestowing on those aristocratic cheeks which Mme. la Guillotine has finally blanched for ever. Like this, you see."

And the inhuman wretch took up one of the round cushions from the nearest chair, held it up at arm's length, as if it were a head which he held by the hair, and then slapped it twice with the palm of his left hand. The gesture was so horrible and withal so grotesque, that Esther closed her eyes with a shudder, and her pale cheeks took on a leaden hue. Merri laughed aloud and threw the cushion down again.

"Unpleasant, what? my pretty wench! Well, you know what to expect . . . unless," he added significantly, "you are reasonable and will listen to what I am about to tell you."

Esther was no fool, nor was she unsophisticated. These were not times when it was possible for any girl, however carefully nurtured and tenderly brought up, to remain ignorant of the realities and the brutalities of life. Even before Merri had put his abominable proposition before her, she knew what he was driving at. Marriage— marriage to him! that ignoble wretch, more vile than any dumb creature! In exchange for her life!

It was her turn now to laugh. The very thought of it was farcical in its very odiousness. Merri, who had embarked on his proposal with grandiloquent phraseology, suddenly paused, almost awed by that strange, hysterical laughter.

"By Satan and all his ghouls!" he cried, and jumped to his feet, his cheeks paling beneath the grime.

Then rage seized him at his own cowardice. His egregious vanity, wounded by that laughter, egged him on. He tried to seize Esther by the waist. But she, quick as some panther on the defence, had jumped up, too, and pounced upon a knife—the very one she had been using for that happy little supper with her lover a brief half hour ago. Unguarded, unthinking, acting just with a blind instinct, she raised it and cried hoarsely:

"If you dare touch me, I'll kill you!"

It was ludicrous, of course. A mouse threatening a tiger. The very next moment Rateau had seized her hand and quietly taken away the knife. Merri shook himself like a frowsy dog.

"Whew!" he ejaculated. "What a vixen! But," he added lightly, "I like her all the better for that—eh, Rateau? Give me a wench with a temperament, I say!"

But Esther, too, had recovered herself. She realised her helplessness, and gathered courage from the consciousness of it! Now she faced the infamous villain more calmly.

"I will never marry you," she said loudly and firmly. "Never! I am not afraid to die. I am not afraid of the guillotine. There is no shame attached to death. So now you may do as you please—denounce me, and send me to follow in the footsteps of my dear father, if you wish. But whilst I am alive you will never come nigh me. If you ever do but lay a finger upon me, it will be because I am dead and beyond the reach of your polluting touch. And now I have said all that I will ever say to you in this life. If you have a spark of humanity left in you, you will, at least, let me prepare for death in peace."

She went round to where poor old Lucienne still sat, like an insentient log, panic-stricken. She knelt down on the floor and rested her arm on the old woman's knees. The light of the lamp fell full upon her, her pale face, and mass of chestnut-brown hair. There was nothing about her at this moment to inflame a man's desire. She looked pathetic in her helplessness, and nearly lifeless through the intensity of her pallor, whilst the look in her eyes was almost maniacal.

Merri cursed and swore, tried to hearten himself by turning on his friend. But Rateau had collapsed—whether with excitement or the ravages of disease, it were impossible to say. He sat upon a low chair, his long legs, his violet-circled eyes staring out with a look of hebetude and overwhelming fatigue. Merri looked around him and shuddered. The atmosphere of the place had become strangely weird and uncanny; even the tablecloth, dragged half across the table, looked somehow like a shroud.

"What shall we do, Rateau?" he asked tremulously at last.

"Get out of this infernal place," replied the other huskily. "I feel as if I were in my grave-clothes already."

"Hold your tongue, you miserable coward! You'll make the *aristo* think that we are afraid."

"Well?" queried Rateau blandly. "Aren't you?"

"No!" replied Merri fiercely. "I'll go now because . . . because . . . well! because I have had enough to-day. And the wench sickens me. I wish to serve the Republic by marrying her, but just now I feel as if I should never really want her. So I'll go! But, understand!" he added, and turned once more to Esther, even though he could not bring himself to go nigh her again. "Understand that to-morrow I'll come again for my answer. In the meanwhile, you may think matters over, and, maybe, you'll arrive at a more reasonable frame of mind. You will not leave these rooms until I set you free. My men will remain as sentinels at your door."

He beckoned to Rateau, and the two men went out of the room without another word.

V

The whole of that night Esther remained shut up in her apartment in the Petite Rue Taranne. All night she heard the measured tramp, the movements, the laughter and loud talking of men outside her door. Once or twice she tried to listen to what they said. But the doors and walls in these houses of old Paris were too stout to allow voices to filter through, save in the guise of a confused murmur. She would have felt horribly lonely and frightened but for the fact that in one window on the third floor in the house opposite the light of a lamp appeared like a glimmer of hope. Jack Kennard was there, on the watch. He had the window open and sat beside it until a very late hour; and after that he kept the light in, as a beacon, to bid her be of good cheer.

In the middle of the night he made an attempt to see her, hoping to catch the sentinels asleep or absent. But, having climbed the five stories of the house wherein she dwelt, he arrived on the landing outside her door and found there half a dozen ruffians squatting on the stone floor and engaged in playing hazard with a pack of greasy cards. That wretched consumptive, Rateau, was with them, and made a facetious remark as Kennard, pale and haggard, almost ghostlike, with a white bandage round his head, appeared upon the landing.

"Go back to bed, citizen," the odious creature said, with a raucous laugh. "We are taking care of your sweetheart for you."

Never in all his life had Jack Kennard felt so abjectly wretched as he did then, so miserably helpless. There was nothing that he could do, save to return to the lodging, which a kind friend had lent him for the occasion, and from whence he could, at any rate, see the windows behind which his beloved was watching and suffering.

When he went a few moments ago, he had left the *porte cochere* ajar. Now he pushed it open and stepped into the dark passage beyond. A tiny streak of light filtrated through a small curtained window in the concierge's lodge; it served to guide Kennard to the foot of the narrow stone staircase which led to the floors above. Just at the foot of the stairs, on the mat, a white paper glimmered in the dim shaft of light. He paused, puzzled, quite certain that the paper was not there five minutes ago when he went out. Oh! it may have fluttered in from the courtyard beyond, or from anywhere, driven by the draught. But, even so, with that mechanical action peculiar to most people under like circumstances, he stooped and picked up the paper, turned it over between his fingers, and saw that a few words were scribbled on it in pencil. The light was too dim to read by, so Kennard, still quite mechanically, kept the paper in his hand and went up to his room. There, by the light of the lamp, he read the few words scribbled in pencil:

"Wait in the street outside."

Nothing more. The message was obviously not intended for him, and yet. . . . A strange excitement possessed him. If it should be! If . . . ! He had heard—everyone had—of the mysterious agencies that were at work, under cover of darkness, to aid the unfortunate, the innocent, the helpless. He had heard of that legendary English gentleman who had before now defied the closest vigilance of the Committees, and snatched their intended victims out of their murderous clutches, at times under their very eyes.

If this should be . . . ! He scarce dared put his hope into words. He could not bring himself really to believe. But he went. He ran downstairs and out into the street, took his stand under a projecting doorway nearly opposite the house which held the woman he loved, and leaning against the wall, he waited.

After many hours—it was then past three o'clock in the morning, and the sky of an inky blackness—he felt so numb that despite his will a kind of trance-like drowsiness overcame him. He could no longer stand on his feet; his knees were shaking; his head felt so heavy that he could not keep it up. It rolled round from shoulder to shoulder, as if his will no longer controlled it. And it ached furiously. Everything around him was very still. Even "Paris-by-Night," that grim and lurid giant, was for the moment at rest. A warm summer rain was falling; its gentle, pattering murmur into the gutter helped to lull Kennard's senses into somnolence. He was on the point of dropping off to sleep when something suddenly roused him. A noise of men shouting and laughing—familiar sounds enough in these squalid Paris streets.

But Kennard was wide awake now; numbness had given place to intense quivering of all his muscles, and super-keenness of his every sense. He peered into the darkness and strained his ears to hear. The sound certainly appeared to come from the house opposite, and there, too, it seemed as if something or things were moving. Men! More than one or two, surely! Kennard thought that he could distinguish at least three distinct voices; and there was that weird, racking cough which proclaimed the presence of Rateau.

Now the men were quite close to where he—Kennard—still stood cowering. A minute or two later they had passed down the street. Their hoarse voices soon died away in the distance. Kennard crept cautiously out of his hiding-place. Message or mere coincidence, he now blessed that mysterious scrap of paper. Had he remained in his room, he might really have dropped off to sleep and not heard these men going away. There were three of them at least—Kennard thought four. But, anyway, the number of watch-dogs outside the door of his beloved had considerably diminished. He felt that he had the strength to grapple with them, even if there were still three of them left. He, an athlete, English, and master of the art of self-defence; and they, a mere pack of drink-sodden brutes! Yes! He was quite sure he could do it. Quite sure that he could force his way into Esther's rooms and carry her off in his arms—whither? God alone knew. And God alone would provide.

Just for a moment he wondered if, while he was in that state of somnolence, other bandits had come to take the place of those that were going. But this thought he quickly dismissed. In any case, he felt a giant's strength in himself, and could not rest now till he had tried once more to see her. He crept very cautiously along; was satisfied that the street was deserted.

Already he had reached the house opposite, had pushed open the *porte cochere*, which was on the latch—when, without the slightest warning, he was suddenly attacked from behind, his arms seized and held behind his back with a vice-like grip, whilst a vigorous kick against the calves of his legs caused him to lose his footing and suddenly brought him down, sprawling and helpless, in the gutter, while in his ear there rang the hideous sound of the consumptive ruffian's racking cough.

"What shall we do with the cub now?" a raucous voice came out of the darkness.

"Let him lie there," was the quick response. "It'll teach him to interfere with the work of honest patriots."

Kennard, lying somewhat bruised and stunned, heard this decree with thankfulness. The bandits obviously thought him more hurt than he was, and if only they would leave him lying here, he would soon pick himself up and renew his attempt to go to Esther. He did not move, feigning unconsciousness, even though he felt rather than saw that hideous Rateau stooping over him, heard his stertorous breathing, the wheezing in his throat.

"Run and fetch a bit of cord, citizen Desmonts," the wretch said presently. "A trussed cub is safer than a loose one."

This dashed Kennard's hopes to a great extent. He felt that he must act quickly, before those brigands returned and rendered him completely helpless. He made a movement to rise—a movement so swift and sudden as only a trained athlete can make. But, quick as he was, that odious, wheezing creature was quicker still, and now, when Kennard had turned on his back, Rateau promptly sat on his chest, a dead weight, with long legs stretched out before him, coughing and spluttering, yet wholly at his ease.

Oh! the humiliating position for an amateur middle-weight champion to find himself in, with that drink-sodden—Kennard was sure that he was drink-sodden—consumptive sprawling on the top of him!

"Don't trouble, citizen Desmonts," the wretch cried out after his retreating companions. "I have what I want by me."

Very leisurely he pulled a coil of rope out of the capacious pocket of his tattered coat. Kennard could not see what he was doing, but felt it with supersensitive instinct all the time. He lay quite still beneath the weight of that miscreant, feigning unconsciousness, yet hardly able to breathe. That tuberculous caitiff was such a towering weight. But he tried to keep his faculties on the alert, ready for that surprise spring which would turn the tables, at the slightest false move on the part of Rateau.

But, as luck would have it, Rateau did not make a single false move. It was amazing with what dexterity he kept Kennard down, even while he contrived to pinion him with cords. An old sailor, probably, he seemed so dexterous with knots.

My God! the humiliation of it all. And Esther a helpless prisoner, inside that house not five paces away! Kennard's heavy, wearied eyes could perceive the light in her window, five stories above where he lay, in the gutter, a helpless log. Even now he gave a last desperate shriek:

"Esther!"

But in a second the abominable brigand's hand came down heavily upon his mouth, whilst a raucous voice spluttered rather than said, right through an awful fit of coughing:

"Another sound, and I'll gag as well as bind you, you young fool!"

After which, Kennard remained quite still.

## VI

Esther, up in her little attic, knew nothing of what her English lover was even then suffering for her sake. She herself had passed, during the night, through every stage of horror and of fear. Soon after midnight that execrable brigand Rateau had poked his ugly, cadaverous face in at the door and peremptorily called for Lucienne. The woman, more dead than alive now with terror, had answered with mechanical obedience.

"I and my friends are thirsty," the man had commanded. "Go and fetch us a litre of *eau-de-vie*."

Poor Lucienne stammered a pitiable: "Where shall I go?"

"To the house at the sign of 'Le fort Samson,' in the Rue de Seine," replied Rateau curtly. "They'll serve you well if you mention my name."

Of course Lucienne protested. She was a decent woman, who had never been inside a cabaret in her life.

"Then it's time you began," was Rateau's dry comment, which was greeted with much laughter from his abominable companions.

Lucienne was forced to go. It would, of course, have been futile and madness to resist. This had occurred three hours since. The Rue de Seine was not far, but the poor woman had not returned. Esther was left with this additional horror weighing upon her soul. What had happened to her unfortunate servant? Visions of outrage and murder floated before the poor girl's tortured brain. At best, Lucienne was being kept out of the way in order to make her—Esther—feel more lonely and desperate! She remained at the window after that, watching that light in the house opposite and fingering her prayer-book, the only solace which she had. Her attic was so high up and the street so narrow, that she could not see what went on in the street below. At one time she heard a great to-do outside her door. It seemed as if some of the bloodhounds who were set to watch her had gone, or that others came. She really hardly cared which it was. Then she heard a great commotion coming from the street immediately beneath her: men shouting and laughing, and that awful creature's rasping cough.

At one moment she felt sure that Kennard had called to her by name. She heard his voice distinctly, raised as if in a despairing cry.

After that, all was still.

So still that she could hear her heart beating furiously, and then a tear falling from her eyes upon her open book. So still that the gentle patter of the rain sounded like a soothing lullaby. She was very young, and was very tired. Out, above the line of sloping roofs and chimney pots, the darkness of the sky was yielding to the first touch of dawn. The rain ceased. Everything became deathly still. Esther's head fell, wearied, upon her folded arms.

Then, suddenly, she was wide awake. Something had roused her. A noise. At first she could not tell what it was, but now she knew. It was the opening and shutting of the door behind her, and then a quick, stealthy footstep across the room. The horror of it all was unspeakable. Esther remained as she had been, on her knees, mechanically fingering her prayer-book, unable to move, unable to utter a sound, as if paralysed. She knew that one of those abominable creatures had entered her room, was coming near her even now. She did not know who it was, only guessed it was Rateau, for she heard a raucous, stertorous wheeze. Yet she could not have then turned to look if her life had depended upon her doing so.

The whole thing had occurred in less than half a dozen heart-beats. The next moment the wretch was close to her. Mercifully she felt that her senses were leaving her. Even so, she felt that a handkerchief was being bound over her mouth to prevent her screaming. Wholly unnecessary this, for she could not have uttered a sound. Then she was lifted off the ground and carried across the room, then over the threshold. A vague, subconscious effort of will helped her to keep her head averted from that wheezing wretch who was carrying her. Thus she could see the landing, and two of those abominable watchdogs who had been set to guard her.

The ghostly grey light of dawn came peeping in through the narrow dormer window in the sloping roof, and faintly illumined their sprawling forms, stretched out at full length, with their heads buried in their folded arms and their naked legs looking pallid and weird in the dim light. Their stertorous breathing woke the echoes of the bare, stone walls. Esther shuddered and closed her eyes. She was now like an insentient log, without power, or thought, or will—almost without feeling.

Then, all at once, the coolness of the morning air caught her full in the face. She opened her eyes and tried to move, but those powerful arms held her more closely than before. Now she could have shrieked with horror. With returning consciousness the sense of her desperate position came on her with its full and ghastly significance, its awe-inspiring details. The grey dawn, the abandoned wretch who held her, and the stillness of this early morning hour, when not one pitying soul would be astir to lend her a helping hand or give her the solace of mute sympathy. So great, indeed, was this stillness that the click of the man's sabots upon the uneven pavement reverberated, ghoul-like and weird.

And it was through that awesome stillness that a sound suddenly struck her ear, which, in the instant, made her feel that she was not really alive, or, if alive, was sleeping and dreaming strange and impossible dreams. It was the sound of a voice, clear and firm, and with a wonderful ring of merriment in its tones, calling out just above a whisper, and in English, if you please:

"Look out, Ffoulkes! That young cub is as strong as a horse. He will give us all away if you are not careful."

A dream? Of course it was a dream, for the voice had sounded very close to her ear; so close, in fact, that . . . well! Esther was quite sure that her face still rested against the hideous, tattered, and grimy coat which that repulsive Rateau had been wearing all along. And there was the click of his sabots upon the pavement all the time. So, then, the voice and the merry, suppressed laughter which accompanied it, must all have been a part of her dream. How long this lasted she could not have told you. An hour and more, she thought, while the grey dawn yielded to the roseate hue of morning. Somehow, she no longer suffered either terror or foreboding. A subtle atmosphere of strength and of security seemed to encompass her. At one time she felt as if she were driven along in a car that jolted horribly, and when she moved her face and hands they came in contact with things that were fresh and green and smelt of the country. She was in darkness then, and more than three parts unconscious, but the handkerchief had been removed from her mouth. It seemed to her as if she could hear the voice of her Jack, but far away and indistinct; also the tramp of horses' hoofs and the creaking of cart-wheels, and at times that awful, rasping cough, which reminded her of the presence of a loathsome wretch, who should not have had a part in her soothing dream.

Thus many hours must have gone by.

Then, all at once, she was inside a house—a room, and she felt that she was being lowered very gently to the ground. She was on her feet, but she could not see where she was. There was furniture; a carpet; a ceiling; the man Rateau with the sabots and the dirty coat, and the merry English voice, and a pair of deep-set blue eyes, thoughtful and lazy and infinitely kind.

But before she could properly focus what she saw, everything began to whirl and to spin around her, to dance a wild and idiotic saraband, which caused her to laugh, and to laugh, until her throat felt choked and her eyes hot; after which she remembered nothing more.

## VII

The first thing of which Esther Vincent was conscious, when she returned to her senses, was of her English lover kneeling beside her. She was lying on some kind of couch, and she could see his face in profile, for he had turned and was speaking to someone at the far end of the room.

"And was it you who knocked me down?" he was saying, "and sat on my chest, and trussed me like a fowl?"

"La! my dear sir," a lazy, pleasant voice riposted, "what else could I do? There was no time for explanations. You were half-crazed, and would not have understood. And you were ready to bring all the nightwatchmen about our ears."

"I am sorry!" Kennard said simply. "But how could I guess?"

"You couldn't," rejoined the other. "That is why I had to deal so summarily with you and with Mademoiselle Esther, not to speak of good old Lucienne, who had never, in her life, been inside a cabaret. You must all forgive me ere you start upon your journey. You are not out of the wood yet, remember. Though Paris is a long way behind, France itself is no longer a healthy place for any of you."

"But how did we ever get out of Paris? I was smothered under a pile of cabbages, with Lucienne on one side of me and Esther, unconscious, on the other. I could see nothing. I know we halted at the barrier. I thought we would be recognised, turned back! My God! how I trembled!"

"Bah!" broke in the other, with a careless laugh. "It is not so difficult as it seems. We have done it before—eh, Ffoulkes? A market-gardener's cart, a villainous wretch like myself to drive it, another hideous object like Sir Andrew Ffoulkes, Bart., to lead the scraggy nag, a couple of forged or stolen passports, plenty of English gold, and the deed is done!"

Esther's eyes were fixed upon the speaker. She marvelled now how she could have been so blind. The cadaverous face was nothing but a splendid use of grease paint! The rags! the dirt! the whole assumption of a hideous character was masterly! But there were the eyes, deep-set, and thoughtful and kind. How did she fail to guess?

"You are known as the Scarlet Pimpernel," she said suddenly. "Suzanne de Tournai was my friend. She told me. You saved her and her family, and now . . . oh, my God!" she exclaimed, "how shall we ever repay you?"

"By placing yourselves unreservedly in my friend Ffoulkes' hands," he replied gently. "He will lead you to safety and, if you wish it, to England."

"If we wish it!" Kennard sighed fervently.

"You are not coming with us, Blakeney?" queried Sir Andrew Ffoulkes, and it seemed to Esther's sensitive ears as if a tone of real anxiety and also of entreaty rang in the young man's voice.

"No, not this time," replied Sir Percy lightly. "I like my character of Rateau, and I don't want to give it up just yet. I have done nothing to arouse suspicion in the minds of my savoury compeers up at the Cabaret de la Liberte. I can easily keep this up for some time to come, and frankly I admire myself as citizen Rateau. I don't know when I have enjoyed a character so much!"

"You mean to return to the Cabaret de la Liberte!" exclaimed Sir Andrew.

"Why not?"

"You will be recognised!"

"Not before I have been of service to a good many unfortunates, I hope."

"But that awful cough of yours! Percy, you'll do yourself an injury with it one day."

"Not I! I like that cough. I practised it for a long time before I did it to perfection. Such a splendid wheeze! I must teach Tony to do it some day. Would you like to hear it now?"

He laughed, that perfect, delightful, lazy laugh of his, which carried every hearer with it along the path of light-hearted merriment. Then he broke into the awful cough of the consumptive Rateau. And Esther Vincent instinctively closed her eyes and shuddered.

# "NEEDS MUST-"

## I

The children were all huddled up together in one corner of the room. Etienne and Valentine, the two eldest, had their arms round the little one. As for Lucile, she would have told you herself that she felt just like a bird between two snakes—terrified and fascinated—oh! especially by that little man with the pale face and the light grey eyes and the slender white hands unstained by toil, one of which rested lightly upon the desk, and was only clenched now and then at a word or a look from the other man or from Lucile herself.

But Commissary Lebel just tried to browbeat her. It was not difficult, for in truth she felt frightened enough already, with all this talk of "traitors" and that awful threat of the guillotine.

Lucile Clamette, however, would have remained splendidly loyal in spite of all these threats, if it had not been for the children. She was little mother to them; for father was a cripple, with speech and mind already impaired by creeping paralysis, and *maman* had died when little Josephine was born. And now those fiends threatened not only her, but Etienne who was not fourteen, and Valentine who was not much more than ten, with death, unless she—Lucile—broke the solemn word which she had given to M. le Marquis. At first she had tried to deny all knowledge of M. le Marquis' whereabouts.

"I can assure M. le Commissaire that I do not know," she had persisted quietly, even though her heart was beating so rapidly in her bosom that she felt as if she must choke.

"Call me citizen Commissary," Lebel had riposted curtly. "I should take it as a proof that your aristocratic sentiments are not so deep-rooted as they appear to be."

"Yes, citizen!" murmured Lucile, under her breath.

Then the other one, he with the pale eyes and the slender white hands, leaned forward over the desk, and the poor girl felt as if a mighty and unseen force was holding her tight, so tight that she could neither move, nor breathe, nor turn her gaze away from those pale, compelling eyes. In the remote corner little Josephine was whimpering, and Etienne's big, dark eyes were fixed bravely upon his eldest sister.

"There, there! little citizeness," the awful man said, in a voice that sounded low and almost caressing, "there is nothing to be frightened of. No one is going to hurt you or your little family. We only want you to be reasonable. You have promised to your former employer that you would never tell anyone of his whereabouts. Well! we don't ask you to tell us anything.

"All that we want you to do is to write a letter to M. le Marquis —one that I myself will dictate to you. You have written to M. le Marquis before now, on business matters, have you not?"

"Yes, monsieur—yes, citizen," stammered Lucile through her tears. "Father was bailiff to M. le Marquis until he became a cripple and now I—-"

"Do not write any letter, Lucile," Etienne suddenly broke in with forceful vehemence. "It is a trap set by these miscreants to entrap M. le Marquis."

There was a second's silence in the room after this sudden outburst on the part of the lad. Then the man with the pale face said quietly:

"Citizen Lebel, order the removal of that boy. Let him be kept in custody till he has learned to hold his tongue."

But before Lebel could speak to the two soldiers who were standing on guard at the door, Lucile had uttered a loud cry of agonised protest.

"No! no! monsieur!—that is citizen!" she implored. "Do not take Etienne away. He will be silent . . . I promise you that he will be silent . . . only do not take him away! Etienne, my little one!" she added, turning her tear-filled eyes to her brother, "I entreat thee to hold thy tongue!"

The others, too, clung to Etienne, and the lad, awed and subdued, relapsed into silence.

"Now then," resumed Lebel roughly, after a while, "let us get on with this business. I am sick to death of it. It has lasted far too long already."

He fixed his blood-shot eyes upon Lucile and continued gruffly:

"Now listen to me, my wench, for this is going to be my last word. Citizen Chauvelin here has already been very lenient with you by allowing this letter business. If I had my way I'd make you speak here and now. As it is, you either sit down and write the letter at citizen Chauvelin's dictation at once, or I send you with that impudent brother of yours and your imbecile father to jail, on a charge of treason against the State, for aiding and abetting the enemies of the Republic; and you know what the consequences of such a charge usually are. The other two brats will go to a House of Correction, there to be detained during the pleasure of the Committee of Public Safety. That is my last word," he reiterated fiercely. "Now, which is it to be?"

He paused, the girl's wan cheeks turned the colour of lead. She moistened her lips once or twice with her tongue; beads of perspiration appeared at the roots of her hair. She gazed helplessly at her tormentors, not daring to look on those three huddled-up little figures there in the corner. A few seconds sped away in silence. The man with the pale eyes rose and pushed his chair away. He went to the window, stood there with his back to the room, those slender white hands of his clasped behind him. Neither the commissary nor the girl appeared to interest him further. He was just gazing out of the window.

The other was still sprawling beside the desk, his large, coarse hand—how different his hands were!—was beating a devil's tatoo upon the arm of his chair.

After a few minutes, Lucile made a violent effort to compose herself, wiped the moisture from her pallid forehead and dried the tears which still hung upon her lashes. Then she rose from her chair and walked resolutely up to the desk.

"I will write the letter," she said simply.

Lebel gave a snort of satisfaction; but the other did not move from his position near the window. The boy, Etienne, had uttered a cry of passionate protest.

"Do not give M. le Marquis away, Lucile!" he said hotly. "I am not afraid to die."

But Lucile had made up her mind. How could she do otherwise, with these awful threats hanging over them all? She and Etienne and poor father gone, and the two young ones in one of those awful Houses of Correction, where children were taught to hate the Church, to shun the Sacraments, and to blaspheme God!

"What am I to write?" she asked dully, resolutely closing her ears against her brother's protest.

Lebel pushed pen, ink and paper towards her and she sat down, ready to begin.

"Write!" now came in a curt command from the man at the window. And Lucile wrote at his dictation:

"*Monsieur Le Marquis*,—We are in grave trouble. My brother Etienne and I have been arrested on a charge of treason. This means the guillotine for us and for poor father, who can no longer speak; and the two little ones are to be sent to one of those dreadful Houses of Correction, where children are taught to deny God and to blaspheme. You alone can save us, M. le Marquis; and I beg you on my knees to do it. The citizen Commissary here says that you have in your possession certain papers which are of great value to the State, and that if I can persuade you to give these up, Etienne, father and I and the little ones will be left unmolested. M. le Marquis, you once said that you could never adequately repay my poor father for all his devotion in your service. You can do it now, M. le Marquis, by saving us all. I will be at the chateau a week from to-day. I entreat you, M. le Marquis, to come to me then and to bring the papers with you; or if you can devise some other means of sending the papers to me, I will obey your behests.—I am, M. le Marquis' faithful and devoted servant,
    *Lucile Clamette.*"

The pen dropped from the unfortunate girl's fingers. She buried her face in her hands and sobbed convulsively. The children were silent, awed and subdued—tired out, too. Only Etienne's dark eyes were fixed upon his sister with a look of mute reproach.

Lebel had made no attempt to interrupt the flow of his colleague's dictation. Only once or twice did a hastily smothered "What the—-!" of astonishment escape his lips. Now, when the letter was finished and duly signed, he drew it to him and strewed the sand over it. Chauvelin, more impassive than ever, was once more gazing out of the window.

"How are the *ci-devant aristos* to get this letter?" the commissary asked.

"It must be put in the hollow tree which stands by the side of the stable gate at Montorgueil," whispered Lucile.

"And the *aristos* will find it there?"

"Yes. M. le Vicomte goes there once or twice a week to see if there is anything there from one of us."

"They are in hiding somewhere close by, then?"

But to this the girl gave no reply. Indeed, she felt as if any word now might choke her.

"Well, no matter where they are!" the inhuman wretch resumed, with brutal cynicism. "We've got them now—both of them. Marquis! Vicomte!" he added, and spat on the ground to express his contempt of such titles. "Citizens Montorgueil, father and son—that's all they are! And as such they'll walk up in state to make their bow to Mme. la Guillotine!"

"May we go now?" stammered Lucile through her tears.

Lebel nodded in assent, and the girl rose and turned to walk towards the door. She called to the children, and the little ones clustered round her skirts like chicks around the mother-hen. Only Etienne remained aloof, wrathful against his sister for what he deemed her treachery. "Women have no sense of honour!" he muttered to himself, with all the pride of conscious manhood. But Lucile felt more than ever like a bird who is vainly trying to evade the clutches of a fowler. She gathered the two little ones around her. Then, with a cry like a wounded doe she ran quickly out of the room.

## II

As soon as the sound of the children's footsteps had died away down the corridor, Lebel turned with a grunt to his still silent companion.

"And now, citizen Chauvelin," he said roughly, "perhaps you will be good enough to explain what is the meaning of all this tomfoolery."

"Tomfoolery, citizen?" queried the other blandly. "What tomfoolery, pray?"

"Why, about those papers!" growled Lebel savagely. "Curse you for an interfering busybody! It was I who got information that those pestilential *aristos*, the Montorgueils, far from having fled the country are in hiding somewhere in my district. I could have made the girl give up their hiding-place pretty soon, without any help from you. What right had you to interfere, I should like to know?"

"You know quite well what right I had, citizen Lebel," replied Chauvelin with perfect composure. "The right conferred upon me by the Committee of Public Safety, of whom I am still an unworthy member. They sent me down here to lend you a hand in an investigation which is of grave importance to them."

"I know that!" retorted Lebel sulkily. "But why have invented the story of the papers?"

"It is no invention, citizen," rejoined Chauvelin with slow emphasis. "The papers do exist. They are actually in the possession of the Montorgueils, father and son. To capture the two *aristos* would be not only a blunder, but criminal folly, unless we can lay hands on the papers at the same time."

"But what in Satan's name are those papers?" ejaculated Lebel with a fierce oath.

"Think, citizen Lebel! Think!" was Chauvelin's cool rejoinder. "Methinks you might arrive at a pretty shrewd guess." Then, as the other's bluster and bounce suddenly collapsed upon his colleague's calm, accusing gaze, the latter continued with impressive deliberation:

"The papers which the two *aristos* have in their possession, citizen, are receipts for money, for bribes paid to various members of the Committee of Public Safety by Royalist agents for the overthrow of our glorious Republic. You know all about them, do you not?"

While Chauvelin spoke, a look of furtive terror had crept into Lebel's eyes; his cheeks became the colour of lead. But even so, he tried to keep up an air of incredulity and of amazement.

"I?" he exclaimed. "What do you mean, citizen Chauvelin? What should I know about it?"

"Some of those receipts are signed with your name, citizen Lebel," retorted Chauvelin forcefully. "Bah!" he added, and a tone of savage contempt crept into his even, calm voice now. "Heriot, Foucquier, Ducros and the whole gang of you are in it up to the neck: trafficking with our enemies, trading with England, taking bribes from every quarter for working against the safety of the Republic. Ah! if I had my way, I would let the hatred of those *aristos* take its course. I would let the Montorgueils and the whole pack of Royalist agents publish those infamous proofs of your treachery and of your baseness to the entire world, and send the whole lot of you to the guillotine!"

He had spoken with so much concentrated fury, and the hatred and contempt expressed in his pale eyes were so fierce that an involuntary ice-cold shiver ran down the length of Lebel's spine. But, even so, he would not give in; he tried to sneer and to keep up something of his former surly defiance.

"Bah!" he exclaimed, and with a lowering glance gave hatred for hatred, and contempt for contempt. "What can you do? An I am not mistaken, there is no more discredited man in France to-day than the unsuccessful tracker of the Scarlet Pimpernel."

The taunt went home. It was Chauvelin's turn now to lose countenance, to pale to the lips. The glow of virtuous indignation died out of his eyes, his look became furtive and shamed.

"You are right, citizen Lebel," he said calmly after a while. "Recriminations between us are out of place. I am a discredited man, as you say. Perhaps it would have been better if the Committee had sent me long ago to expiate my failures on the guillotine. I should at least not have suffered, as I am suffering now, daily, hourly humiliation at thought of the triumph of an enemy, whom I hate with a passion which consumes my very soul. But do not let us speak of me," he went on quietly. "There are graver affairs at stake just now than mine own."

Lebel said nothing more for the moment. Perhaps he was satisfied at the success of his taunt, even though the terror within his craven soul still caused the cold shiver to course up and down his spine. Chauvelin had once more turned to the window; his gaze was fixed upon the distance far away. The window gave on the North. That way, in a straight line, lay Calais, Boulogne, England—where he had been made to suffer such bitter humiliation at the hands of his elusive enemy. And immediately before him was Paris, where the very walls seemed to echo that mocking laugh of the daring Englishman which would haunt him even to his grave.

Lebel, unnerved by his colleague's silence, broke in gruffly at last:

"Well then, citizen," he said, with a feeble attempt at another sneer, "if you are not thinking of sending us all to the guillotine just yet, perhaps you will be good enough to explain just how the matter stands?"

"Fairly simply, alas!" replied Chauvelin dryly. "The two Montorgueils, father and son, under assumed names, were the Royalist agents who succeeded in suborning men such as you, citizen—the whole gang of you. We have tracked them down, to this district, have confiscated their lands and ransacked the old chateau for valuables and so on. Two days later, the first of a series of pestilential anonymous letters reached the Committee of Public Safety, threatening the publication of a whole series of compromising documents if the

Marquis and the Vicomte de Montorgueil were in any way molested, and if all the Montorgueil property is not immediately restored."

"I suppose it is quite certain that those receipts and documents do exist?" suggested Lebel.

"Perfectly certain. One of the receipts, signed by Heriot, was sent as a specimen."

"My God!" ejaculated Lebel, and wiped the cold sweat from his brow.

"Yes, you'll all want help from somewhere," retorted Chauvelin coolly. "From above or from below, what? if the people get to know what miscreants you are. I do believe," he added, with a vicious snap of his thin lips, "that they would cheat the guillotine of you and, in the end, drag you out of the tumbrils and tear you to pieces limb from limb!"

Once more that look of furtive terror crept into the commissary's bloodshot eyes.

"Thank the Lord," he muttered, "that we were able to get hold of the wench Clamette!"

"At my suggestion," retorted Chauvelin curtly. "I always believe in threatening the weak if you want to coerce the strong. The Montorgueils cannot resist the wench's appeal. Even if they do at first, we can apply the screw by clapping one of the young ones in gaol. Within a week we shall have those papers, citizen Lebel; and if, in the meanwhile, no one commits a further blunder, we can close the trap on the Montorgueils without further trouble."

Lebel said nothing more, and after a while Chauvelin went back to the desk, picked up the letter which poor Lucile had written and watered with her tears, folded it deliberately and slipped it into the inner pocket of his coat.

"What are you going to do?" queried Lebel anxiously.

"Drop this letter into the hollow tree by the side of the stable gate at Montorgueil," replied Chauvelin simply.

"What?" exclaimed the other. "Yourself?"

"Why, of course! Think you I would entrust such an errand to another living soul?"

## III

A couple of hours later, when the two children had had their dinner and had settled down to play in the garden, and father been cosily tucked up for his afternoon sleep, Lucile called her brother Etienne to her. The boy had not spoken to her since that terrible time spent in the presence of those two awful men. He had eaten no dinner, only sat glowering, staring straight out before him, from time to time throwing a look of burning reproach upon his sister. Now, when she called to him, he tried to run away, was halfway up the stairs before she could seize hold of him.

"*Etienne, mon petit!*" she implored, as her arms closed around his shrinking figure.

"Let me go, Lucile!" the boy pleaded obstinately.

"*Mon petit*, listen to me!" she pleaded. "All is not lost, if you will stand by me."

"All is lost, Lucile!" Etienne cried, striving to keep back a flood of passionate tears. "Honour is lost. Your treachery has disgraced us all. If M. le Marquis and M. le Vicomte are brought to the guillotine, their blood will be upon our heads."

"Upon mine alone, my little Etienne," she said sadly. "But God alone can judge me. It was a terrible alternative: M. le Marquis, or you and Valentine and little Josephine and poor father, who is so helpless! But don't let us talk of it. All is not lost, I am sure. The last time that I spoke with M. le Marquis—it was in February, do you remember?—he was full of hope, and oh! so kind. Well, he told me then that if ever I or any of us here were in such grave trouble that we did not know where to turn, one of us was to put on our very oldest clothes, look as like a bare-footed beggar as we could, and then go to Paris to a place called the Cabaret de la Liberte in the Rue Christine. There we were to ask for the citizen Rateau, and we were to tell him all our troubles, whatever they might be. Well! we are in such trouble now, *mon petit*, that we don't know where to turn. Put on thy very oldest clothes, little one, and run bare-footed into Paris, find the citizen Rateau and tell him just what has happened: the letter which they have forced me to write, the threats which they held over me if I did not write it—everything. Dost hear?"

Already the boy's eyes were glowing. The thought that he individually could do something to retrieve the awful shame of his sister's treachery spurred him to activity. It needed no persuasion on Lucile's part to induce him to go. She made him put on some old clothes and stuffed a piece of bread and cheese into his breeches pocket.

It was close upon a couple of leagues to Paris, but that run was one of the happiest which Etienne had ever made. And he did it bare-footed, too, feeling neither fatigue nor soreness, despite the hardness of the road after a two weeks' drought, which had turned mud into hard cakes and ruts into fissures which tore the lad's feet till they bled.

He did not reach the Cabaret de la Liberte till nightfall, and when he got there he hardly dared to enter. The filth, the squalor, the hoarse voices which rose from that cellar-like place below the level of the street, repelled the country-bred lad. Were it not for the desperate urgency of his errand he never would have dared to enter. As it was, the fumes of alcohol and steaming, dirty clothes nearly choked him, and he could scarce stammer the name of "citizen Rateau" when a gruff voice presently demanded his purpose.

He realised now how tired he was and how hungry. He had not thought to pause in order to consume the small provision of bread and cheese wherewith thoughtful Lucile had provided him. Now he was ready to faint when a loud guffaw, which echoed from one end of the horrible place to the other, greeted his timid request.

"Citizen Rateau!" the same gruff voice called out hilariously. "Why, there he is! Here, citizen! there's a blooming *aristo* to see you."

Etienne turned his weary eyes to the corner which was being indicated to him. There he saw a huge creature sprawling across a bench, with long, powerful limbs stretched out before him. Citizen Rateau was clothed, rather than dressed, in a soiled shirt, ragged breeches and tattered stockings, with shoes down at heel and faded crimson cap. His face looked congested and sunken about the eyes; he appeared to be asleep, for stertorous breathing came at intervals from between his parted lips, whilst every now and then a racking cough seemed to tear at his broad chest.

Etienne gave him one look, shuddering with horror, despite himself, at the aspect of this bloated wretch from whom salvation was to come. The whole place seemed to him hideous and loathsome in the extreme. What it all meant he could not understand; all that he knew was that this seemed like another hideous trap into which he and Lucile had fallen, and that he must fly from it—fly at all costs, before he betrayed M. le Marquis still further to these drink-sodden brutes. Another moment, and he feared that he might faint. The din of a bibulous song rang in his ears, the reek of alcohol turned him giddy and sick. He had only just enough strength to turn and totter back into the open. There his senses reeled, the lights in the houses opposite began to dance wildly before his eyes, after which he remembered nothing more.

IV

There is nothing now in the whole countryside quite so desolate and forlorn as the chateau of Montorgueil, with its once magnificent park, now overgrown with weeds, its encircling walls broken down, its terraces devastated, and its stately gates rusty and torn.

Just by the side of what was known in happier times as the stable gate there stands a hollow tree. It is not inside the park, but just outside, and shelters the narrow lane, which skirts the park walls, against the blaze of the afternoon sun.

Its beneficent shade is a favourite spot for an afternoon siesta, for there is a bit of green sward under the tree, and all along the side of the road. But as the shades of evening gather in, the lane is usually deserted, shunned by the neighbouring peasantry on account of its eerie loneliness, so different to the former bustle which used to reign around the park gates when M. le Marquis and his family were still in residence. Nor does the lane lead anywhere, for it is a mere loop which gives on the main road at either end.

Henri de Montorgueil chose a peculiarly dark night in mid-September for one of his periodical visits to the hollow-tree. It was close on nine o'clock when he passed stealthily down the lane, keeping close to the park wall. A soft rain was falling, the first since the prolonged drought, and though it made the road heavy and slippery in places, it helped to deaden the sound of the young man's furtive footsteps. The air, except for the patter of the rain, was absolutely still. Henri de Montorgueil paused from time to time, with neck craned forward, every sense on the alert, listening, like any poor, hunted beast, for the slightest sound which might betray the approach of danger.

As many a time before, he reached the hollow tree in safety, felt for and found in the usual place the letter which the unfortunate girl Lucile had written to him. Then, with it in his hand, he turned to the stable gate. It had long since ceased to be kept locked and barred. Pillaged and ransacked by order of the Committee of Public Safety, there was nothing left inside the park walls worth keeping under lock and key.

Henri slipped stealthily through the gates and made his way along the drive. Every stone, every nook and cranny of his former home was familiar to him, and anon he turned into a shed where in former times wheelbarrows and garden tools were wont to be kept. Now it was full of debris, lumber of every sort. A more safe or secluded spot could not be imagined. Henri crouched in the furthermost corner of the shed. Then from his belt he detached a small dark lanthorn, opened its shutter, and with the aid of the tiny, dim light read the contents of the letter. For a long while after that he remained quite still, as still as a man who has received a stunning blow on the head and has partly lost consciousness. The blow was indeed a staggering one. Lucile Clamette, with the invincible power of her own helplessness, was demanding the surrender of a weapon which had been a safeguard for the Montorgueils all this while. The papers which compromised a number of influential members of the Committee of Public Safety had been the most perfect arms of defence against persecution and spoliation.

And now these were to be given up: Oh! there could be no question of that. Even before consulting with his father, Henri knew that the papers would have to be given up. They were clever, those revolutionaries. The thought of holding innocent children as hostages could only have originated in minds attuned to the villainies of devils. But it was unthinkable that the children should suffer.

After a while the young man roused himself from the torpor

into which the suddenness of this awful blow had plunged him. By the light of the lanthorn he began to write upon a sheet of paper which he had torn from his pocket-book.

"My dear Lucile," he wrote, "As you say, our debt to your father and to you all never could be adequately repaid. You and the children shall never suffer whilst we have the power to save you. You will find the papers in the receptacle you know of inside the chimney of what used to be my mother's boudoir. You will find the receptacle unlocked. One day before the term you name I myself will place the papers there for you. With them, my father and I do give up our lives to save you and the little ones from the persecution of those fiends. May the good God guard you all."

He signed the letter with his initials, H. de M. Then he crept back to the gate and dropped the message into the hollow of the tree.

A quarter of an hour later Henri de Montorgueil was wending his way back to the hiding place which had sheltered him and his father for so long. Silence and darkness then held undisputed sway once more around the hollow tree. Even the rain had ceased its gentle pattering. Anon from far away came the sound of a church bell striking the hour of ten. Then nothing more.

A few more minutes of absolute silence, then something dark and furtive began to move out of the long grass which bordered the roadside—something that in movement was almost like a snake. It dragged itself along close to the ground, making no sound as it moved. Soon it reached the hollow tree, rose to the height of a man and flattened itself against the tree-trunk. Then it put out a hand, felt for the hollow receptacle and groped for the missive which Henri de Montorgueil had dropped in there a while ago.

The next moment a tiny ray of light gleamed through the darkness like a star. A small, almost fragile, figure of a man, dressed in the mud-stained clothes of a country yokel, had turned up the shutter of a small lanthorn. By its flickering light he deciphered the letter which Henri de Montorgueil had written to Lucile Clamette.

"One day before the term you name I myself will place the papers there for you."

A sigh of satisfaction, quickly suppressed, came through his thin, colourless lips, and the light of the lanthorn caught the flash of triumph in his pale, inscrutable eyes.

Then the light was extinguished. Impenetrable darkness swallowed up that slender, mysterious figure again.

V

Six days had gone by since Chauvelin had delivered his cruel "either—or" to poor little Lucile Clamette; three since he had found

Henri de Montorgueil's reply to the girl's appeal in the hollow of the tree. Since then he had made a careful investigation of the chateau, and soon was able to settle it in his own mind as to which room had been Madame la Marquise's boudoir in the past. It was a small apartment, having direct access on the first landing of the staircase, and the one window gave on the rose garden at the back of the house. Inside the monumental hearth, at an arm's length up the wide chimney, a receptacle had been contrived in the brickwork, with a small iron door which opened and closed with a secret spring. Chauvelin, whom his nefarious calling had rendered proficient in such matters, had soon mastered the workings of that spring. He could now open and close the iron door at will.

Up to a late hour on the sixth night of this weary waiting, the receptacle inside the chimney was still empty. That night Chauvelin had determined to spend at the chateau. He could not have rested elsewhere.

Even his colleague Lebel could not know what the possession of those papers would mean to the discredited agent of the Committee of Public Safety. With them in his hands, he could demand rehabilitation, and could purchase immunity from those sneers which had been so galling to his arrogant soul—sneers which had become more and more marked, more and more unendurable, and more and more menacing, as he piled up failure on failure with every encounter with the Scarlet Pimpernel.

Immunity and rehabilitation! This would mean that he could once more measure his wits and his power with that audacious enemy who had brought about his downfall.

"In the name of Satan, bring us those papers!" Robespierre himself had cried with unwonted passion, ere he sent him out on this important mission. "We none of us could stand the scandal of such disclosures. It would mean absolute ruin for us all."

And Chauvelin that night, as soon as the shades of evening had drawn in, took up his stand in the chateau, in the small inner room which was contiguous to the boudoir.

Here he sat, beside the open window, for hour upon hour, his every sense on the alert, listening for the first footfall upon the gravel path below. Though the hours went by leaden-footed, he was neither excited nor anxious. The Clamette family was such a precious hostage that the Montorgueils were bound to comply with Lucile's demand for the papers by every dictate of honour and of humanity.

"While we have those people in our power," Chauvelin had reiterated to himself more than once during the course of his long vigil, "even that meddlesome Scarlet Pimpernel can do nothing to save those cursed Montorgueils."

The night was dark and still. Not a breath of air stirred the branches of the trees or the shrubberies in the park; any footsteps, however wary, must echo through that perfect and absolute silence. Chauvelin's keen, pale eyes tried to pierce the gloom in the direction whence in all probability the *aristo* would come. Vaguely he wondered if it would be Henri de Montorgueil or the old Marquis himself who would bring the papers.

"Bah! whichever one it is," he muttered, "we can easily get the other, once those abominable papers are in our hands. And even if both the *aristos* escape," he added mentally, "'tis no matter, once we have the papers."

Anon, far away a distant church bell struck the midnight hour. The stillness of the air had become oppressive. A kind of torpor born of intense fatigue lulled the Terrorist's senses to somnolence. His head fell forward on his breast. . . .

VI

Then suddenly a shiver of excitement went right through him. He was fully awake now, with glowing eyes wide open and the icy calm of perfect confidence ruling every nerve. The sound of stealthy footsteps had reached his ear.

He could see nothing, either outside or in; but his fingers felt for the pistol which he carried in his belt. The *aristo* was evidently alone; only one solitary footstep was approaching the chateau.

Chauvelin had left the door ajar which gave on the boudoir. The staircase was on the other side of that fateful room, and the door leading to that was closed. A few minutes of tense expectancy went by. Then through the silence there came the sound of furtive foot-steps on the stairs, the creaking of a loose board and finally the stealthy opening of the door.

In all his adventurous career Chauvelin had never felt so calm. His heart beat quite evenly, his senses were undisturbed by the slightest tingling of his nerves. The stealthy sounds in the next room brought the movements of the *aristo* perfectly clear before his mental vision. The latter was carrying a small dark lanthorn. As soon as he entered he flashed its light about the room. Then he deposited the lanthorn on the floor, close beside the hearth, and started to feel up the chimney for the hidden receptacle.

Chauvelin watched him now like a cat watches a mouse, savouring these few moments of anticipated triumph. He pushed open the door noiselessly which gave on the boudoir. By the feeble light of the lanthorn on the ground he could only see the vague outline of the *aristo's* back, bending forward to his task; but a thrill went through him as he saw a bundle of papers lying on the ground close by.

Everything was ready; the trap was set. Here was a complete

victory at last. It was obviously the young Vicomte de Montorgueil who had come to do the deed. His head was up the chimney even now. The old Marquis's back would have looked narrower and more fragile. Chauvelin held his breath; then he gave a sharp little cough, and took the pistol from his belt.

The sound caused the *aristo* to turn, and the next moment a loud and merry laugh roused the dormant echoes of the old chateau, whilst a pleasant, drawly voice said in English:

"I am demmed if this is not my dear old friend M. Chambertin! Zounds, sir! who'd have thought of meeting you here?"

Had a cannon suddenly exploded at Chauvelin's feet he would, I think, have felt less unnerved. For the space of two heart-beats he stood there, rooted to the spot, his eyes glued on his arch-enemy, that execrated Scarlet Pimpernel, whose mocking glance, even through the intervening gloom, seemed to have deprived him of consciousness. But that phase of helplessness only lasted for a moment; the next, all the marvellous possibilities of this encounter flashed through the Terrorist's keen mind.

Everything was ready; the trap was set! The unfortunate Clamettes were still the bait which now would bring a far more noble quarry into the mesh than even he—Chauvelin—had dared to hope.

He raised his pistol, ready to fire. But already Sir Percy Blakeney was on him, and with a swift movement, which the other was too weak to resist, he wrenched the weapon from his enemy's grasp.

"Why, how hasty you are, my dear M. Chambertin," he said lightly.

"Surely you are not in such a hurry to put a demmed bullet into me!"

The position now was one which would have made even a braver man than Chauvelin quake. He stood alone and unarmed in face of an enemy from whom he could expect no mercy. But, even so, his first thought was not of escape. He had not only apprised his own danger, but also the immense power which he held whilst the Clamettes remained as hostages in the hands of his colleague Lebel.

"You have me at a disadvantage, Sir Percy," he said, speaking every whit as coolly as his foe. "But only momentarily. You can kill me, of course; but if I do not return from this expedition not only safe and sound, but with a certain packet of papers in my hands, my colleague Lebel has instructions to proceed at once against the girl Clamette and the whole family."

"I know that well enough," rejoined Sir Percy with a quaint laugh. "I know what venomous reptiles you and those of your kidney are. You certainly do owe your life at the present moment to the unfortunate girl whom you are persecuting with such infamous callousness."

Chauvelin drew a sigh of relief. The situation was shaping itself more to his satisfaction already. Through the gloom he could vaguely discern the Englishman's massive form standing a few paces away, one hand buried in his breeches pockets, the other still holding the pistol. On the ground close by the hearth was the small lanthorn, and in its dim light the packet of papers gleamed white and tempting in the darkness. Chauvelin's keen eyes had fastened on it, saw the form of receipt for money with Heriot's signature, which he recognised, on the top.

He himself had never felt so calm. The only thing he could regret was that he was alone. Half a dozen men now, and this impudent foe could indeed be brought to his knees. And this time there would be no risks taken, no chances for escape. Somehow it seemed to Chauvelin as if something of the Scarlet Pimpernel's audacity and foresight had gone from him. As he stood there, looking broad and physically powerful, there was something wavering and undecided in his attitude, as if the edge had been taken off his former recklessness and enthusiasm. He had brought the compromising papers here, had no doubt helped the Montorgueils to escape; but while Lucile Clamette and her family were under the eye of Lebel no amount of impudence could force a successful bargaining.

It was Chauvelin now who appeared the more keen and the more alert; the Englishman seemed undecided what to do next, remained silent, toying with the pistol. He even smothered a yawn. Chauvelin saw his opportunity. With the quick movement of a cat pouncing upon a mouse he stooped and seized that packet of papers, would then and there have made a dash for the door with them, only that, as he seized the packet, the string which held it together gave way and the papers were scattered all over the floor.

Receipts for money? Compromising letters? No! Blank sheets of paper, all of them—all except the one which had lain tantalisingly on the top: the one receipt signed by citizen Heriot. Sir Percy laughed lightly:

"Did you really think, my good friend," he said, "that I would be such a demmed fool as to place my best weapon so readily to your hand?"

"Your best weapon, Sir Percy!" retorted Chauvelin, with a sneer. "What use is it to you while we hold Lucile Clamette?"

"While I hold Lucile Clamette, you mean, my dear Monsieur Chambertin," riposted Blakeney with elaborate blandness.

"You hold Lucile Clamette? Bah! I defy you to drag a whole family like that out of our clutches. The man a cripple, the children helpless! And you think they can escape our vigilance when all our men are warned! How do you think they are going to get across the river, Sir Percy, when every bridge is closely watched? How will they get across

Paris, when at every gate our men are on the look-out for them?"

"They can't do it, my dear Monsieur Chambertin," rejoined Sir Percy blandly, "else I were not here."

Then, as Chauvelin, fuming, irritated despite himself, as he always was when he encountered that impudent Englishman, shrugged his shoulders in token of contempt, Blakeney's powerful grasp suddenly clutched his arm.

"Let us understand one another, my good M. Chambertin," he said coolly. "Those unfortunate Clamettes, as you say, are too helpless and too numerous to smuggle across Paris with any chance of success. Therefore I look to you to take them under your protection. They are all stowed away comfortably at this moment in a conveyance which I have provided for them. That conveyance is waiting at the bridgehead now. We could not cross without your help; we could not get across Paris without your august presence and your tricolour scarf of office. So you are coming with us, my dear M. Chambertin," he continued, and, with force which was quite irresistible, he began to drag his enemy after him towards the door. "You are going to sit in that conveyance with the Clamettes, and I myself will have the honour to drive you. And at every bridgehead you will show your pleasing countenance and your scarf of office to the guard and demand free passage for yourself and your family, as a representative member of the Committee of Public Safety. And then we'll enter Paris by the Porte d'Ivry and leave it by the Batignolles; and everywhere your charming presence will lull the guards' suspicions to rest. I pray you, come! There is no time to consider! At noon to-morrow, without a moment's grace, my friend Sir Andrew Ffoulkes, who has the papers in his possession, will dispose of them as he thinks best unless I myself do claim them from him."

While he spoke he continued to drag his enemy along with him, with an assurance and an impudence which were past belief. Chauvelin was trying to collect his thoughts; a whirl of conflicting plans were running riot in his mind. The Scarlet Pimpernel in his power! At any point on the road he could deliver him up to the nearest guard . . . then still hold the Clamettes and demand the papers. . . .

"Too late, my dear Monsieur Chambertin!" Sir Percy's mocking voice broke in, as if divining his thoughts. "You do not know where to find my friend Ffoulkes, and at noon to-morrow, if I do not arrive to claim those papers, there will not be a single ragamuffin in Paris who will not be crying your shame and that of your precious colleagues upon the housetops."

Chauvelin's whole nervous system was writhing with the feeling of impotence. Mechanically, unresisting now, he followed his enemy down the main staircase of the chateau and out through the wide open gates. He could not bring himself to believe that he had been so completely foiled, that this impudent adventurer had him once more in the hollow of his hand.

"In the name of Satan, bring us back those papers!" Robespierre had commanded. And now he—Chauvelin—was left in a maze of doubt; and the vital alternative was hammering in his brain: "The Scarlet Pimpernel—or those papers—-" Which, in Satan's name, was the more important? Passion whispered "The Scarlet Pimpernel!" but common sense and the future of his party, the whole future of the Revolution mayhap, demanded those compromising papers. And all the while he followed that relentless enemy through the avenues of the park and down the lonely lane. Overhead the trees of the forest of Sucy, nodding in a gentle breeze, seemed to mock his perplexity.

He had not arrived at a definite decision when the river came in sight, and when anon a carriage lanthorn threw a shaft of dim light through the mist-laden air. Now he felt as if he were in a dream. He was thrust unresisting into a closed chaise, wherein he felt the presence of several other people—children, an old man who was muttering ceaselessly. As in a dream he answered questions at the bridge to a guard whom he knew well.

"You know me—Armand Chauvelin, of the Committee of Public Safety!"

As in a dream, he heard the curt words of command:

"Pass on, in the name of the Republic!"

And all the while the thought hammered in his brain: "Something must be done! This is impossible! This cannot be! It is not I —Chauvelin—who am sitting here, helpless, unresisting. It is not that impudent Scarlet Pimpernel who is sitting there before me on the box, driving me to utter humiliation!"

And yet it was all true. All real. The Clamette children were sitting in front of him, clinging to Lucile, terrified of him even now. The old man was beside him—imbecile and not understanding. The boy Etienne was up on the box next to that audacious adventurer, whose broad back appeared to Chauvelin like a rock on which all his hopes and dreams must for ever be shattered.

The chaise rattled triumphantly through the Batignolles. It was then broad daylight. A brilliant early autumn day after the rains. The sun, the keen air, all mocked Chauvelin's helplessness, his humiliation. Long before noon they passed St. Denis. Here the barouche turned off the main road, halted at a small wayside house—nothing more than a cottage. After which everything seemed more dreamlike than ever. All that Chauvelin remembered of it afterwards was that he was once more alone in a room with his enemy, who had demanded his signature to a number of safe-conducts, ere he finally handed over the packet of papers to him.

"How do I know that they are all here?" he heard himself vaguely muttering, while his trembling fingers handled that precious packet.

"That's just it!" his tormentor retorted airily. "You don't know. I don't know myself," he added, with a light laugh. "And, personally, I don't see how either of us can possibly ascertain. In the meanwhile, I must bid you *au revoir*, my dear M. Chambertin. I am sorry that I cannot provide you with a conveyance, and you will have to walk a league or more ere you meet one, I fear me. We, in the meanwhile, will be well on our way to Dieppe, where my yacht, the Day Dream, lies at anchor, and I do not think that it will be worth your while to try and overtake us. I thank you for the safe-conducts. They will make our journey exceedingly pleasant. Shall I give your regards to M. le Marquis de Montorgueil or to M. le Vicomte? They are on board the Day Dream, you know. Oh! and I was forgetting! Lady Blakeney desired to be remembered to you."

The next moment he was gone. Chauvelin, standing at the window of the wayside house, saw Sir Percy Blakeney once more mount the box of the chaise. This time he had Sir Andrew Ffoulkes beside him. The Clamette family were huddled together—happy and free—inside the vehicle. After which there was the usual clatter of horses' hoofs, the creaking of wheels, the rattle of chains. Chauvelin saw and heard nothing of that. All that he saw at the last was Sir Percy's slender hand, waving him a last adieu.

After which he was left alone with his thoughts. The packet of papers was in his hand. He fingered it, felt its crispness, clutched it with a fierce gesture, which was followed by a long-drawn-out sigh of intense bitterness.

No one would ever know what it had cost him to obtain these papers. No one would ever know how much he had sacrificed of pride, revenge and hate in order to save a few shreds of his own party's honour.

# A Battle Of Wits

What had happened was this:

Tournefort, one of the ablest of the many sleuth-hounds employed by the Committee of Public Safety, was out during that awful storm on the night of the twenty-fifth. The rain came down as if it had been poured out of buckets, and Tournefort took shelter under the portico of a tall, dilapidated-looking house somewhere at the back of St. Lazare. The night was, of course, pitch dark, and the howling of the wind and beating of the rain effectually drowned every other sound.

Tournefort, chilled to the marrow, had at first cowered in the angle of the door, as far away from the draught as he could. But presently he spied the glimmer of a tiny light some little way up on his left, and taking this to come from the concierge's lodge, he went cautiously along the passage intending to ask for better shelter against the fury of the elements than the rickety front door afforded.

Tournefort, you must remember, was always on the best terms with every concierge in Paris. They were, as it were, his subordinates; without their help he never could have carried on his unavowable profession quite so successfully. And they, in their turn, found it to their advantage to earn the good-will of that army of spies, which the Revolutionary Government kept in its service, for the tracking down of all those unfortunates who had not given complete adhesion to their tyrannical and murderous policy.

Therefore, in this instance, Tournefort felt no hesitation in claiming the hospitality of the concierge of the squalid house wherein he found himself. He went boldly up to the lodge. His hand was already on the latch, when certain sounds which proceeded from the interior of the lodge caused him to pause and to bend his ear in order to listen. It was Tournefort's metier to listen. What had arrested his attention was the sound of a man's voice, saying in a tone of deep respect:

"*Bien*, Madame la Comtesse, we'll do our best."

No wonder that the servant of the Committee of Public Safety remained at attention, no longer thought of the storm or felt the cold blast chilling him to the marrow. Here was a wholly unexpected piece of good luck. "Madame la Comtesse!" Peste! There were not many such left in Paris these days. Unfortunately, the tempest of the wind and the rain made such a din that it was difficult to catch every sound which came from the interior of the lodge. All that Tournefort caught definitely were a few fragments of conversation.

"My good M. Bertin . . . " came at one time from a woman's voice. "Truly I do not know why you should do all this for me."

And then again: "All I possess in the world now are my

diamonds. They alone stand between my children and utter destitution."

The man's voice seemed all the time to be saying something that sounded cheerful and encouraging. But his voice came only as a vague murmur to the listener's ears. Presently, however, there came a word which set his pulses tingling. Madame said something about "Gentilly," and directly afterwards: "You will have to be very careful, my dear M. Bertin. The chateau, I feel sure, is being watched."

Tournefort could scarce repress a cry of joy. "Gentilly? Madame la Comtesse? The *chateau?*" Why, of course, he held all the necessary threads already. The *ci-devant* Comte de Sucy—a pestilential *aristo* if ever there was one!—had been sent to the guillotine less than a fortnight ago. His chateau, situated just outside Gentilly, stood empty, it having been given out that the widow Sucy and her two children had escaped to England. Well! she had not gone apparently, for here she was, in the lodge of the concierge of a mean house in one of the desolate quarters of Paris, begging some traitor to find her diamonds for her, which she had obviously left concealed inside the chateau. What a haul for Tournefort! What commendation from his superiors! The chances of a speedy promotion were indeed glorious now! He blessed the storm and the rain which had driven him for shelter to this house, where a poisonous plot was being hatched to rob the people of valuable property, and to aid a few more of those abominable *aristos* in cheating the guillotine of their traitorous heads.

He listened for a while longer, in order to get all the information that he could on the subject of the diamonds, because he knew by experience that those perfidious *aristos*, once they were under arrest, would sooner bite out their tongues than reveal anything that might be of service to the Government of the people. But he learned little else. Nothing was revealed of where Madame la Comtesse was in hiding, or how the diamonds were to be disposed of once they were found. Tournefort would have given much to have at least one of his colleagues with him. As it was, he would be forced to act single-handed and on his own initiative. In his own mind he had already decided that he would wait until Madame la Comtesse came out of the concierge's lodge, and that he would follow her and apprehend her somewhere out in the open streets, rather than here where her friend Bertin might prove to be a stalwart as well as a desperate man, ready with a pistol, whilst he—Tournefort—was unarmed. Bertin, who had, it seemed, been entrusted with the task of finding the diamonds, could then be shadowed and arrested in the very act of filching property which by decree of the State belonged to the people.

So he waited patiently for a while. No doubt the *aristo* would remain here under shelter until the storm had abated. Soon the sound of voices died down, and an extraordinary silence descended on this miserable, abandoned corner of old Paris. The silence became all the more marked after a while, because the rain ceased its monotonous pattering and the soughing of the wind was stilled. It was, in fact, this amazing stillness which set citizen Tournefort thinking. Evidently the *aristo* did not intend to come out of the lodge to-night. Well! Tournefort had not meant to make himself unpleasant inside the house, or to have a quarrel just yet with the traitor Bertin, whoever he was; but his hand was forced and he had no option.

The door of the lodge was locked. He tugged vigorously at the bell again and again, for at first he got no answer. A few minutes later he heard the sound of shuffling footsteps upon creaking boards. The door was opened, and a man in night attire, with bare, thin legs and tattered carpet slippers on his feet, confronted an exceedingly astonished servant of the Committee of Public Safety. Indeed, Tournefort thought that he must have been dreaming, or that he was dreaming now. For the man who opened the door to him was well known to every agent of the Committee. He was an ex-soldier who had been crippled years ago by the loss of one arm, and had held the post of concierge in a house in the Ruelle du Paradis ever since. His name was Grosjean. He was very old, and nearly doubled up with rheumatism, had scarcely any hair on his head or flesh on his bones. At this moment he appeared to be suffering from a cold in the head, for his eyes were streaming and his narrow, hooked nose was adorned by a drop of moisture at its tip. In fact, poor old Grosjean looked more like a dilapidated scarecrow than a dangerous conspirator. Tournefort literally gasped at sight of him, and Grosjean uttered a kind of croak, intended, no doubt, for complete surprise.

"Citizen Tournefort!" he exclaimed. "Name of a dog! What are you doing here at this hour and in this abominable weather? Come in! Come in!" he added, and, turning on his heel, he shuffled back into the inner room, and then returned carrying a lighted lamp, which he set upon the table. "Amelie left a sup of hot coffee on the hob in the kitchen before she went to bed. You must have a drop of that."

He was about to shuffle off again when Tournefort broke in roughly:

"None of that nonsense, Grosjean! Where are the *aristos?*"

"The *aristos*, citizen?" queried Grosjean, and nothing could have looked more utterly, more ludicrously bewildered than did the old concierge at this moment. "What *aristos?*"

"Bertin and Madame la Comtesse," retorted Tournefort gruffly. "I heard them talking."

"You have been dreaming, citizen Tournefort," the old man said, with a husky little laugh. "Sit down, and let me get you some coffee - "

"Don't try and hoodwink me, Grosjean!" Tournefort cried now

in a sudden access of rage. "I tell you that I saw the light. I heard the *aristos* talking. There was a man named Bertin, and a woman he called 'Madame la Comtesse,' and I say that some devilish royalist plot is being hatched here, and that you, Grosjean, will suffer for it if you try and shield those *aristos*."

"But, citizen Tournefort," replied the concierge meekly, "I assure you that I have seen no *aristos*. The door of my bedroom was open, and the lamp was by my bedside. Amelie, too, has only been in bed a few minutes. You ask her! There has been no one, I tell you—no one! I should have seen and heard them—the door was open," he reiterated pathetically.

"We'll soon see about that!" was Tournefort's curt comment.

But it was his turn indeed to be utterly bewildered. He searched —none too gently—the squalid little lodge through and through, turned the paltry sticks of furniture over, hauled little Amelie, Grosjean's granddaughter, out of bed, searched under the mattresses, and even poked his head up the chimney.

Grosjean watched him wholly unperturbed. These were strange times, and friend Tournefort had obviously gone a little off his head. The worthy old concierge calmly went on getting the coffee ready. Only when presently Tournefort, worn out with anger and futile exertion, threw himself, with many an oath, into the one armchair, Grosjean remarked coolly:

"I tell you what I think it is, citizen. If you were standing just by the door of the lodge you had the back staircase of the house immediately behind you. The partition wall is very thin, and there is a disused door just there also. No doubt the voices came from there. You see, if there had been any *aristos* here," he added naively, "they could not have flown up the chimney, could they?"

That argument was certainly unanswerable. But Tournefort was out of temper. He roughly ordered Grosjean to bring the lamp and show him the back staircase and the disused door. The concierge obeyed without a murmur. He was not in the least disturbed or frightened by all this blustering. He was only afraid that getting out of bed had made his cold worse. But he knew Tournefort of old. A good fellow, but inclined to be noisy and arrogant since he was in the employ of the Government. Grosjean took the precaution of putting on his trousers and wrapping an old shawl round his shoulders. Then he had a final sip of hot coffee; after which he picked up the lamp and guided Tournefort out of the lodge.

The wind had quite gone down by now. The lamp scarcely flickered as Grosjean held it above his head.

"Just here, citizen Tournefort," he said, and turned sharply to his left. But the next sound which he uttered was a loud croak of astonishment.

"That door has been out of use ever since I've been here," he muttered.

"And it certainly was closed when I stood up against it," rejoined Tournefort, with a savage oath, "or, of course, I should have noticed it."

Close to the lodge, at right angles to it, a door stood partially open. Tournefort went through it, closely followed by Grosjean. He found himself in a passage which ended in a *cul de sac* on his right; on the left was the foot of the stairs. The whole place was pitch dark save for the feeble light of the lamp. The *cul de sac* itself reeked of dirt and fustiness, as if it had not been cleaned or ventilated for years.

"When did you last notice that this door was closed?" queried Tournefort, furious with the sense of discomfiture, which he would have liked to vent on the unfortunate concierge.

"I have not noticed it for some days, citizen," replied Grosjean meekly.

"I have had a severe cold, and have not been outside my lodge since Monday last. But we'll ask Amelie!" he added more hopefully.

Amelie, however, could throw no light upon the subject. She certainly kept the back stairs cleaned and swept, but it was not part of her duties to extend her sweeping operations as far as the *cul de sac*. She had quite enough to do as it was, with grandfather now practically helpless. This morning, when she went out to do her shopping, she had not noticed whether the disused door did or did not look the same as usual.

Grosjean was very sorry for his friend Tournefort, who appeared vastly upset, but still more sorry for himself, for he knew what endless trouble this would entail upon him.

Nor was the trouble slow in coming, not only on Grosjean, but on every lodger inside the house; for before half an hour had gone by Tournefort had gone and come back, this time with the local commissary of police and a couple of agents, who had every man, woman and child in that house out of bed and examined at great length, their identity books searchingly overhauled, their rooms turned topsy-turvy and their furniture knocked about.

It was past midnight before all these perquisitions were completed. No one dared to complain at these indignities put upon peaceable citizens on the mere denunciation of an obscure police agent. These were times when every regulation, every command, had to be accepted without a murmur. At one o'clock in the morning, Grosjean himself was thankful to get back to bed, having satisfied the commissary that he was not a dangerous conspirator.

But of anyone even remotely approaching the description of the *ci-devant* Comtesse de Sucy, or of any man called Bertin, there was not the faintest trace.

II

But no feeling of discomfort ever lasted very long with citizen Tournefort. He was a person of vast resource and great buoyancy of temperament.

True, he had not apprehended two exceedingly noxious *aristos*, as he had hoped to do; but he held the threads of an abominable conspiracy in his hands, and the question of catching both Bertin and Madame la Comtesse red-handed was only a question of time. But little time had been lost. There was always someone to be found at the offices of the Committee of Public Safety, which were open all night. It was possible that citizen Chauvelin would be still there, for he often took on the night shift, or else citizen Gourdon.

It was Gourdon who greeted his subordinate, somewhat ill-humouredly, for he was indulging in a little sleep, with his toes turned to the fire, as the night was so damp and cold. But when he heard Tournefort's story, he was all eagerness and zeal.

"It is, of course, too late to do anything now," he said finally, after he had mastered every detail of the man's adventures in the Ruelle du Paradis; "but get together half a dozen men upon whom you can rely, and by six o'clock in the morning, or even five, we'll be on our way to Gentilly. Citizen Chauvelin was only saying to-day that he strongly suspected the *ci-devant* Comtesse de Sucy of having left the bulk of her valuable jewellery at the chateau, and that she would make some effort to get possession of it. It would be rather fine, citizen Tournefort," he added with a chuckle, "if you and I could steal a march on citizen Chauvelin over this affair, what? He has been extraordinarily arrogant of late and marvellously in favour, not only with the Committee, but with citizen Robespierre himself."

"They say," commented Tournefort, "that he succeeded in getting hold of some papers which were of great value to the members of the Committee."

"He never succeeded in getting hold of that meddlesome Englishman whom they call the Scarlet Pimpernel," was Gourdon's final dry comment.

Thus was the matter decided on. And the following morning at daybreak, Gourdon, who was only a subordinate officer on the Committee of Public Safety, took it upon himself to institute a perquisition in the chateau of Gentilly, which is situated close to the commune of that name. He was accompanied by his friend Tournefort and a gang of half a dozen ruffians recruited from the most disreputable cabarets of Paris.

The intention had been to steal a march on citizen Chauvelin, who had been over arrogant of late; but the result did not come up to expectations. By midday the chateau had been ransacked from attic to cellar; every kind of valuable property had been destroyed, priceless works of art irretrievably damaged. But priceless works of art had no market in Paris these days; and the property of real value—the Sucy diamonds namely—which had excited the cupidity or the patriotic wrath of citizens Gourdon and Tournefort could nowhere be found.

To make the situation more deplorable still, the Committee of Public Safety had in some unexplainable way got wind of the affair, and the two worthies had the mortification of seeing citizen Chauvelin presently appear upon the scene.

It was then two o'clock in the afternoon. Gourdon, after he had snatched a hasty dinner at a neighbouring cabaret, had returned to the task of pulling the chateau of Gentilly about his own ears if need be, with a view to finding the concealed treasure.

For the nonce he was standing in the centre of the finely proportioned hall. The rich ormolu and crystal chandelier lay in a tangled, broken heap of scraps at his feet, and all around there was a confused medley of pictures, statuettes, silver ornaments, tapestry and brocade hangings, all piled up in disorder, smashed, tattered, kicked at now and again by Gourdon, to the accompaniment of a savage oath.

The house itself was full of noises; heavy footsteps tramping up and down the stairs, furniture turned over, curtains torn from their poles, doors and windows battered in. And through it all the ceaseless hammering of pick and axe, attacking these stately walls which had withstood the wars and sieges of centuries.

Every now and then Tournefort, his face perspiring and crimson with exertion, would present himself at the door of the hall. Gourdon would query gruffly: "Well?"

And the answer was invariably the same: "Nothing!"

Then Gourdon would swear again and send curt orders to continue the search, relentlessly, ceaselessly.

"Leave no stone upon stone," he commanded. "Those diamonds must be found. We know they are here, and, name of a dog! I mean to have them."

When Chauvelin arrived at the chateau he made no attempt at first to interfere with Gourdon's commands. Only on one occasion he remarked curtly:

"I suppose, citizen Gourdon, that you can trust your search party?"

"Absolutely," retorted Gourdon. "A finer patriot than Tournefort does not exist."

"Probably," rejoined the other dryly. "But what about the men?"

"Oh! they are only a set of barefooted, ignorant louts. They do as they are told, and Tournefort has his eye on them. I dare say they'll contrive to steal a few things, but they would never dare lay hands on valuable jewellery. To begin with, they could never dispose of it.

Imagine a *va-nu-pieds* peddling a diamond tiara!"

"There are always receivers prepared to take risks."

"Very few," Gourdon assured him, "since we decreed that trafficking with *aristo* property was a crime punishable by death."

Chauvelin said nothing for the moment. He appeared wrapped in his own thoughts, listened for a while to the confused hubbub about the house, then he resumed abruptly:

"Who are these men whom you are employing, citizen Gourdon?"

"A well-known gang," replied the other. "I can give you their names."

"If you please."

Gourdon searched his pockets for a paper which he found presently and handed to his colleague. The latter perused it thoughtfully.

"Where did Tournefort find these men?" he asked.

"For the most part at the Cabaret de la Liberté—a place of very evil repute down in the Rue Christine."

"I know it," rejoined the other. He was still studying the list of names which Gourdon had given him. "And," he added, "I know most of these men. As thorough a set of ruffians as we need for some of our work. Merri, Guidal, Rateau, Desmonds. *Tiens!*" he exclaimed. "Rateau! Is Rateau here now?"

"Why, of course! He was recruited, like the rest of them, for the day. He won't leave till he has been paid, you may be sure of that. Why do you ask?"

"I will tell you presently. But I would wish to speak with citizen Rateau first."

Just at this moment Tournefort paid his periodical visit to the hall. The usual words, "Still nothing," were on his lips, when Gourdon curtly ordered him to go and fetch the citizen Rateau.

A minute or two later Tournefort returned with the news that Rateau could nowhere be found. Chauvelin received the news without any comment; he only ordered Tournefort, somewhat roughly, back to his work. Then, as soon as the latter had gone, Gourdon turned upon his colleague.

"Will you explain—" he began with a show of bluster.

"With pleasure," replied Chauvelin blandly. "On my way hither, less than an hour ago, I met your man Rateau, a league or so from here."

"You met Rateau!" exclaimed Gourdon impatiently. "Impossible! He was here then, I feel sure. You must have been mistaken."

"I think not. I have only seen the man once, when I, too, went to recruit a band of ruffians at the Cabaret de la Liberté, in connection with some work I wanted doing. I did not employ him then, for he appeared to me both drink-sodden and nothing but a miserable, consumptive creature, with a churchyard cough you can hear half a league away. But I would know him anywhere. Besides which, he stopped and wished me good morning. Now I come to think of it," added Chauvelin thoughtfully, "he was carrying what looked like a heavy bundle under his arm."

"A heavy bundle!" cried Gourdon, with a forceful oath. "And you did not stop him!"

"I had no reason for suspecting him. I did not know until I arrived here what the whole affair was about, or whom you were employing. All that the Committee knew for certain was that you and Tournefort and a number of men had arrived at Gentilly before daybreak, and I was then instructed to follow you hither to see what mischief you were up to. You acted in complete secrecy, remember, citizen Gourdon, and without first ascertaining the wishes of the Committee of Public Safety, whose servant you are. If the Sucy diamonds are not found, you alone will be held responsible for their loss to the Government of the People."

Chauvelin's voice had now assumed a threatening tone, and Gourdon felt all his audacity and self-assurance fall away from him, leaving him a prey to nameless terror.

"We must round up Rateau," he murmured hastily. "He cannot have gone far."

"No, he cannot," rejoined Chauvelin dryly. "Though I was not specially thinking of Rateau or of diamonds when I started to come hither. I did send a general order forbidding any person on foot or horseback to enter or leave Paris by any of the southern gates. That order will serve us well now. Are you riding?"

"Yes. I left my horse at the tavern just outside Gentilly. I can get to horse within ten minutes."

"To horse, then, as quickly as you can. Pay off your men and dismiss them—all but Tournefort, who had best accompany us. Do not lose a single moment. I'll be ahead of you and may come up with Rateau before you overtake me. And if I were you, citizen Gourdon," he concluded, with ominous emphasis, "I would burn one or two candles to your compeer the devil. You'll have need of his help if Rateau gives us the slip."

III

The first part of the road from Gentilly to Paris runs through the valley of the Biere, and is densely wooded on either side. It winds in and out for the most part, ribbon-like, through thick coppice of chestnut and birch. Thus it was impossible for Chauvelin to spy his quarry from afar; nor did he expect to do so this side of the Hopital de la Sante. Once past that point, he would find the road quite open and running almost straight, in the midst of arid and only partially cultivated land.

He rode at a sharp trot, with his caped coat wrapped tightly round his shoulders, for it was raining fast. At intervals, when he met an occasional wayfarer, he would ask questions about a tall man who had a consumptive cough, and who was carrying a cumbersome burden under his arm.

Almost everyone whom he thus asked remembered seeing a personage who vaguely answered to the description: tall and with a decided stoop—yes, and carrying a cumbersome-looking bundle under his arm. Chauvelin was undoubtedly on the track of the thief.

Just beyond Meuves he was overtaken by Gourdon and Tournefort. Here, too, the man Rateau's track became more and more certain. At one place he had stopped and had a glass of wine and a rest, at another he had asked how close he was to the gates of Paris.

The road was now quite open and level; the irregular buildings of the hospital appeared vague in the rain-sodden distance. Twenty minutes later Tournefort, who was riding ahead of his companions, spied a tall, stooping figure at the spot where the Chemin de Gentilly forks, and where stands a group of isolated houses and bits of garden, which belong to la Sante. Here, before the days when the glorious Revolution swept aside all such outward signs of superstition, there had stood a Calvary. It was now used as a signpost. The man stood before it, scanning the half-obliterated indications.

At the moment that Tournefort first caught sight of him he appeared uncertain of his way. Then for a while he watched Tournefort, who was coming at a sharp trot towards him. Finally, he seemed to make up his mind very suddenly and, giving a last, quick look round, he walked rapidly along the upper road. Tournefort drew rein, waited for his colleagues to come up with him. Then he told them what he had seen.

"It is Rateau, sure enough," he said. "I saw his face quite distinctly and heard his abominable cough. He is trying to get into Paris. That road leads nowhere but to the barrier. There, of course, he will be stopped, and—"

The other two had also brought their horses to a halt. The situation had become tense, and a plan for future action had at once to be decided on. Already Chauvelin, masterful and sure of himself, had assumed command of the little party. Now he broke in abruptly on Tournefort's vapid reflections.

"We don't want him stopped at the barrier," he said in his usual curt, authoritative manner. "You, citizen Tournefort," he continued, "will ride as fast as you can to the gate, making a detour by the lower road. You will immediately demand to speak with the sergeant who is in command, and you will give him a detailed description of the man Rateau. Then you will tell him in my name that, should such a man present himself at the gate, he must be allowed to enter the city unmolested."

Gourdon gave a quick cry of protest.

"Let the man go unmolested? Citizen Chauvelin, think what you are doing!"

"I always think of what I am doing," retorted Chauvelin curtly, "and have no need of outside guidance in the process." Then he turned once more to Tournefort. "You yourself, citizen," he continued, in sharp, decisive tones which admitted of no argument, "will dismount as soon as you are inside the city. You will keep the gate under observation. The moment you see the man Rateau, you will shadow him, and on no account lose sight of him. Understand?"

"You may trust me, citizen Chauvelin," Tournefort replied, elated at the prospect of work which was so entirely congenial to him. "But will you tell me—"

"I will tell you this much, citizen Tournefort," broke in Chauvelin with some acerbity, "that though we have traced the diamonds and the thief so far, we have, through your folly last night, lost complete track of the *ci-devant* Comtesse de Sucy and of the man Bertin. We want Rateau to show us where they are."

"I understand," murmured the other meekly.

"That's a mercy!" riposted Chauvelin dryly. "Then quickly man. Lose no time! Try to get a few minutes' advance on Rateau; then slip in to the guard-room to change into less conspicuous clothes. Citizen Gourdon and I will continue on the upper road and keep the man in sight in case he should think of altering his course. In any event, we'll meet you just inside the barrier. But if, in the meanwhile, you have to get on Rateau's track before we have arrived on the scene, leave the usual indications as to the direction which you have taken."

Having given his orders and satisfied himself that they were fully understood, he gave a curt command, "*En avant*," and once more the three of them rode at a sharp trot down the road towards the city.

IV

Citizen Rateau, if he thought about the matter at all, must indeed have been vastly surprised at the unwonted amiability or indifference of sergeant Ribot, who was in command at the gate of Gentilly. Ribot only threw a very perfunctory glance at the greasy permit which Rateau presented to him, and when he put the usual query, "What's in that parcel?" and Rateau gave the reply: "Two heads of cabbage and a bunch of carrots," Ribot merely poked one of his fingers into the bundle, felt that a cabbage leaf did effectually lie on the top, and thereupon gave the formal order: "Pass on, citizen, in the name of the Republic!" without any hesitation.

Tournefort, who had watched the brief little incident from behind the window of a neighbouring cabaret, could not help but chuckle to himself. Never had he seen game walk more readily into a trap. Rateau, after he had passed the barrier, appeared undecided which way he would go. He looked with obvious longing towards the cabaret, behind which the keenest agent on the staff of the Committee of Public Safety was even now ensconced. But seemingly a halt within those hospitable doors did not form part of his programme, and a moment or two later he turned sharply on his heel and strode rapidly down the Rue de l'Oursine.

Tournefort allowed him a fair start, and then made ready to follow.

Just as he was stepping out of the cabaret he spied Chauvelin and Gourdon coming through the gates. They, too, had apparently made a brief halt inside the guard-room, where—as at most of the gates —a store of various disguises was always kept ready for the use of the numerous sleuth-hounds employed by the Committee of Public Safety. Here the two men had exchanged their official garments for suits of sombre cloth, which gave them the appearance of a couple of humble bourgeois going quietly about their business. Tournefort had donned an old blouse, tattered stockings, and shoes down at heel. With his hands buried in his breeches' pockets, he, too, turned into the long narrow Rue de l'Oursine, which, after a sharp curve, abuts on the Rue Mouffetard.

Rateau was walking rapidly, taking big strides with his long legs. Tournefort, now sauntering in the gutter in the middle of the road, now darting in and out of open doorways, kept his quarry well in sight. Chauvelin and Gourdon lagged some little way behind. It was still raining, but not heavily—a thin drizzle, which penetrated almost to the marrow. Not many passers-by haunted this forlorn quarter of old Paris. To right and left tall houses almost obscured the last, quickly-fading light of the grey September day.

At the bottom of the Rue Mouffetard, Rateau came once more to a halt. A network of narrow streets radiated from this centre. He looked all round him and also behind. It was difficult to know whether he had a sudden suspicion that he was being followed; certain it is that, after a very brief moment of hesitation, he plunged suddenly into the narrow Rue Contrescarpe and disappeared from view.

Tournefort was after him in a trice. When he reached the corner of the street he saw Rateau, at the further end of it, take a sudden sharp turn to the right. But not before he had very obviously spied his pursuer, for at that moment his entire demeanour changed. An air of furtive anxiety was expressed in his whole attitude. Even at that distance Tournefort could see him clutching his bulky parcel close to his chest.

After that the pursuit became closer and hotter. Rateau was in and out of that tight network of streets which cluster around the Place de Fourci, intent, apparently, on throwing his pursuers off the scent, for after a while he was running round and round in a circle. Now up the Rue des Poules, then to the right and to the right again; back in the Place de Fourci. Then straight across it once more to the Rue Contrescarpe, where he presently disappeared so completely from view that Tournefort thought that the earth must have swallowed him up.

Tournefort was a man capable of great physical exertion. His calling often made heavy demands upon his powers of endurance; but never before had he grappled with so strenuous a task. Puffing and panting, now running at top speed, anon brought to a halt by the doubling-up tactics of his quarry, his great difficulty was the fact that citizen Chauvelin did not wish the man Rateau to be apprehended; did not wish him to know that he was being pursued. And Tournefort had need of all his wits to keep well under the shadow of any projecting wall or under cover of open doorways which were conveniently in the way, and all the while not to lose sight of that consumptive giant, who seemed to be playing some intricate game which well-nigh exhausted the strength of citizen Tournefort.

What he could not make out was what had happened to Chauvelin and to Gourdon. They had been less than three hundred metres behind him when first this wild chase in and out of the Rue Contrescarpe had begun. Now, when their presence was most needed, they seemed to have lost track both of him—Tournefort—and of the very elusive quarry. To make matters more complicated, the shades of evening were drawing in very fast, and these narrow streets of the Faubourg were very sparsely lighted.

Just at this moment Tournefort had once more caught sight of Rateau, striding leisurely this time up the street. The worthy agent quickly took refuge under a doorway and was mopping his streaming forehead, glad of this brief respite in the mad chase, when that awful churchyard cough suddenly sounded so close to him that he gave a great jump and well-nigh betrayed his presence then and there. He had only just time to withdraw further still into the angle of the doorway, when Rateau passed by.

Tournefort peeped out of his hiding-place, and for the space of a dozen heart beats or so, remained there quite still, watching that broad back and those long limbs slowly moving through the gathering gloom. The next instant he perceived Chauvelin standing at the end of the street.

Rateau saw him too—came face to face with him, in fact, and

must have known who he was for, without an instant's hesitation and just like a hunted creature at bay, he turned sharply on his heel and then ran back down the street as hard as he could tear. He passed close to within half a metre of Tournefort, and as he flew past he hit out with his left fist so vigorously that the worthy agent of the Committee of Public Safety, caught on the nose by the blow, staggered and measured his length upon the flagged floor below.

The next moment Chauvelin had come by. Tournefort, struggling to his feet, called to him, panting:

"Did you see him? Which way did he go?"

"Up the Rue Bordet. After him, citizen!" replied Chauvelin grimly, between his teeth.

Together the two men continued the chase, guided through the intricate mazes of the streets by their fleeing quarry. They had Rateau well in sight, and the latter could no longer continue his former tactics with success now that two experienced sleuth-hounds were on his track.

At a given moment he was caught between the two of them. Tournefort was advancing cautiously up the Rue Bordet; Chauvelin, equally stealthily, was coming down the same street, and Rateau, once more walking quite leisurely, was at equal distance between the two.

V

There are no side turnings out of the Rue Bordet, the total length of which is less than fifty metres; so Tournefort, feeling more at his ease, ensconced himself at one end of the street, behind a doorway, whilst Chauvelin did the same at the other. Rateau, standing in the gutter, appeared once more in a state of hesitation. Immediately in front of him the door of a small cabaret stood invitingly open; its signboard, "Le Bon Copain," promised rest and refreshment. He peered up and down the road, satisfied himself presumably that, for the moment, his pursuers were out of sight, hugged his parcel to his chest, and then suddenly made a dart for the cabaret and disappeared within its doors.

Nothing could have been better. The quarry, for the moment, was safe, and if the sleuth-hounds could not get refreshment, they could at least get a rest. Tournefort and Chauvelin crept out of their hiding-places. They met in the middle of the road, at the spot where Rateau had stood a while ago. It was then growing dark and the street was innocent of lanterns, but the lights inside the cabaret gave a full view of the interior. The lower half of the wide shop-window was curtained off, but above the curtain the heads of the customers of "Le Bon Copain," and the general comings and goings, could very clearly be seen.

Tournefort, never at a loss, had already climbed upon a low projection in the wall of one of the houses opposite. From this point of vantage he could more easily observe what went on inside the cabaret, and in short, jerky sentences he gave a description of what he saw to his chief.

"Rateau is sitting down . . . he has his back to the window . . . he has put his bundle down close beside him on the bench . . . he can't speak for a minute, for he is coughing and spluttering like an old walrus . . . A wench is bringing him a bottle of wine and a hunk of bread and cheese. . . . He has started talking . . . is talking volubly . . . the people are laughing . . . some are applauding. . . . And here comes Jean Victor, the landlord . . . you know him, citizen . . . a big, hulking fellow, and as good a patriot as I ever wish to see. . . . He, too, is laughing and talking to Rateau, who is doubled up with another fit of coughing—" ·

Chauvelin uttered an exclamation of impatience:

"Enough of this, citizen Tournefort. Keep your eye on the man and hold your tongue. I am spent with fatigue."

"No wonder," murmured Tournefort. Then he added insinuatingly: "Why not let me go in there and apprehend Rateau now? We should have the diamonds and-"

"And lose the *ci-devant* Comtesse de Sucy and the man Bertin," retorted Chauvelin with sudden fierceness. "Bertin, who can be none other than that cursed Englishman, the — ?"

He checked himself, seeing Tournefort was gazing down on him, with awe and bewilderment expressed in his lean, hatchet face.

"You are losing sight of Rateau, citizen," Chauvelin continued calmly.

"What is he doing now?"

But Tournefort felt that this calmness was only on the surface; something strange had stirred the depths of his chief's keen, masterful mind. He would have liked to ask a question or two, but knew from experience that it was neither wise nor profitable to try and probe citizen Chauvelin's thoughts. So after a moment or two he turned back obediently to his task.

"I can't see Rateau for the moment," he said, "but there is much talking and merriment in there. Ah! there he is, I think. Yes, I see him! . . . He is behind the counter, talking to Jean Victor . . . and he has just thrown some money down upon the counter . . . gold too! name of a dog . . ."

Then suddenly, without any warning, Tournefort jumped down from his post of observation. Chauvelin uttered a brief:

"What the — are you doing, citizen?"

"Rateau is going," replied Tournefort excitedly. "He drank a mug of wine at a draught and has picked up his bundle, ready to go."

Once more cowering in the dark angle of a doorway, the two

men waited, their nerves on edge, for the reappearance of their quarry.

"I wish citizen Gourdon were here," whispered Tournefort. "In the darkness it is better to be three than two."

"I sent him back to the Station in the Rue Mouffetard," was Chauvelin's curt retort; "there to give notice that I might require a few armed men presently. But he should be somewhere about here by now, looking for us. Anyway, I have my whistle, and if—"

He said no more, for at that moment the door of the cabaret was opened from within and Rateau stepped out into the street, to the accompaniment of loud laughter and clapping of hands which came from the customers of the "Bon Copain."

This time he appeared neither in a hurry nor yet anxious. He did not pause in order to glance to right or left, but started to walk quite leisurely up the street. The two sleuth-hounds quietly followed him. Through the darkness they could only vaguely see his silhouette, with the great bundle under his arm. Whatever may have been Rateau's fears of being shadowed awhile ago, he certainly seemed free of them now. He sauntered along, whistling a tune, down the Montagne Ste. Genevieve to the Place Maubert, and thence straight towards the river.

Having reached the bank, he turned off to his left, sauntered past the Ecole de Medecine and went across the Petit Pont, then through the New Market, along the Quai des Orfevres. Here he made a halt, and for awhile looked over the embankment at the river and then round about him, as if in search of something. But presently he appeared to make up his mind, and continued his leisurely walk as far as the Pont Neuf, where he turned sharply off to his right, still whistling, Tournefort and Chauvelin hard upon his heels.

"That whistling is getting on my nerves," muttered Tournefort irritably; "and I haven't heard the ruffian's churchyard cough since he walked out of the 'Bon Copain.'"

Strangely enough, it was this remark of Tournefort's which gave Chauvelin the first inkling of something strange and, to him, positively awesome. Tournefort, who walked close beside him, heard him suddenly mutter a fierce exclamation.

"Name of a dog!"

"What is it, citizen?" queried Tournefort, awed by this sudden outburst on the part of a man whose icy calmness had become proverbial throughout the Committee.

"Sound the alarm, citizen!" cried Chauvelin in response. "Or, by Satan, he'll escape us again!"

"But—" stammered Tournefort in utter bewilderment, while, with fingers that trembled somewhat, he fumbled for his whistle.

"We shall want all the help we can," retorted Chauvelin roughly. "For, unless I am much mistaken, there's more noble quarry here than even I could dare to hope!"

Rateau in the meanwhile had quietly lolled up to the parapet on the right-hand side of the bridge, and Tournefort, who was watching him with intense keenness, still marvelled why citizen Chauvelin had suddenly become so strangely excited. Rateau was merely lolling against the parapet, like a man who has not a care in the world. He had placed his bundle on the stone ledge beside him. Here he waited a moment or two, until one of the small craft upon the river loomed out of the darkness immediately below the bridge. Then he picked up the bundle and threw it straight into the boat. At that same moment Tournefort had the whistle to his lips. A shrill, sharp sound rang out through the gloom.

"The boat, citizen Tournefort, the boat!" cried Chauvelin. "There are plenty of us here to deal with the man."

Immediately, from the quays, the streets, the bridges, dark figures emerged out of the darkness and hurried to the spot. Some reached the bridgehead even as Rateau made a dart forward, and two men were upon him before he succeeded in running very far. Others had scrambled down the embankment and were shouting to some unseen boatman to "halt, in the name of the people!"

But Rateau gave in without a struggle. He appeared more dazed than frightened, and quietly allowed the agents of the Committee to lead him back to the bridge, where Chauvelin had paused, waiting for him.

## VI

A minute or two later Tournefort was once more beside his chief. He was carrying the precious bundle, which, he explained, the boatman had given up without question.

"The man knew nothing about it," the agent said. "No one, he says, could have been more surprised than he was when this bundle was suddenly flung at him over the parapet of the bridge."

Just then the small group, composed of two or three agents of the Committee, holding their prisoner by the arms, came into view. One man was walking ahead and was the first to approach Chauvelin. He had a small screw of paper in his hand, which he gave to his chief.

"Found inside the lining of the prisoner's hat, citizen," he reported curtly, and opened the shutter of a small, dark lantern which he wore at his belt.

Chauvelin took the paper from his subordinate. A weird, unexplainable foreknowledge of what was to come caused his hand to shake and beads of perspiration to moisten his forehead. He looked up and saw the prisoner standing before him. Crushing the paper in his hand he snatched the lantern from the agent's belt and flashed it in the face of the quarry who, at the last, had been so easily captured.

Immediately a hoarse cry of disappointment and of rage escaped his throat.

"Who is this man?" he cried.

One of the agents gave reply:

"It is old Victor, the landlord of the 'Bon Copain.' He is just a fool, who has been playing a practical joke."

Tournefort, too, at sight of the prisoner had uttered a cry of dismay and of astonishment.

"Victor!" he exclaimed. "Name of a dog, citizen, what are you doing here?"

But Chauvelin had gripped the man by the arm so fiercely that the latter swore with the pain.

"What is the meaning of this?" he queried roughly.

"Only a bet, citizen," retorted Victor reproachfully. "No reason to fall on an honest patriot for a bet, just as if he were a mad dog."

"A joke? A bet?" murmured Chauvelin hoarsely, for his throat now felt hot and parched. "What do you mean? Who are you, man? Speak, or I'll—"

"My name is Jean Victor," replied the other. "I am the landlord of the 'Bon Copain.' An hour ago a man came into my cabaret. He was a queer, consumptive creature, with a churchyard cough that made you shiver. Some of my customers knew him by sight, told me that the man's name was Rateau, and that he was an habitue of the 'Liberte,' in the Rue Christine. Well; he soon fell into conversation, first with me, then with some of my customers—talked all sorts of silly nonsense, made absurd bets with everybody. Some of these he won, and others he lost; but I must say that when he lost he always paid up most liberally. Then we all got excited, and soon bets flew all over the place. I don't rightly know how it happened at the last, but all at once he bet me that I would not dare to walk out then and there in the dark, as far as the Pont Neuf, wearing his blouse and hat and carrying a bundle the same as his under my arm. I not dare? . . . I, Jean Victor, who was a fine fighter in my day! I bet him a gold piece that I would and he said that he would make it five if I came back without my bundle, having thrown it over the parapet into any passing boat. Well, citizen!" continued Jean Victor with a laugh, "I ask you, what would you have done? Five gold pieces means a fortune these hard times, and I tell you the man was quite honest and always paid liberally when he lost. He slipped behind the counter and took off his blouse and hat, which I put on. Then we made up a bundle with some cabbage heads and a few carrots, and out I came. I didn't think there could be anything wrong in the whole affair —just the tomfoolery of a man who has got the betting mania and in whose pocket money is just burning a hole. And I have won my bet," concluded Jean Victor, still unabashed, "and I want to go back and get my money. If you don't believe me, come with me to my *Cabaret*. You will find the citizen Rateau there, for sure; and I know that I shall find my five gold pieces."

Chauvelin had listened to the man as he would to some weird dream-story, wherein ghouls and devils had played a part. Tournefort, who was watching him, was awed by the look of fierce rage and grim hopelessness which shone from his chief's pale eyes. The other agents laughed. They were highly amused at the tale, but they would not let the prisoner go.

"If Jean Victor's story is true, citizen," their sergeant said, speaking to Chauvelin, "there will be witnesses to it over at 'Le Bon Copain.' Shall we take the prisoner straightway there and await further orders?"

Chauvelin gave a curt acquiescence, nodding his head like some insentient wooden automaton. The screw of paper was still in his hand; it seemed to sear his palm. Tournefort even now broke into a grim laugh. He had just undone the bundle which Jean Victor had thrown over the parapet of the bridge. It contained two heads of cabbage and a bunch of carrots. Then he ordered the agents to march on with their prisoner, and they, laughing and joking with Jean Victor, gave a quick turn, and soon their heavy footsteps were echoing down the flagstones of the bridge.

* * * * *

Chauvelin waited, motionless and silent, the dark lantern still held in his shaking hand, until he was quite sure that he was alone. Then only did he unfold the screw of paper.

It contained a few lines scribbled in pencil—just that foolish rhyme which to his fevered nerves was like a strong irritant, a poison which gave him an unendurable sensation of humiliation and impotence:

"We seek him here, we seek him there!
Chauvelin seeks him everywhere!
Is he in heaven? Is he in hell?
That demmed, elusive Pimpernel!"

He crushed the paper in his hand and, with a loud groan, of misery, fled over the bridge like one possessed.

VII

Madame la Comtesse de Sucy never went to England. She was one of those French women who would sooner endure misery in their own beloved country than comfort anywhere else. She outlived the horrors of the Revolution and speaks in her memoirs of the man Bertin. She never knew who he was nor whence he came. All that she knew was that he came to her like some mysterious agent of God, bringing help, counsel, a semblance of happiness, at the moment when she was at the end of all her resources and saw grim starvation staring her and her children in the face.

He appointed all sorts of strange places in out-of-the-way Paris where she was wont to meet him, and one night she confided to him the history of her diamonds, and hardly dared to trust his promise that he would get them for her.

Less than twenty-four hours later he brought them to her, at the poor lodgings in the Rue Blanche which she occupied with her children under an assumed name. That same night she begged him to dispose of them. This also he did, bringing her the money the next day.

She never saw him again after that.

But citizen Tournefort never quite got over his disappointment of that night. Had he dared, he would have blamed citizen Chauvelin for the discomfiture. It would have been better to have apprehended the man Rateau while there was a chance of doing so with success.

As it was, the impudent ruffian slipped clean away, and was never heard of again either at the "Bon Copain" or at the "Liberte." The customers at the cabaret certainly corroborated the story of Jean Victor. The man Rateau, they said, had been honest to the last. When time went on and Jean Victor did not return, he said that he could no longer wait, had work to do for the Government over the other side of the water and was afraid he would get punished if he dallied. But, before leaving, he laid the five gold pieces on the table. Every one wondered that so humble a workman had so much money in his pocket, and was withal so lavish with it. But these were not the times when one inquired too closely into the presence of money in the pocket of a good patriot.

And citizen Rateau was a good patriot, for sure.

And a good fellow to boot!

They all drank his health in Jean Victor's sour wine; then each went his way.

Made in the USA
San Bernardino, CA
28 November 2014